Praise for

SHE WHO RIDES THE STORM

"Caitlin Sangster's latest novel is her most ambitious book yet. *She Who Rides the Storm* is a tightly-woven fantasy heist with memorable young adult characters and a killer premise."

—BRANDON SANDERSON,
#1 *New York Times* bestselling author

"Ghosts. Tombs. Betrayals. With multiple unfolding mysteries and complex and varied magics, *She Who Rides the Storm* digs right into a new, imaginative world, leading the reader deeper into the history—and the truth—of a divided land. Nothing is what it seems."

—JODI MEADOWS,
New York Times bestselling coauthor of *My Plain Jane* and author of *The Orphan Queen* and *Before She Ignites*

"The dramatic tension builds to a final plot twist that will delight fans of intricate, complex fantasies. . . . Will leave readers clamoring for more."

—*Kirkus Reviews*

"This heist novel will certainly capture the attention of fans of Leigh Bardugo's *Six of Crows*."

—*Booklist*

ALSO BY CAITLIN SANGSTER

Last Star Burning
Shatter the Suns
Dead Moon Rising

SHE

WHO

RIDES

THE

STORM

THE GODS-TOUCHED DUOLOGY

CAITLIN SANGSTER

MARGARET K. McELDERRY BOOKS

New York London Toronto Sydney New Delhi

MARGARET K. McELDERRY BOOKS

An imprint of Simon & Schuster Children's Publishing Division

1230 Avenue of the Americas, New York, New York 10020

This book is a work of fiction. Any references to historical events, real people, or real places are used fictitiously. Other names, characters, places, and events are products of the author's imagination, and any resemblance to actual events or places or persons, living or dead, is entirely coincidental.

MARGARET K. McELDERRY BOOKS is a trademark of Simon & Schuster, Inc.

For information about special discounts for bulk purchases, please contact Simon & Schuster Special Sales at 1-866-506-1949 or business@simonandschuster.com.

The Simon & Schuster Speakers Bureau can bring authors to your live event. For more information or to book an event, contact the Simon & Schuster Speakers Bureau at 1-866-248-3049 or visit our website at www.simonspeakers.com.

Also available in a Margaret K. McElderry Books hardcover edition

Interior design by Irene Metaxatos

The text for this book was set in ITC Galliard Std.

Manufactured in the United States of America

First Margaret K. McElderry Books paperback edition September 2022

10 9 8 7 6 5 4 3 2 1

The Library of Congress has cataloged the hardcover edition as follows:

Library of Congress Cataloging-in-Publication Data

Names: Sangster, Caitlin, author.

Title: She who rides the storm / Caitlin Sangster.

Description: First edition. | New York : Margaret K. McElderry Books, [2021] | Series: She who rides the storm ; 1 | Summary: Teenaged master thieves Anwei and Knox, aided by friends, attempt to break into the tomb of an ancient shapeshifter king who is believed to have stolen souls from his subjects.

Identifiers: LCCN 2020055230 (print) | LCCN 2020055231 (ebook) | ISBN 9781534466111 (hardcover) | ISBN 9781534466135 (ebook) | ISBN 9781534466128 (pbk)

Subjects: CYAC: Robbers and outlaws—Fiction. | Magic—Fiction. | Fantasy.

Classification: LCC PZ7.1.S263 Sk 2021 (print) | LCC PZ7.1.S263 (ebook) | DDC [Fic]—dc23

LC record available at https://lccn.loc.gov/2020055230

LC ebook record available at https://lccn.loc.gov/2020055231

To my SMB, which I still think is the funniest nickname you've tried to get me to call you.

—C. S.

CHAPTER 1

An Aukincer's Pot

When Anwei stepped into the trade advisor's private study, she smelled death. The odor burned in her nose, the dregs of it seared into the ornate desk chair, the walls. It was rank in the very air.

"Don't touch anything," she whispered to her partner, Knox, as he slipped through the window to stand next to her.

"I thought the *point* was to touch things." Knox looked around the moonlit study. "Stealing usually requires physical contact." He pulled off the scarf covering his face, caught Anwei's pointed look at his bared nose and mouth, and grudgingly replaced it. The last year of working together had taught him to respect Anwei's acute sense of smell, even if he didn't really understand it.

Their contract was simple. Steal the original Trib figurine the trade advisor had acquired through blackmail. Get it to the magistrate by the next day. It had nothing to do with justice for the poor artist whose sought-after work had been stolen, so far as Anwei could tell. City wardens would have been put on the job instead of a thief if that were the case. No, it seemed more like the magistrate, whose jurists sent thieves and blackmailers to the shipping crews every day, just wanted the little

Trib maiden for himself and was angry the governor's trade advisor had gotten to it first.

Anwei walked over to the rose-carved desk at the center of the room, her eyes glued to the small copper pot that appeared to be the source of the noxious smell. Kneeling by the desk, she opened the advisor's drawers one by one to look for the figurine, wishing the magistrate had warned her that this particular bureaucrat was messing around with an aukincer. The concoction in the pot was clearly an aukincer's work—just the smell of it sent prickles down her throat with a silvery, sharp sort of glee, as if even inhaling the air near it would slice her lungs to ribbons. She didn't want to think what *ingesting* it would do. But anyone stupid enough to go to an aukincer for magic instead of a healer for medicine deserved what they got.

Knox slid past the desk to inspect the shelves next to it. "Is that what I think it is?" He nodded to the pot. "You're not going to try to witch the aukincer's residue off me once we get out of here, are you?"

Anwei rolled her eyes. "If 'witching' would fix you, I would have done it a long time ago, Knox." She pulled open the last two desk drawers, her mind jumping to the list of herbs that would best counter the toxic cloud coming from the pot. She closed the final drawer with a delicate click. No figurine.

No figurine—and no sign of what Anwei was *actually* looking for in this house either.

The sky-cursed stench of aukincy made it impossible to smell much of anything else in this room. She stood and turned to check the display behind the desk. If the tip that had led her to this house was wrong, she was going to crack some Crowteeth heads. It had been *two years* since she'd had a solid lead, and if her gang contacts thought they could mess with her—

"Aukincers don't even promise more years of being young." Knox's whisper made Anwei look up. He was by the window, lifting the reed blind to look out. "Just more years—and probably cursed years too, since it's all supposed to come from forbidden shapeshifter magic. If it were between dying when I'm old and bent, and dying when I'm a few years *more* old and bent—"

"We all know how you feel about medicine, Knox. Not that this abomination counts as medicine. Even shapeshifters would turn their noses up at this stuff. Why are you over there?"

"*We* all?" He smirked. "Is that the royal 'we,' or have you started sampling your own herbs?"

"Did you hear something out there?" The beginnings of worry pulled Anwei's limbs tight as he replaced the blind. "We should have three more minutes before the guards do a sweep."

"I thought I heard footsteps." He turned from the window. "Maybe I imagined it."

Knox didn't imagine things like footsteps. "Let's get this done and get out of here, just in case. Help me with these last shelves." Anwei moved toward the case flanking the door, then froze midstep when something other than the stink of aukincy hit her nose. A flare of anticipation burst through her. She stood still, taking a much longer, deeper breath, and sorted through the scents: the sharp bite of ink; the deep, earthy musk of the wooden desk; the sour tang of the wool rug, with coppery aftertones for the dye.

Anwei breathed out. She smelled nothing that mattered.

Barely stopping herself from swearing, Anwei turned her attention to the case she'd meant to search. Two years since she'd found even a *hint* of her brother's killer in this sweltering cook pot of a city. Two years since the letter that had sent her running to Chaol. He'd been here, and then he'd disappeared.

Frustration brewed inside Anwei. The tip to investigate the trade advisor had been so promising—and then she'd gotten a request to take something from this very house. It had been perfect. But *every* lead that came through Anwei's system of contacts throughout the Commonwealth seemed perfect to her. That was what hope did to you. It made you see things that weren't really there.

Arun's face seemed to be imprinted on every surface in the little study—the desk, the walls, the stupid pot—her twin's expression just as aggressively bored as the day he'd tried to persuade her to sneak away from the town council meeting back on Beilda. The last time she'd seen him before the snake-tooth man got him.

Anwei moved away from the display case, then paused again when a new scent rose to the surface, a thin coat of sickly yellow that festered in her nostrils.

Ah, so that's *why he called an aukincer.* The trade advisor was sick.

Of course, she couldn't be sure of specifics of his illness without finding the man himself. She sighed. Rich men were so hopeful and so stupid at once, as if money could solve any problem, including the ones inside you. But an aukincer's elixirs weren't going to help the trade advisor do anything but die faster.

"Found it!" Knox slid over to a side table. Anwei jerked from her train of thought and joined him. The little statue was all cheekbones and full skirts, her coquettish look enough to earn her a place in the lovers' temple next to Freia, their patron goddess. Knox reached out to take the figurine, but his fingers stopped just shy of it. He looked at Anwei. "Is it safe to touch?"

Anwei sniffed experimentally, but it was only for show. The aukincy contamination wasn't so bad on this side of the room. "I think you'd at least get to the door with it. Maybe even out of the compound." She scrunched her nose, looking at the little figurine. It was pretty enough, but thirty bronze coins for a girl made of stone? It wasn't just health that rich men were stupid about.

Knox was still staring at her with a concerned frown, so Anwei gave him a bright smile. At least the magistrate would have his figurine. That meant referrals. More jobs. Money to pay bribes and to buy the equipment that allowed her to search this city house by house for the snake-tooth man's scent. "Don't worry, Knox. I'll carry your body back to the apothecary and put your cut of the money in your grave. Shall we?" There was nothing here for Anwei to find. The lead that had filled her with so much hope was worthless, just like all the others had been.

She strode toward the window and checked the courtyard outside. It was still clear. They had another two minutes before the guard would patrol past the office. When she turned back to Knox, his brow was knotted and he still hadn't taken the figurine. "This isn't one of those times I'm going to be sad that I thought you were joking, is it?"

"It's fine, Knox. We'll just burn all your clothes."

"You know how little clothing I own." He pulled out a handkerchief, wrapped it around the figurine, and shoved the little Trib statue into his pocket.

Anwei's smile strained a bit at the edges. Knox had plenty of money for clothes; he just seemed to like stashing it in the box under his bed better than spending it. One coin at a time until he saved enough to leave this city—to leave this *country*. It wasn't that Anwei *couldn't* do jobs without him, but after so many years of sneaking into fancy houses alone, then going home to sift through the clues she found alone, eating alone, sleeping alone . . . well, that last part certainly wasn't going to change, but having Knox only a room away to worry if she didn't come home was nice. Her contacts in the gangs might notice if she went missing, she supposed, but they'd only come poking around for spoils.

Maybe she should broach the subject again. Convince Knox that staying in Chaol was safer than leaving.

Anwei held the window covering back for Knox to climb through, but instead of doing so, he dove under the sill, pulling her down with him.

"Calsta's breath," he hissed. "There's someone coming."

Fear plucked in Anwei's stomach, the wall hard against her spine. After all her weeks of watching the house, not one of the guards had broken the patrolling schedule. They were supposed to have more *time*. She forced her muscles to relax, her ears straining to hear whatever it was that had alarmed Knox.

But there was nothing to hear.

Still, she didn't move. Just as Knox knew to trust her nose, Anwei had learned to listen when he saw or heard things she didn't.

After a moment the sound of unsteady footsteps tripped across the courtyard, only to stop directly outside the study. A swish of wind blew in through the tightly woven mat covering the window, fanning a sickly scent of decay from outside into Anwei's nose. It had to be the trade advisor himself, unless there were two men in this compound with their stomachs rotting from the inside.

A key rattled in door's lock. *The advisor is just an ailing old man,* she told herself. *This will be easier to get out of than that time Knox accidentally woke the governor's wife with her silver candlesticks in his hands.*

Anwei slunk over to the door, gesturing for Knox to wait. He nodded, ready to move the moment she did. As the advisor lifted the latch, she wrenched the door open. The old man stumbled into the study and landed on his knees. Anwei flitted past him like a breeze, out the door before he could've seen more than her shadow. When she looked back, the advisor was still on the floor and Knox had already disappeared into the night.

Heading toward the compound's outer wall, Anwei skipped from stone to stone on the raised pathway that led through the garden, a crow of success in her mouth.

Then the trade advisor coughed. A wet, ugly sound.

Her feet slowed, and she couldn't help but look back at the bureaucrat on the floor. His shoulders curved down as another cough racked his chest, something inky and red spilling out onto his hands. The sickly yellow smell of his illness spiraled around Anwei. Taking the aukincer's brew had made whatever was wrong with the trade advisor much worse. She slipped a hand into the bag hidden under her robe, wishing she'd brought *something* that might help him—

A pole rapped across her shoulders. Anwei wrenched herself from her relapse into herbs and diseases just in time to block a second blow from the guard aimed at her head. She stumbled to the side, angry at herself for missing the smells she should have been looking for. Now they flooded over her in quick succession: the pork and sugared eggplant that the guard had eaten for dinner; the dusting of geratry root that colored the first two fingers of his right hand gray, the smell like burned pepper; boot polish and a rotten tooth. She dodged the pole's third blow and pushed closer to the guard so she'd be too close for him to use it. He dropped the weapon and slammed her into the wall.

Anwei's eyes swam as her head hit brick, her hands snaking toward her medicine bag just as the guard's forearm pressed into her throat. His body trapped her arms. Fear swarmed inside her as she strained to reach her bag. She fought for air, the scents around her turning sharp, the man's grizzled face like an auroshe with all its teeth bared.

A stone sailed straight into the guard's helmet, hitting with a hollow clang. The guard bit off a curse, and the pressure of his arm on Anwei's throat slackened just enough to let her slide sideways and plunge a hand into the medicine bag. She came up with a handful of powdered corta petals and ground them into the guard's face. He reared back and clawed at his eyes and nose, letting Anwei scramble away.

She ran to the aviary, thanking every star in the sky for the millionth time that she'd stopped working alone. Without Knox, she may actually have been caught that time. Cages of geese, ducks, and sparrows swung in the dim lantern light, the birds agitated to honking and calling, as if they wished to do their part in protecting the trade advisor's home. Anwei scrambled up the cages, swearing when her muscles started burning long before she got to the top. It was at that moment—ducks and geese honking avian obscenities in her direction, the salty ocean wind clawing through her hair—that Anwei smelled it.

The black, empty *nothing* scent of Arun's murder.

She froze even as the shouts and clatter of armored feet on the cobblestones behind her got closer. If the smell *was* here, then—

"*Anwei!*" Knox's voice grabbed her from below, where he was crouched by the wall. Stray hair from his blunt nub of a ponytail hung down the sides of his face as he stared up at her. "What are you *doing*?"

Anwei cast one frustrated look into the compound, then jumped onto the street and ran to catch up with Knox because he'd started walking without her. "They always go for *you*," he murmured when she'd drawn even with him.

"I'm the pretty one." Anwei caught hold of his long tunic and pulled him into an alleyway as shouts from the trade advisor's house spilled out into the street after them. The waterway dividing them from the next cay over was tantalizingly close, but they'd left their boat at home for this trip. The bridge between the two islands was clogged with nobles sporting khonin knots in their hair to mark their status. They glittered, as the rich often did. The trade advisor was on the less opulent side of the Water Cay—he was only a second khonin, the two knots in his long hair ensuring everyone knew—close to the bridge leading to the next island in the river-mouth chain that made up the city of Chaol. Because Anwei didn't feel like a nighttime swim, escape would have to be over that bridge.

Anwei cleared her throat once the guards had blundered past, the feel of that steel-lined sleeve still pressing against her vocal cords. Knox pulled the scarf from his face, snapped his fingers impatiently for Anwei's outer robe, and waited with his hand outstretched until she'd pulled it over her head to bare the more brightly colored one underneath. Guards tended not to see Knox, even when he was right in front of them. It was one of the many benefits Anwei hadn't anticipated when she'd first taken him on.

"If we're going to start comparing who's prettiest, we should probably set some parameters." He stuffed the robe into Anwei's bag.

"Are we talking face symmetry? Body proportions? Are these guards really objective observers, or—"

"I'm sure there are *some* people who think you're prettier. There was that whole incident with the Warlord's Devoted the day we met, don't you remember?"

Knox's head jerked back to look at her, but only for a second. He pulled the medicine bag's flap closed, then went back to watching the street. Regret tasted tinny in Anwei's mouth. Perhaps some things would never be funny.

"Thank you for staying long enough to make sure I got out," she said, changing the subject. "That was a good throw."

"You okay?" he asked, still not looking at her.

"Fine." Anwei coughed, the burning in her throat bringing back the hunched image of the trade advisor, blood on his hands. But she banished that image in favor of the whiff she'd caught of the snake-tooth man's nothing smell. She *had* something at last, which meant she was better than fine. "Let's go."

Anwei slid out from the alleyway, and Knox fell in next to her, draping an arm around her waist in a way she hoped would appear less forced than it felt. They walked past another set of guards in the advisor's colors when they got to the bottom of the hill and started across the bridge. Chaol's dry market glistened with torches and candles from across the channel, the drum tower looming over it all from the ocean side of the island.

"Hey, you two!"

Anwei quickened her steps, her soft leather boots sticking to the still-warm cobblestones. Knox matched her speed across the bridge's huge, weathered stones, the market's tents and booths and chatter waiting with outstretched arms to hide them on the other side. The smell of cook fires and spices from the southern provinces filled Anwei's nose. It took only seconds for her and Knox to lose themselves in the milling sellers and malt-buzzed patrons, all elbows, open sandals, and smoke.

They strolled, watching with concern like everyone else when guards pushed past them through the crowd. Anwei bought a juicy kebab with change from her pocket, though Knox only wrinkled his nose when she offered him a bite. By the time she'd finished it, they'd reached the edge of the market, the crowds thinning around them like watered-down soup. Knox's arm dropped from Anwei's waist, leaving her both relieved and a little cold.

"Another hard day's work complete. And no one poked any holes in us!" Triumph rose like a sun in Anwei's chest, making her want to dance Knox back through the market one playful step at a time. Not that he'd comply. She wouldn't think about the advisor curled up on his own steps. She *wouldn't*. "I'm still hungry. Let's—"

"Watch out!" Knox grabbed Anwei's arm and wrenched her backward into a stairwell. The Trib maiden's angles and curves pressed into Anwei's spine through his pocket. Still elated, Anwei didn't freeze completely until she heard it. The hollow clop of cloven hooves on stone.

An *auroshe*? She shivered at the thought of those monsters with their long serrated teeth and razor-sharp horns—and that was nothing compared with the soldiers who rode them. But there hadn't been Commonwealth soldiers in Chaol since a year ago, when Anwei had first found Knox. Why would they be here now? And would they be ordinary Roosters, or . . . they couldn't possibly be *Devoted*, could they?

The threads of triumph in Anwei's stomach pulled tight, then snapped with a painful twang. She'd run across many Roosters in her travels throughout the country, although Chaol itself was a little out of the way for them to be stationed. But she'd never seen a true Devoted until the day Knox fell into her life with a whole group of them chasing after him like parchwolves hunting their prey.

That's what Devoted did when one of their own tried to escape.

Anwei could feel Knox's breathing slow against her back, her partner going stone still as two auroshes rode into view, one black, one white. Their manes and long tails were tied in intricate knots that mimicked their riders' distinctive braids, the white with one slender horn protruding from its brow, the black with two that stuck out from its head like twin lightning bolts. The sight of the creatures curdled Anwei's belly, but when she spotted their riders, she released a breath. "They're just Roosters, Knox, not—"

Knox's hand slipped over her mouth to stop her from saying more. The Roosters passed by the stairwell, their auroshes bowed and tired. They didn't seem to notice the hush that fell over the closest market stands as they passed, nor the eyes in the crowd that were glued to the Warlord's crest on their uniforms. The two Roosters broke away from the road and hugged the edge of the market, making for the Water Cay bridge, the silence that their presence brought hovering like mist after the riders themselves had melted into the night.

Anwei flinched when the night market patrons began calling to one another once again, drunken students loudly trying out new curses like bits of sugar. A minute passed. Two. "Knox?" Anwei mumbled through his fingers covering her mouth. He still hadn't moved.

"Just . . . wait," he whispered.

She grabbed a handful of his tunic, as if she could anchor him in place. "They weren't Devoted, and anyway, Devoted can't track you unless you use your . . ." Biting her lip, she trailed off, not knowing *what* it was exactly that he couldn't use, because the two of them had silently agreed not to ask questions when they'd started working together. Devoted weren't allowed to say anything about the goddess Calsta or the power she lent them. They had hardly even left their seclusions in the last few years except on the Warlord's business.

Of course, Knox wasn't just a Devoted; he was also Anwei's friend. But even bringing up Devoted magic felt like stepping over a line drawn between them that they had both promised not to cross.

"They can't find you unless you use your *whatever it is* on purpose," Anwei tried again. "Back in the compound, you heard the old man coming before I did. And you got out without a single guard even noticing—"

"I haven't been using it." Knox's voice was choked. He shrank back against the wall. "At least, as much as I can help."

"And the sword?" She hated even thinking about that gods-forsaken thing. "You haven't touched it lately or—"

"*No.*"

Anwei let out the breath trapped in her lungs. "Then we're okay. Those soldiers have no reason to be looking for you." She turned to face Knox when he didn't answer. He didn't look at her, his gaze turned to the crowd, darting from person to person as if he was searching for something she couldn't see. He smelled of the bland noodles and broth they'd eaten before going to the trade advisor's study, hints of smoke and meat clinging to his shirt from the night market. But underneath she could scent the salty odor of an agitated sweat.

"It's been a year since you left them. It's going to be okay." She said it firmly, as if she knew it to be fact.

Knox's eyes refocused on her, one hand coming up to touch the empty space where that cursed sword hilt would have stuck out above his shoulder if he'd been carrying it. Anwei's heart sank even as he changed the gesture to smooth back his dark hair.

"They'll never stop looking," he whispered. "It is *never* going to be okay."

She peered after the auroshes. Even now, out of sight, the soldiers seemed to radiate power, the force of law, the Warlord herself and everything she stood for, almost as frightening as the shapeshifters they hunted. If Roosters were in Chaol, their masters—Devoted— would likely soon follow. Anwei's grip on Knox's tunic tightened, the thought of Knox leaving her sharp in her chest. It was only when one of the students from across the street sent a suggestive whistle toward them that her grip loosened.

Knox was right, of course. The last dregs of triumph from a job well done funneled away as Anwei stepped out of the stairwell. She had known from the moment she found Knox lying almost dead in the street, his head shorn and his hands clutching a shapeshifter's sword like his life depended on it, that nothing was going to be okay.

But the *nothing* smell she'd caught earlier? That could change everything.

CHAPTER 2

More Useful Than Dead Plants

Knox could hardly walk straight as he followed Anwei toward the ladder to the rickety rope skybridge that would take them across the channel to their home on the Coil. He closed his eyes, as if that would somehow shut out the soldiers and their mounts. Devoted could already be here in the city.

Scrubbing a hand through his hair, Knox pressed a finger to each of the scars he'd been given when he made oaths to join Calsta's warriors. He knew a rogue Devoted was a risk the Warlord couldn't take. How could she keep the peace if there were warriors who could move faster, jump higher, hear better—warriors who could defy the laws of gravity and possibly use those powers against her?

I told you to abandon the seclusion. The voice burned through Knox, leaving him charred inside just as it had the first day the voice had spoken to him when he was young. *Calsta.* Goddess of sun and storm. Speaking in his head as she hadn't to anyone else in five hundred years. *I don't really feel like going over it with you again, Knox. Stay clear and they'll leave you alone.*

It was both a relief to hear her voice and a pain. None of the old records talked about how grumpy Calsta was.

No. A second voice that wasn't quite so warm threaded through Knox's thoughts, sending shivers down his spine. *Don't you remember how horrible Ewan Hardcastle was to you and your little Devoted sister, Lia? Ewan was the one they sent to hunt you. Why not find him first? We could end it all now before he does.*

Lia. Knox blotted her name out almost as quickly as the voice said it. The two together—the icy voice and the thought of the best friend he shouldn't have left behind—were too much. They twisted together like poison waiting to be released into his heart.

"Eyes open please." Anwei's husky voice jolted him back to the warm night, the steaming cobblestones, and the little Trib statue in his pocket. "Much as I feel sorry for you, I will not refrain from laughing if you step off the walkway and go headfirst into the channel."

She pulled him to the base of the skybridge ladder. It led to the first island in the cluster that made up the Coil, lamps and torches flickering in the distance from the bridges and underwater tunnels that strung the rest of the little clump of islands together like a necklace. Anwei's fingers still clutched at Knox's shirt as if she were afraid he'd float away. One plait—one of the even hundred that covered her scalp, marking her a healer from Beilda—had slipped free of the scarf covering her head, the braid black against her tawny complexion. Anwei grudgingly let go, then scurried up the ladder, waiting for him to join her. The old wooden rungs creaked under Knox's weight as he followed, the bridge itself swaying when he stepped out onto it. Half the wooden planks were broken and the ropes looked frayed, but short of swimming or hiring a boat, there wasn't another way to get back to the Coil. Before she scurried across, Anwei flashed a grin at him that was directly opposite to the tension he could see riding her shoulders.

"Even with your eyes open, you're still off-balance," she called. "Would it help if I pushed you in?"

"You push me into a channel and you'll wake up with all those braids undone," he returned. But he did reach out to the ropes to steady himself. "You'd look like a . . ." He racked his brain, trying to remember the word. "A *pritha*."

Anwei paused for a second, already starting down the ladder on the other side. "A *pineapple*?"

"Did I mean *printha*?"

"Are you trying to say *priantia*? One of those wandering Trib holy men who spend all their lives hoping Calsta will touch them?" Anwei continued down the ladder to the street below. "Two things: One, I'd make an amazing holy . . . person. Especially if I'm allowed to keep one of those fiery lizard things that the Trib carry around. Two, would you please stop trying to speak . . . well, *anything* but Common? You're good at Common."

Knox sighed and followed her down the ladder. On the ground, he kept close to Anwei, watching for anyone who might be tailing them like he was supposed to. They were only one thin channel past the dry market, but the buildings were much taller and dirtier than the compounds they'd left behind on the Water Cay.

It was the people who were hard to look at, though.

A man tripped past them, a dimmed, distorted aura that matched his wobbly, drunken steps suspended around his head like a globe of light. A wrinkled old woman hobbled by, her aura gleaming the bright, almost painful white of one near the end of her life. A pair of students hopped a narrow spot in the waterway just ahead of them, one not quite making it and falling in with a splash. The one who landed safely on the bank started laughing while his friend pulled himself out of the brackish water. Ripples of fatigue waved through both their auras like antennae.

It took every ounce of concentration Knox could muster to keep himself from looking at any auras beyond those of the people immediately around them. Having taken Calsta's oaths, he couldn't help but see the halo of glowing white energy around each person who passed them. But if he were to use Calsta's power to push his awareness farther—down the street, to the next island over—searching for the gold flecks that would mark a Devoted's aura . . . that would be dangerous. *That* would get him found.

And then there was Anwei, of course. She pulled him down a side street that closed in tight around them, the bricks smelling as if they were wet with something other than water. Unlike the auras bobbing down the waterway and the walkways around it, Anwei's aura was an inky smear where light should have been. At the end of the alleyway, she gave an experimental sniff that sent a shiver of ice down Knox's spine despite the heat still steaming up from the cobblestones. Anwei's nose, however she played it off, was not *natural*. Nor was the inky purple of her aura.

He'd spent most of his life chasing dark auras like hers, before their owners could destroy the people around them.

"Give me the figurine." Anwei held out a hand for the little statue when they got to the bridge leading to the next little piece of the Coil. "You head home to the apothecary, and we'll decide what to do about the Roosters when I get back from delivering the statue to the magistrate."

Knox shook his head. The idea of sitting in his room in the dark waiting for Roosters to find him was more than he could stomach. "How about I deliver the statue? I'll check the drop over at Yaru's temple, too. That way Gulya will be too tired to kill me by the time I get back."

Anwei turned toward him, a dimple creasing her cheek to the left of her mouth when she smiled. "I don't understand why she hates you so much. You pay rent, you haven't broken anything." She caught her bottom lip in her teeth, looking up at him with that quiet way she had, as if she could see more of people than showed on the outside. "You can take the Trib figurine if you want, but don't follow the Roosters, okay? Following them is like betting on that snaggle-toothed auroshe at the fights and not expecting to lose."

Knox wasn't going to go after the Roosters. He hadn't needed Calsta's warning to know better—the goddess's advice was always good, even if he didn't know *why* she'd decided to descend upon him of all people. Still, it was comforting to know a goddess was watching over him in the mess that was left of his life. "Auroshe fights are illegal."

"So is stealing. We'll just avoid the Water Cay until the Roosters leave."

Knox did not look at Anwei's dimple or her mouth. He untangled her hand from his tunic, where it had once again lodged itself. "Fine. We can split at the next waterway. Meet you back at the apothecary?"

She nodded, looked both ways down the channel, then started up the ladder that would lead toward home.

Home. Shoulders hunching, Knox followed her. The word tasted like salt and savor, unsuited for Knox's tongue no matter how much it watered. Why would Devoted come to Chaol *now*?

The only thing he could come up with was that Chaol was the last place Ewan had found traces of Knox. A lot of traces, actually. Knox had been so far spent that day that the people he'd staggered past had seemed to be on fire, the white of their auras flickering and dissipating overhead as if they were all draining into the sky. He wasn't sure why Anwei had stopped when she found him, the backward twist to her aura making it an umbra instead, glowing deep purple black instead of white.

A dirt witch's aura.

He almost drew his sword at the sight of her, even though Calsta had forbidden him from taking it out of the scabbard. If there had ever been a moment for last resorts, that had been it. But then she tucked the braids lining her face behind her ear, and her husky Beildan accent stopped him short.

"I hear Roosters will chase even if you cut their heads off." Her eyes skated over the prickles of hair still too short to hide his oath scars.

Putting a hand on top of his where it gripped the sword, she kept her voice quiet. "If you're game, we can try burying you instead of them."

He wanted to laugh even as the sound of cloven hooves on stone thundered in his chest. She couldn't have heard them, couldn't have seen anything but the panic that had chased him every step he'd taken away from the Warlord, a forbidden sword on his back. Still, Knox followed her across a channel and two streets over to the apothecary, lay down in the room above Gulya's shop, and winked out like a candle for three days.

When Knox finally opened his eyes, Anwei was there, setting a bowl of clear broth next to his shoulder. Alarm flooded him, his eyes full of the bruised purple aura hovering around Anwei where white should have been. "Where's my sword?"

She nodded to the blanket next to him. With shaking hands he pushed back the cover. The blade was underneath, sheathed and shrouded the way he'd left it.

"You need food more than you need that sword." Anwei drew her eyes away as if watching him clutch at the weapon were somehow indecent. He covered the sword, drank down the broth, and closed his eyes, waiting for Devoted to break in through the leaded-glass window. When nothing happened, he followed Anwei's aura downstairs to the apothecary, where he watched her treat a man's blisters, and then followed her again that night on a job that had nothing to do with apothecaries or blisters at all. That was how things had been ever since.

Knox had been buried somehow, just the way she'd said. Anwei had taken him into her potted collection of herbs and remedies, though he liked to think he was more useful than dead plants. Anwei would probably not agree. He *liked* "finding" with her, as she called it, as though they were helping old ladies retrieve their spectacles. *Finding* was a good deal different from *taking* in Knox's mind. But it was easy to forget the sword under his bed and the soldiers on auroshes hunting him when he was sneaking through the city with Anwei. There was something sky-blessedly escapist about helping corrupt, rich, and mighty men stab one another where it really hurt—their art and wine collections, mostly. It was a relief after so many years of finding *people* for the Warlord.

The icy voice hummed happily at the back of Knox's head, as if remembering those bloody days. Knox pushed it back. It didn't really matter if his life was better now. Devoted would keep coming, searching for the gold flecks in Knox's aura just as they had a year ago.

I promised you that if you kept your oaths, I'd help you. Don't make me say it again.

Knox cringed at Calsta's voice. Giving up his oaths to her had never been an option. She'd saved him long before Anwei and had continued to save him over and over, but her voice burned.

Even if he *were* to give up his oaths, it wouldn't fix his aura. The gold flecks would always be there, lurking around him like tattered fireflies, a testament to what he was. Lying low wouldn't be enough if Devoted had figured out Knox was still in Chaol. Not unless there had been something *else* hiding him this last year.

Knox's eyes traced the line of Anwei's back, her confident stride. The darkness of her aura that felt like clenched fists and murder. Only two kinds of people had auras that weren't boring white. Devoted, who were swirled over with Calsta's gold, and dirt witches—*Basists*—who practiced banned magic. They belonged to the nameless god, the very creature who had broken Calsta's mask. The same monster whom the goddess had strangled in her temple.

Anwei abruptly stopped in front of Knox, bringing his thoughts back to the present. She gave another deliberate sniff when he almost bumped into her, though he thought it was mock irritation this time, not whatever darkness flowing through her humors that allowed her to scent impossible things. "Not too close. I don't want any of your Devotedness getting on me."

"It doesn't rub off." He edged around her, looking up the walkway that would lead him toward the Ink Cay, where the magistrate lived—he was only a third khonin, not fancy enough for the Water Cay.

The Trib figurine felt thin and frail in Knox's pocket. He pulled it out, opening the handkerchief wrapped around it to make sure it hadn't come off worse for wear after escaping the trade advisor's compound. "Do I need to wash this thing before I leave it for the magistrate, or are we okay with poisoning him?"

"Just give it a good rub with your handkerchief." Anwei started down the road toward the apothecary, turning toward him to walk backward as she spoke. "And maybe don't handle it directly. I'm okay with the magistrate being a *little* poisoned. Maybe he'll pay me for an antidote." She narrowed her eyes, her feet slowing. "I'll check you over when you get back, just to make sure none of that aukincer's rubbish got inside you. Honestly, the things people will believe when they don't like what a healer says . . ."

Knox started up the hill without answering her, a shudder running up his spine. Anwei probably didn't really know what she was doing with those herbs. He'd never heard of a Basist with a nose like hers— her skill was probably a manifestation of being able to match herbs to illnesses or something like that. She hadn't hurt anyone that he'd seen, but Knox had his history lessons along with everyone else in the Commonwealth. Basists had started just like Devoted. Taking oaths just the way Knox had done with Calsta, giving up parts of themselves in order for their god to give them power. Stories had Basists building castles from rocks that burst from the earth, shaping water into ice and rain, growing flowers and herbs into forests, or even growing someone injured back together.

That was before. At some point one Basist found a way to step around the oaths. To *take* power instead of having to sacrifice for it. A new oath, perhaps, that twisted him into something corrupted and wrong, allowing him to strip energy from the people around him down to their very souls and take it for himself. Basists after him became something inhuman, creatures that were far more powerful than any god's devotee had ever been before, their lives spanning long, their fingerprints more like claw marks on history.

Knox pulled his scarf back up over his nose and mouth, pretending he was no different from any other late-evening walker, trying to block out the smells of smoke, beast, and the ripe fragrance wafting from the canals. Ever since Basists had been banned, aukincers had cropped up trying to replicate the miracle cures of old, but without the power from the nameless god to bond elements together into medicine, it was mostly rubbish, as Anwei had said. Harmless at best, but usually aukincers didn't stop there. Knox had spent most of his time as a Devoted hunting down reports of banned magic only to find a fool like the one who had left the pot in the trade advisor's study.

Anwei, though . . . somehow, oaths or not, Anwei was the real thing.

Breaking into the magistrate's compound wasn't difficult. Those who expected "Yaru" to answer their prayers tended to leave their shutters unlocked—they knew what their offerings to that goddess were paying for. Knox left the little Trib girl on the magistrate's bedside table, the man himself too well fed and accustomed to uninterrupted dreams to notice the company.

Once that was done, Knox headed toward the one drop Anwei let him check. It was on the long, thin island that ran the length of Chaol: the Gold Cay, where malthouses would be open all night. Auras tickled the back of his mind as he hopped onto a ferry to cross—there were no bridges or tunnels to the Gold Cay—and the shore was crowded with white globes of light. When Knox got to the docks, he started for the temple, ignoring the auras glowing at tables with dice and cards and in their rooms above the street.

A fight broke out in an alley just as he passed, knives flashing in the lower moon's pinkish light. He shut his ears to it as best he could, but the slurred shouts and grunts chased him all the way to the little temple where Anwei's clients could bid for her services. Candles glowed red and yellow in the open doorway, and two university students knelt before Yaru's statue inside. A tray of dried herbs burned at her feet, the smell peppery and harsh in Knox's nose.

The little shrine never felt quite far enough from the Temple Cay, where Calsta stood with the rest of the gods and goddesses watching over Chaol. New deities slipped in and out of fashion all the time, so adding Yaru hadn't been difficult, but Knox still tried not to think of the fake goddess as he slipped into the malthouse next to the temple, her statue's hair wild, eyes closed, her hands clenched in fists as if there were nothing in this life she could ever let go of. Anwei had commissioned the sculpture long before she'd ever met Knox, rented the space where bureaucrats went to forget their shipping manifests and trade reports. She'd sent whispers into their ranks inviting patrons to "pray" away their problems, and they'd come.

Knox knew that "finding" for high khonins wasn't all Anwei did as Yaru. He'd seen Yaru's mark down on the Fig and Sand Cays, where gangs held court more freely than Chaol's wardens, but Anwei kept her mouth shut about it, and he didn't feel the need to ask.

Dodging a gaggle of drunken students leaving the malthouse, Knox looked away when they staggered straight toward Yaru's outstretched arms. Some went to Yaru's temple knowing exactly what she was—a confidential way to hire a thief—but there were many who didn't know, and it was they who bothered Knox most. Their hands were clutched just as tightly as the goddess's, people who dreamed only of things they didn't have. After the dreams came wanting; after wanting, a resolution that wanting and deserving were the same; and then, with no more thought than it took to put on a pair of shoes, they went to Yaru. As if she or *any* goddess could make dreams materialize out of thin air.

Giving the malthouse keeper a nod, Knox slid through the clusters of patrons at their round tables to Anwei's rented storage under the malthouse. He dodged the towering crates of herbs and stones and bones that apothecaries seemed to think were necessary but mostly made Knox sneeze. At the back of the room, Knox slid a few boxes back from the wall, then crawled through the tunnel hidden behind them that led to the space under Yaru's temple. Anwei had dug it herself. Probably not with the nameless god's energy, but Knox still didn't like to think about it.

The room beyond was hot and not quite tall enough for him to stand. Knox went to the box of gathered offerings that had been lowered from above by the temple attendant Anwei paid very well for her silence.

There were only a few papers in the box today. One asked for a beautiful wife with small feet, hair past her hips, and hands that could cook and sew at the same time (accompanied by an offering of three fresh palifruits). One asked for a woman to be killed—Knox didn't touch that one or the money attached to it, his skin crawling with memories. Then there was a red-dyed paper with a message written in a student's carefully squared letters asking for passing marks on an upcoming exam—but not a specific class, so there wasn't much they could do to help. (Not that Anwei would have in any case. The student had left only two loose coppers in offering.)

The last piece of paper stuck to the bottom of the box. Knox couldn't quite get his fingernails under it, swearing when the stiff paper cut his fingertip. He was tempted to leave it—there wasn't an offering attached to the paper, and Anwei didn't work for free. After finally managing to peel the paper out of the box, Knox sucked on his bleeding finger as he read the words:

Greenglass Malthouse tomorrow at the third drum. Twenty thousand silver rounds.

Twenty *thousand* silver rounds?

First, Knox bit back a laugh. Was the offer a joke?

Then a sort of hope filled him. His cut of twenty thousand in silver would be enough to bribe his way across the Commonwealth border into Lasei, where Devoted couldn't reach him. He wouldn't have to rely on Anwei, wouldn't have to keep worrying that she'd done something worse than mixing herbs to keep him hidden for so long.

And then, reality. Who would pay twenty thousand in *copper* for a thief? You could buy whatever you wanted with that kind of money. It had to be a ham-handed attempt to unmask Yaru for what she was. The hairs on the back of Knox's neck prickled at the idea of one of Chaol's wardens kneeling before Yaru, trying to see down the drop. Or maybe one of the gang bosses from the lower cays, angry at jobs lost to a goddess. Either could somehow notice the tunnel to the malthouse. Follow Knox home to his room next to Anwei's over the apothecary.

He pocketed the odd note along with the student's coins and snuck back out through the tunnel, the itch of being watched between his shoulder blades. Keeping to the shadowed edges of the malthouse on his way out, Knox grunted as a man in Trib furs knocked into him, scraping his side with the knife handle sticking out over his belt. Ignoring the sting, Knox kept walking, anxious to be gone.

Bad things always came in threes. Roosters in town. A tempting offer that was likely a baited hook. What would it be next?

CHAPTER 3

Tastes like Veil

Lia looked over her shoulder at Chaol's dry market and the running channels beyond before she made herself ride through the drum tower gates. It was hard to see anyway, Lia told herself, trying to squint at the booths and stands through her veil. But even after all these years, she couldn't stop herself from feeling that this city was home.

Vivi nickered impatiently when Lia turned to look one more time, tugging on his reins until she put a gloved hand to his long, dappled neck. He twisted around to lip her skirt, his serrated teeth catching on the fabric. She laughed and gave him a doting scratch, unable to reach the spot he liked best behind the horn jutting from his forehead.

A pair of silenbahks trundled by on the other side of the channel, where the trade road had been built to span Chaol's central islands to the shipping port lodged like a rock in the river mouth. Were creatures so large allowed on normal city streets these days? Lia still remembered her mother taking her up on the river walls to watch the beasts from afar, their armored tails, scaled shoulders, long necks, and even their tusks and trollish faces loaded with tea, spices, and fabrics from faraway provinces.

She could see clear to the Sand Cay walls even through her veil, but no matter how Lia twisted in her saddle, all she could see of the Water Cay was the bridge on the other side of the dry market, the rest of it hidden by the platform stages and hubbub of sellers yelling to passersby. Vivi began pawing the ground, raking the stone with his front hooves as Lia shut her eyes and breathed in deep, greedy for the saltwater scents of her childhood. Her veil sucked up against her nose and mouth, making her gag.

"Are you all right?" Lia tensed at Ewan's voice behind her. "I've never known *you* to sleep in. We agreed to meet half an hour ago." He strode up to stand next to Vivi, giving the side buckles on his leather breastplate an annoyed tug when she didn't answer immediately, as if the effort of having to ask was more important than the answer. "The governor didn't try to keep you, did he?"

"I'm fine. The governor wasn't even home all morning. I promised to write Master Helan when we arrived, and I wanted to make sure the governor's staff posted it before I came here." Lia's teacher had been so quiet when she got her orders to come. Pensive. Unhappy. But he always obeyed, just as she did.

Lia inhaled more carefully, wishing she could pull back the semisheer veil that dripped down her back and over her face, pooling on the saddle's pommel in front of her. Even it couldn't block out the familiar scent of Chaol's fried bread. The smells, the wet drip of the air, the bend of the sunlight itself, made Lia feel as if she were only nine again. Climbing trees in her family's private park, painting horrible portraits of her father, swinging from the knotted rope at their family beach with her mother, tying messy knots in Aria's hair when no one was looking. How old would Aria be now? Lia's brow furrowed as she tried to count.

"Who cares about your stuffy old master? You promised me that you'd look for him this morning. Did you see anything?"

She opened her eyes, lightly tapping Vivi's side with her heel to turn him toward the stables. "Knox isn't here, Ewan."

There would be no ponds, no climbing, and absolutely no dreadful portraits during this visit to Chaol. Not even Lia's annoying little sister could know she was there after so many years, though Aria probably could still use knots in her hair. But Devoted didn't have families, so it would have to fall to the servants to keep Aria in check.

Lia's veil pushed up against her face as Vivi darted toward the groom who waited at the stable door. The sheer fabric tickled her lips as if teasing her. *I'm the only thing that will ever touch you,* it seemed to sigh.

Unless Ewan gets his way.

She pulled Vivi's snapping teeth back from the groom, blanking out the thought before it could take hold. Ewan lurched forward a second too late, as if he didn't trust Lia to control her own mount, his hand groping for her reins and coming down uncomfortably close to her leg. Lia kicked Vivi forward, ignoring the way Ewan smoothed back his cropped hair so the shaved sides of his head would give a clear view of the oath scars that marked him a Devoted. Master Helan didn't like him either—but then the Warlord had sent her away with Ewan, so far away from her teacher. . . .

"Knox *has* to be here." Even Ewan's voice was invasive and coarse as he followed her to the row of stalls specially made for auroshes. "You can't just lose a Devoted—"

"No. *You* shouldn't have been able to." Lia dismounted, grateful for her extra-wide skirts. At least she hadn't been forced to ride sidesaddle after giving up her armor. Vivi nipped at her as she shut the stall's barred door, her auroshe's slitted nostrils flaring as he watched her lock it. Not that it would help him. Opposable thumbs were required to operate the mechanism.

She strode out of the stable and toward the main building, catching hints of the aurafire that littered the streets outside the drum tower gates, their white glow made a dull sort of gray by her spiriter veil.

Those auras would have been out of range for a normal Devoted. Lia was not normal.

The sparks of energy clear to the Sand Cay walls flared in Lia's head. Not just ahead, but behind her and to the left and right, the whole string of islands alight with auras. Lia could look close too, focus on one of those little flares and follow it to the world's end if she liked. Each aura was unique and different, easy to track for a spiriter like her. But no matter how much Ewan complained, ordered, or whined, Knox's familiar, gold-flecked aura was nowhere to be found in Chaol.

"You have to look again." Ewan followed too close behind her, his height and bulk beneath the leather armor disconcerting now that Lia wasn't atop Vivi. She found herself reaching for a sword that she was no longer allowed, like a security blanket that had been taken away.

"I don't *have* to do anything. And looking again wouldn't change the fact that he's not here."

"That's not good enough, Lia Seystone. You came here to help me."

"No, *you* came here to help *me*." Lia turned into the drum tower's entrance, carved with Calsta's brushes, waving for the two Roosters on guard at the doors to stay in place. The smells and familiar streets suddenly felt bone empty. She'd *wanted* to find Knox. Not finding his familiar flecks of gold had felt like missing a stair. No, like falling down an entire flight, and she was still falling. If her Devoted brother's aura wasn't here, then he wasn't anywhere.

Devoted looked like anyone else once they were dead.

It hurt to say out loud, but Lia did it for herself just as much as she did it to make Ewan leave her alone. "He's gone to the Sky Painter."

"That's not possible." Ewan's teeth ground together. "I would have found his body."

Lia gathered a handful of her skirts to keep from tripping over them as she crossed the polished marble floor, pretending she didn't notice when a maid stumbled out of her way. One day Knox had been scheming with her over breakfast about how to sneak bowel softeners into Master Tracy's tea, and then the next he'd been gone, a trail of blood splattered in his wake. Well, that wasn't exactly true. They'd been separated long before that, but she'd still thought about him as if he were behind her, like he had been since they first entered the seclusion. Watching her back.

Why hadn't he told her about his plan to leave? Why had he left at all? Between the two of them, it hadn't been Knox who had dreamed of his life before Calsta.

Ewan crowded in behind Lia as she strode up the stairs, swearing when he tripped over her long skirts. "If we took you to the wall, maybe your view would be clearer—"

"You are wasting my time." She kept her composure, tugging her skirts out from under his boots with a gloved hand, wishing for her armor. Spiriters weren't supposed to wear it. They were above such things. "If I don't read everyone before the Warlord gets here, she could be in danger. The governor sent over the first batch of officials, and the longer they wait, the more difficult they'll be."

Officials. Saying it felt like biting her own tongue. Meeting with these men and women shouldn't matter. By her oaths, it *couldn't*, no matter *who* might be among them. Still, Lia's chest panged.

Calsta did not share her power with Devoted for nothing. It was an exchange. Lia touched her gloved hand to the side of her head through her veil where the oath marks had been burned into her, each leaving shiny bald patches under her hair. The first two oaths granted Devoted aurasight, to go faster, see better, become stronger. The third let them bend their bodies to their will, to push against the laws of nature, like gravity, mass, velocity. But for each power and with each oath, Calsta took something. First, it was strong-tasting and -smelling foods. Alcohol of any kind. Second had been Lia's possessions—she could own simple things but couldn't spend her time trying to get more. Third, Calsta had taken everyone Lia loved and any she might love in the future. Anyone who could possibly divide her loyalty from the goddess. Or the Warlord, who represented her.

Lia put a hand to her chest, her fingers clenched as she tried to dismiss the unhappiness that welled up in her heart at the thought. Here she was in her own home city, her family so close. She hadn't spoken to them since the day she made her third oath.

What office would her father hold now? Was he high enough to be interviewed by Devoted searching for plots against the Warlord?

"You can read all the officials during dinner tonight." Ewan's voice elbowed into her thoughts. He ran a hand along the wall as they climbed, and Lia couldn't help the spark of jealousy at the way he casually touched the stone. The whole world felt like lukewarm soup under her veil and gloves, but the risk of touching someone by accident was too great to do without them. "It's not like either of us will be able to eat. Don't plotting and murder stand out from people's thoughts?" His voice changed a degree, warming. "Making officials wait now just means they'll be all the more . . . intrigued when they meet you later. Anticipation, and all that."

Lia walked a step faster for an answer. She could feel his eyes on her back, and, if only in this isolated moment, she was grateful for her coverings.

She could see what he was thinking when he looked at her.

There were few who could make the three oaths Calsta required of Devoted. No food, no possessions, no relationships. Lia had two scars more than that, though, one of only six in the entire Commonwealth who did. It had been the gloves first. She couldn't *touch* anyone, but she could *track* anyone within a few miles. The veil had come next— her oath said she couldn't look directly at any person, but Calsta let her see into their thoughts. If Lia trained even more, she'd be able to read people's hearts, to the root of what they wanted, who they were. Master Helan had been so worried about letting her come on this trip, especially since Ewan was coming with her. It was odd to feel his worry when she'd never actually seen his face under his veil.

Perhaps as odd as seeing her own face in Ewan's mind—or a version of it, at least. He'd gotten her blue eyes and red hair right, but he'd blanked out her freckles, added pronounced curves where Lia had none, and given her a sultry pout as if he'd forgotten what she looked like in the two years since she'd taken on the veil. Maybe Ewan had never seen her clearly before, only felt her sword at his throat in their years of training together.

"Let's skip the banquet and really let them stew. We could eat together, just the two of us." Ewan stopped, letting her get ahead a few steps. "It would be good for us to talk. *Alone*. Don't you think?"

Lia's refusal choked in her throat when a miniature version of Ewan popped up in his mind and sat down next to the little version of her. The thought-Ewan pushed up against miniature Lia, his hands snaking around her. Then he tore off her veil—

Jerking her attention back to the stairs, Lia took the last three in one jump. Her legs burned to go faster, but she forced herself to walk to the end of the hall, her veil plastering against her face. Did Ewan know how much she could see?

There were strict rules about what it meant to give up anyone who might distract you from the goddess. No physical relationships were allowed at all, no matter how fleeting. *None*.

Except in very specific situations.

How Ewan's aura was still Devoted gold with such images crowding his mind, Lia couldn't fathom. There was a difference between thinking and doing, she supposed, but seeing the thought version of herself in his control with no way to intercede made the space between the two seem very narrow.

She nodded to the Rooster who stood guard at the room set aside for interviews, the shadow in her chest growing darker when Ewan streaked ahead of her, blocking her way into the room.

"Lia, please." He took a step toward her, almost touching her veil where it fell to her toes. He lowered his voice, and his words oozed like cooking fat. "You can't fight me on this. You don't want to, do you? We're supposed to be partners."

Lia gathered her veil around her like the armor she missed, ignoring the way the Rooster's ears perked, the girl's eyes widening as if she wished she had heard the beginning of this disagreement. "It's my choice in the end, Ewan."

"You know it's what the Warlord wants."

She pushed past him into the room. Ewan lurched out of the way, sensible enough not to risk letting any part of him touch her, but she could feel the way it made him seethe. Having to step back, not able to flash his oath scars and expect her to bow to his will as most people would.

But there wasn't much Lia could say. Ewan was right. More Devoted grew ill every day, wasting sickness thinning out their ranks. Lia was the only spiriter under the age of fifty, and the likelihood of finding others wasn't high unless the Warlord could produce more from within the Devoted's own ranks. It still felt like the last thing Calsta could take from her, as if Lia should be promised some sort of ultimate power for having to make such a sacrifice.

Instead, it probably meant more walls around her. More choices revoked, if that were possible. Lia hadn't understood what it meant when Devoted had come to cart her away, hadn't understood everything she'd have to give up—she'd been only eleven.

Lia could barely focus on Ewan, her eyes blurry behind her veil. The Warlord had said Lia could choose the person she was paired with, just the way history books said old Devoted did. But then the Warlord had sent Ewan with her to Chaol, his mind full of the oaths he looked forward to breaking as if she'd already given him leave. "Please. Go."

He smirked. And went.

Lia reached out to the Rooster standing at attention by the door as if the girl could somehow save her, balance her, hold her up like a crutch. Lia Seystone needing a crutch? She'd been the terror of the training yards, the name Basists whispered in the shadows of nightmares. Calsta had taken her family from her, and so Lia had filled the space with forms, swords, and the hunt. Now all she had was a veil.

Lia's fists balled in front of her as the Rooster moved out of reach, just the way Ewan had when she'd almost touched him.

Composing herself, Lia let her hands fall to her sides. "Give me a moment. I'll call for you when I'm ready." She walked into the little office, closed the door behind her, and leaned against it, shutting her eyes. To do her job, she couldn't let herself be muddied by Ewan's thoughts or anyone else's. Not even her own. And so she took a deep breath and let go.

The thought of Knox in a shallow grave. Gone.

The fact that Ewan was a grease fire of an excuse for a human and that the Warlord seemed to be spinning a web that bound them together. Gone.

The familiar smells of Chaol. The faces of her father, her mother. Little Aria with her red curls.

Gone.

This was who she was now. Lia's oaths were made, scarred into her whether or not she'd had a choice in making them. Calsta didn't let her devotees just walk away. Knox was evidence enough of that.

Lia let her eyes drift back open, taking in one last deep breath to calm herself. Once again her veil sucked into her mouth. She tore the thing from her head, threw it on the ground, and stepped on it as she squeezed past the screen the governor had set up in the back corner of the room so she'd be able to interview his officials in comfort.

She sat at the desk hidden behind the screen. Took one last moment to calm her aching insides, because there wasn't room for regret in any Devoted. No room for complaints. Wishes. Dreams. The moment the masters had realized Lia could wear the veil, her future had been set.

This was her life. So Lia found her voice. "Send in the magistrate, please."

CHAPTER 4

Healers and the Naked

When Anwei woke, the sun was already high in the sky, the drummers in their tower rapping out the late-morning hour. She sat up with a groan, her shoulders and arms complaining.

Unbuttoning her high collar to expose her neck and shoulder, Anwei grimaced. The skin over her scapula was a muddy bluish purple where the guard's pole had hit her, the color running under the long, raised scars that marked her from collarbone to shoulder blade. She tenderly touched her neck, wondering if it looked worse. The guard had, after all, tried to strangle her. Hopefully, with her high-necked tunic buttoned, Gulya wouldn't see the bruises.

Flinching, Anwei reached for the pile of letters on her bedside table, correspondence she'd picked up from her lower city drops the night before, but then immediately shoved them back into place. She didn't have to sift through reports to figure out where the snake-tooth man might be. The nothing smell had been at the trade advisor's home last night, and now it was time to trace it back to the murderer who'd left it behind.

"Anwei?" A knock sounded at her door, Knox's voice quiet. "Are you awake yet?"

"Yes," Anwei called. She hurriedly rebuttoned her sleep tunic to hide the scars marking her shoulders, checking her sleeves to make sure the ones that wound down to her wrists were also covered before telling him to come in.

Knox was not so well covered, a sheen of sweat across his bare chest gleaming from doing forms in the apothecary's rear yard. "Gulya thinks I'm trying to steal the chickens again."

Anwei looked down. He had scars enough himself but was proud to bare them whenever possible, it seemed. "You should probably stop doing that."

"I was trying to make her breakfast. The eggs are in the coop."

"When shirtless young men try to make me breakfast, I usually accept." She glanced up, pointing to a new scratch down his side. "Where did you get that, and why do you feel the need to parade like a Tanlir dancer instead of just telling me?"

"Let's not pretend you care about bare chests all of a sudden." He turned away, lines of sweat still running down his back as he started toward his room. Anwei forced her stare back down to her hands, not dignifying that with a response.

"Will you please remind Gulya I'm a paying tenant?" he called. "She was mumbling about calistet."

Anwei sniffed, her nostrils flaring when all she could smell was Knox's sweat threaded through the normal things in her room. Flowery green smells from the herbs filtered up from downstairs, but they were muted from this far away. She couldn't detect the fiery red of calistet, but that didn't mean Gulya hadn't opened the jar. "Everything went smoothly after you left last night?"

"All fine."

"Anything at the temple?"

Knox waved a hand at her before turning into his room. "Just a sad attempt to have you caned. Or maybe hung."

"Wait, *who* wants me dead?" Anwei called, letting herself look up now that Knox was out of sight. He'd come in so late the night before that she'd almost gone out looking for him, something that had not sounded appealing after she'd spent half the night following those ridiculous auroshes to the governor's compound on the Water Cay.

She'd only watched them long enough to see that the Roosters were the last to arrive, not the first. Devoted were already staying at the governor's house.

"I don't know if someone is *really* trying to kill you." Knox backtracked into her line of sight. "There was a job offer—a very well-paying job offer—but only if we meet to discuss it in person."

Anwei frowned and held out her hand. Sighing, Knox came back to her room, pulling one of Yaru's prayer papers from his pocket along with a few coppers. She took the paper, the letters slanted oddly, as if they had been written by someone who did not wish their penmanship to be recognized. "I'll have to ask the attendants who left it. Maybe I'll have to find new ones if there's a possibility someone bribed them into talking."

"What if it's worse than that?" Knox retreated to her doorway. "If the magistrate sent that note, he's probably already watching the temple."

"The magistrate? You think he feels like he overpaid for the figurine?" Anwei kept her carefree tone even as she considered the implications. If the wardens were after Yaru, it might be best to stay away from the temple and jobs altogether for a while.

Of course, there *were* more-dangerous people who could be watching the temple than the stuffy old magistrate. Anwei's stomach lurched at the idea of auroshes pawing the ground outside Yaru's scented hall.

Really, Knox should leave. He should. Anwei knew it in her head, but the idea of his room empty had Anwei reaching out like she had the night before, wanting to take a fistful of his tunic so he couldn't float away and never return.

There were too many people who had left Anwei. Arun, though it hadn't been his fault—dead people don't have much choice in leaving or staying. Her parents, who had had all the choices in the world.

Anwei put a hand to her collar, twisting the button between her fingers, her scars burning with the memories of that day: Her final braid, which Arun was supposed to tie in front of the whole town council. Her twin's blood on the hem of her skirt. A storm gathering in the sky like Calsta herself had seen Arun fall. Arun had known something was wrong and had tried to leave. He'd tried to take Anwei with him, and she hadn't gone.

That couldn't happen to Knox.

But she *couldn't* leave now. Not with the nothing smell wafting from the Water Cay after she'd spent so long searching for it.

Knox's shrug caught her attention as he pointed to the note clutched in her hand. He was still talking about the job offer. "What if the Trib figurine was the first test? To see if Yaru really was what the magistrate suspected. Then he sent wardens to set a trap?"

"The note came after you delivered the figurine?"

"It was there before I got to the temple. I guess that timeline doesn't make sense. Could it be someone from the Fig Cay trying to unmask you?"

Anwei shook her head slowly. She'd been too careful with her contacts in the lower-cay gangs for them to know much more than that the goddess Yaru made poison that left no trace for the magistrate's wardens to find. And that she'd exchange it for information.

Knox licked his lips and looked at the paper in her hand. "It *could* be a real offer."

Twenty thousand in silver. Anwei folded the paper and set it on her bedside table. "Doesn't matter. I don't work with people who want to see my face." She braced herself for what had to come next. "I followed the Roosters last night. I know you don't like talking about Calsta, but we need to make sure you're safe. Devoted are already here."

"In the city?" Knox's head came up. "Are you sure?"

"Yes."

Knox stepped back from the doorway, hands scrubbing through his hair, still short enough to look like he belonged nowhere. Too long to be a servant, too short to be much of anything else. "Did you see who it was? How many?" He swallowed, his Adam's apple bobbing up and down. "Were there any who were . . . covered? Veiled?"

Anwei shrugged. "I didn't see them. I just knew they were there." She could *smell* them inside, the slippery metal tang of Devoted swords, the sweat and leather of their armor.

"Don't go near them, Anwei. It's dangerous for you, too." He rubbed a hand across his scalp again, and Knox's fingers froze in one of the spots she'd seen his Devotion scars before his hair had grown out. Three shiny pockmarks on his skull as if he'd been burned. It bothered Anwei that she didn't know what they meant.

"Sure. Everyone's scared of the Warlord's terror crew, but they leave *most* of us alone. Unfortunately, you're not one of those people, so I need you to tell me whatever you can about them." It felt odd to so casually shed their unspoken agreement as if Anwei were taking off a coat. But she didn't really feel like watching her friend creep around in the shadows until the Devoted found him and then die once they had. "I know there's some weird rule that keeps you from talking about Calsta and whatever magic stuff you do—"

"It isn't called *magic*."

"Fine." Anwei shrugged. "But . . . what are they looking for? We can put them off the scent. Unless they're literally capable of sniffing you out? And I don't mean your *not*-magic. You could do with a bath."

"I can't. . . ." Knox's lips twisted into the serious expression always lurking under his smile. "All I can say is that leaving the seclusions isn't allowed. And I left."

"All right. Any more useless tidbits of information you could share? They're really helping." Anwei held the next suggestion in her mouth, not wanting to let it out even if it was the most logical. Logic and loneliness always seemed to go together in her life. "I don't want you to go, but I don't want to just hope we stay lucky." Her tongue seemed to lock around the words, but she forced herself to spit them out anyway. "Maybe you could get a temporary job with a caravan headed south? By the time you got back—"

Knox shook his head before she could finish. "It's either here or over the border, and I haven't saved enough yet. The only reason I've lasted this long is because I'm with you."

A little warmth bled into her chest at that. "What's that supposed to mean?"

Now he was looking down, one hand sneaking up to his shoulder. To where the sword was supposed to sit against his back. The hairs on Anwei's arms stood up even after he let the hand fall back down to his side. "I don't know."

"So you—the one who turned to stone in the alleyway yesterday— want to just keep your head down?"

"I guess so."

"All right." Anwei wished there were more she could *do*. She was worried if Knox spooked enough, then *he'd* do something, and he wouldn't tell her before he did it. "We'll keep you out of sight until the Devoted leave." Anwei let her eyes drift back down from his face, skipping over his bare chest to focus on the angry red abrasion under his ribs. It smelled clean, like it would heal easily, but it had an odd aftertone, almost like salpowder, an explosive that came from Trib traders. "Are you going to put clothes on, or do you need me to threaten you with medicine before you'll spare me staring at you half-naked?"

"You're the one who's looking." He pushed off the doorframe and headed for his room.

Anwei slid off her bed and stuck her head through the doorway to keep him in sight. "It would heal faster if you would just let me—"

"I'm filling the bathtub, so no surprise witch attacks for at least the next half hour. Otherwise we'll *both* be traumatized." Knox pulled his door shut behind him.

She let her breath out in a huff, sitting back on her bed. *Witch.* As if all the years and knowledge passed down through her family of healers could be distilled into that one ugly joke. Beildans hardly ever left their island, and Chaol was less than a day's ride from the Lasei border, the exact opposite end of the Commonwealth from Beilda. Anwei wouldn't be surprised to find she was the only one within a hundred miles. Two years ago Gulya had jumped at the chance to have Beildan braids sitting behind her apothecary sign, an assurance that in *this* shop, fevers would go down, bones would mend, and the world would be made right. But still, Knox wasn't the first person she'd heard mutter "witch."

Knox was the only one who wouldn't let her fix him when he broke, though, as if medicine were worse somehow than being sick. The winter before, he'd been sick in bed for a week and wouldn't even let her brew him tea, much less examine him. It was only when he was healthy that Knox liked prancing around half-clothed, as if he couldn't see the way it made her look at the floor.

Or perhaps he could see and liked watching her not look. It was hard to tell.

He was right that she'd seen about five thousand bare chests too many in the years since Calsta's storm had chased her away from Beilda in a leaky boat. Men, women, and everything in between. Something about healers made people itchy to shed their clothes, as if Anwei couldn't smell exactly what was wrong the moment they stepped into Gulya's shop. It was as clear as if each one came wrapped in bright silk, a pristine color manifesting for every complaint. Chaol healers looked with their eyes, searched with their hands, listened with their ears, and shirts usually came off before Anwei could stop them.

With Knox, though, it was different. Harder to look away and think only of humors and the way bones and muscles fit together.

Once Anwei had buttoned her gray apothecary tunic up to her throat and donned her favorite green skirts underneath, she went downstairs to see if Gulya really had opened the calistet jar.

The workroom at the bottom of the stairs seemed as if it had switched the floor and the ceiling, herbs hanging in clumps that turned the room into an upside-down field studded with dried flowers. Anwei paused long enough to extract a stalk of linereed, planning to make a poultice for her bruised shoulder and throat.

In the main part of the shop, Gulya stood lecturing a young woman from among the rows of blown-glass globes filled with dried herbs. The herbs seemed almost to sing when Anwei inhaled, as if they were happy to see her awake. Dried linereed, growel, and yuli. Carsom flowers and ground beil. *It's almost like home,* Anwei thought, spoiling the moment of happy.

When Anwei had first left Beilda, healing had been impossible. Eating, drinking, *living,* had been the antithesis of whom she'd become. Her first month in the city across the channel from Beilda was a blur of searching for the murderer's nothing smell. He hadn't just taken her brother. He'd taken every bit of Anwei's twelve years, leaving nothing inside her but a hole. It wasn't until an apothecarist offered Anwei a scrap of bread that she sat still long enough to remember she was hungry. Thirsty. So tired she might as well have been dead.

While Anwei was eating, the apothecarist lamented her empty jar of frelia, because a local gang was hoarding the stimulant and charging ten times what it should cost to street buyers. Anwei sat up, thinking of where she'd last smelled frelia's lemony pepper scent. "I could find that for you," she said.

The old woman smiled. "First eat. I don't want you getting into trouble on my account." But then Anwei did it. Followed the scent to a warehouse, the high windows too small to be guarded. She went in and took enough for the apothecary, and the apothecarist paid her without asking any questions. She tweaked one of Anwei's braids, saying, "You know you could be put in the stocks for impersonating a Beildan."

"I earned these, every one," Anwei whispered.

"Then why don't you stay?" The old woman brought out a crusty roll and a bowl of soup that smelled like safe. "I could use someone like you to help me tell people what to do about the funny bumps on their behinds."

Anwei's stomach turned at that safe smell. The idea of mending funny bumps and rashes and deep humors and holes inside people jolted all the holes inside Anwei loose: Memories of Arun pushing her off the bench at their mixing table and laughing when she kicked the bench out from under him so he landed on the floor next to her. Of lying out under the stars talking about when they would open their own shop, but it would have salpowder explosives and frosted cupcakes. The memory of the apothecary so empty and cold because what had been left of Arun wasn't a person anymore, it was less than a thing. It was a hole in the air, a *nothing* where so much had been before. Anwei's heart, mind, and soul had been braided together with her twin's, as if they were only one person, so when the snake-tooth man had ripped Arun apart, he'd ripped Anwei in two as well.

Then came the memories of Anwei's mother behind the counter, a knife hidden in her skirt and thunder rumbling overhead.

Sitting at that apothecary's counter, the smell of frelia peppery in her nose and soup in her stomach, Anwei shook her head. "I can't work here."

Nodding, the woman let Anwei sit quiet for a moment before smiling. "It's part of who you are, isn't it? It doesn't have to be my shop or my counter. But if you earned those braids, then you're a healer."

Shaking her head again, Anwei ate the last of her bread. She didn't know what she was anymore, but she was fairly certain there wasn't room to be more than a hunter, a finder, an avenger. "Maybe I could find more herbs for you?"

That, the woman took with a smile.

So that was what Anwei had done. Find things. There were people all over who loved a finder once Anwei learned where to look. Tracking down things, people who had become lost. Sometimes helping people to lose the things they didn't want anymore. Every job took her to a new part of the city, then new parts of the Commonwealth, to look for the man who had ruined her life. The snake-tooth man. But she'd always gotten her hair rebraided like clockwork, as if giving up her braids would be too much.

Anwei breathed in deep one more time, trying to love the smell of herbs despite the memories. Chaol was the first place she'd decided to work in an apothecary, after Gulya had made her laugh and then offered her enough money to buy her way past most guards clear to the Ink Cay. But it wasn't the first place she'd healed—that old apothecarist had been right. All the memories of Arun's hands grinding herbs next to hers never did dull. Anwei's nose had always found the funny bumps even when she tried to ignore them. They were always there, calling to her. Her parents hadn't been able to take that away from her, though they'd tried.

Anwei rubbed her scarred shoulder again, checking her collar to make sure it was buttoned tight. Then she curled her fingers through her braids, newly oiled and retied the week before. She'd earned them.

"Don't take it more than twice a day or you'll end up with sores under your tongue," Gulya was calling after the customer she'd been talking to. The woman was young, two knots jauntily placed in the twist of hair lining her face, marking her second khonin. She glanced over her shoulder at Anwei before fleeing the shop, her green eyes familiar.

Anwei blinked with surprise. It was Noa, a high khonin contact she hadn't expected to see for weeks at least. The girl paused in the window, pointing toward the dock outside the apothecary before scampering away to avoid Gulya seeing her. Anwei turned toward the glass globes, hiding a smile at the prospect of talking to the second khonin.

She was always good for a laugh, and something interesting must have happened to bring her all the way down to the Coil.

"And make sure you give an offering to Freia." Gulya had gone to the door to call after Noa, her voice a shade terser than Anwei thought the old woman realized. "Or she'll take it all back!"

"You know most people don't like being commanded to get better, don't you, Gulya?" Anwei grinned at the old woman, picking up one of the oiled bags they used to transport remedies. A good chat with Noa sounded nice, but Anwei had things to do today up at the trade advisor's compound, so whatever gossip she'd brought would have to be quick.

"Sick people are too busy dying for me to muddle through niceties." Gulya raised an eyebrow as Anwei opened one of the glass globes to extract a silvery-white root. "Where are you taking that?"

"To a man with a deteriorating lower humor. He isn't seeking proper care, and I'm going to help if I can." Anwei added the root to her bag, choosing her words carefully. Gulya didn't know why Anwei had agreed to work only a few days a week in the apothecary and spent the rest of her time ranging through the city like a hungry parchwolf, and she didn't want to supply any extra clues.

"That root won't combat stomach issues. You need—"

"He was seeing an aukincer, Gulya." Anwei's smile melted off her face as she glanced toward the old apothecarist, Gulya's mouth open to argue before Anwei could even finish the sentence. "No, I don't want to fight about it. So long as none of that poison is in this shop . . ."

"I've seen positive results, Anwei. There are enough who don't understand your methods who'd find it easy to call *you* a dirt witch." Gulya's words were soft, but still they jolted through Anwei. *Witch.*

The old healer unfolded her sleeves, which she'd tucked back in order to get whatever nonsense herbs Noa had asked for. The noble couldn't have requested her normal order from Gulya. "Sometimes you have to experiment a little. There could be benefits to—"

"No. There couldn't. They *want* people to call them dirt witches because that's what they're pretending to be. Using five-hundred-year-old remedies without the magic that made them work?" Anwei finished adding herbs to her pouch. She buttoned it closed, then crushed it between her fingers, the leaves and dried blooms inside making a satisfying crackle as she ground them together. "That's poison. Also, could you please stop harassing Knox?"

"That boy isn't right, and you know it." Gulya went to the large wooden mortar, opening a packet she'd made of her own, and dumped the contents inside.

Anwei pressed her lips together, walking to one of the two wide windows that flanked the heavy front door, blue swirls of paint marking it as an apothecary. There was nothing *wrong* with Knox. Knox was just difficult to explain. "He does his fair share of work here and—"

"And keeps a *sword* under his bed. Only two places he could have gotten that. Devoted don't need a room over a crumbling apothecary, and apothecaries don't need thieves among their tenants."

It was true. In the Commonwealth, from the northern border with Trib land to the Southern Sea, only Devoted were allowed to carry swords, but there was something very different about Knox's weapon. There was little chance he'd stolen it from his seclusion. The blade had been the reason Anwei had stopped that day in the street. It had smelled like *him*—Arun's murderer, the man who changed faces and had a snake carved into his tooth. It was initially why she'd let him follow her onto jobs, carefully concealing who she was in the hopes that he'd give something up.

Anwei squeezed the packet of herbs a little too vigorously, and the smells from inside blended into a perfect answer to the sickly yellow color of the trade advisor's illness. "I'll only be gone for an hour or so. Will you please refrain from burning any of Knox's things or attempting to give him diarrhea before I get back?"

Gulya's brows drew together as she dug into the wooden bowl

with her pestle, her hesitation evidence enough that at least one of those things had been on the menu for the day. "I need you to go down to the Fig Cay this afternoon, Anwei. There's something worrisome brewing down there—a rash that's putting people in bed. Don't want it to spread. Crowteeth boss asked me special, and we both know you'll figure it out first."

Anwei paused. "What kind of rash?"

"Cross-humor, blotchy bruising. First case is coughing up blood—almost sounds like gamtooth poisoning, though I think I would have heard if we suddenly had subtropical spiders infesting Chaol. I haven't heard tell of random spurts of the truth landing people with the magistrate yet, though I suppose there's still time." Gulya cackled. Gamtooth poisoning, among many things, caused truths to spill out of people before lies could take hold. "You'll find the sick down by Fig's afternoon market. South side, by the waterway. Ask for a man called Jecks."

"I'll go as soon as I deliver this." Anwei tucked the packet into her medicine bag, her thoughts circling the bottle of gamtooth venom she'd extracted for a Fig Cay customer only the month before. The spiders had come home with her on her last trip south, kept safe in a jar under the herb room's floorboards, where Gulya would never know to look.

Mostly, Anwei didn't mind when the Crowteeth or the Blackhearts or any of the gangs who knocked things over in the lower cays used her poisons to clog up one another's humors, but if her poison had accidentally been dumped into one of the dirty waterways that webbed through the Sand and Fig Cays . . . Anwei shrugged off the itch of annoyance at whoever had been so careless. She never sold enough to do too much damage, but it wouldn't be the first time she'd provided the antidote to her own poison.

She walked out the door, something inside her relaxing when she found Noa lounging by Anwei's little canoe where it was bobbing at the apothecary dock. "Sky Painter protect you." Noa grinned, a few too many teeth showing.

"And may she send her storms far from us." Anwei finished the greeting in Elantin, Noa's native language from the south. The high khonin had dark green eyes Anwei had never seen outside the southern provinces, and her dark hair and amber skin made her look like a jewel flashing in the sun. "I'm so glad to see you—everything's been so . . ." Anwei shrugged through the rest of the sentence and the list of things she could never say out loud.

"I know what you mean." Noa's smile twisted. "Where are you headed?"

"I've got business to get to in the Water Cay." Anwei started toward her canoe. "Come with me! I thought I'd have to wait until you ran out of galrot."

"Oh good, you can take me home. I *have* run out of galrot. Can you imagine what that old woman would have said if I'd asked for some?" Noa sighed. "I have something terrible to tell you."

"You're *out*? How many people did you put to sleep, Noa?" Anwei stifled a laugh as she stepped into the boat. Noa had first come to her looking for herbs to sleep. Anwei had seen through her too-casual request in a second and had snatched Noa up as a contact on the Water Cay in exchange for the plants she wanted. It had started strictly as business, but Noa was so full of wicked smiles and gossip and ruining people's days that it had been hard not to look forward to her visits. Even Anwei could do with a laugh now and then. Noa stepped into the front of the boat, keeping her balance as it bobbed under her. "My father is trying to destroy my very existence as usual. I had to put him to sleep every night last week, or I wouldn't have been able to push over that statue at the university with Bear. His father was so angry—I think he might have paid for it. *And* there's a ball in a few days that *requires* a few doses of galrot, or I might actually shrivel up into nothing."

"The governor built a statue of his own son at a university he can't seem to graduate from? And Bear didn't even like it?" Anwei snorted, dipping her paddle into the channel's murky water to push them away from the dock. "So, what's the bad news, and which high khonin ball are we destroying?"

"Oh, the governor's." Noa leaned back in the boat, putting her hands behind her head. "Bear proposed, so I have to get rid of him before my father finds out and makes me marry him."

CHAPTER 5

A World Made of Doors

Knox waited until he heard Gulya's naturally ire-filled tones directed at Anwei downstairs before he shut off the water pipe, leaving the half-filled tub untouched. He crept out of the washroom, still stinking of sweat and dirt from his forms that morning. It was a little embarrassing to sneak behind his partner's back, but Anwei wasn't going to follow up on the mysterious bid from the temple, and Knox couldn't afford to ignore it. He went to Anwei's room and picked up the little folded prayer to Yaru. *Twenty thousand in silver.*

He stuck it into his pocket and turned toward his room. Why did Devoted have to show up in Chaol today? The thought was a black hole of panic inside him, but the promise of so much money—enough he could leave and never see the Warlord's insignia again—was one he couldn't put out of his mind.

What if Lia had been sent to track him, like those karavte hunts high khonins seemed to enjoy so much? He couldn't imagine his best friend—his chosen sister, the only family he had remaining—howling like a parchwolf to the Devoted over his scent. But Lia was still in the seclusion and had no choice *but* to sing when the Warlord pointed at her, even if she hated every note.

The cold female presence that lived at the back of his head—the one that Calsta wanted him to ignore—shifted, as if she could be restless and pacing in her state of . . . nothing. Willow was her name—at least, he still called her that. He wasn't sure how she thought of herself since being trapped inside his head instead of going to Calsta as she should have.

Lia wasn't the only sister he'd betrayed.

Unlike Willow, Lia was still *alive*. Still trapped under her veil instead of outside under the sky as he knew she would have preferred. But she was still breathing, able to feel the warmth of the sun through her veil. Knox had thought through his escape from the seclusion a million and a half times, and he'd always come to the same conclusion despite the thought of Lia at the seclusion alone. His going missing had merited an entire search party of Devoted. Lia's disappearing would have turned out an entire seclusion with the Warlord herself at their helm. Asking her to come wouldn't have been fair anyway—to drag the one person who meant something to him into a life on the run. Knox wished it weren't so, but he knew Lia could take care of herself.

Willow was another matter. When Knox had left her, she'd lost her hands, her voice, her *life*. If Knox didn't fix it, no one would.

Knox went back to his room and pulled on a shirt, grimacing as the cloth stuck to his still-sweaty back. Anwei's laugh rang out from below, Gulya's old-woman cackle joining in. He frowned, splashing some water across his face from the basin on his washstand. Anwei always knew what to say.

Every time he tried to do something nice for Gulya, it made things *worse* between them. Anwei could joke and laugh and quietly close the calistet jar, but Knox only knew how to address the issue directly. Look Gulya in the eyes and say, *"I'm nice!"*

It hadn't worked yet. If Gulya had her way, she'd probably have him cut open like in a backwater purging ceremony, hoping to catch a glimpse of whatever she thought was wrong inside him.

Knox had spent months watching the way Anwei gathered people around her, collecting them just the way she'd collected him. Her world was made up of doors in all shapes and sizes, the people on the other side smiling the moment she stepped through. No matter how hard he tried, Knox's world remained a straight path. It started where he was standing, ended where he wanted to go, and the only time anyone else figured into it was when they stood directly in front of him.

Anwei's confidence always seemed to end with her sleeves, though. Despite the awful wet summer heat in Chaol, Knox had never glimpsed an inch of skin south of Anwei's chin except for her hands.

Not that he *wanted* to see more than that.

Knox reached up to touch the scars marking the side of his head, the oaths he'd made heavy in his mind. It wasn't just Anwei he'd learned to block out, though she probably would have been pretty enough if he allowed himself to look.

That was a lie. He knew she was pretty. Beautiful even, and he wasn't the only one who noticed. Since the first day he'd been well enough to make it down the stairs, Knox had seen the steady stream of young men who stumbled into the apothecary with very large grins and very small complaints, all asking for Anwei. But Knox couldn't be one of them. There was much more than pride for him to lose in looking at *any* girl that way.

Grabbing his shoes from their rug by his door, Knox sat down to buckle them before wrapping a scarf over his face. He slipped his favorite knife into his pocket, then pushed open the window, listening hard when the chatter downstairs went quiet. Anwei would probably take the boat, so he'd have to use skybridges and tunnels all the way to the ferry to get him to the Sand Cay. Anwei didn't want him to check out the mysterious job, but if the magistrate was sending wardens their way, being ready for it seemed like a better idea than ducking when the cudgels started swinging. If it was somehow Devoted who had left the note, Knox wanted to know *now*, not when they came through the windows and the roof, swords drawn. And if it turned out to be a real job?

Knox swung a leg over the window frame, sea air in his lungs.

Willow's freezing whisper chittered in his head. *You're not leaving me here alone again, are you?*

He stopped and looked back toward the dark space under his bed, Calsta's warnings— *Anwei's* warnings—hanging over him like lead.

You need me. Her voice was stronger this time, the shadows under his raised mattress breathing.

Where was *Calsta* when he needed her? Probably sleeping in, if that's what goddesses did. Knox swallowed hard and turned back to the window, Willow's voice a comforting buzz in his head. It made his chest relax, his heart beat a little slower, the threat of Devoted and the draw of the mysterious job fade. His sister's voice had always soothed him when he was growing up. Then the Devoted had come. . . .

Hold me, Knox. We could fix all of this. Your crabby landlord. The Devoted. Your friend's broken aura. Suddenly Knox was kneeling next to his bed, not remembering the space of time between leaving the window and bending down to peer at the huddled blanket lurking in the shadows.

None of them would matter much if you let me have them.

"Hello?" Gulya's voice wrenched Knox back to himself, the stairs creaking under her feet. "Silly little boy, are you up here still? I need your disproportionately long arms to get something stuck in the chimney."

The sword was in his hands, the heavy blanket wrapped around the sheath bulky and awkward.

Wait, in his *hands*? Knox shoved the sword away and kicked the bundle back under the bed. Wrapping his arms around his head, he crouched there on the floor, willing his heart to begin beating again.

Willow's voice crooned in his head. *Knox, please?*

Going for the window, Knox fled the voice just as much as Gulya's knuckles rapping against his door. He jumped to the ground, then slipped through Gulya's courtyard gates. Knox wouldn't let himself run, but his hands didn't stop shaking until he was two canals away, the trade road in sight.

It wasn't just Anwei who had a problem with banned magic.

The Greenglass Malthouse was near the trade gate, where the trade road made a bridge to the mainland, if Knox wasn't mistaken. The name sounded like the Sand Cay, and the color and inclusion of "glass" pointed toward a rough neighborhood near the old city wall built along the island banks. When he finally got to the ferry dock, Knox had to concentrate, putting Willow and the sword out of his mind.

She wasn't really his sister. Not anymore. Willow's croon at the back of his head sounded like skeletons and carcasses and murder, not the girl who had stayed up late telling him boring stories about high khonin ladies falling in love with wandering *printha . . . priantia . . .* holy men who wished Calsta had chosen them. That was before the day Devoted had come to take the two of them away. Willow had started seeing auras almost a year before Knox (they'd terrified her, even after their parents had managed to figure out what was going on and explain it). She was two years older and much more interested in lace and the cobbler's son than becoming a sword protecting the Commonwealth for the Warlord, but when a passing Devoted noticed her and Knox glowing with gold—Willow two whole years past time to enter the seclusions—there wasn't much room to argue.

The Warlord sent a whole group of Devoted to collect them, giving Knox and Willow time to say their goodbyes while the soldiers put on a demonstration for the little eastern town. Their parents wanted them to stay home for one last night together, but Willow knew Knox wanted to go watch the demonstration, so she distracted their parents while he snuck out the window. He sat there on a stone wall, watching the Devoted flip and walk up walls and fight so smoothly it looked as if they were dancing—maybe that would be some consolation to Willow!—thinking how lucky he'd been to have a passing Devoted catch sight of his blossoming aura.

Watching that night, Knox was filled with a fire that only grew as he ran home to tell Willow. But when he came to their lane, the door was hanging open, candlelight leaking out into the darkness like blood from inside. There were two lumps in the entry hall, Mother and Father sprawled on the floor in impossible shapes, completely unmarked, their eyes dull.

Everything turned a bit fuzzy after that. "Willow!" he called into the cold, empty house, running past his parents without quite being able to look at them, pretending that maybe he didn't understand why their auras had disappeared. Willow was on the second floor, her eyelashes still fluttering, a gaping wound in her chest. And the sword—that awful *sword*.

It was bubbling, blackened, *melting* into the floor at her feet. Knox grabbed the hilt to pull the awful thing away from his sister, and it suddenly snapped back into a solid sword shape. Willow convulsed forward when he touched it, then went limp.

And then, her voice. It started in his head.

Knox? she cried. *Knox, I'm scared. A man came and he hurt me. His face was like a snake. Where are Mother and Father?*

Knox tried to drop the sword, but it stuck to his hand like flesh against frozen metal. His heart began to pound, his body started to shake. . . .

And then a new voice. One that *burned*, lighting him up from the inside like the sun, filling him to the brim. *Put it down,* it commanded.

"I can't!" His voice echoed in the empty air, a pained scream of panic because he couldn't, and his heart was flapping, fluttering. Stopping, as if whatever made him *him* was going to be sucked into the sword right alongside Willow.

Don't put me down, Knox. Please, help me. I'm trapped, Willow cried.

Knox. Listen. Concentrate. Let it go. That new voice put space between him and the icy cold of his sister's panic, and the sword dropped to the floor with a clatter. *Find something to wrap it in. It's too dangerous to leave here,* the voice said next, though it didn't say why, nor how . . . nor what Knox should do with his poor sister's body, or his crumpled parents downstairs. So he hid the sword in a blanket, stuffed it inside the bag his mother had packed for him, and then did exactly as the burning voice commanded next: he went to the Devoted.

It wasn't until Knox arrived at the seclusion that the burning voice made sense. He'd been too afraid to question it at first, and then, when they got to the seclusion gates, he knew.

A statue of Calsta was standing there in her broken helmet, her long sword held up over her head, the very goddess his parents had prayed to. The voice didn't speak as he passed the statue, just warmed him inside as he looked at it, as if Calsta was identifying herself.

The thought choked inside him even as it made him sit up a little straighter. Calsta, the goddess herself, had seen fit to speak to him directly. To *save* him from whatever Willow had become.

Not that Willow ever stopped reaching for him. At first she whispered to him during lessons, over meals, when he was trying to sleep in his hard bed in a room full of boys and girls just like him. *Where am I? Please hold me.* And then when he didn't respond, she'd snarl and tell him to use the weapon for much worse things. It grew harder to ignore her every time she spoke, but it wasn't until Knox's body began to obey his sister's voice against his own will that Calsta's voice appeared again, sliding between Knox and his sister's ghost like a shield. That was just about the only time he could count on the goddess: when things were about to break.

Looking up at the sky now, Knox squinted at the sun, flaring like the one behind Calsta's golden helmet. When the ferry came in, he flipped a coin to the captain and took a seat by the rail, testing the walls inside his head that Calsta had taught him to build against Willow. She'd gotten stronger over the years, and it was becoming harder to listen to the goddess rather than the ghost.

When the boat docked at the Sand Cay, Knox pushed out onto the walkway, the other passengers flooding out behind him into the twisting streets and rickety dwellings piled high on top of one another. Three auras from the boat followed Knox toward the trade road. He kept them at the back of his mind, watching out of habit to see if they were going in the same direction or following *him*. Devoted couldn't afford to ignore such things, and thieves couldn't either.

The walkways around the trade road were clogged with beasts and wagons and shouting traders as they always were, though not so bad as the road itself. Knox followed alongside it as best he could, sellers hawking bits of food, phony silver, and talismans to ward off shape-shifters, thrusting their wares toward him with more violence than he could have done with his sword. He was pretending to admire a tray of still-twitching fish when a trio of wardens swept toward him. Flurries of movement down the walkway marked sellers who didn't have proper licenses as they scooped up their wares and disappeared into the alleyways. Auras bobbed around him like fish in the river waves.

They are *beautiful, aren't they?* Calsta's voice. *Now,* she chimed in. *You need to watch it, by the way. Don't let Willow catch your attention. Remember your training. Remember* me.

So beautiful, Knox wanted to snark back. *Almost as beautiful as being alone inside my own head.* How many more years of this would he have to endure? It had been years already, and Knox was no closer to freeing his sister's soul from the sword. Calsta had promised she would help him do it, so long as he kept his oaths.

But just like that terrible night when she'd first spoken to him, Calsta hadn't told him how. Or why. When. Anything useful, really.

Knox knew from all their years together that he could trust the goddess with . . . everything. It *was* everything he was trusting her with. And, somehow, she was trusting him when she hadn't trusted anyone for half a millennium.

Or maybe it was the thing in the sword that had made Calsta wake from her sleep and speak to him.

I'm not a thing. Willow's voice came like an echo from far away. Knox stumbled, accidentally splashing through something that was definitely not water. He clutched a hand to his head at the prickling cold the voice brought, pretending to adjust his scarf when a passing woman pulled her child away from him, her eyes wide.

That was twice Willow had spoken to him from far away in the last two days. And she'd almost made him take the sword from its wrappings back at the apothecary. Had something changed? Knox forced himself to walk, his sensitive ears eating up the trade road's booming silenbahk bugles, clattering horse hooves, and wagon wheels on stone. Not that they could drown out a voice coming from inside his head.

Can't worry about this now. He had to stay alive, and that meant earning enough money to bribe his way over the border into Lasei, which meant finding out if the Greenglass job was real. He turned into the muggy glass tunnel that went down into the water, leading to the other side of the canal. It was close quarters, the tube clogged with merchants dragging their wares and farmers leading livestock. Knox slowed at the tunnel's exit, near the crumbling city wall—a relic of less peaceful times, when shapeshifters had carved the whole of the Commonwealth into little kingdoms that did not get along. "Green" was for the Green Waterway—one of the smaller ones dug across the island itself. "Glass" would be . . .

The three auras he'd been lazily keeping track of were meandering through the tunnel behind him. Great.

Knox slipped sideways through the milling crowd and darted into a side alley that wound between the ramshackle buildings. It was in moments of unexpected trouble that he was most vulnerable—Calsta's power was right there within reach, and after so many years of training with the Devoted, reaching for it was a reflex. A part of him. But Knox couldn't touch it, not unless he wanted to draw Devoted to him like flies.

The three auras started faster, cutting through the crowd to follow. Knox broke into a run, following a lane that twisted this way and that, blocking his pursuers' line of sight. Visions of fancy braids, of swords and Roosters and auroshe teeth, danced through Knox's head as he threw himself into an alleyway piled with trash. He scaled the craggy brick wall and pulled himself onto a windowsill wide enough to shield him from the lane.

This was who he was now. Someone who hid.

The three auras turned the corner and slowed. They were white, untouched by Calsta, so Knox risked peeking over the edge of his perch. Three men walked past the alleyway's mouth, their rough leathers, uneven ponytails, and spurs enough to tell him they were Trib horsemen. He caught a glint of silver at the leader's neck before they passed out of sight.

Trib? Knox waited a few minutes before climbing back down, keeping his aurasight open to make sure they didn't double back. He hopped to the ground, his feet squishing when he landed, the smell of rotting fish and greens filling his nose. The Commonwealth's northern border was shared between Lasei and Trib land—the Lasei enforced their part of the border, but Trib clans didn't so much, mostly staying on their own side, so long as Commonwealth people didn't start building on their land. Even traders who wanted the explosive powder Trib extracted from firekeys that roamed their high mountains had to go to the clans to get it.

What could three Trib want with him?

Knox watched the auras turn the next corner, then fade out of sight on the next street over, before he stepped out of the alley and headed in the opposite direction. Stopping in front of a boy selling silk ribbons, he asked, "Do you know the Greenglass Malthouse?" Wandering wasn't a good idea if someone was after him. The prickly auroshe smell from the night before still sat in Knox's nose.

"What's it worth to you?" The boy's front two teeth were crooked, making him lisp.

"I'll buy the purple one." Knox pointed to a length of silky purple ribbon, flowers embroidered down the middle. Maybe Anwei could use it.

"That'll set you back half a copper round. . . ." Knox scoffed, and the boy smiled. "Okay, fine. Five coppers."

"How about one?" Knox pulled a copper from his pocket and tossed it to him. "Which way?"

The boy smiled and handed over the ribbon. "West side of the gate. Third level up on the wall."

"Thanks." Knox shoved the ribbon into his pocket and started toward the gate.

"It'll look nice with your hair!" the boy called after him. "Maybe after it grows, anyway."

Knox pulled his scarf a little higher over his nose as he walked. At the far side of the market, he found the rows of precariously balanced shops that had been built out over the water to lean against the old wall, a green glass door on the third level, about thirty strides from the trade gate.

Instead of taking the series of ladders and platforms that led up to the shops, Knox strolled past to climb the next set of stone steps that led to the top of the wall. There, Knox walked until he was nearly above the Greenglass Malthouse, then leaned against the parapet, giving the expanse of city a good country stare. There was a girl a few paces down in a university tunic with an easel and a half-painted canvas in front of her. "Nice day!" she said, looking at him expectantly.

"Yeah. Sunny." He licked his lips when she kept looking at him expectantly, as if he hadn't fulfilled some social contract. "Um . . . I like your painting? The colors are nice." From what he could see, she'd made the drum tower an uncomfortably bright shade of pink.

"Thanks. You know, when the light hits that tower, it just . . ." Her mouth stayed open, as if she couldn't find the words. Knox backed away a step, and then another, not sure how he'd gone from standing there, minding his own business, to having a whole conversation.

"I've got to . . . go. Over here." He ignored the odd look she gave him. That was one thing he missed about baring his Devoted scars: people before had left him alone.

There were hours to go before the meeting, but whoever had sent the note would be watching too. With some luck, Knox would see them first. Not that Knox needed luck. He'd spent enough time hunting people to know how it was done. He stared down at the malthouse's dirty roof, watching the people clustered below until—

Until—

Willow suddenly unfolded in a vengeful war of hunger and thirst. Knox convulsed forward, a hand to his head, an *attack* like she'd never tried before. *Finally!* she crowed. *Enough to make me alive again! Finally someone feeds me—*

I've never *fed you. I don't even know what you eat.* He fought her back, his breaths coming fast, sweat dripping in streams down his temples, and his vision blurring. *Why is this happening now? What has changed? Where* are *you, Calsta?* It came out as a snarl inside his head. Willow liked it, nodding in approval. *Yes, where is your goddess, Knox?*

He fought, forcing her back behind the walls in his mind, but it was like trying to pour water into cupped hands, bits and pieces of her streaming through cracks he hadn't known were there. By the time Knox had wrestled Willow out of his thoughts, he was out of breath, his fingers sore from pressing against the stone parapet.

"Are you all right?" The artist was looking at him again, a drop of pink paint dripping from the end of her brush onto her smock.

"I'm . . ." Before Knox could brush her off, he saw them. Three familiar auras at the edge of his range. One stood on the stairs just behind Knox, the other two down the wall less than fifty paces away. Three Trib horsemen.

CHAPTER 6

Gold in the Air

ia drank a sip of her watery tea, sighing in boredom as the second-to-last interview let the door swing shut behind him. Not a single person in this city would so much as frown at the Warlord's carriage as it passed, much less plot against her. The Warlord had been so certain *something* was going on in Chaol, but based on the readings Lia had done from behind her screen, the most likely revolt would be directly related to the subpar refreshments in the waiting area outside her interview room.

Pushing a long red curl out of her eyes, Lia called, "Next please." She fingered the veil where it lay discarded on the desk beside her, ready to be finished with this whole ordeal.

Footsteps entered the room, a man's aura blazing into Lia's mind. His thoughts were focused on the lukewarm tea in his cup and a fond glimmer for a black horse with a star on its forehead. Before Lia could dig deeper than the fleeting images at the surface of the official's mind, a child ran through his thoughts.

She had red hair. Skinned knees. Freckles that Lia could have mapped out herself because it was her own face she was staring at, but young. Lia's gloved hand shook as she carefully replaced her teacup in its saucer, looking down at her notes. No names were given as part of the list of men and women she had to read, only titles. *Valas*. Second only to the governor.

Lia's family had done well in her absence.

Her father's aura had been the first Lia noticed back when she was only six. Startled questions to her nurse about the ghost hugging Daddy's head had gotten Master Helan to come from the Rentara seclusion to test her. The Warlord didn't take Devoted until they were eleven at the earliest, but those five years meant to be a gift to Lia and her family had felt like counting down to her own death, every moment of Lia's childhood seasoned with dread for the man in the veil who would take her away. Her father had cried as he'd hugged her goodbye.

He was remembering that now too, the sight of her riding away with Master Helan, like his life was an embroidered tapestry and the Devoted had just taken one of the threads and pulled, leaving a gaping hole.

"Am I supposed to . . . do something?" His voice was exactly the same as it ever had been, cocoa from the far south.

Just sit still. Let your mind go blank. That was what Lia was supposed to say, but the words were lodged tight in her throat. *I'm right here. I can see you missing me. It couldn't be half so much as I miss you.* But those were the *wrong* words, so Lia gripped the table, forcing herself to focus. *Keep the Warlord safe. Read all the officials' auras. All the servants, the gardeners, anyone who will have access . . .*

"I don't mean to be rude." He was talking again. "I know Devoted can't give out much information, but my daughter went into your seclusion about six years ago. Could you tell me if she's doing well? She was our world . . . and we're so proud," he hurried to add. "If you had news of her, perhaps it would help me to miss her a little less."

Lia tried to breathe, but her chest was knotted tight. One little sob escaped her throat, and the valas's thoughts seemed to go cloudy,

Lia's own emotions too loud for her to read what she needed from her father's aura.

His chair creaked as he shifted in his seat. *"Lia?"*

"You can go." She choked it out, knowing any more would result in consequences.

He sat for a moment longer, her emotions still a swirl of thunderheads obscuring her sight into his aura. But that was worse because she *wanted* to see what he was thinking. To see herself as a little child bursting with light the way he remembered her.

Devoted were supposed to be free from petty society, political marriages, the *world*. But Lia couldn't help feeling the world had been stolen from her instead. That every useless laugh, every moment of wasted time she'd observed from behind her veil, was precious and beautiful. She savored what she'd seen in her father's thoughts, the love that surrounded her in his memory.

The only thing that surrounded her now was a screen.

"It is you, isn't it?" He whispered it. "Are you all right? Are they treating you well? We love you so much, Little Spot."

Her throat clenched. Little Spot. She'd forgotten he used to call her that. "You have to go."

The floor creaked when he stood, but he didn't move toward the door immediately. It was a waiting silence, a drowning one, one she wanted to break with her voice or his.

Then the door opened. Shut. And she was alone.

Lia pulled off her gloves and put her bare hands to her face. Her cheeks were warm and wet, tears like rain on her fingertips. Ewan's aura approached the door outside, so she hurriedly scrubbed them dry and grabbed her discarded veil.

The door opened, Ewan already talking before he was in the room. "Are you going to come out? That's the last one for . . ." He pushed the screen aside without asking, trailing off when he found her frantically pinning the veil back into place. "Oh, sorry."

She could see from his thoughts that he was not sorry.

Picking up her gloves, Lia pushed aside her notes and stood, edging around him to get through the doorway. This time he didn't move to make way for her, her skirts and veil catching on the buckles lining his cuirass as she passed.

Nodding to the Rooster standing guard outside, Lia nearly ran to the balcony door. *I gave you my life, Calsta*. The words anchored her to the earth as she pushed through the door to the open air. *I gave you everything the world could offer me*.

She crashed into the balcony's stone railing, her hands groping for something to hold on to, the city spread out below her, bristling on with life as if hers weren't about to come undone. She'd given everything, but Calsta had given her nothing but emptiness in return. It had been six years since she'd seen her mother's smile. Two since the veil had been settled on her head, turning her into an object of value but kept in a box so she stayed pristine. Gloves were a precaution against touching another human, one Master Helan had insisted upon, and her naked hands felt rebellious. Air gusted up from below to steal inside her coverings as she clutched at the railing, the smooth stone warm against her fingers.

One year since Knox had left. Her brother in the seclusion hadn't even said goodbye before he'd left her so horribly alone.

Sounds filtered up from outside the drum tower compound, the dry market's air crammed tight with laughter, children playing and singing. Friends joking with one another over a fruit stand, a young woman gazing up at a young man in a university uniform, her mind so full of him that Lia couldn't find anything else in her thoughts. In the distance, the city wall stood like the edge of a teacup, and all the deliciousness she couldn't have was trapped inside its bowl so far below her.

Ewan stepped out onto the balcony behind her, his thoughts a salivating mess. The powerful flare of gold around him seemed to be siphoned away a little with every step he took toward her, as if he'd contracted wasting sickness. It probably wouldn't go entirely unless he touched her.

Until he touched her.

Lia shivered.

"Look for Knox one more time. Please, Lia." He bent toward her to whisper it, his lips almost touching her ear. "I swear I'll never ask you again."

Lia scuttled back. Bile rose in her throat at the thought of Knox dead somewhere in the city. She could still remember him arriving the day after she did in the seclusion's primary hall, the way his nose scrunched when he'd taken his first bite of lentils. The hollowness inside him, as if he'd left more behind than his home, his family.

"I'll take care of you," she'd said. "If you'll watch out for me, too." And so they'd eaten, back-to-back, wishing their meal had some taste. Ewan had been there too, loudly complaining about the food and taking it poorly when Knox told him to shut his mouth.

They'd fought, the masters looking on. Knox had won.

When Knox had cut his way out of the seclusion, of course they'd given the search to Ewan, the one Devoted who would have died just to wipe Knox's name from the rosters. Lia had volunteered to help back then, thinking maybe she'd find Knox first.

So she could ask why he'd left.

Why he hadn't taken her with him.

Now Knox was gone, his name on Ewan's glistening mouth. Her parents were gone, out of reach even though they were *right here*. Her sister, Aria, all freckles and bared teeth. Lia would never be bitten by her again. She wouldn't see her sister's first khonin knot tied when she turned thirteen, wouldn't see her graduate from the university. Aria could be dead in the ground for all Lia knew.

Lia chewed on her lip, the coppery taste of blood leaking onto her tongue. They'd taken her sword, exchanged her fight training for mind-reading lessons with old Master Helan, his voice thin and papery and so very *quiet*, as if hearing thoughts made everything else too loud. She was too loud for him, or too young, or too proud, and her first lessons had been tainted by a fierce anger from him that she didn't understand. It was as if her teacher hated Lia under the veil just as much as she did herself.

What else would Calsta take? Was there anything left? Anger churned through Lia, her aurasight lashing out like a monster, its many arms shooting to the farthest reaches of Chaol in one violent swoop. It crawled down the streets, snaked through the boats in the wide canals between islands, sank into the chinks between stones in the wall. It pushed into malthouses, passed over a man on a horse with a little freckled girl in his thoughts, headed toward her family's home on the Water Cay. Every aura in Chaol was white.

But then something changed.

An aura high on the river wall suddenly burst out in flickers of gold. Lia's eyes jerked open. She turned to face the lower cays, where the aura vacillated between gilded and white, so muted and small no one but Lia could ever have seen it.

It was an aura she knew well.

CHAPTER 7

The Fault You Choose

Noa sat primly at the front of the canoe, paddling absently as Anwei steered them through channel traffic toward the Water Cay. Her dark brown hair streamed behind her in a loose braid, the two knots marking her second khonin caught up in a double-pronged hair stick with a lily carved into the end for Falan, the god of performers and thieves. Not that he gave his devotees anything more than advice. It was only Calsta and the nameless god who shared power.

"So, Bear asked you to braid a bridal wreath. The governor's son. The most important and eligible bachelor in this city. He wants to marry you, and you want to . . . poison him?" Anwei asked.

"Only a little." Noa switched to Elantin—a southern dialect Anwei had learned during her first year away from Beilda. Sometimes Anwei thought maybe the reason Noa had glommed on to her so quickly was because Anwei could answer in her own language. It was hard to find Chaol natives who could speak anything but Common outside the docks, and even Noa knew the docks were a rough place for someone like her to go looking for friends. "Daddy's been so smug about the two of us spending time together, and he still won't tell me when we can go back home—"

"I thought you liked Bear."

"I do like him. Vandalizing stupid statues and taking him to street performances when his father isn't looking is fun, but that doesn't mean I want to be shackled in his dusty old house wearing crimson and gold the rest of my life. He's not *that* entertaining."

"The governor's colors?" Anwei maneuvered them to the common dock. "He wouldn't really make you wear them all the time, would he?"

Noa twisted to look at Anwei, the paddle flinging drips of water back to dot Anwei's skirt. "I just want to go home. Or to be *able* to go home without having to ask permission—from my father, from my husband, from my *new* father if I marry Bear. I mean, who needs *two fathers*? One is bad enough." Noa unspooled the mooring rope and threw it to the dock attendant.

Anwei pulled the boat in the rest of the way and tossed the attendant a coin before stepping out onto the dock. Noa's plight—too much money and time, and not as many options to waste them on as she'd like—always left Anwei wishing she could laugh in a way that wouldn't offend the girl, but she didn't let it bother her just then. With the snake-tooth man's scent calling to her, Anwei could almost smell her own future opening up. She started down the dock. "Well, tell me how I can help."

Noa stepped out of the boat after her, the customary smile on her face a little bit strained. "You think I'm being silly."

Anwei stopped and turned to look at her friend, trying to find space inside herself for some sympathy. "No, I wouldn't want to be chained up in some high khonin's house and forced to wear gold either. It would wash me out."

Noa snorted, her smile returning. "Well, the galrot would be a start. If I don't stop my father from talking to Bear's father at that ball, they'll draw up the contracts, sign them, then package me up with pretty paper and a bow and send me over by post before I have a chance to push Bear into the cape for the narmaidens."

"Bear just . . . assumed you were going to say yes?"

"He hardly even asked and didn't wait for an answer. That's how he does everything. That's why he was fun. That's about how I like to do things too, but not *to other people.*"

Noa's scowl nagged at Anwei, surprising her. Noa was a contact. A nice contact, one she liked talking to, but Anwei couldn't afford *friends*. Not outside of Knox, and even him she barely knew. It was jarring to wonder all of a sudden if she was asking questions in order to use the information later or if Anwei just wanted to make sure Noa was all right. The two were very different.

Anwei kept the smile lodged on her face, suddenly anxious to keep moving. "You don't think anyone will notice if the governor's son washes up half-eaten on the beach?"

Noa shrugged, her dimples carving deep lines in her cheeks. "I'd have to find a narmaiden first. They don't usually come this far north."

Adjusting her medicine bag, Anwei glanced toward the trade advisor's compound. She had to stay focused. Friends were probably nice things to have, but nice wasn't a part of Anwei's life. It couldn't be until she'd found the snake-tooth man. "I'll bring you what you want, Noa, so long as you've got gossip for me. Have you heard anything about someone new staying up at the trade advisor's house? I hear the advisor has been seeing an aukincer. Or do you know anything about the Devoted in town?"

"There are Devoted here?" Noa's eyes widened, her teeth clacking together in a diamond-hard smile. "Do you think they'd kill someone for me?"

"Kill someone, probably. For you, less likely. See if you can find out why they're here. I'll come by your house tomorrow."

Noa shook her head. "Come to the Firelily. I'll be rehearsing all morning. And bring the good stuff. In the meantime, I'll dig up everything I can. Maybe the Devoted will be at the ball! Everyone will be too scared to dance or talk or anything else. Maybe I won't even have to drug Daddy! He might just hide in a corner until they've gone." She groaned. "Why don't you come, Anwei? We could send the entire government of Chaol face-first into their coconut cream."

Anwei laughed. "Someday, Noa. I don't know why you're worried about Bear locking you away. *He* is the one who should be worried— that he'll marry you and you'll take this city away from him. You'd make the whole Ink Cay dance for you."

Noa rolled her eyes. "Who would want that? I want to be the one dancing, Anwei. But I want to be doing it because *I* want to, not because someone made me."

Isn't that what everyone wants? Anwei couldn't help but think Noa could hardly see the world around her. Everyone wanted to do exactly as they pleased, only there was bread to be earned, work to be done, revenge to be had, all of which made dancing a little hard. But Anwei kept her sympathetic smile and waved goodbye. When she turned toward the trade advisor's house, a thrill of anticipation mixed with fear inside her. Finally Anwei would be getting the one thing she wanted, but it wasn't going to be much of a dance.

When she got to the gate, the guard sitting just inside threw down a hand of cards. "What do you want?" he growled before getting a proper look at Anwei, his eyes stopping on her hundred braids. She caught sight of the rough circle carved into his canine as he gritted his teeth, the trade advisor's house mark. Rich households had marked their servants since before the shapeshifter wars.

"Pardon my rudeness, healer." The guard fingered the tails of his single long braid, free from any embellishment that would mark high position among his fellows. Two other guards stood to stare at her over the wall. "Are you here to see someone in particular?"

"The advisor sent for some medicine. He's lucky to have such a good-looking group of guards." Anwei pretended to marvel over the not-quite-cleanliness of his armor. The night guards were different from the day, but she still felt a glow of relief that this man wasn't the one who had tried to take her head off. "He's expecting me."

"I doubt it."

"You think I'd lie to someone with muscles like yours?" Anwei inhaled surreptitiously, itemizing the smells and blocking out the ones that didn't matter. The cheery green of grass peeking up through the brittle gray brown of paving stones, the dirt under the guard's fingernails. One dull yellow line of inflammation fuzzed underneath the smells coming from him—a rash of some kind. Her mind flicked back to the outbreak of rashes Gulya had asked her to look into. She'd said it was isolated to the Fig Cay.

Anwei shook her head, focusing. Last night the shapeshifter's scent had been over by the aviary, on the other end of the house. Far enough away that there was little chance of following it without the guard letting her inside. "I heard there was an aukincer working up here. Any chance he's here now? I wanted to check with him to make sure he approves of the remedy I brought."

The man rubbed his neck, and Anwei caught sight of red blotches across the back of his hand. "I promise, your services are not needed, healer."

"Maybe once I'm done helping the advisor, I could check your rash—" Anwei started to point at it, but he cut her off.

"The advisor's *dead*. Now get out of here before I call the wardens."

Anwei blinked, the packet of herbs crunching between her fingers as they closed into a fist. Dead? She'd gone into the man's house. Diagnosed his illness. Stolen his property. Then she'd run, as if sicknesses were something that sat and waited.

She turned and started walking away, a hole inside Anwei opening up. The same hole she'd run from all these years after Beilda. When Anwei used her hands to heal, they touched people. They memorized people's faces, their stories, their families. Their lives. And then, when she couldn't do anything to help them, it somehow felt as if it were her fault.

Just like her twin's murder.

When Anwei stole and poisoned, everything *was* her fault. But it was a fault she chose. Arun had always sat next to her—so much better at pulling apart the flowers to dry the petals, knowing all the hundred remedies and earning his braids a full year before she did, though they were the same age. Born the same day, she with a smile and he with . . .

Anwei closed her eyes and inhaled, steadying herself. In a single moment she was blessedly overrun by Chaol's scents: weeds poking out between the street's paving stones, dog excrement clinging to a passing maid's shoes, dirt, pollen in the air, leaves on the trees, sweat and linen and cotton and leather . . . and that fuzzy yellow line wafting from the guard.

No. Anwei couldn't think about Arun. She couldn't think about the advisor coughing out his last breaths on the stairs. What mattered was the nothing smell. If she couldn't get in the front gate to find out where it had come from, she'd have to find another way in.

"Healer!" The shout brought Anwei back to the present. She turned to find one of the trade advisor's guards running toward her. "You said he was sick. Come quick!"

"Who?" The fuzzy yellow smell grew stronger. The sick guard.

"He's fainted. Please, can you help him?"

In that moment something pulsed. And the smell turned from yellow to . . . *nothing*. A burning hole in the air.

The stink of shapeshifter.

Knox stared at the Trib horsemen who'd found him somehow, the two on the wall walking fast in his direction. The one below stood at the base of the stairs, blocking his escape. Calsta's power flickered inside his chest. He forced his hand away from his shoulder, trying not to grope for the sword that wasn't there. No armor, no shield, no weapon except for the knife in his pocket. *They shouldn't have been able to follow me after I lost them in the alley.* His eyes darted across the battlement, looking for a way out.

What if they were working for Devoted?

"Did you steal something from them?" The artist gestured toward the men with her paintbrush. It flicked droplets of the awful pink across his tunic.

The auras were thirty paces away. Knox could run down the wall toward the gate. They'd only follow. He could face them with nothing but his favorite knife. A knife fight on the wall would attract too much attention.

Twenty paces. Ten.

The shops below, the Greenglass Malthouse . . .

Knox hopped up on the battlement and stepped over the edge.

He caught himself on the stone lip, the battlement giving an ominous groan, bits of chalky mortar peppering his face. If he climbed down to the highest shop, lost the Trib men in the maze of ramps and ladders, then . . .

Then he'd find Anwei. She'd hidden him this long.

At least, that was his plan for the split second before the stone gave a great crack and Knox was in the air. Everything slowed, all of Knox's muscles clenching at once, as if he could somehow grab the ledge that was no longer there. Inside, his mind clenched too, so much closer to touching Calsta's energy than usual that it seemed to reach for him. A tiny fissure opened in the barrier he'd built between himself and the goddess's power, a drip of gold from his aura swirling into his blood like milk in a cup of water.

Knox shoved his hand out, jamming his fingers into an impossibly small chink between stones. His fingers and arm held when they caught his weight, as if he were made of feathers, his body swaying back and forth.

The glow of energy he'd been craving dribbled inside him, a sense of power chasing everything else away. Until he saw the painter gaping at him over the edge of the broken parapet. Her arms were outstretched as if she meant to somehow catch him midfall, horror in her face because she knew there was no way she could, and even more horror layered on top of that when she realized she didn't need to. He was impossibly balanced against the crumbling wall, breaking every law of nature she'd learned at the university.

Hands pushed her out of the way, the two Trib elbowing into view.

Knox's fingers pinched, Calsta's energy thrumming through him with a healthy dose of dread. He scuttled down the wall like a spider, frantically trying to rebuild the wall between himself and Calsta's power, but the break wouldn't close, the drip of golden energy turning into a river. Light streamed into him faster and faster, panic burning through his whole body. They would see. There was no way they *couldn't* see.

The world seemed to quiet around him, narrowing to nothing but the churn of pure light inside him. Knox could feel every line in the stone under his boots, every fiber of his tunic, sunlight burning into the skin on his face and bare arms.

Birds hung in the air overhead, mosquitoes hovered over the cool waterway abutting the wall under the shops, flies investigated beads of sweat pearling on his forehead. It rushed through Knox, flooding all his senses, the city lighting up with energy signatures until his mind was nothing but white.

He started to shake, losing his grip on the wall as the power burned through him, and landed on his back with a thump that tore the breath from his lungs. *"Anwei!"* He choked it out, rolling onto his side. Every time he'd woken from a nightmare of auroshe teeth and spiriter veils, Anwei had been there to assure him he was well and truly safe. But Anwei wasn't here now. What would Calsta think of him calling out for his partner instead of her?

But it was Calsta who was the problem. Her energy roared inside him like a beacon for anyone with aurasight to see.

Lia's lungs froze, the flicker of gold aura on the wall twinkling. Knox was here. He was *right there*.

No. Her mind circled him once, twice. Demanding that he disappear. *NO.*

"What do you see?" Ewan whispered, his breath leaking wet through her veil.

"I . . ." The flicker exploded to a golden bonfire, aura ripples shooting up so high even Ewan should be able to see them.

Feet moving too fast for her skirts, Anwei tripped as she entered the gate, then skidded to a halt at the fallen guard's side. Her fingers shook as she undid the buckles on his armor, shouting for servants to bring water. The guard's eyes had rolled back in his head, faint breaths panting out from his throat. All Anwei could smell was the tiny hint of *nothing* spiraling through him like a worm's hole, thinner than a thread. Blood leaked from the corner of his mouth.

Coughing up blood. A rash.

Anwei pulled a little knife from her medicine bag and sliced open the guard's undershirt, finding the red blotches across the man's stomach and chest. Cross-humor, Gulya had said, and this rash covered three at least. "Has he been to the Fig Cay?" That's where Gulya had said the outbreak was. This man couldn't be the shapeshifter. The smell was like a foreign object lodged inside him. Was this what she had smelled the night before?

What *was* it?

"Pausy moonlights for the Crowteeth. He was down there last night." The guard who had brought Anwei hung back, staring at the rash. The other guard came running with a ceramic jug of water. "Is it catching?"

"I don't know. Give me that." Anwei held her hand out for the jug.

"Excuse me, young lady. . . . " A young man ran toward them, smelling of rinoe, hael, and other aukincer nonsense. "If you could just step back, I believe I can help. . . ."

He had burn marks on his hands that stunk of chemicals—burn marks from his *own remedies.*

Anger boiled up inside Anwei at this man, this guard, this rash, this ridiculous puzzle that made no sense when it was supposed to point to the snake-tooth man. She dug her free hand into her medicine bag, meaning to teach the sham aukincer a lesson, but just as her fingers touched the leather flap, something in Anwei's head stiffened. The world seemed to blur around her, the water pouring from the jug going fuzzy in front of her. The nothing smell receded to make room for a voice.

Anwei! it screamed.

Knox's voice.

Anwei scrambled to her feet, dropping the water jug. It shattered, the pieces skittering across stone as she put her nose in the air, searching for the source of the voice. Only, it wasn't a *smell.* It was inside her, prickling like all of Gulya's knitting needles were under her skin and trying to get out.

The sick guard's eyes flickered open, one hand going to his chest as if his lungs wouldn't inflate. The aukincer skidded to his knees, his hands already greedily groping for some remedy that would, at best, do no harm.

Anwei! the voice pled.

"I'm here," she whispered. But the shapeshifter . . . the nothing smell right in front of her . . .

Knox's voice swelled stronger, and suddenly it was as if she were looking inside Knox's mind, his emotions scrolling along like the narration in a puppet show. Fear. Pain. Fear.

"I'm *here*!" She yelled it this time, stepping back from the fallen guard, though it was exactly what she shouldn't be doing. "What's wrong? Where are you?" The words felt slippery with sweat in her head. The guards were staring. The world had stopped.

She gawked at them, her eyes landing on the aukincer with his hands full of powder. "Don't let *him*"—she pointed at the aukincer— "touch your friend if you want him to get better. I'm at the Coil Apothecary. Tell him to come when he wakes up." Then Anwei hitched up her skirts and ran.

Lia dropped her gloves, one bare hand clawing free of the veil toward Ewan.

"What's wrong?" Ewan's voice pulled tight, his back going unnaturally straight at the sight of her fingers. His eyes were full of her, so full, the explosion of golden energy behind him didn't catch his attention. "Lia, what are you *doing*?"

She clutched her hands to her throat, pretending to choke. She stumbled forward.

Into him.

Lia crashed into Ewan's chest. His arms clutched around her waist to steady her, his heart racing, the cloud of thoughts around his head turning to fire. He was touching her. All the places he *wanted* to be touching her. And, before her eyes, his aura corroded. The golden flecks sickened to a brackish green, then winked out.

Tears burned in Lia's eyes at the feel of another person against her skin, of her face pressed against Ewan's chest, even with the veil and his armor between them. Her bare hand was touching him.

Lia's aurasight was made up of long tentacles and arms that snaked through the city, but with her own two broken oaths—touch no one and let no one see you—they shriveled and writhed, disintegrating into golden flecks on the dirty streets.

Suddenly Lia didn't have to pretend she couldn't breathe anymore. It started with the beacon on the wall, her view of Knox's aura winnowing down to nothing as Calsta withdrew her power from Lia. The wave of darkness crested high, washing out all the little halos between Lia and the wall—the families, the old women, the little children clinging to their parents in the streets—each disappearing one by one until it got to Ewan, whose arms were still tight around her.

Touch no one.

"Lia! What's happening? Are you hurt?"

Then even his thoughts were gone, the world around her silent and dark without Calsta's glow, and Lia was no longer a spiriter. No longer threaded through with Calsta's power. She was only a girl wearing a veil.

Knox felt as if his head were splitting open with Calsta's power as it rushed into him. Willow's bony fingers stabbed into his brain. She was excited, *ecstatic*, but then—

Then—

A net of darkness circled him, dimming the air around Knox. The fingers were gone. Calsta's power was there around him but not burning him from the inside. He could see. He was alive. He was lying on a hot tile roof, the scent of ocean in his lungs. The invisible net seemed to settle across him, like a shield to neutralize his aura.

It was purple. Like Basist auras. Like *Anwei.*

Skin crawling, Knox rolled off the shop roof and tumbled onto the walkway below, narrowly missing a display of pewter mugs and plates. The Trib aura on the street was climbing toward him, and the two above him were running down the length of the wall toward the stairs.

A voice whispered in his head. Not Calsta's burning tongue, nor his sister's ghostly decay. It was Anwei.

I'm coming! she whispered.

Knox forced himself up from the splintery walkway and toward the shop's open door. Willow was still there in his head, but now she was crying. *They're going to take you, Knox. And if they take you, they'll take*

me, too. We'll both die. It's her fault. You saw her aura all around you!
She's been doing it this whole time, touching you with that dirty Basist
magic. She's going to hurt you if you don't hurt her first.

The shop proprietor stood to meet him, a stern pinch to his mouth
telling Knox he wasn't the first person to come stumbling into the
shop as if he'd had enough malt for two.

"Quick." Keeping his voice level, Knox pulled everything he had
from his pockets. A few coins. The purple ribbon. Purple like Anwei's
net of magic somehow looped inside him. He hadn't known. How
could he not have known?

Knox shoved the ribbon back into his pocket and held the coins
out toward the man. "Is there a back way down? I can pay you more if
you get me out of here."

CHAPTER 8

A Hole to Nowhere

By the time Anwei got to the apothecary, she was unraveling inside. Knox's voice in her head had died down, but her mind still felt *crowded*, as if she weren't the only one inside it.

She barely waved to Gulya as she gusted through the apothecary's front room and up the stairs. She didn't know *how* she knew. Her nose had never been able to detect anything beyond what was in her general proximity, but Knox's voice had left an odd residue of certainty that he'd made it back to his room upstairs.

Anwei burst through Knox's door, then froze at what she saw inside. Knox was sitting on his bed, his sword across his knees. The blade was still in its wrappings, but an inch of the pockmarked metal peeked out from its sheath, dull in the sunlight.

Knox raised his head to look at her, sweat dripping down his temples. "What have you been *doing* to me?" he rasped.

Even with the blade inside its wrappings, even trying *not* to breathe, Anwei could smell it—a void in the air where the sword should have been. The cotton blanket's ochre dryness wafted toward her, the air swirled with the murky smell of dirt Knox had tracked in from outside. She could even sense the tie holding back Knox's hair, damp with sweat. But of Knox himself she could smell nothing, because when he held his sword, the void swallowed him, too.

He became *nothing*, just like the snake-tooth man.

Anwei carefully stepped inside Knox's room and closed the door behind her. She moved slow, the sword seeming to watch her from Knox's lap. "I haven't been doing anything to you, Knox."

Knox's neck corded on both sides as he looked up at her, his eyes leaden and black. Anwei's stomach twisted with fear. It wasn't just Knox's smell that disappeared when he held the sword—*Knox* faded too, and something else took over. She forced herself to take a step closer, keeping her eyes on the blade. "You promised me you wouldn't touch that thing while you were here."

His fingers tightened on the sword's wraps. "My energy . . . my aura . . . it all came out. I couldn't stop it."

Anwei edged closer. "I'm not sure what that has to do with swords."

"Anwei, they're *coming for me*." He stood up in one movement that went too quick. Anwei's hand snaked down to her medicine bag to touch the corta petals hidden inside. Corta wouldn't be enough. Its strong smell wouldn't work on someone disciplined, someone trained to withstand surprises. Knox had spent years fighting for the Warlord before he'd ever met Anwei.

At least, she was fairly certain he had. Their no-questions policy had left much up for interpretation.

"I called for help, and then something happened. Your aura—it was all over me." He peeled a hand up from the sword to point at her.

Her *aura*? Licking her lips didn't work because Anwei's mouth was too dry. "The sword, Knox."

"Whatever you did to hide me stopped working. They found me on the wall." Knox tried to swallow, his voice croaking when he continued, "They were after me *before* everything broke. They knew. There were men following me through the Sand Cay—"

"*Who* is after you? Devoted?"

He shivered, his hands picking at the knots holding the sword's covering in place. His eyes looked dead, unblinking and focused on every move Anwei made. "But then it snapped back into place. A shield or a net or . . . I can feel it now. What you're doing." He raked a hand through his hair, pulling at it. "It's in my *head*."

She pushed the corta aside and slid her fingers around the packet of calistet she always kept in her bag for emergencies. "I'm not doing any . . ."

Knox tensed, and her fingers tightened around the deadly packet. *I don't want to hurt you, Knox. Please don't make me hurt you.* There was little chance he'd live if she had to use it. Calistet undiluted would kill.

Instead of coming at her, Knox turned toward the door. "They're here. They're outside."

"I'm going to help, Knox, but I need you to put the sword down first."

Knox looked down at the blade loosely held in his hands, his eyes opening a fraction wider as if he hadn't noticed it was there.

"Put it *down*." Anwei stepped toward him, poison tight in her fist.

Stiffening at the command, Knox held out the sword. Arms shaking, he peeled his fingers open as if he wanted to drop it but couldn't make his hands obey. Anwei leapt forward and batted it out of his hands, and it hit the floor with a leaden thunk at her feet.

Tears stung her eyes as Knox's real smells came back. He had a sticky red cast, sweat and *fear* all over him as if he'd poured a bottle of sugar syrup over his own head.

Fear? Anwei's whole body felt as if it were contracting, trying to make itself small. *I can't smell fear.*

Knox was staring at the sword on the floor, both hands tearing into his hair. "Anwei, I . . . I am so sorry . . . I didn't mean to . . . I promised I wouldn't take it out. I'm sorry."

Anwei sagged back, her spine hitting the closed door, her head lolling to the side as she let the packet of calistet drop back into the bag where it belonged. She slid down to sit on the floor. *Enemies. Calistet is supposed to be for* enemies, *not my own partner.*

Anwei's heart beat against her sternum, shaking her from head to toe. She'd seen Knox go dead like that only two other times: when she'd first found him, and then again when he'd woken up three days later. It stank the way her brother's room had, the panic-tinged memories from that day forcing themselves before her eyes in a flood.

Her brother's murderer hadn't needed a pockmarked sword to turn into nothing. The man *was* that smell. But he hadn't forced his way into her head the way Knox had either. The way Knox was *still* doing, his voice slicked inside her thoughts even now. There was an aftertone of brick and blood to him now that she could smell from scratches and scrapes. But his bones fit together as they should, and his humors were balanced.

He was fine.

Anwei forged her voice into something calm. "You're in my head. Is that something all Devoted can do?"

Knox's face blanched. "*No. You're* in *my* head. I didn't do it. Everyone knows the stories about dirt witches being able to mess with people's minds!"

He stopped when Anwei stood, every muscle in her body taut. *Dirt witch.* "What did you say?"

"I'm saying that whatever is wrong with your aura is—"

"There is nothing wrong with my—what in Calsta's name is an *aura*, Knox?" It came out a little too forcefully, Anwei's hands grazing her high collar and the scars underneath. "I didn't do this. I heard you call. I stopped . . . what I was doing. I shouldn't have, curse Calsta and *every god on the Temple Cay,* but I did."

"I called to you instead of . . . It doesn't matter." He twisted toward the door. "They're downstairs right now. Devoted . . . or people working for them. They were all dressed up like Trib horsemen, but they must be

Roosters. I need . . ." He dropped to the floor, reaching for the sword.

Anwei darted forward, landing on her hip between him and the weapon. Knox's brows came down, his hand halfway to the hilt where it stuck out from the blanket. She curled her legs forward and planted a foot at the center of his chest. "We *will* talk about this later. Now get out of here before they come up the stairs."

His eyes tripped down to the hem of her skirts, where her heel dug into him, exposing the scars curling down her ankle. Gritting her teeth, she pushed him away with her foot, knocking him toward the window's bubbled glass. "Go!"

Knox caught himself on the windowsill, eyes wide.

"I'll take care of this. Wait outside the trade gate." Anwei turned, gathering the sword into her arms. She shuddered, the odd touch that belonged to Knox still lurking at the back of her mind. He hadn't moved to open the window.

"You trust me, right?" she rasped. "Do what I'm saying."

"I don't want them to hurt you instead of me."

"Don't worry about me. I'll meet you before sundown. Even if it's just to bring your money box and . . . this." Anwei clutched the sword to her chest as she stood and walked to the door. It made every inch of her scrunch, skin and muscles rebelling at being so close. "Go!"

She didn't bother to check whether Knox had obeyed. She knew he would. She could feel it in her head.

CHAPTER 9

The Soul Stealer

Mateo stared at the dark hole in the ground. He shifted to the side to try to let a little light down into it and accidentally bumped against his father, crouched next to him. It was early morning, the sun barely peeking over the horizon in the north, the two brother moons, Castor and Jaxom, ghostly and skeletal in the sky. Baskets were laid out in a grid behind Mateo and his father, each numbered and brimming with rock.

"We're not even sure Patenga made it this far north," Mateo whispered.

"Positive attitude, Mateo. We don't know much about Patenga at all, but we can't be choosy. Not very many shapeshifters even had burials—only the ones who let themselves die on purpose and could plan their own honors." Tual Montanne—Mateo had always thought his father's name sounded a bit like fancy cheese—gave the ladder propped up against the side of the hole an exploratory shake, grimacing when bits of rock pattered down into the darkness below. Dust stained Tual's hide boots despite the carpets that had been arranged around the tomb entrance. "It does look very dirty down there, doesn't it?" Mateo's father said. "You're always talking about how you like the hands-on parts of your studies, but I can't agree with you on this one."

Mateo sat back on his heels, checking his set of charcoals, his sheaf of vellum, and the little hand mirror stuffed into the satchel he always carried on excursions like this. "I'd love nothing more than to spend all afternoon down there taking notes on pre-Common-era burials, but you dragged me up here without giving me a chance to do the proper research. This tomb wasn't even on the list of most promising sites to find . . ." His mind went an awful gray, the words suddenly gone. "To find . . ."

It took a moment before Tual looked at him, filling the empty space between them with a solemn frown. "Is it affecting your mind now too?"

"Just because I forget *one word* does not mean wasting sickness has finally come to finish me off." Anger flushed through Mateo, and he stood up, pretending to check the buttons on his coat, the buckles on his shoes, making sure everything was in order. Checking things was easier than staring down into that hole, a maw of what would probably be just another disappointment. Forgetting the name of one obscure Basist compound—even if it was the compound he and his father had been searching for; what *was* it called?—was just because of the heat.

Mateo rubbed a hand through his hair, tipping his wide-brimmed hat back on his head. The moment he'd ridden up to these gods-forsaken ocean cliffs, his brain had clouded over, as if ignorance and stupidity were in the air itself. He bristled at the feeling of Tual's eyes still on him, taking a step back from the hole as if maybe that would give him a better view. He was fine. *Fine.* Mateo had never been exactly sprightly, but there hadn't been any episodes lately—no fainting or bleeding from his ears or any of those first-stage symptoms in more than six months. Father said his studies at the university in Rentara had been good for him. They were, too.

It was just that wasting sickness tended to go quick once you were past the first stage, and it usually set in out of nowhere. Your very life force started draining. You faded—magic first, then your energy, your muscles, skin, teeth, and hair, your very thoughts, scrubbing out of existence until you were gone. A terrifying affliction that had only just appeared in the last decade but had recently taken hold in the Devoted seclusions. Which meant Mateo had what should be a *Devoted* affliction.

The anger in his gut boiled.

Tual was already turning to climb down the ladder. "We can't afford to spend time in dusty old books anymore. Devoted are dying left and right. The Warlord is desperate. *I* am desperate. I don't want to lose you, son." He knocked his own hat back from his head, so that it hung from the cord around his neck. "Patenga is linked to the earliest mention of shapeshifting either of us has found. I only came across his name after a deep dive into some old texts over the border. It's a miracle this tomb is here and intact."

It was a miracle the man had allowed himself to die. Even more of one that some later shapeshifter or even Patenga's own subjects hadn't raided the tomb. Not for gold or jewels, but to stop him coming back. Most people now shuddered at the thought of disturbing a shapeshifter's body, as if going near would wake it back up.

There were enough stories of that being the case that Mateo wasn't sure what to believe. He was, however, fairly certain that *no* amount of magic could bring a skeleton back to life.

Mateo squinted out across the water, ocean wind blowing him back a step. "I still can't believe you asked for funding without telling me."

"The Warlord would fund a sandbox in the Taluth Desert at this point if I told her it might help me find a cure to wasting sickness. And this lead on a caprenum sample is *not* the only reason I dragged you out here. We have to plan out your future, too, not just the present."

Caprenum. The word settled inside Mateo, filling the empty space in his brain where it was supposed to be. *Caprenum.* The missing ingredient to his father's wasting sickness medicine. Shapeshifters had always kept at least one piece nearby, as if it were the key to their soul. Every shapeshifter tomb they'd found had images of the metal prominently displayed like a spoil of war, a trophy, a weapon even. The depictions were always defaced, scratched out. *Burned*. As if the subjects who had survived saw caprenum itself as the reason for their sorrow.

None of it made much sense to Mateo—all records of what made the medicinal compound so important to shapeshifters had been destroyed—but he and his father knew how to follow patterns, and caprenum definitely made one.

Mateo held the ladder steady as it wobbled under his father's weight. "I still don't understand why you won't just try to make it yourself. Why can't we research *that* instead of scouring the depths of every hole in the Commonwealth for treasure?"

Tual looked up at him from the ladder, squinting into the sun. "Basists had been brewing remedies for thousands of years by the time they came up with caprenum. You really think I can reinvent a complicated medicinal compound that probably took years of expert research? The only sample I ever had was long used up before I realized how scarce it is. I don't have a teacher. We don't even have sky-cursed *books* Basists wrote. It was all destroyed." After going down a few rungs, Tual looked back up at Mateo. "Maybe I could figure it out if I had years. A lifetime." He blinked and then continued his descent into the darkness. "You don't *have* years, Mateo. And the Warlord's patience with us isn't going to cover years of experiments. As it is, the only reason we're still alive is because I've managed to reduce the number of deaths in the seclusions. *She* doesn't have much time either. Soon provincial governors will realize there's a pandemic killing off Devoted. The Warlord is using some political trouble to cover up the fact that she's coming out here to inspect our findings." His voice had begun to echo. "I have a good feeling about this tomb, Mateo. We're going to find some caprenum, use it to cure you, and then we can finally disappear."

"If she lets us."

"It's not up to her. I have plans, and not all of them are to do with caprenum."

A fresh surge of anger flushed in Mateo's belly. At his father and his plans—Father *always* had plans—but even more at the fact that they had to go grubbing in old tombs to find the compound at all. Basists had done a lot of good before shapeshifters had ruined everything. But only Basists could become shapeshifters. They'd figured out how to do . . . *something*. Something so horrible it had been stricken from all histories and records, even the name of their god chiseled from every temple, every monument, burned from every book.

Mateo paced back and forth, trying to redirect his anger so it wouldn't touch his father, but it was hard. *Everything* was hard.

One of the few living Basists in the Commonwealth, Mateo didn't need a Devoted to hunt him down and kill him as they had all the others. His own magic was doing it just fine.

"Are you going to hold the ladder or not?" Tual called from below.

Mateo went onto his knees, gripping the rough beams to hold them steady until the ladder stopped shaking, his father safe on the ground. He turned and started down himself, hunching his shoulders as he went through the hole to keep his coat from brushing against anything too nasty. It was new.

The musty air closed in over Mateo's head, morning heat bleeding away as he descended into the cleared chamber. Excitement, *hope*, rose in him with each rung he descended. Maybe his father was right. Maybe this was a completely undisturbed shapeshifter tomb with a whole host of old records showing them exactly how to cure every disease from a cold to a rusty spear through the gut. Maybe it really would be Patenga down here, and his bones would be clutching the last living sample of caprenum.

Tual swore as Mateo stepped off the ladder, something metal tumbling to the ground next to him. The sunlight from overhead came down in a solid beam to form a hard circle of light at the base of the ladder, and Tual had somehow kicked over the huge mirror stand at the bottom, meant to redirect the light deeper into the tomb. Biting back a laugh, Mateo knelt to help his father set it right, the light catching on his father's short beard and the underside of his nose.

Once it was on the stand, Mateo stepped back to let his father reposition it and looked around. The chamber was at least thirty strides tall and about as wide from what he could tell. The beam of light danced across some carvings on the wall across from him, hitting a doorway cut into the stone. Mateo's eyes narrowed, the light jerking this way and that, so his eyes couldn't quite take in—

"What in the nameless god's blasted beard do you think you are doing?" a voice growled from the darkness beyond the doorway. Mateo's heart hiccuped in his chest as a shadow lurched toward him like a thing come back from the dead.

Tual stepped away from the mirror, sliding between Mateo and the shape with a smile plastered across his face. "Hello? I didn't realize anyone would be down here at this hour, but I'm glad to have a tour guide. Tual Montanne, the Warlord's aukincer, at your service. I wrote to say I'd arrive today."

The shape paused just outside the beam of light, seeming larger than life. Dangerous, like the shapeshifter who was supposedly buried here so deep in the rock. Mateo's heart didn't slow as the shape seemed to analyze them, its tongue silent. His legs began to feel weak, his head spinning. *Not now*, he begged. *Please don't faint now. I didn't even try to use my magic.*

"I'm afraid you have the advantage of us." Tual gave a little flourishing bow before turning back to the mirror, wrenching it into place. "You are . . . ?"

The beam of light slid across the shape, revealing a face worth drawing, if only for the sheer silenbahk trollness of it. The man's eyebrows were heavy and scrunched, a day's growth of beard scrubby across his cheeks and chin, his body like a potato-filled sack that could have been muscle or not.

"I'm Brellan Van, the director of this dig." As Director Van put a hand up to block the sudden light, painting shadows across his face, Mateo caught a glimpse of a house mark carved into his tooth, though not which one. A servant who had risen high, it seemed. "The Warlord can't just send *whomever she likes* to trample—"

"Sky-cursed government officials. They never ask for permission, do they?" Tual's smile could have lit a candle. Mateo hid a grin. His father could smooth a charging parchwolf's hackles, given the opportunity. It was the only reason the Warlord hadn't impaled the two of them with her sword the first time they entered her court, spouting aukincer theories and whispering about Basist magic. She didn't know, of course. Nobody knew what Mateo and Tual were, or they'd already be dead. How his father had managed to pull it off with all that Devoted aurasight stuff no one was supposed to know about, Mateo wasn't sure. All he knew was no Devoted had looked at him twice except to sneer at his skinny arms.

"It's dangerous down here," Director Van snarled. "The traps in this room alone injured three men. We've just barely disabled the pressure plates in the connecting hallway, and we're still analyzing soil samples to know what to expect farther down. You could have *died*."

The well of hope inside Mateo seemed to expand. Traps? Pre-Commonwealth high khonins didn't put traps in their tombs; they just had them filled in to protect valuables they were too selfish to pass on. Traps meant this place was something special.

"I don't believe I read about traps in the initial reports." Tual shot Mateo an excited look. "Now, don't worry about us, you won't even know we're here. My son knows how meticulous this kind of work is—he's studying archeology at the university in Rentara and was so pleased to have the opportunity to see a master at work."

The director moved toward the mirror to fix the angle of the beam of light, but Tual didn't make way, forcing Van to go around him. "You could have killed me, taking away my light just now. I've been working since the sun came up to map out the room beyond the antechamber, and I've identified only three potential trouble spots yet, but I'm sure there are more. And that's without workers muddying the air, moving the mirrors, moving the *wrong dirt*." He grumbled to himself before fixing Mateo with a nasty glare. "I don't need an amateur putting us all in danger. So if you don't mind, I'd rather you both left and broke your necks on the way out."

Mateo wasn't sure if he should laugh at the director or run, the ire cascading off him somewhere between comical and a physical assault. But there was something else strange about this man, something that waited in the dark, a bit of reflected sunlight not enough to lay him bare.

"We're only here to do some drawings, cataloguing. Satisfy the purse holders . . ." Tual squeezed Mateo's shoulder as he spoke, an invitation. "Just give us a moment to look around. I promise we won't touch a thing."

"You expect me to stand here and watch you. . . ."

Mateo turned away from the director, tuning out his voice. His muscles still felt oddly weak, as if one of his attacks had come and gone. He breathed in deep, opening his mind to the stone around them. Echoes came back to him from the cavern walls, but he couldn't tell what kind of stone they were made from. It was . . . a combination. A tortured recipe of elements that shouldn't have been able to go together. Mateo's brow furrowed, the mixture unlike any Basist work he'd ever seen. He could feel that the hallway extended another twenty strides and that there were a few rooms to either side of it. The floor underneath them, however . . . Mateo looked down at his new boots, their toes already scuffed. There was something under the floor, but he couldn't *see*, as if the stone itself was blocking his power.

He threw his mind out again, and it snagged on a square of ground in the far corner of the room, far from where any light touched. Something about it wasn't normal. Not even Basist. It was *wrong*. Wrong like shapeshifters.

The tiny effort of extending his mind left Mateo's hands shaking, his body suddenly too heavy and his head too light. A flare of anger burst up inside him when the nameless god's magic drained before he could get a better look at the odd catch in the floor. Why did *his* magic have to be corrupted? Mateo *deserved* the nameless god's power at his fingertips. He deserved to know the oaths, the history, the learning, that had all been lost because of the first Warlord's hunger for power. A life spent searching for the nameless god, trying to clear him of all the blame that had been laid at his feet, and somehow it was Mateo who was dying.

It wasn't fair.

Tual's hand on Mateo's shoulder tightened. It was his cue. Cutting Director Van's grumbling off, Mateo found himself a smile and stepped forward to play his part. "I'm very pleased to see a real dig. I see you're using the Veli method to map the tomb and the places artifacts are found?" He pointed up toward where the numbered baskets sat above on the surface. "Was anything of interest found over here?"

"No. The real work's back in these rooms we uncovered." Director Van suddenly seemed wary, watching closely as Mateo pulled out his hand mirror. Sliding it into the beam of light reflected from the large mirror, Mateo angled it toward the place where his mind had snagged. There wasn't anything there, the ground completely cleared.

"You won't mind if we look, then?" Mateo started toward the corner. The snag was back in his mind, drawing him to one of the many identical stone blocks lining the floor in the corner. Mateo knelt down and smoothed his hands across the floor, the sense of *wrong* tearing little holes in his thoughts. His fingers found something hard lodged between two of the blocks. Digging at the thing—a rock, a nail?—Mateo gritted his teeth as the rough stone blocks scraped at his fingers, when—

Suddenly the ground wasn't there.

It happened too fast for Mateo to process: one second he was kneeling, the next he was falling, and then he was suspended in the air, caught by his new coat's stiff collar. Heart and lungs flapping in a panic, Mateo tried to stay still even as his body wanted to flail for something to grab hold of.

Light beamed down into the hole, his father's voice choking out from immediately above him. "Don't move, son!" Tual, somehow, had caught him. He always did.

The light fell on the ground immediately beneath Mateo, dust kicked up by the trapdoor he'd fallen through diffusing the mirror-light. There was a carving, something huge that took up the entire wall next to Mateo—

Tual gasped. He'd seen it too. "Help me!" he called. "I can't hold him."

Twisting, Mateo jabbed his little hand mirror into the light beaming down into the hold, redirecting it to slice across the huge figure at the center of the carving.

The thing was covered in dark green paint that had peeled and cracked. Its gargantuan face was scaled, with a lizard's bulbous eyes and long snout. Fangs dripped from its jaw, and claws jutted from its fingertips. The carving's chest, arms, and hands were human, but its feet were furry and clawed like a parchwolf's.

"Ready, one . . . two . . ." Stitches popped on Mateo's sleeves as hands jerked him up through the open trapdoor and rolled him onto his side.

"Son." Tual's voice was frantic, the darkness closing in around Mateo. "Son, are you all right?"

"Blasted outsiders breaking things and . . . what is down there?" Van's growl seemed to diffuse along with the light, filling the cavern with an odd mix of anger and curiosity as he peered into the hole.

Gasping for breath, Mateo scrambled back to the opening and dipped his mirror into the chamber to get another look at the figure on the wall. Carvings at the figure's feet were depictions of waves or stones or . . .

Mateo gulped. They were humans. Hundreds of them, tiny and kneeling at the creature's feet. Their heads were bowed, their arms extended upward. Half were painted white, half a deep, bruised purple.

Patenga. A shapeshifter, a *soul stealer* from long before the first Warlord had begun unseating the horde of tyrannical shapeshifter kings who infested the land. Mateo goggled at the intact relief—a shapeshifter wearing an unnatural form—that was completely whole. Not defaced or destroyed by angry subjects or Devoted.

Mateo pulled his head away from the hole and rolled onto his back, breaths shuddering in and out of him. His fingers itched for his charcoals; the art style was like none he'd ever seen before.

"Leave the back rooms," Van's voice rang out. "Hey! Get over here! All of you!" Accompanied by the scuttling sound of feet on stone. "I need lines down, buckets, brushes. . . ."

Tual's hand found Mateo's shoulder again as he and the director stared down into the hole, a single ray of light on Patenga's face. With every tomb they'd discovered over the years, Mateo's hope to live past nineteen had risen and then been dashed to pieces when they didn't find anything. And when hope was gone, Mateo found himself dashing other things to pieces as well, wishing everything he broke would persuade the world how unfair it was that he had the same sickness *Devoted* suffered from when Mateo himself hadn't made a single oath to Calsta.

But now Mateo felt that fragile hope in his chest turn solid.

Tual dipped his own mirror into the opening as workers rushed to the hole, depositing equipment all around them. "Mateo, you need to see this."

Mateo rolled over and looked down into the hole once again. Tual had moved the light up the shapeshifter's arm, the thin beam touching Patenga's hand.

"That's it, son," his father whispered.

High above his head, Patenga held a caprenum sword.

CHAPTER 10

Red Hair, Red Blood

Something sucked up against Lia's nose when she woke. She gasped, jerking forward to claw at her face.

It was her veil. Lia wrenched it from her head, her eyes feeling dry and grainy as they found the vaguely familiar footboard, the chest of drawers in which she had no possessions to place, and the wide windows with the view of Chaol she'd gulped down her first night in town.

"How did I get back to my room at the governor's compound?" she whispered to herself. "I was at the drum tower, by the dry market. There were officials. My father. Ewan standing next to me on the balcony, and . . ."

And Knox on the wall.

Lia clawed the air around her with her mind, trying to find the auras, the fleeting thoughts, even the familiar buzz of Calsta's energy inside her, but it was all gone.

Shoving her veil to the floor, Lia slid off her bed. Breaking oaths wasn't something to be taken lightly. The masters told all Devoted over and over that once Calsta chose you, she would not let you go. That she forgave mistakes, but not easily. Lia shuddered at the memory of touching Ewan, but his thoughts had strayed too far from Calsta when her hands touched his chest. His oaths had been broken too, his aurasight drained just the way hers had been. That was all Lia had wanted.

With his aurasight gone, he hadn't seen Knox on the wall.

What was even more interesting: *Lia* hadn't seen Knox until his aura blew up. She paced to the window, blinking when her mind didn't sail out to look for her old friend again. Knox's aura had been hidden somehow, blanked out by some kind of barrier. It had cracked for a moment, but even before she'd touched Ewan, Knox's aura had begun to dim down to nothing again, as if he'd found a shield that worked against aurasight.

But there *wasn't* a way to hide a Devoted aura. That was why every person in the Commonwealth who was touched by Calsta ended up in a seclusion. At least, all the people whom Devoted passed close enough to notice. If hiding were possible, Lia would have been tucked into bed in her family's home on the other side of the Water Cay, not standing alone in this room with a dirty veil at her feet.

A cool wind slipped through the open window, beckoning Lia to her balcony door. The governor's home was on the far side of the Water Cay, high enough that she could see all the way to the ocean waves beyond the river mouth, the whole world clear without her veil to turn it a dingy gray. Drinking in the greens and blues and hints of copper roofs, Lia pulled off her outer dress, sticky with yesterday's sweat. She stepped onto the balcony in her slip, the sun kissing her bare arms, the stone warm against the soles of her feet. It was the first moment in two years when it didn't matter if anyone saw her.

"Lia?"

Lia startled, wildly searching for the voice, but all she could see was balcony and the ground fifty feet below. She put a hand to her head, the balcony's stone floor almost seeming to bend under her, the vertigo of not being able to immediately place people by their auras making her dizzy.

"Lia!"

Lia peeked over the balcony's rail, an even darker worry muddying her thoughts. If someone could get close enough to speak before she saw them, then Ewan could be anywhere in the governor's house and she *didn't know where.*

Just under the stone rail, a girl was hanging from the wall by her fingertips. A girl with red hair. "Dad said you were here," she rasped. "I couldn't let you go away again without seeing you."

"Aria?" Lia's throat closed like a trap. "How did you . . . ? There are soldiers guarding this house! Don't you know anything about Roosters? They'd kill you in a second for coming up here."

"The ones watching this side of the building aren't very smart. Auroshes are *very* interested in fighting each other. And people. And plants. And puppies—"

"What did you do to the auroshes? Don't you know that *they* could kill you in . . . *less* than a second?"

"They like me." Lia's little sister pulled herself up another foot, peering through the railing. "Are you okay? You look . . ."

"Happy." Lia knelt down, drinking her sister's freckled face in. "So happy to see you."

"I was going to say naked-ish." Aria eyed Lia's bare arms and feet.

Something hot and ecstatic bubbled up in Lia's throat, coming out without asking permission. A *laugh.* She hadn't laughed in—

A fist pounded against her bedroom door, the sound shuddering through her. "Hide!" she rasped at her sister, pulling her up over the railing. Lia shepherded Aria to a potted tree at the corner of the balcony, and her back straightened when the pounding came again, this time even harder.

A voice leaked through the door. "Are you awake?"

Her stomach dropped. It was Ewan. Lia was *blind* without Calsta. "Lia? I'm coming in."

After checking to make sure Aria was hidden, Lia darted into her room and grabbed the first thing that came to hand, a light summer cloak, meant to cover every inch of her. The door slammed open, and Ewan was in the room, crossing the floor, pushing her hard against the wall.

"What in Calsta's name—"

Ewan shoved his lips against hers, trapping her against the wall.

In her mind, Lia's fists balled. Her elbow broke his nose, a punch cracked one of his ribs. She executed a perfect kick to his head and watched his skull slam into the floor. . . . But her actual body, the one being crushed into a wall, had turned to glass. Immobile. Petrified. Seconds from shattering.

He kissed her neck, buried his face against her shoulder, breathing in so deep, it was like he was trying to consume her. "I knew you'd be waiting for me. You want this—"

"N-no!" Lia finally found herself again, squirming as he ground her spine into the wall. "I *don't* want . . ." His hands seemed to be everywhere, as if he'd grown ten extra ones when he walked into the room, every inch of her so very exposed. "Get *away* from me! You forget yourself and your oaths—"

"You know they chose you for me. *You* chose me." He pulled back long enough to look into her eyes. "Our oaths are already broken. *You* touched me. *You* were waiting for me practically naked. . . . It's obvious this is right." His fingers on her shoulder pulled at the cloak until it slipped off. "It doesn't make sense to wait any longer. This is Calsta's will."

Lia gasped as he stuck a hand into her tangled hair, pulling it back from her face. He stared at her, his grease-yellow eyes sliding across her. "You weren't this freckly before, were you?"

The words set her free from the sick paralysis holding her prisoner. Lia knifed her hand into Ewan's ribs and kicked the side of his knee. He reared back, his hold on her loosening enough so she darted under his arm, sprinting for the door. She'd always been fast, even before she'd had Calsta's energy to call on. There would be Roosters *some-where* on this floor—

Fingers grabbed her hair, dragging her back. "If you think fighting makes you more devoted to Calsta—" Ewan's voice bit off with an oath, and suddenly the hand tearing at her scalp was gone.

There was a flash of red hair and a streak of blood, and then a small set of hands grabbing her arm. "Run!" Aria croaked.

Following her sister's pull, Lia stumbled toward the balcony door. She broke off the latch with the flat of her palm, then pulled the door shut behind her, her mind in a panic. A shattered latch wasn't going to stop Ewan. He was trained to do more damage than any common soldier even without Calsta's help.

So was Lia. But it had been two years since she'd been allowed a sword.

She certainly didn't have one now. What had Master Helan said before she left? To remember what she needed. To believe that Calsta knew it too, and then to let go of her fears and wants and needs and trust Calsta to provide. The problem was, letting go meant she had to believe Calsta *cared* what Lia needed, something she hadn't found evidence for in all six years she'd worn the Warlord's insignia.

Aria's thick coppery brows buckled together as Ewan's weight slammed into the door. She looked up at her sister. "What do we do?"

Lia grabbed Aria's hand and pulled her to the balcony rail. With one quick prayer to Calsta asking for forgiveness, she helped her sister over the barrier.

Another slam against the door shattered the window, glass skittering across the stone balcony. But Lia was over the rail and climbing down, Aria just below her.

"Lia!" Ewan yelled from above, bits of glass still flying. He hadn't gotten through yet. Where were the Roosters? They'd brought six warriors with them, and none had even come to investigate.

Lia climbed faster, the rough brick cutting into her fingers. The farther down she climbed, the harder strings binding her to Calsta seemed to pull. So she began to cut. The cold, lonely view. *Snip.* Her veil and gloves in a lumpy pile on the floor. *Snip, snip.* The threads that had kept her from hugging her own father, from even looking him in the eye. *Snip.* Vivi, her one companion . . .

Lia closed her eyes, a tear squeezing out to burn down her cheek. She was not meant for a life bound like a fly, waiting for the spider to come.

Warm air billowed up through the cloak across her bare legs. Aria's red curls beneath her lit like fire in the sun, her sister cackling like an old witch as they jumped off the wall.

The sound of the door crashing open overhead was almost quiet in Lia's ears when she started to run, Ewan's voice a heinous, indistinct roar.

Snip, snip, snip.

CHAPTER 11

The Serpent

Anwei shoved the cloth-wrapped sword under her bed, then wiped her hands across her tunic before sprinting down the stairs. Knox had said there was some kind of Devoted—maybe more than one?—down in the shop. Dipping a hand into her medicine bag, she once again took up the packet of calistet.

At the bottom of the stairs, Anwei sniffed, looking for clues in the herb room's cloud of dry green scents. All she could smell was a hint of parched, gritty gray coming from the apothecary shop beyond the door. A scent like flame—salpowder, perhaps?

Concentrating on the scents was easier than the thought of Knox's face when he'd held the sword. And what he'd said—that something wrong of hers had gotten inside him. And calling her *dirt witch*? She wiped the frown from her face and pushed through the herb room door into the shop.

Gulya was lecturing two men at the counter. The older of the two was wearing an animal-skin vest with a silver Trib medallion square on his chest, the likes of which Anwei hadn't seen since she was in the jagged mountains north of the Commonwealth border. His uneven brown ponytail was absent the Commonwealth's ranking of knots and braids, and Anwei's nose filled with the smell of furs, horse, and that gritty gray that prickled in her nose like an obsidian knife. Salpowder.

The younger man was about Anwei's age, and he focused on her immediately, the fringe of hair cut shorter around his face obscuring his expression. It was him that the powder smell came from, as if he'd stashed a firekey lizard down the front of his shirt. There was nothing Devoted about either of the Trib men.

Anwei looked around the room again, expecting a Rooster's underbraids to pop out from somewhere inside the maze of glass globes, but there wasn't anyone else to find.

Gulya paused her lecture long enough to give Anwei a raised eyebrow—it had been only a few minutes since she'd gone running up the stairs to find Knox. "Perhaps you can help this man. The mole on his chin—"

"I didn't come to ask about a mole." The older Trib's voice seemed to be gaining heat, as if he'd already said as much, perhaps more than once. His accent made the words heavy and long. "The man who lives above the shop—the one who went up the stairs *less than ten minutes ago*—is the person I came to talk to."

"He's not a healer," Anwei cut in before Gulya could say anything else. She smiled at the older man, then switched to the younger one when the old Trib didn't so much as glance at her. "I suppose you must know that. Knox is indisposed at the moment, but I may be able to help. Follow me, we can talk in here." She gestured toward the herb room.

The old Trib flicked a long fringe of hair from his eyes, finally turning to look Anwei up and down. "No. I don't want to talk about moles, or medicine, or—"

"Perhaps I didn't make myself clear," Anwei interrupted, this time in the man's own language. It had been years since she'd spoken Trib, but she liked the way the hard syllables sat on her tongue. The clipped sounds suited her at the moment. "Why don't you come in and tell me what you *would* like to talk about."

Gulya smiled and waved the men along as if Anwei had done something particularly clever. "You won't regret it, sir. Anwei's the best healer in the province."

Gritting her teeth, Anwei held open the herb room door, waiting until the old man grudgingly walked through it. The young man followed, smiling congenially as he passed her. Anwei let the heavy door swing shut on the shop, then unhooked two bunches of herbs to make room for the two of them to sit at the table.

Neither sat. The old man looked impatiently at the stairs even as the younger one grabbed hold of his arm to keep him in place.

Anwei kept one hand in her medicine bag, her fingers finding the button closure to the calistet. "How did you manage to track us down? I'm so impressed."

"What do you mean, 'us'?" The older Trib inclined his head as he brushed the younger man away, an exasperated take on a traditional Trib showing of respect. "I mean no insult, healer. I had an appointment with the man upstairs on the Sand Cay, and . . . something happened."

The Sand Cay? He sat only when Anwei pointed at the bench with her best winning smile. *That was the location mentioned in the ridiculous bid from this morning.* She'd told Knox *not* to go nosing around after that job.

The younger Trib hung back, leaning casually against the wall. Anwei didn't miss the way his hand slid into his vest, but when he drew it out, he wasn't holding a knife or a sky-cursed firekey lizard. It was a figurine of a little Trib maiden. The same one Knox had lifted from the trade advisor's office, then left for the magistrate while he slept. "I don't suppose *you* recognize this? Your friend—Knox, is it?—seemed very interested in purchasing it."

Anwei let herself look at the figurine, her stomach dropping a few inches more. She kept her face smooth. "I never knew Knox to be an art collector. It's very pretty, though."

No one had ever found her, not in the two years she'd been in Chaol. Not her informants, not the gangs who left letters at her drops. No one. It kept her safe from gang bosses who wanted a poisoner to work exclusively for them or no one at all. More importantly, it kept her safe from the snake-tooth man. Arun's murderer knew Anwei, probably moved around erratically partly because of her slowly narrowing search. At least, Anwei liked to pretend it was because of her.

Regardless of who these northerners were, they'd walked into the wrong apothecary.

"You think *she* works for . . ." The older man glanced at Anwei, lowering his voice to a gravelly whisper that did little to disguise his words. "A healer wouldn't have anything to do with Yaru, Altahn. And she's a girl besides."

"Let's talk to her and find out." Altahn's tone was a hair too patient as he tucked the statue away. "She's seen this before."

"You think?" The man's face squished into a pout as he looked at her, as if trying to shove two ideas of who she was into a space that was too tight. "Well, if that's the case, then would you please go get your master upstairs?"

Anwei sat, easing the calistet packet open with one hand and grabbing for Gulya's stack of cheap rice paper with the other. "I wish I knew what you were talking about, but maybe I can ask Knox when he's available?" What would Gulya say when she found two dead men on her worktable? Anwei didn't think the old apothecarist would believe it if she blamed the mole on the older one's chin. "What are your names? I'll pass along your message." She pulled Gulya's inkpot and quill over, dipping the nib.

"Shale Berantiz, kynate of the Verac clan." The man puffed up ever so slightly.

Altahn pressed his lips together, much less happy about sharing the old man's status as clan leader to someone he knew must not care but could use the information against them. He almost patted Shale's shoulder but stopped himself just in time. "It isn't very complicated." Altahn kept his voice light. "We're interested in purchasing another . . . artifact. Like the figurine. There's a tomb being excavated in the sea cliffs outside of Chaol. One of your shapeshifter kings, I think?"

"You want a shovel to go with that pretty statue in your pocket?" Anwei asked, batting her eyelashes. "I don't think they sell things that come out of the ground in those excavations. I don't like the idea of them being dug up at all, to be honest." Anwei awkwardly made a sign to ward off ghosts, dripping ink across the paper with the quill. With her other hand she twitched the packet so the powder was all in one corner, planning. She'd have to use her sleeve to protect her nose and mouth. It might take two throws to get Altahn, and then she'd have to run to Gulya's garden pond to wash off any residue and . . .

"We're after a sword. It belonged to my great-great- . . . *many*-greats-grandfather." Shale glared at Altahn when the younger man nudged his arm hard. "You say she works for Yaru and now you don't want to tell her anything? How's she supposed to steal it for me?" He turned back to Anwei, talking louder when Altahn tried to cut him off. "The dig director probably knows its value, and that's why he's here, the old serpent. It's a miracle he's got enough learning to know."

"Old serpent?" Anwei gauged the distance between her and the stairs, the angle the powder would fly. She took a deep breath and held it in her lungs, about to throw the poison.

Shale pulled his lips back in an old man's indignant snarl, rubbing his left canine tooth with one finger.

Serpent. Anwei froze. *Why did he touch his tooth like that? That's where house marks are carved.*

The memory of the nothing smell seemed to pulse in Anwei's nose. The snake-tooth man had a house mark carved into his canine.

A snake. It belonged to a house long dead, their compound burned to the ground with the family inside more than seventy-five years earlier. That was one of the first bits of information Anwei had hunted down once she got to the mainland.

"The Warlord's had him digging up every shapeshifter tomb she could find. It's been going on for almost three years." Shale looked down at her. "Haven't you seen the notices?"

Anwei blinked. She had seen notices promising a reward for any solid information on pre-Common-era tombs. Altahn was shaking his head, giving up on stopping the old man from spilling everything without a thought to consequences.

"We knew the king who stole the sword was buried near here, so we sent word through the right channels. They found the entrance a few months ago." Shale licked his lips, leaning toward her. "I need your friend upstairs to get in there and take the sword before the archeologists uncover it."

Clutching the calistet packet, Anwei was frozen, unsure for the first time in her whole life. "If you know that much, then why are you contracting the work out?" she asked slowly. "Why not walk in and take it?"

Altahn's head came up, a smile starting on his lips.

"Because I'm not a thief." Shale spat the words out. "The dig is guarded. The tomb itself is fitted with traps and poison and all sorts of other nonsense. And . . ." His hand flitted up to touch his forehead. A gesture to ward off ghosts, like she'd done.

Altahn put his hands flat on the table in front of him. "While I'm sure my dear kynate would like to tell you everything, I think it might be prudent at this point to ask who you are before we speak further. Anwei, right? I don't think a name's going to be enough right now."

The old serpent. Anwei kept her smile pinned to her cheeks, her fingers on the calistet packet trembling. It couldn't be a coincidence. The guard at the trade advisor's compound had been infected with the nothing smell. Then these two with information about a man with a snake on his tooth being in town? Anwei felt light-headed, sick almost. She'd been excited the night before—but *this* wasn't whispers of odd behavior and aukincy. Was it possible that she had finally found not only traces of Arun's murderer but the man himself?

The flare of excitement extinguished in one flash of smoke. It *wasn't* possible. Believing in good luck was like believing in gods who were only carved bits of stone. It was her blasted hope again, wanting to believe without seeing proof in front of her eyes.

But it might be a lead. All Anwei had to do was get information from this old man, his tongue lolling out of his mouth as if he didn't know what happened to people who spoke too much.

"Yes. My name's Anwei." Anwei buttoned the calistet packet and let it drop into her bag. "And . . . I guess I do know a little about Yaru." Saying it felt like prying herself open. When you exposed yourself, beasts came sniffing after the blood. But if it meant finding out something—*anything*—about the snake-tooth man, then Anwei could let the beasts circle a bit closer before she silenced them.

Altahn's smile was a little too cold. "And your friend upstairs?"

"Is unavailable at the moment. So sorry." She smiled her best smile, watching as Altahn's eyes flicked down to her dimple and across her mouth. "Just so I understand the, um . . . message. You need someone to sneak into this dig, get past a few old traps, and bring you a sword that . . . *might* be inside?"

"It's there," Altahn said firmly.

Shale nodded. "They haven't located the burial chamber yet. The moment they do, all the artifacts will be catalogued and taken to the Warlord's seclusion in Rentara, so we'll need this done very quickly—I need you to stress that to your master. Maybe write it in all capital letters?" He craned his neck to get a look at the bit of rice paper Anwei was scribbling on. "And we'd want Altahn right there with him, managing things. None of the dangerous work, of course, just being the leader you unfortunate criminal types need—"

"Based on the reports we've intercepted, the traps they have been able to identify are beyond our abilities to diffuse." Altahn gave his kynate a pained look. "At least, not without destroying the whole tomb before we can secure the sword."

Destroying the whole tomb? Anwei let her eyes rest on Altahn for a moment, flicking across his hands. He had burn scars all across his knuckles, the black, gritty smell of salpowder stinging in her nose. She smiled when she met his eyes, letting her expression empty and shallow, though it was obvious he wasn't buying her act. "Why don't you tell me more about this man we'd be stealing from?" Anwei switched her gaze to Shale, keeping her face empty, impassive. Inside she was nothing of the kind. "The snake. What exactly would we be up against?"

Shale's hand twitched toward his mouth again, as if he meant to once again rub his tooth. This man he was talking about had to have some kind of house mark, even if it wasn't a snake. She only just now remembered how dismissive Trib were of the practice, marking servants as if they were belongings. It could all be hope skewing what Anwei heard into the shape she wanted to see. But it might not be. "He's a tricky man, if my reports are right."

Altahn put a hand on Shale's arm. "I think the kynate would be happy to share more if we knew you were committed to doing the job."

"Yes, when can we talk to Yaru—Knox? Whatever his name is, hiding upstairs?" Shale asked. "I was pleased with his work last night." He poked Altahn. "Show her the figurine! Yes, I was very pleased. I need the sword, and I think he's the fellow to get it."

"She's already seen the figurine." Altahn's teeth barely let the words out of his mouth.

Putting down the quill, Anwei tried not to flinch when Shale bumped a stalk of drying flowers, showering the table with petals. "You must *really* need this sword. I mean, twenty thousand silver rounds is a lot." She leaned forward, watching Shale's face. "What do you want it for?"

Shale started blustering, his jowly cheeks wobbling. "I demand to speak to your superior, young lady. I will not be subject to—"

Altahn placed a hand on the kynate's shoulder, probably to calm him, but the blustering was all Anwei wanted. She could tell Shale wasn't lying, exactly. But also that he wasn't telling all of the truth. Altahn was telling even less of it. So that left the question: What were they really after?

No treasure was worth twenty thousand silver rounds. Which meant there was something else at stake here. And probably no money, which meant Altahn and Shale expected Anwei and Knox to be too stupid or too dead at the end of this job to try to collect.

Maybe this *was* all a front, and the governor was coming for his stolen candlesticks. But if that were the case, why would the governor fabricate such a ridiculous job and reward in order to tempt them out into the open? Altahn already had proof enough in his pocket that Knox was a thief.

Which meant it was probably a trap for Anwei. Maybe not even for Anwei the thief and Yaru, but for Anwei the scared little girl who had found her brother's bed soaked with blood. Anwei took in a long, slow breath, focusing on the smells coming from the two Trib men. Silver. Horsehair. Salpowder and sweat. Not a single hint of *nothing*.

But Anwei couldn't let the thought go. What if instead of Anwei finding the snake-tooth man, he'd found *her*? What if he'd already set a noose and was just out of sight, waiting to pull it tight around her neck and rid himself of her once and for all?

"No, Altahn, I won't be *shushed*." Shale gestured dramatically, petals falling all around him when his open palm hit a clump of dried colis. The smell of blood flooded Anwei's nose, the memory of Arun's room suddenly a stark and fearsome thing in her head. Her hands began to shake.

And Knox. Anwei leaned forward, the medicine bag pressing hard into her stomach. Her brother's blood littered her thoughts, but suddenly it wasn't on his bed and his floor anymore. It was all over the room upstairs, *Knox's* bed soaked in crimson. The snake-tooth man didn't mind death, and he'd already taken all the people she cared about. Arun. Mother and Father. A town full of people who had loved her . . .

The memory crashed around her, wind whipping her braids, waves threatening to swallow her, and rain like icy needles on her skin as she rowed toward the mainland, blood still dripping down her arms. Not all of it had been her own.

An ache deadened Anwei's chest, every inch of her feeling like lead. Knox was all she had in the world—all she'd *allowed* herself in the last seven years, after what had happened back home. Making him go would kill her.

Not making him go might kill *him*.

"Why don't you sit down, Shale." Anwei steepled her fingers, pressing them together to hide the way they shook. When Shale and Altahn finally stopped whispering so loud that she could hardly think, she gave them her best smile. "I'm sure you understand that discretion in our line of work is important."

She waited until they both nodded before setting aside her medicine bag. "Knox will be intrigued. We'll need an advance, of course. All the information you've collected so far. And a promise you will never set foot in this shop *ever again*. Not you or Altahn. Knox would never accept an outsider trying to manage him anyway."

"I beg your pardon?" Shale spat.

"We can do that," Altahn interjected.

"You've got information on the dig itself? The traps they've uncovered, maps? A roster of workers and guards?"

Altahn spoke before Shale could sputter a response. "They're not letting much out of the dig at all. We managed to intercept a few reports about artifacts, and we do have a map of both the compound and the tomb itself as far as it's been explored."

"Guard schedules? Names of the archeologists involved? How many workers and where they came from?"

"We'll provide you with everything we can, of course. Including all the background information we have on the man in charge." Altahn smiled, and Anwei could see he hadn't missed her interest. "But if you aren't willing to work closely with me, then there are some things we can't hand over until you're ready to take the sword. I'll be there outside the compound when you go in and meet you when you come out. Maps, details about obstacles we've managed to identify." He shrugged at her flat expression. "You could take any information we've lifted and turn us in to the magistrate. I'm not willing to take that kind of risk."

Anwei watched his face, his hands, his fingers twitching this way and that. He wasn't comfortable with what they were doing. The thieving, or whatever the *real* purpose of this job was. After all, no employer would want to be at the scene of the crime as it was being committed—the risk of getting caught was far too high.

This was definitely a trap. Definitely dangerous. And Anwei definitely couldn't pass it up. She'd sailed straight into a storm to escape the carnage the snake-tooth man had made of her life. This time the wind, the rain, the thunder and lightning, wouldn't be coming for her. This time Anwei would ride the storm just like the vacuous sky creature so many in the Commonwealth called a goddess.

And Knox would have to leave.

Anwei sat up straight, dipping her quill in the inkpot and putting it to vellum. "Tell me everything you can."

CHAPTER 12

A Soul like Dried Sweat

When Knox finally spotted Anwei's purpled aura in the crush between Chaol's gate on the other side of the bridge, he couldn't help but stand up from his table. His muscles complained at the movement after an hour of sitting fused to his chair outside the riverbank malthouse while he waited for her.

He held himself in check, bobbing forward on his toes and almost knocking his head against the battered malthouse sign, a peeling affair sporting a bloodied auroshe with a broken horn. Running through the crowd to check Anwei for wounds wouldn't do anything but draw attention, but every moment of waiting itched as if he'd swallowed a cupful of spiders.

Anwei walked right past Knox, eyeing a towering silenbahk as it lumbered past, before ducking into the crowd. The riverbank market was clogged tight, and by the time Knox had pulled out a coin to leave on the table, she'd lost herself among the hundreds of traders milling between stalls. He slid into the tide of wide skirts, scarves, dirty boots, and false silver, disconcerted when he couldn't find Anwei's dark aura in the flood. Even more so when following her, despite not being able to see her aura, wasn't a problem, the spot at the back of his head that belonged to her pointing him through the crowd.

He looked back toward the bridge that led to the Sand Cay. He didn't see any familiar auras, and not a single fleck of gold. No one had followed Anwei out of Chaol so far as he could see. How had she escaped?

Knox followed Anwei to the wagon lines at the edge of the market, snippets of her primrose accent easy to pick out from the thistly affectations of the Elantin trader she was speaking to. "You're headed for Gretis?" she asked as he loaded bags of dried barley into the back of his cart. "Just two of us."

"That's a nice little place—right on the ocean. I can get you there in less than an hour." The driver walked around the edge of the cart to check on the animal tethered to the front. A donkey? It had odd twisty horns that made Knox think it was at least part auroshe. "You'll have to walk from the road, though," the man called.

Knox couldn't help himself, pulling Anwei around to face him. "You're all right?" he asked.

"Why wouldn't I be?" Anwei gave him a bright smile, the one she used to wrap people up and make pets of them. He fell back a step, surprised. To most people, Anwei looked soft, small, and bright, but it had been a long time since she'd bothered pretending with him.

"What happened?" he whispered.

Still she smiled. A sharpened blade in a sheath made of wildflowers. "Gretis is the perfect place for us to get away. Finally, we'll get to spend some time alone together!"

Knox's aurasight begged to expand, but he forced himself to fall in with what Anwei was doing, as he had the night before, pretending all he could see was her pretty face when he was looking for guards. The air seemed to hum with violence.

"How are you in once piece?" he whispered.

"Did you expect anything else?" She raised an eyebrow, lowered her voice. "We're getting you out of here."

The old man bumped Knox's arm as he came back around the cart, then lifted another bag into the bed. "It'll be a copper apiece, healer. I'll settle for one and a split if you help me load the rest of these bags."

"Perfect." Anwei stepped away from Knox and hoisted one of the bags up from the ground.

Knox numbly followed her movements, flinching when a deep boom echoed out from the drum tower. He turned to watch the trade gate's heavy timbers on the other side of the bridge shudder and begin to close. Panic of a new kind welled inside him, his mind suddenly full of the pockmarked sword.

Are you going to leave me again? Willow's voice rasped in his head. Knox tried to swallow, his throat dry. He'd left her the day she died. Gone to see the Devoted play-fight in the town square while she and the rest of his family were being brutally murdered.

"Why are they closing the gate?" he croaked.

"I heard someone important went missing." Anwei looked toward the gate, unconcerned.

Someone important. Like a runaway Devoted? Were they trying to shut *him* in and had just missed him?

Anwei touched his arm. "Not you. Someone from the governor's house, up on the Water Cay." She tossed her braids out of her face, bending to pick up another sack. "Are you going to leave all of these for me?"

Knox forced himself to turn from the closing gate. The sword's voice carved lines in his head, crying acid tears. *Anwei doesn't care about me. Maybe* you'll *be safe from Devoted in Gretis, but what will happen if they find* me? *It wasn't enough earlier. It's never enough. Now you'll be far away, too.*

He'd hidden Willow (the sword? Were they the same?) in his bags when he'd left with the Devoted for the seclusion. Buried her in the gardens outside once they arrived because Devoted weren't allowed possessions. But Master Helan had seen Willow in Knox's thoughts that last day at the seclusion. Sky-cursed spiriter. If Master Helan hadn't found the sword in his mind, maybe Calsta would have let Knox stay. Maybe he wouldn't have had to cut his way out, running from his life once again.

Maybe he would never have met Anwei.

He hoped the Roosters he'd fought had recovered.

Knox swallowed, bending to pick up the last sack of barley. "How long are we going to be gone?"

Anwei heaved her bag into the cart with a grunt. She glanced back toward the wall. "You can't be away from . . . *it*?" Her hand strayed to her shoulder in an odd pantomime of Knox's own reaching for the sword. She looked back at him. "Or is it your money box that's got you worried?"

The words were, once again, flower-petal soft. Knox searched through them for thorns. Anwei had found him today with the sword in his hand after he'd promised not to touch it. Was this some kind of . . . ending? His money box was supposed to be his way over the border, but when the Trib had started chasing him, it hadn't been Lasei or bribes he'd been thinking about.

It had been Anwei.

He threw the last sack into the cart, then climbed in and held a hand out to help her up after him. "Please just tell me what is happening. Tell me you're okay."

A shadow crossed her face, softening something in her expression, but then it hardened again. She took his hand and climbed in next to him, waving for the driver to prod the bony mule into a walk. Anwei grabbed hold of the side of the cart as it jerked into motion. "You know I'm okay."

"And?"

"And you are going to stay at the inn at Gretis. I'll get your sword, your money, and let you borrow some besides. I just got an advance on a new job." Anwei's fingers made knots of one another as she crossed her feet at the ankles next to him, holding herself away so there was space between his legs and hers. The air between them felt cold even in the afternoon heat. "It won't be enough to bribe your way over the border, but it'll be a good start. You could go north first and see if the bribe is less if you cross from Trib land."

"Don't firekey lizards infest the whole mountain range? I'd get roasted before I got close." Knox sat back, the cart's sideboards pressing into his spine. Only the night before, when they'd seen the auroshes, Anwei had been full of reasons he should stay. What had changed? "Tell me what happened." He kept his voice low, pitched so the driver wouldn't be able to hear. "Please, Anwei?"

Anwei smoothed braids back from her face, twirling one and then another. Counting them one by one as if she meant to check there really were a hundred. "The men who followed you from the Sand Cay were the same ones who left the bid in the temple last night."

Knox's forehead crinkled. They'd asked him to come to the malt-house, then tried to corner him? "That makes no sense, Anwei. Why would they chase me home?"

"They're very motivated."

"And you're . . ." He watched her face, the way she was looking away from him. "You're taking the job."

Anwei scanned the streams of people parting for the cart as it bumped down the road, her eyes seeming to find every face that passed. Every face but his.

"And I'm being sent to Gretis? You don't want me to help?" he asked.

"Not this time."

"Are you angry at me?" Knox scrubbed a hand through his hair, hating this fake version of Anwei that she was putting up around her like a shield, trying to remember what had happened at the apothecary.

It was murky, full of Willow's voice and the sword. "I know you told me not to go, but . . . it was so much money. And I didn't mean to pick up the sword."

"I know." She arranged a smile on her face, a small, parched thing he'd never seen before. "I'm just beginning to see that I should have asked more questions before inviting a Devoted to live down the hall, that's all."

The words jabbed like bony fingers in Knox's stomach. "Like what?"

Anwei touched the back of her head with tentative fingers, and Knox could feel a sort of echoing twinge in his own head. "It doesn't matter now."

"It does matter. Anwei, whatever is happening—"

"It isn't safe for you in Chaol, Knox." She spoke a little faster now, as if even she was tired of having to put on her pretty apothecary face for him. "I didn't want the cart driver to hear, but whatever that was on the wall—you're only safe because the Devoted were distracted. One went missing, I guess, and they're searching for her. If something happens with you again, you won't have that kind of luck."

"Me? What about you, Anwei?"

"What about me?" She was losing patience.

Knox sat back against the cart's slats, trying to think. Devoted didn't just go missing. Not unless they were him. "How do you know one of the Devoted went missing? It's too soon for your contacts to be feeding you information. The only one you'll see in person is that Neela girl."

"Noa. She doesn't know she's a contact. She thinks we're friends."

"Aren't you?"

Anwei shrugged. "I went by the governor's house to see if you were right about Devoted coming after you."

"You just . . . went back there?" The idea of it sucked the air from Knox's lungs. He touched her arm, trying to give weight that didn't sound like instruction. "Anwei, Devoted will be able to see what you are. You can't—"

"What is that supposed mean?" Knox startled back from the sudden raw sting to her voice. "*What I am.* I'm a person. I heal people. I find things. I'm good at both."

"I know." The rose in her cheeks had darkened, the plum hue in her aura churning around her head. Anwei's teeth dug into her lip, and for a moment Knox wished he could read thoughts, but he immediately regretted such a flippant want. Gifts from Calsta never came without sacrifice, and the ones that went with reading thoughts were the kind he was glad had never been asked of him. "But, Anwei, I thought a Devoted was going to come over the wall with your body draped over his shoulder because—"

"Because *what?*" Anwei turned to face him head-on now. No shielding smile, no soft words, no compliments. Her fingers worried at the top button on her apothecary tunic, tight against her throat. "You've been calling me a witch since we first met. I always thought it was a bad joke. But was it ever? Today it got a little too close. Do you think I don't know what Devoted do?"

Knox suddenly couldn't breathe. Devoted kept the peace. Watched the borders. Kept an eye on the governors.

And they killed Basists before they could become shapeshifters.

He shook his head, hardly able to control the movement. "Anwei, it *was* a joke."

"Which explains why you won't let me come anywhere near you when you're sick. You're afraid I'll *witch* you."

"No. I mean . . ." Yes. In the year he'd been with Anwei, Knox had seen her use her aura. When she was helping sick people, it glowed around her like a plague lantern in the dark. But he knew dirt witches could do more.

"You mean you're worried I'll suck your soul out through your eyeballs? You think *I'm* the reason the Devoted haven't tracked you down, but also the reason they're going to find us now?" Anwei twisted the button at her throat so hard, Knox heard threads pop. "I'm really good at smelling things. That's it, Knox. It doesn't have anything to do with magic or . . . whatever you said today. Auras. Or shapeshifting or anything else." She gave an experimental sniff. "And unless your soul stinks like dry sweat, I can't smell it to steal it."

"I *didn't* mean . . ." Knox shifted against the bags, rubbing a hand across his face, the gritty dirt from the marketplace scratching his skin. "I don't have an excuse. I'm sorry." He tried to sort through the muck that coated the conversation they'd had at the apothecary. He'd handed her his sword, then run because she'd told him to run. And he'd said . . .

Oh, he'd said some things. In exactly the wrong way. The twist inside of Knox wrung tighter. "I am not afraid of you, Anwei." He shivered as he said it, the truth much more complicated. "And I wish you were right about smelling things."

Putting his hands up when she glared, Knox tried to keep his voice calm. "I mean, not about my soul. I wish it were true that you were born with a parchwolf's nose. But that's . . . not a thing. You know it's magic. Don't you?"

"No. I don't know that." Her eyes pinched closed, and Knox began to worry that he'd truly broken something between them. Or maybe that she'd broken something inside herself, and talking about it wasn't going to make it better. But she brushed it away, forcing her eyes open again. "And even if it was, what does it matter? Is my *nose* going to slit your throat?"

The crowded booths had given way to an open road. Fields of some crop swayed beyond that, deep enough to hide just about any kind of monster, a salty wind swishing up from the ocean to ripple through them from the ocean cliffs beyond.

Knox lowered his voice and leaned toward Anwei. "It doesn't *matter* to me that you can do banned magic. You are a good healer. Some of the old Basists were too, before they found the oaths to grow so much stronger. Devoted aren't going to find me because of you, they'll find me because *me*. But if they find me, they'll see you, too. Except for some reason it seems like they can't see us when we're together."

"That makes absolutely no sense, Knox. I wasn't with you on the wall."

"No, but then you *were*. . . . I called out to *you* when I fell. And you answered. And then . . . this happened." He touched his head.

Anwei was shaking her head. "Still doesn't make sense. I don't even believe in any of your stone gods."

"You know what doesn't make sense?" Knox sat forward, trying desperately to make her look at him. "A year ago I was lying in the street, so drained that it's a miracle I was still alive. I wasn't even trying to hold in Calsta's energy. I was on fire. They could probably have seen me all the way back in Rentara. And the one who was hunting me . . ." Thinking of Ewan and the years of bruises and scars that went with him made Knox's fingers clench. Of Ewan spitting on the country boy who bested him in the training yards. Ewan trying to cheat and stab Lia when the masters weren't looking, of broken glass in her sheets, and sugar in Knox's tea. Ewan would never stop trying to stomp out a light that looked even a little brighter than his own. "He never would have stopped looking, not out of pity, not out of a sense of decency. Not for anything. But you picked me up and took me in, and there wasn't anything for him to find."

"I didn't do anything but give you a bed, some soup, and a lousy landlord!"

"Then"—Knox couldn't let her talk over him—"when I panicked on the wall, I lost control and was on fire again. I called for you, and suddenly . . . you were there. Your aura or . . . something. It covered me. It got *deeper*." He shivered, touching the back of his head.

"I didn't do anything." Anwei's brows crunched down, her rosebud mouth flattening into a frown. "I am *not a* shapeshifter."

"I didn't say you were!"

"You of all people should know I'm not. It was a shapeshifter who made that sword of yours!"

"I know!" Knox's stomach pulled, his throat bubbling with bile as his sister's gaunt face reappeared in his head.

"You think I could make something like *that*?"

"No. I know you couldn't. You'd be better suited as a . . . *pri* . . ." Once again Knox couldn't remember the word. "A . . . pineapple."

Anwei stared at him, her mouth hanging open. Then she clapped hands over her lips, her eyes scrunching shut with a laugh she couldn't keep in. When she finally had control of herself, she let her hands drop, the smile still unwilling on her lips. "*Priantia*. Of all the words you could learn in Trib, why is *that* the one you keep reaching for?"

Her smile was a relief, even reluctant the way it was. Knox knew Anwei wasn't a murderer, but it *was* banned magic that had left his parents cold and his sister some kind of ghost festering inside a sword. He tried to find the right words. "I don't think of you as one of . . . one of *them*."

"A wandering Trib holy man? That's probably good, because I think Calsta would be upset with my methods. I've never once tried to give up my food and clothes in order to convince her I'm worthy of power."

Knox shook his head, not wanting to think about the northerners so devoted to Calsta that they attempted to sacrifice the way Devoted did in the hopes she would touch them. "It was my *job* to find people who were using the nameless god's power before. You aren't like them. I mean, I guess you are in some ways. But they were . . ."

"Bad?" She licked her lips and pressed them together. "If there's an 'us' and a 'them' based on whatever you've decided is wrong with me, then why do I get to be part of your 'us' instead of your 'them'?"

"I guess because I know you?" Knox waited for her to look at him. She didn't. The night was cooling, sweat on him drying sticky and uncomfortable.

"Did you try to know any of the other ones you met?"

"They were hurting people, Anwei. And it isn't something I 'decided' about you. Auras don't lie. They only change color if you've been using energy from an outside source. *Magic*, if you prefer. It marks you forever. When you're actively drawing it in, you burn brighter than a normal person. I can see it in you." He looked down, the sinking feeling inside his chest dropping an inch or two. "Those Devoted in Chaol will be able to see it too. Unless there is . . ." He pointed to her and then back to himself. "Something here."

The button on her tunic was about to come off between her fingers. "You don't understand. I *can't*—"

"I'm not going to tell. *You're* not hurting anyone, Anwei." Knox reached out to touch her arm again. "I mean, not really. There are a few high khonin who might disagree with me."

Mouth twisting, Anwei looked out into the fields. Her voice came out in a croak. "I'll meet you at the inn in Gretis tomorrow morning with all your things. You can't stay with me anymore." Then she hopped off the back of the cart.

Knox caught one glimpse of her dark outline against the swaying stalks before she was in the field and out of sight. He breathed in deep, the air around him suddenly so much colder. Then he jumped off after her.

"Anwei?" He plunged into the shivering plants just as a bright light flashed from somewhere across the field near the cliffs—a trail of lanterns moving in a tidy line like ants in the distance. The light blazed in front of Anwei's form ahead of him, the milky yellow making a halo around her face and down her shoulders.

Knox drew even with her, letting her lead him through the maze of stalks toward the ocean, assuming that if he just kept following, she'd either tell him to go away or tell him what they were doing, but she didn't.

"I don't want to go to Gretis without you," he said. "You saved my life a year ago, and you saved me again today."

"The Trib weren't going to kill you."

"We didn't know that. You're the only good thing in my life. I don't *want* to leave. . . ." The words choked in his throat because they were wrong. *I don't want to leave* you. The rest of the sentence sat like a stone on his tongue. He swore at himself under his breath.

Anwei's face was an unnerving blank as she methodically moved through the plants towering over their heads, her eyes never straying from the lights. Auras fizzed into existence when they got closer, arranged around some kind of compound with high walls of wood where field should have been, running clear to the edge of the ocean cliff. Just as Knox was about to speak again, she stopped, sniffing quietly.

"Did you see the guards?" Knox whispered.

"No." She sniffed again. "What are we up against?"

We. Knox felt the tension in his chest lessen a tiny bit. "There are three on this side. But I can't see far enough to know if they go all the way around. If there are only cliffs on the other side, they probably don't watch it as closely."

Anwei nodded, squinting at what they could see of the compound. "Do you trust me, Knox?"

She'd said it back in his room, the sword between them. "Of course I do."

"Then go to Gretis. This job isn't for you."

"*This* is the job?" Knox looked toward the torches. The compound wall was so new that sap wept from the boards. "What inside there is worth twenty thousand in silver? Worth trying to force a thief into working for you?"

"I can't say I understand it, but they need us. Me, anyway." Anwei circled toward the back side of the compound. She sniffed again, her nose wrinkling. "Are those bael wreaths hung under the torches? It's like they're afraid of something in there."

Knox squinted at the herbs strung across the walls, able to see the shape of them, but he didn't know enough about herbs to agree. How could he have been so stupid to think the Trib were working for the Warlord? "What did they do to you? Did they threaten you?"

She shook her head, not quite looking at him. "Bael is supposed ward off ghosts." He could practically feel her rolling her eyes at the idea before she moved on, but Knox's neck prickled, and he barely stopped himself from reaching for the sword that wasn't there. Ghosts weren't so easy to dismiss for him.

Anwei muttered to herself as they circled back toward the compound's gate, stopping every few feet to make notes on the pad she kept in her medicine bag. "Wall is about ten paces high, and it's all lit. . . ." She took in a deep breath as the wind swished over the compound and into their faces. "I can smell fresh-turned clay. Metal and glass—tools probably. And I can see the governor's house mark on some of the equipment out here. . . ." Another gust touched her face, her long braids blustering around her like blades of grass. "Uh-oh."

Knox froze at the same time she did, because the wind had brought something to his ears just as she smelled it. A high, cackling whinny that belonged to no horse. The tall, grassy stalks rustled about thirty paces to the south, an aura suddenly in range and headed toward them.

Bad things always came in threes. "Let's go, Anwei."

"Why are there auroshes here?" Anwei whispered, her brow furrowed.

Panic welled up inside Knox, and he grabbed her arm, meaning to pull her back from the aura steadily pushing toward them through the field, but Anwei halted, her hands flying up to cover her mouth.

A figure had appeared at the top of the compound wall. A hood shadowed his face, his coat rippling behind him in the ocean wind. Though he was too far for Knox to sense his aura, something inside Knox went still, Calsta's energy leaking past his barriers to fill him before he could stop himself.

The torch glow turned the man's hood a fiery red as he scanned the fields. Knox forced himself to let go of Calsta's power, though it was obvious this man wasn't Devoted or he would have seen their auras at once. The patrolling guard was less than twenty paces away and would see them for sure if they didn't move.

"We have to go, Anwei." Knox's arms erupted in goose bumps as the figure's hood swung in their direction. "Now."

Anwei didn't move, eyes stuck tight to the form on the wall, her nose flaring. She sucked in air until Knox was sure she'd implode. He grabbed her hand and pulled her back through the stalks, the spiky leaves whipping across his face and clawing at his sleeves. He glimpsed the woman patrolling the field, a Rooster's three underbraids tight against her head.

Though it was too dark for the man on the wall to see them with torchlight at his feet, Knox couldn't shake the feeling he was watching them go. That there was something very wrong inside that compound, and he didn't like the idea of finding out what it was.

Anwei let him shepherd her back through the field. Just as their feet found the road's pressed dirt, the high whinny sounded again, like teeth scratching on bone. Knox took hold of Anwei's shoulders, all thoughts of swords, the border, even Devoted, becoming unnaturally small in his head. Castor's anemic light painted Anwei's face with purple lines. Her aura was, for once, quiet.

"Who was that?" he whispered.

Anwei dragged her eyes away from the pinpricks of light in the distance. He flinched when a tear ran down her cheek.

"All these finding jobs . . ." Her voice was brittle. "Yaru. Breaking into people's houses." She looked up, finally meeting his eyes, and it was as if her iron coating had cracked and she was letting him see a sliver of what was really inside. "I never told you what it is I've really been looking for."

CHAPTER 13

The Woes of a Wandering Soul

Mateo woke with a wooden spoon lodged between his teeth.

He gagged, and suddenly air flowed into his lungs, as if they'd been empty for hours. Panic spooled tight around his chest when he tried to move his arms and found he couldn't. The spoon disappeared for a moment, then returned to pour hot liquid down his throat. His throat clenched in protest, bile building up and threatening to vomit out.

The sound of a thick slurry bubbling in a pot close by turned Mateo's panic to raging fury. He was broken again, and there was nothing he could do about it.

"Thank the nameless god." His father blew out a breath when Mateo's eyes opened. A metallic medicinal taste coated Mateo's mouth, and he shuddered, swallowing again and again to try to clear it away. "You used your power to look deeper into the tomb, didn't you? You can only use a drop, a *taste*, Mateo, or the sickness—"

"I only looked a little. Nothing more than usual." Mateo choked. He focused on his lungs, each breath wet and unwilling. His heart beat sluggishly. "I didn't feel any different than normal down there, except maybe a little faint when we were talking to the director. I wish you would teach me the oaths so I could just *try*—"

"Don't push yourself. Be calm. I wish I could look for you. . . ."

"But you can't, I know," Mateo finished. "You only do plants and healing and all that." The nameless god didn't hand all talents out to one person. He liked to spread them around.

"That tone of voice doesn't solve anything, but it does make me worried you'll bite me." Tual sighed when Mateo rolled his eyes. "You know that oaths would only open you up further to the sickness. It would make this worse."

Mateo pressed his eyelids shut, forcing himself to focus on the sounds Tual made as he stirred the pot, the compound squelching unpleasantly. If the nameless god had chosen Mateo as a vessel for power, why had he allowed Mateo to crack? He opened his lips for the spoon when it came, and warmth spread through him as the medicine went down despite its awful consistency.

"I've had a letter from the Warlord, by the way," Tual murmured, balancing the spoon across the top of his pot. "She's on her way. I guess her retinue is going to stay in the city to keep up the narrative that this is over the political upset."

A cough tore through Mateo's chest, bending him forward and leaving him with a mouthful of black tar. He spat it out over the side of his bed, his whole body shaking. "She's not expecting us to be involved somehow, is she?" Mateo choked out. "I thought that was why we took a house outside the city. To keep high khonins from poking their noses into things."

Tual once again presented the spoon and waited until Mateo had sipped the medicine before answering. "We can endure a little poking if it means we get what we came for."

"You think so? Or is this some kind of weird checkup because she doesn't trust us? And what will happen once you've cured all her Devoted and she doesn't need fake-aukincer dirt witch trash—"

"None of that, Mateo." Tual sat back, replacing the lid on the pot and carefully setting the spoon on top again. "Pretending I'm an aukincer is the only reason we're still alive. And the shapeshifter kings weren't good people. The reaction to them was warranted, if . . . misinformed. It's not surprising that people still feel worried about people like us."

"Warranted? Thousands of people were *slaughtered*. Both of us should be dead, according to the law." Mateo allowed his father to pull him up, but he took it slow, the comfortable web of anger bright in his mind. "Why should I be held accountable for wrongs done over five hundred years ago? *Anyone* in the Commonwealth could decide to take their neighbor's life. Last I checked, they don't put people to death until they actually do it. Why is the standard different for us? Just because I *could* become a horrible monster that destroys society as we know it doesn't mean I will."

It was an old argument, one his father hadn't bothered to engage with in a long time. "Fear does funny things to people."

"Very funny. Mass murder is hilarious. If only you hadn't shown up before my parents were able to finish slitting open my humors when I was a child. That would have been enough to laugh about for *years*."

He couldn't remember much more than that. A knife. Tual carrying him away. He'd learned enough about purging ceremonies at the university to put the rest of it together and hadn't prodded any further. Not knowing was better than having to think of parents who would destroy their young child—little more than a baby—out of fear for themselves.

Tual settled back on his stool by the bed. "I am your father, Mateo. Blood doesn't change that. Your parents didn't want you and I did. I could see the potential in you, when all they could see was evil. It's like trying to persuade the world there are two moons when they aren't willing to look at the sky. The light is there on their faces, Jaxom and Castor are there for anyone to see, but you can't force people to look up." He shrugged. "Changing things will take time, but we've made a good start. A start that will be much more difficult to maintain if you don't keep that temper in check."

Heat in his cheeks, Mateo nodded, though it didn't do much to stop the resentment built up inside. It was made from reed after reed, small things that had happened over his life, all bound together around his heart until they formed an unbreachable wall. The world would change. He would make it.

He just had to not die first.

"Like I said, I have a plan." Tual stood up and went to the wardrobe in the corner. "Get dressed. We have a house call this morning."

"You're already healing people? We've only been here a few days." Mateo let his feet swing down to touch the floor, his head pounding. Thankfully, his heart was pounding too. It was as if he were a windup toy, only needing a good twist to come back to life. His fingers wanted charcoal and vellum, Patenga's distinctive figure in front of him to draw. "Why do I have to come? I just want to go back to the dig. Anything else will be torture."

"You can't go muddling around in a tomb when you're still recovering from an episode." The smile on his father's face looked positively mischievous. "And I only arrange for the best kinds of torture for you, son. I'll find you a fancy coat to make it more bearable. Something with lace."

By the time Mateo and his father arrived at the house in question, Mateo was dripping with sweat and cross. Chaol was so inconvenient with the separate cays and the ferries and the skybridges and the tunnels—he couldn't even imagine how difficult it had been to navigate between sections of the city before the trade bridge united most of the main cays. Mateo lowered himself onto the edge of the ostentatious fountain in the main courtyard in front of the house, the spray a moment of relief from the wet, heavy heat. Fanning himself, Mateo looked down at his coat. It was, perhaps, a bit too lacy for the weather. His boots, however, were perfect.

Tual crossed from the house's main doors and sat next to him on the fountain's lip. "Apparently, most people need appointments to see the valas of Chaol. Don't worry, though, he won't keep us long."

"Didn't you send word we were coming?" Mateo fanned himself even harder, wishing he could curse the blasted sun. If the grooms or the household were Calsta devotees, they probably wouldn't appreciate it if he did.

"He knew we were coming."

The main doors opened, and a man came storming out. A man with the sides of his head shaved and a sword belted at his hip. The Devoted stalked past them and out the compound gate without even looking in Mateo's direction. A sad echo of aurasparks circled the man, as if to tease Mateo for his lackluster ability to sense them. Mateo turned to look at his father, alarm firing inside his chest. "What is this? You said we're not getting involved in the political stuff."

"Did I?" Tual smiled, but it was the smile that made Mateo want to check his pockets for bees or lizards or something else equally unexpected. "Well, hopefully, we won't be. We should get you inside, though. You're sweating."

"I'm fine. It's not like I'll ever see these people again, so it doesn't matter much if my copious sweating offends—" Mateo broke off as a guard emerged from the house, a second man close behind him.

"Valas Seystone, we are so pleased to meet you." Tual stood, moving to greet the man. Mateo kept his seat, wondering what his father could want with the deputy governor of Chaol. Tual continued without introducing Mateo. "The moment I heard your wife was sick, I knew I had to come."

The valas toyed with the top button of his coat. "Who told you my wife was sick? We're honored, of course, by your visit, aukincer— and the Warlord's visit is much anticipated, I assure you, but . . ." He floundered, pulling out a handkerchief to mop his brow. "I'm afraid this isn't the best time."

Mateo stood, knowing the part he was supposed to play. "Illness is especially uncomfortable in this weather. Could be water related? Lower humors?" He looked at his father, who nodded.

"It is quite serious, but . . ." The man swallowed uncomfortably. "I didn't ask for you to come."

Mateo's father smiled. "And yet, here we are." He gestured to Mateo. "There are important introductions to be made, but my son is recovering from his own illness, so I must request that we find a more comfortable spot to make them."

The valas's face blanched, and he looked this way and that as if there were some way out of inviting the Warlord's personal aukincer into his home. When the valas glanced toward the sky, Mateo had to stifle a laugh, wondering if he was hoping Calsta would help him. No storm clouds rolled in and no lightning struck Mateo or his father down, so the man turned and led them toward the house.

A trickle of sweat wormed its way down Mateo's temple as they stepped into the white marble entryway, but he stopped himself from wiping it away, trying to tamp down frustration at his father's overly large grin. What was Tual up to? If Mateo couldn't go to the dig, he would much rather have stayed back at the house to sneak his father's copy of *A Thousand Nights in Urilia* than watch Tual make yet another high khonin squirm. Why had *he* needed to come?

Tual stopped to ask about the beautiful carvings set into the double staircase leading to an upper level. Mateo rolled his eyes over the valas's jumbled account involving his great-grandfather and a very old salmon—until Tual caught his eye.

Mateo's father looked purposefully at the floor, then looked back up at Mateo. Mateo glanced down, but there was nothing to see but boring black and white tiles. When he shrugged, Tual actually pointed at the floor and had to cover it up by swatting at an imaginary fly when the valas's story stalled in confusion.

"I heard there have been some conflicts between you and the governor, Seystone." Tual interrupted the valas's story, giving Mateo one last meaningful look. "In fact, I heard the Warlord is coming partly to resolve them. . . ."

Great. A government official who needed political help. Mateo waited until the valas looked away from him to glare at the tile again, which was when he saw it. Mateo put a hand over his mouth, sweat dripping down his cheeks.

The valas stopped midreply. "Is . . . there something wrong?"

"No. Of course not."

Yes. There was. Because under the tiles, probably on the floor below, Mateo could just make out the golden flecks of a Devoted's aura. Mateo put a hand to his forehead, wondering if he'd done more damage to himself in the tomb than he'd thought. There was no way a Devoted could be hiding in Valas Seystone's basement.

The aura didn't go away, though. Mateo couldn't see it, exactly. It was more like sunlight on rippling water, there and gone in one second. A famished, withered version of what he should have been able to see, unless it was a fledgling, untrained Devoted.

The thought sat in the back of his mind for a moment, not quite registering. But when it did . . .

Mateo looked back at his father, his eyes wide with alarm.

Tual's grin put Mateo on high alert. The Devoted who had just stormed out of here should have been able to detect any sort of aura. He would have demanded the valas turn whoever it was over, in accordance with the Warlord's mandate . . . but what was a Devoted to a valas when it came to power?

It was hard to tell. It depended on what the Devoted's orders were.

The Warlord, however, wouldn't take kindly to a rich valas hiding a fledgling Devoted. This—whatever it was—was an execution in the making.

But Tual's grin made Mateo think his father saw it as an opportunity. A Devoted potentially separate from any seclusion, any loyalty to the Warlord. What was it Tual had said earlier? *A caprenum sample is not the only reason I dragged you out here.*

The Warlord was always a breath away from discovering what they really were. Devoted hunted Basists every day, so it was a mystery to Mateo how Tual and he had survived as long as they had. Like Tual had said, they had to find caprenum, then disappear. But where was there to go? A place far enough away, independent enough, that they could live without worrying who was watching. Mateo had always assumed that meant Lasei, where they prohibited magic but not the people who were capable of performing it. But now, with so many fewer Devoted to do the Warlord's will, it was much less likely anyone would come looking for them if they stayed in the Commonwealth.

Maybe in a place where Devoted didn't usually go. Like Chaol.

I only arrange for the best kinds of torture for you. We have to plan out your future.

Mateo could see the shape of what was about to happen, and a scowl wasn't a serious enough response. Maybe if he opened his mind and shattered all of the windows or broke the stupid salmon carvings and the stairs with them, but even that wouldn't be enough. Tual had been threatening for *years*. And now he'd found someone with power who was in trouble—someone they could manipulate into making space for them.

His father wouldn't have called it torture unless it was Mateo who was going to be the bargaining chip on the table. Father had dragged him to this ridiculous house to meet a *girl*.

Tual caught his eye and smiled one last time before interrupting the valas's blustering. "I get the distinct impression you're hiding something from us."

Lia huddled in the pantry, her back lodged uncomfortably against a sack of flour. Aria sat squished in front of her with an ear to the door.

Ewan's voice still seemed to weigh in the air, touching everything inside her house even after he'd left.

The Warlord must have told him Lia had family in Chaol—it wasn't that hard to figure out, since she still carried their last name. But being smart enough to check at her family compound couldn't give Ewan his aurasight back to find her hidden in the pantry.

Lia tried to feel jubilant, victorious. Mostly she felt shaken, as though if she made any sudden movements, she'd fall to a thousand pieces.

Aria crept over and wrapped her arms around Lia. "He's gone," her sister whispered against her hair. The feel of arms around her brought tears to Lia's eyes, her sister so soft and good when all Lia remembered of her were naughty faces and play swords. "I would have climbed to your balcony a long time ago if I'd known you Devoted are always attacking each other like that. I'd have ridden straight to Rentara and sprung you right out."

"No one has ever . . ." Lia's teeth dug into her lip as she wondered whether Aria understood what had been happening when she'd raked her fingernails across Ewan's face to help Lia get away. "It's never happened before."

"Didn't they teach you to fight back? I thought that's what Devoted were for. Fighting."

There had been years of training. With Calsta's power flowing through her, Lia had felt invincible with a sword in her hand. But the moment Ewan had touched her, she'd frozen. Like some new kind of magic, one that fed on her surprise, horror, and fear. "I should have fought back better, Aria. I should have been able to."

"I don't see how 'shoulds' have anything to do with it. I'm just glad you're okay."

Footsteps tapped down the stairs toward them. Lia slipped a hand over Aria's mouth. Aria squirmed against Lia's arms as if she didn't like being held quite so tightly, but Lia had a hard time loosening them, her muscles stuck in that one position. Maybe if she never moved, Ewan would never find her. Maybe no one would.

But that wasn't what would happen. Ewan's aurasight would return soon, and then he wouldn't need eyes to see her. Calsta made repentant Devoted work to come back into her good graces, but he could be back to normal in two weeks if he did enough.

Lia wanted to believe there were some offenses the Sky Painter wouldn't forgive. That what Ewan had done would mark him as unfit for Calsta's sword. The memory of his body pressing her hard against the wall shuddered through Lia, and she put a hand up to cover her face. But abandoning the Warlord and hiding in her parents' pantry was breaking an oath too, and it bothered her that she didn't know which one Calsta would count worse.

The footsteps crossed the kitchen, closer and closer. Was it Ewan again?

Lia whispered a curse. She was *blind*. How long could she last?

They'd been sitting at the servants' table only an hour before Ewan had gotten there. Lia's father had sent all the servants away. Mother was sick, apparently, but the idea of seeing her soon had been enough for Lia to smile. Talk. *Laugh*, as if everything were all right. But that was a dream. This nightmare was real life. The Warlord would never let one of her prize spiriters disappear, wouldn't stop hunting until Ewan found a body.

A thin line of light broke the darkness, the pantry door easing open so awfully slow. But then suddenly Lia's father was on his knees beside her. He gathered Lia and Aria into his arms and squeezed them tight. "He's gone."

A hug. Lia began to cry.

"I didn't know." Father was crying too, tears dripping from his chin onto Lia's head. "I didn't know you wanted to escape. I would have come for you. I would have done *anything*—"

Feet padded down the stairs. Lia's father lurched back from her and out of the closet, and slammed the door between them. The footsteps turned into the room and paused just outside the door. Lia held Aria close. "The Warlord's aukincer is here to see you, sir."

"The Warlord's . . . ?" Lia didn't understand the stress in her father's voice. His footsteps paced toward them and then away again.

"Sir, should I ask him to leave?"

"No." Her father's voice was stretched thin, about to crack. "He must have seen the Devoted coming from the house. He'll know we're here." Swearing, he paced away and back again once more. "I . . . I'm coming."

His footsteps clicked across the kitchen and up the stairs. Lia had known the Warlord had an aukincer hidden away somewhere and that he was involved somehow in treating wasting sickness, but it had always been a bit confusing to her. Why employ a man obsessed with the nameless god to help Devoted?

It sounded uncomfortable. Desperate.

Which, considering what the Warlord had wanted Lia to do, was probably accurate. But what hold could such a man have on the valas of Chaol?

"An aukincer?" Aria whispered. "I've *always* wanted to—"

"Shhh. The guard might still be down here." Lia shifted to the side, holding her sister close as she pressed her ear to the door. Lia herself had come to Chaol to help the Warlord uncover some political plot, but no one had told her anything about an aukincer being a part of it.

"That was only Indran," Aria hissed. "He's not going to tell anyone you're here. And he tells the best jokes—"

"We can't let *anyone* know I'm here, Aria. Not even the servants," Lia breathed.

"I want to see the aukincer. What if he has horns like one of the old kings!" Aria's voice took on a certain whiny quality before Lia shushed her again. Maybe the aukincer could miraculously knit bones together the way the old stories hinted, but without the nameless god's power, she doubted it.

And what if being able to reknit bones meant you could break them too? Lia pushed the thought away when it twisted together with the feel of Ewan's teeth against her lip. What chance would she have had if he'd been a basist instead of Devoted? If he'd told the wooden floor to grow into a cage, cracked the walls open, and made them hold her? What if he'd broken the bones inside her, told her muscles them-selves to still?

Everything she knew about banned magic seemed pointed and sharp.

"Want to go spy on them?" Aria's voice broke into her thoughts

"Please be quiet, Aria." Still Lia couldn't let her go, as if Aria were an anchor to this reality and letting go would mean waking up in her bed in the governor's house, Ewan pounding on the door.

He'd find her. Even if she ate animal flesh and drank malt and bought every dress in the Gold Cay, Ewan would look for the last bro-ken bits of gold in her aura just the way he had for Knox, but worse, because he only wanted Knox *dead*.

Maybe if she went back and told the masters what had happened . . . Lia put her hands over her ears and clenched her eyes shut. It wouldn't help. Master Helan might take her side, but the other masters wouldn't push the Warlord's favorite little warrior out of his place among the Devoted. Ewan would always be there. Angry. Watching her. Waiting.

She couldn't go back. *Wouldn't*. The lines were cut.

"What is wrong with you, Lia? Are you okay?" Aria asked.

Lia let the question slide off her, not even sure what it meant to be okay anymore. *Knox* had been the catalyst for this whole mess. She'd seen him there on the wall, but not any of the other times she'd looked. He'd been hiding somehow.

If he could do it, so could she.

The Warlord would be here in two weeks. That was about how

long it would take for Ewan to recover his aurasight, too.

Two weeks to find Knox. He could show her how to hide.

"Lia?" Aria put a hand on her shoulder, her fingers soft. "You're scaring me. You said I can't call a servant . . . do you need to lie down? Mother's healers are upstairs. . . ."

Footsteps sounded, and Aria trailed off to look toward the pantry door. It wasn't just Father this time. There were at least three people approaching.

The pantry door suddenly wrenched open, blinding light assaulting Lia's eyes. She let go of Aria, springing into a crouch, her fists clenched. Her hood blocked most of her sight, so all Lia could see was a pair of very fancy buckles on a pair of very fancy shoes.

"Oh, good." A young man's voice, peeved through and through. "I found her."

CHAPTER 14

The Comfort of Middle Age

T hat man killed my brother." Anwei walked fast between sugarcane stalks, keeping the road in sight. She could feel Knox beside her but couldn't let herself look at him. She should never have let someone follow her around in the first place. It wasn't safe for either of them, and not just because of the snake-tooth man. "You'll be in danger now that I've found him. That's why I want you to go."

"Your brother?" Knox fought to keep up with her.

Anwei put a hand to her nose. The snake-tooth man had been there. Standing right in full view, smelling like the void he was. Shale had led her right to him. She could still feel Arun's laugh ringing in her ears. It sounded just the same as hers.

Her whole body ached, as if finding Arun's bloody bed had just happened. Memories of stealing food off his plate and him slapping her hand only to steal off hers; Arun's fingers gently tying one of her braids in front of the town council when she'd earned it; Arun steadying her when she started crying over a bowl of seeds that wouldn't grind down fine enough, her father waiting outside for the medicine to be ready. "We were like . . . one person. I pretended I'd done half the naughty things that were actually him, and he took canings for half of mine. It was the two of us, toeing the line for my father because he wanted us to learn right, Mother drying all our tears when he got frustrated with us." She took a deep breath, hardly able to glance over at Knox. She felt so, so empty. "He was everything to me. And the snake-tooth man killed him."

"All those jobs we did." Knox's mouth was moving too slow, tasting each word. "All the things we stole. It wasn't for the money?"

"Some of it was. Gulya doesn't pay *that* well."

Knox was so quiet. The sugarcane swayed in the breeze, and Anwei could hear every soft snick her shoes made against the ground, but even Knox's feet didn't make any noise. When he finally spoke, it was low. "You were looking for traces of his smell? And now you've found it. *Because* of this job?" He sped up, darting so he was ahead of her and walking backward, forcing her to meet his eyes. She could see the questions twisting in his mouth, but he kept them inside. No pasts. Only jobs and stupid banter. That was their unspoken agreement.

"I told you I'd bring you your money." She couldn't look at him. "More besides. You can head for the border, or . . ." The "or" came out before Anwei could tug it back.

"You said it was a trap. Someone offers us an obscene amount of money, and this guy you've been looking for is there at the middle of it? Anwei, this is not a good idea."

"The snake-tooth man is working inside the dig, and Shale can help me get inside. He knows who the snake-tooth man *is*." Anwei twined a braid around her finger, trying to remember what it had felt like when Arun first tied it, eli flowers tucked into the leather. One herb for each of the hundred braids. She could remember each of their names, but it was getting harder to remember the feel of him there beside her.

Knox switched to walking alongside her again. The lights grew closer, the night colder. "If there are Devoted inside that compound, I won't be able to help you."

"I know." It hurt even when she said it in a whisper. Why did it hurt? Half an hour ago he'd been accusing her of banned magic. Hours before that he'd been holding that abominable sword, and she'd been clutching the packet of calistet. This should be easy.

"And . . . I explained about auras. Why *you* being near Devoted isn't safe. You believe me?"

Anwei shrugged. Then shrugged again, tears burning against her eyelids. After all these years her scars still stung.

"But I want . . ." Knox tensed, his head jerking toward the edge of the field. "Someone's coming up the road. It could be Roosters. There were enough of them at that compound."

He paused long enough to be sure she was following before he melted into the shadows. It was odd, but she could point to where he was even without her eyes, keeping close behind him until he hopped into the ditch on the other side of the sugarcane field. She lowered herself down next to him and sat on the cold ground, surprised when he leaned toward her, his arm and shoulder brushing hers.

"Listen," he whispered once the hoofbeats had passed. "You've found your murderer. What now? You want to get revenge? Turn him in?" Knox paused, a question humming in his voice. "Kill him?"

She stood, dusted herself off, and climbed out of the ditch. "That last one."

"You should have told me to bring a bow. He'd already be dead."

"It isn't that easy."

"Why not?"

Anwei stared into the lights until her eyes watered. No questions. No history. No friends. No self. No life. Because she didn't have one. Not while the snake-tooth man still lived.

That wasn't what she wanted. To be empty. To constantly feel the raw edges of where Arun was supposed to fit in next to her. This life of chasing and hiding and never letting anyone in because it meant the snake-tooth man might hear she was there looking for him. That he'd do to her what he'd done to her parents, and then . . .

And then . . .

Anwei's face crumpled, and a gasp tore at her throat. She wanted it to be over. And now that the snake-tooth man was there, standing on the wall, real as murder itself, it could be. "An arrow wouldn't work. He's a shapeshifter, Knox—he could probably pluck it right out of the air before it got to him."

Knox stopped halfway out of the ditch, nearly falling back into it. He swore, floundering at the bottom for a moment before climbing out and walking to stand beside her, Jaxom's red moonlight a halo around his head. He stood very still, solidly *there* for once.

"My brother is dead because I was too scared to leave a town meeting. I let him hide at home without me, and I've spent the last seven years of my life trying to fix it." Saying the words out loud was a knife to Anwei's own stomach. "I escaped Beilda on a boat with no food, no clothes, no friends. Barely breath in my lungs."

"Escaped?" Knox's outline flinched, his hands opening and closing at his sides. The stillness of him was unnerving. "You mean you ran away from home?"

"No." Anwei started walking again, deflated, as if the secret had been the only thing holding her spine straight. "Killing my brother wasn't the only thing the snake-tooth man did."

Gretis's blocky buildings beckoned them out of the dark, only a hundred paces down the road. The town square was lit up at the center, people dancing back and forth under the lanterns.

"What more did the shapeshifter do, Anwei?" Knox was suddenly in front of her again, his hand on her arm. "Please, I need you to tell me. What happened?"

She steered him toward the shadows as they entered the town, searching for a red door that would mark an inn. The story bubbled up inside her, the one she could never tell, festering inside her like poison. And here Knox was, asking, as if he really cared.

He *did* care. Anwei could feel it inside her, like she'd had only two legs to a stool and suddenly Knox had lent her a third. "It was the day Arun was supposed to tie my last braid in front of the town council."

Knox took her arm and drew it through his as they walked. Maybe he knew she needed steadying even with those first words.

"Everyone was waiting for us, but Arun wouldn't come. It was like . . . he knew something was wrong." She smiled a little, remembering the way he'd tried to pretend that he was bored, that council meetings were a waste of time, that he'd rather go down to the ocean and search for gulls' eggs. "I got mad at him. I'd worked so hard to earn my last braid—he'd already earned his hundred and was working with my father in the shop—and I thought he didn't care. So I went without him and it stayed with me like a thundercloud. Hardly anyone came to the ceremony, like most of our town forgot I was finally earning my last braid. My father pulled my hair as he tied it. And as we walked home, I came up with all the awful things I was going to say to Arun for making such an important day a bad one. But when I got to his room, I . . . I found him. What was left of him."

Knox tensed beside her, his arm in hers pulling her an inch closer, as if he could hold her there where she couldn't get lost in such an awful memory. But saying it out loud did feel like losing herself. Anwei could still remember the smell of it: the red all over Arun's bed, the breeze from the open window, and the man who had been standing there. A *sort-of* man—hulking in the bright light like a beast startled from its meal, his cheeks streaked with blood. She'd felt something reach out toward her, something hot twisting up inside her brain as he met her eyes, until all she'd been able to do was scream. "I saw him— the snake-tooth man. He ran away from the house and I screamed for my parents, but when they came, they couldn't understand why I was so upset. They couldn't remember they had a son."

Knox's toe caught on a flagstone, and he barely managed to catch himself, swearing under his breath. "How is that possible?"

"I don't know." She could hardly whisper it, the memory still too acid to soak in. "It was as if the moment Arun stopped breathing, some god plucked him out of existence. Out of my parents' minds, from our friends', our entire village's memory. No one believed me that Arun had been killed, because no one knew who Arun was anymore. Not even when I showed them his blood, his fingers still scattered under the bed, where they'd been cut off. It was like they couldn't see any of it. I never even found the rest of his body."

"What did the snake-tooth man do with him?"

Anwei's head shook, her thoughts sticky with red. "He had blood on his face. Around his mouth and all across his cheeks. I don't know what it is shapeshifters have to do to steal . . ."

"Calsta above." Knox's breath was shaky as it went in. "Um . . . there's an inn over there." He pointed to a red door across the brightly lanterned square. It was sandwiched between two malthouses that reeked of dirt and boredom. "Are you all right?"

Anwei shook her head. "No. But I've had seven years of not being all right. Now I can finally do something."

Scrubbing a hand across his face, Knox gave her a gentle pull, leading her across the square and into the light. "Was there a . . . a weapon? Anything else the shapeshifter left behind?"

"A weapon? No." Anwei looked over at him, her mind glomming on to the sword. The day her brother was murdered was the day she remembered *smelling* for the first time. Not the normal scents of toast burning or dirty feet. The world opened up to her like a perfume bottle and presented itself with a curtsy. And all the herbs started shaking in their jars, screaming along with her. . . . Anwei shook her head now, wishing she could banish it all from her mind. "The shapeshifter left *nothing*. A trail of it. He *was* nothing, and he made Arun into nothing. He smelled like your sword."

Knox flinched, the moment of silence heavy. Anwei stifled her nose, setting aside the strong smells of sugarcane and cotton that blew in from the fields, not sure if Knox's reaction was because of the mention

of her nose or of his sword. *There's something wrong with your aura.*
Devoted will be able to see what you are.

But she was not what Knox thought she was. Maybe she could
have been, but not anymore.

"But why leave?" Knox asked. "Seven years . . . you couldn't have
been more than . . . ten?"

Anwei found herself a smile because laughing was always easier.
"You don't know how old I am?"

"Something more happened. What made you run?"

Something more. Every muscle in Anwei's body seemed to contract.
Her scars felt as if they were on fire. Anwei clenched her eyes shut, not
wanting to remember. Refusing. "It doesn't matter."

"How do you figure that?"

Anwei pressed her lips together and looked at him. "Does it matter?"

Opening his mouth, Knox couldn't seem to find words for a moment,
then finally cocked his head. "No, not if you don't want to talk about
it. You've already had to live through enough memories for one night, I
guess. But that was definitely your brother's murderer up on that wall?"
Knox scrubbed a hand through his hair. "What's the job?"

"The compound is a tomb excavation. Some old shapeshifter king.
Shale wants me to take a sword from the burial chamber." Anwei
watched him from the corner of her eye, not sure why he cared. "I
recognized Shale's description of the dig director and came out here to
see if I was right. It is definitely him."

"What could a Trib want with a—" Knox's voice cracked. "A
shapeshifter's sword?"

"What do you want with yours?"

They'd come to the inn door, and Knox stopped with his hand on
the latch, looking down at her, his mouth half-open as if he meant to
answer. But then he only pulled open the door.

Anwei bit back a curse. *No questions.* That was their agreement.

Spilling her secrets didn't mean he was going to reveal his own. He'd called her a dirt witch only a few hours earlier. Maybe this was where they parted ways, not because she told him to go, but because he'd finally want to go himself. She bit back another curse, wishing for the first time in a year that she hadn't picked Knox and his cursed sword up off the street.

Forcing her back to straighten despite the way her insides were caving in, Anwei followed him into the common room. She didn't really wish she and Knox had never met. That thought was almost as lonely as the idea of him leaving now.

The main floor was scattered with round tables, one of which hosted a circle of farmers suspiciously eyeing one another over their cards. A raised bar ran the length of the far wall, mismatched stools pushed up under it, staffed by a barkeep with a long, braided mustache who was reading an illustrated version of *A Thousand Nights in Urilia*.

"A room?" she called, not looking at Knox. She couldn't, the weight of her story unbalancing everything between them. She didn't want to go all the way back to the city alone, though, not with the nothing smell rank in her nose. "Two, if you've got them."

"Only got one that's clean." The man hardly looked up from his book.

"We're not picky." Anwei jumped when Knox nudged her with his shoulder. "Okay, *he* is picky. I don't know why, since he smells like a brickmaker's armpit."

The man set his book down. "Three coppers for two rooms. Four if you want dinner."

The first room smelled clean enough, though the bed linens were stained. The second, however, had a family of rats living in the straw-stuffed mattress and a hole in the floor that had obviously been used as a privy. Anwei looked sideways at Knox. "Just the one room will be fine," she said.

Once the barkeep left them, Anwei let herself slump down onto the bed. Knox took a spot on the floor and leaned back against the wall, watching her every move as if he thought she might sprout fangs or perhaps an extra set of arms.

"I'm not the one who's picky." He said it quietly, carefully.

"Rats spread disease, Knox. You are welcome to sleep in the other room if you want, but you might need healing after, and we both know how you feel about that." The mattress felt hard, as if it were made from gristle and bones instead of straw.

"Fine." Knox knit his fingers together, switching to a businessy tone she'd heard him use only with Gulya. "So, we sleep here tonight. In the morning you can show me what Shale's given you, and we can make a real plan."

Anwei blinked, something like nausea sloshing through her stomach. And hope. Blasted hope. "We?"

"I'm guessing we have a very limited window to get in? Devoted wouldn't be here if things weren't close to being finished. Once the dig closes, you won't know where your snake-tooth man is anymore, so we have to move fast. He's staying inside the compound?"

"I don't know. That's part of the reason I need to work with Shale. He has a lot of information on the dig I can't get without spending weeks watching, if at all. Maps, shipment schedules, labor lists. He knows a lot about the archeologists there, where they're from, where they stay, when they sleep. But he won't give most of it to me until I'm ready to go over the wall." Anwei waited until Knox looked at her. "What's it matter to you? You can't be a part of this, Knox. You said it yourself."

"But we can't trust Shale or this job, so we need to find out how to get access to the people he stole the information from." Knox stood, distractedly picking up one of the pillows edged in yellowing lace, then putting it down again. "The governor's house mark was all over that compound, so that means he's been the one overseeing it until now. I'll bet he's where Shale got all his information."

"You said you can't—"

"He'd have maps for certain. Rosters, supplies, guard rotations. Staking things out at the dig isn't an option, but maybe we could get into the governor's house? We already know the layout and exactly where he'd be keeping records. Breaking in would probably get us everything you need without having to rely on Shale."

"*Knox.*" Anwei sat up, wishing she had the energy to be angry. "Stop. You can't come."

He pivoted toward her, his fingernails scrubbing against his scalp. "I . . . I need the money."

"You just said I shouldn't work with Shale. And even if I do, I doubt there *is* money. He advanced a little, but I'm guessing he means to take it all back the moment this trap, whatever it is, snaps shut." Anwei leaned back against the wall, crossing her arms. "That's a good idea about skimming the governor's records, though." She pointed at Knox. "Noa said there's some kind of party up at the governor's compound in the next few days—she even asked me if I want to come."

"I hate Noa. She's all gold and silver with nothing underneath."

"She has nice things to say about you."

"If I end up snoring in my dinner after she's been by, you can remind me why you like her then." Knox leaned back against the wall and slid to the floor, letting his head hang down. "How come you didn't tell any wardens what happened to your brother, Anwei? Or a Devoted? That's what Devoted do. They *hunt shapeshifters.*" His head came back up, a trace of a smile on his lips. "Seems like a . . . fifteen-year-old . . ." He paused, eyeing her. "A fifteen-year-old would have known to ask for help. Am I getting any closer?"

"It happened seven years ago. You think I'm twenty-two?" Anwei's real smile sparked through her lead coating.

"How did you live?"

Anwei held up a fistful of braids.

"You healed people?"

"Not at first." Knox's face was so impassive; nothing was enough to shake him. Except for the mention of her brother and the shapeshifter. Anwei watched his face as if she could catch him feeling something. "Why does it matter to you?"

"It's nice to have a setting to put you in."

That wasn't enough, and suspicion began to prickle inside her. "Where's *your* setting?" Anwei couldn't look at him, saying it to the ceiling.

"Before we get into that, we need to talk about this shapeshifter—"

Anwei shook her head, staring at the water stains marking the wood panels. "This is my war. You're not invited."

"I'm inviting myself." Knox moved, and Anwei jerked her head down to look at him. He knelt on the floor right next to the bed, the light soft on his face. "You're my friend, Anwei."

The light didn't feel soft on her. It felt like a thousand beetles crawling all over her body. Deciding to risk your life because of friendship didn't make sense. And it hadn't made sense to him, either, not until Anwei told him about the shapeshifter. She rolled over and perched her chin on her hands, their faces even. He didn't blink, the almost-black irises more distracting than his ridiculous guesses at her age—she'd sailed away from Beilda into that storm just before her twelfth birthday. The seven years since might as well have counted as double. But she couldn't afford to pay attention to Knox's eyes, not when they distracted her from the truth.

And the truth was that Knox hunted shapeshifters, had stuck with her for the last year, then done something unnatural to her head. She could literally *smell* the discomfort squirming through him even now, when she'd never smelled a single feeling on anyone until that day. Anwei hadn't remembered until telling her story, but that was what the shapeshifter had done too. He'd messed with all their heads, and it had changed everyone in her family, in her town. But not her. "Tell me the real reason," she said.

Knox's mouth pinched into a straight line, and for a moment Anwei didn't want to hear the answer, not if it made him look as if he were about to kill someone.

But she *had* to know, no matter how much she didn't want to.

Knox looked down at his hands, clenched so the scars on his knuckles stretched. "We have more in common than you think."

"Oh?"

"Yeah." His words came out clipped. "My sister was murdered before I went to the seclusion. My parents, too. About six years ago." He glanced up, not quite meeting her eyes. "When I was eleven, just so we're clear on ages."

"What happened?"

"I'm not sure, exactly. I wasn't there." Knox's face seemed to be leaking color, his fingers flexing and unflexing. He slipped them into his pockets, as if that would make them stop, but then his hands just balled into fists inside. "I found her dead. Holding the sword."

Anwei couldn't breathe for a second, the scales between them sliding back toward something equal. "You think a shapeshifter did it. My shapeshifter?"

"Your story and my story are a little too similar for it not to be."

"They aren't similar. Not really."

"But how many shapeshifters are capable of . . . of . . ." Knox half turned, his eyes pointing toward Chaol. "Of making something like that sword? It takes a long time to learn any kind of magic, shapeshifting included. I'd be much more inclined to believe one very powerful shapeshifter has been able to survive rather than two or ten. They can't hide from Devoted."

Anwei shivered when he turned back to look her up and down, his eyes pausing on something over her head and shoulders that she couldn't see.

"You say *I* can't hide from Devoted, but I've never had problems."

"Your aura is small, and Devoted haven't been searching as far out as they used to. I guess it could be two separate shapeshifters. But the sword has been *different* over the last little bit." He faltered, his voice falling. "Stronger. What if it's because she recognizes her maker is near? What if it . . . feeds her?"

A sword that recognized things. She? *Feeds?* Anwei eased back from him a few inches, wondering how it was she'd lived so long next to Knox and not seen any of this. Her skin prickled as she remembered his empty obsidian stare from earlier that day, the sword in his arms. It was easy to set aside ghosts, wreaths of bael, and Calsta, the goddess who conveniently hadn't shown her face since the first Warlord began killing shapeshifters five hundred years earlier. But the sword? She'd seen what it could do. Gods and goddesses were only made of stone, their altars on the Temple Cay covered in flowers and offerings, devotees with wide eyes and open hearts wasting prayers on their empty stone ears. Magic, though . . . Anwei knew to believe in that.

"Two murders. My brother, your sister." She counted them on her fingers. "Four if he killed your parents."

"I don't know if he did. *She* might have done it," Knox whispered. "She might have . . . sucked them dry."

Somehow this was worse than anything else he'd said. Words caught in Anwei's throat at the expression that flicked across his face before it disappeared. "I'm so sorry, Knox, but you talk about . . . *her*, and I don't know if you mean your sister or the sword."

He pulled one of the lace-edged pillows to rest under his chin. "They're the same. Willow is *in there*. It was . . . a trap, maybe? A soul catcher."

"She's *trapped*? Inside the sword?" Anwei's stomach wrenched, the memory of that nothing scent still burning in her nose.

It made her wonder just for a moment: If shapeshifters stored souls once they stole them, was there a chance that Arun's was still somewhere? Trapped in something stupid like a ring or a cup or a butter knife, turning the air around him empty?

She looked at Knox. "What would finding the shapeshifter do to help you?"

"I don't know. If he's the one who did it, then maybe killing him would undo it. If not . . . he might know how to let her go. Let her die peacefully instead of . . ." Something pained flicked across Knox's face.

Anwei sat up, swinging her legs over the side of the bed next to him. "You were set to enter the seclusion. And you came with a sword instead of a sister. Both your parents were dead. No one asked questions? You didn't tell anyone?"

"I hid the sword. And . . ." Knox's mouth hung open a moment, his eyes flicking back and forth, focused on something in the past. "No one remembered. Calsta told me not to say anything, and no one ever asked."

Anwei closed her eyes. *No one remembered.*

"I . . . I was so upset at the time, I didn't even think about it. Not until now." He hunched around the pillow, the yellowed lace brushing his chin. "Anwei, this is an answer. There has never been anything but questions until now. All she wanted was to become a tailor like my mother and maybe kiss the cobbler's son, if she could get away with it. And now she's . . . something else. A ghost? It was my fault for not being there."

Anwei licked her lips, staring at him. The little bit of him that had burrowed into her head that morning seemed to be off, as if there were some kind of weight pulling it into the wrong shape. A ghost on Knox's shoulder that he couldn't help but reach for.

She grabbed the other pillow and lay down on it, closing her eyes, the cool fabric soothing against her cheek. *Do I look the way he does?* She wondered if she looked misshapen too. *What has this life of hunting made of me?*

"How have we taken this long to talk?" Knox tried to smile, as if he could cover up everything he'd said. He never had been much good at pretending.

Anwei snorted. "I was worried if I told you anything about myself, you'd realize how much older I am than you."

When she opened her eyes, the light in Knox's eyes was suddenly familiar again, the smirk on his lips the one she'd grown so used to. "I was just being nice before. We both know you're well into middle age. That's why you and Gulya get on so well."

She laughed, hugging her pillow so close, she could feel each goose feather inside it. Knox pulled himself up from the floor, letting his pillow fall next to her. The muscles in his arms slid smoothly under the skin as he reached over her to gather up the extra blanket lying next to her. "I'll sleep on the floor."

Anwei shut her eyes, her breath catching in her throat at the way he brushed against her. "You can sleep up here. Just keep on your side. If you kick me in the middle of the night, I'll probably shapeshift and eat your soul." Not everything was resolved between them.

Knox's brows twitched together, his fingers digging into the scratchy quilt's fabric, but he only walked around to the other side of the bed in answer, the pallet dipping toward him when he sat down. It was only after the candle was out that Knox whispered, "I told you I hunted Basists, Anwei."

She bit her lip.

"Killed them."

Her scars burned, her silence burning too. He would have killed her, had they met at a different time in his life. Even though she was broken. Not a Basist. Not a threat. "Children?" she asked.

"No."

"Why not?"

"Devoted children start to see auras when they're young, but it goes away if they don't make any oaths, even the aftersparks in their auras. It must be the same with Basists. I'd like to think if a Devoted saw someone manifest young, they could . . . take them into hand. Watch them. Stop them from going any further."

"But that isn't what Devoted do?"

He didn't say anything for a long time. "I never hurt a child. But if I hadn't gone after the Basists who did make oaths, they could have . . . I don't know, drained their villages. Started stealing souls. Set up new shapeshifter kingdoms again. That's what history says. What *Calsta* says." But then he was quiet, as if perhaps he'd heard the Warlord say it and he wasn't sure if that was the same thing as a goddess.

"You've fought a shapeshifter?" Anwei asked. "Someone who had actually gotten that far?"

"No." He drew breath again. "It was always a fight, though. They would have killed me."

"Was it always a fight because they wanted to kill you, or because they knew you'd come to kill them?" she whispered.

He shifted, the pallet dipping and dragging her toward him an inch. But she stayed on her side, clinging for dear life. When he spoke, his voice was quiet. "I don't know. I wish I did."

"Do you? Or would that make it worse?"

"Worse isn't bad if it means knowing the truth." Knox shifted again, and she could feel his breath against her shoulder. Anwei's whole back tensed, waiting for him to touch her. But instead he said, "It seems like it should be easy to know what is right and what is wrong. But I spent my whole life thinking anyone with a shade of darkness in their aura was evil, until I met you. And even until . . . well, now, I was worried about what that darkness meant, even when I've never once seen you use it to hurt someone."

Anwei made herself breathe. He was so close. "No?"

"You've hurt people before, I suppose. But usually only to stop them hurting you. And you've never used your aura to do it. It makes me wonder how many of the Basists I located over the years were just trying to live. Until I found them."

Anwei let her eyes open and stared at the yellowed lace.

"Do you think it will even be possible to get this shapeshifter to talk to me about the sword? I'm a Devoted. He's going to fight."

She looked over her shoulder to find him looking up at the ceiling, a hand across his forehead. "Is that what you are? Devoted?"

"Yes. Calsta is the only reason I'm still here."

Anwei turned onto her back, staring up at the ceiling too. She wasn't sure what it meant to be Devoted, other than what Knox had said. That people like him killed people like her to protect the Commonwealth. But he hadn't done it. What did that mean? Anwei let out a ragged breath, hugging her arms around her ribs. "I think I can persuade him to talk to you." Her mind flew to the jar under the floorboards in the apothecary herb room. Gamtooth venom made people spill truths at random, but if mixed with some other ingredients into a serum, it could force much more targeted truths from the person who drank it. She didn't mind forcing a few secrets from the shapeshifter before he died. "Yes, I think so. With some help."

"How were you planning to do it?" She felt him turn toward her, the empty space between them tingling. "Kill a shapeshifter? If stories are true, they can take the energy straight from people around them to keep themselves from dying. That's why they shift, I thought. Because when you take from someone else, you become less tied to your own aura. They're . . . distorted. Corrupted. Not quite human anymore."

Anwei turned onto her stomach, burrowing her head between her arms. That was one flaw she'd never been able to see past in her years of finding. The first Warlord had found a way to kill the old kings when no one else had been able to. Whatever she'd done hadn't been shared with the rest of the Commonwealth. Everywhere Anwei had gone in search of the snake-tooth man, she'd searched for an answer—sometimes bribing the university library attendants with love potions and itching powder just to get into the sections that talked about the shapeshifter wars. But in all her years in searching the Commonwealth—down in Elantia, Corosoy, and Prith; to the east in Chiantan and Forge; and even up past the border into Trib lands—all Anwei had ever learned were new words.

Anwei clutched her pillow tighter. "I expect even gods die when you stab them in the heart."

CHAPTER 15

The Worst Swear Words

ateo contemplated the Warlord's double auroshe crest tooled into the toes of his boots and took another bite of cake. Cake was easier than looking at the girl huddled inside her blue cloak opposite him, the hood pulled down over her face like she was about to be executed.

Cake was also easier than listening to the words being thrown back and forth between his father and the valas. Mateo shouldn't have agreed to play, shouldn't have done what his father wanted and followed the girl's aura to the pantry. But he'd done it, and now his life was over. More so than usual.

"I don't know what you are suggesting." The valas was in full bluster, all denial and a bushy mustache. "This girl is none of your concern, and I can't see how you or anyone else could tell just by *looking* at her that she's not supposed to be here."

"Valas Seystone." Mateo's father smiled one of his sad, endearing smiles. "We don't need to dance around this and make idiots of ourselves. I know she's your daughter. I knew the moment she ran away from the governor's house."

Mateo blinked. She'd run from the Devoted who were visiting

from Rentara? So she wasn't a fledgling Devoted. She was a real, sword-stabby, auroshe-petting—

"You're lucky that the Devoted who left as we got here didn't feel secure enough in his authority to do a *real* search of your home," Tual continued.

"I absolutely *refuse*—"

"I also know that the Warlord is coming here personally to reprimand you." Mateo glanced up at that. The girl's head cocked toward his father. "The governor doesn't like that you've been bribing the magistrate to look the other way when your merchant ships neglect to declare their goods properly to avoid taxes. And the shipments of Trib powders you've sold to Lasei."

"But—"

"Or the assassination you had planned. How much worse would it be if the Warlord found you harboring a runaway Devoted?"

Silence. Mateo smoothed a hand across the embroidery edging his coat's sleeve and moved the cake's crystalized-sugar salmon garnish (what was it with this house and salmon?) around his plate with his fork, wishing he could melt into the chair. Have an episode and die, right on the carpet.

"Why are you here?" Seystone finally said, his voice hard.

"He's offering you an exchange." Mateo sighed through it, ignoring his father's amused look. "He can use his influence to make the investigations show that you weren't involved in . . . assassination attempts?" Mateo waited for Tual's affirming nod before continuing. "Maybe even show that all your scheming and bribing was, in fact, a plan to unseat a corrupt governor. . . ." Another affirming nod. "And, I'm guessing, in return we get to keep your daughter."

The girl stiffened in her chair. Mateo looked down at his plate, shifting the last crumbs this way and that.

"My son is not entirely at ease with the idea of an arranged marriage." Tual laughed. "But it's an arrangement I believe could be quite beneficial for both our families. Governors hold quite a bit of power, much of which is outside the Warlord's scope of interest. My son and I find the Warlord's reliance on Devoted to be a bit tiresome." Tual sat forward in his chair. That was his negotiating face; Mateo knew it well. "Something I think you can identify with? If our families were to be connected, we could help you with the Warlord, and we'd be able to move back and forth between Rentara—representing our interests there but spending more time out from under the Warlord's thumb here. I believe the closest seclusion is right on Lasei's border, though I don't know if they're trying to keep us in or a Lasei army out. The Lasei queens haven't looked our direction in more than a century."

Seystone licked his lips. "But what—"

"Devoted don't marry." Mateo looked up at the girl's voice, authoritative and full of violence. His cheeks warmed. They had walked into this house and demanded a marriage alliance, and he didn't even know her name.

"I'm aware of the oaths you've made." Tual's smile was kind, and it made Mateo even more uncomfortable. How many Devoted had this girl killed to escape? Hadn't there been another case like that only last year? Three dead and their killer on the loose.

Tual was still talking. ". . . I'm sure we can come to an arrangement that will fit into your life away from the seclusion. Unless you *want* to be thrown over an auroshe and dragged back to Rentara?"

The girl sat back in her chair, every inch of her tense.

Tual turned back to the valas. "The Warlord pretends that Devoted are meant to keep us all safe from Basists. Mostly they represent the Warlord's interest in keeping the Commonwealth governed from Rentara, something she isn't capable of doing very thoroughly at the moment." He sighed, gesturing helplessly. "She uses them to frighten people like us into compliance. They steal our children for their seclusions and tell us it's an honor. Your daughter is a very accomplished Devoted, I believe. One of whom they asked a little too much." The girl twitched as Tual's gaze settled on her once again for a second. "I would have run away too."

Mateo's blood began to heat, his teeth grinding together at the things his father chose not to share with him. His father had known she would be here. That meant Tual had known her before. Had been watching, *planning* this for a long time. Maybe he'd even suggested that the Warlord send this girl here to clap her own father in irons.

The valas was sputtering something about overstepping, but Tual once again cut him off. "Devoted forces are dwindling. There's an opportunity here to set up a more autonomous region, especially with someone channeling Calsta's power to help us see threats before they come and then to take care of them when they do. We could give the Warlord reason to respect us. It seems like a goal you would share, since the Warlord doesn't have much mercy for those who go against her."

Mateo could hardly stop himself from rolling his eyes. Yes, an autonomous province where the Warlord had less influence would be fabulous. But it was an empty goal if they couldn't find a cure to the wasting sickness, because he wouldn't be around to see it.

"I won't be married off." The girl under the cloak kept her voice calm, speaking fact, not opinion.

"Oh, my dear, I wouldn't dream of doing anything without your consent." Mateo's father turned toward her once again, his smile full of understanding. "We have two weeks until the Warlord comes. I'll give you that time to get to know my son. He's much nicer than he seems at the moment—he even looks quite nice when he's wearing something a little more practical."

Hadn't Tual been the one to pick the coat out? Mateo frowned, rearranging the folds of lace that draped over his knuckles. It was one of his favorites.

"And you might find life here less restrictive than what you endured at the seclusion." Tual returned his attention to the valas. "But I'm afraid two weeks is all we have to decide if this will work for both our families."

The valas sat forward. "With death being the alternative? If you manage to pin an assassination attempt to my name, the Warlord will have me executed."

Mateo watched the girl, her hood swiveling toward her father as he so bluntly spoke of his own end. Her fists were balled up in the fabric from inside the garment, every inch of her hidden.

Why hide? he wondered. Her father was bushy haired, hints of brown showing like rust in his gray eyebrows, his teeth and his stomach both overlarge. Perhaps a cloak that covered every inch of her was the only way this girl could feel confident. Mateo stood, then gave the valas a much more gracious bow than he deserved. "I am planning to spend my time in Chaol at an excavation outside of town. Let me know what you decide. I'll be sure to bow and scrape and hold up the bridal wreath like a good boy."

"This is the attitude we can expect?" the valas growled.

"This is as much of a surprise to Mateo as it is to you and your daughter." Tual laughed again. "Perhaps we should give them a moment to talk?" He turned to look at the girl. "What do you think, Lia?"

She flinched, making Mateo's anger flare again. Tual even knew her name and hadn't seen fit to share. Shifting uncomfortably on his feet, Mateo resisted the urge to storm out, impatient at having her silence holding him in place.

Finally she nodded. "All right. I'll talk."

"Lia, I haven't done anything wrong." Her father stood up from his chair as well. "There's no reason to give in—"

Lia put her hand up, thin white fingers emerging from her sleeve. "The Warlord is coming to reprimand an official here. It seems these men have means to make it appear as if you are at fault, even if you are innocent."

"That's why she sends her spiriters," her father blustered. "To ascertain the *truth*."

"Yes." Lia's voice was quiet. "That's why she sent *me*. But I'm not going to be there to tell her what is true and what is not."

A thread of revulsion shivered down Mateo's throat, and he looked at Lia's blue-swathed form with new eyes. Father wanted him to marry a *spiriter* who could read his every thought? Why wasn't she crying foul over finding two Basists in her living room? It explained why she was wrapped up in her cloak like some kind of worm, flinching away from the tiniest suggestion of light. But it didn't explain the way her aura flickered in tiny, shriveled spurts around her.

Mateo's heart sank. His aurasight must be broken now too somehow. Yet another part of him going haywire from wasting sickness.

"We can agree to see how things go for now." Lia interrupted his thoughts, sitting a degree straighter. "Would you send someone to Aria, Father? She was scared."

"And after Aria has been taken care of, might I look in on Lady Seystone? Her illness concerns me." Tual closed his eyes for a moment, and Mateo knew he was looking for her in the house, perhaps to diagnose her before he even set foot in her sickroom.

Valas Seystone glared at Mateo. "If you so much as touch my daughter—"

"I am quite capable of defending myself, Father." Lia's voice was cool.

Mateo frowned. "And I'm not a piss pot of a human being who takes advantage of anyone unfortunate enough to be alone in a room with me."

"Oh, Mateo. So poetic." Tual was laughing again. He walked to the door. "Come, let us see to little Aria. I have a story or two that would buck her up. I understand she likes pirates . . . ?"

His voice faded as he and the valas went up the hall. Mateo pushed down the momentary stab of concern for his father. If the valas decided disposing of the two of them was a better idea than working with them, his father could defend himself easily enough. It was Mateo who might not survive.

He turned to face the cloaked girl. "Lia, is it?"

"I'm not interested in marrying you."

"It would be odd if you were." Mateo lowered himself back into the brocade chair and looked up at the ornately carved ceiling panels, light from the large windows touching them. "You've been hiding here for less than a day. Seems like you'd have more pressing concerns than getting married."

"You seem less than enthusiastic as well."

"Well, don't get offended. You said it first."

Lia's hood gave a decisive nod. "Then we're on the same side. What's the likelihood of you persuading your father he doesn't want to hurt my family or make us get married, either one?"

Mateo shrugged, lazily crossing his ankles. "Possible, I suppose."

"Let's get to work on that, then." Another nod, as if it were settled between them. Covered head to toe and bossy to boot. "In the meantime, can you pretend to be compliant enough to keep my father from running you through?"

"I'm not planning to come back here, so I don't believe it will be a problem."

"And where are you staying? Not with the governor."

"No, in an old manor on the sea cliffs. About halfway to Gretis, above the rocky coves?"

"The Tulath manor?"

"Probably." He sat forward in the chair, curiosity making him hope for a glimpse of her face beneath the hood, but the blue material wasn't giving anything up. "I'm assuming your status as a fugitive is going to keep you huddled in the pantry rather than coming to visit?"

Lia radiated sullen anger, but she didn't respond.

"Not that it will help you," Mateo continued. "Why did your

partner storm off instead of walking straight to you the way I did?"

She stood with an abrupt speed that made him flinch. "How *did* you know where I was?"

He managed to stay seated despite his heart's immediate gallop, an awful strain after this morning's episode. Mateo's palms began to sweat, but he kept his unconcerned pose. "I'm . . . hyperobservant. A crooked rug pointed straight toward you." He shook his head, massaging his temple. "Wait. No, it was because I could *smell* you. Or maybe it was because we're meant to be. My *soul* led me straight to your door." He ignored her annoyed snort and pointed to his head. "You know how I found you, don't you?"

Her fingers curled up tighter in her sleeves. "What do you mean?"

"I've spent enough time around Devoted to have picked up a few things. Like at least some of what spiriters can do. You said it yourself. You were here to tell truth from lies."

Lia didn't move for a second. Then she pointed toward the door. "You can leave now."

Mateo stood, gave her a stiff bow with, perhaps, one flourish too many. "If you feel the need to throw things, I give you leave to send them in the excavation's general direction. That's where I'll be." Then he walked out without waiting for her reaction, already plotting exactly what he'd say to his father the moment they were gone from this horrid place.

Once they were outside the gate, he'd gotten only as far as "You are the *worst*—" before his father gripped his arm, fingers pressing hard enough to make Mateo pause.

"Her mother is quite sick. A sham aukincer's work, if I'm not mistaken."

Mateo looked down, not wanting to feel sympathy, but he'd seen enough cases to know the tug of worry in his stomach for the woman upstairs was warranted. He chanced a look back at the house and flinched when he saw a smudge of blue in one of the upstairs windows.

"I should be able to help her." His father followed his gaze, giving a jaunty wave toward the house. "But what I really want is to help *you*, Mateo. I want you to have a future that doesn't involve running. I've been running my whole life. I was *alone* my whole life, until I found you."

Mateo's shoulders sagged. "The likelihood of me surviving is so low—"

"No." Fingers closed over both his shoulders, pulling them straight. "We're only working with the Warlord because she has the resources to find what I need to help you. Putting ourselves inside her sphere was a risk, but one worth taking for your sake. Now we need to make sure we can get back out of it." Tual waited until Mateo raised his chin, looking his father in the eyes. "Don't you remember anything from your childhood? You hid in a fair number of closets before I came for you, and several after. It isn't a good way to live, constantly in fear."

Mateo shook his head. "I don't remember—I couldn't have been more than two or three. And you don't need to draw any lines between me and Lia. Her existence isn't illegal. Only her choice in jobs."

"I want you to have a future after getting better." Tual said it as if caprenum and Mateo's sickness were only flies to be brushed aside. "Nothing is ever going to change who we are. *What* we are. This province is far enough from the capital that many already come here to hide, and the Warlord doesn't follow. Far enough that Valas Seystone has been about an inch from toppling the governor for months now, and the Warlord is mostly coming because of the *tomb*." His smile crinkled the skin around his eyes, and Mateo couldn't help but feel the glow of hope inside him as his father started toward the stables. A flurry of movement inside indicated the hostlers had noticed them coming.

"I've heard from her masters at her seclusion that Lia is a very nice girl." Tual's voice was lower now, a hint of pleading making discomfort prickle between Mateo's shoulder blades. One of the grooms appeared in the stable doorway with his little mare, Bella. Something inside Mateo relaxed. Bella, at least, didn't want anything from him.

"If you like her, then this could be a very good situation." Tual's grip on his shoulders tightened. "Please, son. Can you give it a chance? I've even heard she's quite pretty under that hood."

The hood. Mateo pulled away from his father to pat Bella's nose. No matter how pretty Lia was, all he could think of was her long white fingers rummaging through his head. And just in case that was exactly what was happening as she watched them from the window, Mateo thought all the worst swear words he could come up with.

Lia's father waited in the library door, silent until Tual and Mateo Montanne had disappeared through the front gate.

"I need your help," she whispered. "I need to leave before the Warlord gets here."

"I don't want you to leave. Can't you stay here now, where you're safe?" Her father's voice broke over the words. "You were suffering. They hurt you."

Lia stepped back from the window, the shadow of her hood making it difficult to take in her father properly. Years had silvered his hair and filled out his stomach, but his eyes were the same. "There's nothing you could have done."

"You are my child. They took you, and every day I hoped . . . I wondered—"

"We don't have time for regrets. The Warlord will send every Devoted sword she can find after me, no matter what those . . . those . . ." Lia bit her tongue, unable to come up with a word suitable for Tual and his flippant son. "No matter what those blackmailing parchwolf poachers say." She paused, staring up at her father. "Their claims are false, aren't they? I would have seen guilt in your thoughts during our reading." Only, Lia hadn't done a proper reading. Hadn't pressed into his mind past those images of her as a child.

Her father's head drooped.

"Smuggling. Selling explosives to Lasei." The words buzzed on Lia's lips. "*Assassination?* You tried to have the governor killed?"

He shook his head, but it was so slow, it hardly seemed an answer to her question. When he finally spoke, each word brimmed with a horrible apologetic certainty. "It's not that simple, Lia. Lasei is hardly a threat; they haven't been for over a hundred years. They only stockpile powder to make sure the Warlord doesn't get any fancy ideas about crossing the border with her Devoted. And the governor of Chaol is corrupt. Wardens can hardly even walk through the lower cays—it's a miracle the gangs haven't started charging passage on the trade road. If they did, the governor would probably just take a cut. He's letting the water in the poorer cays go foul, driving up the cost of food by imposing unreasonable taxes—"

"The Warlord *is* coming here to censure you?" Lia turned back toward the window, trying to swallow, but her throat was too dry. Her mind seemed to be moving too slow, thoughts flickering in and out of existence. "It doesn't matter. If I don't get out of here before she arrives, harboring me would be enough without whatever else you've done." She clenched her fists, all her muscles wanting to contract, to fight *something*. Only there wasn't anything she could fight with her hands. "And now if I leave, the aukincer will ensure the Warlord believes you are guilty, regardless of evidence. I assume there isn't much, or she'd have just called for your execution." She pressed her lips together hard, pulling her cloak sleeves down over her hands, yearning for the calm of having a weapon in her hand. "I need armor. A sword."

"Lia, that's hardly a good idea. Which of these problems can be solved with a blade?" Her father paused. "Are you someone who . . . solves problems with weapons now?"

"Sounds as if it's a family trait." Lia made for the door, clutching her cloak to her chest. It felt like power, like a plea to Calsta. *I'm obeying. I'm covered. I need you.* And on the other hand: *I don't want this anymore, I don't, I don't.* "We need to plan. Where is Mother? If she's with healers or servants, we need to clear her rooms so they won't see me."

Lia's father caught her arm, trying to meet her eye, but the hood stood between them, transparent enough for Lia to see bits of him but not enough for him to see her. Spiriter garb. "Lia, you can't see your mother. She's ill enough that it's unlikely she'd even know you. And if she did recognize you, she wouldn't be able to keep your presence here a secret."

Putting a hand to her chest, Lia forced her lungs to calm, her brain stuck in fighting mode, looking for paths forward, ways to parry the knives that seemed to be jabbing in from all sides. "What did the auk-incer say about her?"

"He said he can help. But it could just be another thing he's trying to hold over us." Her father's hand on her arm tightened a fraction, and his head bowed. "I hope he's telling the truth. None of the healers have been able to tell what's wrong with her, and some have made it worse. Right now I think the safest thing would be to . . . plan. Hide you in your old rooms, wait for Tual Montanne's next message, and catch him out somehow." Nodding to himself, he started herding Lia up the hall. "We'll get you some different clothes—"

"Father, I'm not a child."

"I know. This is all so sudden." Her father pulled her to him as he had when she was small, wrapping his arms around her as if he could somehow shield her from the world's ills even now. Including the ones he'd created. "I just . . . want to be able to see your face. How could they have hidden you away for so long?"

Lia bristled at first, unused to being touched, being *hugged* no less. But after a moment she let her arms relax, let him hold her close. It was nice having someone who wanted nothing from her. She hugged him back, wishing she could let herself lean on him. Let herself collapse, allow someone else to take the burden. But decisions had never been hers, and if the aukincer got what he wanted or Ewan found her, they never would be. She gently pushed away from her father and secured the hood down over her face. "I have a little bit of an idea, but it's not enough. Not yet."

Finding Knox and learning how to hide herself might keep the Warlord and Ewan away, but it wouldn't stop the aukincer from walking her father to the gallows. When she found Knox, maybe he'd know how to help.

"What if we don't think of something?" her father whispered.

"We will." Lia tried to find a smile for her father before starting down the hall toward her old rooms, her steps soft enough no servant would hear. "There's no other choice."

CHAPTER 16

Calsta's Voice

Knox couldn't sleep, the heat of the room dripping down his neck and chest despite the wind coming through the open window. Anwei had a brother who'd been murdered by a Basist. A *shapeshifter*.

Thoughts of Willow swished around in his head. How she'd pushed him into a pond only days before the Devoted came. How she hadn't wanted to go with them and had cried into her pillow with Mother stroking her hair and whispering that she didn't want Willow to go either. Knox had only thought of swords and shields, of auroshes and armor, of his father telling him stories about Therasian the Stolid, Gelana the Brave, and the first Warlord giving up her name and life to organize an army that could take on Bevanti, a shapeshifter monster with spider legs and fangs.

Swords and stabbing things sounded much better in stories than it ever was in real life.

Is this the answer you've been promising me, Calsta? He buried his face into the pillow as he thought it, almost a prayer, though Knox had never been sure if Calsta listened except when she felt like it. Gods seemed to prefer speaking to listening, bestowing without caring very much about whether or not the recipient wanted what was given. *Was meeting Anwei your doing?* What else could he believe? It was too much to be a coincidence.

If this shapeshifter could tell Knox what had been done to his sister, then could Anwei use her power to help him undo it?

He looked over at Anwei, curled into a ball around her pillow in the very corner of the bed, as if she thought he'd take all the rest of the space. One of her hands held the blanket up to her chin like the prim thing she was, the ends of her braids curling all around her. One for each place she'd lived. One for each of the hundred isles. One for each boy she'd kissed.

Anwei came up with a new answer every time he asked why a hundred was the right number of braids for a Beildan healer, each one a different size, as if earning them had required different amounts of effort. One very small braid was curled across her cheek, and Knox moved to brush it back.

His mind caught up with his hand just before he touched her. Pulling his hand back, Knox turned over to stare at the wall. He knew what it meant to keep oaths—his whole life had been one of looking away, of holding himself aloof, something that hadn't been too difficult with a sword on his back and the Warlord's auroshes on his chest.

Now, though, it didn't seem quite so simple. Giving people up was much harder than never letting them in in the first place. Anwei was already there inside him. Her touch was inside his head. And if he was honest, it hadn't started when he called for her on the wall.

Knox closed his eyes, forcing his mind from what had happened earlier in the day. The way Anwei had come running for him when he'd called, how she'd stood between him and the sword while Willow danced in violent circles in his head, prodding him toward her. How Anwei had tried so hard to tell him to leave because she was worried about what the shapeshifter could do.

The way her breaths rose and then fell in her chest as she slept now.

Eyes shut, Knox concentrated on the aura glows that plagued him despite the wall between him and Calsta's well of energy inside him. The innkeeper downstairs. Four men around a table, probably still playing cards. A few auras walked in and out of his range outside, their globes magnified and distorted with malt and an evening of dancing in the square. But Anwei was there too, her aura a quiet lavender in sleep.

If Calsta minded his partnership with Anwei, the goddess would have taken everything, down to Knox's aurasight. But it was all still there. It wasn't as if friends were not allowed. Knox had been close to Lia for years, the two of them like two halves of a sword, taking turns who was the hilt and who was the blade. But it had never been like *this*.

What had the masters meant, exactly, when they'd burned the third oath into Knox's scalp? Love only Calsta. Knox turned over again, restless. Because he did know what it meant. Sweat dripped into his eyes, and Knox swore at himself under his breath, staring up at the wood-paneled ceiling. After so many years of closing his mind, his heart, everything about him, Knox hadn't even *looked* at a girl in ages—so long that he hadn't realized he'd been looking at Anwei.

He breathed in deep, *not* thinking of Anwei or her hundred braids, or the way she looked so much smaller and softer curled up beside him.

When sleep came, dreams came with it. First of Willow, crying herself to sleep, but when she sat up, she was Lia, the sister who had replaced his murdered family. "You left me just the way you left Willow," she cried, her voice as loud as the sword's. Blood ran down from her chest, out her eyes and nose, covering her like her veil. "You left me when I needed your help the most."

"I'm sorry." He tried to wipe away the blood, but it only came faster, Lia dissolving right before his eyes like a spoonful of sugar under a stream of water. "Lia! No! Lia, I didn't want to leave! I want to help now!" But she melted away.

"What are you doing, Knox?" It was Anwei behind him. Knox looked back toward where Lia had been, but she wasn't there, Willow wasn't there, there was nothing *there* but warm air and the crackle of Calsta in his chest. Anwei stepped in front of him, a flower behind her ear, and her olive cheeks flushed as she looked up at him. "I want you to go," she said, but then she took his hand.

She took it and pressed it to her cheek, kissed his palm with soft lips.

And then he was against her and it was his hands pulling her close. His nose in her hair. His lips against her cheek, his body curving around her as she smoothed her hand up his back . . .

Knox's eyes jolted open, his body filled with a swarm of bees. The room was wrong, Jaxom, the lower moon, peering with his black-and-red-mottled face through the window with a smirk. Anwei had moved, curled up next to Knox, her eyelashes like petals against her cheek. The high collar of her tunic had come undone, the line of her throat and collarbone bared. The end of a scar marked her neck and what he could see of her shoulder, the thin white line disappearing beneath the cloth.

Breathe. Knox sat up and turned toward the wall, his bare feet cold on the smooth floor.

First I gave you my tongue, Calsta. My food, my nose.

Then my things, my bed, my clothes.

Last of all my heart, my body. They are yours.

Breathe.

Lia. What happened to Lia? The thought felt like blood pooled behind his eyes, but he shook it away. Lia was only a dream. He missed her, worried about her, but Lia had always been able to take care of herself.

The last thought that broke through was somehow worse than all the others: *Anwei is your best friend. How she would laugh if she knew what you were thinking right now.*

No, what mattered was what *Calsta* thought. Knox looked toward the window, the heat of the room leaving condensation dripping down the panes. But still it was Anwei's face, the way she laughed, the way she *would* have laughed and then sent him to sleep with the rats in the other room if she'd been awake and able to see into his mind at that moment.

A bloom of fire burst inside his head. *We don't really need to talk about this, do we, Knox?*

Knox curled forward, hands clutched to his head as the words charred his mind. So different from the ice of Willow's death gasps. He sucked in a breath, fingers pulling at his hair.

Calsta. Of course she'd chime in now, not when Willow attacked him or when a sky-cursed shapeshifter peered down at them from the excavation wall.

You know I can hear all of what you are thinking, right, Knox? All of it? Believe it or not, I do have other things to do than watch you scuttle around like a little bug.

Knox tried to push space between himself and her words, holding them at arm's length like a muddy shoe, but her voice didn't recede, scorching holes through him. He thought back to when he'd first tried to tell the masters about Calsta's voice, and they'd all looked at one another with worry. Asked him if he saw things that weren't there, if the voice ever told him to do anything.

Calsta had laughed afterward. *You thought they'd believe that I was speaking to you? I can't guide people whose paths are already set in motion. Yours is a path that might fix a few things if you walk where I want you to. Something you won't be able to do if you get distracted.*

Knox hadn't been confident enough at the time to ask what sorts of things a goddess would need him for, and when he'd asked later, she'd always told him to wait. He'd trusted her, and she'd nudged him along, taking him to Lia, to the right masters, to a safe place for the sword. Her power had made Willow's voice quieter.

He *trusted* Calsta. But he'd always been able to see the shape of what he was supposed to do, until she'd told him to run away. It had been nothing but stumbling in the dark since then, Willow's voice growing louder every day, as if she could shout the goddess herself down.

And now? *It's been a very long day, Calsta.* He looked at the ceiling as if the goddess would come down from the sky and speak to him in person. *Seems like running into a shapeshifter would pique your interest.*

You must be very, very careful. Both about Anwei and otherwise. This is exactly where I need you, but it is very dangerous for all of us. This is the chance I've been waiting for, but I can't tell you any more.

"Dangerous for *you?*" Knox whispered. "The goddess of the sun and storm? You can't . . ." Knox threw his pillow into the wall, but he could already feel the heat receding, leaving him there alone. "What is that supposed to mean, this is exactly where you need me?"

But Calsta, as usual, only answered back when she felt like it. Had she really come down from whatever it was she did up in the sky to reprimand him over a *dream?* The words burned like hot coals against his forehead. Anwei shifted, her hand slipping out to rest next to him on the blankets.

He breathed in. Out. Retrieved the pillow and placed it on the floor next to the bed. Didn't move for a moment, commanding every inch of his mind to concentrate on the way Lia's face had looked as she stared up at him in the dream. The murderous ghost that was all the shapeshifter had left of Willow. The pockmarked sword he needed to destroy. Calsta and her burning words.

Then he stood. Laid himself down on the floor and closed his eyes. But he did not sleep for a long time.

The morning found Knox before it was fair, a hand on his shoulder giving a firm shake.

"Since when do you sleep in?" Anwei's voice was so cheery, he wanted to fight her. She gave his shoulder a slap that was definitely harder than warranted. "Are you all right?"

He sat up a little more quickly than necessary. "I'm fine."

Groaning, Knox stood, his whole body aching from the night on the hard floorboards. He hadn't even taken a blanket, as if sleeping on the floor would somehow atone for his wandering mind the night before. And it had worked, apparently, because Calsta's energy was still there waiting for him. He let out a long breath before looking over at Anwei, angry at himself for letting something so trivial as a dream shake him. "So, we go to the governor's house?"

Anwei's back was to him, her tunic rumpled from sleeping in it. "First I have to go to the Fig Cay. Some kind of plague outbreak." He couldn't help but remember the scar on her collarbone, a thin white line against her amber skin. She turned, arms raised to tie her braids at the nape of her neck. "Then I'll talk to Noa, and we'll plan how to get into the governor's party. Getting in as a servant might not be hard. Getting back out with the governor's logbooks might be more difficult if they're watching the doors." She paused. "Unless you think Devoted will scoop you off the streets before we get there?"

"I don't know. It feels like . . ." He scratched the back of his neck, Anwei a warmth at the base of his skull. If that meant he was hidden, then they were safe. But did it? "I don't know how it works. *When* it works."

"*If* it works." She waved a hand dismissively and started toward the door. "We'll have to be careful today. Let's go."

He grimaced at the bowl of water, the lip edged in grime, but splashed some onto his face anyway. "I'm playing assistant, then?"

"You'll make a good one." She pulled the medicine bag from her shoulder and held it out to him. "You can carry my things and look very worried when I tell people how sick they are and how expensive it will be to treat them."

Knox rolled his eyes but held his hand out for the bag.

She looped it over her own arm instead. "You really think I'm going to part with this when we have Devoted on the loose? You use your weapons, and I'll use mine."

Hitching a ride back to Chaol wasn't too difficult, Anwei flipping a driver some coins and clambering into the back of the cart before it had come to a complete stop. Knox lodged himself between sacks of onions, amused when Anwei covered her nose with one hand, as if the smell was more than she could bear.

The trade gate was open again, but Knox couldn't help but notice a Rooster stationed just inside. He didn't recognize the girl's aura, but he slumped down all the same, keeping out of sight.

When the cart turned off the trade road toward the Sand Cay's main wet market, Knox hopped out and started for the tunnel that would get them to the Fig Cay. Anwei kept pace beside him, waving to farmers and traders rowing their boats up and down the green-tinged channel. On the other side of the tunnel, they followed a little offshoot waterway that snaked through the Fig Cay, the walkway cobblestones sprinkled with last night's malt and, in some places, shards of last night's malt glasses. Men and women with black feathers stuck into their braids sat on street corners, observing the early-morning hawkers shouting to passersby as if they owned them. Knox watched them from the corner of his eye and with his aurasight, waiting for one to challenge him and Anwei. Not many of the lower cay gangs appreciated outsiders barging in. It had probably been years since any warden had set foot in this part of town.

No one stopped them, though, and one of the watchers even went so far as to nod to Anwei. A gesture his partner enthusiastically returned before running to the woman to ask how her new twin grandbabies were faring.

Knox hung back, watching bits of unidentifiable trash float along the ditches of water that ran across the cay from the main waterway. The whole island stank of refuse and urine.

"And who is this you've brought us?" The woman's voice turned Knox back around. She was carrying at least three knives and had a Crowteeth feather in her hair, but she had a smile for him because he was with Anwei. Everyone smiled for Anwei.

"This is my assistant. In fact, we're late—we were supposed to be here yesterday." Anwei looked around. "You've heard about the sickness spreading around here?"

The woman's face blanched, and she grasped the silver amulet around her neck. "The ghost talkers?"

Anwei cocked her head. "I heard it was more of a rash."

"Starts that way. But it's making problems for . . . for people down here, if you know what I mean." The woman touched her gang feather before sitting back down in her chair and pulling out a skein of hairy yarn and a crochet hook. "Best be careful."

"Thank you, we will." Anwei leaned forward to give the old woman a hug. Knox watched the old woman's hands, particularly the one with the crochet hook, but all she did was hug Anwei back. His partner was quiet as they hopped the ditch that connected to a much larger waterway, where stalls selling fruits, vegetables, weapons, and who knew what else were open both to the walkways and to the boats floating by.

"This is it." Anwei looked up toward the two tall buildings leaning tiredly out over the waterway. "Gulya said the south side. . . ." Knox tensed as a man pushed past a pair of students toward them.

"Thank Calsta. You were supposed to come yesterday, healer," the man hissed, snatching Anwei's arm.

Knox grabbed hold of the man's shirt and wrenched him away from her, pinning his arms to his sides. He rooted his feet and held the man fast while Anwei brushed herself off. "Hello," she said, smiling. Always smiling. "You must be Jecks. You asked for a healer?"

The man had only a single braid, a yellow scarf, and knuckles with enough calluses to account for every black eye in Chaol. He squirmed against Knox's arms, his words coming out in a sputter. "My boss doesn't know you are coming. He wasn't going to be here yesterday." Jecks gave a particularly violent jerk to the side and Knox let him go, sending him stumbling clear to the waterway's lip. He teetered on the edge for a moment before he regained his balance, and when he turned, it was fear in his face, not anger. "We'd better get you inside before it goes up the string."

Anwei nodded slowly, her smile dimming. She jerked her head for Knox to follow. "This is a gang plague house? It was all members of the . . ." She looked him over. "You're a Blackheart. Right next to Crowteeth territory?"

Jecks dodged into an alleyway. "Would you move? We don't have a lot of time."

Knox opened his aurasight as far as he could without drawing on Calsta's power, one hand on his knife as they followed the man. No one was lying in wait that he could see, only buildings so close together that sunlight made it to the ground in dapples and strings. Long vines trailed from windowsills above, and clotheslines were strung from window to window in a web that any spider would envy. Jecks turned toward a rickety building with stairs sticking out between floors like old bones. Knox's aurasight flickered, doubling and redoubling. The building was crammed to the brim with people.

Knox put a hand on Anwei's shoulder at the same moment she stopped dead in the middle of the street. The auras inside the building had a sickly, pearlescent sheen. Knox had never been able to tell much about people from their auras—no more than he could probably have seen by looking at their faces—but at least half of the auras inside the building were . . . wrong. Not tainted with lavender and ink like Anwei's, and not buzzing with Calsta's golden energy, either. They were *dimmed* somehow. A dying man would grow so bright, it hurt to look at his aura . . . but this? Anwei's hand snaked out from her wide sleeves to grab hold of Knox's tunic, weighing him down.

The wrongness felt familiar, like something he'd tasted before but couldn't place. "What's wrong with them?" Knox whispered.

Her hand clenched harder and she didn't move, her cheeks paling as she stared up at the building.

"Quick!" Jecks held open the door to let them in and pulled it shut behind them. He started down the hall at a run. "We've probably only got a few minutes before one of the lookouts comes to check in. They're down here—leeches don't know how to help them."

Anwei followed after a little more slowly, a hand covering her nose. Her voice croaked as she pulled open her medicine bag. "Stay close," she murmured to Knox, then walked into the door Jecks held open for her.

Anwei gripped her bag to her chest as she followed Jecks deeper into the tenement hall. Knox followed close behind, coiled as tight as a spring in her head. The wooden floors were soft and rotting, pallets lining the hallway, doors open to sickrooms that were crammed with beds. A lower-cay healer—one of the leeches, as Jecks had called them—stood up from the pallet closest to the door Jecks led them to, interest sparking in his eyes when he saw Anwei's braids.

"This one," Jecks said, pointing to the bed by the door, a man lying pale against his pillow. Anwei knelt beside him, putting a hand to the patient's forehead just as people liked her to do. Then she closed her eyes and took a shallow breath.

The biting cinnamon hue of gamtooth poisoning hovered all around the man, so strong that it seeped out to coagulate in the hallway outside. Gulya was right about the spinner poison, but that wasn't what concerned Anwei. Underneath the smell of poison there was a tiny spiral of *nothing*.

Just like the guard at the trade advisor's home. She hadn't been able to smell any gamtooth on the guard, but it might have already left his system by the time she found him. This man had a rash down his arm and peeking from the collar of his shirt. She pulled up the shirt and found more on his chest.

Definitely gamtooth poisoning. If all the victims were here, where Crowteeth and Blackhearts collided, the likelihood was that the sickness was her fault. Knox touched her shoulder, and she looked up at him before switching to Jecks. "They're all shut in here because they're telling the truth, yes?"

"How did you know?" Jecks knelt down next to her, eager. "You know what it is?"

"Your boss won't be happy you let an outsider in here."

"That's why you need to hurry."

Anwei went to the next bed, occupied by a young girl. She felt for her pulse, swallowing hard at the string of nothing smell coming from her. Unobstructed truth was a little inconvenient if you happened to be in a gang. "You're recruiting very young, it seems?"

"She's not . . ." Jecks knelt next to Anwei to take the girl's hand. He glanced at the man Anwei had just checked. "You can help them?"

"These two aren't Blackhearts. . . ." Anwei stopped, her eyes weighing on Jecks's soft touch on the man's shoulder. "Your daughter and partner?" she asked quietly. "That's why you risked bringing me in?"

"The people upstairs are worse. We've already lost three today," the healer said quietly.

Jecks looked down at the little girl. "Can you help them before they get worse?"

The little girl's eyes cracked open, then widened as they found Anwei hovering over her. She blinked twice, the rash a ruddy band of pustules across her cheek and down her neck. Reaching up, she took one of Anwei's braids in her fist. "Your hair looks like snakes," she croaked.

"Shh, that's not very nice." Jecks untangled the girl's fingers from Anwei's hair, his voice soft.

"It's all right. She can't help it." Anwei stood. "It's two things, if I'm not mistaken. One of them I can help." She had the herbs she needed back at the apothecary to make an antidote to gamtooth venom. "The other, I'm not so sure. Are all the patients from the Fig Cay?"

The healer shook his head at the same time Jecks nodded. The Blackheart blinked, gesturing for the healer to speak. "We just had five people from the Coil dumped on our front step this morning," he said. "Same symptoms. We think the wardens dragged them down here while it was still dark."

The Coil? By the apothecary? Even if someone had dumped gamtooth venom in the channel there, it wouldn't have done much. The water was too deep and clean. Anwei went to the door. "Show me."

Jecks shook his head. "No, I want you to help my—"

"Show me *now*. The poison that did this shouldn't be enough to kill anyone. It doesn't make sense that someone from another cay would have the exact same symptoms, either. Not unless someone is poisoning unconnected groups of people on purpose." That didn't seem possible, because she hadn't sold enough gamtooth to account for two sets of victims, and Anwei hadn't cracked the spinner jar in a month except to feed the little monsters.

The healer bustled toward the door and took her to a set of stairs. Only halfway up, Anwei's knees began to quiver. The nothing smell was stronger here. Not just threads but ropes around the victims inside. She stopped, a hand to her stomach. "Where are the bodies? Have they been burned?"

"Blackhearts carted them out as soon as they died." Jecks peered around Knox, who had followed her up the stairs, and was now standing with a hand to his head as if he was in pain. His eyes were wide, worried.

Anwei gripped the railing, the nothing smell winding its way inside her, making her feel unmoored. The shapeshifter had been here. He'd done something, but she didn't know what.

What she did know: gamtooth spinners weren't common, even in the tropics. The likelihood that anyone other than her and Gulya would recognize the symptoms was very, very low.

But what if the shapeshifter had recognized the poison? Had made up his own batch of gamtooth secretions so that he could use the rash—a very odd and troubling one that most healers wouldn't know how to treat, nor how it was spread—as a cover for something else? Something bad.

An odd mass sickness like this could have looked like an opportunity for him, to poison more people so he could put those nothing spirals in them, counting on the fact that no healer would even be able to recognize what the rash had come from. But what was he *really* doing?

Stealing souls? He'd stolen hers.

Not like this, though. When the snake-tooth man had taken Arun, there hadn't been much left.

Anwei only glanced into the first two rooms, pausing when she saw the guard who had collapsed at the trade advisor's compound the day before. Knox hovered close beside her, tensed as if he thought fighting would be a good answer to the situation. The nothing smell had begun to curdle inside her, making her dizzy. "Come on. We have to go." She started for the stairs.

"Wait." The healer darted to block her. "You aren't going to examine them? You haven't said what we can do."

"I have some recommendations that should help."

"But—"

"We have to leave." Anwei pushed past the healer and Jecks, striding toward the door as fast as her feet would go without breaking into a run.

"Healer, when can we expect—" Jecks's voice came at her, panicked.

"I'll send someone with the herbs today. Don't worry, your husband and daughter will be all right for that long at least." She pushed through the front door, gasping down the muggy, corrupted air outside. But at least it wasn't full of nothing.

Knox followed her down the street as she headed toward the canal. "What is wrong with them?"

"You could feel it too." She threw a glance over her shoulder at the plague house, wondering if the shapeshifter was there even now. "Could you see anything in their auras?"

"Not like . . ." Knox glanced around them, lowering his voice. "They're not different the way we are—their auras have no color. But there's something wrong. I feel like I've seen something like it before—it's as if they're fading away."

"Dying?"

"No. Like they're *leaking*. Can you help them?"

"I can heal the rashes. But more than that?" Anwei hazarded one last glance at the building before turning into Crowteeth territory. Jecks was still standing in the doorway, his shoulders slumped. "They've all been touched by the shapeshifter."

CHAPTER 17

Aggressively Outgoing People

Even after the plague house was out of sight behind them, Anwei walked as fast as she could to get out of the Fig Cay's winding streets, silently willing Knox to wait until they were clear before speaking any more. Knox seemed to understand, watching the streets around them with a sharp undercurrent of worry that stabbed through the bond between them. When they got to the island's western side—a mishmash of rotting docks, most of which were carved with Crowteeth feathers—she stopped only long enough to gauge the distance to a ferry navigating the clogged waterway toward the pier, the Ink Cay only thirty feet of dirty water away.

Anwei took a running jump, barely clearing the ferry's low railing. She ran with her momentum, hopping to a smaller fishing boat next, and then a high khonin's glistening barge, only one of the boat owners getting close enough to take a swipe at her before she made it to the docks on the other side. Knox landed just behind her.

"Do you think he was in there?" he asked quietly, nudging her to get moving as the dock attendant came storming toward them.

"I don't know." Anwei couldn't stop her skin from crawling. She wanted to wash whatever had happened to those people out of her mind. She walked straight past the dock attendant, pulling back her scarf to show her braids. The attendant missed a step but didn't stop muttering about Fig Cay rats. "It doesn't change anything. We get Noa to sneak us into the party, we steal the dig plans, we get rid of the shapeshifter, and it solves everyone's problems. The Firelily's only a few minutes' walk. Let's go."

"But what exactly is happening to those people?"

"I don't know." The theater was on the other side of the Ink Cay, standing a head above the squat government buildings that made up most of the island. It stared across the channel toward the Gold Cay as if it could see more promise in the glittering malthouses and shops than in the life that held its dreary neighbors bound. Gritting her teeth, Anwei breathed a sigh of relief when the theater came into sight. "You said you've seen sickness like that before."

"It's like . . ." Knox slowed a step. "I do know where I've seen it."

"Where?"

"I'm not supposed to talk about it, but not because of an oath, I guess." He licked his lips, looking back toward the rotted buildings they'd come from. "It looks like wasting sickness."

Anwei's brow furrowed. *Wasting sickness*? "What causes it? Does it pass between people?"

"No. It only happens to Devoted. Victims' connection to Calsta gets . . . eaten up by something. It drains them—like there's an imbalance. Something siphoning their energy from the inside, and there isn't a cause or cure that I know of. I've never seen anything like it among normal people." Knox stiffened, glancing over his shoulder. "Someone is following us."

Anwei looked back before Knox pulled her along, forcing her to keep walking. "Jecks?"

"No." He put a hand to his forehead. "Calsta above, I'm so tired— how did I miss that? It's an aura I've seen in the past few days, but I don't remember where. Maybe more than once over the last week."

"And you're only now bringing it up?" Anwei pressed her lips together, pushing herself a little faster. So Knox could recognize specific people based on their auras? See things *wrong* with people too? Anwei added it all to her mental list, along with the slipping into shadows, hearing a little too well, and seeing things when she couldn't. Jumping a little too far, moving a little too fast. A panicked buzz trilled along her arms and back at the idea of someone tailing them—that would be twice in two days someone had managed to latch on to Knox, when it had never happened before.

She didn't like the idea of this wasting sickness either—something that wasn't caused by a particular thing inside a person, but was just *there*, eating away at them? Anwei's hands tightened around her medicine bag strap. Wasn't that supposed to be what shapeshifters did? Steal energy?

And if that's what the snake-tooth man was doing, and he was involved at the plague house, then maybe it was him following them. Maybe he'd been following them for days, weeks. . . .

Knox touched Anwei's arm, attempting to draw her down an alleyway branching off from the road, but she resisted, pointing at the Firelily's black dome. "Whoever is following us isn't going to go in there after us—how would they hide?" She lowered her voice. "We can leave the back way once we've talked to Noa. If there is one."

Knox let her pull him toward the theater, his eyes stopping on the sign over the Firelily's door. It was carved with gaudy flowers and glittering paint. "I hate this place."

Anwei paused, her hand on the latch. "You've been to the Firelily?"

"No. But I'm sure it's full of aggressively outgoing people who will want me to like them."

Anwei stifled a laugh that felt more like a pain in her side. Her fingers dug into Knox's arm as she pulled him through the open door to the outer gallery with its paisley curtains and gold paint, heavy drumming echoing from deeper inside. Passing the curtains, Anwei stepped into the circular theater itself, narrow benches arranged in neat rows around a square wooden stage at the center. On the stage, five men leapt to the time of a deep-voiced drum, the drummer sitting on the theater floor to the side. The men swung weighted tethers in quick circles around their heads and bodies as they danced, the blackened tang of salpowder wafting from the stage. Each of the tethers was coated in it.

Knox tensed, pulling away from her to draw his knife.

"Knox, what—"

Suddenly Anwei could hear it, the groan of chains and gears. She put a hand on his arm, coaxing him to lower the knife as a trapdoor opened at the center of the stage. The top of a woman's head rose through the hole, the stage mechanism lifting her. She tossed her hair and began spinning before the platform had brought her all the way up, her wild brown waves held back from her forehead by a brightly striped scarf. Noa.

Noa always looked most herself when she was dancing. Her peacock-blue and green skirts were divided, so they swished around her legs as she ran to one of the men, who boosted her into the air—there was a burst of sticky black and gritty rose in Anwei's nose—and the weighted tethers in Noa's hands ignited. The flames twirled around her as she spun in the air. She landed lightly on her feet, then tossed the tethers into the air, spinning them up over her head.

"Noa!" Anwei called, moving closer to the stage. The dancers circled around Noa as if they were worshipping her—Anwei wouldn't have been surprised if Noa herself had added it to the choreography—then each of them flipped up from the stage, their tethers igniting into purple flames. "Noa! Come down!"

Noa stopped midspin, peering out into the benches. "Anwei?" She dropped her flaming tethers and ran toward Anwei's side of the stage, ignoring the other dancers, who continued to twirl. One of them stopped to stomp on Noa's tether where she'd left it burning merrily on the wooden stage.

"Sky Painter protect you, Noa," Anwei called out in Elantin.

"May she send her storms far away from us," Noa sang out. She hopped off the stage and grabbed Anwei's wrists, kissing her forehead to finish the greeting a little more enthusiastically than she usually did. "What's the matter? You look like you stepped on a ghost."

"Just about." Anwei returned the gesture, raising a hand to point at Noa's colorful scarf. "No knots? What would your father say? And are those pants you are wearing?"

"I won't tell if you won't." Noa laughed, pulling the scarf back to reveal two braids wound into tight knots on top of her head. She produced a wooden hair stick from her pocket, twisted her long, blustery waves into a tight bun, and jammed the prongs into her hair to keep the bun in place. "I thought you weren't going to come! What have you got for me?"

"I don't have everything mixed yet. Maybe I could give it to you right before the ball? It's in the next few days, right?" Anwei led Noa back into the benches, out of earshot of the other dancers. Not that they were paying attention. They probably couldn't speak Elantin anyway. "Like you said, together we could take out the entire government of Chaol."

Noa froze for a split second, her face going blank, but then she smiled twice as wide, as if she could cover it up, squealing like a pig headed to the slaughter pens. "You want to come to the governor's *ball*? It's tomorrow. Will you be able to get the herbs mixed in time?"

Anwei didn't answer for a moment, wondering if she'd imagined Noa's chagrin. "It seemed for a second like you didn't want to go anymore."

"Of course I want to go. This is my dream come true! We are going to have so much fun."

"I'm glad to know you dream about a healer helping you make people sick." Anwei noticed Knox cocking his ear toward them, as if listening closer would rearrange the syllables from Noa's native tongue into Common. "But I need a little more than that."

Noa's smile faded a hair. She sat down on a bench, holding her shoulders a little too straight. "*You* need something. From me? Other than gossip."

"Nothing too terrible." Anwei felt a twinge of discomfort when she sat down, though she couldn't think why. Noa had always just been a contact, and sometimes contacts needed to be pressed. But she didn't like the sudden tiredness in Noa's eyes. "What's the matter?"

"Same things as usual." Noa wrapped her arms around herself, rubbing her arms as if she was cold. "I was thinking of pretending to be sick that night. But if you're coming, then it won't be so bad."

"Why? I thought the whole point was to make your minders sick so you could have fun."

"Yes, well, my minders have minds of their own right now. And know a little too much."

"Did your father find out about Bear proposing?"

Noa's nose scrunched. "He's never going to let me go home to Elantia."

"Bear or your father? No, never mind, I think I've got something that will cheer you up." Anwei's insides twisted; she wished she had time enough to let Noa talk, but Noa's problem of marrying a boy too rich to care that she hadn't agreed to the wedding and too dumb to know she'd do as she pleased felt a bit small, what with someone following Anwei and Knox through the streets, the Trib trap, the shapeshifter finally within reach after so many years. . . . Anwei pushed on, even as she saw Noa's face fall a little. "How would you feel about skipping mild poison and haunting the ball instead?"

Anwei and Knox had talked about it on the cart ride from Gretis to Chaol. They needed a distraction to ensure they could get into the governor's study to take maps and documents related to the dig without being interrupted. The dig itself was draped in so many ghost wards that choosing an appropriate distraction had been almost too easy.

"A haunting?" Noa's chin came up, her voice losing its raw edge. The fire dancers behind her were now trying to push one another off the raised platform while whooping loudly. The tether Noa had abandoned in the center was still smoking a little, and Anwei could smell the burned herbs on Noa's hands. "You want to scare the entire Water Cay into thinking the governor's house is haunted? *Yes.* A thousand times yes." She stood up and started for the door. "This will take planning. Costumes. What else? . . . I'll be back in a minute, boys!" Noa yelled the last in Common toward the dancers, hurriedly gesturing for Anwei to follow her to the theater door. "Come on! This is going to be the most fun I've had in weeks!"

Knox appeared at Anwei's side in that way of his—sliding into existence as if her eyes had somehow missed him until the moment he wanted to be seen. "We need to go. Whoever is following us just walked into the entrance hall."

"Anwei." Noa was peering past the curtains into the entrance hall. "Your little friend who pretends he's your shadow—the pretty one. Did you bring him? Because I think he . . ." She turned back to look at Anwei and jumped when she saw Knox, both hands clapping over her mouth. "Falan's flowers, you scared me. Were you here before?" she giggled, switching to Common. "But if he's in here, then who is out—"

Anwei darted toward Noa, linking her arm through the dancer's, pulling her toward the stage. "Where's the back way out?"

"Oooh, someone followed you here and you don't want to see him?" Noa dug in her heels, craning her neck to see past the curtains. "He loves you, but you love this one." She pointed at Knox. "Oh, and he's come to fight for your heart! You look like you know how to fight." Noa looked him up and down.

"That's not it at all, Noa." Anwei couldn't help but laugh through the tension twisting her shoulders tight. "A back way out?"

"Oh, fine." Noa skipped toward the raised stage and pushed through a door at its base. "If it's not a fight to win your heart, then what *is* all this about? People following you. Haunting the governor. I always knew there was more to you than herbs."

"Not really." Anwei ducked into the narrow opening and followed Noa down the dark, dusty steps under the stage, the light blue smell of canvas, dirty ochre of wooden sets, and vermilion bursts of pigment in oil touching Anwei's nose in quick succession. "A few archeologists from that shapeshifter dig on the cliffs stiffed me payment for some herbs, and I wouldn't mind watching them scream themselves hoarse, is all. Unless all the Devoted are going to be there. They'd probably stab us through before we could do any proper howling."

"Shapeshifter dig?" Noa paused, the darkness under the stage hiding her expression, before she pushed her way into the shadows. Anwei almost felt Knox stiffen behind her, ready to defend against some kind of attack. She *did* feel it, a tautening in her mind, as if it were her own muscles winding tighter than a spring. "A live one?"

"No. A very, very dead one, so I'm told." Rubbing at the back of her head, Anwei tried to banish the sensation, only to feel threads of worry drip down her own back. Noa wasn't quiet, Noa didn't think. Noa just was.

But that wasn't what the second khonin was doing now. Anwei *couldn't* see what she was doing, the girl's lemongrass scent laced with salpowder too strong to know exactly where she was in the darkness. Groping for her medicine bag, Anwei felt her heart begin to race before she could think. When her hands closed around the corta, her mind caught up with the rest of her. Noa wasn't a threat.

But Knox thought Noa might be a threat, and he was in her head, making her think it too.

A door opened in the darkness, sunlight making Noa's silhouette too long and thin, as if she were half spider. Anwei recoiled, her eyes clenching shut at the sudden light, and she could feel Knox bracing for something to happen, thinking that no one would blind a Devoted like this unless it was to gain an advantage in an attack. . . .

"Sounds like the type of people who would feel a little worried about ghosts, no?" Noa's voice was still shadowed, the light behind her making her impossible to read. After a moment she stepped back, revealing a quizzical expression on her face. "I thought you were in a hurry? Unless you *do* want the man in the entry hall to catch you. I wouldn't mind if he caught me. He looked handsome."

Anwei felt her insides unwind, and she pulled her hand from her medicine bag. Knox was coiled tight, ready to attack if Noa put a foot wrong. She tried to wall off the spot he'd claimed at the back of her head, but nothing changed.

Knox's hand touched her arm as if to calm her down, and Anwei jolted to attention, realizing that if she could feel so much of what he was feeling, then it probably went the other way too. "Are you all right?" he whispered. "This . . . connection stuff is getting worse."

Anwei turned back to Noa, her cheeks hot. "About the haunting . . . ," she started.

"Yes, we have to get you in." Noa leaned against the door as she waited for Anwei and Knox to follow her. "They're blocking all traffic from crossing the Water Cay bridge, and you'll need an invitation to get past the governor's gates. I asked Daddy about the Devoted after you mentioned they were in town, but he says they're not doing anything until they find the one who disappeared." Her brow furrowed. "I heard she can look into your mind. Bothersome person to lose if she doesn't want to be found. She'd always know you were coming."

Anwei didn't like the way Noa's words twisted Knox inside her, as if they meant something to him. She shook the feeling away, lining the plan back up in her mind. If the Devoted weren't going to be there, then nothing could stand in their way.

"I'm not worried about getting in. Knox and I can dress as servants. They'll let in cooks, musicians. Florists?"

"Earlier in the day, I suppose." Noa nodded. "But they'll check anything you bring in—every basket, every bag, every flower. I guess there was some kind of break-in at the governor's compound a few months back, so he's gone a bit funny about those things."

Anwei and Knox exchanged a glance. Stealing those candlesticks hadn't been easy, but it meant they already knew the layout of the compound, the way the guards moved, where they could get in, and where the governor's papers would be.

"So what kind of haunting did you have in mind?" Noa was all smiles now.

"The kind with salpowder." Knox's voice was a hair too quiet from behind Anwei. "Seems like you wouldn't have a hard time using it, what with your dance routine?"

Noa's smile grew. "None whatsoever."

Anwei stepped into the blinding light, making sure her grin was in place. If they were searching servants' bags on the way in, they'd certainly be searching them on the way out as well. "They aren't going to rifle through *your* things when you come, are they? I'll bring you some supplies to drop off inside the compound. Knox and I will find our own way inside"—Noa's eyes flicked over to Knox, as if weighing him, and Anwei caught herself moving to stand between them—"and perhaps you could sneak us out when you leave? They won't be counting invitations on the way out."

The light slithered across Noa's face as she looked toward the Water Cay thoughtfully. "They'd notice if I suddenly had a Beildan and a man with no khonin knots in my carriage." Her eyes slid over Knox's hair. "We'll have to dress both of you up to fit in."

"Might be a good idea anyway, so we can help you play ghost without anyone noticing us."

"Me?" Noa put a hand to her chest, her voice rising. "You want me to *play the ghost*? Anwei, if you were a man, I'd propose."

"I know how you feel about proposals, so if you did, I'd know to watch my back."

The high khonin's grin was a little too sharp. "What do I need to do?"

It wasn't until Noa had skipped back into the theater that Knox emerged from the shadows in one sudden jerk that sent Anwei teetering back on her heels. "Our tail managed to follow. He's out there."

"Or she." Anwei flinched as a shadow darted across the alleyway's mouth. She stuck a hand into her bag, fishing for a tiny bottle of special malt, less than a knuckle's worth inside. Then she pulled out her package of ground lysander. "How much do you think they heard?"

"They were outside my range until just now, so I don't know. Maybe everything."

"I'll take this side." Anwei put her back to the alley wall, extracted the wooden funnel from her bag, and carefully poured the powder into the bottle's narrow mouth. She plugged it with a cork, then gave the bottle a brisk shake to mix the powder and malt. Knox took his place on the opposite wall, his eyes flicking between her and the alleyway's mouth.

"Ready?" he whispered after a moment.

She put up a hand to wait, giving the bottle another shake. He nodded toward his side of the alley to let her know their follower was closer to him, hidden only by the wall. Anwei swirled the bottle one last time, then held it up to the light, waiting until the smell turned from a combination of citrine and fiery red to a burnished, sickly gold.

She nodded to Knox, and he darted out of the alleyway, a stifled yelp echoing back toward her before she followed him. But instead of Knox holding their tail, Anwei found Knox on the ground, rubbing his ankle.

"He wasn't where I thought he was. Which should be impossible." He pointed down the street. "There was a . . . a little *thing* where his aura was. It scorched me and scampered off."

"A thing? That scorched you? What does that even mean?"

"A *lizard*. That doesn't matter, though. I've never seen someone throw his aura like that—it wasn't in the right place. I did get a look at his face, though."

"Is it someone we need to worry about?" Anwei tucked the bottle back into her bag. The concoction wouldn't work if it wasn't used within moments of mixing. She could already smell the burnished edge tarnishing, the gold fading to an ugly mustard. It could knock a person out, even stop a charging silenbahk if she mixed enough of it, but only if it hit skin inside the right time frame. It was useless now.

"I know where I've seen his aura now." Knox smiled grimly up at her, massaging his ankle.

"Stop pretending you didn't trip and just tell me."

"I *didn't trip*. I've never tripped in my life. There was a *lizard*."

"Sure. A lizard wearing a man's aura. I believe you." Anwei's throat suddenly clenched. "Wait, do you mean—"

"No, it wasn't a shapeshifter. It was like the man was using the lizard as a puppet. But here's the thing: he was one of the men at the apothecary yesterday when I went out the window. And I think he was at the temple the other night after we stole that figurine. The scratch on my side? He pushed past me in the malthouse, and I came out with this. He's *Trib*."

"Trib? One of Shale's clan? So . . . there were men who chased you back to the apothecary . . . but this man wasn't one of them. He was already there outside the apothecary, waiting." Anwei's chest tightened. She held a hand out to help Knox up, her eyes straying down the deserted road to where the man had disappeared. "But he's *not* a wandering holy man? No pineapples today, Knox?"

Knox gave a half-hearted laugh at the joke, but he was staring down the road just as hard as she was. "Maybe. I've never seen a trick with an aura like that before. And I'd never seen his face before—he's young. And yes, definitely at the apothecary yesterday. I didn't realize he was with the other Trib."

Anwei immediately knew who their tail was. The young Trib who'd been with Shale—Altahn—had been much more aware and concerning than Shale himself.

More than ever Anwei could feel a trap's wicked teeth all around her, waiting to spring shut.

CHAPTER 18

If the Sky Painter Cared

Lia's father gave her a long blue scarf to cover her face at her request and a closet full of plain servant's dresses without any request at all. The scarf was tighter than her veil, knotted across her forehead, nose, and mouth, like some people wore in the eastern provinces. Much less worthy of notice than a full veil, though it left Lia's eyes exposed.

Somehow the scarf felt hotter, more intrusive because she'd never had less reason to cover herself than now. But Lia loved the way it felt against her skin. It covered how frightened she was.

Maybe Calsta would see the scarf instead of the terrified creature who had always been lurking inside Lia, waiting for an excuse to run from her oaths. Maybe the aukincer and his bratty son would see it instead of a girl they could use. Maybe it would keep Ewan from seeing a single one of her freckles ever again. Lia had detested the veil every moment she'd worn it because she hadn't wanted the power, hadn't wanted the authority, the prestige. She'd wanted her friends, her family. But now that she had them again, she was back to hiding.

Hiding itched. And it wouldn't last. But the next part of her plan required finding Knox and his hidden aura, which required leaving the compound, something her father wasn't willing to sanction. So Lia drummed her fingers on the desk pushed up under her old window, waiting for the guards on the ground to patrol somewhere else so she could climb out.

The guards were dawdling by the pond. The familiar sight of it sparked memories of the time Lia had tried to send Aria out onto the water on Mother's best silver tray. The memory tarnished almost before it unfolded, though.

Father still wouldn't let Lia near Mother's room.

What are the guards doing? Splashing each other in the fountain? Lia paced across the room to wrench open the wardrobe. Next to the maid livery, it was full of little dresses, ribbons, petite shoes in neat rows. All for a child who didn't exist any longer. She threw the doors shut, her insides seeming to swell too large to fit her outside any longer. Nothing about her old room showed who she was now. No leather cuirass or blade from the seclusion; no Vivi, who was probably wasting away, missing her now that she hadn't brought him fresh meat for two days. No . . . what? What was she now that she wasn't doing as Calsta asked? What *should* be in her wardrobe?

Lia wasn't sure.

She crossed back toward the bed, stopping to look at a little gilded ball sitting on the bedside table. Enough gold for armor? Boots? A proper set of clothes that didn't involve long skirts?

It was hard to know. Lia had never used money. As a child she hadn't needed to, and as a Devoted she hadn't been allowed. She picked up the ball but then dropped it, bile rising in her throat. Lia didn't want the afterlife of hollow darkness that waited for those who betrayed the Sky Painter.

She paced across the room again, hoping whatever Ewan was going through was ten times worse. He was probably pretending his aura was still gilded and hoping for Calsta's energy to return before the Warlord came. The thought of him sat in her stomach like three-day-old fish. Surely, regaining favor with the goddess would take more than keeping to flavorless food and a hard pallet. Calsta *had* to see there was something *broken* inside him, that he wasn't worthy of her favor.

But Calsta had allowed him to rise high among the Devoted in the first place. If he was broken now, hadn't he been broken the whole time? Maybe not.

Finally the guards disappeared around the side of the house. After checking her scarf one last time, Lia vaulted over her windowsill and clambered to the ground. Her heart didn't slow, not when she got to her family compound's wall, not when she was three streets away, not even when she got over the Water Cay bridge and onto a ferry that would take her to the lower cays, where she'd seen Knox glimmering on the river wall. The drum tower's high-noon rat-tat-tat made her jump as it echoed over the dry market, the passengers around Lia giving her and her scarf odd looks. Maybe because it covered her hair and forehead, not just her mouth and nose like theirs.

Lia elbowed her way to the ferry's front to sit on a bench where she could see but no one would be able to see her very well, her eyes flicking from boat to boat in the crowded channels and across the different islands' packed docks, the water smelling of refuse and animals even through her scarf. Once they docked in the Sand Cay, Lia started toward the river wall, forcing her mind to skip over the fact that he could be *anywhere* in this city and that she had no real way to find him.

She soon reached the trade road, spilling across the edge of the cay, towering silenbahks, horses, donkeys, and carts rattling by like ants taking food to their queen. Lia watched the traffic pass, her mind whisking with it. If she couldn't see Knox, maybe she could make sure he saw *her*. He must know there were Devoted in town, had maybe heard a spiriter was missing. If she made a big enough stir—even if she had to make it every day for the next *week*—he'd come to investigate.

Wouldn't he? They'd always been so close.

But what were the odds Knox would come looking before Ewan did?

Lia pushed that thought away, refusing to be frightened. If Ewan came, she'd deal with it. She always had before, at least until . . .

Until . . .

Pulling her scarf tighter, Lia pushed her way down the crowded walkway to the edge of the bustling road. Without thinking, without breathing, she threw herself out into the rush.

A wagon driver veered to the side, passing so close that Lia teetered forward, lurching into the path of a hunchbacked silenbahk. The driver shouted in fear, swearing at her when she jumped out of the beast's lumbering path.

It was a dance. Two years of being locked inside her veil, and suddenly Lia was in the sunlight, dodging between heavy carts as if they were assailants. Donkeys and wagons veered away from her as she twirled across the road, life burning inside her. A horse reared only inches behind her, his hooves lashing toward Lia's face, but the creature was nothing more than a poor imitation of Vivi, the rider shouting at her as if a little, tame horse could harm an auroshe rider.

Lia wove between the animals and riders, obscenities shouted at her like a warm cloud of recognition. Tomorrow she could come again, and the next day and the next day, until Knox heard about the girl with the scarf, a death wish, and feet too quick for a mere mortal. He'd come see in a few days. Maybe a week or—

Lia threw herself to the side as a cart swerved too close, an exhilarated laugh bubbling up from deep inside her, and wondered if the angry drivers were *trying* to hit her out of spite.

"Hey!" a familiar voice shouted from behind her. "Are you drunk? Get out of the road!"

Lia turned to find a man in a lacy coat bearing down on her, the Warlord's crest silvered across the toes of his riding boots. His horse swerved alongside her, and in the split second the man had stolen from Lia's attention, a cart clipped her elbow, knocking her into a silenbahk's scaled leg. Lia bounced off, only to be brought up short, her scarf pulling tight around her neck. It had snagged on one of the buckles securing the load to the silenbahk's back and legs.

The lacy-jacket man continued to yell at her, wrenching his horse to a halt directly in the stream of fast-moving carts, giving Lia a bubble of space as she tried to tug the scarf free. The silenbahk continued down the road, the scarf cutting across Lia's windpipe as the thing dragged her along behind it. Lungs burning, Lia tried to pull herself free, her sandals sliding across the paving stones.

Suddenly the silenbahk gave an angry bellow, as if it had finally noticed Lia attached to it, metal pots tipping from the wide trough strapped to its back to rain down around her. Its front legs lifted off the ground, dragging Lia up into the air.

"Let go of the scarf!" the man yelled.

It's tied around my neck, you idiot! Lia choked on the words, her vision starting to swirl. Grabbing hold of the length of scarf above her, Lia kicked her feet up, jammed them in one of the silenbahk's tethers, and hung upside down. Her vision crackled at the edges as all the blood ran to her head. Lia arched her back, reaching for the buckle where the scarf had snagged, her fingers rubbery and soft, her head full of flies. Straining, she looped a finger through the buckle and managed to tear her scarf free.

Lia flipped down, landing lopsided and stumbling as she clawed at the knots that had pulled so tight around her neck. The road was a circus of shouts and curses, the silenbahk rearing, horses slamming into wagons, donkeys braying—

Two more silenbahks emerged from the haze of Lia's vision. They were off kilter, angry, and charging directly toward her. Horses, messenger beasts, donkeys, people on foot, all ran helter-skelter in a panic to get out of the way. The air roared in Lia's ears. She frantically groped for Calsta's energy, sagging sideways when there was nothing there. The two silenbahks' knobby heads jerked against their riders' reins as they lumbered straight for the monster rearing behind Lia. They were going to slam straight into it, with her smashed in the middle.

The shouty rider's horse danced into her vision, the creature wide-eyed and trying to bolt. Holding the poor thing in check with a steady hand, the man yelled something useless about getting out of the way. Lia grabbed hold of his saddle's high pommel and jammed her foot into the stirrup, on top of his fancy boot, pulling herself off the ground. The horse wheeled to the side with her clinging to its shoulder, the rearing silenbahk's feet crashing back down just behind them. Fear shriveled Lia's heart, and she kicked one foot over the saddle and sat, her knuckles white on the pommel. It would have been simple with Vivi. Vivi knew her. Vivi wasn't afraid of anything.

And Vivi's saddle wasn't occupied by a blackmailing aukincer's son.

Mateo's arms jerked around Lia, trying to get the reins over her head even as his mare reared. Lia plastered herself forward, Mateo pressing in tight behind her to keep in the saddle, the reins slack in his hands. Once the horse came down, he kicked her through the mayhem to the side of the street, then into a branching alley clogged with people, who threw themselves aside to make way for the horse. The thunder of silenbahk feet and their angry bugling rumbled through Lia's chest, the whole world rocking back and forth beneath her.

They burst out into the open end of a water market, the floating walkway bobbing this way and that, Mateo's mare startling back and beginning to rear again. People skittered away, watching them with wide eyes, except for one woman with fists like great hams who shook an empty basket at them, a pile of spilled apples on the ground at her feet.

"What in Calsta's name is wrong with you? I thought Devoted abstained from alcohol," Mateo snarled in Lia's ear, his hands on the reins to either side of her more gentle than the tone of his voice. "No, I'm *not* going to bruise all your apples and steal your children!" That last was directed to the old woman shaking the empty basket. It had probably been their fault.

Lia dry-heaved, her fingers still pulling the scarf from around her neck. She turned in the saddle, attempting to dismount, but her skirt was twisted around the saddle's high pommel. After pulling it free, she kicked her foot back over the saddle, then slid to the ground. A thread of remorse needled her chest when the mare startled away from the sudden movement, so she gave the creature an apologetic pat on the shoulder before walking deeper into the market.

"Hey! *Lia!*" Mateo's voice chased after her. The apple seller's shout swelled up to check him, though. "No, I told you, I'll only pay for the *bruised* ones," he shouted back. "*No*, I can't carry them away with me!"

Lia slid through the narrow spaces in the crowd. The earth still seemed to rock back and forth under her feet, sending her stumbling to the side.

A hand on her arm pulled her to a stop, Mateo's smell of stone and dust and some kind of flowery cologne washing over her head. "You can't even walk straight. You could have killed yourself. You could have gotten *me* killed!"

"Well, I almost lost my scarf, so we're even." Lia pushed away from him, blinking until the ground and sky righted, her mind racing. Knox would definitely hear about this. So would everyone else in the city, including her father. And Ewan.

Mateo grabbed for her arm again, but Lia blocked it and spun toward him, jabbing him hard in the ribs. The aukincer's son hunched over, his eyes bulging.

"Touch me again and I'll cut off your hand." At least her voice was calm. Inside all she could feel was Ewan's hands grabbing her, his breath in her face.

"I believe you," Mateo croaked, clutching his stomach. There were mud stains on his fancy boots, and he held one of the bruised apples in his hand. "Why aren't you hiding in a pantry up in the Water Cay where you belong?"

Lia rolled her eyes. She hadn't hit him *that* hard. "Thank you for your help. I'll leave you to your . . . apple buying? Good luck getting all those home." The angry apple seller was scooping every single fruit to her name into a sack, one eye on his horse as if gauging how much the creature could carry and still fit Mateo in the saddle.

"Wait." Mateo put a hand up, still breathing heavily as he straightened. He was a good foot taller than she was even without his ridiculous hat. "You didn't break anything, did you? You're all right?"

"We aren't actually getting married, so you can stop pretending to care." She put a hand to her burning throat as she turned to walk away, almost crashing into a man with a barrel under each arm who had obviously been listening.

"Looks like he has money, lass. Might want to rethink your attitude." The man gave her a knowing leer. "Unless he's the one who did that?" He nodded to her throat.

"I would *never*—" Mateo broke off, suddenly looking over his shoulder. "Lia, we have to go."

Lia pushed past the man with the barrels, anger foaming inside her. "*We* don't have to do anything."

"But he's coming! He was at the dig with me, and now he's . . . he's on the road."

Lia stopped, the sun beating down on her shoulders. "Who are you talking about?"

"Come on. Come *on*!" Mateo was already pushing to the other side of the market. "What's your range? Can't you see him? Unless you *want* to go back to the seclusion? I assumed the pantry act yesterday was because he was looking for you before I got there."

The pantry act. Because *Ewan* had been looking for her. Lia suddenly felt as if she were floating away. She could feel Ewan's teeth on her lip, his breath in her ear.

"Lia, are you coming?" Mateo was staring at her from beside a table covered in sadly gasping fish.

She started after him, her head down, her blood frozen in her veins. He led her across the market walkway to where the canal opened up, boats skimming by almost nose to tail.

"Are you sure you aren't injured?" Mateo asked over his shoulder, his comically thick eyebrows ratcheted up as high as they would go. "I've seen people jump from boat to boat. Maybe if we're quick, we could get out of range."

"He . . ." Lia's feet stalled, and she looked back over her shoulder. There was nothing to see, no auroshes, no shiny cuirass, no sword drawn and swiping at the apple lady or any of the street sellers gaping after her and Mateo. "Where is he?"

"On the trade road. You Devoted can see one another from what, eighty paces? A hundred?" Mateo swallowed. "I don't mean to be rude, but both of you are very, very scary, and I don't really want to watch you fight to the death. Especially since you seem . . . completely unarmed?" The last came out like a question, as if Mateo couldn't fathom a Devoted without her sword.

Lia couldn't either. Yet there she stood.

But Ewan's aurasight was gone. She'd taken it herself with one touch of her hand against his skin. It shouldn't have worked on any Devoted but a spiriter, but his crass thoughts about Lia had been draining him already, and her touch was enough to tip him over the edge. Touching him had broken her oath. Ewan touching her back when he wanted to so very much had broken his.

Something she was pretty sure he'd continue to try if he found her.

Lia instructed her heart to stop pounding, her hands to stop clenching into fists, though her body didn't listen. "Ewan won't be able to see me from the road right now. He's diminished, Mateo. You falling into a canal instead of making it across the boats would just attract attention."

"If *I* can see him . . ." Mateo's mouth pursed, cutting off the words.

Lia choked down her bad memories and concentrated on the way Mateo's eyes traced the air over her head. Where her aura would be. "Wait, *you* have aurasight? *That's* how you found me?"

"Diminished . . . like he broke one of his oaths?" Mateo licked his lips, his head dipping forward so his hat's outlandish brim hid his face.

"He probably won't have his aurasight back for a few weeks at least. He wouldn't realize who I am unless he came over here and ripped off my scarf." Lia batted the hat off Mateo's head. "You, however, managed to see me just fine. I was in this city for days before I lost my aurasight. I didn't see a single auraspark in this city. *Nothing*. If you can see auras, where is *yours*?"

Mateo started to shake his head, but Lia didn't let him speak. "You found me in the pantry. You recognized me on the road. And now you know Ewan is in the street behind you more than a hundred paces away. *How* are you not locked up in a seclusion somewhere? And you're standing there in . . ." She gestured at his ornamented boots, the lavish embroidery on his coat. All things a Devoted couldn't have. "I saw you eat enough cake yesterday to sink the Commonwealth fleet. Why aren't *you* diminished?"

Mateo eased back. "You know, it's hard to read your expression when you're all covered that way. It almost sounds as if you're accusing me of something."

"You're hiding your aura. You're keeping your powers without doing *anything* Calsta wants." She closed the space between them and took hold of his ridiculously embroidered coat. *"How?"*

The people milling by had slowed their steps to stare. Mateo's eyes darted from side to side, as if he were hoping someone might take pity on him and intervene. Lia grabbed another handful of coat, giving him a shake. *"Tell* me, you useless *butterfly."*

Mateo's mouth gaped open in what she thought was going to be argument. Instead his eyes rolled back in his head, and he drooped to the ground, his dead weight pulling Lia down on top of him.

Lia rolled off him, jerking her skirts out from under his less than impressive bulk. "If you think going boneless is going to save you . . ." Which was when she saw the saliva dribbling from the corner of his mouth, Mateo's eyes vacant.

Then he began to convulse.

CHAPTER 19

Butterflies

You say he just collapsed?"

The voice echoed in Mateo's head as if it were coming from down a long stone corridor.

"Right in the middle of the market. I was yelling at him. What is . . . how . . . what can I do to help?"

"You've already done quite a bit. It was lucky he told you where we were staying." That was Tual. Mateo couldn't help but hear the croak in his father's voice as it came out. This was not good. "I've given him his first dose, and that will get him awake enough to take the rest. If you hadn't brought him here . . ." The words died into nothing. A hand settled on Mateo's shoulder. "I can't thank you enough, Lia."

Lia. A familiar anger budded inside Mateo even before his eyes would open. Lia, the girl he was supposed to drop everything and marry right before he dropped dead. "Butterfly," she'd called him.

How appropriate. Beautiful. Fleeting.

"You two arranged to meet today?" The note of hope in his father's voice made Mateo's teeth grind together. "Wait, he's moving! Thank Calsta above."

The hand on Mateo's shoulder pushed him onto his side, scratchy upholstery itching against his cheek. He forced his eyes open just in time for the spoon to shove up against his lips, hitting his teeth.

"I'll help you." Lia's voice. Her hands grasped his shoulders, pulling him gently into a sitting position. When Mateo's eyes opened, Lia was there right in front of him. The blue scarf still concealed her nose and mouth, but a red weal peeked out from between the loosened knots at her neck.

"You'll stay for the evening meal, won't you, Lia?" Tual's relief seemed to flood every inch of the room, cool and grateful where Mateo was burning up with rage. *This never happens. Two episodes inside of two days? It should be Lia lying here. A* Devoted *dying from wasting sickness. Not me.* Mateo managed to open his teeth, letting the spoon past to drip medicine down his throat.

"No, I can't stay." Lia's eyes followed the spoon, her fingers pressing harder than was strictly warranted where she held him up. Mateo wanted to squirm away from her, but his body didn't care much what he wanted. "I have to get back before Father finds my room empty."

"In that case, I have something for you. I sent Mateo into town with medicine for your mother—such a sly boy, he didn't tell me he was going to try to see you, too!"

"He wasn't. We only bumped into each other by accident."

"A happy accident, I hope? It's fairly important your mother gets this medicine soon—I'll go get it. It was in his coat, I think." Mateo's eyes followed his father as he left the room, then appeared through the window in the courtyard outside, where Mateo's horse was standing unattended. *How did Bella get back here?*

How did I get back here?

Embarrassment curdled inside him. *Lia* had brought him back. Saved him like he was a helpless princess in a fairy tale.

"Are you all right?" Lia whispered, easing him back down onto the couch.

"No." Mateo was proud of his mouth for being able to form the word.

"If I had any doubts about what you are, wasting sickness proves it. You're Devoted." She picked up the spoon, turning it over in her hands. "But this medicine . . . it helps?" There was an unholy note of hope in Lia's voice.

"No. Go away. Go *home.*"

Lia moved to the chair across from him, fists on her knees and her back straight as if she meant to kick the low couch out from under him if he didn't answer her properly, but she kept still until his father walked back into the room. Tual held out the cloth-wrapped package he'd given to Mateo once he'd finished his morning at the dig.

Lia took the package and tucked it under her arm.

"Are you going to be in trouble if your father finds you gone?" Tual's voice dripped with sympathy. "Why isn't your father allowing you out of the compound? I suppose he must be very worried about you."

Mateo let his head fall back on the pillow, exasperation sour in his mouth. Leaving *any* card on the table was beyond his father. He would use every strategy, every argument; every string that could be pulled would dance under Tual's fingers. It was the only reason they were still alive, but Mateo didn't much like having it used against him.

Standing, Lia started for the door. "Save your sympathy for someone who can't see through it." And she walked out.

Thank you! Mateo gripped the sofa hard, relieved that Lia wasn't letting his father manipulate her.

But then Tual started laughing. He leaned over to brush Mateo's hair out of his eyes. "I like her! Don't you like her?" His expression faltered as he looked Mateo over, and suddenly Mateo didn't have room for annoyance or anger, because if Tual was that worried, that meant even more was wrong than he knew. "I'll be back in a minute."

He followed Lia out of the room, his voice muffled when he caught her in the entryway. "At least take the horse. I'll send Mateo for her when he's feeling better."

"No!" Mateo struggled to sit up, the muscles in his neck straining. "She can't have Bella."

"If he's so sick, it's not safe for him to be out alone, is it?" Lia's voice was almost too low to catch.

"I'm afraid this is all quite new, so it's hard to say." Tual looked back at Mateo through the open doorway, and Mateo leaned sideways, trying to coax his body into getting up. To stop Tual from telling the killing machine in the entryway everything about him. The lean was all he could manage, and it unbalanced him so much that he tumbled off the low couch.

Couldn't you have at least let me land on the rug? he complained to the nameless god as he tried to roll over. The flowered decoration on the rug whirled in dizzying circles, his vision burning at the edges as if the sickness were eating away at him from the inside. *Eletoria flowers and plince vine, purple and blue . . .*

Tual ran to his side. "Easy, son. There's no need—"

Mateo shuddered, his anger shaking him now. *I'm going to die, and somehow my brain is calling up the names of obscure flowers on the rug?* "I wouldn't want to be rude." His voice was coming back. "Got to walk Lia out. Wave goodbye and smile while she steals my horse."

Lia, framed so prettily by the front door, gave a very unladylike snort.

She did give him one last concerned look before walking out. To his horse. Which she took.

It wasn't until hours later, when Mateo was capable of sitting on his own and halfway through a goat cheese and onion pie, that Tual found him in the kitchen.

"I stayed at the dig after you left this morning, and it's a good thing we had you roped into a harness instead of touching down in the new room. They didn't find any traps on the ground, so they sent workers in." Tual dumped an armful of reports onto the table, drawings and notations from the team of archeologists gray against the vellum. "Three of them collapsed before Van realized the floor was coated in poisonous paint. He managed to get them out in time for me to help, luckily. It's some kind of byanti concoction, meant to slow people down in smaller doses, but Van had them down there for hours. It was lucky I got to them so quickly."

"It's on the floors?" Mateo grimaced, putting his spoon down.

"See for yourself." Tual pushed the drawings toward him and sat down at the little table Mateo had appropriated despite Hilaria, the cook, threatening him with rat ears for dinner if he didn't get out of her way. Mateo pulled the topmost roll of vellum closer. It was one of his drawings of the new room, with all the reliefs and statues. The extra notations around the outside marked paint and wear, symbols with speculation about what they could mean, and there at the bottom, capital letters noting poison contamination across the floors and up the walls.

He pointed to the back wall. "There's a door through here."

Tual squinted at the drawing, pulling Mateo's satchel from his shoulder and setting it on the table. "You felt it while you were down there?"

"No." Mateo's humors tingled. While he'd been at the dig that morning, he hadn't dared use the nameless god's power. Using it to watch Ewan's aura ride by must have been what made him collapse directly into Lia's arms. "It was just a hunch. I'll go back later today and . . ." His eyes blurred. Blinking, Mateo tried to force his eyes to focus on the drawing. It didn't work. His head began to pound, the edges of his vision blackening. He closed his eyes and tried to breathe.

"Mateo?" Tual's hand was on his shoulder. Then a spoon was at his lips.

Mateo opened his mouth and let the foul stuff slide down his throat. When he opened his eyes, they were still blurry.

He pushed the drawings away from him, the top few sliding off the table and fluttering to the floor.

Tual watched them fall. "Son . . ."

Picking up the next illustration in the pile, Mateo couldn't quite make the lines unblur, though he'd drawn them that very morning. He remembered Patenga, the burnished gold paint edging the shape-shifter's likeness, which Mateo had spent an hour matching. And the sword, the beautiful *sword* . . . Mateo balled the drawing up and threw it across the kitchen, barely missing Hilaria's frizzy head. She turned to glare at him.

"Mateo!"

Mateo grabbed his drawing satchel next. Lia must have brought it with her when she'd carried him in. His life was made up of moments where other people had to decide to help him. A life of depending on everyone else's charity. A life that would *end* no matter how hard they searched for an answer. Mateo upended the whole bag, his charcoals and inks skittering across the marble floor and rough vellum fluttering like birds' wings.

"One little episode is not worth this tantrum." Tual's voice was quiet. "We're so close to finding what we need. If we can persuade Lia to—"

"I've never had episodes so close together." Mateo's hands clawed through his hair as he searched for the power that was supposed to be his, sweat dripping from his nose, down his cheeks, cold drops plinking on the floor as he groped for the nameless god and his magic. But there was nothing. Not even the salty aftertone of Devoted aura on the air, not a single song of stone or herb, not a whisper from the wood. He was blocked off from it after wasting all his energy to track Ewan's aura from the gate and down the road, all to protect Lia, who didn't need protecting.

At least she'd given him one answer. He'd thought her aura—

Ewan's, too—had looked starved and sad because he was rubbish at magic. But no, they were diminished. For once he wasn't seeing it wrong. Mateo looked at his father. "What if the caprenum isn't down there? What if we can't even find the burial chamber?"

Tual pressed his lips into a thin line. "We will find it, Mateo."

"Good. Then stop pushing me at the Seystones, and let's go to the tomb." Mateo couldn't help that his voice was getting louder. Hilaria suddenly found reason to go into the pantry and shut the door behind her.

"You need to rest. And Lia . . ." Tual licked his lips, looking down. "I love you, son. I want you to be all right. She plays a larger part in this than you think."

"The only thing I'm interested in right now is not dying."

"Yes. She plays a larger part in you not dying than you realize."

"You think she's going to be the one to pull a caprenum sword out of the tomb?" Mateo shook his head, the room whirling around him. "Is that some shapeshifter trap that I don't know about—it has to be a Devoted who goes in?" Lia had latched on to the idea that he was a Devoted. For someone who was supposed to spend her life hunting Basists, she was pretty terrible at it. The whole court was.

Tual didn't say anything, his brow knotted.

Mateo was too wound up to stop. "And even if that were the case, which it's *not*, you think the only way she'd do it is if we're bound together legally in *marriage*? Even if Lia and I fell *madly in love* the moment we set eyes on each other—something that hasn't technically happened on my side unless you count blue scarf as a facial feature—you'd be making a widow out of her before we braided our wreaths. Even if I had *years* to look forward to, I'd want to choose who and what were in them."

The words felt final. Horrible. Real in a way his sickness never had before because there *were* no choices. There was no future. All Mateo had was right there in front of him. A dangerous tomb sketched across a collection of crumpled papers with no direct path forward. A tear etched a line down his cheek, burning like acid.

Tual slid off his chair to gather the littered papers and pencils. "I won't stop fighting until—"

"Until *what?*" Mateo pushed back from the table, his insides churning. He wanted to make his father say it.

His father looked up at him, tears glossy in his eyes. "Until you are well again. I'm not letting go of you, son. You're all I have."

"I'm going to the tomb." Mateo started toward the door, stumbling into the wall when his knees turned to jelly. "I am the only reason they found the lower room. Maybe I'll find more. Are they covering the floors, or did you take something down to neutralize the poison?"

"Mateo—"

"I can't lie in bed and wait. I'm going."

"Studying these would be more help." Tual held up the crumpled pages. "Besides, Lia has your horse."

"Then I'll take *your* horse." Mateo slid along the wall, barely making it to the door, his boots' soft soles too quiet to satisfy him as he tried to stomp out.

He stopped just outside the doorway, his lungs like wet paper, each breath tearing them a little more. Walking was hard. Breathing was hard. Even standing in the hallway, his back to the wall, was like trying to balance on a single suspended rope. Mateo closed his eyes and waited for the dizziness to fade.

Tual came out of the kitchen, his arms full of reports. He stopped when he saw Mateo, his face lanced through with real fear. But he recovered himself and held up the reports once again. "I really could use your eyes on some of these. I think you'll find the one of the wall you mentioned of particular interest. I'll put them in the office for you." He smiled. Then left Mateo to battle alone. Tual knew him well enough not to hover.

It took the better part of fifteen minutes for Mateo to manage another step, tears burning down his cheeks. Another half hour got him to his father's crowded office. Inside, he flopped into his father's chair and stared at the pile of drawings. Comparisons to past tomb structure, parallels to known burial ceremonies of the time, sketches of artifacts . . . he swept them all from the desk's surface and let his head rest on the polished wood, his heart still thumping too slow.

This was the end, wasn't it? Maybe not today, but soon.

One paper was still on the desk, partially under his cheek. His eyes tried to focus on the words: "Dark or corrupted auras . . . or any manifestation of unexplained power even without an augmented aura . . . I will provide restraint until they can be evaluated. . . ." Mateo sat up and wiped the tears from his face. *Dark auras.* That's what a Basist aura was supposed to look like, though Mateo had never seen one. It was part of the nameless god's many quirks—Mateo could see Devoted, but not the aura hovering around his father. Maybe his father had done something to hide their auras, or maybe not all Basists had them. It was even in this letter—unexplained powers with no aura augmentation. It was hard to know.

Mateo's fingers brushed across the document, fiddling with the blown-glass paperweight that had saved it from being swept off the desk. It was signed by one of the seclusion heads. "All potential candidates will be referred to Tual Montanne . . . special attention to any unhealthy attachment to objects, including, but not limited to, unauthorized weaponry."

Candidates. With a dark aura. A corrupted aura—Mateo didn't know what that meant—or *no* aura and magic. Like Mateo.

You're all I have. That's what Tual had said.

But Tual said a lot of things. Tual had smiled through that interview with the valas as if he were not threatening to have the whole family killed if they didn't do as he wished. He always had plans, then backup plans.

That was why they were still alive.

But what would Tual do if Mateo weren't still alive? What would his backup plan be then? He always talked about how he'd been so alone before Mateo, unable to feel safe in a country where his magic—wanted or not—was a death sentence. The two of them together, working together, studying together, planning together . . .

And here Tual was looking for other Basists. Candidates to replace the faulty one he was stuck with.

The paper crumpled in Mateo's fist, his teeth grinding tightly together. There was a deeper violence, a deeper anger, clawing at his arms and hands, twitching in his legs.

We will find it, Mateo.

Son. Adopted son. He seemed so sure they'd find caprenum before Mateo succumbed to wasting sickness. Tual had been alone before he'd saved Mateo as a young child. He'd be alone again if Mateo died.

A possibility Tual seemed to be taking very seriously.

CHAPTER 20

The Many Names of Calsta

Knox looked up at the drum tower as the late-afternoon signal rapped out across the city. From his spot in the alley behind the silenbahk milk booth, he could just see the governor's roof sticking up from the other side of the Water Cay. Barriers had been set up along the Water Cay bridge to keep unwanted carriages out, just as Noa had promised.

Anwei's shoulder pressed into Knox's side as she leaned forward, a cascade of sparks sizzling up Knox's torso. *Sky Painter,* he whispered inwardly to distract himself from the feel of Anwei against him. *Storm Rider. Cloud Weaver.* Counting off Calsta's names very loudly in his head wasn't helping, so he tried to edge away, but the brick wall was against his back. There was no escape.

Problem was, Knox didn't exactly want to escape. "You're sure about this?" he asked.

"It's all we've got." Anwei moved away from him, hands smoothing down her disguise to give it one last check. Her torso swelled out in front of her under a ridiculous frilly apron—the perfect disguise, she'd said. No one suspects a pregnant woman. "One Devoted-free party."

Knox nodded, not bothering to add that there was another Devoted—a *spiriter*—who had somehow become lost in the city.

There were only so many spiriters, and he couldn't help but think that Lia could be here.

Here and lost didn't really make sense, not for any spiriter.

Here and hunting him, however . . .

The former made him want to drop everything and start looking for glints of red hair. He'd missed Lia every day he'd been gone, missed the seclusion, missed the simplicity of being told what to do, doing it, and knowing he was on the right path, rather than this muddle he was in now.

The latter—that Lia could be hunting him—made Knox want to run. If anyone could find him, it would be Lia.

He pushed away both ideas. Any spiriter hunting him would be bad, and the Warlord wouldn't have sent Lia to Chaol to find her closest friend—it would be too much to ask of any Devoted. The spiriter who was here could be anywhere. Running away like everyone seemed to think. At the party. Over the border in Lasei. If the spiriter had come to find Knox, there wasn't much he could do about it dead. Knox stopped his hand before it could reach for the sword, and a warm glow bloomed at the back of his head as if Calsta was trying to offer comfort. Or maybe that was just Anwei. Because, for whatever reason, with Anwei, no spiriter would be able to find him.

He hoped.

From Willow, Knox had heard nothing. Anwei had stashed the sword somewhere, but when he'd asked what had become of it, his friend had shrugged and instructed him to help her gut slugs for some poor, unsuspecting customer.

He wasn't entirely certain slugs had guts. It had all been about the same when he'd done the job. Mushy. The space inside his head had changed, though. The pull of the sword was still there, but Willow's voice was gone, and he couldn't pretend he wasn't relieved.

Anwei gave her huge belly a fond pat, as if it actually were some sort of growing spawn attached to her, before she walked out of the alley. Knox followed, dragging a wagon of freshly cut blooms behind him. The florist's apron obscured the straps that held the fake baby against Anwei's stomach, but it was so . . . *there*. He knew it was just her medicine bag—padded to make it look less like a bag and more like a life waiting to spill out of her—but it still made his insides go all funny.

Turning to look at him once the guards had waved them over the bridge, Anwei asked, "Any sign of our little pineapple friend?" She twisted the top button on her florist's tunic, every single button done clear to her throat, unlike any florist Knox had seen. He'd always wondered why she felt the need to cover every inch of her body, but after glimpsing the scars on her shoulders, he supposed he could understand. Sort of. Anwei wasn't shy about much of anything, so hiding scars seemed odd.

Remembering the scars made Knox's eyes fix on that button twisting between Anwei's fingers, made him remember her shoulder, her collarbone. And the dream of Anwei kissing him. The one where he kissed her back.

Ageless One. Bright One. Honest One. Knox turned his eyes to the guards checking the small line of people waiting to enter the governor's compound and made them stick.

"Knox?"

Knox blinked. She'd asked him a question. About pineapples? If he'd seen the Trib following them. Altahn. "Not today."

Anwei seemed to catch herself fiddling with the button and forced her hands up to check the western-border scarf she'd twisted around her braids. "We'll deal with it. Whatever comes."

"We always do." Knox stepped forward in line, his voice low. Anwei did her part, and he did his. He shook his head, thinking of Noa's belly laugh and the way she'd dropped her blazing tethers at the Firelily, leaving the flames for someone else to put out. "I just don't like relying on someone who isn't you."

Anwei smiled. He could feel it in his head better than he could see it from behind her.

Two more guards were standing watch at the governor's gates, the first asking Anwei to turn out her pockets, a second coming to kneel by Knox's wagon.

"Auroshe handler?" The man looked up at him for confirmation, the thick leather Knox had spent hours stitching into the neck and arms of his uniform setting him apart from other hostlers. Knox nodded, hoping very much that he wouldn't be asked to perform any actual auroshe-related duties while inside the grounds. His own mount, which he'd left behind at the seclusion with little remorse, had always seemed to think Knox wouldn't notice if he nibbled off one of Knox's toes.

"And you're feeding those things . . . chrysanthemums?" the guard asked, glancing down at the red flowers.

"They're actually begonias." Anwei pushed between him and the wagon, her perfect smile contagious. The guard fell back a step, making way for her overlarge belly. "He was so kind to help me when he found me struggling to get the wagon across the square. When I realized they weren't letting any vehicles past the bridge, I thought that was the end for me."

One of the guards gave her a small smile. "What florist would have allowed someone"—he faltered, eying her belly—"someone in your *situation* to drag something so heavy all the way from the lower cays?"

"Oh, I'm fine." She smoothed a hand across her ridiculous apron. "Got to earn my wages so I can spoil the little monster rotten." Anwei gave a little spin that was unbalanced enough it almost ended with her on the ground. Knox picked up the wagon's handle, hoping the movement hid his involuntary smile.

"You'll help me get it into the house, won't you?" Anwei grabbed hold of Knox's arm and turned her pretend gaiety full force on him, her chest and shoulder pressing into him as she started to pull him past the guards.

Protector of Souls. Blue Mage.

"Wait." The second guard blocked their way. "We need to check under the wagon." He bent down and pulled up the side. Flowers spilled onto the cobblestones.

"No! You're ruining them!" Anwei threw herself to the ground, trying to hold the rest of the flowers in place even as they spilled into her lap. Tears were suddenly streaming down her cheek, as unexpected as a bolt of lightning. "If we lose even *one*, Madame Geller will flay me alive. . . ." She tenderly picked up the nearest fallen flowers and clutched them to her chest.

Knox knelt next to her on the ground. "Let me, you shouldn't be doing that in your *condition*. . . ."

"I'm not in any condition," she snapped. "Babies are *normal* and *natural* and *beautiful*!"

The guard not searching the wagon fell to his knees next to them, gingerly gathering the blooms. When the other guard finished his inspection, he grudgingly helped them gather the last of the flowers and resettle them in the wagon bed.

Anwei's tears were falling in earnest now. "Some of them are bruised." She gave a pitiful sniff.

"Chin up. You know, I've got two little babies at home myself, and I couldn't bear to think of their mother being so badly treated as all this. We'll walk you in." The first guard gave Anwei's shoulder a fatherly pat. "Make sure your master understands it was our fault."

Anwei gave him a very brave look, her lip trembling. Knox barely succeeded in keeping his eyes from rolling. "Would you?"

The guard gave Knox a dismissive wave. "You go on now. We'll take care of this."

Knox hunched his shoulders and nodded. Anwei had known the flowers and tears would be enough to keep them from patting her down. He didn't know *how*, only that she was usually right, deciding how people would act before she'd even seen them, as if they were her puppets on strings. He started across the paved courtyard toward the stables, the house with its three stories and gabled rooftop just the way he remembered it.

Anwei's loud talk of flowers and wages and babies passed out of his hearing as one of the guards led her toward the main house. Even if the actual florist was waiting in the kitchen, Anwei would say something that would make them all laugh and believe her place was there. She always did.

Which was why Knox had been the one assigned to pick up the bag Noa had left for them in the stables while Anwei drew attention away from him. He walked past the wide-open doors at the front, where hostlers were gathered for some kind of scolding before guests began to arrive. Knox circled around to the back side of the two-story building, running a hand along the stone walls carved with dragonflies and water lilies.

At the back of the building, where the thatched roof dipped almost to the ground, Knox slipped through the much smaller door into the room where saddles and tack were stored, the inside pleasantly cool after the blazing afternoon sun. He scanned the building for auras, finding all but two of the hostlers clustered together at the front. One was working in a stall just past the tack room, and the second was on the upper level.

Knox left the tack room, walking purposefully down one of the aisles between stalls. There were three long rows of open stalls and stairs leading to the second floor, which covered about half of the building. His destination lay at the very back, past a reinforced barrier where the ceiling was high, skylights sending columns of afternoon light down to the bales of hay below. Against the wall, well away from the other animals, there were six completely enclosed stalls. Metal bars reinforced the barriers, the interiors marked with long, ugly gouges. The smell of blood was rank in Knox's nose.

Three of the stalls were occupied. Some of the Roosters would be at the party, then.

Knox shuddered as he approached the auroshes. Even after years of riding them as a Devoted, he was still terrified of the beasts. They flicked their ears back as he walked closer, but none of them looked his way, as if they could lull him into believing they weren't dangerous.

The one closest was the first to break the charade. Her skin was white with patches of brown, a single horn protruding from her forehead. She didn't lunge or scream, just raised her head, black tongue flicking out to clean her long, jagged teeth.

The other two auroshes waited until Knox walked past them toward the stairs leading to the loft. The one in the center charged at his stall bars, mouth opening unnaturally wide as he tried to snap at Knox. He was a black bay, two spiky horns jutting from his skull. One of the two Knox had seen that night after the trade advisor job. Watching the creature carefully, Knox was on the first step before he really looked at the third auroshe.

Knox stumbled, barely catching himself.

The thing was silver with dappled spots down his shoulders and haunches. A single white horn twisted gracefully from his forehead, almost a thing of beauty until you saw his wicked black eyes. No pupil, no iris, just inky black. The creature's teeth were jagged and white, his mane plaited more intricately than the other two.

Vivi. Lia *was* here.

Knox clenched his eyes shut, forcing his thoughts calm. His brain wouldn't obey, though, splintering at the edges, begging to expand his aurasight. He didn't know if he wanted to find her or run away before she found him.

When he opened his eyes, he found Vivi had crept to the edge of the enclosure. The creature pressed up against the bars as if he recognized Knox, wanted to reassure him. Vivi cocked his head, retreated a few steps—

Then darted forward, his long fangs silvered in the dim light as he snapped at Knox's arms.

Knox jerked away and stumbled up the stairs. Vivi went still, his black eyes following as Knox climbed to the loft, his long, twisted horn pointed directly at Knox's heart. The other auroshes wound their heads to track his movements, the straw that littered the ground around their hooves stained brown with old blood. Brownish-red clumps were caught in the fur across the paint's muzzle and down her chest.

Knox shuddered, quickly moving to the supply shelves. If Lia was here at the governor's house, then he and Anwei were done for. His hands shook as he pawed through the clay jars, the hooks and spiked halters, the bloodstained buckets that sent flies erupting into the air. How had Noa come up with *this* as a perfect place to stash their supplies?

The auroshes ensured not many people would come close, but the feeding loft was the only thing in the open second-story space, exposed for anyone to see.

It wasn't until Knox got to the large clay waterpot between stacks of hay that he found Noa's bag lodged between the pot and the wall. He half expected Noa herself to jump out from behind the haystacks and push him down into the stalls with a delighted cackle, just to see what color his blood was.

Maybe it wasn't so odd that Noa had chosen the auroshe's feeding loft. She seemed the type who'd like things with teeth.

As Knox looped the bag's leather strap over his shoulder, his mind caught on one of the hostler auras moving in his direction. He looked up to find the man emerging from the first row of stalls, his chin tipped up to stare directly at Knox.

Knox dislodged a section of hay and dumped it into the first auroshe's enclosure. The paint keened up at him as the dry stalks rained down on her, her black eyes following when he started down the stairs. She bared her teeth, as if memorizing his face for later retribution.

"I thought those things didn't care for hay." The hostler looked Knox up and down, eyes snagging on the reinforced collar of his jacket. "I haven't seen you around here before, have I?"

"Sometimes they need something to settle their stomachs." Knox pointed a thumb at the paint, flinching when she gave an angry screech. She started pawing at the hay, crushing it under her divided toes. "She's been off her feed since we arrived. Went up to check her lines from above, but nothing seems amiss. Must be her gut." It came out a little fast and dry.

The hostler shrugged, happy to look away from the beasts. His eyes slid down to the bag under Knox's arm. There was a bit of silvered fabric sticking out of it, but Knox started walking before he could ask any more questions.

Outside, the sun was waffling just above the horizon. Servants coursed by in droves now, arms full of fabric, food, and various pieces of furniture, all dancing to the shouts of the woman Knox recognized as the housemistress. No carriages yet. Knox slipped back into the stables and found a dark corner where he could watch and wait.

He could see the auroshes, the bay and the paint pawing at their stall doors and snuffling at the ground in that alert, agitated way auroshes always had. Vivi was quiet, though, his head snaking over to look at Knox with those wide, dark eyes. He looked lonely.

Knox's stomach clenched, twisting so tight he couldn't breathe. Lia, who had talked him through so many lonely days and nights. Lia, who knew about his parents, his sister. Lia, who had cried herself to sleep every night for their first year at the seclusion, wishing for nothing but her own bed.

Lia was in Chaol. And Lia was *missing*.

Knox hid in the tack room until the brother moons had risen. Castor looked a bit blue from his spot higher in the sky, the two almost in line. Carriages had started arriving, announced by the clatter of wheels, horses huffing at one another, and hostlers leading them into the long lines of empty stalls.

After creeping out the tack room door, Knox followed the faint sounds of music coming from the house, candlelight blazing from the two-story windows. The shuffle of dancing and talking from inside was soft enough even he couldn't hear much. Rounding the side of the house, he walked toward the west wing, where everything was dark.

Once Knox had ducked behind an ornamental shrub, he waited for a guard to pass before he started counting second-floor windows. The one he wanted—the lady of the house's office—was completely exposed, but a tree grew a few windows down. When he and Anwei had been here last winter, they'd used this same entrance, but since the candlestick incident, the governor was said to have added locks to all the windows. The guard who had passed moments before was certainly a new addition.

Knox slunk across the lawn to hide in the shadows at the tree's roots, waited for the guard to pass again, then ran at the wall. He launched himself upward, grabbing hold of the second-story window ledge with one hand. Dangling, Knox grabbed the sill with his other hand and pulled himself up. He didn't need Calsta for something this simple.

Two windows down, the pane swung open. Knox jumped to the next sill and, using his momentum, continued into a leap toward the open window, grabbing the window frame to change directions, and slid in feet first. He rolled once to absorb the momentum.

"Flashy. As usual." Anwei had retied the scarf binding her hair, the side artfully arranged to mimic a first khonin knot. Her medicine bag was still buckled tight over her stomach, the dreadful bulge jarring enough that Knox had to force his eyes away. Anwei didn't seem to notice as she closed and locked the leaded-glass window, then dropped to her knees to open Noa's bag. Knox let her take it, dusting himself off. The whole *room* was dusty, long unused.

"Noa set some curtains on fire during dinner and loosed some rats among the musicians, so the guests were already on edge when I came up here. The ghosts should be starting about now." Anwei dug past the ruffles of silvery fabric in the bag and pulled out the envelope of lockpicks stuffed at the bottom. They'd been too heavy and too incriminating to risk hiding on their persons on the way in. Next Anwei pulled out the swaths of silvery fabric, which turned out to be the dress Noa had insisted was necessary. Anwei held it up, looking it over with a sort of trepidation Knox didn't understand.

"Don't like the cut?" he asked.

She ignored him, squishing the ruffles back into the bag and going to the door to check the hallway. Knox pulled off his hostler jacket, turning the sleeves inside out to bare the side that was made to look like the uniform of one of the governor's house servants.

"The guards have been cleared?" He finished buttoning the coat to his chin, then smoothed down the gray front, hoping his black hostler pants would pass muster.

"Noa should have started by now, so hopefully they'll all be running toward the ballroom. I'm going to open the door. Keep watch for me down here."

The governor's study was at the end of the hall, so Knox took his position just inside the office while Anwei knelt before the locked door. She pulled out two different picks, then shoved the first deep into the tumblers. Knox's ears seemed to hum, searching for evidence that Noa had started screeching ghostly threats at the guests, but there wasn't anything to hear of ghosts or otherwise. After a moment Knox slid into the hall and backed his way toward Anwei, eager to be finished with the job.

When he got to the study door, Anwei was sticking her tongue out the side of her mouth in concentration, breathing in softly as if she could somehow smell the lock open. Knox looked away when a dark tendril of purple bled through her aura, blocking her eyes.

She's doing it again. Right in front of you.

Willow's voice slipped into his mind, a whisper. So she wasn't gone.

He recoiled, pushing the voice away. Fenced it off in his head, built a wall of brick and stone and ivy and iron around it, but still he could feel his fingers twitching for the pockmarked sword. Calsta's power had shielded him from that voice for so many years, but lately the goddess's fire had been too weak in the face of Willow's ice.

Just stand a little closer, Willow hummed. *That's all I ask. Her aura is right there. . . .*

Knox took a step forward.

Calsta's voice warmed his thoughts, but it was as if she was far away. *Stay where you are, Knox.*

Knox looked down at his hands. They'd come up, stretching toward Anwei. He reached for Calsta, for her burning fire. *Help me!* he called.

Her voice was barely a whisper. *I can't help you now. That's why I brought you to Anwei.*

Anwei? Knox couldn't focus his eyes, Willow like a frozen blade stabbing into the center of his brain. *Calsta . . . please . . . you know what is going on. You know how to stop Willow. Why won't you just tell me? Why don't you just* fix *it, the way you promised back when I first found Willow with the sword!*

But Calsta was only a flicker of flame, not the burning wall that had protected him from his sister at the beginning. So he tried to do as she said. Knox grasped for the spot of Anwei in his head, hiding underneath it just the way he'd hidden under her aura that day on the wall.

Immediately Willow's claws of ice seemed to melt away. Not erasing her—he could still hear her muttering at the back of his head, but a weight had been pulled from his hands and arms, as if Willow had been trying to wrest control away from him, and he'd noticed only when she couldn't touch him anymore.

Anwei looked up abruptly, sending a flutter of alarm through Knox. He was wearing her like a coat, hiding under her like a blanket, and she was just looking at him, confused. "You all right?" she asked, the lock clicking open under her fingers.

"I . . ." Knox's whole body was shaking. Anwei suddenly felt altogether too close, too intimate inside his mind.

The night before last, Calsta had been painfully direct in telling Knox not to let himself get distracted by Anwei, and now she was saying this mind-bonding awfulness had been the plan the whole time? That somehow the goddess was losing the battle with Willow in his head, and so she was tying him to a Basist instead? How was that supposed to work?

Knox gritted his teeth as he pushed through the governor's study door. The problem was, that seemed about right for Calsta. It was like she had an entire plan for fixing Willow, fixing Knox, fixing the *world* maybe, only she hadn't told anyone and was doing it backward.

The study was crowded with the rich purples and reds of old leather. Shelves of books lined each wall, the old tomes interspersed with little bits of pointless junk that only rich men seemed to find interesting. The governor's desk squatted at the center of the room, bent under the weight of scrolls and a thick sheaf of vellum. While Anwei locked the door behind them, Knox went to the desk. He flipped through the loose sheets for anything about the dig, uncomfortable even looking at his friend.

"I don't see anything here. . . ." Knox glanced up to find Anwei pulling the florist's tunic over her head. He dropped his eyes, concentrating on the letters in front of him. Something about fish. Lake fishery quotas. Fishhooks. Fish . . . food?

"It doesn't have sleeves." Anwei's voice caught.

Knox chanced looking up again. Anwei was holding the silvery-gray dress to her shoulders, ruffles cascading to the floor from the waist. She was still wearing a long-sleeved undertunic that covered her up to her neck and down to her wrists, the medicine bag with its extra padding discarded on the floor next to her.

"I told her it had to have sleeves. . . ." She poked the neckline, which appeared to be slit clear to the knees.

Crouching, Knox started opening desk drawers. The first was full of inkwells and quills, weights for scrolls. "Wear your tunic under it." That would be better for him as well. Much less to look at.

Anwei pulled the cascade of gray-silver ripples over her head. He glanced up when she started laughing. The dress had thin straps that hardly seemed capable of holding the weight of the ruffles, the neck plunging down to Anwei's waist. It was made from a shiny fabric that was creased and rumpled by design, her undertunic a glaring white against the silvery color. It looked, at best, awkward. "We're supposed to *fit in*, Knox."

"You look fine. No one is going to be paying attention to dresses when we meet up with Noa. They'll all be screaming about ghosts. Are you doing the shelves?"

He could almost feel Anwei rolling her eyes at him before she moved to the other side of the room, where the shelves were stacked with papers rather than books. Turning back to the desk, Knox found the second drawer full of vellum bound into ledgers. Shuffling through them, all he found was house logs and inventory lists. The third drawer was locked. The fourth was full of odds and ends. No dig reports.

"I need you to do this drawer with your picks when you're done with those shelves. Unless you find something first." Knox pointed at the locked drawer, making sure Anwei saw it before he moved to the shelves opposite her. He ran his fingers along the books' spines, searching for anything that looked official, but there was nothing except for a complete history of the Commonwealth, several guides to Elantin sculpture, a beautiful atlas, and three separate copies of *A Thousand Nights in Urilia*. One of them had been shoved hurriedly behind a row of books, the scandalous drawings inside hidden from view.

"About twelve minutes left, including the walk to the entry hall," Anwei said from where she was crouched in front of the desk, jamming her picks into the drawer's lock. When she pulled the drawer open, Anwei gave an aggravated sigh. "Nothing in here but a report about some kind of assassination attempt . . . some letters . . ." Her voice caught. "Letters from the Warlord."

Knox spun around. "What?"

"Knox, she's *coming here.*" Anwei held up a sheet of rice paper, her eyes wide. But then she looked at it again, her mouth pursing. "Maybe it's not so bad."

Panic was like a wild thing inside of Knox. "Not so *bad*? Anwei, if she comes to Chaol—"

"To discipline the valas?" Anwei waved the thin paper at him. "And to inspect the dig? She's not here for you any more than the Devoted are."

"It doesn't matter *why* any of them are here." He forced his hands to keep searching. The Warlord. She was coming. "They'll find me."

"Honestly, you aren't that self-centered, are you?" Anwei was using that playful tone that stung the most because she wasn't trying to hurt him as she teased, but it still sort of did. "They probably haven't given you a second thought. You're *free.*"

"Free Devoted aren't a thing." Knox went to the next shelf, frantically looking for anything that might be of help. Only, he knew what was going to help: finding the shapeshifter.

She's going to try to take me away. Willow's voice slunk through a crack in the defenses he'd made of Anwei. *Master Helan probably told her all about me, so she knows why you ran away. . . .*

"Are the reports in there?" Knox asked, his voice a croak. Lia was here in Chaol. And she'd disappeared. What had seemed like an impossible circumstance suddenly bloomed into all his worst nightmares. Everyone knew Lia hated the seclusion. He would at least have stopped to listen if she'd shown up at the apothecary door asking for help, and the Warlord must have known it. Lia missing *had* to be a trap.

The thought twisted like a knife in his gut. Lia wouldn't be party to such a scheme, not if it meant he'd die. Would she?

"No reports . . . oh, wait a second." Anwei's voice turned him around. "This thing has a false bottom. But why would he hide . . ." She grunted. "Come help me."

Knox walked back to the desk to kneel across the drawer from Anwei. She pointed toward the far side, gesturing to the wooden drawer bottom. "I think if you pull up while I press here . . ."

Jamming his fingers into the tiny gap, Knox pulled up the bottom with a jerk. A spray of dust jetted out from the opening directly into his face.

Anwei froze, her hands groping for her medicine bag. "Knox, don't move."

Knox obeyed, his muscles going taut. The dusty smell crawled up his nostrils, then wormed down his throat and into his mouth. He sneezed.

Anwei pulled out three separate envelopes from her bag, muttering angrily to herself. "The nameless god must be laughing." She threw one of the packets back into her bag and grabbed for another one. "It's poison, Knox, and I didn't smell it. How could I not have smelled it until it was *in the air*? I knew something was odd down there, but it was *masked* somehow . . . the dirt on these papers, or . . . it shouldn't have been enough to *block poison*." She swore, dumping little red petals into another of the envelopes, purple strings twisting through her aura like little worms.

"What is it?" Knox kept his voice calm.

"Does it matter? I don't have the right things to get rid of it. Best I can do here is slow it down."

The feeling of fullness in Knox's nose and mouth began to press against the back of his throat, the skin and tissue stretching tighter than a first khonin's purse. Anwei extracted what looked suspiciously like bug legs from the third envelope and added them to her mix, then began furiously kneading the little pouch with her fingers. The purple strings in her aura thickened, turning syrupy and grotesque.

"Anwei." Knox choked on her name. Willow was breathing in his head, pulsing bigger at the sight of Basist magic coursing through the air. "You can't . . . you can't *do that*."

Anwei's fingers stopped, and her eyes narrowed when she saw him looking at the envelope. A cough bubbled up from Knox's throat, tearing out of him like a fistful of gravel. "Just so we're clear, you'd rather *die* right here in the governor's study, where they'll strip you down and give your body to the wardens to use for target practice, than let me help you?"

Willow began pushing against Knox, testing the barrier Anwei made in his head. *I'm so hungry, Knox.*

"That's n-not what I . . . m-meant," he stuttered. He could barely speak, his hands flexing and clenching. His throat was burning, the roof of his mouth on fire. The purple strands congealed, turning opaque around Anwei's face, and his connection to her seemed to fray, Willow seeping through the holes. *Shapeshifters. My job is to stop them. If I let Anwei do this* . . . He *couldn't* let her use the nameless god's magic on him. And if he did, what would Willow do? She'd talked about hunger, about *feeding*, and now she was suddenly stronger. *What do I do, Calsta?*

But Calsta wasn't there. As usual.

Anwei was staring at him, rage and sadness like a war in her eyes. The thoughts in Knox's head turned gummy, melting together. Anwei was beautiful. Anwei was made of purple smoke. Anwei was the nameless god's. He shook his head, trying to clear it. "For Calsta's sake, just fix it."

Then her fingers were in his mouth, pushing his tongue up and emptying a foul-tasting powder underneath. He gagged, sagging to the ground.

"Hold it in your mouth until I tell you. Then swallow." Anwei's arm threaded under his, guiding him back until his spine hit the desk. She moved next to him, but his eyes were underwater, all of him was underwater until she thrust something into his face. A small glass bottle from her bag. "Open and swallow."

The word settled in his head, the meaning taking a beat too long because Anwei pressed a hand on his cheeks, forcing his mouth open and emptying the vial inside. He swallowed it gratefully, the taste of glass on his tongue.

"You'll be clear for a few minutes—it might come and go, but if we don't get you back to the apothecary in the next half hour, you'll die." Anwei's cheeks were pale as she dove into the locked drawer, pulled out a book, and flicked it open. The first page seemed to be a map of some kind. The rest were sketches and lists that swam before Knox's eyes. "This is exactly what we were looking for. He'll see if it's gone . . . but we don't have time . . . and he'll see the poison was triggered even if I put it back. . . ." That seemed to decide it for her. She grabbed Noa's bag and the padding she'd had under her tunic and threw them into the drawer. The book and the lockpicks went into her medicine bag, though they hardly fit, the seams on her bag straining.

The burning in Knox's throat had begun to recede. Anwei rammed the false bottom back into the drawer, dropped the letters on top of it, then slammed it shut. She grabbed Knox's arm and helped him up, his head spinning. The floor seemed to be washing this way and that under his feet like a beach in the tide.

She's right there, Knox, and I need her. I need more *or I'll be gone forever. You have to take her.*

Willow again.

Knox screwed his eyes shut, pressing his hands to both sides of his head until it began to hurt. The ghost's voice was running through him like acid, and he didn't even know what she was asking. *"Go away,"* he murmured to himself. The connection with Anwei had helped, so he concentrated on her warm glow once again. Willow's icy cold drew back a hair.

"Knox? We have to move. You have to *walk.*"

A flare of energy blossomed next to him, Anwei crowned in purple as she pulled him toward the door. Knox opened his eyes to look at it. It was beautiful, her magic. The thought felt wrong, like watching a thousand murders only to find one performed gracefully and calling it art.

It wasn't murder, though. She wasn't murder. She was Anwei.

Willow shrank back with a cry as the bond seemed to grow, burning up inside of Knox. But then he was too close. He could feel Anwei's concentration as she forced his stumbling feet past the desk. He could feel her fear, the weight of him pulling her sideways as she tried to support him. Anwei looked up at him suddenly as a swirl of inky purple washed across her face, and she jerked back in alarm, swatting at the insubstance of her own aura as if she was seeing it for the first time.

Knox hurriedly pulled his mind back from his partner, closing his eyes and concentrating on making his feet move toward the door. But there was something wrong. A sound like tapping coming from outside that shouldn't have been there.

Anwei grabbed for the door latch just as the sound pushed through the fuzz stuffing Knox's head. He lurched forward, knocking her hand away. "Someone is coming!"

CHAPTER 21

The Voice of a Dead King

Anwei pulled out from under Knox's arm, her ears straining for the sounds of footsteps he could hear but she couldn't. All she could smell was the cinnabar stench coming from Knox, the edge only barely taken off by the herbs she'd jammed down his throat. Everyone should have been running out of the ballroom by now. Who would run this way?

She hitched up her skirts and cinched the medicine bag's strap tight around her hips, letting the bag itself hang against the backs of her knees, where it would be hidden under the long gown's ruffles. Knox stumbled toward the window, one hand against the wall for balance.

Anwei beat him to it just as the first footsteps in the hall reached her ears. The door jiggled and she was glad she'd thought to lock it. Anwei hopped up into the deep window well and stood between Knox and the leaded glass, the sticky, clotted red of his breath still harsh in her nose. "We can't get out this way," she whispered. "You can hardly walk."

He tried to pull himself up next to her but tipped sideways and stumbled, as if the earth had suddenly tilted under his feet. "We can't fight them." He swallowed loudly. "They'll see we took . . . the book. Shapeshifter will know . . . we're looking for him."

His words slurred and fell apart at the end, and he put a hand to his forehead as if his neck could no longer hold up his head. Anwei cursed the weight of her medicine bag under her skirts as the doorknob rattled. So many useful things inside, but no way to use them. Knox falling out the window to his death wasn't going to help anyone, though, so she stood her ground in front of the window, batting his hands away when he tried to unlatch the fancy new lock on the frame. They didn't have much time before the poison would eat him through.

A key slid into the door's lock.

Knox managed to pull one of the windows open. Anwei could *feel* the confusion in his mind, the frustration of his body moving too slow. The book she'd gotten from the secret drawer weighed on her, begging to be taken back to the apothecary. She'd only been able to look at the first pages—a map of the tomb, tiny notations showing where traps had been set—but the book had to contain the worker lists and guard rotations they were after.

The door cracked open, the hinges squeaking.

Getting caught wasn't an option. But neither was leaving Knox. So Anwei did the only thing she could think of and kissed him.

Or she tried to. She grabbed a handful of his hair and shoved her face toward his. Knox jerked back, pushing Anwei away hard enough she almost fell through the open window. He staggered backward, toppling off his feet to land on the floor, knocking his head against the ornate desk.

Three men stood in the doorway, their mouths open. The one in front seemed to have frozen, his hand fused to the latch, key clenched in his hand. "What . . . ," he sputtered. "What in Calsta's name are you doing in here? This part of the house is not open for . . . for . . ." His cheeks went cherry red as he found the top of Knox's head, the only part of him visible from the door. "For *entertainment.* How did you get in here?"

"We wanted a place to talk, is all." Anwei whispered it, hardly grateful for the heat blooming in her face, because it was real.

Knox clapped his hands over his ears as if she were speaking too loud. His face had turned an awful, embarrassed red under his light brown skin, his expression about ten degrees worse than horrified as he stared up at her.

"Well, I'm sorry to inform you, but the governor's personal study is not a suitable place for trysts, young lady." The man brushed away the guest behind him who pointed to the single knot in Anwei's scarf, his lips peeling back to show the governor's house mark on his left canine. "No, I don't care who she is. In fact . . ." He squinted at Anwei, and she drew herself in, trying to decide how she could get to her herbs under her skirt. "I don't recognize you, young lady. I hope you know impersonating a first khonin will get you two days in the stocks." He strode forward, edging around the desk to get a look at Knox. "And this young man . . . that's not a real house uniform." He pulled Knox up by his collar, and Anwei willed Knox to be still as she felt his fists clench. "It's not even the right color. You"—he pointed at one of the two men still standing in the door—"bring me two guards. And then inform the governor of this breach."

"Yes, Master Gein." The man took off down the hall at a run.

Master Gein. The governor's house steward. That explained his single braid and house mark somehow paired with so much authority. Anwei pushed between the steward and Knox, thrusting a hand into one of her dress pockets. She tore through it, and her fingers glanced across the calistet bag with its distinctive button. Shoving it aside, Anwei grabbed the bag of corta leaves instead. She wrenched them free and threw them in the steward's face, though without being ground up, the petals weren't smelly enough to do more than make him rear back in alarm.

But it was enough of a distraction. Anwei bowled into the steward's stomach, knocking him into the desk. His head hit the edge, and he fell to the floor. The man in the doorway surged toward her, fumbling for the knife in his belt. Anwei threw herself behind the desk, the bag knocking into her knees and throwing her off-balance. Her knees hit the floor just as the man swiped with his knife toward her neck.

But then Knox was there, popping into existence where he hadn't been before. He batted the knife away, sending it through the air to stick, trembling, in the governor's ornate bookcase. Knox crashed into the man, slamming his head into the wall, then jabbed his knuckles into the man's airway. The man fell to the ground, limp.

Knox turned to face Anwei, standing straight, as if there weren't a single ounce of poison in his system. In that second Anwei thought she saw a sort of glow about him, golden flecks skittering across the air like sparks around a bonfire. Even the connection she felt to him seemed to have cleared a little, the poison smell in her nose dulling to a tarnished rose. The herbs she'd given him had taken full effect, but they wouldn't last.

Anwei jumped up from the floor, skipped over the fallen man, and grabbed a fistful of Knox's jacket, then towed him out of the room behind her. It only took a few steps before he started stumbling again, the slick, silvery red showing through. She pulled him down the hall toward the main wing and settled him behind a column in the candlelit entry hall. All was calm, the sound of music and laughter echoing from the ballroom. None of this was right. What had happened to Noa and her ghosts?

"Stay here," she told Knox, her stomach lurching when he began to laugh.

"I . . . I don't think I can move my legs." He giggled. "Why are you holding me like this? It reminds me—"

"You have to be quiet," she whispered. "Stay still, so the poison doesn't spread as fast. Can you do that?"

"This is like my dream." He grinned, looking up at her, his face completely open. "You kissed me. But it wasn't against the rules."

A spark flared in Anwei's chest, something inside her unlocking.

Knox had dreamed about kissing her? And . . . there were rules? There had always been rules between them, but she didn't remember that one coming up. Was *that* why . . . She shook the thought away, holding him up against the column, her hands starting to shake. "Shut up and sit still, Knox."

"Why?" His words slurred, his eyes glazed and unfocused.

Because you could be dying. Anwei's fingers pressed hard into his shoulders, her stomach sick. "Because if we don't get Noa and ride out of here in the next few minutes, the governor is going to find two unconscious men in his study and shutter the whole compound. *Don't move.*"

She left him there in the shadows and ran toward the ballroom, her bag hitting the backs of her legs with every step. After skidding to a stop in front of the ballroom's ridiculous, gold-mottled doors, Anwei forced herself to walk in, her chin held high. The dimly lit room was full of clothing meant to glitter in candlelight, horned and flowered headdresses, red-heeled boots and peacock plumes imported from the west, and so much alcohol that the air seemed to distort over each guest's head, as if the room were full of ghosts. Anwei tried to focus her nose, to shut everything else out but Noa. She had to find Noa. But there were only traces of Noa's lemongrass perfume in the air, leading Anwei nowhere.

A buxom first khonin—Lady Brehlan, whom Anwei had relieved of a very muscular clay rendition of the magistrate only last year—stumbled into Anwei, spilling her goblet of amber malt across Anwei's silvery dress.

"Oh, my dear child, you were standing right in my way!" the old lady began, but Anwei couldn't hear anything else because a sudden, animalistic keen filled the air.

The lines of couples dancing at the center of the room floundered to a stop, bumping into one another as people looked up to find the source of the noise. Knox burned at the back of Anwei's head, a sudden flare of pain rocketing through her.

No. Noa was starting *now?* Anwei turned away from Lady Brehlan, frantically looking for stairs that would lead to the upper balconies.

"Six hundred years he slept." The voice hissed out from above. The musicians' instruments screeched to sudden silence, matched by the stillness of five hundred people all holding their breath.

An otherworldly shriek rocked the air, and a bloom of flame spurted up from each of the four corners of the room. Anwei searched wildly for the men who had done it. Noa said she'd bring people from her fire-dancing troupe to help. . . .

It was too late to stop it, but maybe Anwei could finish it early. Before the governor came storming in with guards, looking for thieves. Before Knox crumpled to nothing in the entry hall. She stuck a hand into the pocket she'd torn through to get to her bag. Another screech echoed from behind the musicians, and there was another bloom of flames.

"Six hundred years he lay buried in the ground," the voice from above cried. "Who dares to wake the shapeshifter? Who *dares* to wake the nameless god's servant who devoured so many of my brothers and sisters . . . ?"

Anwei found the leftover cluster of oil-soaked capsules she'd concocted for Noa, the smell of them charring in her head when she pulled them out. She'd kept back only a few, but they would do.

"Let him sleep, or he will return. *He will return!*" Noa's voice rose to a ghostly shriek. Anwei purposely bumped into Lady Brehlan to cover her movement as she threw all the little capsules. They ignited in sparks and skittered across the floor with ugly hisses, issuing black smoke. A flash of flame flew from an upper alcove like a firebird, soaring across the ballroom to crash into the table behind Lady Brehlan.

Anwei hadn't given anything *that* big to Noa.

She sprinted for the door, barreling past merrily burning drapes, a cluster of the little pellets she'd made dead ash underneath them. In her head, Knox seemed to be on fire too.

"I'll visit you in the night." This time a man spoke, a laugh bottled up behind the words. Anwei couldn't stop to listen, but she knew Bear's voice. A new line of trepidation lanced through her as she ran—of all the silly things Noa could have done, she'd brought in the governor's own blasted *son*? The very same man she was trying to escape from?

"I'll make your eyes bleed, your cheeks hollow, and your bones turn brittle. . . ." Bear's voice trailed off into a ghostly wail that chased Anwei and the other fleeing high khonins down the hall. "I'll eat your souls!"

Anwei sprinted to the sitting room just off the entryway where Noa had agreed to meet her. It was empty except for two long white couches before the blazing fire. Anwei forced herself to stand by the stone fireplace, the yellow green of burning pine blocking out all the smells threatening to overwhelm her. She counted the quills and books carved into the stone, the homage to the scholar god Castor keeping her mind focused as she waited one minute. Terrified guests were running into the entryway. During minute two Lady Brehlan stumbled past the sitting room door with her makeup smudged, a yellow malt stain on her dress, and her attendants crying. By minute four the guards patrolling outside had come running into the house, heading for the ballroom.

But no Noa.

Without Noa there was no way out. Not with the book.

Had the governor found his steward in the study? How long could it have taken for that servant to fetch him? They'd lock the whole compound and interrogate guests one by one until they found her and Knox.

And by that time Knox would be dead.

The medicine bag felt too heavy, the straps pulling against Anwei's hips. The book inside was all they needed to find the snake-tooth man. To end him.

But Noa wasn't going to come. Not in time.

The heat of the flames burned into Anwei's skin. She reached into her pocket, unknotted the medicine bag's strap, and let it thump to the floor around her ankles. Then she wrenched the book open and flipped through the pages. She ripped out something that looked like a map. A list of shipping notes, a ledger with names . . . scholar, scholar, archeologist, Director Brellan Van. The name was at the bottom of the page, in normal ink, as if it didn't belong to a murderer.

Anwei folded the pages and stuffed them down her undertunic, then threw the bag, the book, all of it, into the fire.

The smell of charcoal burned in Anwei's nose as she shouldered her way through the stampede of frightened high khonins and servants to where Knox was hidden behind the column. His face was pale, but his eyes were sharp, taking in the pandemonium. The poison was pulsing inside him, her herbs muting its effect on his mind for the moment. "How long do we have?" he rasped.

"Maybe twenty minutes?" Anwei helped him up from the floor, barely managing to pull his arm across her shoulders before he fell. He was heavy, his arms limp and his head lolling to the side. Easing him toward the doors as high khonins crowded around them, Anwei got her first view of the gates.

A line of guards stood at attention, barring the frantic crowd from leaving the compound.

"We can't go that way. We have to get out of here." Knox veered to the side unexpectedly. His face had gone pale, the air around him hard and bright somehow, as if, for the first time, she were seeing him completely out of the shadows.

"Could you possibly try to balance on your feet—"

"No. We have to *run*. Ewan Hardcastle is coming."

"Who?"

"The Devoted who chased me here a year ago. He's *coming*."

Anwei shoved herself past a weeping high khonin, an army of maids clustered around her with handkerchiefs. The gates were closed. Maybe they could get over the wall.

Knox sagged forward, all his weight threatening to pull Anwei over as she dragged him toward the compound's ten-foot wall. It took to the count of thirty before she heard cloven hooves ringing against stone. "Come on, Knox. . . ." He wasn't helping at all, his feet skidding across the cobblestones. She could hear the auroshes panting, snapping at one another.

"Out of the way!" The Devoted's voice cut through the crowd like a storm just as Anwei tugged Knox into the wall's shadows. She huddled next to him as a monster cantered past her, high khonins screaming as they threw themselves out of the way. Two more auroshes followed, but it was the first beast's rider who drew Anwei's eye, his hair pulled up to show off the shaved sides of his head. Three burn marks marred his skin just behind his ear on the right side.

Knox had said Devoted would see them. That any Devoted would kill them both the moment they saw their auras. Anwei suddenly couldn't stop thinking about the gold she'd only just seen sparkling in the air around Knox when their minds had rushed together for that one frightening moment in the governor's study. The purple mist that had folded across her vision, as if she were seeing herself through Knox's eyes.

One hand fisted in Knox's shirt, Anwei pressed him against the wall to keep him upright. To keep him *there*. Did shadows help disguise an aura?

The Devoted wheeled his auroshe to the side, the man himself dismounting in one fluid movement, the two Roosters following. He walked toward the stables. Or maybe he was walking toward Anwei; she couldn't tell.

Anwei's fingers dug into the stone, into the ivy clinging to its face. She could smell every stem, every leaf, the purple blooms that had closed for the evening. Earwigs and ants, a hunting spider. And Knox, inside her head.

Ewan Hardcastle. His name sounded like vomit in Knox's thoughts. A storm they couldn't weather. The Devoted walked toward them, his auroshe snuffling from side to side, sending frazzled servants and high khonins darting out of the creature's reach. Closer every step. She'd burned her medicine bag. Now she had no weapons. No way to fight.

They can't have Knox. It was a clear thought in her head. *If Knox is right and I'm somehow still connected to a god somewhere . . .* She looked up, around, down at the ground, not sure where the nameless god was supposed to be. *Now would be a really good time for some help, nameless god, whoever you are!*

Knox jerked to the side, pulling away from her as something dark snaked across her vision. The plants behind her almost seemed to sing, all their voices coiled together, answering her call for help, their smells turning sharper than swords.

Ewan drew the sword at his back, his eyes sparking. The auroshe tried to rear, but he pulled it down with his lead, and the creature pranced forward with flecks of rosy spittle raining from its mouth. Knox pushed himself hard against the wall, and a shower of stone and dust trickled around him, the dull brownish gray of earthen brick and mortar crumbling in Anwei's nose.

Anwei gasped as the bricks gave way behind her, leaving a thin opening between the fingers of ivy that had slithered straight through the wall. Looping Knox's arm over her shoulders once again, she dragged him through the hole. He collapsed on the other side. She propped him up against the wall and stood over him, fists clenched, as if she could somehow fight off a Devoted holding a sword.

One second. Three.

Nothing came through the hole after them.

Breathing too fast, Anwei hauled Knox and his drunken steps down the road to the water, frantically waving once they got past the barriers to where carriages for hire were clustered. Their boat was moored clear down in the Ink Cay, where they'd thought wardens would be less likely to take note of it. Getting Knox to the apothecary was impossible; it was too far, and there wasn't a ferry that would take them directly to it. Any other apothecary would be closed at this time of night. And that Devoted—

A carriage separated from the others to meet Anwei's wave. The driver hopped out and opened the door to help Anwei lift Knox inside. "Too much to drink?" he asked.

Knox tensed, bending forward to dry-heave. He grabbed at Anwei, his eyes bulging. Ten minutes, that's all Knox had. Anwei could trace the lines of his humors, the paths of his airways, the blood pulsing inside him as if it had all come alive.

"Yes. Too much to drink." Anwei hopped into the carriage and pulled from above while the man lifted from below to get Knox onto the carriage floor. When the driver climbed back into his seat, she handed coins over the partition. "Gold Cay, please, as fast as you can—the Broken Arrow Malthouse. You can get across the channel?"

Knox curled toward her, his hand circling her ankle. "He's . . ."

"Don't try to talk." Anwei's voice shook. "We're almost there."

"He's . . . a . . . pineapple."

The word jabbed in her brain. *Pritha* in the northern language. No, *priantia*. A Trib holy man. A *Trib*.

Altahn.

The driver's nose and mouth were covered by a scarf, like so many workers in Chaol, and Anwei couldn't smell anything past Knox's poison. But she knew to trust Knox.

Climbing onto the seat, Anwei reached over the partition and locked her elbow around the driver's neck. He let go of the reins to pull at her arm, the horses continuing haphazardly down the road. Something inside his coat twitched, and then it was scurrying up her arm. Anwei held her grip around the man's neck firmly, grabbing hold of the thing climbing toward her shoulder. Out of the corner of her eye she saw horned scales, long claws, and—

Flame bloomed from its mouth. A *firekey*. Anwei swore, not letting go. Instead she groped with her other hand, took the thing by the neck, and threw it from the carriage, then batted at her smoldering sleeve. Altahn struggled, trying to loosen her arm, but Anwei held firm until his head drooped and his arms went slack.

She had to squeeze to get over the partition, but Altahn's hands and feet weren't so difficult to tie with strips of Noa's ridiculous silver dress. His dead weight strained her muscles as she flopped him over the partition into the carriage. She didn't look at the burn, her sleeve charred and the skin under it red. It was nothing to Knox's poison.

After driving the carriage to the Gold Cay ferry and then to Yaru's temple, she tied up the horse behind the malthouse. Knox's skin was hot where she touched his neck, his eyelashes fluttering only inches from her face.

"Lady of Blue. Queen of the Sky," Knox whispered, turning his face into her shoulder as she helped him out of the carriage. His breath was hot through her thin sleeves.

"You should probably wait until you're not dying to start thanking Calsta," Anwei whispered, ignoring the Trib, who was still a boneless heap on the floor. As she dragged Knox into the malthouse and down the stairs, she tried not to think of the bricks, the plants growing and twisting through the wall, and the Devoted with his sword flashing, because it was impossible. It had been since the day of the storm. The same day she'd decided that gods were no more than stone and stories made up by people who wanted to feel like there was someone watching over them, keeping them safe.

But a plea still bubbled up inside her: *Please. If you're listening. Please help me get this poison out of him.*

It was impossible. *Gods* were impossible, but for one fleeting second Anwei wondered if Knox had been thanking the wrong one.

CHAPTER 22

Most like an Auroshe

Lia was more than cross by the time she and Aria arrived at Mateo's gate, Aria's little voice an unending stream of ridiculousness. She scowled at the Montannes' house. Who chose to live on the edge of a sea cliff, nothing but wind, sea spray, and a deathly drop? In an attack the only place you could go would be over the cliff and into the angry waves below.

"I just think you need to consider it, Lia." Aria was still talking as she directed her horse into the courtyard, wind coming off the sea making a riot of her red curls. "If you're going to get married, a duel is *necessary*. Just to make *sure* he isn't a sissy. And if Daddy won't do it, it has to be me."

Maybe normal people didn't think about attacks. The wind smelled like salt, picking at Lia's scarf as she followed her sister through the gate on Mateo's little mare, her head ducked as if she were a servant. Aria impatiently adjusted the large hat and scarf Lia had insisted she wear, because if Ewan was going to remember anyone, it was the little girl who'd manage to bloody him. "I don't see why any of this is happening anyway. You just got home. Surely, you don't need to get married right *now*."

"If anyone duels Mateo, it will be me." A stinging bead of sweat slid down Lia's temple, and she glared up at the morning sun. How could it be windy and hot at the same time? She swung her leg over Bella's saddle and slid to the ground, then handed her over to the hostler who'd come out to greet them. "I've taken care of her," she said quietly to him, "but please be sure to check her over for me?"

The hostler gave a curt nod and took the horse's lead. Lia gave the mare a fond pat before the man led her away. Mateo's mare was the most placid little thing Lia had ever ridden. It made her miss Vivi and his penchant for attempting to bite passersby even though he knew she would never stand for it—one of the many games he liked to play.

Maybe there was a way to extract Vivi from the governor's stables? Lia sighed, letting her auroshe sit at the back of her mind as she looked up at Aria. "Father's only going to be busy at the governor's compound for a few hours—until the governor is done blaming him for whatever happened at his party last night, I guess. We have to do this quick, so keep your mouth shut and don't embarrass me."

The hostler waiting to take Aria's horse looked down, uncomfortable.

"Embarrass you?" Aria slid off her horse, then took off her hat and scarf with a smirk. "Didn't cross my mind even once."

"Right. You're officially restricted to this courtyard. Do not move, I'll be back in a minute."

Just as Aria's lip began to protrude in a pout, the manor's front door creaked open, and Tual Montanne himself came out onto the steps. "Lia! You're so kind to come check on my son."

Lia swallowed, ignoring Aria's goggling eyes looking up at her. Checking on Mateo had not been her purpose at all—they had *things* to discuss, namely how he was hiding his aura from the sky-cursed Warlord and the entire rank and file of Devoted—but saying so out loud seemed rude, so she met Tual on the stairs. "How is he doing?"

"Much better, thank you. Won't you come in?" His eyes moved to

Aria, and he put a hand to his forehead. "Oh dear, I'm being unpardonably rude. I don't know how I could have missed seeing you there, Miss Aria. Your hair stands out like rubies set in gold."

Aria wrinkled her nose.

"Too much?" Tual smiled. "I appreciate a girl who can't be flattered into good humor. Come along! Let's see if apricot biscuits and cream will do the job."

Inside, Tual left them in the sitting room where Mateo had lain like a corpse the day before. Aria settled on the blue paisley couch next to Lia, her feet kicking at the expensive Beildan carpet as she took everything in.

"He may have let you inside, Aria," Lia growled out of the corner of her mouth, "but you aren't allowed to say a word."

"How else am I going to find out if you've kissed Mateo yet?"

"Gross." Lia shuddered.

"So you have?"

"No!"

"Like I can trust *you* to tell the truth."

Lia opened her mouth to ask why Aria was so interested in kissing, but Tual came in before she could, a tray with apricot biscuits and a bowl of cream in his hands.

Mateo trailed in after him, dark circles under his eyes. His face seemed as if it had been shaved down an inch or two since the day before, his cheekbones sharp. His hair was perfectly combed, and his shirt and unbuttoned coat had more color in them than all the sitting room furniture combined.

Aria's eyes went wide. "You're much floppier than I remember. Is Daddy really going to make Lia marry you?"

Lia bit her tongue, blood coppery in her mouth.

Mateo moodily threw himself into the chair farthest from them, then crossed his ankles and let his head loll back. "That's what I hear."

"Well, you don't have to be so snooty about it." Aria frowned.

"Believe me, I can be much snootier than this."

Tual laughed, setting the tray on the low table in front of Aria. "Now, Mateo. If you hadn't been with Lia yesterday—"

"I know." Mateo took in a long breath and let it out with a huff. Sat up. Looked directly at Lia. "Thank you very much for dragging my limp body back here, Lia Seystone. I owe you my life. May all our years together be littered with similarly embarrassing incidents."

Lia rubbed a hand across her face, fingers meeting the cloth of her scarf. In all her years of being a Devoted, no one had spoken to her with so much wounded pride and so little respect. She had to hold herself very, very still in order to keep from laughing.

"You're right, Lia." Aria took a biscuit and crammed half of it into her mouth, dribbling crumbs down her front as she tried to speak around it. "Dueling him would be mean. He probably can't even pick up a sword."

Mateo groaned, pulling himself up from the chair. "I'm going to the dig." He pointed at Lia. "That's really why you're here, right? You brought my horse back? I've been trapped here for almost a whole day."

"Yes, I brought Bella." Lia sprang to her feet, wondering how to get Mateo on his own so she could bully him into telling her what she needed to know. "She's a good little horse. Made me miss my mount."

"Your . . . auroshe?" Mateo squinted. "Not quite the same thing, is it?"

Lia blinked, suddenly feeling teary. They'd hardly let her ride Vivi once she'd begun studying with the spiriters two years before—it was only because no other Devoted had managed to bond with him that she'd been able to keep visiting him at all. She'd been allowed to brush and feed Vivi. Take care of him. Watch as Devoted took him out and tried the dominance ritual over and over, attempting to get close enough to touch the base of his long, twisted horn and only getting bucked off, chased out of the arena, and sometimes gored for their trouble. They were alike, she and Vivi.

She shook her head, starting for the door. There must be something she could do to get Vivi back. "Stay here for a second, Aria. And you"—she pointed to Mateo—"I'll walk you out. I need to show you—"

"Where my horse is? At my own house?" Mateo followed her, though.

Pausing in the entryway, Lia waited while Mateo took his hat from its peg before opening the door to the courtyard and walking out onto the veranda. The hat had a dirt spot on the back from where his head had hit the ground the day before.

"I need your help." She said it as quietly as she could manage, looking over her shoulder to make sure Tual was too far to hear. Not being able to sense people made everything two steps harder than it should have been. "You fainted very conveniently yesterday when you were supposed to be telling me how you hide your aura."

"I don't know why you can't see my aura, but I'm not doing anything to hide it, so you can stop trying to browbeat me into telling you. Harlan!" He waved to the hostler, who came running from the stable, a gust of wind almost taking his hat before he clamped a hand down on top of it. "I really do have to go to the dig, so you and your sister can scamper off now. This tomb might mean the difference between a lot of people living or dying, so . . ."

He trailed off, turning to look over his shoulder at the gate.

"We need Mateo's horse," Lia instructed the hostler, and waved him off before he could speak, then whirled to face Mateo. "I can't see your aura because I'm diminished. There will be at least six other Devoted with the Warlord when she comes, but that doesn't seem to matter to you or your father. They *can't see you*. How?"

Mateo's back suddenly went very, very straight. "Lia, get lost, would you?"

"Excuse me?" She took a step toward him, and he stumbled back, his spine hitting one of the veranda supports. "Your father said he'd cause trouble for me and my family. Seems like I could hurt you just as easily if I wanted."

"The Warlord already knows everything she needs to about me, but thanks for asking. And she's going to know about you, too, if you don't *get out of here*."

"Is that a threat?"

Mateo pointed toward the road, and suddenly Lia heard the distinct scratch of auroshe hooves on dirt. She turned, and there they were on the road: three Roosters headed for the gate. She grabbed Mateo's ridiculous coat. "Did *you*—"

"I didn't do anything. Come on." He darted into the stable, and Lia followed, her mind flicking through calculations of where they'd go, how she could get out . . . but Aria was inside. She couldn't leave Aria, no matter how bratty she was.

They ignored the waving hostler, Lia keeping right on Mateo's heels despite her sinking heart. The Warlord already knew about Mateo? That still didn't account for how *she* hadn't seen him when she searched the city twice. Could he be naturally hidden somehow? Maybe something to do with his diet, or something Tual had done accidentally with medicine? He was an aukincer, after all, and no one really knew what those old remedies did.

Mateo dove into a box stall at the very back of the stable and ducked down into the hay. "They won't see us back here."

"They won't see us . . . ?" Lia groaned, looking around the little stall. She'd thought he was taking her to a back way out, but no, Mateo meant to *hide* here. Maybe aukincers' sick sons skipped the don't-trap-yourself-in-small-quarters-when-fleeing-an-enemy lesson at their fancy universities. She peeked up over the edge of the stall's barrier, catching a glimpse of fancy braids and auroshe teeth outside. The worst fight Mateo had been in had probably involved the peacock he'd denuded to trim his coat.

She could fight Roosters easily enough—at least, she could have with Calsta's power flowering her aura. Now, after two years stuck under the veil without training, and Calsta leaving her a dry husk? Lia's jaw clenched. She would not go back to the governor's house. She would *not* go back to Ewan.

The stable door slid open, and the hostler threw himself inside, the Roosters just behind him. He ran to the horses stabled near the front. ". . . it isn't fair to the other animals!" he was saying. "This isn't at all how things are usually done. . . ."

Ducking back down, Lia hissed, "Is there another way out?"

The horses began to snort, the sound of their fearful shuffling loud in Lia's ears. Mateo looked up from where he was slouched in the hay. "Hiding in here will be fine. We wait until they leave, and—"

"They're going to stable the auroshes back here, Mateo."

"They wouldn't *dare*. . . ." Mateo sat bolt upright, his brim catching on the wall and knocking his hat into the hay. His little mare began to scream. "Those sky-rotted, bloodthirsty—" Lia grabbed hold of Mateo's coat before he could launch himself into the aisle to yell at the three Roosters leading their mounts into the stable. It went against the rules to put auroshes with just about any other kind of livestock without proper barriers, but she'd broken the rules enough times herself to know most people wouldn't argue too much with Devoted. A wooden thump echoed through the stable as one of the horses threw itself against its stall door in an attempt to escape.

Lia slipped through the box stall door, towing Mateo behind her past the rest of the enclosed compartments. The place had open rafters and high windows set into the wall, but no way to get to them without putting themselves on complete display. A loft . . . She redoubled her grip on Mateo's arm. "Where are the stairs to the loft?"

"You're inviting me up into the hayloft? When my horse is *right there* screaming her head off? I'm not sure how I—"

"If you say another word, I will break your skull." She wrenched him around the corner just as the first Rooster stepped into the area in front of the box stalls. His auroshe looked right at her and gave a nasty chirp. "Show me how to get up there."

Mateo breathed in, his head cocking to the side as if he was giving himself some kind of internal pep talk. The air was full of frightened horse noises and the hostler's low voice as he tried to soothe them. One of the Roosters laughed as he led his mount into a stall, an ungrateful, callous sound—it was Balan, she thought. All muscle and furious nods whenever Ewan spoke.

Lia hated him for it.

Finally Mateo started down along the other side of the stalls, casting a concerned look toward his mare. But he turned into a small passage with stairs at the end.

"Was someone back here?" Balan's voice rang out. "There's a hat. . . ."

Both Mateo and Lia froze, Mateo reaching up to touch his head as if he could somehow make it reappear where it was supposed to be.

"I saw Master Mateo come in with his lady friend. But if they were still here, he would have come out to help his mare," the hostler yelled over the horses' noise.

Lia bolted for the stairs, Mateo a clomping signal flare behind her. One side of the loft was covered, shielding them from sight, but she could feel the auroshes quieting, their eyes all pointing toward where she and Mateo slid to a stop against the loft's enclosed railing. The roof was thatched, so maybe if she pushed her way through . . .

"There's someone up there."

"Well, I did say Master Mateo came in with his lady friend. . . ."

Mateo's face twisted. "Great. As if I need my father to hear—"

"We'll need to clear the area to ensure the safety of the household." The Rooster's voice quieted, speaking only to the other Roosters. "You two go talk to the aukincer. I'll bring the little master in."

Lia swore under her breath, climbing up to where the straw roof met the wall.

"What are you doing?" Mateo rasped.

"Trying to make sure they find you alone." The straw bit at her fingers, too tightly tied to get through without a knife. "But our conversation about aura hiding isn't over. I'll be back tonight."

Footsteps rang out on the stairs. Balan wasn't even trying to be quiet. And there was no way out.

"Do you have a weapon, Mateo?" Lia snarled. "Anything?"

Mateo dug a hand into his satchel, coming up with a selection of pencils.

"Here." She held out her hand, catching them when he threw them over.

Balan faltered when he got to the top of the stairs, his gaze darting to Mateo, who was pressed against the wall, then coming back to her. "Is that . . . Spiriter Seystone?"

Lia's heart fell at what she'd have to do. "I'm sorry," she whispered. She let him start to draw his sword, his hesitation both sweet and unfortunate, because it was exactly what she needed. Lia was on him before he could get it free.

Her foot snapped against his ribs and then into his stomach, though it didn't do much good through his leather armor. At least he was wearing only light riding leathers. Lia spun, swinging her other foot up to crash into his jaw.

Balan staggered back into an aggressive stance, but he'd been trained to fight *with* Devoted, not against them. Against shields and spears and people in armor who moved a hair too slow. Lia had never been a hair too slow, even without a drop of Calsta's gold.

She heard Mateo gasp as she rolled to the side, kicking Balan's front leg out from under him, sending him staggering toward the rail. His sword was out now, held in front of him with a snarl. He lunged, and Lia darted closer, turning her shoulders so it swished by her ribs, her dress ripping on its blade. But then she was close enough, rapping a fist against his bicep to make him drop the sword, then skewering the pencils toward his throat.

He blocked the sharpened pencils just in time, grabbing hold of her wrist and throwing Lia to the floor. Her head and back hit one of the railing support beams, knocking the breath from her lungs. Lights popped into existence at the edges of her vision, but Lia forced herself up, spun a kick into his knee, then reversed into a jab to his throat.

"Lia!" Lia looked up in time to see a thin razor between Mateo's fingers, suited for sharpening pencils. And ending this fight.

She turned into Balan's chest, stabbing under his arm through the gap in his armor with the pencils. He yelped as they pierced his armpit, hunching forward over Lia and gasping for air. His hot, awful breath was in Lia's nose, gusting across her cheeks, trapping itself under her scarf to strangle her. And one horrible image flickered across her vision.

Ewan. Ewan with his hands on her.

She froze, Ewan's awful smile like an ice pick in the middle of her brain. *This* was what she should have done to *him*. This was—

"Lia!" Mateo's voice sliced through her thoughts, jerking her back to reality just in time to see the blunt hilt of Balan's sword swinging toward her face. She ducked, stumbling toward the railing.

"I . . ." Balan's voice was thick. Pained. "I don't want to hurt you. We need to get you back—"

Lia surged forward, slamming Balan's head into the support beam. "Throw it!" she yelled at Mateo, opening her hand for the thin razor. "Do it."

"You want me to throw a razor at you while you're . . ." Mateo gestured quite vigorously.

"For Calsta's sake! If I move too far away from him, he'll be able to use the sword. Throw the sky-cursed razor!"

Mateo tossed the tiny blade toward her, not nearly enough force behind the throw. Lia ducked Balan's arms grabbing for her and dove for the razor, snagging it between her fingers. Rolling out of the dive, she latched on to one of the support beams and swung around it, then landed light on her feet behind the Rooster. Slashing the razor at his cuirass buckles, she managed to detach two. She followed his movements to keep behind him, slashing the third and fourth buckles before he could get around, leaving his side exposed. Lia snapped a kick into his bare side, then swung the second into his spine. He tried to stumble away, but Lia kicked up off the floor, meaning to lock her knees around his neck. If she could knock him out, he might forget—

Her skirts caught on his gauntlet, twisting tight around Lia's leg as her flip turned into a fall, slamming her to the floor with a spine-shattering thump. *May Calsta destroy all skirts.*

She groaned, hands going to her head. The razor had made a bloody mess of her hand. Balan's outline was blurred as he lurched toward her. Head screaming, Lia pulled her knees in and arched up from the floor, landing on her feet. Something fluttered through the air—did Mateo just throw *hay?*—into Balan's face. The Rooster jerked back just as she barreled into his legs, cutting them out from under him. His back hit the rail. Which snapped.

And he went down. Right into the auroshe stall beneath them.

A horrible snarl filled the air, and a frantic scream. A second auroshe began to keen, the awful sound pulsing in Lia's head. She couldn't look—Balan's own auroshe would try to protect him, but he must have fallen into a different auroshe's stall. Auroshes were loyal only to their master and skittish enough that falling down from above was enough of an invitation.

The scream cut off in an awful gurgle.

"You . . ." Mateo was still gasping as if he couldn't breathe. "You just . . ."

Lia couldn't move. She hadn't *meant* to kill him, but that didn't change the wet tearing sounds coming from below.

Who else in this place would kill a Rooster and risk the Warlord's wrath? Who else even *could?* Ewan would know she'd been here. Lia pulled herself up and started for the stairs.

"You kill a man and run?" Mateo was huddled in the straw, hands over his face as if he couldn't accept even his own small part in the fight. "What happens when the other Roosters come out here and find . . ." He gulped, pointing straight down. *"That."*

Lia's chest was made of iron, welded shut. "I don't know. I have to get out of here. Come with me so they don't think—not that they *would* think you could do this."

Mateo was staring at one of his pencils, bloodied on the tip and lying dead in the straw.

The stable's main door cracked open, light flooding into the darkness. Lia dropped down beside Mateo as two forms entered: Tual and Aria.

The auroshes screamed.

"She's supposed to take it every morning with some food." Tual's words barely filtered through the noise, the auroshes lunging toward Balan's body, the one on the very end striking at the door's lock as if it could open the stall to save its rider from the others. "Make sure her attending healers know," Tual continued even as he ran a casual eye across the back of the barn, weighing first on the auroshes and then on the loft, where Lia and Mateo hid. He turned his attention back to Aria, pulling out a packet of what looked like herbs. Lia's chest panged. They'd been inside discussing her mother and medicine? While she'd been doing what Calsta had taught her to do.

Calsta. Lia sent her thoughts up toward the sky. *Balan served you. He was trying to take me back to where you probably want me to be. But is that really what you want for me? Every moment before Ewan attacked me made me unhappy. And after . . .*

The next thought clenched inside her, twisted tight with desperation. *What am I supposed to do now? And is it the same as what I think you'd ask me to do?* Lia tried to breathe, but it was like she couldn't get enough air. There was blood dripping down her hand.

"Mother's already looking a little better," Aria's little voice piped up, so much more serious than Lia would have expected. "Daddy won't even let Lia see her yet, she was so bad. But I think maybe soon . . ."

Mateo leaned a little closer, listening.

But Aria didn't continue, looking up when one of the auroshes crooned in her direction. The creature had turned away from the meal it couldn't reach, poking its horn out of the stall toward Lia's sister, trilling as if it meant to sing to her.

Grip on the railing painful, Lia tried to see how she could stop Aria from coming any closer. She'd see the Rooster, the blood. . . .

"I wouldn't." Tual casually stepped between Aria and the closed stalls. "They're vicious creatures, even if they are beautiful. It's always beauty that fools us, isn't it?"

Lia could almost hear Aria rolling her eyes. "If you say so. And you're sure Lia went into town with Mateo? Without even telling me she was going to abandon me here?"

"Young love. You'll understand someday."

Lia could feel Mateo gagging next to her, though it was hard to tell if it was over the dead man or the sentiment. Once Aria was on her horse and out of the stable, Tual turned to face the auroshe stalls. He walked back slowly and stopped in front of the stall with the dead man and the creature that was eating him.

Finally he tipped his chin up toward the loft. "Let's get you out of there, shall we?" he called softly.

Lia felt a tear burn down her cheek.

"Get who out of where?" Mateo called back. "I wish you'd come to save me ten minutes ago, before Lia . . . destroyed three of my favorite pencils." He looked quite pale in the dust-flecked beams of light coming through the thatch, the back of his hand to his mouth as though he might vomit.

Lia's stomach was similarly unsettled. She offered a hand to Mateo to help him up, not understanding his grimace until she looked down and saw the blood dripping from the razor cuts on her palm. "Sorry," she whispered, switching hands. It was oddly gratifying when Mateo accepted the help up, though his legs were shaking. Poor butterfly boy with his peacock wars and his coloring pencils.

"What happened?" Tual took in the sight of the dead man and the snarling auroshe with a sad eye, flinching when the creature charged at him, stabbing through the slats with its two horns. "No, I don't want to know." He looked back up at Mateo. "The rest of the Roosters are inside waiting. Would you please keep them entertained for the next half hour so I can . . . take care of this?" He frowned down at the body. "Apparently, Director Van has discovered something new, and he's coming to appreciate your special talents, Mateo. Say I sent this one"—he gestured toward Balan's body—"on an errand or something, and I'll be sure his auroshe is gone when they come out. They came to escort you to the dig, and the other two can do it just as easily."

Take care of it? *This one?* Lia hugged her arms about her middle, still unable to make herself look down at Balan. Tual was so *cold*. Was her own father this bad? He *had* tried to hire someone to murder the governor. Lia's arms squeezed tighter. Killing people was Devoted work, work she'd hated. But those fights had always been dangerous—kill or let yourself and everyone else be killed by dangerous magic. This was different.

And why was everything centered around this dig? Ewan had been there, according to Mateo. The Roosters were going today. How was it she hadn't heard a single mention of the place, not even in Ewan's thoughts . . . though she supposed he'd been quite preoccupied for most of the trip. She shuddered and leaned back against a supporting beam, her breaths still coming too fast. *I'm sorry, Calsta. I'm supposed to hunt Basists, but what do I do when my fellows are hunting me?*

Tual jabbed his chin back toward the house. "Go on, Mateo. I'll take Lia home in the skiff after I deal with . . . everything." He didn't look back at Balan's body.

Mateo did not look down at the bloody stall either as he brushed the straw from his coat and trousers. He saluted Lia and turned toward the stairs.

Something inside Lia softened just a little. He'd been scared and tried to help anyway . . . and this was *awful*. Watching had to have been awful. She couldn't blame him for not looking at her as he walked away.

But she also couldn't let him walk away. Not now. Balan disappearing would only make the hunt for her intensify—might even focus it on Mateo's house. Now it was twice as important that she find a way to hide, to run, to fight. . . . If only she had Vivi, two of those things wouldn't be so hard.

Perhaps getting him back would be a good start.

"Tonight," she whispered, wishing she didn't mind the way his shoulders tightened at the sound of her voice. "In your courtyard." Maybe he really didn't know how his aura was hidden, but he *could* do one thing: get into the governor's compound, where Vivi was stabled. "Sundown. If you don't show up, I'll drag you out of your window." She was proud of how calm she sounded, every inch a Devoted. "You know I could."

She thought she saw Mateo shudder before he disappeared into the stairway's shadows only to reappear in the light of the main door. Tual spared a smile for his son as he passed. "Bring some of your medicine to the dig with you. And don't let Van keep you down there for more than an hour."

Mateo nodded, not looking back even once as he walked to the stable door, stopping only to pat his frightened mare. Once he was gone, Tual tipped his chin up to look at Lia once again. "Seems like you have a stomach for politics after all, Lia Seystone. Why don't you come down from there? I think it's time we talked, just the two of us."

CHAPTER 23

A Circle of Cracks

Despite his father's instructions to go with the Roosters to the dig, Mateo didn't relish the idea of trying to ride Bella between their auroshes, not with the sound of the dead Rooster's scream so firmly lodged in his head. He made excuses for the missing Rooster, made buffoonish attempts to show them he wasn't quite ready to leave, and sent them ahead of him once Tual's requested half hour had passed. They went, eyes rolling, but they didn't come back, so Mateo supposed his father had been successful in removing the dead man and his agitated auroshe.

And cleaning the one that had killed the man. Mateo's stomach squirmed.

When he got to Bella in the stable, she nosed her way into his shoulder as if she meant to cry until she felt better, a sentiment he could echo.

All evidence of blood in the back stall was gone, the ground lined with new straw, though Mateo wasn't sure how that was possible, even for his father. He would have had to get rid of the body, get rid of the straw, get rid of the auroshe. . . . He must have had Lia and the hostlers do some of it—Harlan had been with the family so long, he would do anything for Tual, even throw a body over the cliffs. But where could

Tual have sent the mourning auroshe? Over the cliff with its master? To the underground fights? Mateo had heard of wild auroshes on the eastern plains, but the idea of those creatures running in packs across open farmland left him feeling sick.

Mateo held on to Bella, breathing in her honest horse smell, and she breathed back as if her nose in his shirt blocked out the scent of auroshe. Lia had killed that man right in front of him. With *his* drawing tools. That he'd given to her. That razor was for sharpening pencils, not . . . He closed his eyes, blocking out the images, but they only burned brighter in the dark. Death wasn't new to him—he'd seen Devoted wasting away in their little rooms in the seclusions, some not waking up in the morning when he went to check on them for Tual. But those sad, starved deaths were different from the vibrant color of life that had been fighting for existence one moment and then gone the next.

Yet another idea he was a little too familiar with.

The Rooster would have either killed Lia or taken her back to the War-lord, Mateo told himself. She hadn't *meant* to kill him—the railing had broken. But if killing him hadn't been her strategy, then what *had* it been? Was her life at the seclusion really so bad that killing was justified in order to escape?

Bella pressed up against him, and Mateo sighed out all the tightness in his back and neck, the warmth of his horse like a comforting blanket. He clutched Bella tighter. If it had meant the difference between his own life and death, between finding caprenum and not, maybe he would have done the same as Lia had. But who knew why she had done it? Maybe she was just . . . violent. Like the rest of the Devoted, locked away in their seclusions until the Warlord whistled for them to dispose of the people she thought should not exist.

People like him.

It wasn't hard to imagine Lia turning those pencils on him if she found out what he was.

There were flowers carved into the back of Bella's stall, and Mateo stared at them until a kind of calm washed across him. *Valtri blossoms,* he thought. The horse tamer's blessing. The knowledge made him feel grounded. He was still alive, and they were on caprenum's trail. All this other stuff could disappear.

Mateo waited until Bella was done shaking before saddling her and following the Devoted to the tomb. When he got to the compound gates, however, the air seemed just as tense as it had back at the house. The guard at the gates waved him through, and the hostler who took Bella didn't quite meet his eyes, though he did tie her well away from the two auroshes scratching at their leads at the other end of the hitching post. The Roosters themselves had disappeared—probably gone to talk to Director Van or any other archeologist aboveground. Based on Mateo's interactions with Ewan and his little tagalongs, they didn't like the idea of digging up a shapeshifter any more than the workers did. Mateo did hope they were occupied with the director, because the man gave Mateo the creeps.

"Ah. There you are." The voice made Mateo jump. Luck really wasn't on his side today. Van stepped out of one of the artifact sheds and slid the door closed behind him before Mateo could get a glimpse inside. "I was wondering when you'd come." He smiled, a hint of a house mark peeking out from his canine. "Shall we? I need your help with something."

"*You* need *my* help?" Van had done nothing but glower every moment Mateo had been at the dig. "With what, exactly? Father mentioned you found poison in the new room I uncovered." Mateo didn't miss the way Director Van's smile widened at his ownership claim on the room, and little flickers of anger started in his belly. Was Van laughing at him? "Did my father tell you my hunch about where the next door is?"

"Yes, and we found it." Van nodded to workers as they passed with wheelbarrows, some with shovels propped up on their shoulders or buckets in each hand. He stopped one worker with a pan containing a human skull, each tooth dipped in gold. "Where are you going with that? It should be in shed *six*." He pointed back the way they'd come. He turned back to Mateo and led him along the path between sheds and past the shaded baskets of fill, workers sorting through them with wire screens. "So, your door: there are stairs beyond the wall. The two workers who got it open set off a mechanism in the floor that dumped them down to the next level, and we haven't heard from them since."

Van pushed through the crowd of workers around the tunnel opening. Two men were lying on the ground, another kneeling next to them. Mateo almost stopped when he saw blood stippling the fronts of their tunics. "Are they . . . ," he started.

"Oh, fine, fine. They're just reacting to the poison in the statue room—can't have them down there more than an hour, even with the carpets, before that starts happening. They slow down, and then the bleeding starts. It's not serious—the effects go away. Your father can give them what they need to get them back up to speed."

"I thought precautions had been taken—" Mateo startled back as one of the workers went into a fit of coughing that bent him over. "Father's not even planning to come here today. Have you sent him a messenger yet?"

"Precautions *have* been taken. They're fine, Mateo." Director Van grabbed hold of Mateo's arm. "Come on, now. We've got more-important things to talk about."

Mateo struggled to keep up, his drawing satchel flapping against his side as they snaked through the crowd of workers bringing buckets up from the tomb opening. Van kept talking as they walked. "We've managed to cut the wires and pulleys so the mechanism by the door can't engage again. But I'm worried every single stair is some kind of pressure plate. There are holes in the walls, and we aren't sure what is going to come out of them. We must be close to the burial chamber, so whatever it is, if it hasn't rotted away, can't be good. And . . ." Van stopped by the tomb's mouth, the ladder jutting out of it like a needle in mid suture. He flicked a glance over his shoulder at Mateo. "Listen, it's important for you to keep your mouth shut about what happens in here. The entire dig. That it even exists."

"Keep my mouth shut?" Mateo extracted his arm, stumbling back a step, suddenly not sure he wanted to go down into the tomb. Director Van had done nothing but try to get him away from the tomb until now, but suddenly he wanted Mateo down there? With workers coughing up blood left and right? He could feel the pull of the tomb, of caprenum, but Van was pulling awfully hard too.

"We've had some problems with people talking about the tomb, and you're one of the few people allowed outside of this compound. Oh, you don't know what I'm talking about?" Van pointed to the ladder. "Go down."

The tomb's mouth seemed to breathe, ruffling Mateo's curls, the awful smell of *wrong* bristling in his nose. Director Van watched him, his eyes a hair too eager.

"What did you need my help with?" Mateo asked very slowly.

"Your father is so set on getting to the burial chamber as soon as possible—a goal I share, even if we have to sacrifice a few things here and there." Van didn't look back at the workers huddled at the edge of the pavilion, but Mateo could still feel his skin begin to prickle. Van couldn't be saying *Mateo* was disposable, could he? The director knew who his father was, that he would be angry if he disappeared. "I'm surprised to find you less interested. Were you planning to just watch from afar today? Maybe from the wall with your Rooster friends where it's light?"

Mateo stiffened. "No."

"So what's the problem? *Go.*"

Clutching his satchel to his side, Mateo put his foot on the ladder, running through the logic of the scenario in his head, hoping it would calm the irrational spikes of fear skewering him through. *Director Van works for the Commonwealth. He's not going to just murder people at random. If he wanted to kill you, it would be much easier down here, but what reason could he have for doing it?*

The ladder twitched as Van climbed after Mateo, pebbles and dirt raining down on Mateo's face when he looked up. Once they both got to the bottom, Van led the way to the spot where Mateo had fallen, several of the stone blocks now removed, a ladder leading down into the hole and a pulley system perched on its lip. Workers were taking turns hauling buckets of dirt and rock toward the entrance.

"Now." Director Van gestured to three workers sitting at the edge of the hole, and they brought a rope and a harness. "It seems like you've got a knack for this work, Mateo. An *extra sense* for it, if you know what I mean. Here, put this on." He held the harness out to Mateo.

The hairs on the back of Mateo's neck stood on end. *Extra sense?*

The director was still talking. "I've come to the realization that your extra sense here is going to get me to where I need to go. The way you found this trapdoor. The hidden entrance in the statue room. All your doing—it's almost like *magic*."

Mateo couldn't see Van's face in the dark, only a hulking shadow. Tual had been accused of Basism enough times—he always laughed it off because the Warlord's might was enough to protect him from any purging rituals that might have left him without ears and a nose, or even with his guts spilled onto the ground, depending on where the accusers thought he kept his magic—but no one had ever looked twice at Mateo. Mateo could sense rocks and minerals, and if he'd taken oaths, he would have been able to move them. Combine them. Change them, much the way his father did with herbs. But without oaths, all he had was dodgy aurasight and enough sense of rocks and minerals to know how much he was missing. Neither tended to alert the witch hunters.

Van continued. "Like I said, we've run into some problems with people talking."

"Talking? Who would care? Why are you telling *me*?" Mateo stepped back from the hole. "And I don't need a harness. There's a ladder."

"Can't see what I want to show you without hanging."

Hanging. Van leaned forward into the mirrorlight, daring him to argue. His eyes looked oddly black. Mateo's humors hummed as one of the workers came forward, hands outstretched to help him put on the harness. "You shouldn't go down there," he whispered in Eastern Forge.

Mateo knew the workers had been shipped in from far away but hadn't known they were from the east coast. He'd spent a whole summer searching for caves on that coast, so the dialect was familiar. "Why shouldn't I go down?"

The worker startled back as if he hadn't anticipated Mateo understanding his warning. But then he leaned closer to feed the harness straps around Mateo's legs and waist, his voice low as he said, "The ghosts are angry."

Ghosts? Mateo blinked, and suddenly everything looked normal again, the shadows only a normal sort of black, the hole nothing more than an entrance to a place he really wanted to go. The key to his future. He wasn't afraid of superstitious nonsense. The only things down there were one man's self-centered tribute to himself and a lot of old bones. If he could find the burial chamber and Patenga's caprenum sword, Mateo could leave behind his sickness, these new episodes, Lia the murderer, all of it. He moved to the hole's edge, his toes peeking out over the black drop beneath. Mateo looked Van in the eye. As best he could. It was dark. "What did you want to show me?"

Van gestured for him to go in. Gritting his teeth, Mateo leaned back against the rope and walked over the edge, letting the workers lower him down. Catching light with his hand mirror, Van directed it onto the wall below. It was so dark—*why* was it so dark, hadn't workers been down here only moments ago?—that Mateo could see only the tiny spot of mirrorlight reflected, glossing over carvings of vines, flowers, mountains, and constellations up near the ceiling, all coated in bright colors of peeling paint. Without thinking, Mateo reached out with his mind, feeling the echoes of precious gems set into the stone. Until the light stopped on an ugly section of broken rock just next to Patenga's largest relief.

Mateo's stomach sank. "I thought this tomb was untouched."

"It was, until last night."

Van's mirrorlight flipped back to shine directly in Mateo's face. Mateo's hands shot up to block it.

"Someone came in here last night right after all the commotion up in Chaol." The director's voice was cold.

"Commotion?"

"*Ghosts.* Attacking the guests. Setting fires. Telling the whole Water Cay that we're digging up their master."

Mateo tried to look past the light, his vision nothing but bright spots. "So you're worried the high khonins of Chaol are going to show up here to cut off our heads and skewer them on poles outside to satisfy some stupid archeologist's idea of a prank?"

"No one has left the compound except you, your father, and the Warlord's representatives."

"Aren't there people delivering food, supplies . . . what about the governor?"

"They've brought word of a plague in the lower cays, Mateo Montanne. Ghosts in the governor's house. All my workers are scared half to death, and there are artifacts missing from my sheds and *bloody chunks of the wall gone.*" Van's voice rose to a roar. "*Who* did you tell about the jewels? About the shapeshifter, about the *dig?* No one is supposed to know we are here. Even the Warlord is pretending we don't exist!"

"What's a plague got to do with . . ." Mateo's hands were shaking, the rope swinging back and forth as if the workers holding him were slipping. He couldn't see the ground, only awful blackness that seemed to go on forever beneath him. "I didn't tell anyone!"

"A plague, ghosts, and a dead shapeshifter king. You don't see any connections? My workers do. People in the city already do. What happened to the subjects that the shapeshifters drained to keep themselves alive, don't you remember?"

They died. Just as from a plague. "So . . . you're worried people will come break down your walls and fill the dig with seawater?" Mateo craned his neck, his heart racing even as he tried to hang on to his jaunty tone. "I didn't do it, and I don't see how hanging me down here is going to help anything now."

"True. And not everyone's scared. The thieves who chiseled out artifacts down here were dressed like ghosts. It's not just violence I'm worried about. It's the art. Untouched, and in the one and only undisturbed shapeshifter tomb we've ever found. Why do you think the Warlord sent Roosters and Devoted to protect it—Roosters who got called away the *second* the governor cried for help at his ball?"

"So you're worried about thieves now?" Mateo gestured helplessly. "Which is it? This is ridiculous. *Let me back up!*"

"You are the only person who has connections in the city, the only person who has even *been* to Chaol other than me to deliver reports. My guess is you told the right people, then used the distraction to come in here yourself."

"I . . . I would *never* . . . !" The babbling came out as if Van had a knife to Mateo's throat, and he might as well have with the mirror-light shining in his eyes, a pit of poison at his feet, and three workers who were scared enough just standing in a shapeshifter's tomb. They weren't going to do anything but run if something bad happened. "This is a unique find. We could learn so much . . . not to mention the value of the burial chamber contents—was anything else taken?"

"Yes. Two of the sheds were raided—they took everything with gold or precious stones and left all the pottery." Van let the light slide down, so instead of blinding Mateo, it sank into the gloom below them. Mateo tried to grab hold of the rope, thinking perhaps he could climb back to safety, then despaired immediately because the tight arms of his coat wouldn't let him reach high enough even to try. "I heard you and your father talking about the burial chamber. You know what's down there. You knew where the doors were. You know a lot for a teenager who should be drinking tea with the Rentara University head and thinking of the largest words possible to include in your next essay. You know more than anyone is supposed to."

More than anyone is supposed *to*. Mateo tried swinging to the side, wishing for even a teaspoon's worth of Lia's spidery, flippy, sword scariness. But then the rope jerked, pulling him back up toward the opening.

"Seems like kind of a risky business, knowing so much about shapeshifters." Van's whisper snaked down into the darkness, a light suddenly illuminating him as he adjusted one of the mirrors. He helped Mateo back up into the antechamber, his grip crushing Mateo's thin artist's fingers even after he'd found his feet.

"Stop!" Mateo cried. "*Stop*. You think the Warlord won't hear about this?"

Van grinned, the light catching in his mouth, making it look misshapen and feral. "You want to get to the burial chamber. *I* want to get to the burial chamber. And I think we both know your special knack is going to get us there faster."

Heart burrowing up to his throat, Mateo fell back a step. How could Van know what he was? Could he see it like a Devoted? Mateo stared at the air over Van's head, but it was empty of any kind of aura, much less Devoted gold. If he'd taken oaths, though . . . Could Basists identify other Basists? Every Basist had slightly different powers, and little was known about them, so he supposed it wasn't impossible. What if this man had some kind of affinity that wasn't for stone, but he still knew the value of caprenum?

There weren't many in the Commonwealth who would seek an assignment digging for old shapeshifter kings. And Mateo wasn't stupid enough to assume he knew all the uses for caprenum.

"Let's go down." Van's voice was scaly and sleek as he gestured to the ladder. "There's a safe path to the lower doorway, and I'd appreciate your thoughts on the stairs and how I might get down them without having my throat cut."

"I'm not going to help you raid this tomb before the Warlord gets here, Van." Mateo stepped back from the hole, wondering if he could make it up the ladder and to Bella before the man grabbed him with his big, meaty fists.

"Raid this tomb?" Van laughed, the sound echoing unhealthily. "How about this, Mateo. I'll help you get out of this bed you've made for yourself. You help me get to the burial chamber, and I'll try to make sure it happens before the people in Chaol decide which of us seems most likely to be Patenga come back from the dead. I don't think the Warlord would even intervene, what with her trying to pretend she isn't a part of it. Do I make myself clear?"

Patenga back from the dead. Most of the workers knew that Mateo had been the one to uncover the trapdoor, and he'd sent more than one report to the director about the door in the relief room, his own name at the bottom. And a *plague* beginning in Chaol? Had Father heard about that yet? It wouldn't be hard at all for Van to connect the dots for frightened workers and people up in the city.

The air around Mateo pressed in on him, the stone *pulsing* with wrongness. If people thought there were shapeshifters in Chaol, and the dig director pointed at Tual, the Warlord's aukincer . . . at his poor, sick son, who knew *so* much about rocks . . .

People would believe it.

Mateo swallowed. Then started down the ladder.

CHAPTER 24

The Hunt

When Knox's eyes opened, everything was a dull, dusty dark. The air smelled of smoke and herbs, and his mouth, throat, and stomach felt raw. Whispers of chanting touched his ears, but they were muffled, as if from the next room.

His mind seemed to fuzz at the edges, circled in purples and blacks that pulsed and shuddered . . . until he realized it wasn't something wrong with his eyes. It was Anwei's aura, swollen up so large that it filled the room like a thousand-legged spider.

Knox gasped, the air burning clear down to his lungs. "Anwei?" he choked out.

"I'm here." A hand appeared in front of his face, holding a spoon. "Drink this. Don't move."

"Where . . . ?" he croaked. His mind flashed back to what he could remember. The governor's study, a cloud of powder in the air. Anwei stumbling as she tried to support him. She'd been crying.

"We're under the temple," Anwei's voice whispered.

The grasping bits of Anwei's aura crept toward him. Knox closed his eyes tight, breathing deep to calm himself, but it didn't shut the purple tendrils out, his aurasight making the edges of her magic glow like stained glass. Willow breathed inside his head as if she wished to speak, but then she didn't. She *couldn't*. A panicked desperation that was only partly his began to fill Knox, as if Willow were banging on a door between them that hadn't been there before, blocking off her voice. Knox felt for the sword, frantically needing to touch it. "Where is my sword?" he moaned. "Where did you put it?"

"Don't move, Knox. Open your mouth, you need—"

"No, I need *my sword*! What did you do with it? I need it *now*." His voice crackled in his throat as Willow twisted inside him, her claws digging into him. It hurt, every corner of his head frosting over, energy draining from his limbs.

Anwei's hands grasped his shoulders, her nightmare aura clouding in around them, the feel of her *inside* his head a warm, expanding glow. The crackles of ice receded even as Willow raged. But she couldn't speak. She couldn't *speak*.

"Knox, breathe with me." Anwei's voice was both in his ears and in his head. "We're safe. You're going to be all right."

Forcing himself to inhale, Knox felt Anwei's calm spread through his mind like a mouthful of hot water going down his throat on a snowy day. Each breath he took with Anwei thinned Willow's screaming until he couldn't feel her anymore. Until all that was inside him was his own breath. His and Anwei's.

Suddenly Knox's mind was *clear*, as if he'd been seeing the world through a dirty window—or perhaps through a ghost's shroud—and now, with Anwei's help, it was clean.

I can't help you now. That's why I brought you to Anwei. An echo of the goddess's words from earlier warmed his chest. When Knox let his eyelids crack back open, Anwei's face was above him, her smooth cheeks and deep eyes a spot of calm at the center of a storm of pulsing purple energy. His back was against the wall, and both of Anwei's hands pressed against his shoulders to hold him there.

"What happened?" Ewan had been there, his aura diminished to less than that of a new initiate with a sweet cake hidden in his cheek. "The Devoted was coming."

"What is happening right now?" Anwei's voice croaked.

"It . . . there's . . . it's hard to explain. Ewan. How did we get away from Ewan?"

"He rode right by us. And I . . . got you away."

Knox shook his head. That wasn't what had happened. The ivy on the wall had swollen up, flowered, and pushed through the brick itself, giving them a way out. And Ewan had been too diminished to see the swell of Basist magic right in front of him. He'd just been riding to the stables, delighting in the terror on all the high khonins' faces.

Brushing Anwei's hands away from his shoulders, Knox hunched forward, covering his eyes even as the purple ink swirled in closer. Memories of what had happened were a knife in his stomach, sparking memories of other moments in his life when that swell of murky color had meant a Basist was trying to kill him. Saying he didn't mind Anwei's magic was a good deal different from sitting at the center of it like a fly caught in a web.

Back then the outcome had always been the same. Him and his sword cutting it all away.

For the Commonwealth. To protect the people.

But this time he'd been the one running. The one hiding under a veil of purple. And it had saved his life. "Was it always a fight because they wanted to kill you, or because they knew you'd come *to kill* them?" Anwei had asked.

"Tell me what is happening to you, Knox. *Something* is happening, and I can't . . ." Anwei's voice was ragged. She'd dropped her spoon, new tears marking the old trails of salt on her cheeks.

"I'm . . ." He breathed in long and deep. It burned, but only in the spots the poison had touched him. "I'm alive."

She tipped forward, her forehead hitting his shoulder, her arms wrapping around him. He didn't have the energy to push her away, didn't *want* to push her away, which was wrong on all the levels of his existence. "No, I can smell the sword on you—I can *feel* something—"

"I was going to die last night." Knox looked up at her aura, the tendrils slipping down around her like a crown. "I could feel myself fading away."

"But you stayed." She sniffled, her breath hot through his tunic. "I had to leave my bag—it didn't have the things I needed anyway. There's a store of herbs here."

"You saved me. With your power." He stared hard at her aura. It had already begun to spool back up over her head, growing smaller now that she wasn't actively using it anymore.

Anwei abruptly pushed away from him to grab the spoon from the ground. She turned to a little pot over a tiny flicker of flame and dipped in the spoon, then held it out to him, one hand under it to keep the mixture from spilling. She wouldn't quite look him in the eyes. "*Drink it.* You're lucky I earned my hundred braids."

She was more than her Beildan braids. Both of them knew it, even if she wasn't able to say it out loud. Knox stared hard at the spoon, feeling the purple afterimages of her magic all around him.

Then he opened his mouth, letting her dribble the medicine onto his tongue. The herbs tasted bitter, but he swallowed, and all he felt was sorry.

Six years of hunting people touched the way Anwei was. One year watching Anwei from the corner of his eye as if she'd suddenly sprout claws. But *he* was the one with a ghost living in his mind who was trying to make him drag everyone into the darkness with her.

"I'm . . . sorry." Speaking took his breath, making him feel starved for air.

"Don't apologize. You're alive."

"No, I'm *sorry*, Anwei. I've been . . . awful to you." He'd been doing what he'd been told, *believed* what he'd been told. *Calsta!* he asked. *What does this mean?*

Calsta sighed in his head, answering for once. *I can't, Knox. Not right now.*

Then when? he wanted to shout, still feeling shivers of revulsion at the touch of Anwei's magic. Was it the magic itself that was wrong? That couldn't be it. He knew that wasn't it. It was just what he'd been taught his entire life, because Basism led to shapeshifters and shapeshifters had ruined the world. All Basists had gone that way before the first Warlord. At least, it seemed like that was the case according to what he'd been taught, starting long before he entered the seclusion.

But had Knox ever actually met a shapeshifter in all those years of hunting purple auras? He didn't think he had. So did Basism *really* always lead to shapeshifting? Did just having the *potential* for evil actually make someone evil?

It didn't seem that way right now. Which made him a murderer. Clear and simple.

What if . . . what if he'd been the one doing the evil?

Anwei blinked at Knox and set down the spoon. She didn't acknowledge the apology, moving on smoothly as if he'd just stayed quiet. "We have to figure out how to get into the dig before the wardens track us down. A lot of people saw us last night, and the governor will be missing his book."

Knox tried to shake the fog of blood and auras and swords from his brain, but it wouldn't quite go. He put both hands to his face, speaking through them. "Now that we have the book, getting in won't be difficult. We can do it . . ." He felt Anwei go still. Peeking through his fingers, Knox sagged back at her expression. "We don't have the book."

"I have a few pages." She shook her head slowly. "But I had to burn the rest."

"You had to *what*?" He coughed, the force of the words too much for his lungs.

Anwei reached for a small pile of folded vellum on the floor. One looked like a map, one a list, and one . . . a letter perhaps. "I had to get you out, and Noa wasn't coming. I took what I could." She spread the papers out before him. "The rest—I thought there was still a chance he wouldn't find the missing book for a few days. If he found it in his entryway with pages ripped out, he'd know for sure someone was going to break into the tomb. We have to do this fast and then get over the border."

"With what money?" Another cough ballooned up inside of Knox, cutting through the words. "We both know Shale won't give us twenty thousand in silver for that sword."

"Yes. But we might be able to get something. Now we have leverage."

Knox blinked at her, unsure of what she could mean. Until he looked past her aura to where she was gesturing. There, hidden in the tunnel between the malthouse and the temple, was an aura slippery with some kind of sedative.

The pineapple.

Walking wasn't as difficult as Knox expected, but it wasn't easy, either, his breath short. The blistering morning sun made his eyes ache. On their way out, he eyed the carriage and horse Anwei had paid the malthouse owner to store in the back courtyard, but he knew they couldn't use it. Not if Shale was looking for where they'd stashed his spy.

Knox took Anwei's arm when she offered it, letting her lead him across the island where the canal ran between the Gold and Ink Cays. Anwei hailed a boat headed toward the trade gate and paid a loose copper for them to sit at the prow until they got to the Coil.

"We have a map of the tomb's upper rooms and a staff manifest." Anwei sat up a little straighter. "If Shale does care about his spy, we can put the pressure on him to give us the rest. Before they double the guards on the compound, and before the Warlord comes."

"So within the next few days?"

"It'll have to be. I have some ideas—we can talk them over once we're home." Anwei fumbled in her pocket, then pulled out one of the papers. She glanced over her shoulder at the oarsman before holding it out to Knox. The Warlord's signature was at the bottom. "Do you know what this means?"

Knox stared at the paper, addressed to a name he'd heard but couldn't place. It had dates, symptoms . . . and suddenly it made sense. "The Warlord is sick, Anwei. This letter is to her aukincer." Knox had heard of the aukincer—that he'd helped ease and lessen wasting sickness in the seclusions.

If the Warlord was wasting away, who would take her place? The last time a Warlord was chosen, Lia and Knox had hidden in the seclusion kitchens for most of the fighting and wooing and politicking, emerging to smile and nod only when the new Warlord gave up her name. Now, though, all the masters were so old, and many with influence and support enough to have succeeded in taking over had been pruned away by the wasting sickness. Who would maintain the borders if Devoted all died off? Who would keep the governors from fighting one another?

Would shapeshifters return if there was no one strategically hunting down Basists? Knox glanced sideways at Anwei, who was still bristling over the letter.

"An aukincer? Surely, the Warlord couldn't be so stupid. . . ." She cleared her throat, tucking the letter away. "Well, more information is good. We have a dying woman coming to town, so desperate that she'll call in an aukincer. Maybe I should stay long enough for her to arrive just so I can help her."

Every inch of Knox went taut. "No."

Anwei looked up. "No?"

Knox glanced at the oarsman as they pulled up to the Coil dock. He stepped out of the boat, hating the way Anwei had to hold him up when his head began to spin. "Do you not remember what happened last night?"

"I do remember." She linked her arm through his and started down the walkway toward the apothecary. "I managed to help you because I'm a really good healer. The kind the Warlord should call on instead of a charlatan wannabe shapeshifter."

"You broke a wall! With *plants*!" Knox stumbled and had to catch himself on a brick wall. The apothecary's blue door was in sight ahead, a blessing from Calsta because he wasn't sure how much farther he could walk. "I was about two breaths from *dead* last night, and now I'm not. You may have learned the best medicine on this side of the Castal Sea, Anwei—"

"The best in the *world*."

"—but last I checked, flower petals aren't enough to bring someone back from death's pit once they've already jumped over the edge."

Anwei dropped his arm, pushing away to fiddle with the scarf covering her braids.

"You saved me. I'll never run from your herb pots again, Anwei. Why does it matter—"

Her head jerked up, her eyes narrow. "Yes, why *does* it matter?"

Knox swallowed, his throat ablaze. "Because no matter how much you don't want to admit it, putting you in the same room as the Warlord could be a death sentence. No matter how good you are or how many people you save, all she would see is your aura."

Anwei blanched. But she didn't fly at him. Didn't deny it. She just linked her arm back through his and continued toward the apothecary door. "We need to concentrate on getting into the dig, not any of this aura nonsense. How long do you think Shale will wait before attempting to get Altahn back?"

Knox pointed to the shop. "He's in there waiting for us right now."

Gulya found extra skin folds to make a properly disgusted scowl for Knox as he and Anwei walked in. He compulsively glanced at the calistet jar, relieved to see the heavy clamps shut tight.

"You have a client waiting, Anwei." Gulya's hand jabbed toward the herb room door, through which Knox could see Shale's aura. "The stupid one. With the mole. He needs a calfel tincture or it will begin to grow its own face." She carefully turned one of the glass globes, brushing off some imaginary dust. "Where have you two been? This man is not the only client who has asked for you since yesterday. I got word from the Fig Cay that your visit was brief and insufficient and that *he* was with you. People are dying, Anwei."

"I know. It's not behaving like a normal sickness, Gulya. I'm going down again today. Nothing else too serious?" Anwei's smile was the exact right portions of sweet and worried, as if she'd measured them out and ground them up in one of those medicine bags for Gulya. She waited for the old woman to shake her head before turning to the herb room. "I'll just go take care of this mole, then."

Gulya's withered hand shot out to grab Knox's, to stop him from following his partner. "What have you gotten her into?" she growled.

"Nothing?"

"Knox was helping me gather lilia blooms outside of town." Anwei paused in the doorway, Shale's aura shimmering just behind her. "You know how hard they are to get at full bloom. . . ." Anwei snapped her fingers, spinning to point at the old apothecarist. "A *lilia* infusion for the mole. That would help combat the—"

"The risk of warts! But wouldn't it interfere with the calfel's—"

"Not if we use a half-malt base."

A surprised smile gleamed out from between Gulya's wrinkles. More a baring of teeth than anything else. "You are a treasure."

She didn't let go of Knox, watching the door swing closed behind Anwei before she pulled him around to face her. "You make sure she gets home at night. That she eats and sleeps. No more of this running away for days at a time, do you hear me? She looks *sick*. What are you worth if you can't even get her to eat?"

"It's my job to make sure Anwei eats?" Knox looked Gulya full in the face, trying to listen to what was happening in the room through the door at the same time. "Anwei's been taking care of herself for years, Gulya. Why would she need me?"

"Exactly." Gulya frowned. "She's talented. Brilliant, even. She doesn't need a rock like you to drag her to the bottom of this pond."

Knox breathed in long and slow as he'd been taught, then let it out. "I'm not dragging her anywhere. If you need assistance with herb gathering or anything else, I'd be happy to help you, too."

"I don't need help from a loose-copper mercenary who can't get a job. A *thief*. I know about the sword you keep hidden up there." Gulya glanced up at the ceiling toward his room. "I bet the Devoted in town would be very interested to hear about it."

"You've been searching my room now?" The idea of the old apothecarist pawing through his things grated at Knox. He shook off his annoyance, though. There were bigger arguments to be had. "I promised to help Anwei." Knox held up the bag of herbs Anwei had shoved into a box to bring with them just in case he had some kind of relapse between the temple and the apothecary. He hoped they looked like lilia petals, whatever those were. "So I'm going to . . . go?"

His mouth stalled, the auras milling outside the shop suddenly coming into sharp relief. One in particular, sparkling with Calsta's energy. A Devoted. Another *depleted* Devoted.

Lia?

Knox let whatever Gulya was snarling about slide off him as he ran for the herb room door. He slipped through and pulled it shut after him, keeping his back to the wood. Anwei and Shale looked up, the two of them glaring daggers at each other across the table. Well, Shale was glaring, one hand fingering his long tail of hair, the other on his belt knife. He did have a mole, though Knox didn't think it was worth all the rancor and disgust Gulya had given it.

Anwei looked as chipper as she ever did, as if she were about to bring out a copy of *A Thousand Nights* and laugh with the Trib over the naughtiest illustrations.

"Thank you for finally joining us." The man stood, silver jingling at his throat. "I told her I wouldn't deal with a flunky anymore. I bring you a job and you *kidnap one of my men?*"

Lia's aura didn't walk past the shop. It paused, then came in.

"I'm not . . ." Knox's breath caught. He gulped down his panic, forcing himself to focus on the Trib as the old man advanced on him. "I didn't kidnap anyone."

Anwei stood up from the table and walked over to Knox with false nonchalance. Her hand snaked down into the box he was holding and the herbs inside. "You send a tail after us, you come back here after I expressly told you not to—"

Shale drew his knife, holding it downward like a man who knew how to use it but hadn't decided whether or not he was going to do so. "You tell me where my son is, or I'll kill you both."

"Your *son?*" Anwei's rosebud lips curved in a smile, and she withdrew her hand from the box, crumpling the leaves in her hand. Knox could almost feel her mind turning, the celebrations that would be had later. How could Shale have been stupid enough to leave his son out where Anwei could find him? She turned back toward Shale. "If you run me through, you'll never find him, will you? Please"—she gestured to the table—"let's talk."

Knox's brain felt split in two, trying to watch the knife and Anwei's casual air, which was not casual at all, while also trying to listen to Lia on the other side of the door. Another aura walked into the shop, hovering next to Lia's, white and unremarkable. A male voice rumbled through the door, asking for specific herbs. A healer? What would she be doing with a healer?

Anwei sat down, clasping her hands in front of her. "Your son is safe. I'm sure we can resolve this in a way that works for both of us. Why were you watching us?"

"You're *thieves*." Shale kept the knife out, looking between Anwei and Knox before going to the table as Anwei had asked, though he did not sit down. "I was right to watch you. You went to the dig last night after you took Altahn, and now there's no chance we'll get in."

The dig last night? Knox forced his eyes to focus on Shale, but then Lia laughed, that familiar I'm-not-actually-amused-but-I'll-humor-you chuckle ringing bells in his memory every which way.

"You're watching the dig, too? Interesting." Anwei leaned forward, cocking her head. "Why exactly do you think we raided the tomb last night?"

"*Everyone* knows. Ghosts, just like you did at the governor's party. You used the information I gave you, told me you'd help me, stole my gold, stole my *son*, took valuable artifacts from the dig, and now you're going to, what? Use him to extort money out of me? Calsta's *teeth*, how did I let myself get mixed up in all this?" He growled the last into his own fist, so low Anwei might not have heard.

Anwei blinked once, confusion she wouldn't show radiating toward Knox. They had taken Shale's son, but they hadn't been to the excavation compound the night before. Knox almost wished they had, since it seemed whoever had gone over those walls had been successful. Shale had had his son tailing them, so he had to have known what their plan was, or Altahn wouldn't have been there with the carriage the night before.

And yet the same day Knox and Anwei had unleashed ghosts on the governor's friends, thieves pretending to be ghosts had haunted the dig, too? That was a little too much of a coincidence. Anwei's eyes flicked over to Knox, one eyebrow rising a bit. He jerked his head toward the shop, trying to convey that Shale wasn't the only threat at hand. Her gaze moved to the door, then back to him, her brow furrowing. But he didn't know what to do further—Lia wasn't coming in, and Knox liked knowing where she was much more than the idea of running away and not knowing—so Anwei turned back to Shale's growling. "What kind of ground worms are you two? The sword is the only thing worth its metal in that tomb, and it would take a miracle to get it now. Give me my son, or I'll hand you over to the magistrate."

Knox closed his eyes, trying to concentrate on both Shale and Lia in the shop. Lia wasn't speaking. Wasn't moving. Her aura was just hovering there on the other side of the door. Had she come with a knife or for explanations?

"We didn't go to the dig last night. Who have you told that we are working for you? You knew we were going to haunt the governor and whoever you told did too." Anwei's voice was deathly quiet as she stared Shale down.

Lia's aura suddenly moved toward the herb room door. Knox tensed, waiting for her to slam the door into him, maybe to not bother opening it, just stab her sword straight through the wood into his back. But she didn't.

Was it possible she didn't know he was here? Her aurasight was gone, but there was no way that of all the apothecaries in Chaol, Lia had walked into Gulya's by coincidence.

Shale was still glaring at Anwei across the table. "I haven't told anyone yet, but that is going to change if you don't give me my son *now*."

"You're willing to give up on getting your sword back? After offering so much money? After already paying me some of it?"

Shale paced up and down the length of the table. His jaw twitched, his fingers clenching and unclenching around the hilt. "I'll hire someone else."

"We are the only people in this city who can get to that sword, Shale." Knox pitched his voice low. Quiet. Wondering if Lia would hear it through the door. "And we didn't go to the dig—which means Anwei is right. *Someone* knew what we were planning to do and copied us. All the people who knew on our end are accounted for. . . ." His mind stopped on Noa for the first time since the spray of poison the night before. Noa *wasn't* accounted for in all this. But Shale didn't need to know that. "Your son must have heard us planning. Either he told someone or you did, which is how we find ourselves in this situation."

Shale kept pacing, one hand pulling hard on the silver necklace until it dug into his skin. "This . . . this is a problem."

"We're going to do the job, Shale. We'll give you your son along with the sword once you've paid us." Anwei stood, her voice brisk. "If you tell the magistrate, he's dead. If you follow us from now on, he's dead. If you come back to this shop? Dead." She smiled, the sharp one that made Knox feel antsy inside, wondering what she would do next. "You've kept back information on the dig, and I want it now. Maps? Guard schedules? The archeologists in attendance? Here, let me give you an example." She cleared her throat, putting her hands up and staring off into the distance like some kind of orator. "'Anwei, the *Warlord herself* will be here in less than two weeks to take the thing I want you to steal.' *That* is the kind of information that would have been helpful from the first day you came in here."

Lia was now standing between Gulya and the other aura that had come in with her. Were they talking about . . . fish bones? Knox cracked the door open, wanting to see with his own eyes. She was by the counter, in a dress of all things, her wrists and hands showing and everything. She'd wrapped her face and hair in an eastern-province-looking scarf, but when she turned from the door to speak to the man beside her at the counter, Knox saw her eyes for the first time in two years. Blue, like so many who lived in Chaol.

Knox scrubbed a hand through his hair. Lia was *from Chaol*. How had he forgotten that?

"All I have is a rough log of items going in and out and a map from when the compound was first being built." Shale's voice was hollow. "Everything is different inside now—we only got maps of the first rooms they uncovered. That's why I hired you. So *you* would figure out how to get in."

"You *don't* have a map? Delivery schedules? You promised me both."

Lia had a familiar sharp look to her eyes, as if she were unpeeling everything around her to get a look at what made it work. The man with Lia laughed, a great booming that sounded too jolly to be real. He was wearing an expensive coat, dirt-smudged boots, and an expression that seemed altogether too good-natured considering the fact that he was speaking to Gulya. The man reached a hand out to Lia as if to draw her into his animated conversation, and Lia stepped forward, accepting the unspoken invitation.

It was all very confusing.

"Are we boring you?" Shale's voice lashed toward him.

Knox pulled away from the crack in the door to meet Shale's glare. The old man sat down at the table like a king on his throne. "There are customers in the apothecary. This is the sort of conversation I'd rather not have overheard."

Shale rolled his eyes, turning back to Anwei. "I want proof my son is alive."

"I want proof you have twenty thousand silver rounds," Anwei countered. "Also, if you've been watching the dig, you have more than lists of items going in and out, and if you don't give it to me, you can say goodbye to your son. I want guard schedules. Numbers of workers. Typical delivery days, anything special about the way the dig functions—do they all stay in at night? Do the archeologists leave? Don't try to tell me you don't know."

Knox squinted at his partner, the knife's edge in her voice different from anything he'd ever heard. Anwei didn't threaten, usually. At least, not when he was around.

"I'll give you what I have, but there is no map. There are no comprehensive lists of workers. I can only give estimates, and no names."

The man who'd come in with Lia spoke again, pulling Knox's attention back to her. His only family, so close and yet so very far away. "I gave him three knuckles' worth, and *still* he couldn't see straight for a week," the man laughed, and Lia joined him. Lia *laughing*. It made Knox want to smile too. "They expect aukincy to come with magic. As if I can snap my fingers and all their bones will unbreak."

Anwei's voice: "I'll meet you down in the Fig Cay near the plague house tomorrow after the seventh drum. I assume you know where that is, since your son followed us there?"

Lia's attention wandered past the counter, trailing across the glass globes of powders, flower petals, and leaves long dead. Slowly but surely creeping toward the cracked-open door where Knox stood. Knox tensed, whispering inwardly, *She's diminished. Ewan was diminished. I could use my aura to run around Chaol twice without a boat, then hang upside down from the drum tower, and they wouldn't see me.* But still her eyes slid toward him.

". . . substantial proof of our fee and the information I asked for. For every day you make me wait past tomorrow, I'll take one of your son's fingers. Do you understand?"

Shale's voice was faint. "I thought *he* was Yaru."

Knox's eyes focused on Shale as the Trib looked him up and down. "You'll never get anywhere close to Yaru," he said quietly. Not that diverting Shale mattered much now; the damage was already done. *This* was why Anwei used the temple and drops and sneaking behind the scenes. People who knew where you lived tended to feel the lack of coin in their purse once they'd paid.

Anwei rolled her eyes behind Shale's back as he stood up from the table. Knox opened the door for him, shielding himself by staying behind it. Anwei, however, skipped forward to lead Shale out into the apothecary, pulling herbs from the globes as she went and shoving them into one of the herb packets. She buttoned the packet closed when she got to the counter, gave it a vigorous knead, then held it out to Shale. "Here's everything you'll need. In a half-malt, half-acidic-fruit-juice base with that lilia infusion, twice a day. You can pay Gulya."

Through the gap by the door's hinges, Knox watched her pass by Lia, his breath catching when Lia's hand slipped into her sash. He knew from experience that she preferred larger weapons, but a sash that size could hide a knife or two or five, and Lia was deadly throwing or fighting in close quarters either way. If she was here for him, knew his connection to Anwei . . .

Shale tossed a few coins on the counter with a bit more force than necessary. Lia watched him curiously, the man she'd arrived with stopping his story long enough to smile at Shale.

"You'll be pleased once that unsightly thing is gone." Gulya slid the coins into a little pile with a satisfied smile.

Shale put a hand up to cover the mole on his chin and stalked past Lia to the door.

"Be sure to apply it at least twice a day!" Gulya called, looking as if she meant to run after him. Anwei helped to count the money as Lia's companion paid, then waved them out the door.

Before Lia could get too far, Knox went to the herb room window and climbed out.

CHAPTER 25

The Goddess You Serve

Lia could feel the apothecary building staring after her as she and Tual loaded their purchases onto his little skiff. She stepped into the boat and sat. Tual took up the oars, moving across the channel into the traffic of boats bobbing toward the dry market. Looking back at the apothecary's blue-painted door, Lia wished buildings could give up their secrets the way people did. Something there was amiss.

A dark shape flashed over the garden wall even as she watched. Lia blinked, then blinked again, but her eyes wouldn't quite focus on the dark smudge, and then it was gone. The hairs on her neck stood up. It reminded her too much of the first time Master Calfor had demonstrated bending Calsta's light around herself to smudge her appearance. She'd faded right into the shadows, Lia's mind skipping past her as if she hadn't existed at all.

It could have been a trick of the light, but Lia couldn't stop looking, trying to pinpoint where the shadow had gone. If the Warlord had sent more Devoted ahead of her without notifying anyone, her plan to escape before Ewan regained his aura would be useless. Or . . .

Knox. The boat rocked under Lia's feet as she stood up, looking down the deep channels separating all the little islands of the Coil.

Something caught her eye, another shadow whisking out of sight on the skybridge overhead that led to the little island in the Coil's string. It *had* to be Knox.

Which meant he'd seen her. But he hadn't come out to meet her.

A surge of fear replaced the stirring excitement and anticipation in her chest. If Knox thought she knew where he was, that she was some part of a trap meant to bring him in—

"Are you all right?" Tual looked up, dipping an oar to steer them into the channel traffic, the blue-painted apothecary door disappearing from sight. "I wanted to give you time to think through whatever happened in the stable, but—"

"Get us off the channel. Now." Lia dropped down into the boat, wishing the vessels around them carting piles of vegetables and squirming fish were large enough to block them from sight. Not that it would have mattered. Knox had his aura. He'd see her aftersparks no matter what she did. "Take us over to the Ink Cay. We'll go on foot."

"You're a very industrious young lady, I'll give you that, but *I* do not relish the thought of carrying my parcels all the way to the Water Cay using skybridges and tunnels."

"If you don't want this boat to sink with you in it, then get us to land."

"Is that *you* threatening me, or am I missing something?" Tual squinted at her, leaning against the oars. But then he gave a curious look around and steered the boat's nose toward the Ink Cay docks on the other side of the channel. "Your sister told me what happened to you the day you ran away. What she understood about it, anyway."

"That's what you want to talk about? After you find Mateo and me standing over a man being eaten by an auroshe?" Lia's eyes flicked from bridge to bridge, sweat making her scarf stick to her forehead and temples. The bridges stuck out like spider legs across the whole Coil, the tiny cluster of islands linked together like a badly patched quilt. Knox wouldn't try to kill her, would he? Not after everything they'd been through together. If he could just show her how to hide, then they could hide together.

"I know my son well enough to assume he did little more than cover his face and hope you didn't step on him. And in the context of what Aria told me . . ." He looked up at the clouded sky. "I understand, Lia."

"You *understand*?" Lia's eyes froze on a face looking down at them through the ropes of a skybridge. It disappeared into the crowd the moment she focused on it. Knox had hurt people on his way out of the seclusion when they'd tried to stop him from leaving, and she still didn't know what had caused his sudden departure. They hadn't been able to talk much after Lia had gone under the veil. It panged inside her again, everything she'd had to give up. Even her friendship with Knox. Which, if he thought she was there to drag him back to a traitor's death, might not be in effect.

What if it wasn't him at all?

Lia cursed her skirts, her lack of weapons. Her body still ached from the fight back at the Montannes' stable. She'd done the same as Knox had that day he'd left—made sure no one could take her back. He'd do the same now if he thought she was a threat.

"Aria said that that other Devoted in town—Ewan—attacked you. That you were scared of him and nothing else."

Lia's attention jerked back down to Tual even as the boat knocked against the dock. She climbed out, meaning to bolt, but Tual's hand on her arm stopped her. He shoved a basket into her arms. "Would you help me with these? I'm an old man."

Swallowing down a swear word, Lia looked around the dock. Knox wouldn't outright attack her here where anyone could see. He was trying to avoid notice too. Tension pulled tight through her chest like puppet strings, threatening to break. And Tual, the way he so casually mentioned Ewan and Aria . . . sickness bloomed inside her. What could he understand about any of it? What had happened was an explosion, an earthquake, the world breaking under Lia's feet, and she was still falling.

Tual spoke as if she'd scored poorly on an exam and he could understand why she might be disappointed.

The aukincer clambered to the back of the boat, then threw her the mooring rope. Nerves on fire, Lia found herself reaching out with her mind again, as if Calsta hadn't taken away her ability to see auras, to see into people's thoughts. If only she could see into Tual's right now, if only she could pinpoint *Knox's* aura—but instead she tied the rope to the pylon with her free hand.

When Tual climbed out of the boat, he cocked his head, looking down at her. "Lia, you shouldn't have had to run, but the facts are what they are. Calsta is supposed to protect you, and she didn't. The *Devoted* are supposed to protect you, and it was a Devoted who scared you away."

"I have to go." Lia thrust the basket toward him, but he didn't take it. She couldn't stomach the pity in his eyes.

"The Warlord asked me to observe you, starting about a year ago. She worried your behavior indicated sickness."

"She thought I had wasting sickness?" Lia paused for a split second before shaking her head. "No. I don't care."

"You just murdered a Rooster, Lia. You think you can just walk away from me and hope no one ever finds out?"

"I did *not* . . ." Lia's breath caught in her chest as she put down the basket. "It was an accident."

"Something I'm not going to hold over your head, because if my partner had attacked me, tried to . . . I wish there had been an auroshe handy when . . ." Tual took a shaky breath and looked down at his shoes. "That's probably unhelpful, but I am so sorry, Lia. I'm on your side."

"I'm going home." Lia pushed into the crowd, her mind spinning. She just had to make it through the main glass tunnel that connected the Ink Cay to the dry market, then over the bridge to the Water Cay. From there . . . she started walking faster, forcing her mind to focus on Knox. Knox was a problem she could solve.

There were fewer people wandering around on foot in the Water Cay—most of the compounds had their own personal docks and housing for their servants. If Knox was going to attack her, that's where it would be. So, where best to make sure he couldn't attack without talking to her first? Lia pushed her mind as far from Ewan as she could, looping it around the path she could take, the places Knox would think he was hidden but she would know—

"I knew it was going to happen." Tual's voice trailed after her, breaths coming fast as he tried to drag the two baskets of herbs through the crowd. "Maybe not the way it did, exactly. So many Devoted have fallen to wasting sickness over the last few years, and it's only getting worse. High khonins are beginning to notice that the Warlord has been sending fewer Devoted to keep the peace. They aren't always sharing when their children are touched by Calsta because there aren't any Devoted to catch them at it. In the outer provinces children go completely unnoticed, Calsta and the nameless god shining inside them with no consequences at all. How long before the Trib start pushing the border south? Or the queen of Lasei decides conquering us would be better than continuing to shut us out after all the shapeshifter wars?"

Lia ran down the ramp into the glass tunnel toward the dry market, immediately regretting the choice when the crowd bottlenecked inside. Tual's voice drew closer. "You weren't sick like she thought, though. You were unhappy."

"No one cares if Devoted are happy or not, Tual. They serve Calsta." Lia bit on the words as she said them. *They.* As if she was no longer Calsta's.

"I care." He said it a hair too loud as Lia pushed her way through to the other end of the tunnel. "Please stop, Lia. For once someone is trying to help you. I know you didn't go willingly into the seclusion, that none of this has been what you wanted." He swore when she still didn't slow, dropping one of his baskets to grab her arm.

Lia pulled away, falling into a fighting stance. "Do not touch me. No one has dared touch me in two years—do you really want to see why?"

"Until the Warlord told Ewan to try it?" Tual's teeth gritted, his normally good-natured smile lost in a scowl. "Listen to me, Lia. Mateo is not my son by blood."

"Who cares? I guess you can't blame yourself for his personality."

"It matters because he's special like you." Tual stood there, herbs trailing out from the basket still in his arms. His face was so lost without its smile, all edges of ugly memories that seeped out of him like an aura. The appeal in his voice was worse than a sword. It wasn't violence or even politics and threats. It was a peek into something deeper, as if Tual had cracked open a hard shell she hadn't known was there and was letting her see his soft insides.

"I know he can see auras." She looked him up and down. "I wondered if you could too—you saw me in the loft before you should have been able to. It was you who brought Mateo to my house and pointed him toward the kitchen pantry."

"Mateo is strong like you, Lia. I had to step in when he was young. His parents . . . didn't want him." The flash of anger and misery in Tual's eyes was real. "I read through the Warlord's reports and recommendations for your future."

Lia gulped, hating that he knew. That he'd known the eventuality of Ewan cornering her in a room long before she'd come to Chaol. Hated how it made her feel muddy and soiled, hated that Tual wouldn't look at her as he said it.

But then he did look. He raised his head and met her eyes. "When I look at you, I see Mateo as he was as a child. Defenseless. No way to fight back against the people who should have been protecting him.

They would have killed him if I hadn't been there. What will happen to you if you don't let me help you? I *want* to help you."

Lia took a step closer to him, fury rising in her like bile. "You threatened to have my entire family executed for treason if I didn't marry your son. Don't pretend this is a rescue mission. You have some half-brained political goal to set up your own space here away from the Warlord, using my father's clout."

"Not *my* space. A safe space. A place for people like you and me." A ghost of a smile swished back into place. "Mateo's not so awful, is he? Apart from his taste in clothes, I suppose. I've been able to keep both of us safe from the Warlord all these years." He took a step toward her. "What makes you think I can't do the same for you?"

Lia suddenly felt sick. She turned away from him and pushed toward the dry market. It started as a walk, then turned into a run when Tual called after her, and she wondered how fast she would have to go for him to stop following.

"You have been taught for years that your life belongs to a goddess and if you so much as sneeze at the wrong time, she'll punish you now and forever. Your teachers taught you that every word they said about you, about the world, about people, was all straight from the goddess's lips. How is anyone supposed to argue with that?" Tual's words came patched together as he tried to keep up with her. "Lia, I see an opportunity here. Your father's political failings, our arrangement with the Warlord—all of us could be *free*. I want my son to have a life that has nothing to do with scars and robes and serving a goddess who hasn't spoken to anyone in half a century. I need you, Lia." He reached out and grabbed her arm again just as she felt sunlight on her face through the scarf, wrenching her to a stop. "We both do."

Lia glared down at his hand. All these men seemed to think she belonged to them, that they could touch her whenever they wanted.

"Think of it this way," Tual said through winded breaths. Keeping up with her hadn't been easy for him. "You've been alone for the last six years."

"And?"

"Do you really want the *rest* of your life to be alone? No family. No friends. No choices." He let her go and dropped the abused basket, bending over to catch his breath. "I want this to be your choice. That's why I'm talking to you, not your father. He's the one trying to keep you locked in the house. Your father would have signed this contract without even asking you."

"He would not. The first thing he said after you left was that he wasn't going to force me into anything."

Tual looked down, an unhappy smile on his lips. "You believe that? When you have to sneak out your own window to get out of your family compound?" He swallowed, clearing his throat. "Aren't you sick of people seeing you as a thing to be used rather than a person to bring to their side?"

Lia forced herself to look into Tual's brown eyes. They were calculating but not hard. "I don't belong to my father."

"Tell him that. I need an answer soon. I can't stretch my neck far enough to protect your family if you aren't going to help us in return, Lia." He pulled himself back up, brushing away the leaves and flower petals that had stuck to him from the basket. "I can promise you the trouble your father is in will destroy him. It will destroy all of you."

She could hear a threat in those words. *I could destroy all of you.*

Lia turned on her heel and walked away, but his words shadowed each of her steps.

It wasn't just Tual's words following her. She could feel Knox watching. Waiting.

CHAPTER 26

The Veil

Lia walked through the dry market as quickly as she dared. Past heaps of crusty fish and jeweled craycrabs and little furred mockturtles, their sea coats slippery with salt. When she got to the bridge, she could still feel Knox there behind her, a shadow at the corner of her vision that slipped away when she turned to look. It wasn't until she'd gotten to the guard's blind spot on the wall around her father's house that he finally strolled into view.

Lia put her back to the wall. Her eyes wanted to slide off him, but she held them firm. Knox didn't attack, keeping his distance as he looked her over, a rangy, scrappy version of her friend who'd left her with more questions than breath to say them. His hair had grown out to make a blunt ponytail at the nape of his neck, his cheekbones had hollowed, and his skin was a milk tea color that said he'd been spending less time outside.

"You come for me now?" she whispered. "You should have done it a year ago."

"You left me first." He shook his head, as if he wanted to pull the words back. "That's not what I meant. I'm not here *for* you. I saw Vivi at the governor's house and heard you were missing, and I was worried. . . . Why are you here?"

Lia pressed her lips together tight, then turned to face the wall and began to climb. "Come inside."

Why was she here? That question was much better than what Lia had been expecting—*no* questions and a knife in her back. Knox had left without so much as a goodbye . . . but he was right. She had gone first, though it hadn't been her choice. Lia clenched her eyes shut for a moment, then resumed climbing with a violent burst, not wanting to remember the day she'd left Knox—not that he'd ever needed her as much as she'd needed him.

She'd been sitting outside Vivi's stall one morning, feeding him bits of dried meat, when Knox had come to tell her Master Pel wanted to see both of them. It had been a year or more since she'd made the third oath, Lia's family a scab that still bled when she prodded at it, though being allowed out into the Commonwealth to hunt Basists and scare province officials helped.

She still remembered the exact way Knox had wrinkled his nose as she put the rest of Vivi's treats on her palm and held them up over her head for the auroshe, Vivi's long teeth catching in her curls as he gobbled the meat.

They walked together to the masters' hall. Master Pel was waiting for them with a lumpy armful of stained fabric. White that had long gone gray.

"Weapons and leathers off." She waited patiently as Knox and Lia stripped off their swords and outer armor, Lia's fingers moving slowly, as if she could stave off what she knew would come next.

Knox put a hand on her shoulder when Master Pel turned away to put their swords under her desk. "It's just the spiriter test, Lia. We'll have our next assignment before you know it."

He'd always been so solemn. Pious. Ready to do his part in the fight against the nameless god. But even he shuddered as Master Pel settled the cloth over his head and handed him a pair of gloves.

The veil felt like a weight on Lia's head and shoulders, blocking out light, breath, the last bits of human contact she still had inside the seclusion.

"This week will be one of meditation and stillness," Master Pel said. "Give yourself to Calsta, tell her you are sacrificing your connection to others that comes from direct eye contact and touch. Few can learn to track, and Calsta rewards even fewer beyond that with the capacity to read thoughts. Do not aspire. Be humble. Look inward. Allow the hostlers to care for your auroshes. There will be no training, no assignments. Your meals will be brought to your rooms. Take this opportunity to rededicate yourself to the oaths you've already made to the Sky Painter. Master Helan will be observing you from his room for signs of capacity."

Lia shuddered at the idea of the old spiriter who had brought her to the seclusion when she was a girl. He'd frightened her then just as he did at the beginning, sitting up in his tower, watching her, reading her thoughts from under his thick veil. Knox squeezed her hand once through their gloves before they parted.

"See you in a week." Lia said it as if it were a truth. A conclusion already made. A future that she could count on in a life of futures being chosen for her one after another. "It'll be over soon."

The first day sequestered in her room was boring. With no Vivi to brush, no sword to sharpen, and no armor to oil, Lia felt as if she were disappearing. As if she'd become nothing but a loose conglomeration of annoyance and bitterness covered by a bit of tatty cloth. She pushed her mind out past the confines of her room, wondering what Knox was doing. Promises to Calsta were not said, not even one.

When she found Knox in the male barracks with her mind, she amused herself by watching his aura sit there, as bored as she was. Itching for his sword.

The last thought, the one about the sword, seemed to stand up over his head, dancing through his aura like a wicked little imp, much deeper inside him than she would have expected. External and yet a part of him. Then she saw his boredom turn to thoughts of lunch. She felt him make a decision. The boy who never, ever broke the rules left his room, went to the eating hall, filled a tray with food, and started in her direction.

By the time he got to her room, Lia had torn off the veil and gloves and curled herself up in the corner. When Knox saw her, he dropped the tray and pulled off his own veil.

"Lia?" He was scared too.

Master Helan came in right behind him, ghostly and mysterious under the crisp white folds of his veil. As the man held out his gloved hand to her, Lia could feel everything about her that mattered draining away. Playing with Vivi. Sparring with Knox. Conditioning her armor and mending the padding, weeks on the saddle. Fighting, sweating, pushing herself until she couldn't remember anything but what it felt like for her muscles to burn.

There was no such thing as family, homesickness, or sadness when you were on fire.

Now, when she got to the top of her family compound's wall, it was almost a shock to place the Knox who was standing with his arms crossed as he watched her, no intention of following, next to the memory of him standing in her doorway, his veil on the ground and tears on his cheeks. His openness, his desire to live a simple life doing what he was told, seemed to have vanished into something much more complicated.

"I'm not working with the Devoted. I want you to show me how to hide from them too," she called. "Come inside before someone sees you."

The bite of caution didn't leave him. He looked down the street, then back up at her, then very slowly began to climb. Once they were safe on the other side of the wall, Lia tried to find the right thing to say as she watched for the opening between guards. "What . . ." There *weren't* words to express what was inside her. "Where have you been for the last year? Why did you leave?"

Knox shifted restlessly, all his muscles tense. "Who else is here other than Ewan?"

It looked like the old rivalry between him and Ewan was still in full force despite how trivial it seemed now. Perhaps it didn't feel trivial on the wrong side of a manhunt. "Six . . . I mean five Roosters." A twinge of nausea bubbled up inside Lia at the thought. She watched her friend's face, anger and worry an odd mix across his features. "You didn't tell me you were going to go," she said. "I would have come with you."

"Why are you here, Lia?" He whispered it. "Please tell me this is a coincidence."

"*You* followed *me*. *I'm* the one who didn't turn you in when you blew up on the wall."

"You saw that?"

"And made sure no one else did."

"How did you pull that off?" A slight smile. "Did you put sugar in Ewan's tea?"

"No." Lia swiped at her cheek, wishing tears didn't sting. "Your aura wasn't here when we first got to Chaol and then it *was*. Show me how to hide like you, and we can leave together before the Warlord comes." The simple plan tasted like a dream. A leftover of her past life. But she was just like Knox: a much more complicated version of what she'd been before. Hiding would be only one step of many with Tual breathing down her neck.

"I can't."

"You can't?" Lia took a deep breath, and then another one, feeling as if he'd slapped her. She started toward the house, weaving between hedges and plants until she got to the trellis under her window. "You really are going to leave me behind, then? *Again?*"

"It's not like that, Lia." His chin tipped up to follow her as she scaled the wall and slid through her open window. It took only a moment before he was pulling himself up after her, landing lightly on her bedroom floor.

Knox's eyes widened as he took in her little room, the bed hung with blue fabric, the flowers on her dressing table. So unlike their stark, cold rooms at the seclusion. "What was your plan when you left?" he asked.

"It wasn't a plan. It just . . . happened. And I can't go back. I *won't*." She sat on the chair in front of her dressing table, jumping when her reflection in the mirror moved. Her eyes looked red against the blue of her scarf. Swollen, though she hadn't been crying. "I need your help, Knox. I always did."

"I couldn't help you when the spiriters took you." He said it quietly, as if he'd felt that moment of their makeshift family being pried apart just as keenly as she had.

"I know. I don't blame *you*. How could I? But we can help each other now."

"I can't show you because there's nothing to show. It's . . . complicated. All you ever wanted was to come home." Knox looked around her room once again. "I can understand why now, I guess. This looks like a home." There was an odd hitch in his voice, as if he'd found something he wanted more than Calsta. Lia couldn't imagine what that would be. He smiled, an old smile that sent a nostalgic warmth through her chest. "I can't say I expected so many ribbons."

"A girl can like ribbons *and* stabbing things—"

"Lia!"

Knox and Lia both froze at her father's shout from down the hall. Lia jumped up to close the door. When she turned back to show Knox where to hide, he was already gone. She darted to the window and stuck her head outside to find him on the ground below her, shadows clinging to him like ink.

"Lia, are you in there?" Her father's voice was just outside.

"Please," she hissed toward Knox. "Don't leave."

"You went into the city, Lia?" Her father burst through the closed door without knocking and, finding her at the window, rushed to pull it shut with a snap. "When I got home, Aria was putting her horse away. She tried to lie and say you were in the garden." He leaned against the wall next to the window, his hands covering his face. "How am I supposed to keep you safe if you won't stay here?"

Lia sat on the bed, not sure what she was supposed to feel. Like the daughter he thought he needed to protect? It didn't quite fit after so many years of protecting herself. "Has Mother shown any improvement? Tual sent another batch of medicine with Aria."

"You went to see him?" At her pained expression, he sank down on the bed, letting his hands drop. "She is doing a little better, and normally I'd . . ." He looked up at the ceiling. "I still think you need to keep your distance from her. If she has to lose you again, I think it will kill her. So until I decide what to do about you—"

"What to *do* about me?" Lia stood up, every inch of her bristling.

"It's either send you back to the seclusion you hate so much or let the Warlord find you and take the consequences." He swallowed, his fingers digging into his skin. "Or the aukincer. Those are our only three options."

"How can you say that?" The images she'd seen of herself in her father's thoughts had been like a dream, proof he'd been missing her as much as she'd missed him. But now, inside the house again, it seemed much less nostalgic. She still was that little girl to him. A responsibility. A problem. "Were you yelling for me because you were angry I left the house, or did you actually need to speak with me?"

Her father caught her hand in his. "I don't like it any more than you do, Lia. I don't want you to go back, and I don't want the Warlord to find you. That means I have to seriously consider Tual's offer."

Lia pulled her hand free. "*You* have to consider? This isn't at all what we talked about before."

"I don't like this. I *hate* it, but I've spent every minute of the last few days trying to come up with a way for us to stay together and not die." He rubbed a hand across his forehead and looked at her. "Little

Spot, I can't see another way. We have to deal with the aukincer."

"You haven't even asked me what I've been doing. What plans *I* have."

"All right. What plans do you have?" Lia's father sat forward. When she didn't immediately speak, he shook his head. "Lia, you're a child. You came to me for help, and this is what I have. I'm going to go speak to the Montannes in the morning."

Lia, you're a child. Tual's words about her father sat there at the back of Lia's brain: *I want this to be your choice. Your father would have signed this contract without even asking you.* "What about what I want?"

"You don't want to go back to the seclusion?"

Lia shook her head.

"And you don't want us to be hung when the Warlord gets here?"

Lia blinked. Then shook her head again.

He breathed out, his mouth pinching. "I sort of hate that I'm saying this, but I need you to be a resource, Lia. Not a weight."

A resource. Lia walked across the room and lowered herself into the chair as far from her father as she could manage. "If I don't do what Tual wants, then he won't have to do *anything* to destroy our family. Because you already did. If I hadn't shown up, you'd be scrambling to cover up an *assassination attempt*, among other things. But now that I'm here, you've got an extra resource, a blessing from Calsta that will allow you to fill the hole you dug for yourself?"

"It's not that black and white, Lia." Her father stood and paced past her to check the hallway. "If you had stayed here instead of going to the seclusion, your role in our family would have been to make political alliances. You can protect our family. You can protect this city from the governor—he's turning a blind eye to everything that doesn't immediately put silver in his coffers. There's a sickness spreading from the Fig Cay as we speak—"

"But I *didn't* stay here. I'm not a normal part of the family to be sold off to whoever will help your career the most."

"But you're here *now*." He looked at her. "And Tual has the Warlord's ear. He can save us *and* you. It's not about politics. All you have to do is—"

"Give up everything I am. And everything that I want. *Again*." Lia tugged at the scarf over her face, her breath hot against her cheeks.

"Please, Lia." Her father's voice snapped, as if asking for anything physically pained him. He'd grown used to power; she could see it in the way he held himself. "Talk to the boy. Spend some time with him and his father." He swallowed, turning away from the door. "I suppose when you say you have plans you mean you could save yourself. You could run from here, be hunted like a wild beast for the rest of your life. The rest of us can't do that."

"Why not?" she whispered. "We could *all* leave. Start a new life somewhere else."

"You mean you could keep that scarf on? Put on a veil again, and use your power to . . . make other people believe the things we want them to?" He looked around the room as if there might be some merit to this plan. "We could set up in a city across the border, you could help me gain influence . . ."

Lia's throat closed. Put the veil back on? On her father's command instead of the Warlord's? Was that better? Would Calsta even stand for it?

Could Lia? Calsta was supposed to protect the Commonwealth, her worshippers all doing their part to build society. Devoted were given extra power to protect everyone else. If Lia used it for herself and her family, what did that make her?

Her father was still talking. ". . . But even a scheme that takes us over the border seems impossible. Your mother wouldn't survive the road right now."

Lia forced her shoulders to straighten and looked her father in the eyes, the way she did an auroshe. An enemy until it saw you as an equal.

He didn't flinch, staring straight back. Lia wished for her armor. For Vivi and his long teeth, a sword to hold back the threats of the world. She wished she didn't see her father as anything other than the man who had sheltered her in his arms when she was young.

How, in a world that seemed bent on tearing her to pieces, had Father ended up opposing her? How did he become a person who demanded sacrifices like a god rather than volunteering his own sacrifices for the people he loved? She could still feel his arms around her, the way he'd hugged her when she'd stumbled into the house. Could that man really exist in the same space as the one in front of her? Or was it someone else inside him talking? A man who was trying to shelter a girl long grown and doing it exactly the wrong way?

How she wished Calsta were with her just then so she could see the truth in her father's mind and not the story masking it.

"I'm going to meet with Mateo tonight," she finally said.

Her father nodded. "I think that's best." And then, as if the world, Lia's life, all of it, were decided, he left the room and shut the door behind him.

The window squeaked as it opened.

"I was a good Devoted, wasn't I, Knox?" Lia could barely make the words come out.

"Calsta favored you," Knox said quietly.

She turned to face him, his outline framed in shadow despite the afternoon sun. "But I've left her."

"Have you?"

"I took off my veil. She took her power back." Lia slumped in the chair. Knox had been taught the same oaths, and the same frightening promises of what would happen if he abandoned them as she had. What would it mean if Lia died and had to face the Sky Painter herself with a string of broken promises circling her throat like a chain? The seclusion had always felt like a mouth closed around Lia, the oaths like teeth, power a boon that didn't mean much while trapped on a monster's tongue. But trying to leave only meant the monster would swallow you down.

"I could become a murderer." She shuddered, thinking of the stable. Balan wasn't the first person she'd killed. All the others had been trying to kill her at the time of their demise, but they still stuck with her, every one. "Or a thief. I could protect my family with my life now or let them all die painfully one by one, and it wouldn't matter either way unless I let Calsta put that veil back on my head." The words choked in her throat and she covered her face with her hands. She didn't want a veil on her head, never, ever again. "It doesn't matter what choices I make anymore because I'm already lost."

"It would matter to your family." Knox moved to sit on the chair's arm, leaving space between them as if they were still at the seclusion, every rule about how they could speak, how they could play, talk, and fight burned into his bones. "But I don't believe Calsta is who you think she is. . . ." He hesitated for a moment, then said, "It was Calsta who told me to leave the seclusion."

"*Calsta* told you to leave?" Lia pulled her hands away from her face to look at him. "The goddess. Calsta?"

"Yes."

"The goddess who hasn't spoken to anyone in more than five hundred years? Did she . . . speak directly into your head? Maybe she brewed up a storm and rained down some words? Or did she actually appear in her broken helmet and press that sword of hers to your throat?"

"Lia . . ."

"No, I'm sorry. I . . ." Lia took in a deep breath. Knox had never lied, had never made up stories that weren't true. Why would he now? "Are you sure? How is this possible? How did the masters not know? Wouldn't they have shoved you into a room and never let you out?"

Knox licked his lips, looking down at his clasped hands. "The masters didn't believe me. Calsta's been speaking to me my whole life. She told me to go to the seclusion after . . . you know how my family was killed?"

Lia nodded.

"Calsta has been right next to me—well, when she feels like it—from that day until now. Even when I'm not doing what the masters want. I don't think she's locked in step with the Warlord the way the masters made it seem. She *made* me leave. Told me to come here. And she's kept me safe."

"Your aura. *Calsta* hid it?" Lia bit her lip, wondering if all really was lost. She hadn't thought hiding an aura was possible, but Mateo and Knox—Tual, too—had all somehow received the goddess's favor despite breaking her rules. Maybe she only liked men. The thought twisted inside Lia, cold, hard, and wrong.

"No, Calsta didn't hide it. I'm still not sure how it works, exactly, or even when it works. But Calsta is the one who led me to the person who has been hiding me." Knox shifted uncomfortably, continuing before Lia could ask whom he was talking about. Ask if whoever had helped him would be willing to help her, too. "That man you were with in the apothecary—your father wants you to marry his son?"

"Yes." It came out bitter. Tual seemed so reasonable, and yet he was the one who held the knife to her throat. If he really cared what happened to Lia, he would help her whether she tied herself to Mateo or not.

"I saw his name on a list of people involved in an excavation outside of town. Tual Montanne?"

Lia stood up and paced across the room, everything so tight inside her about to explode. "So?"

"I told you I'm not sure about hiding auras, but I *am* planning to leave here soon. It doesn't sound like your father is interested in abandoning Chaol, but I could help *you* get out of here. Your mother, your sister. Even your father, if you think he'd come around."

"Where would we go? The Warlord isn't going to give up hunting me."

"Lasei. Where Devoted can't go."

Lia stopped. Turned to stare at her friend. "That border has been closed since the shapeshifter wars. I don't even know what's on the other side of it, except for Urilia and some writer who had a lot more imagination than he had access to real women."

"The border's not closed if you have the money to get across." Knox looked around at the room, the ribbons, and the silky bedcover. The smile unfolding across his face was utterly foreign, utterly unlike the boy she'd known before. "Seems like someone in your family might."

"You heard my father. Mother is too sick to survive a trip."

"My partner is a Beildan healer."

"Your *partner*? The same one who is hiding you?"

A faint pink painted across Knox's cheeks. "She can take care of your mother. But we can't leave until we've finished something." He sat forward, his fingers digging into the bedspread as he looked up at her. "Your friend Tual has access to an excavation outside of Chaol. What are the chances you could get him to take you inside?"

CHAPTER 27

A War between Moons

Mateo sat on a bench in the manor courtyard watching waves crash high up on the cliff below him. Down the coast, little torch flares made tiny spots of orange in the evening's purple and gray where the dig site sat perched on the cliff. As Mateo squinted at it, his insides roiled like the waves below. How could he stop Van from taking everything he and his father had been searching for?

Tual hadn't been home all day, but he'd know what to do about the director's threats. Breathing in hurt as Mateo switched his gaze to where Jaxom had risen, the moon mottled black, gray, and red. The ghost of his brother moon, Castor, was bluish and angry above him in the sky, the two aligned for the night. Story went that the scholar god Castor was jealous that his sister, Calsta, had seen fit to hang him so much farther away than his brother, Jaxom, and they fought whenever their paths crossed, making the sea jump its shores. It was their fault the waves were so high.

It was their fault people were extra worried about shapeshifters in their midst.

Everyone knew wars between gods were bad luck. Though it

happened only once or twice every decade, Jaxom always won when he crossed paths with Castor, blocking the higher moon's blue light. That didn't stop their devotees from brawling in the streets. Jaxom was the patron of warriors, and Castor that of scholars, so the fights were, perhaps, a little unbalanced.

Mateo sucked in a breath as a spot on Jaxom's red-and-black surface suddenly swirled with white and blue, almost like smoke from a salpowder explosion. The sudden change chilled Mateo, the gods and their wars too large and too far away for him to understand. Everyone knew that when Jaxom changed color, the warrior god was about to launch some kind of attack. Even if the god did mean for it to warn off Castor's icy glare, it would be the Commonwealth that saw the effects in a few days, leftover bits of the gods' war streaking across the night sky like hundreds of burning arrows. . . .

And Tual would probably want Mateo to stand out here with Lia when the streaks painted a map between the stars. As if staring up at godly carnage next to a killer would be romantic.

She'd be here soon. She'd promised.

Threatened, really.

A lantern flickered to life inside the house. Mateo lurched up from his bench and threw open the door, wondering how his father had managed to sneak in past him. He ran to his father's office and burst through the door, Tual jumping back with a hiss. Quickly covering his surprise with a smile, Tual waved the still-lit tinder he'd used to light the lantern. "What are you doing here? I thought you were meeting Lia."

"Something happened at the dig. Things were stolen. *Burned.* Director Van thinks I'm a shapeshifter, and he's going to tell all the angry people in Chaol if I don't get him into the burial chamber soon. He's *not following proper archeological protocols.*" Mateo dragged in a breath when he ran out of air. "Father, I think he knows we're after caprenum. I think he might be after it too."

"Wait, slow down." Tual set the smoking tinder in a dish on his desktop, then sat in his leather chair. "Artifacts were stolen from the dig?"

"The workers think it was spirits of the dead, and apparently, there's a *plague* in Chaol? And some kind of 'ghost attack' at the governor's house? Everyone's ready to cry shapeshifter, and Van is going to point them toward me."

"Ghost attack?" Tual sat back, putting his feet up on his desk and crossing them at the ankles. "I do know about the plague. I was in the Fig Cay today, and it's like nothing I've ever seen before. I'm going back in the morning to study it further." Tual frowned. "And you say Van suspects you. Because of everything you've found?"

"He practically threatened to turn me over to the magistrate."

"That's a pretty good play, you know?" Tual tapped a finger against his lips. "People are already wary of aukincers, why not just confirm their bias? Very well done indeed." He took off his hat and set it on the desk. "But what would Van want with the burial chamber or caprenum? Hardly anyone knows of its existence, much less its value."

Mateo slumped into a chair. "Who else would need it except for another Basist? Or . . ." He blinked, sitting up a little straighter. "Or a shapeshifter? That sickness in the Fig Cay—you said it's like nothing you've ever seen. I have an episode every time I go to the dig. If shapeshifters feed on energy, and all of us touched by Calsta or the nameless god have extra . . ."

"Mateo—"

"I thought it was because I've been trying to use my energy down there." Mateo sprang up from his chair, hope rising in him like the explosion of smoke that had burst out from Jaxom above. "Devoted have fits just like this when their energy starts siphoning away from wasting sickness. What if Van is *taking* it?"

He paced the room, trying not to feel the deathly silence emanating from Tual. Mateo wanted it to be true, *wanted* to find a sky-cursed shapeshifter despite all the damage they'd done to Basists. Because if his episodes were caused by a shapeshifter, that meant they weren't part of his sickness.

It meant he wouldn't die. Not yet, anyway.

He'd have enough time for his father to melt the caprenum sword into whatever it was that would cure him, and he could be a real Basist. A real person. Not half of one, only one foot in life, the other sliding inexorably toward a black sky full of dead stars. "*Something* down there isn't right. Even the rocks feel wrong, like they're in pain somehow. If Van has made oaths to the nameless god that let him steal my energy—"

"Mateo, stop." Pulling his coat open, Tual took out his blacknut pipe. A little ceramic box came next, which he opened to smear a bit of the nutty paste into the bowl of his pipe. He extracted a bit of tinder and held it to the lantern's still flame, watching as it flickered to life before holding it to his pipe. "Even if, somehow, Van is a shapeshifter, we need to focus on the issues at hand: namely, getting caprenum and getting Lia." He puffed once, a cloud of smoke streaming from his lips. "Who thinks you're a Devoted, by the way. We should probably hold on to that as long as we can."

"Oh, you mean I *shouldn't* tell the girl who just killed a Rooster that we don't have as much in common as she thinks?" Mateo looked back toward the window. Where was she? She'd said she would come at dusk, and dark had already fallen.

Tual sat back in his chair again, chewing on his pipe stem. "Mateo, why do you think Lia ran away?"

"What do you mean? Who wouldn't want to, given the opportunity?"

"You know spiriters aren't allowed to let anyone touch or see them. . . ." Tual waited until Mateo nodded before blowing out a ring of smoke. "Unless their numbers grow so small that more little spiriters need to be made."

Mateo stopped in the doorway, turning to look at his father. "Devoted don't—"

"No, Devoted don't. Calsta doesn't give power to those who divide their attention from her. I can't think that all Devoted from the beginning of time have lived their lives that way, though. How else do we explain so much Devoted blood in the population, Calsta's little minions cropping up throughout the Commonwealth without any obvious Devoted ancestors."

"You mean people don't get magic from being touched by the gods?" Mateo frowned.

"Some do, probably. But I think the chances are much higher if they have drops of magical blood in them. And the Warlord knows it." Tual puffed on his pipe, then pointed it at Mateo, blowing out a stream of smoke. "In fact, all this seclusion nonsense seems awfully convenient for the leader of our country—keeping Devoted from getting married and having families. Any Devoted with divided loyalty from Calsta is a Devoted who might have divided loyalty from the Warlord. Every person with Calsta's power in the Commonwealth is directly under her control. Either that or hunting down the ones who *aren't* under her control. But with wasting sickness, she doesn't have the resources to go find all the little children manifesting Calsta's power."

"Great. Fine. What does that have to do with Lia killing one of her own people today?"

Tual's heavy brows folded together. "I think you noticed Ewan, the other Devoted? He's missing his aura, the same way Lia is."

"So?"

"Do you think they both came here on the Warlord's business that way?" Tual waited until Mateo was looking at him. "He knew that Lia had been set aside by the Warlord for some of those little Devoted babies."

Mateo's stomach twisted, because he could see what was coming. He could see it and he didn't want to look. "You think he . . ."

Tual shrugged, looking out at the sea.

"You don't know." Mateo swallowed, leaning against the doorway, suddenly not sure he could bear all his own weight. The wild look in Lia's eye came back to him again, the way she'd fought after the Rooster had said all he wanted was to take her back, but he shook the thought away. His father could come up with whatever theories he wanted, but Mateo knew what his father really was after—he wanted Mateo to go along with his plan. "Even if Ewan did try something, Lia ran away. She *got* away and she probably left him less a few fingers and toes. She's all right."

"I suppose you could put it that way, though I wouldn't, personally." Tual shook his head. "She's had a lifetime of people telling her what to do with no option to refuse. Even her auroshe—the one thing she did like, if you haven't noticed from talking to her—was gone from the governor's stables as of this morning. Probably sent to the fights, since auroshes turn into berserking monsters when their owners disappear, unless someone new manages to bond with them. I had to send that dead Rooster's auroshe there myself today. Everything Lia knows and loves has been taken away from her. Perhaps bear that in mind when next you speak."

"She's not the helpless little victim you are making her out to be, Father." Rebellion boiled up inside Mateo. "Her life hasn't been so different from what we—"

"No, it's *very* far from the life you've led, Mateo. You are sick, and that is difficult, I know. But we're here, free to look for the medicine that will cure you. We're going to be all right. You've gone to the best schools, had food, water, nice places to sleep, and the ugliest clothing I've ever seen in my life to wear." A trace of a smile turned up his lips, and Mateo couldn't help but smile back. A smile that vanished when his father continued. "You have a choice to love or not love Lia. Your body doesn't belong to a goddess who feels free to share it around."

Mateo swallowed his anger, though it didn't want to go. It burned him down to his stomach, and he couldn't help but wonder why they had to compare hardships at all. So Lia had run from something terrible. It didn't change the fact that living under a cloud of inevitable death hadn't exactly been easy for him, either. Were the two even something you could stack up next to each other?

"Lia's outside." Tual looked down at his pipe, gesturing half-heartedly toward his window and the fields beyond it, the long-stemmed crop beyond their gates shuffling in the wind. "I know staying in Chaol linked to a girl you met only a few days ago isn't ideal. But the lives we have been given don't contain as many options as others. We have to take what's in front of us." He looked Mateo in the eye. "It could be so, so much worse, son."

Mateo reached out with his mind to find Lia's aura before he went outside, glad despite what his father had said that it was a sad, diminished echo of what it should have been. He sighed and opened the door. No one would be clawing their way into his mind uninvited that night.

Lia was dismounting just inside the gate. As he walked toward her, she stroked her mare's neck and laughed when the horse swiveled her head to gum Lia's fingers. The scarf was still tight over her nose, mouth, and forehead.

"Good evening." Mateo gave a beggar's imitation of a bow when she stepped past the horse to greet him, though he doubted she would know the difference. "Where are we off to? I assume I'll need my horse?"

Lia fidgeted with the horse's reins. "We're going to the governor's mansion."

"We're . . . what?" The moons overhead were midclash, washing Lia's face in red and blue light as she stared at her boots, eyes flicking back and forth as if she were composing a poem of hatred to recite for him. "Why?"

"Because Vivi is there, and I want him. My auroshe. You can get inside, and I can't."

Mateo's stomach turned to lead, his mind going to Bella in the stall behind him. If someone told him she'd been sold off to fight for her life while people watched, he'd . . .

He'd do *something*. Writing a very angry letter didn't seem quite enough.

Mateo reached for her horse's reins and started toward the stable. "Vivi isn't at the governor's mansion."

Lia darted forward, blocking his way. "I'm not arguing about this. I want him, and the only way—"

"He isn't there. My father just told me." Mateo stopped, his heart beating sad, heavy thumps. "He said they probably took him to the fights."

It was awful, watching her scarf blow in and out against her mouth, her eyes tear, her hand pressing against her cheek. "That's not . . . they *wouldn't* . . ." The sparks in Lia's aura weakly spat and stirred around her head. But then her chin snapped up. "The fights are probably in the Sand Cay, or maybe the Fig? One of the lower ones. We're going to get him."

"What are you going to do, stick your head in every door across two gang-infested islands?"

She took the reins back from him, stuck a foot in her stirrup, and mounted the horse. "I'll wait while you get Bella."

"I guess . . . my father might know where they are." Mateo turned uncertainly toward the house. "I'll ask for you, if you like, but after that—"

"You're coming."

"You need *me* to spring your monster horse out of a violent killer gambling ring? Me?" He put his arms out, giving her a spin so his jacket flared around him. It was green and the perfect texture to catch moonlight, so at least he looked nice. "Think very hard about this, Lia. I'm an *artist*."

"Then you can draw mean caricatures and pretend to get drunk to distract everyone while I get Vivi."

"Caricatures? What exactly do you think happens at auroshe fights, Lia Seystone?"

"Are you telling me *you* know?"

Mateo tried not to fume when she shooed him back toward the house.

Tual was waiting at the door, clearly having been eavesdropping on the whole conversation. "On the far side of the Ily Canal. East side under the private docks. Take the skiff, follow the green fairy lights." He raised his voice, waiving to Lia. "He could use a little trouble! Bring him back in one piece, please!"

"I hate you so much right now," Mateo growled.

Mateo tried to hold his balance against the way the skiff lurched this way and that, the trade road looming overhead as they rowed up the Ily Canal. Lia pulled the oars like a dockworker, assuming everyone in the boat knew how to swim. Regret for his moment of weakness in thinking about how Lia might feel missing her auroshe was firm in Mateo's chest.

"So, I've been thinking." Lia's voice was unnervingly cheery.

Mateo looked around to see if there was a whirlpool handy that she meant to push him into. "About something other than your blood-thirsty monster horse?"

Lia's laugh rang out, and Mateo sat back a bit, wondering if she'd been at her father's malt before riding over to the manor. Hopefully that was it, because it meant her aura would stay gone. "No. You're studying to be an archeologist, right?"

"Yes?" They rounded the edge of the Sand Cay, the city wall looming tiredly above them.

"This dig you came for must be really important." Lia's voice was stilted, as if she was trying to sound eager but didn't know how to lie very well. "It was mostly undisturbed, wasn't it? Early shapeshifter?"

"One of the few shapeshifter tombs ever found, the only one intact.

There are some lights up here." Mateo leaned out, swearing inside his head when his fingers began to tremble. He still wasn't back to normal after mucking around in the dig all afternoon. He hadn't collapsed this time, but his head still rang with the wrongness of the place. "There's the first dock."

Lia glanced over her shoulder, adjusting their trajectory with one oar. "I'd love to see it if you can take me. Most shapeshifter things were destroyed after the first Warlord started striking the nameless god's name from records, weren't they? Tombs. Temples. I hear there are traps?"

No. Not you, too. The one thing he'd actually liked about Lia so far was that she'd put his father in his place as surely as she'd done to him. Mateo jumped from the boat almost before they were close enough to the dock, the skiff jerking out from under his feet. Stumbling, he grabbed one of the pylons and immediately regretted it, sticky tar coming away on his hands. "Stop it, Lia."

"Stop what?" She brought the boat in close and threw him the mooring line.

Mateo put out a sticky hand to help her out of the skiff, but she didn't take it, jumping onto the dock herself. "Stop pretending you are nice and that you're interested in the things that I'm interested in."

"I didn't say I was interested in—"

"You're not. I know. So don't playact about wanting to see the excavation or that you're interested in archeology beyond destroying any evidence that anything came before the Commonwealth. All you Devoted are the same." Mateo started down the dock, the whole length of it bristling with boats. Under the swell of water noise and the chatter from the higher docks built up above the water level, he thought he heard a muted, feral screech. "I think we're here. Now how do we get in?" The tremble in his hands had turned to a shake, and his heart had begun to beat in triplicate, each third beat aching in his chest. He shouldn't have looked for Lia's aura before going out to find her. It was a stretch, what with whatever Van was doing to him at the dig.

Lia's voice took on a much more familiar salty edge. "My mother is dying," she said.

"My father's helping her recover." He offered her his arm because that's what gentlemen did.

She didn't take it. "I want to be here when she's better. Not back at the seclusion trying to forget I have a family at all."

"Maybe this way?" He followed the glow of green lanterns to a set of stairs that seemed to go directly down into the ground. Shivers of anticipation ran up his arms as he descended, the walls turning to glass. This place had been made by Basists before the shapeshifter wars, like all the glass tunnels crisscrossing the cays. "Did my father get to you? Maybe he threatened you on that chummy ride you took together earlier? Or he wrote you a scary note, or—"

Lia put her hands up as if in supplication. "I need you to understand—"

"Understand what?" Mateo wasn't in the mood to be supplicated. Chatter from the bottom of the stairs filled his ears. "Didn't you *leave* because the Warlord tried to match you up with Ewan? And now you're letting my father do the same thing?"

They turned a corner and suddenly there were people, *so many people* all lined up in their not-quite finery. The room went back about twenty feet to where an open arch led to another room, the space from Mateo to the arch squished tight with tarnished silver collars, limp feathers stuck in khonin knots, and the jarring smell of raw malt. Beyond the arch Mateo caught a glimpse of a sunken, sawdust-strewn ring.

He turned to help Lia down and saw that the few visible inches of Lia's face had gone dead white. Her palms went to her cheeks, the scarf pulling sideways, so he got a good glimpse of brownish-red freckles clustered across her cheekbones and down the bridge of her nose.

She took his arm, her fingers gripping the crook of his elbow too tight, all fingernails and bones. "What exactly do you know about Ewan?"

"Nothing." He pulled her through the crowd to where a man stood checking a list of some kind. "But it does seem kind of odd you'd let my father bully you into running from him to me. Especially when I wasn't offering."

Her silence was awful, as if he'd broken something inside her, and the aftermath of it left him wishing he hadn't spoken.

He tried to shunt the regret aside, tried not to see the way she was still pressing a hand to her cheek, all the words his father had said bombarding him. *You have a choice to love or not love Lia. Your body doesn't belong to a goddess who feels free to share it around.* It left him grasping for an apology, for anything that might give her an inch of solid ground to stand on rather than pulling it out from under her.

But then someone from the crowd shoved into them, knocking Mateo. Lia pulled her arm away just in time to let him fall. Then left him there in the middle of the floor. It was the first time Mateo thought maybe he'd deserved it.

"So sorry," the man who'd bumped Mateo blustered down at him, looking like an overripe tomato, only with an unconvincing mustache. A single khonin knot sat just behind his ear, the rest of his hair twisted into a simple braid. He held out an unsteady hand. "Up you go, little man. You just got here? I hear they've got some fresh blood for the later rounds. Not those old nags from Borlouth."

"Right. Not interested in nags." Mateo allowed the man to pull him up but pushed his hands away when he produced a handkerchief to dust Mateo off. Anger writhed inside him just behind the regret, and it was funny both to feel sorry for Lia and to want to shove her into the channel for going against their plan not to humor any more talk of the ridiculous marriage idea.

He forced his knees to unbend and started to walk, only to have the overripe man pull him back. "Not that way, son. Come on, let me make it up to you for pushing you over." He snaked a hand up his sleeve, scratching at his arm, and Mateo spied a patch of red, flaky skin peeking out from under his cuff.

Steeling himself, Mateo refrained from wiping his hands on his coat and followed, the tomato man looking both ways before taking him to a disguised break in the wall that Mateo would never have been able to find on his own. At least, not without magic. "Where does this go?" he asked.

"Down underneath, where the real cream watches. Your lady friend coming?" The high khonin jerked his head toward Lia, who had made her way through the arch that led to the ring. Her head twisted around when she got there, looking back toward the assembled guests with what Mateo thought might have been rage. It was hard to tell under that scarf.

Mateo peered into the opening, the draft from below ruffling his curls. They had come to find an auroshe, not bet on one, but maybe there was a way to access the pens from below.

The tomato man flapped an arm in Lia's direction to get her attention, then jogged Mateo's shoulder. Sighing, Mateo joined him in waving until Lia finally saw and began picking her way through the crowd toward them, a scowl on her face that Mateo could see even through those layers of silk.

"You've money, yes?" The man's breath made the inside of Mateo's nose burn, but he nodded, hoping his face held some kind of compliant smile. He'd brought a few silver rounds just in case he had to bet, or possibly bribe captors out of a hostage situation.

"Good, good. You look very clean, my boy. Latch on to your lady and let's go." The man barely waited until Lia had made it to them before grabbing Mateo by the shoulders and dragging him into the opening. On the other side he pulled open a heavy, brass-banded door and picked up a lantern, revealing a long, narrow hallway that cut deeper into the rock. One wall was glass, a ragged school of bioluminescent fish swimming in the murky water on the other side, giving the place an unnerving greenish cast. The inside wall, ceiling, and floor were all slick stone, and the awful malt reek of the man's breath was replaced with blood, unwashed animal, and misery. A guard stepped out of the shadows long enough to look their guide up and down before letting them past.

Lia slipped in next to Mateo when a curdling sort of squeal wafted up from below. Her hand clutched at his arm, and Mateo couldn't help but clutch back. He didn't much like auroshes, but the thought of Bella down there left his heart with something new to boil over. The tomato man gestured for them to follow him when the hall split. Mateo could see hulking shapes in the dark down one path, but the high khonin took them the other way, leading them to a cozy little room crammed with tables and booths where people spoke in hushed tones over fried bread and drinks.

"You do realize," Lia hissed in his ear, "that your father threatened to have my entire family *killed* if I don't at least try to make something work between us. And that he'll hand me straight back to Ewan if I don't do what he wants."

"My father wouldn't . . ." But Mateo couldn't say the words. Tual was already looking for a replacement son to sit in Mateo's chair once the sickness took him. And it hadn't been a dance across a ballroom that got them into the Warlord's inner circle, either. Tual Montanne was a loving father, a sympathetic, dynamic man full of smiles and jokes until he wasn't. Mateo pushed the thoughts away, trying to focus his blurry eyes in the darkness of the room. "I fail to see what any of this has to do with me." Anger had taken hold of him again, each word feeling heavier and dirtier than the last, plunking out of his mouth and leaving a coppery tang on his tongue. They were easier than the image of her bloodless face from his words before. "I'm sorry your father decided to try assassinating the governor, but I don't really feel the need to assassinate myself by going along with any of this."

"I didn't want to braid a bridal wreath, you idiot. I just need you to help me buy some time. Help me make your father believe we're going along with his plan so he'll protect my family from the Warlord. If I have to go back . . ." She swallowed, looking down. "Mateo, if I have to go back, Ewan—"

"You don't have to tell me." Mateo shook his head, because that wasn't quite right. "I don't *want* you to tell me."

"Why, because it will make you realize there are other people who exist on this planet who aren't *you*? I wasn't *planning* to run away, Mateo. But then . . ." She swallowed, her voice hitching. "I . . . I *froze*."

Mateo watched the people as they walked by, focusing on a beaded scarf, a pair of leather boots with jeweled buckles, some battered and fried squid on a plate, anywhere that wasn't Lia. "Could we stick with you manipulating me into helping you find your bloodthirsty horse thing for right now?"

"Right. Perfect. Let's do that." Each of Lia's words splintered with fury. "You go with . . . whoever that is." She jabbed a finger at the high khonin leading them through the tables. "I'll look for Vivi." One second she was there and the next she was gone, leaving Mateo with the overripe-tomato man who wanted to be sure there was money in his purse.

Sweat beaded under his shirt, soaking him. *If I come out of this with a stained shirt and coat, I'm going to—*

"Here we are!" The man led him to a booth. There were heavies with scuffed armor plates sewn to their tunics just outside, all with a scraggly black feather stuck into their braids, which probably meant something, but Mateo didn't know what. Inside the booth, a little man was hunched over a pile of silver, his eyes yellowed and his fingers long and spindly like spider legs.

"Reathe?" He arranged the little pile of silver coins into a tower in front of him. "I thought you were cleaned out for the night."

"This one wants to look the beasts over, Bastion. Give them a good inspection before he chooses." Reathe presented Mateo to the man with a bow that befitted a very low stable boy. "Come on now, I know you can get us back there."

"Not without money." Bastion sniffed, wiping his nose with a finger.

Mateo shuddered. But Reathe's drunken, almost puppylike hope was too much. He sighed, reaching into his pocket for a single silver round, and slapped it on the table in what he thought was a very rakish manner. Bastion merely slid it away from Mateo, flipped it up from the table, gave it a flick to hear it ring, then stowed it in his money bag. He stood, gesturing back toward the hallway they'd come from. "This way."

"Oh, *I* don't need to see them." Mateo's mind caught up with what exactly it was he'd just paid for. Lia would be in with the auroshes, and Mateo didn't like the look of Bastion's nails, much less the look of the men hulking by the doorway, their battered armor glinting in the candlelight. "I mean, not right now. Maybe later, when I've had a chance to—"

"You *want* to see them early in the night, son," Reathe broke in. "I got you down here, and I'll lend my expertise, of course, in choosing which one to back. We'll split our winnings—I'll only take seventy percent, and you're welcome." His brow scrunched. "Where'd your little lady go?"

"She . . . saw someone she knew." Mateo cleared his throat, trying to breathe through his mouth at the sudden onslaught of malt breath. He turned to Bastion. "I heard something about new blood in the stables. I'll put my round on—"

"Does the new one have one horn or two?" Reathe burst in. "Branded or straight from the Devoted? Those Devoted beasts have practically forgotten how to fight another of their kind. . . ." His voice took an abruptly grumpy turn. "Calsta burn it, we *paid* to see the beasts, and I—"

"*I* paid to see them." Mateo clutched his drawing satchel to his stomach. "And I just realized I haven't brought my scented handkerchief, so perhaps you could just return my silver round—"

"Listen to your friend, son." Bastion sniffed again and started down the hall.

"Well, all right, I guess." Mateo tried to keep his voice from becoming shrill when Reathe grabbed hold of his sleeve and towed him back through the smoky cubbies toward the auroshe stalls. Lia was in there doing Calsta knew what, and Mateo couldn't imagine what would happen if Bastion found her. "Hang on, I think I know someone over . . ." He tried pointing into the formless gloom of money and illegal betting, but Reathe hardly broke his gait, dragging Mateo after Bastion past the two guards standing to either side of the hall. How had Lia gotten past *them*? They both seemed to have their throats intact.

Mateo pretended to trip. "Oh dear, I think I've scuffed my shoe!" But Reathe towed Mateo into the long hall beyond the guards with a loud hiccup that smelled like onions and malt. The hallway opened into a narrow room, both walls edged with iron bars, the awful smell of blood and unkempt animal thick in the air.

They were stalls, each with an angry auroshe staring at Mateo from behind the bars. Reathe dropped Mateo's arm, striding deeper into the cages, but Mateo couldn't make himself move until the creature in the cage to his left lunged at the bars, long tongue licking toward his arm. He jerked away, trying to stand exactly in the middle of the space between cages, where the beasts couldn't reach him.

Where was Lia? Mateo threw his aurasight as far as he could into the stalls, despite the way it made his knees wobble, feverishly looking for the spiriter. Her aurasparks were no more than fifty feet away. Only a few more steps and Bastion would see her.

"Calsta above," Mateo said a touch too loudly, hoping she would hear. "Is it stuffy in here or is it just me?"

Reathe hardly looked back, his eyes measuring horns and fore-locks and tooth length or whatever it was he wanted to see as he followed their guide. Bastion. Who was muttering the exact wrong thing: "Someone's upset my ladies. Those sky-cursed guards aren't worth half what I pay them."

Lia's aurasparks darted about, but before Mateo could see where she went, his magic winked out and threatened to take him with it.

Bastion stopped dead at the partition that led to the next row of stalls. It was dark on the other side, the gloom skittering with little movements. "Only way out's into the ring or through me," he shouted into the dimness beyond the partition. "Were you hoping for a knife in the gut or a horn through your chest?"

Mateo hurried to catch up, his skin prickling as the beasts to either side of him knickered and twisted to watch him as he passed. He stumbled when a horn sliced between bars toward him, his wobbly knees almost dumping him to the ground. "Wait." He grabbed for Bastion, who had pulled out a knife. "I think maybe this might be some kind of misunderstanding."

A person stepped out of the shadows to face them, only it wasn't Lia. It was a young man, embroidered neck to waist and malted up enough that he was leaning against one of the cage doors, the auroshe inside making frenzied attempts to bite his hand through the bars.

He burped. "Hello there. Wasn't I just talking to you?" He turned himself in a circle. "I was just talking to you. But you were a girl."

Mateo cleared his throat, trying to look around without making it seem as if he was looking around. Where had Lia gone?

"If you like your head attached to your neck, you'd best get out of here." Bastion adjusted his grip on the knife.

"I do like my neck." The high khonin stretched up his chin and framed the body part in question with his hands. "Just look at it. Rosalyn was saying just yesterday . . ."

Reathe pushed past Mateo to stand in front of the last auroshe cage, ignoring the only half-intelligible argument blossoming between Bastion and the high khonin. "This is the new one, isn't it?" He peered into the darkness behind the bars, muttering to himself, "Double horns, and he looks healthy enough. He—whoops." Reathe darted back as a horn jutted through the bars, barely missing him. "He hasn't been here long enough to be mopey."

Mateo turned around slowly, eyeing the stalls. Surely Lia hadn't gone into one of them to hide. But there wasn't anywhere else she could have gone.

A muted auroshe squeal filtered in from somewhere beyond the end of the enclosed stalls, and a sliver of light appeared on the floor as if a door had been pushed open by the wind.

"That door shouldn't be . . ." Bastion left the high khonin, who was now sniggering into his elbow, to stare down the flood of lantern light and the series of grates beyond the door. "Did someone go out there? There's a fight happening right now."

A sudden roar of applause flooded the room, jeers and screams of laughter skewering Mateo in the stomach.

He turned and ran back the way they'd come. Because for a moment, with just one flicker of power, he'd seen Lia's aura. And it was in the ring.

Spider Milk

Grating snapped shut across the doorway before Lia could back out of the ring. Pulling at it, she could see the door inside the grate still hanging open, but the barriers weren't meant to be opened from her side. She put her back to the grate, her heart deflating in her chest. Across the arena, two auroshes were screaming at each other, one on the ground, the other stabbing its horn into the first's tender underside.

Her eyes darted up, the too-smooth, Basist-made arena a reminder of days before shapeshifters. People hung over the railings at the top, some screaming at her to run, some to fight, some that they'd help her, while others laughed, crowing that they wanted to see what happened next.

The standing auroshe—a beautiful silver paint with broken teeth—pulled its horn from the downed auroshe's side, nostrils flaring as it swiveled around to stare at Lia. It had an odd, unbalanced look, one horn dripping red, the other broken off near its skull. It took a curious step toward Lia.

"Get out of the ring!" an onlooker shouted.

Lia rattled the grate as the creature's muzzle wrinkled in a snarl.

Vivi would have torn apart anything that came into his space except for Lia herself, or maybe a hostler bearing food. But Vivi had good manners for an auroshe, while this one had been abused, starved—

"Open the grate!" Lia yelled. She'd been talking to someone inside until a man with a knife had started toward them, sending her through the door. Dodging a knife sounded a lot better than dodging an auroshe's horn. "Let me out!"

The door beyond the grate pulled shut in answer.

The creature was now zigzagging toward Lia, pink foam dripping from its bared teeth. Lia's sweaty fingers went to the knots in her scarf, but she couldn't make herself pull it off, so she undid her belt and stepped out of her overskirt, leaving her underskirts bare in the yellow torchlight. Someone in the crowd catcalled, sending a torrent of laughter through the arena.

Whipping its tail, the auroshe bolted forward, but Lia was ready, holding the overskirt out and darting from behind it. The auroshe crashed into the wall, its one intact horn taking the brunt of the charge, snapping off to a jagged nub.

"Lia!" a voice called from above. "Try to reach!"

Lia's eyes darted up to find Mateo hanging over the railing, his hands open as if he thought she could jump into his arms. *Stupid, useless boy. At least he's trying to help, I guess.* Maybe if Lia had had help from Calsta, she could have jumped to him, but Calsta was, as she had been since Lia touched Ewan, silent. Lia ran along the wall looking for cracks in the slick surface, but there was nothing to find. Not even the spot the auroshe had crashed into was marked, as if whatever the Basists had used to make this place was indestructible.

The auroshe had recovered and was watching her closely, head tilted as it eyed the skirt trailing from her hand. Lia cursed inside her head. She wouldn't be able to use it the same way again. Auroshes were too smart.

"Here!" Mateo called, pulling something from around his shoulders and hanging it down toward her. His drawing satchel. "No, wait, look out!" he cried.

Lia turned just in time to dart out of the auroshe's way. The creature changed direction midcharge, snaking its head around to bite at Lia's legs. Lia kicked it under the chin, then spun to kick it again where the auroshe's jaw met its skull. The auroshe skittered backward with a hiss.

The only way to end this was to get close enough to touch the auroshe between the horns. That was how Devoted tamed auroshes and won their loyalty. It was a declaration of dominance that auroshes understood, a show of skill that proved they were worthy riders. No one had managed to claim Vivi from Lia after two years of trying. For this beast Lia would have to do it in one try with no help standing by. And with nothing from Calsta.

"Drop the satchel!" she yelled to Mateo. If only she could get to the creature's head, then—

Mateo let the bag go just as the auroshe charged again. Lia turned away, holding the skirt behind her like a cape as she bent her body forward. She flipped backward, tucking so she was out of the way when the auroshe's broken horn sliced through the skirt.

As Lia landed next to the creature, the skirt caught and she jerked the beast's head toward her, the thing's wide, bloody mouth snapping at her neck. Skirt wound around her arm, Lia yanked the auroshe's head toward her again, delivered one kick to the soft underside of its throat, then rolled into a second kick, which landed on its front knee. The auroshe reared above her, its cloven hooves cutting toward her. Lia rolled out of the way as the auroshe came down, biting up a mouthful of her underskirts.

Lia found her feet, but the thing jerked backward, dragging fast enough to pull her off-balance, though not so hard that the skirt tore. The auroshe watched her, its black eyes calculating.

"Lia! I'm coming—"

"You come down here and we both die, Mateo." Trying to control her breaths, Lia matched her steps to the auroshe's measured tread before the creature could pull her over, then threw her weight to the side. The auroshe lunged with her, letting go of her skirt.

Lia dove into a roll, changing her direction, then arched up into a flip that landed a heel kick just over the creature's eye.

The crowd screamed in appreciation.

Lia's insides twisted. These people were all here to watch a bloody fight, the poor auroshes with no choice but to provide one. Mateo was up there too, both too soft to have kept the auroshe master out of the stables for a few minutes and too hard to want to help Lia out of a difficult situation even when it would cost him *nothing*. And Vivi. She'd looked through all the stalls inside. Vivi wasn't here.

As the auroshe shook its head to shed Lia's overskirt, Lia leapt away from it and snatched up the satchel, slinging it over her shoulder. She wanted to scream. At the world. At these awful high khonins. At Mateo. At the auroshe she didn't actually want to hurt.

The creature came at her again. This time Lia dodged to the side, grabbed across the points of its shoulders, and flipped up onto its back. Rearing, the auroshe screamed.

Before the creature could roll, Lia pulled herself into a crouch on its withers and crawled forward so her weight was on its neck, forcing its head to dip toward the ground. Then she whipped the satchel off, looped the strap over the auroshe's head, and twisted it tight around its jagged mouth, trapping it closed.

Lia jumped off the creature's back before it could react. She wound the satchel strap around its mouth again, then tangled it on one of the auroshe's forelegs when it tried to rear. The auroshe screamed, stumbled, and went over.

Lia ran to the auroshe's head. Placing a hand between its broken horns, she breathed into its long, slitted nostrils. The thing went stock-still.

Just the way Vivi had.

"I'm sorry." She breathed again into its nostrils, pressing hard between its horns while she stroked its cheek. Auroshes were loyal creatures. Submissive even, if you could get close enough to show them you were worth following. Not many knew it. Not many had the skills to try even if they did know.

The auroshe lay frozen for a second longer, then all at once it relaxed, curling toward Lia to rest its nose against her knee.

She'd done it. Without Calsta's power.

The grate creaked open, and a man with a torch raised in front of him like a sword poked his head out. The auroshe twitched at the sight of flame but didn't move.

"What in Calsta's name have you done—" he started.

"And *that's* a true victory!" Mateo's voice rang out above. The man's head jerked up toward Mateo, who stood at the railing, his arms raised. "If you want to meet the warrior herself, she'll be outside, signing autographs. If you're lucky, we'll tell you when she'll be appearing next. . . ."

The man lowered the torch so it was between him and Lia. "You get up. Come with me."

Lia patted the auroshe's cheek and got to her feet, waiting while the creature slowly rose behind her. She undid the satchel strap around its mouth and leg, and it nosed her shoulder once when she rubbed a hand under its jaw. It had mites, poor thing.

Shrinking back, the man raised the torch even higher. "What are you, a dirt witch?"

Lia's fists clenched, and she could feel the man looking at the auroshe behind her as if it were her shadow—her true shape revealed.

A flurry at the grate caught her attention, Mateo spilling into the arena with the odd man who had brought them down to the lower level, his single khonin knot twisted behind his ear and a cloud of malt fumes hovering about him.

"I discovered this girl," he was slurring, his hands raised to the crowd. "I found her, I put her in the ring. I knew she'd win, and now at ten-to-one odds . . ."

Mateo ran to Lia, very obviously trying not to care about the auroshe looming just behind her. He grabbed her hand and thrust it up into the air with a cry of triumph. "The one and only lady brave enough to enter a ring with an untamed beast. Come back soon, and we'll have more tricks to show you!" Mateo tried to steer her toward the open grate.

Lia resisted, stroking the auroshe's cheek when it put its head down on her shoulder.

The high khonins hanging over the railings screamed and yelled. Lia hated all of them.

"She'll be great for business, don't you think, Bastion?" Mateo said, pulling at Lia's hand in earnest. "There are guards waiting for you just outside," he whispered into her ear. "We're going to have to run." He kept the smile pasted on for the man with the torch. "I'll send over a proposal, and we can talk about percentages." Pointing at her scarf, he grinned. "Nice touch, eh? So mysterious. People are lining up just to see her leave."

Lia pulled away, the auroshe flinching when the man with the torch took a step in its direction. She couldn't leave the poor thing here. "Can you mount without a saddle, or do you need a boost?" she murmured to Mateo.

"A *boost*? Lia, if you think—"

Lia spun around and vaulted onto the creature's back. "Which is it, Mateo?"

Mateo climbed up beside her, and Lia kicked the auroshe forward, letting it snap at the two men blocking the door to get them out of the way.

High khonins were flooding the cages, so Lia gave the auroshe its head. The creature rushed the crowd, scenting the fresh sea air above, sending the high khonins screeching in all directions to avoid its sharpened hooves. Mateo clung to Lia's back until they'd gotten past. The high khonins began to laugh and clap, and Lia felt Mateo sit up and wave to them as if it all had been some kind of stunt.

The auroshe didn't go the way they'd come in, but took a different hallway to another metal-grated door, the other side of it a Sand Cay alleyway. "Open it!" Lia called to the guard, who, in the face of a crowing auroshe, pushed open the grate and pressed himself against the wall.

On the other side, the auroshe practically danced, giving playful little leaps down the alley that made Lia want to laugh. When the auroshe threw its head back and crowed up at the night sky, Lia joined it, something inside her suddenly free.

When they got to the road, Mateo cleared his throat. "What's the plan now?" His voice was strained.

"You get off. Take the skiff back, and I'll . . ."

". . . find somewhere in your father's stables to hide this . . . thing?" Mateo shook his head behind her. "Take the trade road and try to look like a Devoted."

"Try?" Lia wanted to laugh and cry all at once. But no one challenged them when they got to the last dregs of the day's traffic, the trade gate looming ahead. It was closed.

Lia clenched her eyes shut. Father had said they were closing it at night because of *her*. "How do we—"

"Just keep riding," Mateo said.

When they got to the gate, he pulled open his satchel, which was still looped across Lia's shoulders, and extracted a few coins. "Official business," he said to the guard who came out of the gatehouse. "We'd appreciate it if you don't mention it around."

"I can't open the gate." The man scowled, but Lia could feel him fidgeting, pointedly not looking at the raggedy auroshe. He couldn't possibly believe they were official anything—Lia in an underskirt with most of her face covered, Mateo with his fancy boots, like a dandy who'd just found a new mistress.

"I could probably knock him unconscious before anyone else comes," Lia whispered. "We can go through the smaller gate the guards use."

"*What?* No." Mateo cleared his throat, then raised his voice to the guard again. "I think I've met you before, haven't I?" He dismounted and gave an overly flourished bow. "I guess I wasn't being exactly honest just now. This lady is the star of . . . well." He lowered his voice. "You haven't heard of the fights, have you?"

The guard's scowl deepened. "The fights? What did you do, steal one of the beasts?"

"No, she defeated it. She's the newest thing on the circuit. No more auroshes fighting each other, my friend—that's boring. This girl can subdue an auroshe with her bare hands. No weapons, even." Mateo sounded like a market hawker attempting to sell the guard a moldy wheel of cheese. "I could get you in. Front-row seats. Maybe even set your first bet, because I know you'll win."

The man squinted. "I *am* off tomorrow."

Lia's mouth fell open. Was it really so easy to bribe a guard in Chaol?

Her father had said the governor let the lower cays fend for themselves.

The auroshe's head jerked to the side at some loud laughter down the street. It shuffled its feet, and Lia began to worry it would bolt before any doors actually opened. "Mateo . . . ," she whispered.

"Perfect, then we'll see you there?" Mateo pulled himself back onto the auroshe, though Lia could feel the tense set to his muscles, as if he'd found himself astride a very large and hungry snake. "If you could just open the door, I'll get this girl—both these girls—to where she can rest."

The guard laughed, then went back to the gate and opened a

smaller one set right next to its gargantuan hinge. "At least a silver round on the table for me tomorrow night, you hear?"

Mateo dug a hand into the satchel once again and took out another coin. "You won't have to wait until tomorrow, friend."

And, just like that, they were past. No swords, no auroshe teeth, and no blood. Lia started laughing once they were through the gate and on the bridge to the mainland, the sea breeze threatening to push them into the river. "How did you do that?" she asked. "You did it back in the arena, too. They would have swarmed me and never let us go if you hadn't been there—you just started talking, and people listened instead of trying to stab you."

"Is that what you want to do when I talk? Stab me?"

"Usually."

He chuckled, swaying behind her. "Thanks for not letting this thing bite me when I got off. What are we going to do with it?"

"I think you were right about 'it' being a 'she.'" Lia gave the auroshe a fond pat on the neck, barely managing to pull the mare back from a table laden with raw cuts of pig. "I'm going to call her Rosie."

"Of course you are," Mateo sighed.

"She's got kind of a pinkish tint, don't you think? That's pretty rare." Lia leaned down to put her cheek against Rosie's neck. "And she's so placid. It's like she's relieved I found her, and now all she wants to do is go lie down somewhere. Like your little mare. Bella, right?"

She felt Mateo nod behind her as Rosie darted toward a donkey cart, the donkey letting out a bloodcurdling bray before Lia brought the auroshe to a halt.

"Placid. That's just what I was going to say."

"In need of some training, sure. But she's had a hard life. The fact that she hasn't tried to eat you yet is actually quite commendable." Lia tried not to be too amused when he stiffened behind her. But the joke faded almost before she'd finished saying it. How could she train Rosie? How could she even keep Rosie? She was leaving.

The elation of getting away died inside her. She'd gone to the fights to get Vivi, and Vivi hadn't been there. What now?

She was supposed to be persuading Mateo to show her around the tomb so she could map it for Knox. Then she and her family could leave. Be free. Hugging her arms around Rosie's neck, Lia tried to hold back the tears that were suddenly burning in her eyes. She'd be free, but Vivi wouldn't be. He'd be killed. Sent to the fights. Maybe another Devoted would bond with him, but even that felt like a future she couldn't stomach.

"Are you all right?" Mateo's voice was too quiet, as if he wasn't sure he really wanted to ask.

"I think I ruined your satchel," Lia said, and sniffed. "I'd get you a new one, but then your father might think it's a sign that he should start choosing flowers for our bridal wreaths."

Mateo laughed again. "I have this rule against asking people who can take down an auroshe with their bare hands about paying for things they ruin."

Lia looked up into the sky, trying not to feel small. If Vivi wasn't at the governor's house or the fights, what had Ewan done with him? "I thought the auroshe master was going to torch me right there in the ring."

"People like something new. Something impossible." Mateo shifted behind her. "It was pretty impressive, what you did in there. Terrifying, sure. But impressive."

"You could have just let the auroshe gut me, and all this talk about marriage would be over. I wouldn't have been able to get to her head without your satchel."

"If that's your version of a thank-you, then you are very welcome. We make a good team." He bristled when she stifled a chuckle, but he thought it was mostly show. "You *just said*—"

"Yes. You're right. We're a good team. You can be my weapons handler anytime. Next time bring me a sword, would you?"

"I'm assuming there was no sign of Vivi down there?" Mateo gave her scarf a tug. "Um, this is coming undone."

Lia's heart skipped a beat, her hands rushing to the blue silk and finding curls spilling out from where a knot had come loose. She rewrapped the ends of her scarf a little too hurriedly, her hair pulling tight against her scalp. "Thanks. And no, he wasn't there."

"You know," he said, "if Vivi didn't get sold off to the fights, that means we have a mystery on our hands here. How are we going to figure out where he really is?"

Lia's fingers tangled in the ends of her scarf as she finished tying it. "We?"

"And I suppose it wouldn't be *so* inconvenient to take you to the dig. Maybe. Only if you're actually a tiny bit interested, though. I'd like to see you try one of those flips against Patenga's traps."

A smile bloomed under Lia's scarf before she could stop it. She turned as best she could, the worst of the crowds having given way to fields, so there wasn't as much for Rosie to attack. "You'll help me? You're going to be *nice*?"

His eyes skittered to the side, then slowly slid up to meet her gaze. "You know I'm sick, right?"

"It was a little hard to miss after your episode in the marketplace."

"Right, well, it seems like we've only got a few days left between us, and you're a pretty good fighter. I already said I'd rather we were on the same side, and I . . . can see where you're coming from with the pretending-to-go-along-with-it stuff. And there's actually something you *could* help me with at the dig."

Something she could help with, like an exchange? Lia let that sit, breathing in deep as if suddenly, for the first time in years, her lungs were clear. "All right."

When they got back to the cliff house, Mateo pointed to a little path that led to the beaches below, and they rode down. The waves left barely enough black sand for Rosie to walk across, making her skip and twist.

"Here." He pointed to a cave that drilled back into the rocks. "No one else comes down here and . . . I can feed her, I guess. Until we come up with something else? You can come too and we'll call it romantic walks on the beach."

"I like the idea of a romantic walk that involves carting raw, bloody meat down a cliff." Lia dismounted but held on to Rosie's mane until Mateo had gotten off. "Come here."

Mateo cleared his throat, edging back. "I'd rather stay away from the toothy end of that thing, if you don't mind."

"Come here." Lia grabbed his arm and hauled him over, taking his palm and pressing it between Rosie's horns. The auroshe's eyes glazed, then she sighed and looked lovingly up at the two of them.

"See, now she won't bite you. Probably. She should be able to find her own food, so you don't need to feed her."

"Not . . ." Mateo looked back up the cliffs toward his house.

"Fish, not people." Lia laughed. "But you'll keep an eye on her until I figure out what to do?"

"Of course I will." He smiled, not quite looking at the auroshe.

It would have to be enough. It *was* enough. A surprise, coming from Mateo, but he'd been full of surprises all night.

Mateo looked out into the waves, his nose wrinkling. "The marriage part of all this *is* a ruse, right? You don't secretly want to marry me for my beautiful coats? I wouldn't blame you."

There were a thousand jokes Lia could have cracked, a thousand laughs they could have had, but Lia wasn't ready to laugh about this. Not yet. "It's only until the Warlord leaves." Really, only until she got inside the excavation compound. After she bled Mateo of any information he could give her, and Knox did . . . whatever Knox was going to do at the dig site. Then Lia and her family would be gone, out of reach for Tual and the Warlord both, and none of this would matter. "We'll have to fake my death or something so your father doesn't report me to the Warlord the minute we break things off."

"As long as it involves narmaidens and lots of pity presents sent to me from the high khonins here in Chaol." Mateo smiled again, and it was oddly attractive, his thin face alight. He held out a hand as if he wanted to shake on it.

It was naked, no gloves, no nothing. Lia steeled herself, wondering what it was Calsta was hoarding when she forced her spiriters to refrain from touching skin. Whatever it was, Lia wanted to keep it all inside, never give a tiny bit of it away again.

But when she touched Mateo's palm, all she felt was rough skin. She blinked down at their hands, wondering how his wasn't as smooth and preened as the rest of him. Mateo noticed her surprise. "You didn't expect me to have calluses. No one ever does."

"I guess not." Lia smiled. Back when she'd been allowed to shake hands, no one had expected her to have calluses either.

Before the sun was properly peeking out from the horizon, Anwei rose from her bed and went to the loose floorboards in the herb room. Gulya wouldn't wake for at least another hour, so Anwei pulled out her secret jar, thick inside with gauzy web. Gamtooth spinners enjoyed the dark.

Shuddering, Anwei pushed the jar down the workbench so she didn't accidentally touch it, then scanned the other jars in her hidden treasure trove, inhaling slightly to find hints of flaring red between the browns and greens. Bright yellow spiky leaves of barin, orange nalitria flowers, and black solomen roots. All deadly. After pulling out the jar of the knobbly, dirt-encrusted solomen, Anwei went to the table, laid out her tools, and put on a pair of thin leather gloves.

Something in the next room scraped against the stone floor. Anwei stilled, listening. Someone was in the shop.

Opening the solomen jar's clamp with a flick of her fingers, Anwei turned toward the door. The roots had been steeping long enough to make a base for the gamtooth serum she'd promised Knox, but in its current state, the liquid would burn any low-life thief or . . . Anwei's brow furrowed. Devoted? Ghost? Entire company of Trib riders looking for their missing lizard wrangler?

Shapeshifter?

Her hands paused as she remembered Knox's question from the night they stayed in Gretis. *How were you planning to do it? Kill a shapeshifter?* Would poison hurt him? Arrows, knives?

When the door opened, the budding sunlight flashed across two khonin knots and a hair stick with Falan's lily. Noa.

Noa slid into the room, her cheeks drawn. "I've been looking for you. You disappeared the other night."

Anwei lowered the jar, letting the breath held inside her lungs huff out. "Where were *you*? We needed you, and you brought *Bear* into it? I thought he was one of the people you wanted to scare."

"And *I* thought we were just going to scare people, not break into the governor's study." Noa lapsed into Elantin, but her tone stayed neutral.

Anwei held very still, her hand twitching toward the solomen roots.

Noa settled onto the bench, her back altogether too straight and her smile missing. "Bear caught me in the hall right before I went up to start the ghosts. He noticed I'd been avoiding him and . . ." She licked her lips. "Anwei, he already went to my father. They're drawing contracts. The door to my cage is closing."

Blinking, Anwei sat down in front of her friend. "And?"

"And I tried to get away from him, but he wouldn't go, like he had a right to stand right by me for every moment of the evening. I knew you were up to more than scaring people at that ball, and that distracting the guests was important, so . . . I told him. Otherwise, I wouldn't have been able to do it at all."

"We didn't break into any offices, Noa. It was to scare those archeologists, like I said."

"You are lying, Anwei. Usually I don't mind lying because most people do their fair share, but you can't lie to me today. I need your help. You're the only person I can trust."

Anwei couldn't help the glow of warmth at her saying that. Anwei had never stayed anywhere long enough for friends. She'd hardly known she wanted one until she met Noa. Knox. Even Gulya.

"You're the only person I know who does whatever you want and . . . I've seen Yaru's temple. I've heard the governor and the magistrate whispering about her, and I've seen you down in the Fig Cay with the Crowteeth and the Blackhearts." Noa licked her lips and finally let her eyes meet Anwei's. "You wouldn't be doing something out in the open like what we did at the ball unless you were planning to leave soon—it's too risky for your line of work."

This was why having a friend wasn't something Anwei could afford. Not until after the snake-tooth man was dead. After he was gone, Anwei wouldn't have to sneak, steal, find. She could just *live*.

Sitting back, Anwei folded her arms, looking Noa up and down. "That's quite an accusation for someone who sees an apothecarist once a week for poison." She didn't like the way the words tasted but didn't take them back.

"I'm not accusing you of anything. I wish I could *be* you, Anwei. Running around, telling handsome young men to do my bidding, stealing things, scaring people? Maybe you don't see your life as a dream, but it's mine." Noa clasped her hands before her, no dramatics for once, no silly jokes. "I want to be able to leave my house without my father asking me where I'm going. To speak to whom I wish, to marry because I find someone I can't stand to be without rather than because someone finds me vaguely amusing and has enough money to catch my father's eye."

Shaking her head, Anwei stood up, gathering the jar and the roots, wanting to laugh at all the things Noa didn't understand.

"Please, Anwei, whatever it is you're doing, let me be a part of it.

Take me with you when you leave." The waver in Noa's voice made Anwei look up.

A tear rolled down her friend's cheek, her eyes turning an unbecoming red. She was serious. Anwei set aside the jar once again, leaning forward on the table as she tried to come up with the right story, the right lie, and suddenly found she didn't want to.

She liked Noa. The sight of her friend in pain hurt Anwei, like the bond between her and Knox, only there was no magic here to make her feel it. Like there was a bond between them made with words and laughter and time spent not worrying about anything. Noa knew nothing about Anwei, wasn't part of any of the things that were important to her . . . and it made it easy to be with her because there was nothing deadly at stake.

But that didn't mean she could spill out her heart and plans onto the table between them. She'd barely managed to tell Knox, and he already knew the rest of what made her up.

"Listen." Noa snuffled. "I know you wanted ghosts at the ball because you couldn't have the governor walking in while you stole documents from his study. Documents about that dig outside of town you mentioned. The dead shapeshifter? I was in the next room when the governor realized they were gone. Don't lie anymore, I'm not going to tell anyone." She smiled, a sad attempt at her dimpled, roguish visage. "How can I help?"

"I have no idea what you are talking about." Anwei pursed her lips. "You want to help . . . what?"

"I've been wondering that myself. What could you want from a tomb? Gold and jewels? Shapeshifter bones to make special poison? Does that boy who follows you around need something?"

"I . . . can't . . ." Even that was an admission Anwei wanted to bite back, as if she'd lost control of her mouth. Like she'd lost control of so many other things when Knox started mattering to her. She extracted one of the long solomen roots and set it down on the table too. "You can believe whatever you want, Noa. I can't help you."

"You're taking something from the dig, and it's so big, you'll have to run away. I need to run away too, Anwei. I'll bring money. I'll do whatever you want. You can trust me."

"Trust you?" Anwei blinked, truth spilling out of her before she could stop it. "Trust you like I did at the ball? Knox almost *died* because you weren't there when we needed you, Noa."

"Beildan!" a voice whispered from the back window. Anwei turned to find the Blackheart from the plague house hunched in the open window—Jecks. His eyes stopped on the squishy roots at her fingertips and he shuddered, suddenly looking as if his message wasn't as important to deliver as he'd thought. He glanced toward Noa. "Not a good time?"

Turning from her friend, Anwei smiled at Jecks, happy to have something so much more straightforward to deal with. "I was going to come check on you and your family today. How are they doing?" She arranged the root's squished innards in front of her, then picked up the paring knife.

"They're worse. The wardens are dumping victims from all the way up in the Water Cay—some of them from the governor's house itself—and they're paying off my boss to take care of them. He's keeping the money, while we can hardly keep everyone fed. Please. You have to come. My daughter . . ." He took a ragged breath. "We need you."

Victims from the governor's house? Anwei held up her knife to the light, checking the edge before glancing at Noa. The high khonin looked down, her hands tightly knit in front of her. She already knew.

Anwei turned back to Jecks. "Your daughter is getting worse? What about your husband?"

"The medicine helped for the first day, but he's worse again. Not as bad as Kaylie."

Anwei began cutting the roots into neat slices. "I'll be there this afternoon. I need your help with something, though." She set the knife back down on the table.

"You need . . . what?" Jecks's eyes went to the roots, one of his hands pulling at his yellow scarf. "Nothing unnatural?"

Anwei rolled her eyes. "I'm a healer, not a witch." She glanced at Noa again. "Let's talk outside, Jecks."

She could feel Noa's green eyes on her as she went into the courtyard and shut the door behind her. Next she went to the window and shut that as well, before turning to Jecks. "There's a Trib clan staying somewhere in this city with a leader by the name of Shale. I want you to tell me where they are lodged. Where they go. What they do. Who they talk to. I'm meeting Shale on the way to the plague house this afternoon, so if you follow me, I can make finding him easy for you."

"And . . . my family?"

"I'll do everything I can for them."

His brow crinkled. "You wouldn't otherwise?"

"I'll treat them *first*. This sickness came from somewhere, and I'm wondering if the Trib brought it with them into the city. If you could help, I might be able to identify what exactly we're dealing with a little faster."

"I can do that. This afternoon?"

Anwei nodded, waving him out the courtyard gates. She waited until they had swung shut before going back in to her solomen roots and Noa. The girl didn't say anything as Anwei picked up her knife and cut off a section of the rough, barky outsides. Black sap bled out of the root's flesh into the dish. She needed a whole cupful for the serum that would make the shapeshifter talk.

She'd seen her father make it once. The memory pricked as she went over it in her mind, remembering the steps one by one. Gamtooth venom had been the second step.

Noa sat forward, clasping her hands in front of her. "You're involved in treating the plague spreading through the lower cays?"

"Maybe you should tell Bear and the governor so I can help who-ever's sick at their house."

"I can't go back there, Anwei. I need to hide. Like you. Can't I hide here?"

"Noa, I'm . . ." Anwei looked up at the girl, the air tense between them. "I wish I could help you."

The words seemed to sit on Noa's shoulders. She reached up to toy with her hair stick, the ends sharpened to points. "You *could* help me. But you won't. There's a difference."

Knox's mind suddenly yawned open above Anwei, blooming in her head where a moment ago there had been nothing. Her hands twitched, the knife slicing too deep into the root. She swore and put the knife down.

"What's wrong?" Noa stood, looking around the room.

Anwei placed the root back in its jar and packed it into a sack with the gamtooth spinners. "I'm really busy today, is all." She hated saying it, but she couldn't see another way. Maybe once all this was done, she'd find another friend like Noa in another city. Another life that didn't hold any memories from this one. "Maybe we can talk next week." By next week she'd be gone.

Noa's eyes narrowed, from sad to calculating in a blink. "I'll show you that you can trust me. That the ball was a mistake I'm not going to repeat. If I prove it to you, can I come stay here? Leave with you when you go?"

"I can't talk anymore. I'll see you soon, Noa." Anwei hardly looked back before running up the stairs to rap on Knox's door, waiting a sec-ond before she pushed it open. He was standing next to his bed, his tunic only half-buttoned.

Knox's fingers froze, and he turned away. Embarrassed? Since when had he cared about being modest?

"Um . . ." Anwei's stomach fluttered at the odd feeling between them, some of it echoing from inside her head. *You kissed me. But it wasn't against the rules.* That's what he'd said, drugged to the eyeballs and giggling about a dream he'd had. A dream about her. Them. Directly after almost pushing her out the window for *trying* to kiss him, though it had just been business. She cleared her throat, looking away until he was done buttoning his shirt. "You need to get back into bed."

"I can't. There's too much happening." He had fastened an extra button on his tunic, his collar done clear up to his chin. It looked a little silly.

"But it's not things you need to help with. I'm going to check on our pineapple, then pick up a few things before I get all the information on the dig from Shale."

"I'm fine." He cleared his throat, wrapping his scarf over his mouth. "Temple first, then . . . ?"

Hesitating, Anwei sat down in the chair by his washstand. She didn't really want to let him out of her sight. He wasn't fine. She could still smell the acrid tang the poison had left inside him. "After Altahn, I'm going to the docks. Here, you can carry this." She smiled, holding out the bag containing the roots and spiders.

He took it, his hand brushing hers. She could feel him thinking about the touch, even if she couldn't feel *what* he was thinking.

Anwei wanted to know, the touch lingering in her mind too. She stood. "Let's go."

When they got downstairs, Anwei was both relieved and sad to see that Noa had gone, the smell of the girl's tears still haunting the herb room.

Altahn was curled around the little pot of simmering herbs Anwei had left, the smoke nearly gone. She sat him up, and Knox arranged the assortment of food they'd picked up on the way there.

The Trib's eyelids began to twitch the moment she pulled the pot away, his breaths coming in long, deep gasps. His hands went to his throat, where bruises from Anwei's assault had turned an ugly purple. Anwei offered a tumbler of water from the malthouse above. "Thirsty?"

He blinked at her, head lolling to the side. "You . . ."

She held the tumbler to his mouth, the watered-down scent of gamtooth venom in the cup twitching in her nose as he drank it down. Not a foolproof truth serum like she would brew for the snake-tooth man, but it would open Altahn's lips. And, perhaps, a few boils on his arms.

"Remember me? I'm Anwei. That's Knox." She pointed to her partner, who pushed the plate of food toward Altahn. "Nice to meet you again."

His brow furrowed, and he sat up a bit straighter, blearily looking around the room.

"You've been a wonderful guest so far, but if you try to hurt us, we will probably kill you, so just take things slow. Once the herbs are out of your system, we can chat, all right? I've got lots of questions." Anwei gave him her best smile before turning to Knox. "This serum needs two days to steep. Would you grab a board from the stacks in the storeroom and another glass from upstairs?"

Knox nodded and crawled back through the tunnel, then returned with the items she'd requested just as she pulled open the drop. The mirrored, false-bottomed box captured light from above and shot it down into the hiding place. Shuffling over to where the beam of light made a harsh rectangle on the floor, Anwei held her hand out for the board. Knox placed it in front of her, set the glass on top, and knelt on the opposite side. She placed the other supplies she'd brought along the edge—a sanded-glass magnifier and some corked tubes and dowels—then tied a scarf across the lower half of her face.

"Cover your mouth and nose." Anwei waited until Knox had pulled up his scarf. He grudgingly slid over to Altahn next, to pull his shirt up over his nose before Anwei extracted the little packet of calistet from her bag. She slipped on her gloves, picked up the glass, and breathed a mouthful of hot air into it. After carefully opening the calistet packet—there was only a pinch in the very bottom—she swiped one gloved finger across the opening, then flicked the tiny bit of powder into the tumbler. The bloody smell tore at her nostrils as the little granules stuck to the condensation from her breath. She handed the glass off to Knox. He hurriedly placed it facedown on the board while she rebuttoned the calistet packet and stowed it away.

"So, tell me, Altahn." Anwei glanced over at the Trib. The gamtooth poison would have spread enough by now to make him talk a little. "Why did your father ask you to follow us?"

"Had to make sure . . ." Altahn swallowed, then tried to stick a crust of bread into his mouth, though his shirt blocked the way. "See what you would do."

"And report it to whom?" She pulled out the jar filled with spiderwebs and gestured to Knox, lowering her voice. "I need your help."

The light dusted his forehead and the bridge of his nose as he leaned forward over the board, making little circles across his cheekbones. Anwei looked down. It was her job to look down.

Or was it? Knox had started looking down too.

"We tried . . . couldn't find a way past the traps. Don't even know where the tunnels go," Altahn continued, his voice meandering this way and that. "If *you* show us . . ."

Sliding the web-filled jar to sit next to the board, Anwei pulled out a set of heavy leather gloves for Knox. "Shale really does want the sword, then. You wanted us to figure out where it was so you could steal it yourselves without having to pay us?"

Altahn's eyes widened. After a moment his head bobbed forward in a nod. He managed to pull his shirt down off his nose and chin, and successfully shoved the bread into his mouth. "We needed you to get in, though. And out." His head lolled to the side against the wall, his eyes glazing.

Why not pay a little money for method rather than offering a lot for the whole job? Shale didn't know that Yaru was mostly separate from the Blackhearts and the Crowteeth, but pretending to offer money for a service and then stealing all the preparation in order to do it yourself was enough to get your name on a death list with any of the gangs.

Could it be this *wasn't* a trap? Just incompetence from a clan chief unused to working with criminals?

"Can I ask him a question?" Knox whispered.

Anwei shrugged. "Why not?"

"How come your aura was in the wrong place when we saw you by the theater? It was like you had a fake one attached to a puppet."

"Gash . . ." Altahn's chin dipped down to his chest. "Firekey."

Knox looked at Anwei. "He had a firekey lizard . . . but don't they just blow fire?"

"To be honest, I don't know much about firekeys or auras, either one. Narmaidens make thought connections with humans—that's how they manage to get sailors to jump into the ocean, where they're easier to catch. Maybe firekeys can . . . pretend to be people? In any case, we can't test it now because I threw his little pet out of the carriage." Anwei picked up the gamtooth jar. She pried open the clamp, leaving the glass top in place before pushing it toward Knox. He pulled on the gloves, his face wary.

"There are three very dangerous spiders in here." Anwei tapped against the glass. "And I need to milk them."

"Milk?"

"For their venom. We need it to make the snake-tooth man tell the truth about that sword of yours."

Knox bent to look at the opaque mass of web. "And you saw me involved in this . . . how?"

Anwei found her sweetest smile. "Oh, I just need you to pull them out one by one." She'd done it many times herself, but she always ended up squishing at least one of them, and gamtooth spinners took a long time to reproduce. "I'll stun them."

He straightened. "Why do you need *me* to pull them out?"

"I hate spiders. A lot."

It took a second before Knox inched the jar closer and looked down into the mess of cottony web. "Fine."

She glanced back at Altahn, who seemed to be snoring against the wall. "So, here's the new plan—"

Knox looked up. "We have no map, don't know what Shale has for us, and you already have a plan?"

Anwei paused, the glass cold between her fingers. "We have a sketch of the tomb interior from the governor—some of it, anyway. People are still talking about the fire at the ball, and odd things have been happening at the dig, so I think if we add a few frightening events, everyone inside the excavation will run the moment someone screams 'ghost.'" She pushed the gamtooth jar a little closer to Knox, ignoring the tentative way he reached out to pull it toward himself. "That's why I want to go to the docks. One of my contacts mentioned Trib powder has been leaving the harbor illegally and sent me a shipment schedule. Some is supposed to go out today. We can't get anything but watered-down salpowder—nothing better than those little fire bursts I made for the governor's house—without stealing it from one of those ships or from the Warlord herself, and I don't like that second option."

"Why do we need more-potent salpowder?"

"Because then we could make something a little more complicated. We could fix it so the ingredients combine over time, so we could drop it in a food shipment, then have it explode once it's already inside the excavation compound."

"You know how to do that? You know which powder we'd need to steal? They make so many different kinds . . . though I don't know how. They all come from the same lizard things that apparently can throw auras."

"Firekeys." She didn't touch her arm where Altahn's little monster had burned her. "And no, I don't know which kind of powder we'd need, but Altahn will."

Knox looked toward the Trib, whose head was still lolling against the cave wall. He had burn scars all over his hands, and he'd reeked of salpowder the first time he came to the apothecary, as if he'd blown something up on the way. Or maybe it had been his pet the whole time.

Anwei cleared her throat. "Minerals don't make sense to me." They were just *there* in her head. They didn't fit together like herbs and illnesses did. "I learned how to make little bursts and noisemakers like the ones I did for the ball while I was up in Trib country a few years ago, but anything more complicated than that would take some guidance. Once I see it, I can do it." She nodded to Altahn. "And I'm fairly certain he can show me."

Knox's lip curled as he looked down into the gamtooth jar. "Why *wouldn't* Altahn help us? We only drugged him and left him here for . . . how long has it been?"

"Two days, if that. He wants the sword, Knox. I think he'll help once he understands why we're asking. And also that we won't give him back to his father unless he's compliant."

Wrinkling his nose, Knox stuck one gloved finger into the jar.

"Spinners are very aggressive, so—" Anwei broke off as Knox jerked his hand out of the jar, a black body the size of her thumb latched to the end of the glove.

Anwei lifted the lip of the calistet-laced tumbler and Knox shoved his finger under it before the spider could wriggle down to bite his wrist. The little creature bit furiously at Knox's gloved finger for another second before its frantic attack slowed. After a moment it stopped moving entirely. Anwei slid the cup off Knox's finger, replacing the rim against the board to keep any of the powder from escaping. Knox gently detached the spider's bulbous black body from his glove and placed it on the board next to the cup, bright yellow stripes like lightning bolts down its back, the creature's long, reedy legs splayed limply around it.

Knox's normally stoic expression wrinkled with disgust as Anwei positioned the magnifier over the spider. She glanced up at him. "If we scare the excavation workers bad enough to run, maybe we'll have enough space to wander around inside until we find our way through the tomb? If only Shale hadn't lied about the maps. Do you think if we bribed a worker . . . ?"

"Wait, we're stealing the sword now? I thought we were just going to find the shapeshifter and get out."

"The Warlord is coming, like you said. And I can't help but think I don't want to be here in the Commonwealth where she can find me any more than you do. Shale might not have twenty thousand silver rounds, but he'll give us something."

"And you want to do the job rather than just ransom Shale's son?"

"I guess." Concentrating on positioning the spider, Anwei was glad not to see his face as she continued. "That, and . . . seeing it might help us figure out what to do with yours. Right? Another shapeshifter's sword."

Her skin prickled when she heard Altahn stir. It didn't matter if he heard their plan, exactly. Altahn couldn't be allowed to leave until Knox's money box was a good deal heavier and a shapeshifter's severed head was buried in the fields.

Anwei was surprised when Knox merely nodded, as if that made all the sense in the world. "We don't really have time to bribe a worker to map the compound. I think I've got it taken care of, though."

Anwei looked up from her tools. "What?"

"My friend showed up in Chaol. She has a connection to the Warlord's aukincer, who is part of the excavation crew. She's going to get him to take her in so she can map it out for us."

"You . . . have a friend?" The words came out disjointed, Anwei's stomach dropping as if she'd missed the last step in a long staircase. "Here in Chaol?"

Knox's head dipped forward in a nod, a strand of hair pulling free from his ponytail to hang in his face. "Lia. She's, um . . . the lost Devoted. She came into the apothecary yesterday while we were talking to Shale."

"The *missing Devoted*?" Anwei's brain hummed. Knox could have friends. Parts of life that didn't involve her. That was fine. But bringing someone else in on the plan? A *Devoted*? She adjusted the magnifier over the spider, bringing the light from above to a single bright, burning circle over the thing's mouth for a split second of intense heat. When she pulled the magnifier away, a drop of venom had appeared at the very end of one of its long fangs.

Rolling the collection vial between her hands, Anwei opened her mouth, then closed it. She couldn't find words. "Are you sure she's not . . . ? She isn't here to . . ."

"I'm *not* sure." Knox fidgeted with the jar clamp. "But she asked me for help, and she's in a position to help *us*, so . . ."

"So another trap waiting to spring." Anwei used a thin wooden dowel to nudge the spider's pedipalps back to let the venom drip into her vial.

Knox's face twisted. "She's like my sister, and if anyone would try to escape a life of Devotion, it would be her. When she told me she could get into the dig, I just thought . . ." He scrubbed a hand through his hair. "I'm sorry. I shouldn't have done this without asking you."

"I don't know. I've just . . ." *Lived for years in hiding. And you were the only person I let in. I didn't realize you'd let in others, too.* "I just don't like relying on someone other than you."

The same words he'd used before about Noa. *Noa*, who had promised she was trustworthy, then left them no way out of the governor's house. "If *you* trust her, Knox . . ."

"I don't want to believe that she'd hand me over, but yes, I'm . . .

aware of the risk. If she comes through with maps . . ." He looked away, tapping at the spinner jar, his hair obscuring his expression. "The difference between knowing the layout in there and not could be the difference between us living and dying. Especially if she can show us where the director sleeps."

It felt like adding narmaidens at the bottom of the cliff edge they were already walking along. But Anwei trusted Knox.

She did.

So she nodded. "All right. We have to let the serum steep for two days, so we'll give her that long to get us maps. And if she doesn't come through, we'll go in anyway. Even a map isn't going to change that we don't know exactly what we're walking into down there."

Knox nodded, glancing at Altahn, who had begun to hum one note over and over again. "Either of us can get through traps. You'd be able to smell them, and I'd be able to see or hear anything down there. One of us can grab the sword, the other one can deal with the shapeshifter, and then we can both get out of this city for good."

We. Anwei made herself focus on the magnifier.

"The serum will help me get what I need, but we still don't know how to kill him, do we, Anwei?"

"Killing is easy work, Knox." She harnessed the light, warming up the spinner's mouth once again.

"That's not what history books say."

"We'll have him subdued. I'll have time to come up with something. That can be the first question we ask him when he's got serum on his skin. 'How do we kill you?' He'll have to answer."

In truth, the question still writhed inside her, worse than any gamtooth spinner. Anwei frowned as the venom stopped bleeding into her vial. The spinner wasn't producing as much as normal. She set the vial aside and looked at Knox, his face still puckered with worry. "Would you put the spinner back for me?"

Knox lifted the little thing out from under the magnifier, cracked open the jar, and slid it inside. Then he looked back at her. She could feel his eyes glued to her shoulder, the side of her neck, drawing lines down her back. *The rule has always been to look away. We look away.*

Anwei turned her chin, locking eyes with Knox. He didn't look away.

Altahn's voice slurred between them, and Knox's eyes skittered away from Anwei to focus on the jar. The spiders. "Father can't wait to get out of this place either."

Sneaking Altahn to the boat launch wasn't so hard. They carried him on a stretcher covered with bundles of what looked like dried petals and weeds to Knox but were probably cures for gout and the mange. Knox set Altahn in the middle of Anwei's little canoe, rolling his eyes when she gestured for him to take the front paddle, as if giving him the easy end of the canoe was the only way to stop him from keeling over and drowning in the river.

Truth be told, he did feel a little weak.

Truth be told, your insides are all scraped raw like a baby who tried to swallow sand. Calsta and her little jokes. But Knox felt something inside him unwind at the sound of her voice. She was still there. Still watching over him.

"Two things," Anwei said once she'd sat down. She extracted a little glass canister and a tube from her medicine bag. "Salpowder will be in the barrels on the dock farthest out into the gulf. They're all sealed, but if you dip this pipe into this mixture"—she gave the canister a little shake—"then press the pipe up against the wood, it'll react with the tar and burn a hole through it. Easy way to tap in." She pulled out two small leather bags next. "And these are dry bags to put the powder into."

"So when you said I should take it easy, what you meant was I should swim through choppy ocean water and . . . steal things from armed soldiers?" Knox held his hands out over Altahn to take the supplies.

She smiled at him, handing them over. "We both know you're much better at the sneaky stuff. And I'm much better in the distraction role."

Knox stowed the bags, the tube, and the glass canister into his pocket, hoping a concoction capable of making tar burn would not also make explosive powder burn. He sat down and took up his oar, and together they rowed out past the Bell Cay and the dry market toward the wave break. The water went choppy, peaking and swirling as seawater met river, making the canoe bob. It took a few minutes of following the boat traffic weaving between the pylons that held up the trade road and fighting crosscurrents before they came in sight of the last island in the chain that made up Chaol—the Dock Cay, where the gulf docks were located. Three huge sailing ships were on the riverside moorings, sailors running supplies up and down the gangplanks. Anwei veered toward a smaller barge docked on the gulf side, away from the others. Three guards with high khonin insignia stamped on their shoulders—it was some kind of fish; a salmon?—stood at attention in front of it.

Salpowder barrels. Knox watched as a woman rolled one of the barrels into the ship's belly. Completely illegal to send them across the gulf, though it was obvious things had been trickling through. Knox dipped in his oar, following Anwei's steering to keep in sight of but not get too close to the dock. "What now? They'll probably kick us in the teeth if we try to get any closer."

The mass of herbs piled on top of Altahn suddenly twitched. The boat tipped as he tried to roll to the side, clawing the blanket off his face. Altahn sat up with a gasp, only to gaze around himself in shock. His fingers were white where they gripped the canoe's sides. "What . . . where . . ."

He swallowed hard, looked forward at Knox, then slowly, so very slowly, turned his head to look back at Anwei.

"All right?" Anwei asked, and Knox almost believed she was

concerned, at least until she dipped in her oar to adjust their course. "Glad to see you awake."

The Trib's jaw was so tight, Knox fancied he might break a tooth if he didn't open it soon. Waves bucked under them, washing the canoe to the side. Altahn stared at the section of rope twined between his wrists, loose enough he could move, but not so loose he'd be able to swim. When he finally spoke, his voice cracked in the briny wind. "Well, I'm not dead, I suppose."

So calm. Knox was both proud of him and a bit unnerved.

Anwei dipped her paddle in deep, steering them toward the bustling docks ahead. "I have a job for you."

"I thought I was paying *you* to do a job."

"Your father is. But if you want it done right, then you'll help us get the necessary materials." She nodded toward a barge at the far end of the dock. "They're loading barrels of salpowder and glass and . . . I don't know what else." Knox caught her sniffing the wind, but she covered it nicely. "You're going to show us what we need to make some things explode, then Knox and I are going to steal them. We need a timed sort of explosion. Limited in scope, more smoke and flash than harm done. Also, salpowder that will burn brighter but less hot, maybe with some interesting colors? Thanks in advance for your help."

Altahn blinked only once. "This is for the dig?"

"Yes."

"An explosion could take the whole thing down. We'd have done that ourselves if it meant we could get the sword that way."

Anwei shrugged. "Didn't I say smoke and flash? We don't want to disturb anything inside the tomb itself. It's more to prime the pump, encourage the workers they'd rather be anywhere but inside the excavation compound before we go in."

Altahn blinked through that as well. But then he nodded. "All right."

Deep inside, Knox's humors twisted. All right? Just like that?

Something caught at his attention from the stream of boats swishing under the trade road and over to the riverside docks. A familiar aura. His eyes snapped shut to give it a better look, then cracked back open. Why would *Noa* be out here, so far away from the malt fountains and parties and forbidden, pants-wearing dance performances that made up her existence?

Anwei squinted at Altahn for a moment, but then her bright smile came out. "I like a man who knows how to make decisions. Let's go. Any funny business and you go headfirst into the brine."

"Understood." Altahn frowned at the barges. "I can tell from the barrel fittings which ones we want, but how are you going to get them? How are you even going to get onto the dock?" He pointed to the lone worker pushing yet another barrel under the close eye of three guards. "They don't look like they tolerate gawking."

"Which barrels?" Anwei prodded.

"Those middle ones are salpowder. And the ones on the end are another incendiary . . . two knuckles of either would be enough to blow the whole tomb to sand. Mixed and modified, and I think we can put together something flashy and toothless for you."

"Perfect. Knox?"

Knox craned his neck to the side, wishing there were some way not to be talking directly over their prisoner. Noa's aura had drawn closer, her boat almost at their heels. She'd messed things up badly enough at the ball. What were the odds that she'd show up here just in time to mess this up too? "I don't like this."

"After a year of complaining that I spend too much time planning? What do you think? Underwater?"

"The powder can't get wet. Kind of important," Altahn interjected.

"Are we worried about any boats? Maybe the one behind us, Anwei?" Knox turned just in time to see Noa's pretty little skiff slick by them, four men rowing. She was seated on the prow, the governor's son, Bear, at her feet, offering her a bowl of grapes. Flowers poured from the prow to dangle into the water around them, a sharp contrast to the line of fishy, weather-beaten boats headed for the docks.

Anwei's smile disintegrated, making Knox's stomach lurch. So there was something to be feared from the second khonin. Noa seemed not to notice them, her servants rowing the skiff so slowly that the boat hands around them swore under their collective breath, but not loud enough for the first and second khonins to hear. They were headed for the smaller tie-ups on the close side of the dock.

"Who is *that*?" Altahn's voice was altogether too appreciative.

"Just ignore her," Anwei said over Altahn's head, a trace of exasperation needling through the bond that Knox didn't understand. That was better than fear, at least. "You have the dry bags I gave you?"

He pulled one out to show her.

"Good. Altahn, move up and take Knox's paddle. I'm going to need you to dig deep. Find your inner disgruntlement with society." The canoe rocked a little as she stood up. "Ready, Knox?"

Knox nodded, eyeing the forty strides' distance between them and the dock. An easy swim, so long as the guards and their spears had something other than his head to look at when he came out of the water. Anwei had moved them a little outside boat traffic and let the canoe's nose wander, so the waves were sloshing around them.

"You're going to have him swim over and just . . . try to take salpowder right out from under the guards' noses?" Altahn's voice crackled with disbelief. "Yaru's supposed to be the best."

"You underestimate us." Anwei flashed a smile toward Knox, the secret happy one that he'd only ever seen her point at him. She dipped down to pick up the blanket that had covered Altahn at the same time Knox climbed onto his seat, flipping the fabric so loose flower petals danced up into the wind. Under cover of the blanket, Knox dove head-first into the sea.

The cold water pressed against Knox. Opening his eyes underwater only made a blur of the pylons and gray depths, but he couldn't rely on his aura to clear it up for him. At least, he didn't want to—he had drawn on Calsta's power the day he'd followed Lia, and he could still feel the weight of it flickering behind the wall, calling to him. It hadn't been safe that day despite all the Devoted being drained, and it wasn't safe now.

Kicking toward the barge's rounded underside, Knox swam beneath the wide dock and hovered below the water's surface, grateful there were a few things Calsta would always help him with whether he wanted her to or not. Being able to stay underwater longer than a normal person made it so Anwei could stop the boat well outside the area the guards would be watching. Calsta sighed at the back of his mind, annoyed. *Why aren't you taking in power, Knox? This should be easy.*

If I wanted to get pinned down by the sword of every Devoted within miles, then get eaten by an auroshe, maybe. Lia and Ewan are diminished, but what if the Warlord sent Devoted ahead of her?

I wish I could explain to you how this works, but you know I can't.

Explain what? When have you ever explained anything?

I can't tell you everything, Knox. It's too dangerous.

Dangerous? Knox listened for a moment, hoping she'd expound on that very intriguing detail, but she didn't. He waited a count of ten. Twenty. Thirty. Then he finally surfaced to hear Anwei in fine form on the other side of the dock. Slithering through the water, Knox peeked up over the edge.

"I give my *life* to curing the sick, and you sell this godless stuff across the border? They're using it to *kill people*." She was throwing flower petals and stems, as if they were the worst sorts of weapons. "I demand you stop this shipment immediately. Only last year a member of my order was *blown up* during a disgusting *dirt witch* purging. . . ."

Altahn was holding the boat steady behind her, doing his best to look angry despite the fact that he was trying not to laugh. The guards had all gravitated toward Anwei, watching her with an odd combination of respect for her braids and amusement for . . . well, everything else. Knox pulled himself up onto the dock, then slunk over to the line of unloaded barrels. He ducked behind the closest one on the gulf side so that it blocked the guards from seeing him. Even the woman moving the barrels had stopped midroll, her mouth hanging open as she stared at Anwei in the boat.

Knox pulled the dry bag from his tunic, unrolled the top, and—

A guard turned toward him, signaling to the woman moving the barrels to carry on. His eyes caught on the dock beside Knox. Knox's shadow flared out long and dark on the boards, the sun behind him giving him away.

This is the kind of help you give, Calsta? Why don't you send clouds instead of sun to light up my hiding spot?

"What the—" Before the guard could finish, a multicolored streak skipped across the dock, a rain of flowers ghosting along behind it. It was Noa, twirling and dancing, a low voice egging her on from farther down the docks. Bear.

Knox pulled out the pipe and the canister Anwei had given him. Perhaps Noa was good for something, even if it was an accident that she was shielding him from attention. He popped open the canister's clasp, and an acrid smell hit Knox's nose. He thrust the pipe into the jar, then stabbed it into the side of the barrel.

Tar immediately began to bubble and boil around it, and the wood began to smolder, then crackled into nothing, so that the pipe pushed all the way through. Knox held out the little bag just in time for the whitish powder to begin pouring inside.

The guards were shouting, and Noa was laughing, but just as Knox pulled the bag out from under the stream of powder and folded it down, he saw a knife flash.

"Hey!" Anwei yelled. "You stab that girl, and her father will have your head on a platter quicker than . . ."

Knox pulled the pipe free and crawled to the other barrels Altahn had pointed to. He dipped the pipe back into the canister for good measure, then stabbed it into the side of the barrel.

There was a cry and a splash of water. Knox's stomach twisted and he pulled himself up far enough to see Noa floundering in the waves, guards clustered around the spot where she'd fallen. She was laughing. "Remind me never to ask *any* of you bumbling idiots to a ball—"

"I'll invite you!" Bear called. "Wait, let me help pull her out."

Knox rolled his eyes and stuck a hand into his tunic for the second dry bag, his stomach twisting at the fumes. His eyes began to water, and he looked down at the spot of bubbling tar, pushing the pipe in a little harder. The smell hadn't been so awful the first time.

Wind gusted over him, dragging his hair from its tie, as if Calsta wasn't done playing with him yet today. But then the breeze fell off, a little stream of black smoke suddenly issuing from the wood around Knox's pipe. Was it supposed to smoke?

In less than a second, the smoke went from a little trickle to a boiling river, the smell making Knox gag.

"Go!" Altahn's voice came spearing through the wind. "Nameless god curse it, *get out of there*!"

The guards turned to see whom he was yelling at, only to find smoke billowing up from the salpowder barrels. Some of the powder inside Knox's barrel had emptied into the dry bag, so Knox hurriedly tied it off, stuffed it into his pocket, then jumped off the dock just as the guards rushed toward him.

Before he hit the water, a *force* slammed into Knox's back, the crack of a thousand thunderclaps tearing through his ears, and slapped him belly-down onto the waves. Calsta was with him before he could even think, helping him to remember his lungs didn't need air, that he could wait. That the water was *supposed* to be a foamy mass of broken boards and limbs going this way and that.

He dove deeper, Anwei a warm dose of panic at the back of his head. After kicking under all the bubbles and flares of golden fire, Knox surfaced over where the boat had been. Anwei waited only long enough to see his hand was on the prow and he was breathing before she started rowing.

Knox let the boat tow him clear to the bridge between the Water Cay and the dry market, where the drum tower stabbed the sky. Anwei slowed, then moved forward to help him in.

"You're all right?" Altahn's voice cut through them. "Gods above, was that *planned*? Blow up the dock so they think it was an accident? I mean, it didn't quite come off, but that was . . . interesting, anyway."

Anwei cleared her throat, not disabusing Altahn of the notion as she dragged Knox over the side of the boat and made him sit back against the rear seat. Knox dug down into his tunic and pulled out the two dry bags, holding them up with a grin.

A smile cracked Anwei's face too. "Well, that's one thing done."

At the back of Knox's head, Noa's familiar aura appeared once again. He twisted to look at her, sopping wet and laughing so hard it seemed like she might fall off the boat. She'd made it off the dock, at least, though Bear seemed not to have been so fortunate, because he wasn't anywhere to be seen. When the skiff swung past them, Knox didn't understand the way Noa sat up, her face changing for a fraction of a second when she looked at them.

No. When she looked at Anwei, behind him. Noa's expression cleared, as if she were taking off a mask, and she pointed at Anwei like she was asking for an answer to a question or perhaps driving a point home. But it lasted only a split second, and then Noa was back to laughing with her boat hands, the skiff headed toward the private Water Cay docks.

When Knox turned back to Anwei, she was shaking her head, almost laughing. All the traces of fear from before were gone.

Altahn waved to get Anwei's attention. "Seriously, who is that?"

He swiveled to look at Knox when Anwei didn't answer. "Was she a part of this too?"

Anwei finally reached out and took the two dry bags from Knox, looking them over as if she were inspecting them for holes, but Knox could feel her thinking. Deciding something. When she finally looked back at the Trib, Knox knew something had changed. "Of course she was. Didn't your father tell you we're the best?"

Anwei swaddled Altahn in the blanket before any spies from his clan could spot them on the way back to the apothecary, then stayed in the apothecary itself only long enough to be sure he was locked in Knox's room before heading out to meet with Shale. She couldn't bear to look Knox straight in the eye. Her heart had stopped the moment that barrel exploded. The guards were supposed to have been the danger, not the powder. And then Knox had just swum back to the boat, calm as you fancy, handed her the bags, and waved at Noa as she went by.

Noa. *Blasted* Noa. She *had* been a help.

Shaking her head, Anwei couldn't help but laugh again. Noa had caught her red-handed, and the idea of her being a part of this felt . . . different.

Exciting, as if Anwei were gathering her favorite things around her and getting ready to do something new. Not the way she expected to feel only days away from finally destroying Arun's murderer—with hardly any information and plans that depended on maybes and perhapses. Anwei had been planning every moment of every day months in advance for years, never entering a house until she knew for sure what she'd find inside, and all of it had been thrown out in favor of . . . *this*. Altahn locked in Knox's room, Noa twirling in and out as she pleased, and Knox staring into her eyes under the temple, his gaze flickering down to touch her lips . . .

Anwei forced herself to step into her canoe and untie it from the dock. To sit down and dip her paddle into the river, pointing herself toward the Fig Cay. Everything was out of control.

And deep in her heart Anwei knew she liked it better than any of her years alone.

But that didn't mean it would get her what she wanted. Everything itched like the new medicine bag she'd bought, which sat weirdly across her body and was soft in all the wrong places. Anwei cleared her head one thought at a time as she paddled through the crowded channel, thinking of Shale waiting for her by the plague house. *He* couldn't know that things were leaping in her hands like a live fish attempting escape.

When Anwei tied up her boat at a rotting Fig Cay dock, she waved to the Crowteeth lookout before walking to the wet market. The kynate was waiting for her next to a palifruit stand in the shadow of the plague house, the building casting a long shadow across all the little stands as if it were watching, waiting for its next victim to swallow. Anwei strolled along the floating walkways to pick up one of the round palifruits, testing its skin with her fingers before handing it to the seller to cut. Shale pulled a packet from inside his vest and slid it into her bag. It was heavy, clinking as it settled atop her herbs. A sheaf of vellum came next, which he held out for her to take.

Accepting the sheets, she nodded to the alleyway behind the stand. "There's a loose brick seven in, three up from the ground in there," she murmured. "I'll leave the time, date, and address for you to meet us when we have the sword. It'll be within the next few days. We'll bring the sword, you bring the rest of the money, then we'll tell you where your son is."

"You just want me to check that alley every day until . . ."

Anwei smiled at the seller as he held out the cut melon. She put her coins on the table, gathered the juicy pieces to her chest, then walked away without saying anything else. A flicker of yellow scarf caught her eye as she walked toward the plague house. Jecks had seen Shale and had promised to follow him, so she'd soon know if Altahn had spoken true—if Shale was a silly old man who didn't know how to deal with a thief or if there was more to this deal than she could see.

When she reached the plague house, Anwei handed the palifruit to the surprised leech sitting just inside the door. He didn't protest when she went straight to Jecks's family's room. Her nose curled with the scent of so much *nothing*—it was significantly worse now. Anwei opened the door to the sickroom and knelt beside the little girl's bed. She smelled more of nothing than gamtooth now.

A familiar panic began to build inside Anwei, her hands shaking.

Her hands, which could do nothing.

"You can help us, healer, can't you?" Jecks's partner rolled over in his bed, reaching out to touch his daughter's arm.

Anwei licked her lips. And went to work.

CHAPTER 29

The Last Thing You'll See

Y ou're sure Ewan and the other Roosters are off somewhere else?" Lia's heart sped up at the sight of the excavation's rough lumber walls.

Mateo grinned, spurring Bella forward the last few steps to the compound. "They're not due back until tomorrow. The dig director is out as well, so I can show you inside the tomb. It's gorgeous. And . . ." His smile faltered. "I mean, don't touch anything down there or it might kill you. Or you could damage something. This is a unique find. The art, the artifacts . . ."

For a moment Lia mourned the loss of her power, being able to see thoughts dancing across people's brains perhaps even before the people themselves realized they were there. But in the next moment she was grateful her power was gone, because she could see almost as much in Mateo's reverent expression.

He loved this. Digging up the dead. "I would *never* destroy the last remnants of your murderous shapeshifter king," she said lightly.

"Good." Mateo pulled Bella to a stop and dismounted in one graceful step, which Lia suspected he'd practiced before bringing her here.

"How's Rosie doing?" she asked, dismounting. The thought of

the tattered auroshe left her longing to comfort the poor creature and made her doubly miss Vivi, wherever he was.

"Oh, I . . . I've looked in on her. She seems to like her little cave. She's fishing, based on the bones I've seen, and I left water. . . ." Mateo pushed back his wide-brimmed hat. "What kind of answer are you looking for here? She's still raggedly terrifying, but it seems like a slightly happier sort of ragged and terrifying?"

"Good." Lia followed him toward the excavation's wide gates, Mateo's trousers dusted with what looked like actual dirt on the knees and cuffs. There wasn't a stitch of embroidery to be seen the whole length of them, which seemed more interesting than the hole in the ground they'd come to see. His boots made her want to laugh again, though. Coming to know him a little better over the last few days had made her realize that comfortable shoes, for Mateo, was one sacrifice too many.

Not that it was a bad thing. Mateo wasn't jumping through martial forms and practicing with a sword, so she supposed if he didn't mind blisters after crouching in a dusty old tomb all day, she couldn't fault him. Since he'd agreed to play at being an interested suitor, Aria especially had become taken with him. He'd come to the house with what sounded like an invitation to make sweet rolls and ended with the three of them hunkered down in separate corners of the kitchen in forts made of chairs, lobbing missiles made of honey and flour at one another.

Lia had won, of course. It had been *fun*, something she didn't remember being allowed to have.

Father had come in on them right before dinner, but he'd only frowned at their white-speckled, sticky faces for a moment before Mateo had started telling the story of their food fight as if it were an epic battle like the ones he'd studied at the university. Father had immediately been transfixed, especially when Mateo had started talking about tombs.

Even Lia had found herself listening with interest to his descriptions of the reliefs he'd found in Patenga's tomb—the differences in style from other burials he'd studied from the same time period—and of the stigma against shapeshifters that had destroyed almost all art and written information about them.

Lia could feel excitement building inside her now as they approached the walls, Mateo's enthusiasm contagious.

But seeing old carvings and paintings wasn't the real reason Lia was here, and she knew it. Leading the horse she'd borrowed from her father's stables—with his blessing this time—she walked through the compound gates. *At least six strides tall,* she thought, starting a mental list to give to Knox. *Two guards at the gates.* "You said the dig director is off site right now? Is that usual?" she asked. *Van, wasn't that his name? Knox said I had to find out where he and the other archeologists are staying. When they're here, when they're not . . .*

"Meetings with the governor, I guess. He's . . ." Mateo's voice cracked, and Lia gave him a sharp look, but he gathered himself together and shrugged. "He probably wouldn't have let me show you anything interesting. That's why I couldn't bring you until now."

Lia handed off her reins to the waiting hostler, wondering what exactly it was Mateo was lying about. But then they went through the gates, and she was too busy cataloguing buildings, memorizing pathways, and counting workers to think about Mateo.

The dig made a bowl in the ground that was nearly twice the size of her family's compound, the wall running clear to the cliff's edge. Ramshackle buildings made rows across the space, the chaos interspersed with pavilions and baskets of dirt and rock. It was difficult to see far through the lines of workers milling this way and that, everything circling around and pointing to the center of the compound like water swirling down a drain. Would her memory be enough?

She ticked through the things that she'd seen so far, lining them up in rows to draw later. It would *have* to be enough. Knox had said he could get her out of here if she brought him a map of the compound, so that's what she was going to do.

"You said you wanted to meet the archeologists working on the dig? They'll probably be scattered all through here. Usually everyone is locked in—this is the first time Van has left since I got here."

"No one can leave except for you and your father?"

"Yes, except for us." Mateo drew her down a well-worn path across the bald rock, leading her toward the center of the swirl of activity. Lia's stomach bubbled and squeezed for some reason. A shapeshifter was down there. She'd hunted Basists and murderers and bad people of all kinds, but the man under all this rock had killed hundreds of people. Thousands. "Most of the archeologists will probably be busy, but we might be able to sit down with a few of them during the afternoon meal. Unless they all hide in their cabins."

"The director . . . he'll be back soon, you say?" Lia glanced toward the rough-hewn cabins Mateo was gesturing to, just past the horses along the northern wall. "I'm surprised all these fancy people from Rentara are willing to stay in a place so rough. They don't *ever* go into Chaol?"

"No. Van snagged the largest cabin, of course, but the rest of them haven't complained when I could hear." Mateo offered her his arm. "When people are passionate about something, they'll give up a lot for it, don't you think?"

Lia barely kept herself from glancing down at his shoes before she took his arm, stiffly walking beside him as if there were something natural about limiting your movement so drastically. "You said you wanted my help with something here. What was it?"

"Well . . ." Mateo looked around as if someone might overhear, then dropped his voice. "You used to hunt shapeshifters, right?"

"Yes, I did. Why?" She kept count of the sheds lining the pathway, all of them filled with tools and rough cloth and wheelbarrows that blocked sight of much beyond.

"What did you look for, exactly? I mean, I know you look for auras, but what else? What are the signs?"

"You're worried that the one buried here is going to come back to life?" Lia peeked through a gap in the sheds to see a long, shaded pavilion near the center of the compound. Baskets were set up on a grid underneath, each one sectioned off and numbered. *Knox wanted to know where the dirt goes. Where the workers and the guards are housed, any guard checkpoints, eating areas . . .*

Noticing where Lia was looking, he explained, "That's where they deposit the fill coming from inside the tomb. The numbers correlate to the map we've drawn of the rooms so we know exactly which area, which floor, it's come from. . . ." Mateo's voice became more and more animated as he led her past the baskets of rocks toward the center of the bowl, where all the worker ants were swarming. There was a break in the crowd, and suddenly Lia saw the hole in the ground, a ladder poking out from the earth like a knife in a wound. She slowed without meaning to.

What could Knox want from down there?

"To answer your questions, I'm not particularly worried about Patenga coming back to life. We hardly knew anything about the man before opening this tomb," Mateo went on, "only that he was in this area at the very beginning of the shapeshifter period and he liked wearing a lizard head. But how did he come to power? What did he do while he was there? Was his entire life bent on becoming a soul-stealing king? How could he have become something so terrible, and why did people let him?" Mateo's cheeks pinked when Lia looked up at him, but maybe it was just the heat.

"Why the lizard head?" Lia eyed a box emerging from the tomb's mouth on some kind of pulley contraption, swinging back and forth on the rope until workers secured the box and took it over to one of the sheds lined up on the other side of the tomb.

"Yes, exactly." Mateo really did smile then. "Why a lizard head of all things?"

"So if you're not worried about Patenga bursting up through the ground, why do you want to know about shapeshifters?"

"Um, call it a suspicion? The dig director has been behaving oddly, and I just wondered . . ." He blushed. "It's probably silly. It's just, my episodes have gotten worse here, down in the tomb especially, and shapeshifters are supposed to steal energy."

"You can see auras, though. It's pretty easy to tell, isn't it?"

"I can't *always* see auras."

"Because you're sick?" Lia counted every structure as Mateo led her around the edge of the open space surrounding the tomb, assigning positions and occupants as best she could inside her head. They walked past a well and what looked like an outdoor kitchen with tables set up around it. The scent of fried dough lingered around the site. "I guess I don't know much about that. I never caught a shapeshifter stealing energy. And I thought your episodes were from wasting sickness."

Pausing, Mateo tipped his hat so she couldn't see his face for a second. "They . . . probably are. I guess. Just . . . would you let me know if you see anything?"

Lia finally let all her attention settle on Mateo, stepping forward so she could see his face. "You're really worried about this."

He looked up at the sky. "I mean, a little. Yes."

"A lot."

Mateo bit his lip and finally looked at her. Nodded.

Unease prickled across her skin. A shapeshifter here? But then Lia shook off the feeling. She hadn't seen a single glimpse of dark aura before she'd touched Ewan. And Knox—Knox would have seen it if he'd come out this way, and it sounded as if he had. "I'll let you know if I see anything suspicious." Smiling was a little harder than it should have been.

"Thank you." His smile was reluctant too, as if there were more riding on his request than he could say.

She changed the subject. "You mentioned an afternoon meal. Are we going to be staying for it?"

"Do Devoted eat?" Mateo asked. "I always assumed your lot subsisted on . . . I don't know, moon milk or something."

"*Moon* milk?" A laugh bubbled up inside Lia, taking her by surprise. "Technically, I'm not a Devoted at the moment."

"Then why the scarf?"

"What's it to you if I wear a scarf or not? Lots of people wear them to keep from breathing dust and smelling"—she gestured back toward Chaol—"everything."

"But people don't wear them the way you do—covering every inch of you. Seems like you'd stick out less if you weren't pretending to be allergic to the sun."

"You sure you aren't just curious?"

Mateo's mouth twisted upward into a real smile. "You're right, I am curious about what you look like. But I'm more worried that you *know* wearing a scarf makes you stick out, which means you're wearing it for a reason that outweighs the danger of being noticed." He pulled her through the line of workers to the hanging contraption poised over the hole. Lia's insides went cold as she looked down into it, as if it were one large, blinking eye. "My guess is it's a weapon. Your father won't let you out with a sword, so you've resorted to strangling people."

Lia snorted, trying to hold back her laugh. "An I'll-let-you-see-my-face-but-it'll-be-the-*last*-thing-you'll-see sort of thing?" She started toward the ladder. "I get to go inside, right?"

"Absolutely." She wasn't sure whether he meant she must be using her scarf to murder people or that she got to go down the ladder. "Come over this way." Mateo's hand tugged her to where the workers had clustered around the hole, the contraption suspended over the opening dragging baskets up from the dark. The light glistened over bits of broken glass and pottery amidst the dirt and rock. Lia frowned, her eyes catching on something brown-stained and bone-shaped poking out from the middle.

Once the workers had pulled the load onto the ground, Mateo

let her hand drop from his arm and gave his hat to a worker. "They finally got past the stairs on the second level—they were all fitted with pressure plates that ejected darts from the walls! It's spectacular, the technology. Probably all uses Basist magic, because I've never seen anything like it. I'm anxious to see what they found on the next level." His voice got quieter as he started down the ladder.

Lia followed, once again wishing for her aurasight. Mateo's questions about shapeshifters made her wish she could see for sure that the shapeshifter in the tomb was well and truly dead.

The air turned muggy and hot as she descended. When her feet finally hit the ground, she almost knocked into the large mirror shooting light from above to another mirror across the room, the mirror there directing it down into a hole in the stone floor. There was another contraption set up next to the hole, long ropes feeding into the open tomb.

Mateo descended the second ladder, and when Lia followed, she felt trapped in the column of light shining from above, more blinded by the brightness than she'd ever been by dark. About halfway down the ladder, Lia caught a breath of movement. There was something lurking in the darkness on the other side of the ladder.

Lia squinted at the wall, her heart beginning to pound when she realized there were eyes there watching her. Bared teeth and claws. A monster.

"Don't be frightened! It's just a relief!" Mateo called up to her, his voice echoing. "Be careful when you get down here. Stay on the rugs."

Descending a little more quickly, Lia stepped onto the ground and hardly even minded when Mateo touched her arm. "Are you all right? I forgot to warn you. Patenga's a little shocking."

Lia stared up at the carving, the shapeshifter so large that he took up most of the wall, the bottom five feet depicting little people bent down to worship him. She shuddered.

"Come on." Mateo pulled her along the rugs, bright red splashed on the stone to either side. "I want to see what they've uncovered."

There were other carvings of Patenga throughout the cave, all of them four times the size of a man and grinning down at her, their eyes following as Lia passed. Lia's stopped at the wide opening to the stairs, framed by what looked like beaten gold. She slowed, looking up at the curved top, the shape odd. "Is that . . . a shield?" she asked.

Mateo squinted up at it. "I have a sketch of it at home, but I haven't been able to cross-reference it yet. It could possibly be some homage to Basism, or perhaps to the nameless god? It's hard to know, since most depictions of him were destroyed. Stay close when we get down the stairs. I don't think they've finished clearing the room of fill, much less any traps. Two workers fell down when they first opened this passage, and we haven't found them yet."

Goose bumps needled out across Lia's arms as she walked under the golden shield. The staircase walls were strangled by carvings of vines, roots, and flowers, and the air felt heavier and hotter in Lia's lungs. Every few feet there were holes in the walls that the carvings couldn't quiet disguise, where darts must have shot through. The stairs themselves were in deconstructed pieces to stop the pressure plates from engaging, it seemed, only gritty nubs left over to hold the mirrors. Lia almost tripped over a loose stone, not sure if she wanted more light to see what was coming or less.

Mateo was practically jumping up and down by the time they got to the bottom of the stairs, almost waltzing her through the door at the bottom, which was surrounded by a gold shield like the one above. Beyond it, a cluster of workers huddled by the closer wall, carefully moving bits of rock and who knew what else from the floor of the cavern to their baskets.

Pulling out a small mirror, Mateo stole some of the light glancing down into the room and redirected it to move across the designs on the wall. Near the corners of the room where the walls met the ceiling, the carvings seemed as if they didn't quite match up, as if whoever had planned them had misjudged the height and had to cut out a section. There were long cracks in the ceiling, the worst bits at the edges. Lia followed Mateo's mirrorlight with her eyes, the little circle catching on carvings of what looked like feathers, clouds, rain . . . a sword?

"Give me that." Lia grabbed the mirror, throwing light onto the very center of the ceiling. There, carved into the rock, was a woman. She held a long silver sword aloft, the other arm looped around a small figure in her lap. Surrounding her was a riot of color, jewels of blue and gray and green, and above her head, a burst of gold that flickered in waves like fire around her broken mask.

Calsta.

Calsta in a shapeshifter's tomb.

"What in the history of sky-blasted . . ." Mateo's whisper was hoarse. "Look, she's holding Patenga."

"They're surrounded in gold." Lia shifted the light so it sat on the figure in the goddess's lap, so small he looked like a doll. He was wearing a golden crown and holding a little sword of his own. "Why would he be surrounded by gold?"

"Maybe it's supposed to be an aura?"

Lia looked at Mateo, lowering her voice. "You've never seen a Basist aura? They aren't gold."

Mateo kept his eyes on the goddess, an angry bend to his eyebrows. "Do all Basist auras look the same?"

"Of course they—"

"Master Montanne!" The shout erupted from the crowd of workers, a figure breaking off to walk toward them, speaking quickly in what sounded like one of the eastern-province dialects.

Mateo's chin came up as he listened, and he looked around the room as if he were smelling sour milk and couldn't tell where it was coming from.

"What is he saying?" Lia asked.

"That they found something." He looked at her. "Is it just me, or is it cooler down here? Is there a draft?"

"I can feel it too. Where is it coming from?" Lia closed her eyes, feeling the brush of air on her skin. It shut out the image of the goddess staring down at her through the cracked mask.

"I can't tell, but maybe . . . well, maybe the rooms down here aren't as secure as we thought. There must be another way in. The whole site could be compromised." Lia's heart sank at the tinge of disappointment in his voice. "But this . . . even if this is all we find . . ." His face lit up as he looked up at the goddess. The worker gestured for Mateo to follow, so Lia did likewise, using the mirror to gloss over the reliefs, her confusion growing every second.

"Calsta's mask is broken." Mateo's voice was breathless. "All our histories say it broke in her fight against the nameless god, but this tomb predates—gods above and beneath," he gasped, pulling Lia's attention down to the floor where he was standing. "Everyone off. Get back, away from it!"

The workers scurried out of the way, and Mateo redirected the main mirror to touch the center of the floor. An awful darkness peered up through the bits of stone and dirt, sparkling in the mirrorlight. As Lia's eyes adjusted to the glare, she found arms, a head, rocks and leaves and trees twined around the figure on the ground. There was a circle around his head, much the way there was around Calsta's, though it seemed to be plain stone.

The nameless god.

He was holding a small figure just the way Calsta was. A man with a golden shield like the one marking the doors.

Lia stepped back, not sure how she felt about seeing the nameless god there right in front of her. Stricken from history books, his very name lost, and there he was, depicted as something to be worshipped, not the creature made of dirt and vines Calsta strangled in her temple.

Mateo walked around the carving, then around it again, his hands caught up in his hair. "This is . . . this is . . ." He grappled for his satchel and pulled out a sheet of vellum. "Lia, this is *huge*. I've only ever seen one other depiction—wait." He stopped, staring down at the sinuous vines and roots twining around the god's arms and legs, little pockmarks in the stone all around his head. "This is fresh."

"Fresh?" The worker who had addressed them in Elantin switched to Common. "Sir, how could—"

"Not the carvings. *This*." Mateo's fingers stabbed toward the little holes. "There are fresh tool marks."

Lia went to stand next to him, looking at all the chipped bits in the stone. It was as if the nameless god had been surrounded by a bed of burrowing worms. But then her light caught on a tiny sliver of blazing lilac. It was a loose gemstone, just sitting on the dirty floor next to the nameless god's ear. "Purple. He had purple stones all around him. Like Calsta's aura. Someone stole the nameless god's aura," she whispered.

"Who could have done this?" Mateo's voice cracked. He looked up at the worker who had brought them over. "Was it like this when you opened the room this morning?"

The man murmured something, touching his forehead, then his chest. A warding sign against ghosts.

"You said two workers disappeared down here." A breeze touched Lia's scarf, making the fringe play across her shoulder. She stilled it, a flicker of unease in her belly. "Maybe it was them?"

"No. There's something . . ." Mateo stood up and circled around the carving once more, then stopped at the nameless god's feet. He pulled out a stick of charcoal, but it broke between his fingers, sending bits skittering across the carving to rest on the nameless god's face.

Whoosh. Lia tensed as all the air around her seemed to suck away. A beam of light shot down from above, the ceiling suddenly alive with gold and white that seemed to be coming directly from Calsta's broken mask. It shone down onto the nameless god's head, shards of purple that had been left behind glowing like purple fire. The carvings around his eyes bled dark, some kind of jet stone behind them drinking in all the light.

The mirrorlight from upstairs suddenly extinguished, leaving an ethereal and *impossible* glow that emanated from Calsta, an echoing slam juddering through the whole room. All of Lia's body prickled over and she slowly turned toward the doorway. It wasn't a doorway any longer: a golden sheet of rock had slid down to block it off.

Above her, the rock seemed to groan, as if Calsta were summoning one of her storms from the cliff itself. Lia looked up, dust raining down on the exposed bridge of her nose and cheekbones.

The ceiling was inching down toward the floor.

Knox eyed the wagon piled high with supplies just outside the dry market. "You're sure this is the right one?" he made himself ask as he turned back to the alley, not liking that he had to.

Because he wasn't out with Anwei. He was with Altahn. And *Noa*, who had suddenly moved into Anwei's room like a little fire-dancing leech.

Looking over when Altahn didn't immediately answer his question, Knox hated everything all over again. The Trib had pulled down the scarf Anwei had made him use to cover his face. He dragged it back into place when Knox glared at him.

Altahn's voice was muffled through the fabric. "Of course I'm sure this is the right wagon. This is the weekly order they take out to the excavation. Father's been watching them since we got to Chaol."

Noa sidled up behind them, making Knox grit his teeth. "Come on, the driver's almost here." Her voice held about twelve too many notes of fun, as if she thought this were some kind of performance that she'd get a standing ovation for at the end. Altahn would probably be the one giving it, if his sidelong glance at her was anything to go by.

Balancing a tray of sweet buns on one hand, Noa craned her neck to catch sight of the wagon driver. "Okay. You two are ready?"

"You need any help with those?" Altahn asked.

"You do your job, I'll do mine." She flashed a smile at him that set Knox's teeth on edge, waiting until the wagon driver began tying down his load before she walked out of the alley with her tray. "There you are!" she said, her huskily accented Common sweeter than the icing drizzled across her tray of sweet rolls.

Knox pressed a hand to his forehead. A year of running around with Anwei, the two of them poking at each other and laughing as they barely kept a few steps ahead of the magistrate and now . . .

This. He was hiding in an alley with a Trib and a fire dancer. Watching Altahn ogle Noa as if it didn't matter who knew he thought she was pretty. Maybe for normal people it didn't. That made Knox's head ache even more.

Noa's husky laugh rang out from down the street as she picked up one of the sweet rolls and offered it to the wagon driver.

"You're *sure* he's the one with the sweet tooth?" Knox whispered.

"What are you talking about? The man is literally eating out of Noa's hand." Altahn clapped his hands as Noa pulled the wagon driver around the side of his vehicle and out of sight. "Where did you dig her up? She's brilliant."

"You really want to know?" Knox asked, voice flat. "She's second khonin, so try to keep the drool inside your mouth."

"She really is? I thought that was just a costume to distract the guards at the salpowder barge."

"It wasn't. And watch out, she doesn't like boys."

"Really? I got the distinct impression that wasn't the case." Altahn peeked around the corner one last time to make sure the wagon was clear. "Let's go."

Knox moved out of the alley, lugging the basket they'd brought. Altahn darted around him to the back of the cart and pulled out the basket of cloth-wrapped breads and then the package of fresh herbal ghost wards underneath it. "Exactly the same order as every other week," Altahn whispered. "As promised."

Trying not to roll his eyes, Knox lifted the replacement basket into the wagon bed, Noa's laugh floating back toward them along with the driver's delighted muttering as he tried to choose between apple cream and lemon sage. The new basket held all of the same breads that had been ordered for the dig, but Anwei had added a layer of marble-sized explosives at the bottom that she and Altahn had concocted together. They were supposed to last for the ride to the dig, slowly heating in the sun so they'd explode sometime after the wagon rolled through the excavation's gates. Smoke and flash, Anwei had said, and Knox hoped for the wagon driver's sake that smoke and flash were all that would come out of it.

Of course, Anwei had also thought burning the fresh ghost wards the director had ordered would be particularly unnerving, especially if they caught the food and wagon, too, so there would be some fire.

She and Altahn had lain belly-down in Knox's room for three straight hours, sweating over little ceramic trays with tweezers. Altahn had sworn at the little grains every two minutes until finally he'd sat up, pushing aside the bowed glass that magnified the tray. "It's not going to work. It could all go up in a second if the sun's too hot or it gets jostled too much. Maybe if we used a weaker catalyst?"

"It'll be unstable." Anwei put a hand to her forehead, and Knox felt her thoughts twisting. Plants fit together like a puzzle in her head, but rocks and minerals usually just told her where they were, not what they could do. "Let me look at it again."

Knox stepped back from the door, realizing that in a moment Anwei's place in his mind had gone from a blur of emotions to actual thoughts he could understand.

Calsta? What is going on in my head? I haven't made the oaths to open minds.

But Calsta only loomed in the background, moody and silent.

Something was itching at the back of Anwei's nose as if she were searching for a smell, the one that would complete the picture the sal-powder was supposed to make. It was just out of reach, like a forgotten name.... *Curse all minerals!* The words were so loud in Knox's head, they hurt, swirling around the answer that Anwei *knew* she knew some-how.... Purple color clotted and streamed across her aura, darkening the whole room.

Knox entered the room to kneel down next to her. "Are you all right?" he whispered.

"Shhh, be quiet."

"I mean, can't you feel . . ." *Calsta, I didn't ask for this. How can* Anwei *not feel this?* It was like spying. But then something clicked inside her mind, and Anwei hopped up and ran from the room, surprising a squawk from Noa, who'd been sitting halfway down the hall in a sulk because there was nothing for her to do except take up space now that she'd left Bear, her father, her house, and gods knew what else behind.

Anwei tore through the drawers downstairs, opened jar after jar as she searched for the smell she knew would make the powder into what she wanted but couldn't quite place.

"You're working on my tethers, aren't you?" Noa called through the open door to Altahn, smiling at him much more sweetly than Knox thought was honest. "I showed you how to ignite them, didn't I? We just need them to burn a different color."

A burst of triumph erupted in Knox's head that didn't belong to him. Anwei had found what she was looking for.

Altahn crawled over to speak to Noa through the open door. "I still don't believe you're a fire dancer. Your hair would go up in a second."

Noa shook her head. "I'd show you myself if you were allowed to come with us to the dig. But *someone's* not very trustworthy."

Grinning, Altahn opened his mouth to respond, but then Anwei was back among them, herding him into the room. Knox watched as his partner grabbed a trivet and placed a clean ceramic dish on top of it, her thoughts moving through calculations he didn't understand as she moved a few grains of the white powder into the dish with tweezers. She pulled out a little bag she'd brought from downstairs and poured something from it onto another tray. Sand?

"Whatever you came up with, it's not going to—" Altahn broke off when Anwei slid a candle under the dish. "Wait, you can't," he sputtered, suddenly moving quick.

Knox darted forward, grabbing Altahn before he could touch Anwei. "If she heats it up, it'll explode!" Altahn hissed. "I thought we were trying to *avoid* holes in the floor. Or in *us*."

Fumbling, Anwei lit the candle. Altahn's voice grew louder, all the geniality dripping out as the grains heated, and Knox could feel the smell turning a bloody red that slicked down Anwei's nostrils like knives. Almost . . .

She reached out and touched Knox's bare foot, and something solidified between them. Willow roared to life, battering the barriers in his mind as if she could see Anwei's aura growing in front of her.

There. Just before the grains erupted into flame, Anwei sprinkled the sand over the top.

And then it was done. Anwei receded in his head, the touch of her a light hand on the back of his neck instead of the tidal wave of her before. She pulled her hand back from his foot and picked up the dish, presenting it to Altahn. "I think I've got it."

"That's not possible." Altahn wrestled free of Knox's grip. "What you just did was *not possible*."

It hadn't been.

And now, lugging the stolen basket from the wagon to the alley, Knox could still feel his hands shaking, though it had happened hours ago. What Anwei had done *wasn't* possible.

Even thinking about it made Willow rear up in his head like the specter she was, her long, knobbled fingers groping for him, for Anwei, for both of them maybe, lurking like a parchwolf outside a mouse's hole for him to peek out. Still she couldn't speak, but her presence loomed stronger than it had the day before, stronger than she'd ever been.

As if something was *feeding* her. But Willow was more walled off from Knox now than Calsta had ever managed, so what had changed?

Altahn set the replacement basket of bread on top of the doctored box of herbs, then scattered a few more of the little incendiaries into the wagon.

"What are you two doing back here?" The driver poked his head around the side. "Put out your hands. What's that you've taken?"

"Nothing." Knox forced himself to snap to the present. "Your bread was about to fall off . . . we were just trying to help." He tried to smile, but lying didn't come easy to him. Altahn grabbed his arm and pulled him away into the market. Noa met them at the boat, picking up the last sweet roll with her fingers and offering it to Altahn, but when he reached for it, she leaned forward to take a bite of it herself, smirking at him with sugar dusting her lips and chin.

Knox groaned, wishing he could push them both into the river. He stepped into the boat and picked up the paddle, nudging aside the pile of lanterns and the packages of herbs Anwei had sent them out to get. There were still hours of errands to finish before they could go back to the apothecary. They'd traded the carriage stashed at the temple for a wagon, but it wasn't in position yet. Knox hadn't picked up the goats Anwei had insisted were necessary, and Noa had to go to the Firelily to collect her face paint and dancing friends.

A whisper broke through the protective barrier Anwei had made in his head as he sat down. *Find me, Knox.*

Knox froze, gripping the paddle to his chest.

Find me, Knox. We have to fix you and Anwei.

CHAPTER 30

A Truth Unacknowledged

Mateo stumbled back from the carving of the nameless god, an impossible thing no one had ever found intact in years. Something that wouldn't matter when he was squashed flat by the ceiling sinking toward them. He stared up at Calsta's mask, which was reflecting sunlight from . . . somewhere? That meant there was a way out of this room; he just had to find it.

Lia grabbed his arm, hauling him to the edge of the room even as Mateo pushed his mind into all the nooks and crannies of stone, finding little vents and passages for the light and air to filter through but nothing big enough for them to escape out of. Half of it he couldn't see properly because it was so *wrong*, twisting inside his head. Not normal stone, but a tortured leftover, like a body that had been sewn together with another body and told to live. The ceiling, a good ten feet over their heads when they'd walked in, was now only about four feet away. But then Mateo felt something beneath them shift. The nameless god's mouth opened, and something rose out of it, slow and poisonous like a snake.

He grabbed Lia's hand, pulling her toward it. The thing rising from the floor was linked to something below; he could feel it. Another room, another . . . *something*. It snagged in his mind, just the way the trapdoor up in the antechamber had. Staying off the reliefs while running was impossible, and Mateo felt his heart crack as stone crunched under his boots. Lia was right with him, every bit of her clenched as if she meant to fight.

There wasn't anything to fight.

The stone rising from the nameless god's mouth was painted black, a little platform at the top stark white in the light blazing down from Calsta. Mateo climbed onto the platform, the ceiling lowering to press down on his head and shoulders. All of these traps, everything in this tomb, were meant to warn him away from something, which only served to beckon him on.

The pedestal jerked under him as if the nameless god himself were awakening.

"Mateo!" Lia screamed, her hands clawing at his legs.

But he had come here looking for answers, and he wasn't going to leave without them. He reached out with his mind again, and he could feel the pressure plates engaging beneath him. The feel of something unfolding below, and then . . .

Lia hauled him off the platform and onto the ground. "No!" he cried. "There's a place down underneath—it's the burial chamber! He's down there!"

Something swung by him, rushing past in a whistle of stone and metal, a horrible crash filling Mateo's ears. He lay on the ground, cheek against the rocky fill, the smell of bone in his nose. When Lia finally tugged on his arm, he sat up to find two horizontal columns of stone slowly ratcheting back into their positions on opposite sides of the room. They'd crashed together right where he'd been standing on the platform, the gnarled spikes on the ends stained with old blood. But it wasn't *that* old.

Mateo thought he knew what had happened to the two men who had fallen down here. But where had their bodies gone?

"Look," Lia breathed, pointing to the black column.

Sitting the rest of the way up, Mateo stared at the ring of floor around the black column where the nameless god's head and aura had been. The stone floor had segmented like a meat pie, dropping down to reveal a black hole.

The groans of rock lowering from above had stopped, and there was nothing to hear but the dark splash of waves coming from the pit.

Sounds began to come back, pleading sobs from the workers, Lia's frenzied breaths, and the whoosh of brackish sea air streaming up from below. Mateo shakily stood, swearing when his head hit the ceiling, low enough that he had to crick his neck a little to one side.

"The burial chamber is down there," Mateo whispered, the black maw calling to him. "I feel . . ." He looked around at Lia and the workers, shutting his mouth before he could spill out any more about the jagged edges of shapeshifter-hewn stone he could feel below. It was too dark to see anything down there, too dark for any human to know what they'd find. But Mateo knew.

There was a door. It was calling to him. The long-dead king? Or maybe it was caprenum beckoning him deeper.

"When the light was still shining . . ." He looked at Lia, flinching when he saw the dirt splashed across her scarf in the dribbles of light still filtering down from Calsta, blood oozing through the fabric over Lia's nose. "I saw it. The burial chamber door is down there. Are you . . . all right?"

She twisted to look at the walls where the spiked columns had returned, her shoulders hunched. Then to the hole. "You almost died just now. You like this kind of work?"

The weight of what had just happened—almost being crushed, almost falling into the dark hole—hit Mateo. Lia's hand was still firm on his arm. He reached out and pulled her closer into a hug. "Thank you for what you just did. If you hadn't grabbed me—"

Her fist rammed into his stomach. Mateo's knees wobbled, and he hunched forward, gasping for breath, just in time to catch her elbow snapping across his cheekbone. Suddenly he was on the ground, ancient dirt in his mouth and stone digging into his side.

And Lia just stood there over him. Glowering. "Do not touch me."

Mateo stayed down, almost too surprised to feel the pain cracking out from his stomach and down his cheek. Almost. "I'm . . . sorry? I was just trying to say thank you."

"Just say it, then, Mateo." A flicker of embarrassment crossed her face as he gingerly stood up, and she looked away, pointing toward the pit. "You're not going to try going down there right now, are you?"

"Lia, you just . . ." Mateo coughed, gagging a little at the pain in his stomach. But then he rolled over and made himself stand, not sure what to say. Lia was fun to talk to and nice to have behind him in a fight—or doing all the actual fighting in a fight—but when it came down to it, all either of them had ever wanted was to see the back of the other. Mateo dusted himself off and started toward the hole, trying to think of the nameless god's face and aura that had been there instead of Lia being awkward just behind him. Excitement had filled him to the chin only moments ago, but Lia had managed to knock it out of him. It was enough to know the burial chamber was down there, but he had to tell his father before Van found out. They had to get in first.

That was it. That was all he wanted.

"I don't mean to be ice in a cook fire, but would you mind terribly if we . . . ?" Lia pointed to the door, which had opened again but was now partially obscured by the lowered ceiling. All the workers had already run back up the stairs, leaving them behind with the gaping hole.

"Yes, of course." Mateo coughed again, mildly gratified when he managed to play off his undignified hunch around his stomach as a result of the low ceiling. She went first through the golden door, the slab of rock that had fallen down to lock them in pulled back into the wall once more. Bits of the mechanism, whatever it was, flickered in Mateo's mind. He hadn't seen it on the way in. He should have been looking.

But he'd been so excited about what they'd find, excited to show Lia, too. And using his magic meant risking episodes . . .

All the excuses poured through him, giving his thoughts a fiery, annoyed edge. Van wasn't here, so episodes shouldn't be a problem anyway. He'd used his aura when he'd looked into the rocks, and nothing had happened to him, so that proved his theory, didn't it? Van was a shapeshifter who sucked the life out of him whenever he came here.

It wasn't until Mateo got to the antechamber—Lia practically ran past him, making for the ladder—that he noticed the flurry happening around them.

"What is it? What's wrong?" he asked a worker in stumbling Eastern Forge. He understood more than he could speak.

The man shook his head, pushing past him. "I don't understand what you're saying."

Another worker waved, a helpful smile plastered across what was obviously fear underneath. "They're clearing the stable. You and your lady had best go move your horses."

Mateo's insides went tight. They cleared the stable only when auroshes were coming. "Lia, stop!" He tipped up his chin, his stomach still hurting like the nameless god had pulled out his insides with one stone fist. She looked down from her spot halfway up the ladder, her scarf turning bright blue in the column of light. Blue spotted with blood. "You have to hide."

Mateo swore as Lia darted past him into the maze of sheds that had been built for restoring and preserving artifacts from the tomb. He tried to run after her, his lungs tightening with every step, his limbs already starting to shake. *No. Director Van wasn't here! This shouldn't be happening.* An attack now wasn't *fair.* Especially after Lia's unprovoked fist to his stomach.

When he caught up to her, Lia was hiding behind the toolshed that bore burn marks. From the ghost attack, Mateo realized. It was the same shed Van had blocked Mateo from seeing inside the day he'd taken him down into the tomb and threatened him.

"I'm sure it's just Roosters," he gasped. "Come on. I'll take you out the side gate, then double back for the horses."

Lia didn't respond as if she'd frozen there. Mateo peered around the corner of the shed to find a man tying a dappled auroshe in the stable. Little golden flecks erupted around him in a flurry that made Mateo swear inside his head. It was Ewan.

Bella and the mare Lia had ridden were shuffling at the extreme other end of the enclosure, whites showing around their eyes.

"He won't see us. You don't need to fight him like . . ." Mateo pitched his voice low, trying not to think of the Rooster Lia had left broken on his stable floor. "This one's easy, Lia. He can't see auras, so we'll just sneak out. Come on."

The auroshe gave a keening wail, throwing its head back toward the sky. Ewan swore, jerking the creature's lead so it bowed before him. He thrust a hand against the auroshe's forehead just under the horn with an air of great frustration, as if he'd done it a thousand times before.

Mateo squinted. That was what Lia had done to tame Rosie, what she'd had him do to keep Rosie from attacking him. The mare—all teeth and skeleton under a stretched hide—always seemed to smile at him when he went to check on her. Why would Ewan need to calm his own auroshe again?

"He . . ."

Mateo's attention jerked back to Lia, her voice scraped thin.

"He *took Vivi*."

"That's Vivi? *Your* auroshe?" A burst of anger on Lia's behalf flamed up in Mateo's chest as he took in the creature, silver-dappled and fierce—a lion next to Rosie's slightly rabid house cat. But causing a stir would only call attention to Lia. "Now's not the time to fix it." He prepared himself to stop her from barreling out toward Ewan, maybe with a shovel or a particularly sharp excavation brush. . . .

Lia put a hand to the blood-speckled scarf covering her mouth, shrinking against the shed wall. Wholly unlike the girl who had just pulled him from the brink of death with a war whoop.

"Lia?" he breathed. "Lia, what's wrong?"

She was *terrified*. "He's riding . . . how *could* he . . ."

The auroshe screamed again and lunged in Bella's direction, but Ewan grabbed hold of the creature's horn and forced his head down once again. Bending to put his cheek next to the auroshe's, Ewan began murmuring softly to the monster, running a hand possessively down his neck. The auroshe began to shudder, his head dipping until his single horn was grounded, though his teeth were still bared. His long tongue flicked out to taste the man's boots. Lia was shaking, just like her auroshe.

"Lia, please," Mateo whispered, both exasperated and torn. Obviously, taking someone else's auroshe was not done, but it wasn't worth getting dragged back to the seclusion over. "At least we know where Vivi is—we'll figure out what to do about that later. Right now we need to *get out of here.*"

Lia still didn't move, the fingers pressing against her mouth turning white. Like she was frozen.

Mateo looked from her to the Devoted. Ewan was just standing there, jabbering at the foul auroshe as if he were a kitten that had done something especially charming. But something was wrong. Really wrong. Lia had *attacked* Mateo just because—

Because he'd touched her.

Oh, gods above and below. Mateo's breath caught in his throat, everything his father had said rushing back to him in one poisonous wave. Father had said it as if it were a theory. A possibility Lia had run away from. But here she was, her feet merged with the ground as if she'd melted into a statue of a girl instead of the one who could stand her ground in front of a charging silenbahk, flip onto Mateo's horse at the last second, then insult him as they ran away.

"I froze," she'd said. Even Lia had tried to tell him.

Mateo slipped between her and the Devoted, bending down to block her view. "We're going, Lia."

She blinked once, her eyes focusing on him. He smiled, gesturing toward the path behind her. "This way."

She let him herd her around the back of the shed, craning her neck to keep the Devoted in sight when they got to the other side. Just as she peered around the corner, Ewan looked up.

Lia flinched, and the Devoted's eyes focused on her, her scarf a spot of blue in a sea of brown dirt.

She bolted.

Mateo ran after her. She went against the flow of people toward the compound's back wall, darting between workers and upsetting a wheelbarrow full of dirt into the path. Mateo swore, cursing his heavy shoes when the toes caught in the dirt, tripping him.

In the split second he was looking down, Lia disappeared. Ewan was nowhere to be seen. Twisting around, Mateo could see only workers milling past him as if they couldn't feel the frantic chase happening in their midst. Mateo closed his eyes, searching for her aura, the faded golden twinkle leading him to the worker barracks on the southern wall. He found Lia curled just inside one of the rooms, much the way he'd found her in the pantry the very first day in her father's house.

"You're the one who taught me that hiding is a bad idea. There's a back way out of here." He held out a hand to her. She stared at his palm without taking it, as if she'd forgotten what the gesture meant. "If there's something you want me to do other than getting you out of here, then tell me."

That, where nothing else had worked, jolted her from her state. "You?" She took his hand and let him pull her up from the ground.

"What would you do, throw those ridiculous boots at him?"

Mateo gritted his teeth. "There's the Lia I know. Come on." He started toward the large tables where the artifacts were cleaned. He could feel Lia less than a step behind him, practically clinging to his coattails, her breathing rusty and sharp. Two archeologists piecing together a small statue of a silenbahk looked up as Mateo broke into a jog to get to the cover of dirt mounds around the refuse gate.

"Where is he?" Lia hissed.

"He saw you behind the shed, but I don't think he came after us." Mateo forced his aurasight to open again, the effort causing beads of sweat to blossom across his forehead. Ewan's sickly aura appeared in his mind at the middle of the compound, near the tomb's opening, as if he was casually trailing the path of Lia's flight.

"Wait, is he following—"

Lia pulled Mateo to a stop when Vivi's sickly caterwaul shot up through the air from the stable, the sound sending the horses into fits of frightened squeals that carried across the entire compound. Mateo could almost feel the air twisting around Lia, as if it could sense her getting ready to run again.

"Don't." Mateo carefully placed a hand on each of her shoulders, and her attention jerked away from the stable to meet his. "I'm sorry." He pulled his hands away. "You don't want me to touch you, so I won't. But please let me help you?" She was so *short*, and where before she'd been a solid block, a wall, Lia had suddenly become insubstantial, as if she'd forgotten how to exist. "Listen to me. The side gate is just on the other side of this building. You get out of the compound. I'll get the horses and meet you outside the gate. It's going to be okay."

Lia closed her eyes and shook her head, a frantic movement that was wholly unlike her. "You have no idea what you are talking about."

"That's usually true, unfortunately." Even as Mateo led Lia to the large piles of dirt waiting to be carted outside, he could feel Ewan's aura drifting past the barracks where Lia had hidden, then turn past the artifact sheds.

The dirt piles were, mercifully, deserted, though Mateo thought it less a mercy when he saw the heavy iron lock on the gate. A guard standing on the upper walkway stared down at him.

Ewan's aura marched closer.

Bumps breaking out across his neck and arms, Mateo pulled his focus away from Ewan's aura. Away from Lia grabbing hold of his hand, her fingers crushing his, away from the smell of dirt, the tickling hints of minerals registering in his mind, to the lock on the door.

"Where is he?" she hissed. "I can't see *anything*."

"Coming. He's coming." Mateo pushed his mind into the lock. Iron, as he'd thought, with brass decoration. He could feel the pins and tumblers inside, but he could also feel the energy streaming from him every second he tried to look at it, as if he'd sprung a leak. Lia let go of his hand, but he didn't look up, forcing his mind to focus, to find every detail, every notch, every sliver of metal.

His knees wobbled.

I know I haven't made the proper oaths. I would if I were able. But let me move the pins in this lock. Please. It isn't for me.

He pulled on the lock, praying, *willing* it to open. But it didn't move. "Lia?" he whispered. Her aurasparks were no longer beside him.

"What are you doing?" Ewan's voice lanced through Mateo.

Mateo forced himself to turn. The Devoted stood there, made from leather and muscle. Three white scars marred the side of his head, his hair shaved to show them as if they were trophies. Mateo flinched as Ewan casually placed a hand on the hilt of his sword. The Warlord's crest was tooled into his leather cuirass, two auroshes with their horns crossed.

Ewan himself smelled like auroshe, an awful mix of horse and dried blood.

"What are *you* doing inside the compound?" Mateo drew himself up. "I was under the impression that all Devoted were with Director Van in Chaol."

"I was under the impression that all Commonwealth citizens answer to Calsta's Devoted." Ewan didn't even bother to take on a mocking tone. "Why are you trying to break open that gate?"

Mateo cleared his throat. "Van will be angry when he finds out you came when he wasn't here. He can be quite fussy about who walks into his dig. Especially if they leave great big bloodsucking beasts near his horse."

Ewan's hand tightened on his sword, but he didn't draw it. Mateo breathed out a sigh of relief. Whatever assignment he'd been given, Ewan clearly wasn't allowed free rein to deal death in the compound as he liked.

"Who are you?"

"Mateo Montanne."

Ewan sniffed. "There was a girl with you."

"My . . ." Mateo racked his brain. "My assistant?"

"Where is she now?"

"I'm not sure." Mateo gave the lock an annoyed rattle, swearing at it, at the nameless god, at Calsta, and every other god he could remember. "I'd prefer it if you didn't murder her when you've managed to track her down. She has admirable penmanship."

Ewan stepped into Mateo's space, grabbing the lapels of his coat and pulling him in so only his toes touched the ground. His breath snuffed on Mateo's face like a bull ready to charge. "Where did she go, Mateo Montanne?"

Mateo wrenched back his head, hating that Lia was watching him dangle from Ewan's fists like a broken doll. His mind flicked through all the elements present: dirt, clay, the brass buckles on Ewan's armor, the steel of his sword. The old Basists could tear stone from the ground with their thoughts, strangle a man with his own necklace, turn a sword against its bearer. But Mateo only bled, his energy and life streaming out of him. "Why don't you ask your goddess?" he finally choked out. "Or doesn't she help you harass girls?"

Ewan threw him down, Mateo's already weak knees buckling under him so he landed in the dirt. A flicker of movement above them on the wall registered at the corner of his mind, the guard set to watch over the gate slipping away from his post and the violence he didn't want to witness.

The Devoted drew his sword and held the point at Mateo's chin. "Refusing to help me is refusing to help the Warlord. I'm only going to ask you one more time—"

"I'm here on the Warlord's behalf." Mateo tipped up his chin, meeting Ewan's eyes. "Or don't you want us to find a cure to the wasting sickness?"

Ewan's eyes narrowed.

"The Warlord is only digging this place up because of me and my father. We're looking for ingredients that could stop your kind from dying their horrible, slow deaths." Mateo tried to sound nonchalant, but the proper cadence was difficult to produce with a sword at his throat. "So I'd think twice before threatening me any more. The Warlord would be more upset about me disappearing than you."

Ewan lowered the sword to rest on the ground beside Mateo. "You really believe some medicine is more important to the Warlord than my sword?"

"If my father wrote a letter asking the Warlord to burn those scars off your head, I think she'd listen. She'll be here soon, so we can test it, if you like. You're already going to be in trouble for losing her spiriter."

"What do you know about spiriters?" When Ewan stepped back, a smile flickered across his face. It was a horrible, violent thing that was worse than the sword. He sheathed his weapon and crouched down next to Mateo. "You tell your 'assistant' that I know the way she walks. The way she runs. I like that she's hiding. I'm not in a hurry to find her. Wherever she is . . . out there in a field of sugarcane. Running as fast as she can back toward Chaol. Huddled in a ditch. I'm coming for her. I want her to know that."

Fear twisted in Mateo's belly. "Is terrorizing archeologists something you normally do? And do you have an immediate superior I could notify of such erratic behavior?"

An impossibly loud crack shattered the air. Ewan and Mateo both twisted to look toward the sound, a narrow plume of black smoke shooting up into the air over the stable. Mateo's eyes froze on the ashy trail blustering into the sky. A second explosion sounded, and then a third, coming from the general direction of the archeologist quarters.

Ewan started toward the smoke, hardly looking back at Mateo to say, "Tell Lia that Vivi sends his love. I only had to use a razor bit the first day."

Mateo couldn't understand the shape of the smoke pouring up into the sky, only glad it hadn't come from the tomb or any of the artifact sheds. Hopefully, no one was hurt, but his father could fix burns, not destroyed artifacts. He picked himself up from the ground, anger building inside him at whoever was stupid enough to mix anything dangerous inside the compound, because it was easier than facing what had just happened. Being knocked to the ground. Threatened.

What Ewan had said about Lia. *I know the way she walks.*

Mateo dusted off his pants and closed his eyes to look for Lia's aura, but everything inside his head wavered, his eyesight crackling with darkness at the edges. Leaning with one hand against the wall, Mateo took a long breath, willing his body to remain upright when it so very much wanted to collapse.

Lia exploded from between two piles of dirt, her scarf wet with tears and a shovel in her hand. Her eyes darted past Mateo to the catwalk above, to the piles of dirt surrounding them. "What . . . where . . ." She wiped a hand across her eyes.

Mateo couldn't quite control his breathing. "He's gone."

Lia raised the shovel blade and lurched toward him. Mateo sagged against the wall, laughing at himself for pitying her—were all Devoted completely unbalanced? But she slammed the shovel's blade against the lock, once, twice, until the metal crumpled and it fell to the ground with a dead thud.

Throwing down the shovel, Lia pushed open the gate. She grabbed his arm, her fingers pressing painfully into his skin as she dragged him through.

It took more than an hour to walk home, winding through the fields with Lia's sharp eyes on the road. Once they got back to the cliff house, Lia didn't even speak. She just went to the stable, saddled Tual's horse, and mounted.

Mateo could hardly hold himself up. *This happens every time I go to the dig. But Van wasn't there today.* "Wait." He grabbed hold of the reins. "We need to talk about this," he said, his words slurring as if an episode would come at any moment.

Lia shook her head, silent, as she had been since they left the compound.

"Ewan knew you were there. He knows you're connected to me now."

She looked up at the sky as if to ask for some kind of help. "So we have to put the bridal wreaths aside until he's gone. It's fine." Reaching up to brush away a tear, Lia tried to kick the horse forward, but the mare was old and more interested in gumming Mateo's arm than listening to a rider she didn't know. "For my own safety, right? At least until your father tells the Warlord my father's a traitor."

Mateo shook his head. "That crackpot is *hunting* you, Lia." Every word out of Ewan's mouth had been caked in a noxious confidence, an improper delight in standing over another man and pressing a sword to his throat. He seemed to relish the thought of Lia huddling in a ditch praying that Calsta would slow his feet, and absolutely certain the goddess would do no such thing.

"My father wasn't lying about being able to protect you. Maybe it would be safer for you to stay with us until the Warlord has come and gone."

Lia's head was already shaking. She pulled the reins out of his hand. "You just said Ewan will know to look here."

"But he's just a Devoted. If he tries to search our house or goes against my father, he'll be creating huge political problems for himself, and he knows it. We can figure out the rest later." He put out a hand to steady himself against the horse. "You'd be safer here even if Ewan saw you standing in the window."

"I have to go." She dug her heels into the horse's side, urging her forward, and galloped out the gate.

Mateo staggered after her, propping himself up against a gatepost to watch her disappear into the dust hanging over the road to Chaol. Was that panic? A rejection? For some reason it felt like both.

Hoofbeats pounded the road behind him. Mateo turned to look, barely in time to catch the auroshe as it blazed past, Ewan on its back.

Mateo ran to the stable, but Bella was still at the dig. Lia had taken his father's horse. Harlan and the other hostlers had beasts here, and Rosie was down on the beach. . . .

Harlan appeared in the stable door, two maids flanking him. "I need you to come inside, sir." He kept his eyes down.

"No, I need a horse. I need—"

"I'm sorry, Master Montanne. Your father gave strict instructions that you stay here once you got back from the dig. He told us we were to stop you leaving, even if it gets messy." The hostler swallowed, moving to block the door. "I don't want to, but those were my orders. I'm sorry."

Mateo's gut clenched at the thought of two scrawny maids and a hostler being able to keep him from going after Ewan and Lia. Anger burst out inside of him, but anger had never done much for him. His hands were shaking, the *world* was shaking, and Lia was out there with no idea Ewan was right behind her. He had to be like Lia. No stern words, all action. "I'm taking one of the horses. You get out of my way, or I'll run over the top of you."

"I'm sorry, sir." Harlan finally looked him in the eye, and all Mateo wanted to do was take his apologies and burn them. "But I'm not going to let that happen."

Knox wiped the sweat from his forehead as he pulled the boat in after the last of the errands and hopped onto the dock to tie it. What would Anwei say if he told her he had a ghost in his head?

That the ghost wanted him to kill her?

That the connection between them had pushed the ghost away . . . but now Willow was getting too strong, even for that?

Noa had gone to the Firelily, leaving Altahn less talkative as he helped unload the last of the supplies—a small recurved bow and blunted arrows, the extra herbs, the *goats*, one of which kept butting Knox in the leg. Knox was supposed to be watching Altahn, but instead his feet took him to the stairs. To Anwei's door. He opened it and there she was, her braids pulled up high on her head and sweat across her forehead as she crouched over the trivet.

Willow glimmered in his mind. *Please, Knox.* There was an undercurrent of a growl he'd never heard in her voice before, as if she was growing, transforming into something new and even less human. *Find me.*

"Success?" Anwei asked, looking up from the bubbling pot. She smiled when he nodded. "Good. Come in and sit down, I need to check you over. You've been improving, but if I can't get you to rest—"

"I need to talk to you." He hung back in the hallway, nodding to Altahn when he went into Knox's room to prepare the rest of the supplies for their planned assault on the dig the next evening.

Anwei came to the door and held it open so he would come inside. He hesitated a moment before crossing the threshold. He could keep

Willow down. He had to, if only for the next few days, until they'd gotten the shapeshifter. Then he'd be able to get Willow out of his head once and for all.

He stepped into the room, keeping a healthy distance between himself and his partner. The easiness that had always been between them seemed to have shattered, as if this job, the shapeshifter, all of it, had irreversibly destroyed the comfortable partnership that had asked so little of either of them.

Knowing more about Anwei made him like her more. Notice her more. Made *Willow* notice her even more than she already had.

And Anwei knowing more about Knox had made everything trickier, too. She wasn't supposed to know anything about him at all. It was in his oaths.

Maybe that was why Calsta was pulling back. The oaths were there inside him, Calsta's *power* was still there, waiting for him to take it. But maybe he hadn't kept them well enough, and so the goddess herself was gone.

Anwei sighed, sinking onto the bed and pulling out her new medicine bag. "Come over here. That poison pushed all your humors out of balance, and if we're going to go steal a sword and destroy a shapeshifter, I kind of need you to be healthy."

"I haven't heard from Lia."

Hand pausing, Anwei sighed again, then opened her bag. "I know. I haven't heard from Jecks, either. We're going to have to make do with what we have. Going into the tomb with nothing but Shale's less-than-helpful maps seems . . ."

"Like a death wish?"

"Sort of. But we can't wait any longer. Every second we hold Altahn, especially with the Warlord arriving soon, is dangerous. We have to get the shapeshifter and the sword *now*."

"I just can't shake the feeling that Altahn's extreme helpfulness will evaporate in the middle of the night and—"

Anwei stood abruptly. She reached out, her fingers brushing lightly across his neck. Knox froze, holding his breath. Her fingers stopped on the pulse jumping at the base of his throat, her eyes glazed as she started counting. Oblivious to the way her breath brushed his collarbone . . .

"Your pulse is too fast." Her brow furrowed. She bent down and shoved her head against his chest. "Breathe in."

"But you're right, we can't wait any longer." He forced himself to keep talking, frantically looking at the ceiling, the door, the medicine bag, anything not to look down at Anwei's cheek against his chest. There were so many walls inside his mind, it felt impossible to tell where one started and the other ended. The one between him and Calsta's energy. The one between him and Willow. And the one that held the other two up, the wall between him and Anwei. "I've lived my whole life at the beck and call of a bloody sword. . . ." The words spilled out, not even making sense. "A *ghost*. Trying to follow my Devoted masters, who may or may not have been speaking for Calsta . . ."

Anwei's hand squeezed his arm, pulling him closer. "Breathe, Knox."

But he couldn't, speaking quickly as if he could build the wall back up with words. "I need this to be over. The only decision I've made for myself in six years was to stay here. With you."

Knox pressed his lips together. *Calsta* had told him to stay here. *She'd* hinted that Anwei was the answer to the sword and Willow and all of it, so he'd stayed. Set up in a thief's house, followed her on jobs, watched her Basist glow.

He'd obeyed. But that wasn't the real reason he'd spent the last year climbing walls and stealing high khonins' ugly art. The reality of it burned in his chest, the truth he wasn't allowed to acknowledge.

Inside him, Calsta's power seemed to waver. He put a hand to the wall, his heart beating erratically. Anwei's hands dropped to her sides, her expression almost frightened. "What's going on, Knox? I can't . . ." She dove for her medicine bag on the bed. "I can't . . . I can't smell it. You have to tell me where it hurts."

"I'm fine." He wasn't. The glittering inside him guttered like a campfire in high wind.

Focus, Calsta hissed inside his head. The flicker of energy didn't siphon away. But even the momentary lapse had left him feeling as if he'd skipped a stair.

Anwei pulled him toward her desk and sat him in the chair. She barely had time to say "Don't move" before she ran from the room.

Knox grasped inside himself, filling himself with Calsta's energy and holding it tight. His eyes pinched shut, and every muscle seemed to clench, as if he could hold the Sky Painter inside him. *Please. You put me here with Anwei. I've devoted my life to you for the last six years. I've never so much as smelled a caramel cake or looked at a pair of fancy shoes. Help me.*

I can't right now, Knox. I can't, or he'll see.

What is that supposed to mean? Who will see?

Why do you think Willow has grown so strong inside you, Knox? He's close. If she tells him even a little . . . I can't say. Anything is too much.

Holding all that energy forced Knox's aurasight out beyond the room—Altahn's aura sat on Knox's bed, Anwei's was darting between jars downstairs, with Gulya's aged aura following her worriedly, and the surrounding alleys and canals were littered with globe after globe of white.

Until his mind latched on to one globe that was not white.

It held a trace of gold in it. Lia.

And there was another one trailing after her. Ewan Hardcastle.

Lia was nearly to the apothecary gates, Ewan on the skybridge between islands less than a hundred paces behind.

Knox forced Calsta's energy back to her side of the wall and stood. Lia was coming. Lia wasn't supposed to come here. She wasn't even supposed to know where to find Knox. But there she was, outside. With *Ewan* in tow.

Knox pushed through Anwei's door and sprinted down the stairs, his legs wobbling with every step, though whether it was because Calsta was distant, because of what he'd said to Anwei, or because of poison, it was difficult to tell.

Bursting into the herb room, Knox found Anwei furiously grinding something in a stone bowl, her knuckles white. "You weren't supposed to move!" She inhaled deep, her nose wrinkling. "I can't smell *anything* on you—"

"Lia's coming this way," he interrupted.

Anwei's fingers didn't stop grinding, her face pale. "Sit down, Knox."

"She's with the other Devoted, Anwei! Doesn't seem like she's bringing a map."

"What is going on?" Altahn asked from the top of the stairs.

"So it *was* a trap." Anwei's fingers slowed. "Is that why everything is going all haywire inside you? I could hardly even read your pulse." She dropped the mortar and pestle and grabbed her medicine bag. "Doesn't matter. You sit down, I'll take care of it."

Willow perked up inside him. *You need me for this. You needed me when you escaped the seclusion, and that was just Roosters.* Knox tried to push the voice back, hating that she was right. He *had* used the sword to get out of the seclusion. But he didn't *want* to ever again. He'd never wanted to use any sword. What Lia wanted might be something else entirely.

Knox followed Anwei to the other side of the table, not wanting to believe that Lia, his closest friend for so many years, his *sister*, had learned to lie.

He *needed* the sword. Knox couldn't tell if the thought was his or Willow's. "Where is it?" The words came out too quickly, and Anwei turned in surprise. "The sword. Where is my sword?"

She brought the stone bowl up to her nose to smell. "You drop this in a knuckle of boiled water and don't move until you feel steady again."

"I'm not sick." He grabbed the bowl away from her. "Where is my sword, Anwei?"

She shouldered her medicine bag and streaked for the back door. "You think I can't take on two powerless Devoted on my own?"

"Devoted are coming here?" Altahn asked, quite a bit louder than before. He rattled off a string of words in Trib that Knox didn't understand.

"Watch your mouth," Anwei hissed at Altahn before going to the door. "Where is Lia now?"

"Where is my *sword*?" The need for it itched and burned inside him. He couldn't let Lia or Ewan in here. Either of them could destroy the whole place without a single spark of Calsta's power. It was a righteous need. One that Calsta would approve of.

Was it Willow or he who thought that? Which was it?

Anwei's hand caught his own and held it still, though he hadn't realized he was groping for the sword in the first place. Suddenly he could feel the force of her inside his head, and the need for the sword dulled and then winked out. "You can't have it, Knox," she murmured. "Now *sit*."

Knox breathed in, embracing his aurasight, and almost startled to find Lia hopping over the back wall into the courtyard. Ewan was following the canal walkway, steadily coming closer. "She's in the courtyard."

"Stay there." Grabbing something from her bag, Anwei shouldered her way through the door without waiting to hear any more. Knox ran after her but stopped himself short when he could see properly outside.

Lia was sitting just inside the gates, her back against the stone wall. Some of her bright coppery curls had slipped free from the scarf over her face. Her long skirts were muddy at the hems, and she was curled over her knees, hand covering her eyes as if she was crying.

"You must be Knox's friend." Anwei's voice was about three times warmer than it should have been, breaking Knox from his momentary surprise. His partner was holding the little envelope of who-knew-what behind her back.

"Get down, Knox." Lia hiccuped. "Hide!"

Knox could feel Ewan's aura stalk near . . . as if he was *chasing after* Lia, not the second arm to an attack.

If Lia didn't want Ewan to find her, why hadn't she dragged him up a skybridge ladder and taken care of him? After years of fighting Lia, Knox knew she was capable of killing with her bare hands if needed, but instead she was here, folded in on herself as she had been the day Master Helan had come for her. Terrified.

What did Lia have to be terrified about?

Knox stepped past Anwei, putting a hand on his partner's shoulder. Since seeing Lia a few days before, he'd hated the way this new life of hiding had turned his mind into a horrible pool where suspicion sat like stagnant water. But what else could Lia be doing here other than helping Ewan complete the hunt he'd failed a year ago?

"I tried to lose him in the tunnels. Had to leave my horse. But he left Vivi and ran after me. . . ." Lia's whisper was a knife in his stomach.

Ewan's aura gusted into the street fronting the apothecary, then stormed by and turned the corner to where the courtyard wall stood between the road and Knox, Anwei, and Lia. Knox slipped down, the top of Ewan's head just visible over the wall.

The Devoted stopped outside. Hands knotted around her scarf, Lia watched Knox's face as if she could somehow steal his aursight and see where Ewan was. Anwei looked between them and slipped out through the outer gate.

Her voice came over the wall, cheery and all too helpful. "You're looking for the apothecary? The entrance is just around that way. Oh,

I can tell from your look . . . no, you don't need to be so embarrassed. Come with me, we have all the herbs you could need for those *downstairs* problems of yours. . . ."

It was only a second before Ewan's aura stormed the rest of the way down the street, then up a skybridge to the next island in the Coil's little chain, disappearing from Knox's aurasight. Anwei's aura returned via the shop's front door and walked through the herb room, and then Anwei herself appeared on the back step, an herb envelope clutched in her hand. "What in Calsta's dirty bathwater is going on right now?" Her cheery tones had faded, her eyes sharp as she looked between Knox and Lia.

"Yeah, I'm confused too," Altahn said over Anwei's shoulder, looking Lia up and down. "Hi. I don't think we've met before."

"Get upstairs *now*, Altahn, unless you want to end up asleep for another week." Anwei gestured menacingly with the envelope. The Trib put his hands up and retreated back into the room, but Knox could see his aura hovering just inside, well within earshot.

But Lia showing up here was too big for him to process, her crumpled form looking far too helpless for the girl who he knew could slit grown men's throats.

"Why are you here, Lia?" His voice broke a little. "Please tell me something I'll believe."

Lia swallowed. "Where is Ewan now?"

"Gone." Anwei walked over to crouch next to Knox. "And you'd better do as Knox said or you will be too."

Lia let her hands sink away from her face, the whites of her eyes stained red from crying. She focused on him. "I ran away because they wanted me to have a child, Knox. Master Helan always seemed a little unhappy about it all, but he never stood up for me. And Ewan was the one the Warlord wanted. I went to the dig like you asked, and Ewan caught me out in the open. . . ."

It felt as if all of Knox's muscles had gone soft, leaving him to sag to the ground. He turned and sat next to her, back against the wall. "They asked you to break your oaths?"

Lia's hands covered her face again. "Ewan knew, and it was killing his aura. My touching him was enough to make him lose it entirely, and I did it so he wouldn't see you up on the wall."

"That's why *your* aura is gone? *Storm Rider*, Lia, why didn't you tell me before?"

"After our auras were gone, he . . . attacked me." Lia's words came out sharp; each of her breaths shuddered in and out. "I should be stronger than this. I *am* stronger than this." Her eyes pinched closed. "Why does this hurt so much? Why couldn't I have just *killed* him when I saw him at the dig? I've killed before."

"Will someone please translate?" Anwei's hands were still full of herbs.

Knox reached for Lia's hand. She let him take it, squeezing his fingers hard. Her palms were wet from tears. "I don't know what's wrong with me." Her breaths were coming too fast, almost like hiccups. "Seeing him shouldn't matter. I got away. But then I saw him following me, and he's hurting Vivi, and he told Mateo he was going to hunt me down, and—"

"Lia, calm down." Knox moved closer, kneeling in front of her.

Lia contracted forward, one of her hands digging into her chest. "I *can't*."

Knox twisted toward Anwei to plead for help, but she was already barking at Altahn to do something, running after him as if the nameless god himself were in her shadow. Lia's fingernails were digging into Knox's hand, pulling him closer.

"Lia, listen to me. Ewan didn't see you come in here. Even if he tried to hurt you, I would . . . *you* could . . ." The sentences were hard to form, images of Ewan tearing off Lia's veil stuck in Knox's brain. His sister, offered to a man as if she were some kind of bargaining chip to keep Devoted alive.

"I can't . . ." She tried to gulp down a breath of air. "I couldn't." Another gasp. "That day . . ." Gasp. "I just stood there. . . ." Gasp. "And he was hurting me. . . ." Gasp. "Aria surprised him. . . ."

And then Anwei was pushing Knox aside, holding one of the soft leather bags from the apothecary up to Lia's mouth. "Hold it over your mouth and nose." Her voice was calm, soft, but brooked no argument. "Just breathe into the bag. Take it slow. Breathe from your stomach instead of your chest. Six deep breaths into the bag, okay? I'll count."

Knox felt as if he was hovering at the edge of something extremely important but couldn't figure out how to make himself useful, so he just held Lia's hand. Anwei was so calm and convincing, looking right into Lia's eyes as she counted out breaths.

"All right. Now take the bag away. Purse your lips and breathe in. From your stomach. Slow." Anwei took Lia's other hand and placed it over Lia's stomach. "Feel it go up and down with every breath."

Lia's eyes closed and she breathed, air flowing into her slowly and then out again. When she finally opened her eyes, her breaths had slowed. Knox waited for Anwei to say something Anwei-ish, like how Lia looked nice in that color of blue. Instead she met Lia's eyes straight on. "Whatever that boy did, it wasn't your fault. Not being able to fight wasn't your fault. You aren't to blame. Ewan is the one who has something wrong with him, not you."

"But I got away." Lia's face crumpled, and Anwei folded her arms around her, pulling her close as she cried. "I could fight him now. But . . . I *can't*. Why can't I?"

Watching Anwei prop up Lia despite the fact they'd never met before warmed Knox's chest. He still remembered the feeling of her hand on his shoulder as she helped him to sit up in the street a year ago. *We can try burying you, if you're game.*

When Lia's tears had stopped, Anwei settled in next to her against the wall. "Even if it wasn't as bad as it could have been, it was still bad." She took Lia's other hand, so the three of them were linked in a row.

"You can't compare what did happen to what could have happened. What you should or shouldn't feel. Your feelings are your feelings, and that's all there is to it."

Lia's hand tightened around Knox's again, but she didn't say anything for a minute. When she finally did, the words were still wet, squeezed so much smaller than he'd ever seen from her. "You're Knox's partner. He told me about you."

Anwei smiled, but it wasn't her carefree, happy smile. Despite what she was doing for Lia, it was makeup, a mask, a lie. Knox caught her eye and nodded. She blinked and reset her shoulders, as if that nod had been enough to make her open the door.

Anwei lived in a world of open doors, but most of them went only one way—she pranced through other people's lives but didn't allow them to follow her back to her life. Her space. Her heart. But in that moment he could see her cracking it open a little just because he'd asked her to. Because somehow Knox was on the same side of the door as Anwei. After a year of pretending they were separate, suddenly he could see just how ridiculous a fantasy it was.

This time Anwei's smile was much smaller, but the hint of it was real, not a mask. "Yes. I'm Anwei. We met the other day when you came in with that aukincer. You're Lia?"

Lia nodded. "I grew up with Knox at the seclusion."

"But you left. And you're going to map the dig for us?"

Lia sat up from the wall, wiping the tears from her eyes. "I went to the excavation compound today. I can draw it out right now if you let me come inside."

Anwei barely glanced at Knox before standing, offering her hand to help Lia up from the ground. She kept her head down as she led Lia toward the workroom. But once they were inside, a sheet of vellum with ink and a quill before Lia on the table, Lia did not begin to draw. She looked at Anwei instead, her eyes focused hard. "What are you doing for Knox? It has to be you who is hiding him."

Anwei shrugged. "He's been lucky. It doesn't have anything to do with me."

Lia's eyes narrowed a fraction, and she glanced at him from between swollen lids. Knox shrugged the way Anwei had, not sure what there was to say. The moment Lia recovered her aurasight, she'd be able to see for herself. Or . . . maybe she wouldn't. Because if Anwei was hiding his aura, perhaps he was hiding hers as well.

"You aren't counting on him staying lucky." Lia's voice was too steady and calm. She'd always been good at hiding behind whatever it was she was supposed to be doing. "You're leaving here once whatever you're doing at the dig is done, and Knox said you'd be able to bring me and my family with you."

"Did he?" Anwei glanced at Knox, and he nodded.

"She's family, Anwei."

Altahn settled at the other end of the table, and Knox could feel Anwei's fingers tensing, one hand twitching toward her bag. It was difficult to know what Altahn had gleaned about them since joining the household or what he'd take back to Shale once they set him free.

Anwei didn't open her bag to threaten Altahn away, allowing him to stay at the table as Lia started talking again. "I'll draw you a map, but I need a promise, an *oath* even, that when you leave, we'll be with you." She toyed with the vial of ink. "You're getting something valuable from that dig. Getting paid for it?" She looked from Knox to Anwei to Altahn. Knox tipped his chair back and laced his fingers across his stomach. Since when had Lia become a bargainer? "You're going to take the money and leave the country, go where Knox will be safe from the Devoted, and you . . ." She cocked her head at Anwei, narrowing her eyes. "I wish I knew why you want to leave. But you definitely do."

Knox shivered a little. Even he hadn't liked the idea of Lia reading his thoughts. He was glad she was out from under the veil for more than one reason.

"My mother is sick and will need a healer to take care of her." Lia traced her eyes over Anwei's Beildan braids. "My father might need to be drugged to get him out of this place, but I'm not above that. And my sister is young, not even thirteen. Over the border she might have a chance at a life that is free."

Knox's heart broke as Lia's voice did over the word. *Free.* Calsta's rules had always felt like a framework of strength to him. A code that kept him focused, that kept his feet on a path that was going to lead him to the places he wanted to go. Protected by a goddess who had the world's best interests in mind, even if she was kind of mouthy in person. But he'd always known Lia didn't see things the same way.

Anwei's face remained unreadable, but he could feel her mind swirling.

Not just her mind. Swirls of purple darkened in her aura. They almost seemed to reach up toward the leaves, the petals, the stalks and flowers all around them. Anwei's weapons of choice.

You'll have to help Anwei. Calsta's voice crackled in Knox's head as he stared at the purple fronds of aurasparks flowering around her like tree branches. *She still believes she's broken, and if you cannot help her use her power, you will fail.*

Fail? To get the sword? Knox went still, a thread of panic running through him at Calsta's words. She'd said she couldn't help, couldn't tell him anything, so why was this so important even with the apparent risk that someone would hear? *Fail to find the shapeshifter?* he asked. *Or do you mean he'll find us first and grind us between his snake-carved teeth?* But Calsta's burning voice didn't speak again. *And what do you mean Anwei believes she's broken?*

Anwei's chin tipped up as she looked into her garden of remedies and back to Lia. There were things in this unnatural forest that could encourage Lia to help them—poisons with antidotes only Anwei knew, herbs that caused pain or took away too much of it. The gamtooth serum they were preparing for the shapeshifter himself that would make anyone tell the truth. But just as the purple filaments swelled around Anwei, she looked at Knox the way she had when Lia had finished crying. It was a question.

Knox nodded, only enough for her to see. He didn't believe Lia was going to trap them or use them. Only that she wanted to escape. That was all she'd ever wanted.

Altahn's chair squeaked as he leaned on the table, watching all of them with his button-black eyes. "I think I can help with this, actually. If you want."

Knox let his chair fall to the floor, turning to the Trib. Altahn's excessive team play was beginning to grate on him. It wasn't normal to volunteer to help the people who had kidnapped you.

Lia's eyes flicked over to the Trib. "Who are you?"

"No one important. But I could get all of you to the border safely. Trib trails will get you through firekey breeding land near the border. They don't watch things quite as closely up that far north because the lizards take care of most threats, and Trib don't cross lines they've promised not to. You haven't promised, though."

Anwei pushed one of her braids back behind her ear. Knox could feel caution seething through her, reaching out to meet his own. "That's a very generous offer, Altahn. Though I doubt your father would feel inclined to participate in a plan that involves helping us after we kidnapped you and held you here against your will."

"Is that what you're doing? I thought he tried to place me here at the beginning, when we first started talking about the job."

Knox's stomach twisted. Anwei hadn't mentioned that. But it would change a few things so they made sense. What if Altahn had a way to communicate that they didn't know about? What if everything they'd done would end in a prison cell under the drum tower, Ewan standing over them with Willow's sword in his hand?

"You know," Knox stood, "I think it's getting a little crowded down here. It's way past your bedtime anyway, Altahn."

"It's midafternoon. And Father only wants the sword, so if I can help get it . . ."

But Knox herded him toward the stairs, and Altahn argued only for as long as it took to get him to the first step, before compliantly walking up to Knox's room. From the top of the stairway, Knox caught the end of Anwei and Lia's conversation, barely loud enough for him to hear.

"You help us, and I'll do whatever it takes to get your family out of here," Anwei was saying. "You have my word."

"When?" Lia asked.

"Get them as far as Gretis by the time Jaxom's at his apex tomorrow night. We'll all leave together. Now start drawing."

CHAPTER 31

Find Me

That evening, Anwei spread the tomb maps across her bedroom floor, looking up when Knox appeared in her doorway. "Has Noa come back yet?" Anwei asked.

"No. She said she'd meet us at the wagon tomorrow before we leave."

"Interesting." Anwei's brow furrowed. "And Altahn? You dragged him all over the city today and he . . . did nothing?"

"He's always there. When I'm awake. When I'm asleep. Watching."

Anwei shrugged, looking back down at the maps. "You're always welcome to sleep on the floor in here. So long as you don't snore. And leave when I want you to." Smoothing her hands over the vellum, she traced the bold strokes Lia had drawn. Walls, barracks, a side gate. The inner tomb, the traps she'd seen, and the cave beneath the drop that the aukincer's son had been so sure of.

It was everything they needed. Everything they could get, anyway. There were probably more traps to reckon with, but they would get the shapeshifter, bleed the information they needed out of him, then kill him. Somehow. Arun would finally be avenged, and Anwei would be . . .

A pit opened in Anwei's stomach. She would be someone new. Someone without a ghost chasing her ever deeper into the dark.

"Go over this with me one more time," she said. "We drug Altahn and leave him with Gulya. Drug the goats."

Knox flinched. "I'm still so confused about the goats."

"We can't look the same going out of Chaol and then coming back in." She shifted forward, smoothing the map Lia had drawn of the dig. It was very detailed, with labels, arrows pointing out the more congested paths, and names on some of the cabins. Anwei's fingers stopped next to a very small and cramped notation that read, *Director Van*.

She looked up at Knox. "We'll meet up with Noa at the Ink Cay ferry launch. Take the wagon down the trade road dressed like workers headed up the coast. We leave the wagon by the road, sneak up to the dig, and distract the guards by burning the bael wreaths on the western wall. The main gates will be shuttered, closing everyone in—workers and archeologists alike—so no one will be able to get out once the panic starts." Most people involved with the dig had been stuck inside the walls since the moment they arrived, according to Lia, including the director. Which meant the snake-tooth man would be stuck there with everyone else.

Knox crouched down next to Anwei, his arm brushing hers. Anwei automatically edged to the side to make room, but then stopped. He was the one who was touching her. He was the one who had been looking back at her down in the temple.

He moved away himself, his fingers glossing over the wall on the cliff side, the one they were planning to climb. "I'm not sure how Noa and company are going to handle this."

"She's excited about it."

"A little too excited."

Anwei nodded. "I'm not sure how seriously she's taking any of this. It's like she thinks she's running away from home but could turn around and go back anytime she likes. Maybe she's testing this life out to see if it fits."

Knox licked his lips, glancing up at her. "I'm not complaining, but the last time she was involved didn't exactly go well."

"The ball? She did okay with the salpowder, though I suppose we didn't ask her to do that." Anwei looked down at the old floorboards, tracing the grain of the wood with her fingers. "I should be doing this alone. Then we wouldn't need a huge distraction. I probably wouldn't be going into the tomb at all, I wouldn't need the gamtooth serum—this has all gotten so complicated."

Knox snorted, a smile touching his lips. "You just don't want to fix the sword for me, do you?"

"Fix the sword?" Anwei stared down at the paper, her eyes blurring. "What do you mean? How am *I* supposed to do that?"

"We're going to get the shapeshifter to tell us how to let Willow out of the sword, and then you . . ." Knox looked at her, his chin jutting forward. "Anwei, how else did you think this would work? You said you could get the shapeshifter to tell the truth, not force him to perform some shapeshifter ritual to undo the soul trap my sister is stuck inside. I thought you understood what I meant when I asked—"

"When you asked to be a part of this?" Anwei pushed back from the map, finding her feet. "Knox, I'm not a shapeshifter. I don't trap people in swords. I don't do any—"

"I know you don't. You heal people, and you are capable of—"

"No, Knox, you don't understand. Maybe once, a long time ago, I might have been able to help you, but . . ." The horrible storm reared up in her head, thunderclouds and lightning. Rain beating on her back, blood streaming down her arms and legs. Anwei pulled her sleeves down, her scars burning. "It's not there anymore."

"Anymore?" Knox stood too, looking quite cross. "Anwei, you've never lied to me before. I mean"—he put a hand up, closing his eyes—

"you've said plenty of things that weren't true. But not about the important things."

"I *can't*, Knox. These powers you're so sure I have—they don't exist."

"They did that night at the governor's house or I'd be dead. You did it with the salpowder—didn't you see Altahn's eyes bugging out while he tried to figure out what you had mixed in to do the impossible? It *was* impossible. But you changed it somehow. Like the nameless god can."

Every word pounded into Anwei like an accusation, just like the ones that had been thrown at her after Arun died, her mother and father looming over her, the town council already at their house, as if they'd known what was coming. She shook her head. "The gamtooth serum will be done stewing by the time Jaxom rises tonight. We'll have just enough time for it to set before we leave tomorrow. You'll look for the shapeshifter while Noa scares the workers. I'll go down into the tomb—"

"You were the only one who could make that powder—to bond it together or whatever it was you did. Have you thought that maybe you're the only person who can open the tomb, Anwei? Lia said that there was something wrong down there, that it affected the workers and the aukincer's son. What if only someone touched by the nameless god could make that tomb, and only someone with his power can break it open?" Knox's voice was rising. "You know that's probably what we're up against. It's the only reason I agreed to this plan, because I thought you *knew*—"

"I'll get the sword," she continued, her voice getting louder, as if it could drown out what Knox was saying. "And we escape through the refuse gate. Lia is going to drug her father and load him, her sister, and her sick mother into a carriage to meet us in Gretis. We exchange Altahn for the money in Gretis, keep the shapeshifter drugged and stuffed out of sight until you get what you need from him, and then take care of him. Once we've got Lia and her family and Shale's money, we'll be over the border within a week."

Knox fell back a step, his face pale and his fingers twisting in his hair. "*Please*, Anwei. The two of us working together is . . . big. Special. Like Calsta and the nameless god have somehow struck a truce for the first time in more than five hundred years." He leaned back against the door, folding his arms across his chest. "If you won't try, then how is anything ever going to change?"

"Is that what we're supposed to be doing? Changing things?" she snapped. There was a weight to what he was saying, but she could feel only the heftiness of it, not the reasons behind it. "I *can't* do what you are asking. No more, do you understand me?"

"No more? Anwei, this is our lives. How are we going to *kill* him—a shapeshifter, who can't *die*—unless we—"

"I'll figure it out." Anwei pushed past him and ran for the stairs.

Anwei's absence from the room pressed on Knox, as if that moment of anger between them had somehow lessened her hold in his mind. Willow was waiting to fill the void.

Find me, she hissed. Her voice burned—not the way Calsta's did, but with ice and acid instead of honest flame. He shrank away from her, head in his hands, but couldn't help looking around the room. Checking under the bed. Checking the floorboards for loose sections.

Knox. Calsta's voice came, but it was quiet, overwhelmed by the flood of Willow in his mind. *Knox,* stop. *Listen to me—*

Find me, Knox.

"Can't you *tell me* where you are?" he snarled, his temper spiking at the growing burn inside him, Willow's fingernails in his brain.

"What are you doing?" Knox looked up to find Altahn standing in the doorway.

Something snapped back into place in Knox's head, and he found himself with Anwei's blankets wadded together in his arms. The drawers in her desk sagged open like broken teeth, and her bed frame was pulled out from the wall. Altahn's brow furrowed as he looked around the room.

"You're not supposed to come out of my room." Knox carefully set the blankets back on Anwei's bed. Groping inside his head, he looked for Anwei's warmth and the haven it had provided over the last few days. The moment Knox concentrated on Anwei's bond at the back of his head, Willow's outline receded, but she laughed as she went.

She had always cried before.

Knox followed Altahn to his room, then locked it after the Trib was safely inside. He leaned against the door, breathing in deep and letting it out slow.

Anwei wasn't going to help him. Anwei *couldn't* help him.

She'll help you, Calsta's voice whispered. For the first time the goddess sounded unsure. *She has to, or all of this will be for nothing.*

CHAPTER 32

Stuck

You can't keep me in here forever!" Mateo called through his bedroom door, anger a pulse inside him. It had been more than a whole day since he watched Lia tear down the road on his father's horse. Outside his bedroom window, the road snaked toward Chaol, a ghost of Ewan chasing after her playing at the edges of Mateo's mind every time he looked. He paced to the door and back again, his eyes heavy from a night of no sleep.

He'd tried to take a horse, almost managed to get into the saddle before the hostler had dragged him off. And then he'd run to the gate only to have one of the maids tackle him to the ground. *Master Montanne wants you to stay here. It's not safe. We're so sorry.*

Not as sorry as they were going to be once he got out of his room. Whenever that would be. Tual hadn't come home that night or at all during the day, so the dogs were still on guard.

Mateo shoved all his blankets on the floor, then upset his bookcase, glorying in the noise of leather and vellum hitting the boards. A few of his own sketches landed on top of the pile, the rendition he'd done during the night of Patenga and the man with the shield staring up at him. He sighed, wondering who the man could possibly be, before gathering the drawings up and placing them carefully on his bed.

By the time Mateo heard hoofbeats in the courtyard, the light had begun to fade. He rushed to the window, hoping for Lia but finding Tual somehow on the horse Lia had taken, two hostlers riding the ones from the dig right behind him.

"Sorry, sir." The maid cracked the door open. "We didn't want to lock you in, but your father said—"

Mateo pushed his way through the door and past her. "I'll take it up with him!" His head pounded, his knees wobbling as he ran down the stairs and out through the entryway, making for the stable. His father's hat was lying on the cobblestones outside the stable door, the wind twitching it this way and that.

Inside the stable, the two hostlers from the dig were dismounting. Tual was already on the ground, headed for the courtyard, one hand on his naked head. "Mateo? What's wrong?"

"Where's Lia? You must have seen her, otherwise you couldn't have . . ." Mateo's fingers shook as he pointed toward his father's horse.

"I found poor Lucky tied up just past the southern waterway in the Sand Cay." He nodded to the hostlers as they walked out. "Thanks for your help. Get some food from the kitchen before you walk back." He turned to Mateo. "I take it your outing to the dig didn't go well? Or went . . ." He eyed the two horses Mateo and Lia had abandoned at the excavation compound. "Extremely well?"

Mateo sagged against the wall. "Ewan must have found her. Where in Calsta's name *were you*? I tried to go after Lia, but the blasted *help* locked me in my room." He gripped the stable's leaf-carved doorframe, suddenly feeling unsteady. Panic stole oxygen away from his lungs, the edges of his vision going dark. *Trine and holl*, his brain provided as he clung to the sight of the leaves etched into the doorframe. A tear rolled down Mateo's cheek when a trickle of oxygen finally pushed past the block in his chest. *Medicinal plants.*

Signs of the horse handler god . . . what's his name? Used to treat mange.

How do I know that? A flicker of rage burned through him. *Who cares about the horse handler god?*

Hands gripped his shoulders, his father holding him up. "Mateo, you're all right. I'm here."

Mateo finally managed to sip down one inadequate breath. Then another that was a little deeper. He sagged against the doorframe, a cold sweat breaking out across his forehead. What was happening? He hadn't been to the dig today. He hadn't been doing anything at all.

It didn't matter. He stumbled toward Bella. The hostler who was in the middle of pulling off her saddle eyed him warily. "Put it back on," he shouted. "I have to go."

"Mateo." Tual's hand grabbed his shoulder, spinning him around. "I don't mean to imply you aren't a fabulous communicator, son, but I'm struggling right now. What is going on?"

"Ewan chased Lia from the dig. She took Lucky into Chaol, and if you just *found* Lucky wandering around, that means Ewan's got Lia and she's locked up somewhere." Mateo's head seemed to burn. Lia had been so scared back at the dig. . . . "And you had the maid lock me in my room. What is wrong with you? Hilaria made me eat cold soup."

Tual's shoulders relaxed, and he let go of Mateo, stepping back to wipe a hand across his face. "I . . . may have asked some of the help to keep an eye on you, what with the number of attacks you've been having." He took a deep breath, leaning back against the stall and looking up at the ceiling. "I'm sorry. I was worried about you."

"Where *were* you? You just were going to let them keep me locked up for days at a time?" An ugly realization burst in Mateo's chest as he went to Bella, pushing the hostler out of the way to buckle the saddle. "Were you interviewing new assistants for after I'm dead?"

Tual went still. "You've been reading my papers. And horribly misinterpreting them."

"Is that where you were? Because now all our plans are done. Van probably already got into the burial chamber, Lia is *gone*—"

Moving quickly, Tual grabbed hold of Mateo, wrapping his arms tight around him. Mateo sagged against him, anger spilling a gush of hot tears down his cheek. "Breathe, son. Calm. You have to stay calm."

Mateo buried his face in his father's shoulder. He'd tried to help Lia, and he'd failed. She was stuck again, just the way he was.

"I was in town this morning, and if the Devoted had caught their spiriter, I would have heard about it," Tual murmured. "I'm sure Lia is just fine. Probably sitting in her room at the valas's compound, coming up with new ways to tie that scarf of hers. You say you located the burial chamber?"

Mateo's voice was muffled against his father's coat. "Yes."

"Good, that is good. Van has needed your help every step of the way so far, so the likelihood of him being able to get in without you now seems laughable, don't you think? He wouldn't have threatened you if he didn't need you."

"I guess." But Mateo couldn't believe it. He could feel the world disintegrating around him.

"Unfortunately, there is another problem we need to address."

"What *now*?"

"Apparently, the governor has been intercepting our mail and didn't care to pass along the fact that the Warlord is arriving ahead of schedule. This evening, to be exact."

Mateo pushed away from his father, another gasp racking his lungs as he stalked over to Bella and shoved a foot into her saddle's stirrup.

"What are you doing?" Tual's voice pounded at his eardrums.

"I have to know if Lia is okay." Mateo pulled himself unsteadily into the saddle, his sight going double for a second.

"But what about—"

"And if she *is* all right, I have to warn her. The Warlord isn't drained the way Ewan is. She'll see Lia's aura." He blinked away the double vision and gave Bella a kick.

Tual grabbed Bella's reins, holding Mateo in place. "Aren't you on the edge of another episode? It isn't safe for you to be out alone. Why do you think I sicced the help on you in the first place? Wait a minute, I'll saddle Lucky."

"You can't come. She won't listen to you. She already thinks . . ."

Tual leaned against Bella's withers, his mouth suspiciously tight. "What? That I'm an old man who will see her married or see her dead? What's changed here, Mateo? A few days ago you would have been dancing in the courtyard if you heard the Warlord was about to surprise Lia with a new set of shackles."

"Nothing has changed." Mateo stared at Bella's ears as they flicked back and forth, his placid horse cagey with all the noise. "Do I have to want to marry her in order to try to prevent something terrible happening to her?" He gave Bella another kick, dislodging his father as she headed toward the wide door.

Tual followed him into the courtyard, triumph rolling off him in droves. "You must be all right, or you'd be angrier and less cheeky."

"You haven't won," Mateo called over his shoulder. He gave Bella a sharper kick, starting her into a run.

"It's not me who's winning." He could hear the grin in his father's voice. "Go to your lady love! Fly like the *wind*!"

There wasn't time to swear at him. Mateo had never been able to force the world to hand over his due—what any person was due. A fair chance at life, at love, at learning, at growing old. But if the gods wanted to hand the same fate to Lia, at least he could do something about it.

Lia checked the whole west wing before heading toward her mother's room. Without her aurasight, she had to do it with her own eyes, like a child sneaking tamarind paste from the larder. Father was downstairs with guests from the Ink Cay, along with most of the servants, and Aria, to the best of Lia's knowledge, was in the kitchen covertly smearing chili paste onto the new trade advisor's currant buns.

Tonight they were all going to escape.

First, Lia had to take care of Mother, figure out how to get her into the carriage without hurting her. Anwei had given Lia some herbs for Father—they'd go into his evening malt, and Aria would be so intrigued by a plan that involved drugging Father and stashing him in a carriage that getting her to come along would be easier than stealing a first-year Devoted's sword.

If only Father had listened to Lia, they'd already be gone. Over the border. Maybe fathers wanted their children to believe they had everything in hand. Maybe he even believed it himself, as if the gods owed him a happy and prosperous life.

Prosperity and happiness didn't appear like flowers in spring, though. They weren't inevitable. Lia had decided that happiness was something hunted in the night, something you subdued with a sword in hand, then locked up inside your chest before it could fly away. The Warlord had taken her life. Ewan had tried to take her body. He *had* taken her only friend left—Vivi. Hunting for your own happiness meant pinching and prying, running, *killing* if that's what it took, and then you treasured whatever you found, even if it wasn't everything you'd hoped for.

You had to *take* what you wanted for yourself and the people you loved because no one else was going to hand it to you. And Lia meant to take it now.

Stopping in front of her mother's door, Lia reached for the latch.

"What are you doing up here?"

Lia jumped at her sister's voice, finding Aria licking her honey-covered fingers down the hall. "You are getting very good at sneaking." Lia kept her voice calm.

"Dad said you can't visit her yet." Aria shrugged, sucking on one last finger before stepping up next to Lia. "But I think that's stupid. She's hardly ever awake anyway." She pulled the latch open.

Lia followed Aria into the room, her heart pounding. Finally she'd get to see Mother. She put a hand to her scarf, meaning to pull it aside—she didn't want her mother to see her for the first time as a masked stranger—but then she let her hand fall away. It still felt too dangerous, exposing her face, her skin. Mateo had been right when he'd said she was hiding. The scarf made her feel as if she somehow still had Calsta on her side of the battle, and the fight wouldn't be done until she was over the border.

Aria walked to the bed and slipped through the curtains, just as Lia remembered doing so many times herself as a child. Jumping on the bed to wake her parents, only to have her mother grab her around the middle, pull her under the blankets, and pretend to fall back asleep. The curtains were drawn against the night now, keeping everything out instead of welcoming everyone in as they used to.

Lia reached to open the curtain, but her sister called a warning before she could. "The light bothers her! Leave them closed."

Swallowing hard, Lia slipped between the curtains into the bed's gloom. An awful smell of sick hit Lia's nose, panic welling up inside her at the sight of the frail form lying under the blankets. Mother's eyes were closed, her freckled cheeks waxy and pale, almost translucent, as if her body had already been peeled away to leave nothing but a ghost. Her hands lay limp at her sides, her body slanted toward Aria's small form, huddled next to her.

Lia reached out to brush back strawlike coppery strands of hair from her mother's face, the shiny curls Lia remembered so well a thing long dead. "You said she doesn't wake often?"

Aria shook her head. "Started a few months ago with her feeling poorly. Took to her bed within a week. After that . . ." Lia leaned forward to take her sister's hand, then groped to find her mother's. Her long, lovely fingers were cold and shriveled.

"And nothing has helped?"

"Dad brought healer after healer. Ruined a few of them, he was so angry when they couldn't help. But this last week, since the aukincer man came, she started waking up again. She actually ate a whole piece of toast yesterday, Lia." Aria looked up hopefully. "Tual can make her better, can't he? He said he might be able to."

"I don't know." Lia's heart seemed to be beating in her ears, blood pounding to all the wrong places in her body. The aukincer had been able to do what healers had not, but Anwei and Knox had both seemed confident that Beildan medicine would be enough for her. Maybe even enough to cure her. When Lia bent to kiss her mother's freckled cheek, tears pricked in her eyes at the feel of her mother's burning skin. Mother breathed in, one tiny inhale that brought a tinge of pink to her cheeks and punched a hole in Lia's gut because she hadn't realized her mother hadn't been breathing. There was no way Anwei's medicine would be enough, not if Father had already scoured the whole city for help.

If Lia tried to move her mother, it would be her fault if she died.

If Lia stayed, it was her own life that would be forfeited. Was there no way to win?

"What would you do?" she whispered against her mother's hair.

The door clicked open. Aria scrambled to the curtains and slid out, standing before the opening. "Daddy!"

Lia's stomach clenched. She could hide or face it, and Lia didn't like all the hiding she'd been doing. She pushed the curtains aside. Her father's eyebrows rose, his forehead knotting as he took her in, sitting next to her mother on the bed.

"You . . . you disobeyed," he stuttered.

"Of course I disobeyed." Lia kept her voice as calm as she could manage. "I don't belong to you. I wanted to see her."

Her father blinked, then looked down, slumping into the chair by the bedside. He put his face in his hands.

"Close the curtains. The light bothers her," he whispered.

Lia couldn't move for a second, waiting for the fight she was sure would come. But when it didn't, she slid to the edge of the bed and closed the curtains.

"I want to survive, Lia. I want to live." The words came out muffled between his fingers. "I want our family to be all right, for Aria to grow past twelve."

Aria's eyes widened, and Lia wished she could stop her father from scaring her. But she couldn't. Couldn't stop him from trying to enact any of the stupid plans he'd come up with, forcing her to save the family behind his back. "I want all those things too."

"So why are you—"

"Because I won't be your bargaining chip!" The words exploded out of her, Aria stumbling back. "You can't keep me from Mother, and you can't hand me off like a cream puff in exchange for becoming governor of Chaol. I am not a toy, not a trophy. I'm a person, and I get a choice."

He looked up at her, tears in his eyes. The silence was electric, burning like a fire in Lia's lungs because it didn't matter what he said; she'd take her family to safety. But it also *did* matter what he said, because even if he had been acting like a master, he was her father. She loved him.

A tear spilled down her father's cheek. "I have missed you every moment since sending you away."

Lia's insides wanted to melt, tears coursing down her own cheeks. "I don't want anyone to get hurt, and I think if we just *leave*—"

"You were always so passionate. So free. Full of love and full of energy. Ready to take over the world." He buried his face in his hands, his shoulders shaking. "I want you to be happy, Little Spot. I don't want to *make* you do anything. I don't want you to be unhappy or stuck under a veil. Or behind that scarf. I don't want . . . any of it."

Lia reached inside the curtains, searching until she found her mother's hand to hold. Her skin felt too soft, as if it would melt away.

"I just thought if we could stay, your mother might have a chance.

After I saw how much better she was with the aukincer's help, I saw this future for us here. One where she recovered, I kept my position, you stayed here with us and didn't have to go back, and Aria got to kick every guard from here to the governor's house in the kneecaps. . . ." Lia's father swallowed, looking up at her. "But your happiness matters too. Reality matters too." He gestured to the bed, hardly able to look at the blue curtains, tears still streaming down his face. "Even *with* the aukincer's help, she might never recover. And staying here on the charity of a man who started by blackmailing us seems risky at best. We'd all benefit for a while, but who knows for how long? And you'd suffer the whole time. Again." He swallowed once more, wiping away his tears. "The first question I should have asked was what you want. So I'll ask now. What do you want to do, Little Spot?"

Lia looked down at her hand in her mother's, the frail, cold fingers interlaced with hers. She thought of Tual, his fluffy exterior barely concealing a blade underneath. Mateo, who was prickly on the outside but all fluff at his center. Knox and Anwei, who were leaving that very night. Her mother's awful condition.

Anwei had said she could help. So Lia took a deep breath and looked at her father. "I have a safe way out of here for all of us. With people I trust."

Her father smiled. "Then I trust you. We'll do what you say." He opened his arms, beckoning her to come.

Inside Lia's chest, a knot untangled. A memory of that golden glow she'd seen in her father's thoughts when he'd first walked into her interview room filled her to the brim. It wasn't just for her. It was for their whole family. And after so many years of not being touched, she stepped into her father's embrace and felt safe. Not because he was protecting her, but because they were going to protect each other.

The door slammed open, a servant's furious blustering filling the air. "You can't go in there, sir, I'm sorry, but—"

Lia's father pulled away from her, and she jumped behind the curtains. "What in Calsta's name—"

"Lia! I know you're in here." Mateo's voice cut through her father's growl. He pushed past the servant blocking the door and stumbled into the bed, accidentally parting the curtains and exposing her. Breaths wheezed out of him, his cheeks an unhealthy red. "She's coming. She's going to be here *tonight*. She might already be in Chaol."

Lia's mother let out an awful groan, her eyelids fluttering in the sudden light. Lia snatched the curtains shut. Of all the nights for Mateo to barge into her home. Did he know she was planning to leave?

"Leave at this moment," her father yelled.

"You have to come with me, Lia." Mateo put his hand out but stopped, as if he meant to grab her arm but knew better. "I don't know if she brought any spiriters, but it's your only chance—"

Lia straightened. "What do you mean?"

"The Warlord is going to arrive here tonight. The cliff house is far enough from the road that she won't see your aura. You *have to come*."

Tonight. The Warlord. All the plans with Knox and Lia fell away. If the Warlord brought Master Helan, it was over.

The moment Master Helan knew she was missing, he'd close his eyes and send out his mind to find her. Latch on to her. Track her across the world if the Warlord asked him to.

Ignoring her father's blustering, Lia slid through a crack in the curtains and bent to kiss her mother's cheek. Pulling back, she grasped Aria's hand and gave it a squeeze. "I've got to go. Get Mother and Father into a carriage to Gretis. A boy with a short ponytail and a Beildan will be there waiting for you." She looked deep into Aria's eyes, unable to let her fingers release her sister. "I'll meet you there."

Lia ran from the room, hating the rest of that sentence. *I'll meet you if I can. If it's safe.* Knox would take care of her family if it wasn't. She trusted him.

Mateo lurched down the corridor after her, swearing when they got to the stairs. Lia could hardly hear through the film of panic coating her every thought until she realized he wasn't close behind her, Mateo hardly even able to walk.

Was he having an episode?

Lia ran back to him, shoved her shoulder under his arm, and supported him down the stairs. Through the entryway, down the front steps, past the fountain to where Bella was waiting. Lia helped Mateo into the saddle, then climbed up in front of him, and they were off.

"I saw Ewan follow you into town. I tried to come after you, but . . ." Mateo's heart was fluttering hard, but not hard enough, like a butterfly's wings in a gale, against her back. "I couldn't leave, and all day I was worried he'd caught you."

"No." Lia thought of Anwei's arms around her, tears pricking in her eyes. "He didn't catch me. Why did you come here? You're about to fall off Bella!"

"I couldn't let the Warlord find you."

She started to turn but then forced herself to concentrate on the gate, the road. "Just hold on."

He didn't speak until they were clear of the gate, the question hanging in the air over their heads. "You don't like that I came?"

Lia shook her head, tears burning in her eyes. There wasn't anything to like or not like. She didn't *understand*.

Finally, once they were past the outer market and the road was open, stars overhead, Mateo spoke again, his voice so quiet, she wondered if he was ashamed. "Would you rather have not known? Or was it because I'm the one telling you?"

"I'm glad you came, Mateo, but if she finds us together, you're the one who's going to be hung. Maybe your father could keep Ewan from coming after me at the cliff house, but the Warlord herself? Both your heads will end up on spikes if she catches us. I'm not your problem."

"You don't deserve the life she'd give you. Not any more than I deserve to die."

"This wasn't supposed to happen. I was supposed to have more time!" Lia's whole body ached. Why did the Warlord have to come *today?*

And what was Mateo playing at in helping her? He was even holding himself up in the stirrups, gripping the sides of the saddle behind him instead of grabbing her. He knew she didn't like being touched.

He knew and cared enough to do something about it. He'd stood up to Ewan even with a sword pressed to his throat. He'd tried to come after her to make sure Ewan didn't find her. He'd risked being named a traitor tonight. . . . Lia bit her lip, feeling bad about the way she'd been thinking of him while she was talking to her father. Mateo wasn't fluff. *You don't deserve the life she'd give you. Not any more than I deserve to die.*

She didn't know what he was, but Mateo didn't adhere to rules as she understood them.

When she finally spoke again, Lia's voice cracked. "You're not going to die, Mateo. You're going to find whatever it is you're looking for in the tomb. Your father loves you too much to let you die."

"If only he'd stop trying to arrange the rest of my life so I wish I were already dead."

Lia laughed, the sound echoing hopelessly up into the air. There was no end to her problems. She was riding out to stay in the aukincer's home, right in the spider's trap. Her way out of the city was leaving that very night, and her mother was half-dead, with Tual perhaps the only healer capable of saving her. "Don't die on my account. Of everything that has happened this week, I mind you the least. Strangely, you're a bright spot in a sea of mud."

"The bar must be very low—" His voice choked. "For this . . . to . . ." Mateo's arms seemed to slacken, and his body bobbed behind her in the saddle. Lia pulled Bella to a stop, barely managing to catch Mateo before he fell off the horse.

CHAPTER 33

The Girl with No Knees

Knox hopped off the driver's seat of the wagon when Noa and her three friends tried to climb up next to him, singing a bawdy song about a girl with no knees. He went around to sit in the wagon bed, lodging himself between the wall and one of the hay bales. Five little goats lay in a cluster at the center, fast asleep. Drugged, so they wouldn't wake up and call attention to the wagon on the road. Based on the way they'd bleated the whole way to the apothecary, Knox could appreciate the need for herbs.

"Come on, Knox!" Noa twisted around to look at him in the wagon bed. "Sing with us!"

Knox found an approximation of a smile but didn't join, not that Noa or the others cared. They were loud enough to outbleat a whole herd of goats. The three dancers around Noa were laughing so hard, it hardly counted as singing anymore.

Screwing his eyes shut, Knox pulled the bow and the sheaf of arrows Anwei had doctored for him into his arms, hugging them to his chest. She was late. His life, *Anwei's* life, hung on this job going well, and he was sitting in the back of a wagon with Noa and her troupe straight out of *A Thousand Nights in Urilia*.

He could feel Anwei getting closer in his head, and he *thought* at her to move faster. Willow stirred in interest, as if she were analyzing this new thing in his head and how she might go about destroying it. Or eating it. He couldn't tell.

Anwei's purple glow appeared only a moment before she vaulted over the back of the wagon. "Let's go!" she called in a singsong voice before kneeling next to the goats to pat one on the head. "You're supposed to be put away," she whispered, lifting the trapdoor they'd made in the floor, and set the goats one by one into the compartment hidden under the wagon. It was big enough for a person, or two if those people were small.

Altahn wasn't so small, and it was hard to know what size or shape Anwei's snake-tooth man would be, but they'd both have to fit.

Noa took up the reins and flicked them against the horse's back. The wagon lurched forward as Anwei snapped the compartment door closed, smoothed some hay across it, then wormed her way in next to Knox. There shouldn't have been room for more than just him beside the hay bale, but Anwei managed to rearrange him so they both fit, just like she always did. He breathed in deep, worried about their argument the day before and how they hadn't spoken since she'd stormed away from him. The flood from their bond ever since had been angry. And sad. And angry.

"Did Altahn go down okay?" he asked quietly, not sure how to speak to her.

She fussed with her bag, not looking at him. "Facedown in his tea. I tied him to your bed. I told Gulya I'm observing one of the Fig Cay plague victims upstairs, so hopefully she'll stay clear. If she goes sniffing around up there, she might have questions for you when we get back."

"Hopefully, she won't ever see us again."

The flash of sorrow that came through the bond took Knox by surprise. Anwei was going to miss Gulya, if he wasn't mistaken. It didn't show on her face, though. She squinted at the wagon bed, then rapped her knuckles against the floor. "This thing isn't going to fall to pieces before we get there, is it?" It had taken him and Altahn most of the afternoon to exchange the carriage for the wagon, and then to build the compartments.

"Might be good to go quickly while we're carrying two people under there, but yes, I think they'll hold for now." Knox contemplated the wagon bed between his feet.

Anwei pulled open the flap of her bag and extracted a small jar of white paste, looking up as a flurry of lights streamed across the sky like stars falling. The clop of the horse's hooves changed to a muffled thud when the road turned from stone to packed dirt. They were already to the fields, it seemed. This was going too fast—and too slow, too. He hated the way there seemed to be so much more space between him and Anwei than usual. "Why were you late?" he finally asked. "I was worried something happened."

After unscrewing the lid from the jar of white paste, Anwei stuck her fingers in, wrinkling her nose. "The truth serum took more time than I expected to drain."

Knox held his breath a second, waiting for Willow to begin screaming at him—that he was betraying her by trying to find the shapeshifter, that he was trying to kill her *again*. But instead she was just a cold shiver that listened. Waited.

She wouldn't be waiting long. After they had the sword and the shapeshifter, after Knox's deal with Calsta was done and Willow was untethered and sent to her afterlife . . . after he and Anwei were on the road . . .

What then?

Knox focused on the paste on Anwei's fingertips, the way the jar sat in her hands, leaving no room to finish that thought. Calsta's energy seemed to flare inside him, a grim approval of his decision to chop that line of thinking at its base. This wasn't over yet.

And Anwei was angry enough at him that he wasn't sure there *would* be an after.

"What is that stuff for?" he asked.

Anwei turned toward him, one hand darting out to grab his chin. She swiped her fingers across his cheekbone, leaving the sticky feeling of paste. "It's your ghost makeup."

Knox bit his lip, looking up at the sky as Anwei smoothed another gob across his forehead, her fingers rubbing it down his temples and along his chin. "I'm sorry about earlier. You don't have to—"

"You're sorry for what?" She dabbed more across his forehead and between his eyes.

"Sorry I pushed you, sorry for *everything*. I just want things to be right between us again."

"Are you just apologizing so you don't have to wear face paint?"

Knox pulled back, swearing when his head slammed into the wagon's edge. "Yes, so I *don't have to wear face paint*. That makes the most sense for sure." He rolled his eyes. "Anwei, I didn't mean to make you upset. I just think we're going to need you before this is done."

"You're going to need a monster, you mean. You want my claws to come out. But I don't *have claws*." Her fingers on his face poked a little too hard.

Knox put his hand over hers, flattening it against his cheek. "Anwei, honestly, you used to scare me. What you can do. Maybe even up until a few days ago."

She pulled her hand, trying to get it away from him. "I *can't do* what you want."

"But I'm not scared anymore. If you don't want to be a Basist, then fine. You're just the Beildan who saved my life. And the best thief on this side of the Commonwealth. The pretty healer Gulya wants to save from me. But can't you just . . . keep an open mind tonight? Just in case? I'll help you if I can."

She raised an eyebrow at him, but her eyes twitched toward her hand against his cheek, and he could feel the hum of something new coming from the bond. "You think I'm pretty now?"

Noa tumbled backward into the hay, almost hitting them, in a burst of giggles. She hoisted herself up onto the hay bale next to where they were sitting and peered down at them. "That face paint's nice and messy! Don't hog it all. We're the main ghosts, after all."

Anwei looked away, pulling her hands back from him and wiping them along her robe. "I think Knox is done. I'll need your help with mine, though."

Knox's chest was so tight he could hardly breathe. *The pretty healer . . .* How had that come out of his mouth? "Why do you need help with your makeup?"

Anwei grinned, the toothy one that showed all her sharp edges. She relished the words, watching him, as if his reaction would fail or pass a test. "Because I'm going to be dressed as the shapeshifter king."

The walls seemed to stand twice as high as Anwei remembered, the air holding a chill that didn't sit well with the late-summer weather. She breathed in deep as they approached the cliffs from the shelter of the sugarcane field, searching for hints of the nothingness the snake-tooth man left in his wake. All she could smell was wood and dirt, cut sugarcane stalks, the sticky brown clay of the paint on her face, and the wintry green of the bael wreaths hung up to ward off ghosts. She looked over at Knox, then had to look away, still a bit angry. "You see anything?"

He shook his head. "There are people in the buildings just inside the wall—worker barracks, Lia said. But I can't see much farther than that."

"Not even if you . . . do whatever it is to make yourself see farther? Ask Calsta for more energy?"

Knox shifted. "No. I'll let you know when I see . . . him." He glanced back at Noa, who had gone very quiet and was sitting with her eyes closed, her three friends arranged to either side of her. "Are you all ready?"

"Shh. Let us focus." Noa didn't open her eyes. "We have to get into the right mindset. Ghosts are very nuanced, especially victims. It's got to be a perfect balance of despair and thirst for revenge—"

"Ethereal but dangerous," the one on her left interjected. "We need to spark pity, but more terror than anything else for this to work properly. Otherwise, they'll catch us."

"We can't get caught." This one was a dancer Anwei recognized from Noa's troupe. He pitched his voice empty and low, as if he'd already begun his ghost routine. "A true haunting requires a repeat performance."

Anwei couldn't help but laugh, glad to have a moment to smile before going inside the compound.

"Are we ready?" Knox nudged her, pulling out one of the arrows she'd made for him. There was no arrowhead, just a few grains of calistet mixed with some other herb in a bag, ready to mist out and incapacitate the guards they chose. Anwei had promised it wouldn't kill them.

"Are the guards in place where Lia said?" With the torches, she couldn't see anyone on the walls, the hirelings lurking behind the blaze of light.

Knox nodded, apparently seeing auras where she could see only darkness. Anwei pointed to the spot in the center where a guard was supposed to be. Knox pulled the arrow on its string to his cheek and sent it lancing toward the wall. The moment it hit, she fancied she could smell the calistet in the air, poison dusting over the man as he slumped to the ground. Anwei waited until Knox gave a confirming nod that the man was down before he did the other two guards.

The moment the second arrow was shot, Knox launched into the naked area around the compound, scurried up to where a bael wreath hung, and shoved one of the slow-release incendiaries she and Altahn had made among the leaves. Not so slow as the ones they'd sent into the compound, but these would give them a few minutes.

Knox immediately took off around the side of the compound, more bael wreaths to burn. Anwei shepherded Noa and the others toward the cliff's edge but stayed inside the shelter of sugarcane. "You have your fire-dancing gear ready?" Anwei hissed.

Noa rolled her eyes. "You focus on whatever it is you are doing, Anwei. Leave the rest of it to us." She pulled the hair stick from her bun, her hair falling in long, stringy clumps around her. She kissed the flower, offering a prayer to Falan before turning to the wall.

After a few minutes a rope dropped down the exposed wall perched above the cliff, rapping against the wood. Noa ran out first and stuck her foot in the loop at the bottom, then gave an elaborate salute as Knox began to pull her up. By the time it was Anwei's turn, all she could smell was fire and bael, as if it would somehow ward her away. She stuck her foot into the loop and held to the rope with both hands as she slowly rose. At the top she pulled herself up over the wall's lip, while Knox disassembled the pulley he'd rigged and stuck it back in his bag. Noa and the others had already climbed down off the barracks roof.

Most of the compound was dark, except for the walls and the catwalk around the top. Torches flared at the main gates across the compound, lighting a line of horses and a few smaller buildings. The workers seemed to be congregated in a cleared space that was brightly lit in the left-hand corner of the compound, as far as possible from where the tomb entrance was marked on Lia's map.

The tomb opening was where the most light came from, torches in a blazing circle around what looked like a hole to the center of the earth. Anwei flinched when Knox touched her arm. He pointed to the wall a bit farther from where all the people were congregated, a little gate surrounded by piles of dirt. Their escape route.

"Do you see the shapeshifter's aura yet?" she whispered.

Knox gave the whole area one more scan. But he shook his head. Anwei blinked twice, trying to find some kind of calm. The shapeshifter was here. He *had* to be. She'd seen him. Smelled him.

What if he was down underground? Inside the tomb itself.

"I'll find him. Then we'll meet outside just like we said," Knox whispered. "The doors are already barred for the night, but I can make sure the stops are jammed as I go by." He nudged her toward the edge of the roof. "Calistet?"

"You're sure you're going to find him first?"

"He's not going to be down in the tomb. They rely on the sun to light the place, so it'll be pitch black. You do have something to subdue anyone you come across down there, just in case?"

Already this wasn't going to plan. Anwei extracted a packet of calistet-laced corta from her bag, hesitating only a second before she handed it to her friend. "I still don't like splitting up," she murmured.

"I don't like anything about this job. But it's all we have. We decided—"

"I know what we decided."

On the ground beneath them, a flare of unnatural fire bloomed. It lit Noa's ghostly painted face, spun up over her head, then twisted around her like a live snake. She had cricked her head awkwardly to one side, her eyes wide and her voice vacant. *"Save us!"* she moaned. *"Save us from the king!"*

The three dancers lit their fires behind her, spinning their tethers in long, lazy circles above their heads.

Immediately in front of them, the workers began to scream.

Anwei watched the flames flare, shadows dancing around Noa and her friends like ghosts waiting to feed as they pushed the workers tighter into their corner, away from the tomb. Anwei glanced over at Knox, his eyes reflecting green flame, his hair tied back tight, white paint smeared across his cheekbones and forehead in the shape of her fingers.

He looked at her, and for a split second she knew he could feel what she was feeling. Despite their argument, she loved that he was here.

Knox gave her a tiny, hopeful smile, and she returned it. "Ready?" he whispered.

Anwei nodded, turning to gauge the ghosts' progress before she started climbing down. The sight of Noa twirling around like the free thing Anwei wished she could be sat in her chest, like a promise to herself. She was glad the high khonin had elbowed her way into their job.

A loud crack shattered the air, and renewed screams came from around the corner as Anwei's feet hit the ground, and she couldn't help but grin. It helped that Noa knew how to put on a show.

Anwei started into the darkness between buildings. She had a tomb to rob.

Past one group of horses. Two, three. Mateo curled in front of Lia on the saddle. Lia held tight to the reins as she kicked Bella faster, gasping when Mateo listed to the side, his weight almost pulling her off the horse. He was a lot sicker than she'd realized.

She pulled him back into place, praying that the Warlord's retinue wouldn't appear, then wondered whose side Calsta would be on if it did. A ripple of nausea washed over Lia at the awful realization that reaching for the goddess she'd followed for so many years was pointless. Calsta wanted servants who did her bidding, and Lia was definitely not doing that. She spurred Bella even faster.

If the Warlord had brought Master Helan, then there was no future for her. It was over. She was caught.

Mateo was hardly breathing by the time she rode through the Montanne house gate, Tual waiting for them just inside. He held out a hand to help Lia down, a sly smile on his face until he caught sight of his son.

"Help me!" she yelled.

Mateo tipped off the horse, Tual barely catching his shoulders and head while his legs twisted awkwardly on the saddle. Lia threw herself off Bella's back, grateful the little marc was so well behaved, standing there so patiently while she and Tual dragged Mateo the rest of the way out of the saddle.

"Help me get him into the house." Tual looped one of Mateo's arms over his shoulders, impatiently waiting for her to do the same. Lia grabbed Mateo's hand and pulled it around her neck, his coat gritty with dirt from when he'd been on the ground.

"We're doing this again?" Mateo murmured. "Why don't you just let her carry me, Father? Women really love that whole vulnerable, gentleman-in-distress bit. . . ." He spasmed forward, a horrible racking cough rattling his entire frame. Lia put an arm around his waist to steady him, finding Tual's joining hers from the other side.

"Don't talk." Tual started moving faster, Lia's muscles bunching and straining to keep up. "We need to get *both* of you inside."

"Is he . . ." Lia shut her mouth when Tual waved her off.

When they spilled into the entry hall, servants suddenly appeared from all sides. One moved in to take Mateo's weight off Lia's shoulder, two others immediately unbuttoned his jacket, and a third pulled off his boots. Tual pointed at a younger servant hovering just inside the doorway that led to the sitting room, then jabbed his finger at Lia. "Take her to the blue room."

"But . . ." Lia hesitated, then took a step back from the ants' nest of people crawling all over Mateo. His eyes had closed entirely, his breaths coming in jerky gasps. Tual was helping to lower him onto the floor, unbuttoning his collar, then putting an ear to Mateo's mouth.

"Lady?" The servant touched her elbow, and Lia startled away. That someone would touch her without asking . . .

Lia took a deep breath, the air sticking inside her. She wasn't Devoted anymore. She wasn't a spiriter anymore. The scarf she wore was no armor. She couldn't do anything, and her presence in the hall would just be in the way. So Lia let the servant pull her away from Mateo and the crisis hemorrhaging on the floor, heat climbing up her neck and into her eyes the farther she got. He'd come for her—come for her even though he was sick. Dying. About to fall off a horse. What friend did that? He wasn't her father, her lover, her family at all.

What did he expect in return?

Lia climbed up the stairs into the gloom where torches hadn't been lit, the hallway musty, as if the windows had never been opened. This had to be the end for her. For all Tual's talk of protecting her, what could he really do? The Warlord was practically here. Ewan had seen her with Mateo. They'd know exactly where to look even if Master Helan hadn't come.

The servant opened a door on the landing, then stood with her hands folded and her head humbly bowed. "In here, Lady."

Lia couldn't make herself look at the woman, frightened and angry all at once and not able to trust herself to be civil. "Does he . . ." She swallowed, looking back toward the stairs. "Has he been this bad before? This attack? Is it worse?"

The maid inclined her head. "It's hard to say." But she left without another word, a taste of blame in the air behind her. If he'd been here at home where he belonged, maybe it wouldn't have gotten so bad. Maybe he'd be better already.

Maybe he couldn't get better now, and it was her fault.

Lia walked into the room, ignoring the beautifully draped bed to open the window that looked out on the courtyard. Jaxom hung low in the sky, two hours from his apex, when Aria and her father would meet Anwei. Castor peered down from so much higher, the stars between them like arrows shot in an impossibly slow war. Shocks of light streaked across the sky.

It wasn't their war that worried Lia. Aria would get Mother and Father to safety—away from the Warlord and Tual both. But Lia didn't have a road to escape down. She couldn't fight against a goddess who wanted her and had a whole army to do her will. And she didn't *want* to fight Calsta; she wanted the goddess to understand. "How can you ask me to go back, Calsta?" Lia whispered. "The path you gave me is death. I cannot follow it."

"Is that what you think Calsta wants?"

The voice froze Lia's humors to ice. Every inch of her went solid, every muscle tensed. She wished for a sword, a knife, a shield, a rope. *Anything*. None of it would help anyway.

She turned slowly. Faced the figure shrouded in a white veil who sat on the bed, not an inch of his skin showing.

"Hello, Lia." Master Helan's voice was so soft and fragile, but she could almost feel his mind prying into hers. "I've been looking for you."

CHAPTER 34

Burning Scars

Knox waited until Anwei was off the roof to take the bow from his shoulder and pull out three more of the arrows she'd made for him, though these ones didn't contain calistet. The first screaming workers had gone running toward the bright lights that marked the excavation mess area, and the ripples of panic had already begun. Noa and her friends lurched closer until their fire brushed the torchlight.

"He took us. Trapped us in between death and the eternal sky, sipping on our souls. . . ."

Shouts for help had brought guards, though the rattled commands Knox heard over the screams from the workers as they ran for the front gates were shaky at best.

"Save us from him. A thousand years under stone . . ."

Knox raised his bow as Noa ignited a second flame, her chant rising to a strangled scream.

Anwei's dark aura flitted under the pavilion around the center of the compound. The guards gave the order to take aim with their bows, so Knox pulled the arrow back and let it fly to the dry grass behind Noa.

The arrow exploded with a loud squeal and a shower of sparks, sending a wave of heat through the air. Noa seemed to grow, unfolding as she threw down one of her blazing tethers. It erupted halfway between her and the crowd in a fountain of green fire.

Screams cut the air, feet pounding against the ground as workers fled, even the guards on the catwalks disappearing in a rattle of loose boards.

Knox took two more of the fire arrows and nocked them together. They arced over the top of the camp, then thunked into the wooden base of the main gates. Flames burst out to lick at the wood, but Knox didn't stop to watch; he hopped off the roof on the far side and melted into the shadows as a group of workers sprinted past him. Pushing his aurasight until it strained, Knox looked in every building he could reach, inspected every flare of white for the shallowest hint of purple. He ran with the workers, circling around until he came upon where the director's lodgings were.

No one was inside.

Knox checked the buildings on either side, but there were only tired archeologists who were peering out their windows for a look at what was the matter. The shapeshifter was supposed to be here. Lia had said it. The papers they'd stolen from the governor had said it. . . .

At the back of his mind, Anwei's aura flickered by the tomb's entrance. Then it went out.

Knox stopped dead, spinning toward the pavilion, trying to see and hear past the clamor of workers and of Noa and her friends' crying as they herded people toward the main entrance.

But Anwei was gone. She hadn't *died* or flown off or run away. Her aura had disappeared right over the tomb entrance. If she'd gone underground, then that meant the tomb itself was blocking her aura from him.

A substance that could *block auras?*

The director's empty room behind Knox seemed to grow, to echo, to roar. If the shapeshifter wasn't aboveground, and the tomb walls could somehow hide an aura . . .

Knox dropped his bow and ran for the pavilion, breath caught in his throat.

Anwei climbed down the ladder. The tortured ghost cries and clamor of shouts dimmed as if she were going underwater. Breathing in carefully, Anwei searched for a hint of nothingness that would say the shapeshifter had been down in the tomb, but the air smelled only sweaty and stale. Her nose filled with the nutty cinnamon-brown scent of new wood mixed with the dusty gray of old, the cocktail of odors peeking from behind the heavy scent of stone. Hushed pricks of color punctuated the hulking weight of the tomb's smell—gold, silver, jewels, and paint. And . . .

Anwei breathed, filling her lungs. And *something*. A familiar something she couldn't place.

She hopped to the ground and took out her lantern, flint, and steel. Once the wick was lit, she held up the lamp, finding the tomb much as Lia had described. A main room with a doorway that led to nothing, a hole in the floor. Anwei went down the ladder, and the *something* scent grew stronger—worse than any kind of aukincy, worse than poison because it wasn't so blatant. It *waited* at the bottom of the ladder, prickling in her throat like a knife.

Her last step off the ladder was almost too careful, the rug under her feet muting the smell. Lia had said there was something wrong with this room and that the rugs were there to protect workers, but it was like nothing Anwei had ever smelled before—an impossibility, like a spider milking its own poison, then waiting in a web to throw it. She pulled her medicine bag to hang across her chest so she could easily reach her herbs or the explosives she'd brought, but for the first time in her life, Anwei couldn't smell the answer to this poison. Her herbs were helpless.

A sudden movement caught the corner of her eye. Anwei stopped dead.

Silence.

As she lifted the lantern toward the place where she'd seen the movement, her golden light bled across a section of carved stone, a lizard head snarling at her from the body of a human man. Anwei put a hand to her chest, laughing to herself. The light must have touched the carving to make it look as if it were moving.

She followed the carpets to the doorway Lia had told her about, not even the smallest glow from her lantern penetrating the black beyond it. *A stairway. Then a room where the door slams shut, the ceiling lowers, and the center of the floor has fallen away.* Anwei pulled out the coil of rope she'd brought in preparation. At the bottom of the stairs, she knotted one end of the rope around the golden column inside the stairwell and looped the rest over her shoulder. The ceiling on the other side of the doorway was low—lower even than Lia had said, making Anwei wonder if she and the aukincer's son hadn't been the last people to trigger it. She went down on her hands and knees, forced to crawl just to get inside. There were baskets filled with rock and shards of pottery clustered around the entrance, making it difficult to slide into the room. Anwei held up her light once she was inside, the relief of Calsta on the ceiling glaring at her through her mask of gold. The center of the floor, where there was supposed to be a pedestal with a hole around it, was solid, a relief glittering darkly in the light. Anwei paused, looking around to make sure she hadn't gotten it wrong, but there was no pedestal, no hole. Only the nameless god staring up at her.

It must have closed again. Well, Lia told me how they opened it the first time. Touch the nameless god, the floor falls in. . . . Anwei looked around once more, trying to take in all the things that were different from what Lia had said. The ceiling was much lower than she'd made it sound, the hole was gone, and there were cracks in the ceiling and wall, chunks of rock missing from the far side, where a fabric sheet had been hung in the corner, hiding the worst of the damage.

Lia didn't mention that, either.

Someone had been down here.

Anwei stared at the sheet, a breeze pushing at the fabric from the inside, making it flutter. *A breeze?* That meant there was another way out of the tomb Lia didn't know about. Maybe another way in and out of the whole compound. Which meant . . . *Maybe the snake-tooth man won't be here?* What would they do if he wasn't?

But then she shook her head. *I have to do my part here. None of it will work without the sword.* So Anwei crawled toward the center of the room, where the nameless god waited. The room smelled . . . wrong. Like no stone she'd ever smelled before.

The lantern light flickered over the banned god's arms and legs, his face so calm and benevolent. He held a man in his lap who was holding a golden shield. *This* was the god who had apparently touched her? The one every Devoted had hunted, befouled, destroyed? Anwei paused, looking him over as if something made of stone could speak. Could confirm the snake-tooth man had been his monster, a thing he had allowed to destroy her life.

She could almost feel an emptiness underneath the nameless god's image, as if whatever made the shapeshifter empty lurked on the other side. Anwei shook her head, unwinding the rope from her arm. Whatever was down there was a thing made by men, not by stone gods, no matter whom the Warlord had chosen to blame.

Chest clenching, Anwei crawled closer to the vines twisting around the nameless god like snakes. Lia had said the moment anything touched him, the floor would—

A furious scratching of stone echoed through the tomb.

Anwei curled down around her lantern, almost burning her wrist on the heated metal when she blew it out. The scratching came again, this time with the sound of pebbles showering the stone floor.

It was coming from the hallway.

Clutching the medicine bag to her chest, Anwei pulled the scarf around her neck up over her nose and mouth, and groped for the packet of calistet she'd diluted to make Knox's arrows. Her fingers were slippery with sweat inside her gloves.

A footstep dragged across the gravely floor. And then another.

"Anwei?" Knox's voice echoed.

"Calsta pin you to the sky, Knox." She swore, sliding the poison back into her bag and pulling down the scarf. "You scared me. I thought we were meeting outside. Where's the snake-tooth man?"

Now that she was paying attention, she could feel Knox's presence in her head. It had been muted, far away until he'd walked within sight of the doorway. Now it was once again a warm glow approaching opening. Warily, as if he could see something she couldn't. "Is he down *here*?" she hissed.

"I'm not sure." Knox's glow crouched down in the awful dark and crawled toward her. "He's not aboveground that I can see."

"Well, what do you see now?" Anwei tried to tamp down her relief, ashamed of herself for being frightened.

"There's something about this stone that hides auras."

Fumbling for her lantern, Anwei found the flint and steel once again and lit the wick. A bloom of light pushed back the darkness, washing across her friend's face. "You think he's waiting down there?"

Knox nodded, his face like stone.

"It *blocks* auras. Does it block my sense of smell, do you think?" Anwei had known finding the snake-tooth man down here in the dark was a possibility, but she hadn't thought through how it would feel to face him on her knees, palms sweating. Talking nonsense was easier than facing it. "I couldn't smell the poison in the governor's study until it was out of the drawer."

"I don't know. It could."

Anwei's teeth ground against one another. "Well, I guess we should go down."

Once Knox had stuck his foot into the rope's loop, Anwei forced herself forward and touched the nameless god's relief.

The ceiling began to groan, lowering so it touched Anwei's back, then forced her down onto her belly. The pedestal started pressing up from the floor into her shoulder.

"Anwei? Are we sure—"

She caught a whiff of sea, and then the floor fell out. They slid headfirst into the opening. Knox's arms were around her, and she clung back, the rope giving an awful snap as it caught their weight. They swung, and Anwei slammed into a wall before they swung back the other way.

A loud crack rang in her ears as the spiked stones Lia had warned them about slammed into each other above them, the crash making the walls shudder. She twisted to see and then wished she hadn't, the thick columns' points covered in old blood. Even as she watched, they ratcheted back into place above.

"Are you all right?" Knox yelled.

"Are you all right? Are you all right? Are you all right?" Knox's voice echoed, but then somehow it *wasn't* Knox's voice, instead turning into a slippery, slithering thing. Knox held her close, his arms so tight around her, she could hardly breathe. "Anwei?"

Anwei's fingers were numb, barely holding on to the rope. She'd dropped the lantern, and her head *screamed*. And the odd smell she couldn't place . . .

"I'm okay." Anwei swallowed, trying to get her bearings as they kept swinging. The lantern was still merrily burning below them somehow, illuminating sea-carved rocks. And there was a rush of air, water—

"Are you all right? Are you all right? Are you all right?" The echo swelled again, prickling Anwei's skin. Her nose curdled with a musky, wet, animal smell. She'd smelled it only once before. Looking down at the flickering lamp, Anwei thought she saw something move.

"There's a door here," Knox said. "You still have the incendiaries?"

"Yes." She craned her neck to see what he meant, the rope spinning. "Don't listen to the voices, Knox. Can we get to the door?"

"The voices?" Knox shifted as another wash of whispers spread out underneath them. The words had changed to *"It's not all right. It's not all right. It's not all right."* He swore.

Swaying together, they made the rope swing them toward the door, and Anwei finally caught sight of it, the shapeshifter king's ugly face snarling at them from the stone. The whispers flowed up higher, taking on a singsongy quality that tugged at Anwei's chest. *"I'm here. I need your help."* When she glanced below, her eyes had adjusted enough to see a single, sinuous coil of scaly skin only a few feet from the lantern. *"Please help me!"* it sang.

Knox reached out and snagged the stone doorframe with his hand. Groaning, he waited for Anwei to hop onto the ledge, her heart pounding. She reached out and caught the rope, and Knox grabbed the ledge with his other hand, then dropped to stand next to her. She wound the rope on a curl of stone jutting out from the relief, testing to make sure it wouldn't break before letting go of it.

She caught the smell of stone, but it was wrong. Stronger somehow, *changed* into something more. But the smell of salt and scales was too sharp to dig deeper.

"I'm all alone, and it is so dark. . . ." The whispers echoed this new line, and Anwei caught sight of sinuous coils writhing between the rocks.

"I thought narmaidens didn't come this far north." Knox's voice was rough. Anwei could feel it too, the pull of the words.

"I think it's nesting ground. New babies. No fully grown adults here right now, or we'd already be down there," she whispered, trying not to think of the fanged sea snakes. The last time she'd encountered one, the fully grown snake had lured three sailors off their ship before the crew realized what was happening. Narmaidens could get into your mind, take the saddest, most frightening images from your head, and sing them back to you inside your thoughts, planting themselves at the center of a story that had you believing that you needed to save them from your own worst fears. She'd heard only one line of song before plugging her ears, already bogged down with images of a young girl, alone, broken, and stranded in a storm that was filling her boat with water.

Anwei wondered what these little ones were singing to Knox now. It would be different for him, and she couldn't feel it even through the bond. "Help me set the incendiaries before the mother comes back," she whispered as a new wave of singing crowded inside her head. *"Please, I'm scared down here in the dark. . . ."*

Knox held out his hands, Anwei passing him two of the devices she'd made after Altahn had explained to her how it was done. She pulled out a spool of twine she'd treated with salpowder and linked the four packages together, then unspooled the rest of the twine, letting it hang loose from her hand. She grabbed hold of the rope, stuck her foot in the bottom loop, and let Knox ease in closer, sticking his foot into the loop beside hers. Once he was ready, Anwei launched back out into the darkness, holding the twine in her free hand.

"Please save me. I've done nothing wrong. They loved me. They were supposed to love me. But they left me here to die. . . ."

"What are they saying to you?" Knox whispered.

"That's a very personal question, don't you think?" she hissed back. "You want to know what I'm most afraid of?"

"No one else will come. The only person who loved me is dead. You have to help me."

"I just thought if you were talking to me, I wouldn't be able to hear *them*."

Anwei could feel a thread of panic flowing from the bond, though she couldn't feel any of what they might be saying to him. "Go back up, I'll do this."

She looped an elbow around the rope and groped for her flint while Knox climbed. When he stuck his head back up through the hole, he cleared his throat. "The room is tall again, but . . . the hole in the floor is closing, Anwei. Hurry up."

Anwei swore. Lia had said it was still open when she left. Why was it closing so fast this time? She struck the fuse alight, then began to climb.

"Please." The voice tore at her chest as she pulled herself up toward the chamber above, the sound of the fuse flickering in her ears. The voice sounded like her own, scared and young, begging for help as the waves knocked her little boat this way and that. She shut it out, trying to remember narmaiden teeth, their glowing eyes. There was no little girl who needed saving in this pit. And nothing could have saved Anwei back then anyway.

Knox grabbed Anwei's arm and hoisted her past where the floor was closing. It clicked back into place, blocking out the narmaidens' song. The ceiling had receded enough she couldn't touch it even if she reached up over her head.

Boom. The floor trembled.

After a moment Knox looked at her. Anwei groped deep in her bag, fingers finding the wax candle she'd left in the bottom just in case. She lit it, and then in the dim light she extracted a packet she'd filled with rocks and threw them onto the nameless god. As the ceiling began to lower once again, something came up from the center through the nameless god's mouth, and Anwei saw the pedestal Lia had mentioned, clearly this time. Keeping hold of the rope, Anwei ran across the nameless god to press against the pedestal once again, immediately ducking at the memory of the spikey columns. She ran back to Knox just in time for the floor to open and the columns to smash together right where she'd been standing.

Below them, in the flicker of lantern light, the lower door was still closed.

Scorch marks decorated the base where they had placed the

explosives, and shattered bits of rock on the ground had peppered the doorway and walls, leaving long gray scratches in the gold-painted stone. But the door was still there.

"No." Anwei put a hand to her cheek. "That's not possible." Grappling for her bag, she felt for the explosives she hadn't used yet.

"Please, I'm all alone. My family didn't want me. No one wants me. . . ."

Knox's hands came down on her shoulders, pulling her back a step. "What if—"

"We have to get through, Knox." She darted away, fumbling to get her flint and steel out again. "No sword means no money, which means no border crossing. And if he is *in* there somehow—"

"What if Patenga built himself a tomb that only a shapeshifter could open?"

Shapeshifter. The word hissed through the air.

"No, Knox." His hands were on her shoulders again, soft and solid all at once. "You don't understand. *I can't.* Maybe I could have back before . . ."

"Before what?"

Anwei couldn't make herself speak, memories of home, of the little shop she'd worked in with her mother, her father. Her mother's slightly crooked front teeth, her father's long, smooth braids.

Knox's hands on her shoulders tightened, and the spot that he'd taken in her head seemed to flare, warm and bright. The bond between them seemed to deepen, as if he were reaching across it. "I said I could help maybe. I know the magic is in you."

"I thought you said it wasn't magic."

Knox took her hand, squeezing it tight. "Please, Anwei. You don't have to be scared. I'm going to be here for whatever happens. Please, just try."

"Please, don't hurt me," the narmaidens sang. *"I didn't know it was inside me."*

Anwei closed her eyes, her scars burning. But Knox's hand seemed to calm the storm roiling up inside her. *I'm going to be here for whatever happens.* He'd been here since the moment she found him. He wouldn't leave her. Not like everyone else.

Something whisked across her vision, though her eyes were closed. Something purple and wispy like smoke. She knew she was seeing something that Knox could always see, as if the bond between them was forging them together to form something new.

The purple haze around Anwei condensed, and a warmth inside her grew out from her core, climbing out from her chest, down her arms and legs. Fusing her to that bit of Knox inside her head.

Suddenly she could smell it. Not just the stone. But the way pieces of stone fit, bits of a puzzle bonded together instead of one solid whole. Behind the sheet there was an awful crack in the rock. Below them, the door and the burial chamber behind it were completely solid, immovable. She couldn't even see past them to what was inside.

Anwei looked at Knox. He was glowing, the bits of light scattering across him like the spark of flint against steel. The gold running through him reached out to twine around her, as if she were stealing his energy. But a line was running from her toward him as well, replacing spots of gold with hints of purple. Knox gasped, and suddenly it was like he was touching every inch of her.

Anwei's mind was too full. She grabbed madly for Knox's hand, as if he could somehow keep her from getting lost, forcing her mind toward the burial chamber so far below them.

Break, she told it.

It didn't move.

Something fell behind the sheet in the corner, jerking Anwei out of the trance. She found Knox's arms wrapped tight around her, the only thing keeping her upright. Both of them stared toward the darkness of the corner.

The candle snuffed out.

And then a slithering sound, like scales against stone.

It wasn't the narmaidens.

"You dare disturb my rest." The voice crumpled like old leaves and rot.

Anwei groped for her bag and pulled out her packet of calistet, but there was nothing to see, nothing to smell, nowhere to look. Just dark, dark, dark all around them. Knox's hand closed tight around her waist, holding her close. She could feel him reaching out with that golden glow in his mind, straining to find the source of the noise.

Something shifted behind the sheet, the bulk of a large creature waiting for them just out of sight. Knox's arms stiffened around Anwei, and suddenly the nothing smell was all around her, so strong her knees buckled.

It was coming from Knox.

Anwei's insides shriveled. *But he doesn't have the sword.* A frantic protestation that didn't matter because it was happening anyway. *I would have known if he'd found it in the shed.*

All the gold and purple light around them was sucked back inside of him, and the bond between them was stabbed through with thorns of ice. A low growl filled the room, growing louder and louder every second until it roared in Anwei's ears, leaving no room for any thought.

"I'll eat you whole!" the voice snarled, the darkness coming alive.

Anwei grabbed Knox's hand and pulled him toward the stairs, but he stumbled like his legs were heavy. The sword wasn't here, but somehow Knox was still not himself. She lurched away from the voice, only it was everywhere, all around them, inside of her, tearing her apart. "Get out of here!" she screamed at Knox, pushing him up the stairs. "Go!"

Light seemed to explode out from every side, as if Calsta had mounted her storm and brought them the sky. Anwei clenched her eyes shut in the assault of smells—fire and stone and poison.

A sharp sting wheeled across Anwei's side like the crack of a whip just as they made it through the doorway. She staggered off the carpets, her hand coming down on the carved, supplicating face of a worshipper at Patenga's feet. The stone crumbled between her fingers, and the poison seemed to leap up from the floor and out from the wall, coating her hand and shoes.

Knox's hand closed over her other wrist. The spot where Knox was in her head, which had only moments before been warm, now grabbed at her with razor-sharp fingers, radiating an inhuman nothingness that screamed *murder*.

Anwei tore her wrist free and ran for the ladder, a numbness spreading up her arm from where she'd touched the wall. Hand over hand, she forced herself up to the top of the ladder and rolled out onto the ground, panting. Shouts cluttered her ears, punctuated by a deep, fiery boom that shook the ground under her.

Knox exploded out of the tomb behind Anwei. She scrambled to her feet and ran toward the side gate, where they were supposed to meet Noa and the others, crashing into workers headed in the opposite direction. Now the numbness was spreading over her feet and up her ankles, as if the poison had sunk through her shoes. Knox was just behind her, stalking her. Anwei could feel that black void reaching for her, begging to consume her.

Anwei's numb hand clenched as she ran, her fingers contorting and her arm going limp. She thrust her clean hand into her bag and pulled out one of the crackling sparklers she'd made for Noa, then lobbed it over her shoulder toward Knox, hoping it would distract him.

The movement made her stumble, and suddenly there were baskets all around her full of dirt and loose stone. Knox dodged the bloom of fire and continued after her, his walk slow and deliberate. Anwei darted around the closest shed and blasted through a stream of workers fleeing toward the front gates. The murderous sheen to Knox's mind made her gag as she tried to run, the numbness of her hands and feet forcing her to lurch this way and that. She rounded a building and found Noa and her friends dancing just in front of the side gate, cackling and moaning as they twirled their flaming ropes.

Anwei tripped forward, her knees giving out and dumping her on the ground. Noa was right there, and yet a million miles away for all the good it did her. The circle of sparkling light their tethers made was just beyond Anwei's reach.

Knox stepped in front of her, blocking the light.

"Knox . . ." Anwei swallowed, her eyes glazing as the poison, whatever it was, made its way deeper through her humors. Knox bent down and grabbed her by the shoulders, his cold hands like claws.

Anwei's hand jabbed toward her medicine bag, but her arms wouldn't work.

Knox reached for his shoulder, for the sword that wasn't there. When his fingers closed on nothing, he froze for a second. Then he reached for the knife he kept at his belt. The icy awfulness of his mind was creeping into hers as if he meant to drink her down.

"Knox!" It was harder to get his name out this time, Anwei's head swirling with the awful closeness they'd shared only moments ago. He'd told her to look inside. To forget the past. To trust him.

She'd done it. Years of armor, of hiding, of staying in her shell, stripped away. Anwei had reached out, let him hold her up.

And now . . .

Anwei's scars burned.

Knox drew the knife, his fingers digging hard into Anwei's shoulder. She reached vainly for anything—a tool, a rock, *dirt*—to throw in his eyes, but her bones were rubber. Useless. *I can't die this way. I won't.* She reached for what she knew was there inside her mind, the core of him, the warmth buried beneath the ice.

And there, huddled at the back, she found a little marble of heat, the touch of familiar thought. Knox froze, the knife in his hand twitching just as it touched her chin.

Please, Knox. I know you're in there. Anwei shut her eyes, thinking of that golden glow around him, and the purple darkness that had been around her, the way they'd spun together.

A high-pitched, inhuman cry tore through the air. Knox dropped the knife, the hilt hitting Anwei's sternum. The keening whinny repeated, followed by flickering echoes, like wolves on the hunt.

Not wolves. Auroshes.

Knox's brow furrowed as his nothing scent faded into something warm and familiar and *him* again, though Anwei wasn't sure if it was the auroshes that had brought him back or if she'd managed to reach him in his mind. Knox's hands shook as he looked her up and down, as if trying to figure out how he'd gotten there. Fear jolted down Anwei's spine that was not her own—embarrassment, anxiety, a whole cocktail of not-her-emotions. "She's here. They're *all* here."

Anwei slumped against the ground, her muscles completely giving out. Knox had never changed into a nothing creature unless he was holding that blasted sword. It had been hidden under the floorboards out in the shed ever since the day Shale chased Knox back to the apothecary.

What was different about tonight? It had started after the voice screamed at them down in the tomb, right after they'd . . . bonded or whatever that was. She'd felt it in his mind like a shard of ice, as if the sword were inside him and not just a thing he carried. Anwei flinched as Knox grabbed her arms, trying to pull her up from the ground.

"Anwei? Anwei, what's wrong? What happened?" His voice was panicked, as if he couldn't even remember the knife he'd held to her throat only moments before. "You have to get up. *The Warlord is here.*"

The traces of god-given energy Mateo had drawn inside himself the moment he realized Lia was in danger wormed their way out of him, leaving him in a boneless heap in the front hall. Every episode he'd had before had started with weakness and ended with him waking up to a wooden medicine spoon in his mouth, but this one was different, his mind trapped inside as every other aspect of him bled away.

The familiar feeling of rage welled up (why him? He didn't care much for Calsta or her Devoted; his life was dedicated to righting the wrongs done to the nameless god's chosen, so how could the nameless god let this happen?), but it wasn't enough to fill him.

At least Lia was safe.

The anxious shuffle of feet and abrupt explosion of orders told Mateo his father was in the room. But it was only when the liquids in the pot were bubbling that Tual began to mutter to himself, only snatches loud enough for Mateo to hear. ". . . can't believe I was so stupid . . . but unless we *find* it . . ."

Find caprenum. That's what they had to do. Mateo clung to the thought.

The spoon brushed Mateo's lower lip, but there was nothing in him to make his mouth open or to stop the dribble of medicine burning down his cheek. Tual tipped his head up and opened his mouth, dripping the liquid onto his tongue.

"She couldn't have stayed. She *couldn't* have." Tual swore under his breath as he pulled the spoon back from Mateo's face, then turned away so his mutters were too quiet to hear. Only a few more words filtered back over the bubbling of the aukincer pot. ". . . still linked all these years . . . proximity, though . . . I have to find her. We'll need to act quickly." The words were edged with steel, every syllable razor sharp.

The energy hemorrhaging from Mateo's aura slowed as the medicine worked its way down his throat and into his stomach. *She couldn't have stayed.* Whom could his father mean? The Warlord? Lia? Neither of those made sense.

Then Mateo remembered the papers he'd found, his father's search for Basists. What if he'd found a Basist here? A woman whom he'd warned to leave, perhaps, because of the Warlord's imminent arrival?

Not a new son, but a daughter. A daughter who would obey when Tual pointed at whom she was to marry. A daughter who wasn't dying.

The rage in Mateo felt as if it had gained a life of its own, growing in a hot, spewing mess to fill his whole skin. The incessant *sucking* at his essence was easing but did not go away. It felt like a bottomless chasm that hungered for him. It felt like *nothing*.

We'll need to act quickly. Tual had said it with such rancor. Whom was he going to act against?

Not knowing left Mateo cold in the chest. When he could finally open his eyes, his father was crouched next to his bed, worry lines stark on his face.

"If you keep frowning like that, you'll start to look your age, Father," he croaked, unwilling to share the awful concoction of anger and fear battling for his soul. What if his father planned to run? To give up and leave the country, caprenum or no. "You haven't given up on me, have you?"

"Oh, my boy." Tual scrubbed a hand through his hair, leaving the carefully combed part awry. "You know I'd give anything for you to stay here with me. *You'd* give anything, wouldn't you? To live."

The tendril of hope stretched almost to breaking. *You know I'd give anything for you to stay here with me.* But there wasn't anything Mateo *could* give up, not in life, not in death, not to any god.

Mateo forced his head up from the bed to meet his father's eyes, searching them for any hints. Tual only looked sad, anxious. But Mateo knew his father well enough to know the outside didn't always represent what was going on in his head.

Mateo's words felt like fire in his humors, strength in his muscles. "I would give anything. Take anything. *Do anything* if it means I continue breathing."

Knox was hardly breathing. One moment he'd been down in the tomb, his mind entwined with Anwei's, the feeling of it still a bonfire that reached to his fingertips and toes. *Sky Painter. Storm Rider.* But there wasn't time for centering himself. How had he gotten to the open area before the refuse gate? Anwei sagged against him as if she were made of hollow bones. She was empty-handed, no sword, nothing from the tomb at all.

"Anwei?" He cast his mind out, looking for some clue as to what could have happened, but there wasn't anyone close by, no auras but Noa's and her backup ghost dancers and the streams of frightened people trying to get out of the flaming compound gates. He pushed farther, looking for the purpled aura that was the *point* of all this, but there was nothing to find. The shapeshifter was gone. Something had happened down in the tomb. But what? "Anwei, talk to me!"

An inhuman scream split the air, horribly familiar, as if it were an echo of one he'd heard in a dream moments earlier. A second scream followed, the auroshe demanding a fight with the first. Knox froze when he cast his mind wider and saw the auras. Bright gold. Five of them. They were in the fields, streaking toward the compound.

The Warlord and four other Devoted, full to the brim with Calsta's power. They closed in on the compound as if they could feel him quivering behind the walls, a mouse caught in their trap.

But what had happened to Anwei? She wasn't moving.

He scooped her from the ground and ran past the packed hills of dirt flanking Noa and the others, their chants burning the air. "You cannot wake our master!" Noa screamed with fiendish delight just as Knox got to the gate. Anwei was heavy, her head flopping to the side as he set her down against the wall, frantically looking for the broken lock Lia had promised him. "You cannot wake our master! He will come for us all!"

The gate was locked. And not just with the latch Lia had described, but reinforced across the wall in five different places. They'd fixed it.

He knelt by Anwei, frantically attempting to hold her up straight. She was alive, he could feel it inside him, but something was terribly wrong. "What do I do, Anwei? What happened to you? I don't know how to pick locks, and they're coming."

"I touched the poison." Her head lolled to the side, her braids a wall between the two of them. "Something was down there."

I was down there, Willow whispered.

Knox brushed the braids back from Anwei's face, her skin too hot. Two of her collar buttons had broken, leaving her neck bare. Light-colored scars cut through her skin along her collarbones on both sides. "Please, Anwei. Tell me what you need."

"Corta," she mumbled.

Letting Anwei sag forward against his shoulder, Knox wrenched open her medicine bag, spilling the envelopes inside. One crunched when he picked it up, the rank, acid stench of corta blossoming in his nose. He tore it open and held it up to Anwei's face.

"Our *master*!" Noa chanted in her singsongy ghost voice, edging back toward the gate. She and the dancers were supposed to dive behind the piles and out the gate while Anwei gave an explosive finish as the shapeshifter Patenga. Instead they'd be cornered against the locked gate and killed, one by one. "The king will make you wish you'd never been born!"

The corta leaves seemed to twitch inside the envelope. Suddenly they flew up into the air and crumbled to powder, forming a haze around Anwei's face like a cloud of gnats. Knox dropped the envelope with a yelp as Anwei breathed in deep, her back arching against the wall's wooden slats. He stared at her, holding his hands over his nose and mouth, wondering if the powder itself would attack him the way it seemed to be doing to Anwei. "Anwei? Are you all right?"

Anwei's head jerked back, slamming into the wall. She gasped for air, her eyes suddenly wide. Knox grabbed her shoulders, coughing as bits of corta stung in his nose. "Anwei?"

Noa had started again. "These years we slept underground, feeding him. Now he will come for you." The ghosts were about to pull back, expecting the explosive display to cover their retreat. And the gate wasn't open.

Anwei wrenched herself upright, Knox's hands slipping from her shoulders, her eyes wide. Every inch of her shook. "The gate . . ." She grabbed at the bars, pulling against the locks. It didn't budge. "I can't pick these. I've never even seen a lock like this."

Knox set his hands next to hers, drawing deep on Calsta's power when it still didn't move. The bars bent a little under his strength, but the gate held.

"Maybe if we climb?" Knox rasped. There was no way Anwei could manage it, shaking the way she was. Maybe not even on a day when she felt well. Noa and the dancers definitely weren't up for a climb, though Knox was less fussed about them getting caught. No one would hurt a second khonin, even if she did have a ghost posse.

Noa's swinging lights extinguished, her voice a skin-prickling caterwaul. Anwei's cue. Anwei turned toward them with a terrifying slowness, her arms outstretched, to stare into the last streams of terrified people who had been bottled inside the compound.

"Patenga," they whispered when they saw her painted face. "Shapeshifter."

The Warlord's aura edged into the compound, the barred doors finally open. A different kind of agitation and tumult began as workers fled, ducking to escape the five auroshes storming through the flaming gates.

Knox dumped Anwei's bag. He pulled out every single explosive packet Anwei had prepared and shoved them in between the bars on the gate, next to each locking mechanism.

"*I'll eat your souls!*" Anwei screeched, her voice breaking painfully over the words. A shudder broke out across Knox's skin. Willow chuckled inside his head. He threw one of the smaller sparklers so that it hit the top packet of explosives, igniting the outer protective layers in a shower of sparks and pops, which spread to the one below it and then the one below that. Smoke welled up around the gate, bringing tears to Knox's eyes.

The Warlord was almost to the toolsheds just inside the main gates. The only things between her and them was the pavilion covering the rows of baskets, the artifact sheds, and the compacted dirt waiting to be carted out the smaller exit. There was no way she and the Devoted hadn't seen Knox's and Anwei's auras.

But they weren't coming straight toward them. How was that possible?

Knox grabbed Anwei around the middle and dragged her to the opposite side of the dirt pile, pressing hard against her when the explosives ignited. A white-hot flash rocked the ground, dirt peppering Knox's back. Anwei gasped, though he took the brunt of the explosion. His ears singing only one high-pitched note, the air still clouded with dirt, Knox picked Anwei up in both arms and ran for the broken gap where the gate had stood. Noa and her friends pushed along behind him, giggles crackling across them like an electrical storm, as if they didn't know lightning was about to strike.

Golden auras sputtered just past the buildings behind them, an auroshe's whinny chasing after them.

"They went out the side gate!" a voice cried over the screams. "Find them!"

Lia stood stock-still, as if Master Helan wouldn't be able to see her through his veil in the darkness. Betrayal felt like weight on her shoulders. "Did Tual Montanne invite you here?"

"No one knows I am here." The spiriter's veil ballooned out with the words. "No one will remember *you* were here either. At least, they won't once I am done with them."

Anwei's mind was swimming with the corta flowing through her bloodstream. Knox's arms were tight around her, sugarcane stalks blowing madly in the wind all around them, his heart pounding hard against his sternum.

Down in the tomb he'd been inside her skin and she inside his, the two of them twined together so tightly that it had felt blushingly close. And now he was setting her into the wagon's hidden compartment, squeezing in next to her. His arms around her, his breath on her neck. The starlight winked out overhead as he pulled the door closed over them.

She shut her eyes, trying to ignore the trills running down her arms and back. Knox had disappeared in that tomb just as fast as those stars did behind the trapdoor; one moment the two of them had been joined together, and the next he'd been something else.

Like the night they'd stayed in Gretis. One moment he'd been lying close, and the next he'd been asleep on the floor. He'd almost thrown himself out a window rather than kiss her. She couldn't lose Knox, and giving in to feelings of . . . *anything* . . . would crack them into pieces.

Anwei took a shallow breath, her mind catching on everything around her: the overwhelming smell of *goat*, the muddy brown of the clay stuck in her boots, the spicy-sweet green that was cut sugarcane on their clothes, the charcoal gray and black that was salpowder, and an acidic torched cinnamon of poison on her skin. She concentrated on those scents instead of Knox's arms around her, burning through the last moments of clarity that the corta was going to give her. The poison was easier to pull apart now that it was on her skin, working through her body. It was meant to slow her down, make her sluggish and easy to catch. And eat, perhaps? She'd thought shapeshifters were only supposed to eat souls, but who really knew?

That voice down in the tomb. Anwei didn't believe in ghosts, but she knew a good performance when she saw one. Was it possible the shapeshifter had been down there waiting for them? Even if the tomb hid his aura, how could he have hidden his nothing scent? And if the snake-tooth man had been down in the tomb the whole time, why hadn't he attacked when Anwei first entered? He'd waited until the very end, when they'd been about to open the burial chamber.

Knox shifted behind her, his arm pulling tight around her ribs, her spine against him.

She whipped her mind into submission. *The burial chamber . . .*

An auroshe scream cut through the night, shouts carving through the harried breaths hot against her neck. "It's her," Knox whispered, not bothering to elaborate, and Anwei's thoughts swam around whom he might mean. Even those were too blurry. "Stay quiet, they can hear even better than I can. And stay close to me if they open this up. Maybe we can—"

"What is going on here?" A woman's voice cut through his almost-silent whispers, pitched so not even a Devoted would be able to hear.

A Devoted.

Her.

The Warlord.

Anwei's fingers curled tight around Knox's wrists. *Stay here,* she pled silently at Knox. *Don't disappear again.*

It would fall to Noa, a job Anwei knew the high khonin to be capable of. She thanked all the stars in the sky that they'd brought her along.

"Wh-wheel's bad, Your Warlordship . . . ma'am." The actor they'd left sitting on the wagon seat stuttered as he spoke, an admirable mask of fear. Or maybe it wasn't difficult to mime fear when speaking to the head Devoted of the Commonwealth.

A dry, reptilian nicker set the hairs across Anwei's arms and neck prickling. Knox's arms tightened around her, his face buried in her shoulder. His breath was against the side of her neck, her ear. Anwei swallowed, clenching her eyes tighter. *The tomb.* She made herself think it, *forced* the thought to replace the tickle of Knox's hair. Something had been down there. It had smelled familiar and had filled her to the brim, as if it had been waiting for her since the day she escaped

Beilda, still bleeding. Like . . . not home, exactly. Like something inside her she couldn't place. *That* was why she couldn't give in to Knox's breath sending shivers down her arms. Because no matter how much it seemed like people might care about her, Anwei knew better than to trust people who knew what she was.

"Your wheel is bad?" The auroshe sniffled at the wagon's wooden slats.

Noa's voice piped up, her native Elantin accent layered on thick. "Yes, and our shipment was due before dark, Your Lordship. I don't suppose you could help us?"

"I'm sorry for your trouble, but I'm afraid we lack the supplies and time to help." The Warlord sounded . . . dry. Unsure. Faint, even, as if there was only a very small person to fill her larger-than-life armor. "You haven't seen anyone on the road? Or in the fields?"

The Warlord—all the Devoted—were supposed to see auras. Knox had spent many moments curled in the shadows, as if he meant to disappear rather than let himself be found. How many times had they argued in the past week over Anwei's aura and how the Devoted would *know* what she was?

But clearly they didn't know. Why didn't they know?

"Some wagons went by not too long ago. Didn't so much as slow down when we waved for help. Could you at least help us boost the wagon off the bad wheel? Our lifter broke when *this* one"—a thunk reverberated through the wooden boards just over Anwei's face as Noa must have aimed a kick at one of her friends—"let the goats chew on it."

She was certainly taking this well. Lying to the Warlord's face. Anwei wanted to smile, but her face wasn't quite working.

"What is wrong with these goats?" Another voice inserted itself.

"We like to keep them comfortable on the journey. They don't fuss so much if they're subdued, you know," one of the dancers piped up.

"Well, may Calsta's light shelter you from her storm. I'm sorry we can't be of more help."

The sound of leather boots in stirrups, the creaking of saddles and swishes of tails. Hooves on the dirt. Then they were gone.

Knox waited a long, long time to speak. Long after the last auroshe scream had faded. After the wagon—which wasn't really broken—had lurched back onto the road. "I thought . . ." His whisper broke, his arms so tight around Anwei's ribs that she had to squirm away. "I couldn't carry you fast enough . . . and I was *sure* . . . Devoted don't ask questions when they see a Basist's aura."

The trapdoor overhead pulled open, and there was Noa grinning down through the gap. "You didn't tell me we were going against the Warlord herself!"

Anwei tried to sit up, but every muscle in her body was tired, her mind sluggish and slow. Knox pulled away from her, his hands gentle as he tried to help her up too. "Anwei got hurt. We need to get back to Chaol as quick as we can."

Chaol? What about the exchange with Shale?

They had no sword.

What about Lia?

They had no money.

Noa's face swam in front of Anwei's eyes, a rush of nausea flooding Anwei's stomach when the girl leapt back into the driver's seat. Serious for once. If coming face-to-face with auroshes and the sky-cursed Warlord herself didn't faze Noa, at least the prospect of Anwei being hurt did. A little rush of warmth threaded through Anwei's chest at her friend's concern. She was glad to have her there, just as she had been at the beginning. A bit of class and a bit of outlandishness—just enough to make their team complete.

Knox tried again to coax Anwei up from the floorboards, but she waved him off, and he gave the sugarcane fields another fearful look.

He didn't reach for the sword, though.

"I thought she was coming for *us*," he whispered. "Why else would the Warlord have come straight to the compound?"

It had been pure panic gushing from Knox's pores as they'd run—he'd practically melted at the sight of Roosters alone the week before. But still Knox had carried her. Stood inside the gate while they came, when he and Anwei both knew he could have climbed it and escaped by himself.

Knox had risked getting caught just to make sure Anwei wasn't found.

He'd helped her to do magic down in that tomb. And then the sword or the shapeshifter or *something* had changed him. But he'd come back to her from the nothingness.

Knox had stayed. Even though he knew what she was. He was watching her now as the wagon bumped into Chaol. The same direction the Warlord's auroshe had gone.

Anwei let herself feel the press of his hands against her wrists, the weight of his attention, for a split second, too scared to let herself think more than that. To *want* more than that.

Knox wasn't like her family. He did know what she was, and he'd stayed.

CHAPTER 35

But Calsta

Lia could sense the room's every possible exit even without Calsta's help. The two large windows, one looking east and one south. The door she'd just come through. Mateo so very close downstairs and yet so far away. She sank to her knees, knowing it was hopeless. That if Master Helan was here, there was no escape. Not until she somehow scrubbed Calsta's touch from her aura or stopped breathing.

The window was open, a breeze blowing at her scarf.

"You were given to Calsta when you were eleven." Master Helan's voice crackled like old leaves, his veil masking any hope she had for mercy.

"Yes, Master." The words caught in Lia's throat, strangling her.

"Our order of Devotion does not allow us to be seen, to touch, to feel. We are apart from the world, and yet you stand before me unveiled. You left the Devoted sent to protect you, and you choose instead to shelter with . . ." He paused, his veiled face turning an inch toward the door but not truly away from Lia. "People I wouldn't have expected."

Lia looked at her hands clenched tight into her skirts. Tual was downstairs too. Perhaps if she screamed . . . ? But even Tual Montanne, the all-powerful aukincer, couldn't fight the Warlord by himself.

Where *was* the Warlord? Sitting downstairs? In the dining room, eating one of Mateo's favorite sweet rolls as she waited for her young spiriter to be subdued?

Spiriters were too valuable to kill. Lia shrank inside herself another inch, missing her armor, her auroshe. Her sword. Feeling as if she were already shackled in a white room with a white veil, her entire life gone. Ewan waiting outside her door. No.

No.

She slipped a hand up to the scarf, pulling the knots loose.

Her face would be the last thing Master Helan saw.

"I can see your mind, child. . . ." His voice rattled, one hand shaking as it came out from under the veil, his gloves worn and soft.

Lia ripped the scarf from her hair, tears burning down her cheeks as she leapt toward him. Praying she'd reach him before he could call for the other Devoted who had to be here. Praying to Calsta, the very goddess to whom Master Helan meant to return her.

"And I do not blame you." A dagger flicked into Master Helan's hands, nothing there one moment, the wicked blade glistening in the moonlight the next. "Stay where you are, child, and listen. I do not wish for you to die."

Lia froze, the flat of the dagger pressed against her stomach. The scarf fluttered around her like she was caught in a windstorm, her curls blowing this way and that.

"What was done to you was an abomination, Lia Seystone." Master Helan slowly stood, keeping the dagger at her. "Not only what I see Ewan has attempted, but your life from the moment you entered the seclusion. Calsta does not compel Devotion." He sighed, his head bowing. "The Warlord is losing her people. She chooses not to ask, but to command."

"Why are you telling me this?" Lia demanded.

"Our order used to be a sacrifice of years, not life. A desire to be close to the goddess and to serve her if you had the talent. A desire you could take up and then give back once your service was done. All Devotion was done in the service of the goddess, an exchange that taught those with power what it meant to suffer, so we would not forget what it meant to be poor, hungry, without family, forgotten." He touched his veil, his old gloves slipping against the fabric. "What it meant to be isolated. Alone. Servants serve better when we truly understand those we serve. We served until we could bear it no more, until we were ready to return to the world, our places given to others who had not yet had the chance."

Lia's hand went to her head, the oaths scarred into her skin. "Calsta does not forgive broken oaths."

"No, my child. Calsta sees Devotion in seasons, our service taking different forms that are appropriate to our place in life—our oaths are supposed to be a choice. It is the Warlord who cannot afford to forgive. When the first Warlord made an army of Devoted, those soldiers chose to be Calsta's blades. They chose to save the people who were hungry, their strength stolen by thieves who called themselves kings, their children eaten one by one."

Master Helan sighed again, looking down at his knife. He withdrew it from Lia's stomach but held it ready in his fist. "In the years following the wars, it became increasingly difficult to control those with power, despite the sacrifices Calsta decreed to keep her Devoted in check. Seclusions were born. If you wished to practice Devotion to Calsta, it was under close supervision so Devoted did not become the new shapeshifters. Using their power to hurt, to steal, to terrify and destroy."

"Like Ewan Hardcastle."

"Yes. Like Ewan Hardcastle." Master Helan's veil twitched in the breeze, moonlight still bright on the knife. "The Commonwealth rests on Devoted shoulders, but Devoted are dying. The Warlord grasps, her soldiers falling between her fingers like sand as the wasting sickness takes them. She worries for our country." He sat back down, cocking his head. "So she has accepted sacrifices from Devoted like Ewan Hardcastle. She took your life without even asking. I have been watching you, child. I have been afraid for you. I followed the Warlord's company when they left Rentara, staying out of range so they would not stop me coming to help you."

Lia stumbled back into a chair, grasping the scarf to her chest. "You . . . you knew all this? You never said anything. You never told me—"

"There was never anything I could do. For me, Devotion to Calsta is my life. It is what I've always wanted. I serve those who cannot choose to be hungry as I have. They cannot choose their hard beds as I did. They did not choose to leave their families as I have. I give up my life for them." He slipped the knife into his pocket. "Your life was taken, not given as Calsta asks. You are my only student, and this opportunity could not be missed. I came here to set you free."

Calsta's power seemed to burn in the air around Lia, swirling just out of reach. If only she could read Master Helan's mind. If only she could know for sure he was telling truths, not stories that would weave a new web around her. She couldn't even sense him there, Calsta's energy a smell in the air when she needed to drink it down. Lia covered her mouth with both hands, jumping when her fingers touched her lips and chin instead of the scarf. Her last bit of armor, finally pulled free. "How can I believe you? The Warlord isn't going to stop hunting me."

"You have not learned all that Calsta can do, child. Thoughts are finicky things that can be moved and reshaped." Master Helan knelt before her chair, reaching out to touch both her shoulders with his gloved hands. Even with gloves, his hands felt warm and soft. "You don't have to believe me. All you have to do is run."

Knox couldn't remember anything except for Anwei limp in his arms. His thoughts seemed to tighten around her as he sat down next to her on her bed. Her eyes were still glassy, a funny smile on her face as he pulled the blanket up over her. "I'm going to get Gulya."

"No." She grabbed his wrist before he could stand. "She can't see me like this."

"If there are lasting effects . . ."

"It's going away." Anwei waved dismissively, her eyes wide as she looked up at him. "I'll probably have a headache in the morning, but I'm fine." She squinted down at her robe, her undertunic buttons ripped open at her throat. Her fingers slid up to touch the scar that ran the length of her collarbone, following it to her shoulder, where it disappeared beneath her tunic. Knox watched, unable to tear his eyes away. "Thank you for carrying me out. You should probably go meet Lia. Tell her it's all gone wrong. Check on Altahn. And then we have to come up with a new plan."

Her other hand still circled his wrist, holding Knox there even as she ordered him away. All her braids twisted around her head like snakes, the scarf she'd worn to hide them lost down in the tomb, and her shapeshifter face paint was smudged so it was just a muddy swirl of color against her tawny skin.

Knox pulled against her grip, looking away. "Let me get a towel and some water—"

Her fingers tightened. "I saw something in that tomb. Felt something. But it didn't smell like the snake-tooth man. What else could all that have been?" She tried to cover the white scars bared across her shoulders. Her sleeves were torn and muddied, revealing the end of another scar on the back of her wrist. "What happened to *you* down there, Knox?"

But Knox couldn't answer, could only see the scars. One of her shoes had come off. . . .

He pulled his wrist from her hand and slid to the end of the bed to pull off her other shoe. His fingers found the line of yet another scar that cut deep across the top of her foot. And suddenly he knew what they were.

"Someone tried to cut your aura away." The words were filled with fire and acid and the sharp sting of a blade. "One of those backwater purification rituals."

She tugged her foot from his hand and buried it in the blankets.

"Anwei." He looked at her. "Just tell me."

When her mouth opened, it was like in the cave, the way it had started at the beginning, as if the two of them had somehow bled into each other.

"The shapeshifter killed my brother." Her voice was so quiet, he shouldn't have been able to hear without Calsta's powers.

The bond between them mirrored everything back at Knox—he could feel his own fingers where they touched Anwei's ankle, and the way his touch made Anwei's skin trill. He could feel the way she liked it, that she didn't want to but she did.

Lady of Blue. Queen of the Sky. She Who Rides the Storm.

"The day my brother died, my family didn't remember him," Anwei whispered. "I tried to tell them. I tried to *show* them. I dragged my father into the room, and my mother started screaming, but it was because she thought there was something wrong with *me*. They saw the blood and thought it was mine, couldn't even remember they had a son to worry about. They were yelling, and I could smell everything in the room when I'd never been able to *smell* before, and there was blood and bone, and the *nothing* scent from the shapeshifter was eating the air, and . . ."

Her fingers had linked together tight against her chest, her knuckles white. "And then the jars in my father's shop started shaking. I could feel their insides, and suddenly they could feel me, too. We were angry, and so they shook like me."

Knox could feel her tensing, the drug in her system loosening something that had been welded shut inside her. "My parents dragged me out of Arun's room, and they wouldn't listen, and my brother was gone . . . *dead*. . . . " Her voice cracked. "And all the jars of herbs started falling off the shelves. Something fell on my mother, and the herbs were trying to help—swirling through the air, pushing us back toward my brother's room. I made them do it. And then my father grabbed me, and . . ."

Her voice petered out, her eyes closing.

Knox had seen scars like Anwei's before, though never so extensive. He moved her robe an inch or two, the scar twisting up her leg. His whole body prickled as he realized what he was doing and took his hand away.

He'd seen scars like that on a new Devoted who had come to the seclusion near the time he'd left. She hadn't flinched when they branded her scalp with the first oath, a resolution in her face that had made his skin crawl.

And he'd seen them in a village where he'd followed a Basist's trail. The townsfolk had tried to cleanse their potential shapeshifter. It hadn't helped them.

"And they tried to take your powers away," he whispered. "What . . . happened?"

"The whole village was there. When they cut me, something inside me broke." She blinked, a tear running down her cheek. "And the grass started growing, and there were tree roots coming out of the ground, making holes and moving rocks. It swallowed everyone up, fighting for me until there was almost nothing left of me. Of them. And there was a storm." Anwei licked her lips. "That was the only time I believed in Calsta, when that storm blew in out of nowhere, stopped anyone from following me. I ran to the beach and got into a boat. And all of them . . ."

All of them died. He could feel it in her thoughts. All of them were dead because they'd tried to kill her. The only people she'd been worried about following her were from the next town over. The Devoted, when they heard. But the storm had stopped anyone from knowing exactly what had happened, and her body hadn't been missed among the dead.

Knox set himself on the floorboards next to her. He could feel the terror in her mind, and the fear that maybe they'd been right to try to destroy her. That her power had made her a monster.

Willow crackled in Knox's head, but there wasn't room for her just now. His mind was full of Anwei.

"I'm so sorry." He propped his chin up on her bed so their faces were even. "You've known what you can do all along. And . . . now you don't want to do it ever again."

"No, that's not it. I *can't* do it. Not on purpose. Though tonight, in the tomb . . . I was close." She stopped, staring up at him. Her eyes moved down his face, pausing on his lips. Something in him ignited, and the forbidden well of feelings burst open, flooding him even faster than it had down in the tomb. The air between them seemed to be on fire, her hand lifting to run through his hair.

Knox. Calsta's voice exploded in his head. *Who is this for?*

The stark strangeness of the question jolted him up so fast that he almost slammed his head into the bed frame. Anwei blinked, her hands falling limply to the bed beside her.

What did Calsta mean, who was it for? Did it have to be for someone other than him and Anwei?

"What's wrong?" Anwei's face was flushed, her lips still parted, and there wasn't a single piece of Knox that wanted any space between him and her. Every inch of him burned.

And Calsta was in his mind. The space she'd taken had left a crack, Anwei's presence giving way to Willow's wicked laughter.

"I can't do this," he whispered.

"You can't?" Anwei's face closed. "You've always acted like . . . but you *wouldn't* . . ." She closed her eyes tight, her hands moving to cover them. "Just say what you mean, Knox." She shook her head, her fingers pressed hard against her face. "No, don't. Go away. Get out of my room."

"You don't understand."

"I understand enough. If you don't want to be in here, then *go*."

"Calsta above, Anwei." Knox groaned, the sound bitter and awful even in his own ears. "I *do* want to be in here. If it were up to me, I'd . . ." And then he had to stop because there were so many things he wished, but even thinking was crime enough for Calsta. Talking about it should have been more than enough for the energy inside him to drain until he was a husk. By all rights, Calsta should have drained him dry *weeks* ago, and he didn't know why she'd been so lenient. Because she could see he was trying, perhaps? In that moment he didn't want to try anymore. He didn't *want* Calsta's muscle, her hearing or sight. What had they ever done for him?

I'm going to save your sister, Knox. Calsta's voice was soft, consoling.

Willow cackled even louder. *I don't want to be saved. Do you love me, Knox? Do what* I *want.*

Knox shivered.

I led you here. I led you to Anwei. Your oaths aren't so I can control you. They aren't to make you miserable. There's a reason. Do you trust me?

"You'd what?" Anwei's voice was quiet. There was a tiny space in her armor, the same tiny space she'd always given him, asking him to be a part of her world.

But it wasn't a gap he could walk through right now. It took everything to breathe in deep. And let go. "Anwei, I care about you. You are one of the closest friends I've ever had."

The gap snapped shut. She shifted, staring up at the ceiling. "Okay."

"I thought you knew about—"

My oaths, he was about to say, but Anwei cut him off. "You don't have to explain yourself to me. I thought . . . but I thought wrong. I'm sorry."

Knox grabbed her hand and pulled her back to face him, all thoughts of letting go suddenly scorched to ash in his head, because this was a door Anwei wasn't going to open again. "You weren't wrong. It's just that right now—"

Anwei jerked her hand away from him. "Right now what? Right now you care about an invisible being who may or may not be real more than you do about what you actually want? A *sky goddess* no one has ever seen who gives you special power to kill people the Warlord doesn't like. I understand *completely*." She turned over to face the wall, her back a beautiful curve through her robe. Knox forced himself to look away.

"She's not fake, Anwei. She's been taking care of me my whole life. She *talks* to me, Anwei. I care about you, but I have to keep my oaths, or—"

"You've been hearing voices?" Anwei tensed.

"No. I mean, yes, but—"

She shook her head. "No, I can't. . . . Just go. We can talk about . . . voices and the dig and everything else tomorrow."

Knox closed his eyes. "It's not like that, Anwei. Please, if you just let me explain—"

"Why did it have to be the one time I don't have my medicine bag that you *refuse to leave my room*?"

Knox couldn't look at her. He forced himself to stand. "I have given up everything for Calsta. Food and comfort. Every possession. My family." His throat closed. "Love."

She rolled onto her back, looking up at him. "You aren't a Devoted anymore."

"I've kept my oaths, Anwei. My sister, the one who was *eaten* by that sword, is trapped between here and the sky. Calsta promised me if I kept my oaths, then she would help me set her free. And she led me to you. A Basist who could help me."

Anwei's face crumpled for a split second, as if a crack had appeared in her armor, letting him see to her core. But then it was gone. "That's why you've stayed with me, even when the Devoted came? And tonight. You carried me out of the dig because your goddess needs me alive?"

"No." Knox's stomach twisted. "I can honestly say I haven't thought about Calsta at all tonight."

Until now. Now Calsta burned like an effigy in his head, her energy swirling around him like an invitation waiting to be accepted. Willow flickered in the shadows Calsta cast.

Waiting.

Calsta had taken Ewan's power just for even thinking about breaking his oaths, so what was this game she was playing with Knox now? She had to know what was in his heart, what he wanted. So why hadn't she withdrawn?

A gust of wind wafted in through the window, touching his back as if Calsta herself were there behind him. *You don't understand everything yet. You will.*

"I have to go." He whispered it, hating every word. He said other things in his head to Calsta directly, but her presence didn't dim, no matter how much he cursed.

Anwei's expression broke him, her eyes no longer glassy but full of something dusty and cold. It was the face she showed her contacts, the gangs from the lower city. Yaru's face.

It wasn't Yaru who had dragged him off the street and made him her partner. It wasn't Yaru he'd eaten with, stolen with, laughed with, ducked Gulya with. And it wasn't Yaru he'd carried out of the compound.

Anwei was his best friend. She was . . . everything.

He retreated to the doorway, trying to anchor himself to the ground as he touched the cool wooden lintel. Yaru didn't have friends.

Devoted didn't either.

"We're going to come up with a new plan. We'll finish this, and then . . ." He didn't know what to say, if he was even allowed to think beyond the next day. Not until Willow was no longer a monster inside a sword.

"And then *what?*" Anwei's voice rasped. "It'll just be the next thing your invisible god needs from you, and then the next after that. Gods who demand you to give up your life aren't going to nicely hand it back when you ask. Isn't believing in right gods and wrong ones what gave me these scars?"

Knox couldn't find any words to say. None that were safe.

"Once all this is done, you're going to disappear." The words held a raw hurt that echoed across their bond. Years of loneliness and scars that stung.

"I'm not going to disappear." He stepped back, pulling open the door's latch. "But I have to save my sister." It shouldn't have been hard to say it, but it was harder than watching the veil settle over Lia's head and having no power to stop it. Harder than leaving the seclusion with nothing but a sword on his back and auroshes on the road behind him, screaming for his blood. "To save my sister, I have to keep my oath to love only Calsta. And every day I'm with you, I break it."

"Anwei!" Gulya's voice rapped against Knox's ears. The door slammed into his back as she burst through it. The old apothecarist stumbled past him, her face growing hard when her eyes found Knox. She turned on her heel and rushed to Anwei's side. "That boy, that Trib you were quarantining up here? You could have warned me he was an unruly patient—Anwei?" She put a hand to Anwei's forehead. "What is wrong with you?"

"Unruly?" The hairs on the back of Knox's neck stood on end, his aurasight suddenly pinging in his head. He hadn't been paying attention, his whole mind full of Anwei. But when he looked into his room just on the other side of the wall—

Knox bolted past Gulya, pushing her hands away when she tried to grab hold of his tunic. "Don't think I don't understand what's going on in here!" Gulya's voice slapped at him as he ran. "You leave me with a violent man who comes down the stairs like the nameless god himself, hits me over the head, and runs away as if he was some kind of prisoner. Then I find poor Anwei like this? What have you done to her?"

He wrenched open his bedroom door to find Noa sitting cross-legged in the middle of the floor, his money box in her lap. There was no sign of the Trib.

"Where is he?" Knox demanded. He pushed open the leaded-glass window, staring out at the dark street.

"I came in here hoping to find out the same thing." Noa had the courtesy to flinch when he rounded on her, eyeing the box in her lap. "There's no need to be so angry! You promised me a drugged boy." Noa pouted, clutching the box to her chest. "I can't help that I got bored! Just think of all the funny things he might have said."

"Knox?" Anwei hollered, her voice hoarse. "No, Gulya, I'm *fine. . . .*"

"Don't get up," Knox called, fingers tearing through his hair. Noa pushed the money box back under his bed frame, her ears a little too sharp for him not to notice. "Altahn is gone."

Mateo woke to morning light on his face. The curtains were open, and there was a book positioned on his bedside table as if someone had placed it there hoping to entice him back to life. Pulling himself up from the pillow, Mateo groaned. His muscles were all stiff, and his lungs seemed to have shrunk two sizes, but at least he wasn't draining away to nothing as he had been the night before.

He picked up the book from his bedside table, then almost dropped it when he caught sight of the title: *A Thousand Nights in Urilia* in garish purple. A piece of paper had been shoved between the pages, his father's measured handwriting peeking out from the cover. Mateo slipped it out and replaced the book on the table.

I'm not certain how much of our conversation last night you remember, Mateo, his father wrote. *The Warlord has called me to her side, and I fear you will wake up angry, so I want you to remember this until I can get back: you said you would do anything to survive this sickness.*

You also do not care to be commanded. This is something I

understand. But I wish to present you with the solutions to our plight as I see them:

Caprenum, of course. There remains a possibility that it will be corrupted, insufficient, or simply not there in the tomb.

Mateo let the letter crumple, his arms too tired to hold it up any longer. It had always been his job to doubt. *His* job to despair. If his father was giving up now . . .

But there was more. Inching the paper up, Mateo forced himself to continue reading.

There is another way to save you, I hope. One I feared to tell you.

It has to do with your magic and the nameless god. His magic is dangerous for you to use—I fear the wasting sickness has turned you into a drain. I can feel the way it pulls your energy. It is an emptiness, a nothing that desires to consume everything around it.

Wasting sickness untethers those with magic from this world, but if we can find you another anchor, all might not be lost. I've discovered evidence that Basists and Devoted have not always been at odds—that they joined together long before they were enemies. Perhaps to combat this very problem? All I have are theories.

But when my son is at stake, theories are what I work with. This is why I introduced you to Lia.

Mateo's fingers balled into fists before he could stop them, the paper tearing. *This* was why his father had introduced him to Lia? *This* was why he'd threatened to have her whole family killed if she wouldn't marry his son? Mateo's fingers shook, unwilling to relax until he forced them open, then tried to piece the torn paper back together.

There is a bond. One that comes only to a Devoted and a Basist when they trust each other. When they grow close. Love each other—not always in a romantic way. Any sort of love will do, so long as you are willing to sacrifice yourself for the other. They need to be the person you reach for in a moment of crisis, someone you trust as much as a god. I believe if you could form that kind of bond with a Devoted, then your episodes would end.

Lia is the only Devoted I could find who wanted to leave the Warlord and could be put into a position forcing her to give you a chance. If the two of you bonded, you would stabilize. Both you and *Lia would be safe.*

Eyes blurred, Mateo let the note's pieces fall onto his chest. Was his father going to claim they'd talked about this the night before? All he remembered was his father swearing over finding someone. *Lia* wasn't lost, which meant there was someone else caught up in this mess whom he hadn't even met yet. More scheming, more threats, more lies.

But even still, the idea of living sounded good. *Very* good. Mateo sagged back against his pillow, clocking the irregular beat of his heart. Then he picked up the bits of paper and willed his eyes to focus. There was only one line left to read.

Are you willing to at least try *to give Lia your heart if it means it will continue beating?*

Mateo let the papers flutter to the floor next to him. Forced his head up from the pillow, his spine to sit straight. He eased his legs over the side of the bed, shoved his feet into his favorite silenbahk-fur slippers, and pulled on the robe draped over the chair by his bed. Caprenum had always seemed like a too-simple answer to a complicated problem. A mythical substance that could cure him? Maybe it was just a distraction, something for Tual to throw Mateo at until he'd found a Devoted suitable for this new plan. One who had stepped past her oaths—or perhaps had been pushed past them?

This had always been about Lia.

Mateo tested his legs, his knees still shaky and his body made of lead, but he could stand. Walk. He stared at himself in the mirror, his cheeks hollow and his hair an ungodly mess. There were still smudges of dirt on his hands and face from lying in the entryway, bits of horse-hair stuck to his neck, and the bitter taste of aukincy in his mouth.

Lia had gotten him that far. To the courtyard. Of course, she was the reason he hadn't been at home in bed in the first place. Because . . . why?

"Go to your lady love!" Tual had yelled after him, as if he'd *wanted* a good punch to the jaw. Years of research, years of digging, of cozying up to the Warlord, fixing Devoted with the wasting sickness, spending years evaluating tomb sites, and this was what his father had come up with. And now Tual was hiding with the Warlord somewhere instead of facing Mateo head-on as he dropped this crucial bit of information.

At least his father loved him enough to look this long. To come up with a solution at all. He'd adopted Mateo, put himself at risk for so many years to find something that would heal him. The thought warmed in Mateo's chest even as he scrubbed a hand through his hair. He wished he'd been the one to figure out that there were more options than caprenum. That way, it wouldn't have felt so *imposed*. How was he supposed to force himself to love someone? *Bond* with the first girl his father thrust at him?

Mateo tried storming toward the door, and when that didn't work, he trudged with great disdain. He slogged down the stairs, refused to accept help when the upstairs maid offered him her arm. It wasn't until he got to the kitchen and could lean on the doorjamb that he called out to the cook. "Hilaria! I need sweet rolls immediately!"

His voice died in his throat when it was Lia's face that poked out from behind the wall enclosing the little area where the servants took their tea. Well, some of her face. Most of it was concealed behind the dark blue scarf. Swearing inside his head, he looked around the open kitchen, hoping the cook would appear. "Have . . . have you seen Hilaria?" he asked.

"You're all right!" She slid out from behind the table and almost skipped toward him, her eyes wide. A red curl had escaped the scarf at her cheek, as if she'd tied it in a hurry. "I thought . . ." She looked him up and down when she got to him, her eyes sticking on his furry slippers. "Well, it looked bad. How are you feeling this morning?"

"Fine. Yes. All fine." He cleared his throat, wishing he'd changed out of his silk pajamas. Then aggressively not caring that he was wearing pajamas, because he didn't want to impress Lia. Impressing her would probably have required killing someone with his drawing pencils anyway.

"You wanted sweet rolls?" she asked, looking around. "The kitchen staff all left so I could eat." She touched her scarf. "It was kind of them. You almost caught me without this."

"You don't magically absorb food through your hands? That was my vote." Mateo inched past her into the kitchen, looking wildly about for anything edible. If he could just grab something and run—well, plod—back up the stairs, then he wouldn't have to think about this right now. But Lia seemed to have swelled to twice her size, taking up far too much room. This girl whom he was supposed to magically fall in love with and somehow convince that she felt the same.

That was the worst part about all this. If Tual was right, it wasn't as if Mateo could create a list of things to accomplish, set goals and then work toward them. Relationships weren't a matter of studying all the right sources and digging until you found the prize. *Lia* would have to decide she liked Mateo enough to keep him alive. He doubted you could fake it, come up with a way to make the gods believe you were doing what they'd asked, the way he and Lia had tried to fool their parents over the engagement.

Lia stepped around him, hand darting out to take his arm when he sagged against the counter. "What is wrong with you? You look like you just swallowed a dead frog."

"That's . . . very specific. I don't eat things that are slimy."

"I don't eat things that taste good. Maybe I should try frog." Lia smiled up at him, or her eyes did, anyway. He couldn't see her face under the scarf. "Come sit down—I don't feel like dragging you back up to your room if you collapse again. I'll pour you some tea."

Once he was situated at the table, with a sweet roll found in the cupboard on a plate in front of him and a steaming cup of lavender tea in his hand, Mateo finally let himself look at her. Lia. With whom . . . he had not hated spending the last few days. She was outlined in sunlight, an unfinished crust of bread on the plate before her and her tea cold in its cup. She didn't reach for either, the scarf tight around her nose and mouth. She kicked her feet absently as she looked out at the cliffs beyond the window. The waves had gone down, Jaxom and Castor's battle dying away until they came too close to each other yet again.

"What's wrong with you?" Mateo asked, setting the cup down. "You're all . . . *happy.*"

She snorted. "Sorry, I'll go somewhere else if I'm spoiling your morning sulk."

"No. I'm . . ." The words came before he really thought about them, but they were true, so he let them spill out. "I'm glad you're here. I'm glad you brought me back last night. That you're safe."

"And that you are too?" That smile again, hidden behind her scarf.

"I am very glad to not be dead on the roadside, yes." He took another sip of tea, nodding to her bread. "Don't skip your breakfast on my account."

She rolled her eyes.

"My father didn't try to tie a bridal wreath around your head while you slept, did he? He left me a rather alarming note that made me wonder if all the ceremonies had already been performed."

"If he did, I slept through them too. I suppose we can ask when he gets back." Lia watched Mateo sip again, a hint of furrow in her brow. "I was really worried last night. Thank you for coming to get me before the Warlord came. And for doing it when you were so sick. It was a risk, and I'm grateful you took it, or I'd be . . ." She looked down, a trace of the statute girl she'd become around Ewan sliding across her face. "I don't know where I'd be."

A flicker of anger sprang to life in Mateo's gut about the fact that Ewan even existed as a human being.

"I've been wondering about that, actually." Lia looked back up at him, all traces of stone gone. "When we were at the compound, you lied to Ewan for me even though he had a blade to your throat. And then last night . . . you know the Warlord could kill you just for helping me, don't you?"

"Well, we're supposed to like each other, right? You're the one who asked me to play along." Mateo had to fight hard to hold her gaze and not look down into his cup.

"You aren't playing anymore. Tell me why." It was an order. From a Devoted to a . . . whatever he was. A hiding Devoted, she thought, not a dying Basist—a boy she would have killed without a thought if she'd had her full range of powers. Lia didn't break his gaze either, her fingers twisting the end of her scarf. Her voice softened, and there was no mocking lilt. For once, she was just looking back. "Please tell me?"

Mateo's mind was made of white milk, of white bread innards, of other horribly blank things. It was a good question. The reason wasn't so complicated, and it didn't have much to do with Tual or his sickness, either one.

Lia was terrifying. She was a sky-cursed Devoted who could pry open your mind and gobble up your bloody secrets one by one. But if the answer to his sickness lay in Lia, then whether he lived or died was out of his control. It was like the rest of Mateo's life, his very existence depending on someone else's favor. It felt like a crimp inside him, that Lia could be in charge of his fate, but he couldn't be angry at her for it. He hadn't even minded the last few days they'd been thrown together. They had been . . . *nice*.

"You know, I like you, Lia." Mateo put down his tea. "I wasn't expecting that."

It was an experiment. A tentative step forward. Mateo sat back in his chair and watched her reaction. Her face changed beneath the scarf, a flicker of eyebrow peeking out from under the band of fabric shrouding her forehead. Then she sat back in her chair, cocking her head and watching him just the way he was watching her.

Then she laughed.

She threw back her head and *laughed*, a clear bell of a sound that was completely without restraint. It was as if she'd been wearing armor up until this very morning, her hand on the hilt of a nonexistent sword. Now it was gone. All except for the scarf. "I don't think anyone has made liking me sound so painful."

"Because they were too worried you'd stab them." He picked up the sweet roll and took a bite that was far too large. The rest of what he meant to say came out a little squashed and crumby. "Or make their brains bleed out of their eyeballs while you read their minds."

He was glad, at that moment, that Lia's aura was so diminished.

"I'm never reading another mind. Never again." The laugh in her voice stayed. It wasn't Mateo's imagination—she *was* acting differently. Had Tual chatted with her last night too, only he'd said she was free to go and become a silenbahk farmer or a fire dancer or whatever it was Lia wished she could do with herself? Not a plea to save his son. To *love* his son and keep him tethered to the earth when Calsta and the nameless god had both forsaken him.

"No mind reading?" He pointed at the scarf with his roll. "What's that for, then?"

"Calsta requires that spiriters not see or touch anyone directly. I wore gloves and a veil for two years." She touched the long fringe trailing over her shoulder. "At first it just felt . . . more normal. Then I told myself I was wearing it so Ewan wouldn't see me."

"But neither was true?"

"No, I think it was because I was afraid."

Mateo swallowed his bite, his chest suddenly feeling tight. This had suddenly become a serious conversation. And he was torn between wanting to end it and wanting to continue. Refusing to see more of Lia because that's what his father wanted, and actually wanting to see more of Lia. Heart picking up speed, he took another bite of the roll, not quite able to look at her. "Afraid of what?"

"Afraid . . . Calsta would see who I really was. That she'd know my heart was broken every day that I couldn't talk to my family. That she'd see how glad I was to be away from the seclusion and back with them. That my father would see how angry I was at him. That Aria would see how scared I was. That your father would see something in me he could use. And that you . . ." She leaned to the side, toying with the end of the scarf. "That you'd see my face and decide being married to me would be easier than fighting off your father. That you'd go along with it, I'd lose you as an ally, and then we'd be stuck together for the rest of our lives."

Mateo almost choked, clearing his throat once he managed to swallow. "Are you trying to tell me that you're very, very pretty under that scarf?" The flippant answer slipped out, but Lia laughed. "You were right to be worried. I am definitely that shallow. Can't resist red hair."

Her hand jerked up to the scarf, finding the solitary curl that had escaped. She started to tuck it back but then lowered her hand. "I have been hiding for so long. Behind Vivi, my sword. My armor. Until they took it all away." Her fingers went to the scarf's knot. "Then it was my veil."

Mateo's stomach lurched as she began to untie it. "What are you doing?"

"I think . . ." She pulled at the knot until it came undone. Pushed the scarf back from her forehead, down from her lips and chin. She let it slide to the kitchen floor. "I think I'm done hiding."

CHAPTER 36

Our High Khonin Friend

Jecks, the Blackheart from the plague house, tapped on Anwei's window as she packed the last of her herbs. Every movement still felt as if she were underwater, the tiredness of a night without sleep sitting heavy on her eyelids.

Knox couldn't find a single trace of Altahn. He'd ranged out through all the Coil, down through the Sand and Fig Cays. He'd even gone to Yaru's temple. The Trib's aura was nowhere to be found. The maps and the last of the explosives were missing too.

Anwei pushed open the window for Jecks, hardly remembering what she'd asked him to do for her.

"They're outside the city," Jecks whispered, holding himself back from the window. "Near that dig everyone is talking about."

"The Trib clan?" Anwei blinked slowly, trying to think what that could mean. "What are they doing?"

"Digging. There are others with them. I think they might be wardens."

Anwei's mouth went dry. Wardens? Why would the Trib involve wardens in a plot to steal from the Warlord? She blinked at Jecks, pulling all her emotions in check. "Perfect. Thank you for your help. How is your family doing?"

A smile cracked his lips. "Better. Most of the quarantine seems to be a little better. You really are a miracle worker."

His eyes touched her braids but then dropped down to the floor, the stink of superstition enough that Anwei could almost smell it. She frowned, thinking of the quarantine. When she'd been there the other day, the nothing smell had been stronger than ever, and none of the patients had looked as if they were getting better. She'd done all she could to get food and water into Jecks's daughter and partner, but curing a sickness that wasn't attacking a person's physical body wasn't something Anwei knew how to do.

Jecks continued, scuffing a foot against the ground. "I guess they're confining any other sick people they find to their cays. The Warlord herself is here and shuttered up in some high khonin's house, hoping she doesn't catch it. Even the governor is in bed with a rash."

"The governor?" Anwei looked up in alarm. Gamtooth poisoning didn't spread between people. It was a poison, not a sickness. Even if someone had dumped gamtooth poison the whole length of every canal, it would have been long gone by now. Which meant she'd been right. The shapeshifter had to have seen the original mass poisoning down in the Fig Cay, then used it as a cover to . . . do whatever he was doing. Burrowing into people, taking from them, the effects being blamed on a sickness that had started before he even came back to the city. Then, when those initial victims weren't enough, he'd poisoned more people so it looked like a spreading plague. But *what* was he doing?

Last night he hadn't been at the excavation, unless he'd learned how to mask his smell. There had been only a voice, that whip against her skin, and *Knox*. . . .

Anwei's stomach twisted.

Jecks squinted at her. "You didn't know it had spread so far? The Warlord is only going to be here for the day, I guess. She's going to go out to the shapeshifter tomb to cleanse it of any foul presence, so they say. Hopefully, that will take care of the sickness once and for all."

Nodding, Anwei looked away, trying to let the thoughts about last night drain before they could form. *I have to keep my oath to love only Calsta. And every day I'm with you, I break it.*

What goddess commanded you to love her and no one else? That wasn't even possible, not if you had a single human relationship. The link to Knox felt tenuous in her mind. She could feel him coming from the direction of the Sand Cay just then, bone tired and worried.

And angry. Hurt just as much as she was. It made her cross—*he* wasn't allowed to feel hurt or angry. *He* was the one who had said . . .

No. Anwei took a deep breath, forcing herself to focus on the Blackheart standing before her, an odd expression on his face. Knox was her partner. She needed him. Not just for the shapeshifter and the sword. He was her only friend.

Well, that wasn't true. Noa had proved to be more than a contact. It had been almost a relief to have her here in the apothecary. But Noa hadn't almost kissed her and then rejected her.

Why had Knox's being anything other than her partner occurred to Anwei in the first place? It was ridiculous to realize how much she'd wanted Knox, because she'd thought he was saying yes, but he'd said no instead.

Anwei's chest seemed to squeeze. Everything was falling apart.

She forced herself to focus on Jecks, his eyes shifty as he edged toward Gulya's outer gate. "You say the Warlord is going to the dig today?"

The man nodded, inching back another step. "If you aren't needing anything else . . ." He was already halfway to the gate, as if he could creep away from Anwei and her scary healing abilities before she called up the earth to swallow him down. *Dirt witch.* She could almost see the thought on his face.

"Anwei?" Gulya's voice called from the apothecary. "The governor himself wants you to come! Something about the plague—apparently, you're the only healer who managed to help?" The woman appeared in the doorway. "What an honor, the governor knowing your name!"

Anwei blinked, the beginnings of a plan starting in her head. "Yes. What an honor. I'll . . . go as soon as I'm done with . . ." She looked down at the blank table. "Something very important."

Gulya's mouth squished into an unpleasant sort of smile, but she returned to the apothecary, calling to a customer who must have just come in.

"You cured the plague?" Noa's voice made Anwei jump.

She turned to find her friend on the stairs, hair tousled by the night's sleep. "You scared me. I thought you were asleep, Noa."

Noa wound her hair up on top of her head and stuck that double-pronged hair stick of hers into it, Falan's flower jauntily poised above her ear. She hopped down the last steps to sit next to Anwei at the table. "I'm surprised you are awake." Noa's nose flared as she looked Anwei over. "You look better than you did last night. What happened down there? And then Altahn . . . what happened to him? All I found in Knox's room was that box full of money."

Anwei snorted, trying to cover it with a cough. So many questions, just like Noa. "I'm feeling better, thank you."

"Good." Noa didn't speak for a moment, as if she expected answers to the rest of the questions, but Anwei only smiled. "So when do we head back to the dig? It's going to be today, isn't it?"

The dig. Today. Anwei was so tired, she had a hard time finding a smile for her friend. "What do you mean?"

"Well, you and Knox went down into the tomb and came out with nothing to show for it. The Warlord is probably here to *purge* the whole place." Anwei glanced at the window where Jecks had been, wondering how long Noa had been standing on the stairs. How she could have known about the shapeshifter purging unless she'd grown ears as sharp as Knox's. "And after whatever performance the Warlord puts on with her Devoted, she'll bundle up the prize they were digging for, then leave." Noa's eyes glinted, and the back of Anwei's neck prickled. "Taking with her whatever it is you've been risking so much over. Right?"

Anwei hadn't told Noa anything to do with the dig other than needing ghosts to scare the workers. Not about the Warlord or time frames or any of it. And yet Noa knew. Altahn had spent enough time looking at the dancer out of the corner of his eye—he could have told her. But when? And why would he?

Altahn was *gone*.

Noa was still talking. "I mean, if you'd gotten what you were after, we'd all have left already. That was the plan."

The tone of her voice felt so eager, so full of things she wasn't supposed to know. Exactly as Noa always sounded, like she was about to take a bite out of something, but suddenly Anwei felt as if the target was *her*.

"Are you worried your father is going to find you?" Anwei asked slowly, standing up from the table. "Or did you decide poisoning people at balls is more fun than having to hide all the time?"

"Oh, Daddy's never going to find me here. I'm sure he already stormed the Firelily and probably tried searching Bear's house, though I suppose they wouldn't have let him in."

Because his father's taken sick. Like all the other people around Noa take sick. The thought struck Anwei hard. It had taken Anwei almost five years to confide in anyone what she was doing. To include Knox in her missions. She'd known he wasn't a threat long before she'd allowed him even that close.

But Noa . . . Noa was a *contact*. Anwei usually didn't even meet with contacts in person, and yet she had with Noa. From there, Noa had wormed her way into Anwei's circle awfully quickly. Had seemed to put together all the pieces of Yaru and the tomb when no one else had.

"So if you're safe, what's it to you if we stay a few more days?" Anwei asked, reaching up to extract a few stalks of linereed to cover her confusion.

"Nothing at all, of course. I just want to help. I want to know what we're after and how we're going to get it." Noa looked around the workroom with such interest, as if she could divine exactly what each herb was, where the doors and windows were, where the secret panels might be. She'd already gone through the upstairs, if Anwei wasn't mistaken. Knox had found her sitting in the middle of his floor with his money box open in her lap the night before.

Noa's Firelily theater was right there next to the Fig Cay plague house. She'd been in the governor's house, where Noa had particular reason for rancor. In the Coil, where all the different gamtooth cases had popped up. Anwei's own stash of gamtooth spinners had been producing less than they should, as if they'd already been milked.

"I'm still thinking about what we should do. I've got an idea, but I have to talk to Knox about it first." Anwei shook away the ridiculous line of thought, arranging the linereed stalks on the table so they didn't touch, then gathered them up together again. The spinners produced differently every time; it had to do with time of year, the heat. . . . Her eyes touched Noa's hair stick as the high khonin reached up to pull it out, twine her hair into a bun, then stick it back in. The two prongs seemed altogether too sharp for something anyone should like stuck in their hair.

Two prongs. Like a spider's bite.

A shapeshifter could change. The only things that had ever stayed the same about the leads she'd tracked were the nothing smell that followed the shapeshifter and the snake on his tooth—it was as if he couldn't change his bones, just rearrange them, make them swell and shrink. Would Noa show her teeth if Anwei asked?

Anwei shook her head again, wondering whether, if she lost another night of sleep, she'd start believing Gulya was the shapeshifter next. Noa didn't have a dark aura or Knox would have noticed. She didn't smell like nothing.

"Are you feeling all right?" Noa stood up and leaned across the table. "Is it whatever happened down in the tomb? How can I help?"

"Nothing. I'm fine." Knox's smell wisped by Anwei's nose, and the back door opened behind her. Anwei swallowed, keeping her eyes on Noa. What *had* happened in the tomb last night? She'd been attacked by something with no special smell, no aura. . . .

Noa had been at the dig that night. Just like she'd been at all the other places where gamtooth poisoning had appeared.

All these years Anwei had been chasing her brother's murderer. What if the snake-tooth man had gotten tired of it and decided to stay in one place? Wait until Anwei wasn't paying attention, then slip into her life, gain her confidence, and . . .

Knox stepped into the empty space beside Anwei, spoiling her concentration. *And what?* Anwei laughed at herself, rubbing her temples. Why would the shapeshifter want to get anywhere near her?

Why had Noa wanted to get near her?

Why had the shapeshifter killed Anwei's brother in the first place?

The problem was that Anwei didn't know. And questions—maybe it was because she was tired—but they hit one after another, ringing with clarity. Years and years had gone by without Anwei letting a single person into her house, into her heart. Then Knox had come with his nothing smell, and she'd treated him like a lead until it became obvious he wasn't. Then Noa . . . but there had been no reason for Anwei to grow close to Noa. Yet here the girl was, *living in her house*, twisted up in the one thing that could give Anwei her life back.

How had it happened? It was almost as eerie as the idea of her parents forgetting they had a son despite his blood spilled across their floor, their minds and memories changed into something new. The shapeshifter had done that.

What if . . . what if Noa *was* the snake-tooth man? Bent into a new shape. Watching Anwei for the better part of a year. What if she'd been wrong about the dig? Wrong about Director Van?

"The whole governor's house is infected with the plague." Knox cleared his throat, grabbing one of the apples at the center of the table and biting into it. Noa's presence seemed to darken as she looked between Anwei and Knox. She'd already known about the governor.

Was Bear one of the victims? Or had all that gossip and angst over forced marriage contracts been a story for Noa to present like a treat, because she knew Anwei would swallow it?

"And Lia's family didn't go to Gretis last night. The Warlord is staying in their house," Knox continued, then took another bite of apple. But she could feel him tense next to her, all the thoughts running through her head manifesting as fear to him through the bond.

Anwei felt the soft connection between them twinge. He wanted to know why she was afraid. Wanted her to look at him. But Noa was standing there like a shadow. Like a great big *nothing* darkening the workroom.

"What about Lia? Is she safe?" Anwei drew the words out slow, sending her mind into the flowers and leaves hanging from the ceiling. Her medicine bag with the gamtooth serum, the corta, and even her tiny pinch of calistet was upstairs.

Knox shook his head, giving Noa a quick glance. "I didn't see her at the house." Her aura was what he meant. Noa probably already knew about his aurasight, his sword, that the Devoted were hunting for him, too. "There were Devoted guarding the gates, the windows. They didn't see me, same as last night." He cleared his throat. "What's wrong, Anwei? Last night . . . didn't go well, but—"

"It's not you." *Didn't go well?* As if it were as simple as cross words that they could leave behind them. But there were bigger things to worry about. Anwei couldn't pull her eyes away from the hair stick jutting out from Noa's bun. Such a simple weapon. Beautiful. Unremarkable. Underestimated.

Noa suddenly moved. Anwei jerked forward in anticipation, grabbing hold of Knox's wrist as if she could force him to come to attention. He sprang up, confused, as he looked at Anwei. "Well, what is it, then?"

The sudden movement had only been Noa reaching for a stalk of pretty dried flowers. She paused before touching them. "These won't give me warts or anything if I touch them?" She looked from Anwei to Knox, then pulled the stalk down. "She's worried about how we're going to get into the dig, Knox. I have some ideas. But the secrets need to stop. If I don't know what we're after, then how can I help, really?"

Anwei stood slowly, energy arcing painfully down her muscles. Knox's arms tensed, his head slowly turning to look between Noa and Anwei. Flexing her hands, Anwei gathered up her branches of linereed. Not poisonous. Not even prickly. But they were the only thing vaguely weaponlike within reach. "You're a lot more interested in the dig than I would have expected, Noa."

There was no denying she'd sensed the shapeshifter there at the dig that first night. Or had she?

"It's interesting." Noa shrugged, picking the flowers apart and letting the pink petals rain down on the table. "A real shapeshifter is down there, and you want something from him." Noa looked up, the light sick on her face. Her smile prickled, but it wasn't wide, because Noa never smiled big enough to show anything but her front teeth. Never wide enough to reveal a house mark. "You're a puzzle, Anwei, and if I'm going to be a part of your group here, I want to know more of the pieces."

What if the nothing smell didn't follow the shapeshifter himself, like Anwei had believed all these years? What if it marked where he'd been, the scent of energy being stolen and the void it left behind?

"You're right. If you're going to be a part of the group, you should know." Anwei's mind raced. "We'll show you once we're done at the dig today. I think I'll need your help to get in."

Knox's head swiveled slowly to look at her, confusion on his face going from thin to thick.

"Do I need my friends from the Firelily?" Noa's dimples creased her cheeks.

"No. I need you to set the wall on fire. The southern end, where we were yesterday. I'll be coming with the Devoted."

Knox's chin shot up, alarm in his eyes.

Noa flinched. "You're coming with the Warlord? She saw me last night, so if she sees me at the dig as well . . ."

"Show me, Noa. Show me I can trust you."

"I *did*. I helped you steal salpowder. I went into the excavation last night dressed as a ghost, lied to the Warlord's face. What is setting a fire going to do to help you?" The girl swallowed, all affectations and laughter suddenly scrubbed from her countenance.

"It's a distraction. You're so good at distractions." Like pretending all she wanted was to be free. Just like Anwei wanted. To be free.

The snake-tooth man could rearrange people's minds. Had he looked inside hers to see what she wanted most, then used it to make her feel sorry for him? You didn't watch the people you felt sorry for as closely because it was easy to think you knew exactly what they wanted.

A plan was beginning to whirl in Anwei's head. "I want you to set the fire right after the Warlord goes inside the compound. Her retinue won't see you that way."

Noa licked her lips. Drew in a shaky breath and touched the hair stick, Falan's rose peeking out through her fingers. The god of actors. Of thieves. Of gamblers.

If she was the shapeshifter, then what was this gamble?

Nodding ever so slowly, Noa backed out through the door and shut it behind her.

Anwei threw herself onto the bench, unable to meet Knox's eyes. "I think Noa might be the shapeshifter."

"*What?*" Knox's voice hollowed down to nothing. He slumped next to her at the table, as if every bit of his energy had been sucked clean from his bones. "I mean, she's annoying, but not . . . what about the dig director?"

"I don't know. She was *there* last night." The muscles in Anwei's throat clenched as she whispered. "She knew about the dig. She was even already playing ghost. Do you remember Shale getting angry at us because someone broke into the dig dressed as a ghost? It happened the same night as the governor's party. Noa didn't get us out of the party like she was supposed to, she disappeared. What if she went to the dig instead, then blamed it on Bear?"

"What would she want at the dig? Besides, her aura isn't marked."

"*Our* auras aren't marked either, Knox. At least, no one else can see them." Anwei looked at him, tears dry in her eyes. "I don't know what she'd want at the dig, though. Something a shapeshifter needs. Why would Director Van want to open the shapeshifter's tomb? Why would the Warlord? There's something down there—"

"The sword, probably. If it's anything like my sword, I don't know why anyone would want it, but it does seem like a lot of very important people are digging in the same place." Knox shook his head. "But you saw the shapeshifter at the dig the first time we went out there. Noa couldn't have been there then."

"I could *smell* him. I can smell him all over this city, Knox. I've smelled him on *you* when you're holding the shapeshifter sword. I don't think the nothing smell is from the snake-tooth man. I think it comes from his *victims*."

Knox's eyes traced around her, looking at the aura he could see but no one else could. "What do we do?"

"We need the sword, and we need the shapeshifter. We're going to the dig today because the Warlord is going to open that room, and the shapeshifter has definitely been involved there . . . whether it's Noa or Director Van or someone else entirely. He'll be there."

"You're not sure."

Anwei breathed in, hating everything. "I'm not sure about who. But I have to believe I'll know when I see him."

"Will you? Right now you don't know if it's the flighty noble who has been sleeping on your bedroom floor. Even if you do suddenly recognize him, then what? Are you going to throw serum all over him and drag him away while the Warlord is watching?"

"I'll have to! This is our last chance." She slammed a fist against the table. "This is *my* last chance. I've been following this monster for more than seven years with nothing to show for it. If I don't get to him today, he's going to get *me* or he's going to disappear forever. Gamtooth serum will slow him down enough that I'll have time to figure out the killing part. If you don't want to come—"

"You always say that. As if you think I won't follow you." Knox's voice was so soft. "You have a plan. What is it?"

Anwei forced herself to look up, to meet his gaze head-on. "The Warlord's worried about her Devoted getting the plague."

"And?"

"I can make sure they *do* get it. It's just gamtooth venom that causes the rash, and I'm the only healer in the city who's been any help. The governor himself sent a message for me to attend him."

"You managed to cure people of whatever the shapeshifter did to them?"

"No, they started getting better on their own, but no one else knows that. I'll go present my services to the Warlord when her Devoted start showing symptoms, and from there I'll figure out how to make sure I'm one of the party going to the dig."

Knox closed his eyes, his hands coming up to rub them. When he opened them again, the air seemed to crackle between them. His body tipped toward her, waiting for something to happen.

Every day I'm with you . . .

He looked away.

Anwei forced herself to breathe. "She knows your face, so you can't come. I'll meet you in Gretis. By then I'll know how to fix your sword and how to kill this monster . . . it'll all be done."

Knox stood, shaking his head. "Anwei, *no*—"

"Can you think of another way to find him?" Her voice broke. "This is how we save your sister. How you get away from the Warlord forever. You won't need . . . whatever this is anymore." She pointed between them, the bond turning to an odd mix of stinging and soft.

Knox's face twisted, but then he nodded. "I'll come with you to Lia's compound and help poison the Devoted if I can. I'll make sure they don't see me. Then I'll go find Shale outside the dig and stop him from interfering. And after . . ." He trailed off.

Anwei looked away. Maybe there was no after. Knox was Calsta's, and the goddess didn't seem to be the type who shared her spoils of war.

That, by itself, was an answer. Knox was here to lay his sister to rest. Anwei was here to do the same for her brother, and nothing else mattered.

It couldn't. Because it didn't to him.

Anwei traced the shape of Knox's face in her mind, the tilt to his shoulders, the straightness of his back. His hair too short to stay in its tie. The lines that crinkled his mouth and eyes when he smiled. Anwei let it fill her to the brim.

She took the image of him, so carefully preserved, and set it on fire in her mind. Let it burn. He didn't belong to her, and he'd end up abandoning her like everyone else in her life had the moment Calsta asked. That was her lot, it seemed. She'd taken him in, and that deviation meant she'd have the shapeshifter now. She just . . . wouldn't have anything else.

Anwei stood from the table, trying to ignore the ashy hole in her chest, as much a void as what the shapeshifter himself had left her. "I'll get the serum from upstairs and all the leftover venom. And while I'm at Lia's family compound, I'll see if I can find out what happened to her."

"This is going to end badly," Knox whispered. But he followed her out the door, as she knew he would. The connection between them felt like a fungus that had spread from her mind down through her humors, invading her heart.

An infection she'd had before—her parents had left a much larger, bloodier hole. And she had yet to sniff out the complement of herbs that would close it.

She stopped as Knox stuffed a hand into his pocket and drew out a long purple ribbon that sparkled with beads. "I bought it for you a while ago." He handed it to her. "I guess the color reminded me of . . ." His eyes traced around her, the ghost of what she was. "It reminded me of you. I'm . . . sorry. About everything."

Then he left.

Anwei held the ribbon. *It reminded me of you.* The idea made her glow inside for a split second, a sparkling hint of a future that could include things like ribbons when she hadn't worn something so pretty in years.

A new life. With Knox.

But his future didn't look the same as hers, not with his Devotion to the goddess. So it wasn't real. And Knox might say he was there, that he was by her side, but in reality, her biggest threat the night before had been him.

The only thing she could rely on was her own two hands.

She left the ribbon in a sad bundle on the table and walked out.

CHAPTER 37

We'll Fix Everything

The moment she entered Lia's street, Anwei knew something was terribly wrong. It wasn't the chittering of bored auroshes needling the air or the Devoted clutching their sword hilts before the gate. It was the smell.

A nothing smell wafted from the upper windows of the house, so strong that Anwei's throat convulsed.

"Knox," she whispered as her partner fell into step with her, the top of Lia's house barely visible over the wall. "Something . . . terrible is inside. Maybe he's in there right now, or maybe . . ."

"I can feel it too." Knox peered down the road. He'd already been tense, but now he seemed to clench together, turning from her friend into something predatory and wholly *other*. Anwei's skin pebbled over at the sight, remembering his knife at her chin the night before. Whatever the sword did to him, it was *inside him*. She'd sensed it, like a briar strangling his soul.

He seemed normal now. But what if he changed again?

Knox looked at her, blinking as if he could feel her sudden doubt. "Remember how back at the plague house I told you the victims' auras looked like they had wasting sickness? There's someone inside that house with almost *no* aura, like she's in the final stages. There's only a tiny bit left of her."

Anwei's stomach roiled at the nothing smell washing over her. "So if the smell is the result of a shapeshifter draining someone . . ."

"Is it possible that wasting sickness is because of a shapeshifter? That Devoted are being killed off one at a time by . . . him? The snake-tooth man. Or a group of them, or . . ."

"That's what shapeshifters did, supposedly. Steal power." Anwei stared forward, everything finally clicking into place. "You said wasting sickness is killing Devoted left and right?"

He nodded.

"He drained my brother, then. That's what I smelled that day." Anwei shook her head. "Why would he do that? My brother wasn't a Devoted."

"Neither are any of the victims down in the plague house. Neither is the woman in there." Knox pointed toward the house. "Maybe when he doesn't have access to power from gods, he steals it from normal people, and has to take from more of them because they don't have as much energy as Devoted." He shook his head. "It looks like every Devoted in there has been . . . not diminished, but *preyed on*. Just a little bit from each one. Could that be why the plague house got better suddenly? He has access to Devoted again?"

"Do you think Noa could have come up here?" Anwei whispered. Noa could have done anything—she'd been face-to-face with the War-lord herself and all these Devoted the night before.

"The dig director could have too," Knox whispered back.

The gate opened when they were only halfway to it, a man on a horse emerging from the compound, his clothes dusted in dirt. He pulled the horse to a stop and looked back. "I'm not certain we'll be able to get the wall down before the evening drum. If we can't—"

"That's when she'll be arriving, Director Van." A Devoted stepped out into the road, peering up at him. "So I suggest you do what you can to make sure she isn't disappointed."

Director Van. Anwei stared hard at the man as he rode away. He smelled of nothing too.

"Did you see that?" she whispered to Knox. "I don't understand."

"All we can do is go to the dig, like you said. Whoever it is wants that sword." Knox pulled out the little blowpipe he'd grabbed on the way out of the apothecary. "I'll distract them." He walked into the alley between compounds, fading into the shadows despite the morning sun.

Anwei clenched her teeth. Took out the bottle of venom. The distilled serum was safe in her medicine bag, ready for . . . whom? She didn't even know now.

Gripping the last bottle in her fist, Anwei walked to the open gate. "Sir!" she called to the Devoted just inside. "The lady of the house, sick in her bed—I've just been made aware of her symptoms, and I'm afraid it may not be safe for the Warlord to stay here."

Watching Anwei dab poison on the Devoted's hand made Knox smile all the way back to the apothecary. Even Devoted could be distracted by a pebble to the neck.

At least, he smiled until he remembered Lia. Her aura hadn't been inside the house.

He hoped she was safe.

Knox walked through the apothecary's back gate, the horse they'd taken from Altahn raising his head placidly to look at him. A swaybacked old thing, suited more to chewing grass in a field than pulling carriages or wagons, much less carrying Knox on his back to watch Shale's camp. It didn't fit. Just like him.

Only, Knox did fit. He fit too well in this place he wasn't meant to be. The place he *wanted* to be. The pain in Anwei's face last night had left a hole inside him. She'd been clinical and cold all morning, as if their partnership, friendship—whatever it wasn't allowed to be—had dissolved.

How will this ever be fixed? Knox thought it toward the sky as he climbed onto the horse's back. *You don't care, so long as I dance to your tune.*

For once, Calsta answered. In a voice not of scathing flame, but of soft candlelight. *She loves you. You love her, too. But it is too dangerous for love right now—everything has been wrong for hundreds of years, Knox, and it is in your hands to fix it. Your tiny, insufficient, human hands.*

There's a vote of confidence.

Another war could very easily start, Knox. Or things could go back into balance. I want you and all your little human friends to be happy and stop killing one another, and I have done everything in my power to make it so. Stop wallowing and try to understand that there is an order to these things.

He stared up at the sky, anger building inside him. "Is that order that I can never have anything that I want?" he said out loud. "That I give everything to you, serve my whole life, and—"

I led you to Anwei. You love Anwei. How is that not something you want?

"You made me promise that I couldn't love anyone but you long before you sent me here."

There are still oaths to make, Knox. There's more, or none of this will work. Power is not something to be given with no promises in return.

"None of *what* will work?" Knox stopped in the gate, the horse nipping at his sleeve. "Why can't you just tell me what I'm supposed to do? *More* oaths?"

What else did Calsta want to take away from him? He'd already proved that he didn't have what it took to be a spiriter. Not everyone could do more for Calsta. He wouldn't have liked to live with a veil over his head, but he would have done it, because he believed that Calsta knew what was best. What would be best for him.

But it didn't feel that way right now.

Oaths are not shackles to be dragged behind you and mourned every day. Devoted have forgotten their true meaning. Please, focus. I cannot tell you everything because I am not the only being peering into your mind right now. He might not know it yet, but our time grows small, and I can't give him any more tools than he's already discovered.

Knox's skin went cold. "The nameless god? Is that what is wrong with Willow? And what happens to me? That's him taking control of me? Trying to kill Anwei and . . . anyone else he can?"

Calsta was there, a tinder and flame at the back of his head, and her silence was heated. Angry, as if this were the stupidest explanation Knox could have come up with. But she didn't answer.

Shackles. At least with shackles someone else was putting them on you. Knox had put these ones on himself, and he had to keep putting them on every day, choosing the weight, the boundaries, the loneliness.

You do not understand, Knox. But you will.

Gulya appeared in the herb room door, her ancient fingers knuckle-deep in some concoction of leaves and malt. "I have words to speak with you, thief," she called.

Knox waved, giving the horse a kick to get him walking, but the thing only started toward Gulya's herbs. He kicked the horse again, wishing he knew how to politely tell Calsta to get out of his head. Swearing to himself when the horse didn't move, Knox dismounted and grabbed hold of the creature's lead to walk it out of the gates. Oaths had never been hard before. He'd relished in the control, in his ability to go to Calsta for power. But now they felt like his own version of Lia's veil, and he couldn't find a way to take it off. As if he were serving a goddess who didn't care much for him and wanted everything he had in return for her lack of interest.

The oaths were never meant to be worn like a shield between you and the world. Only to give you a way to see what you could not otherwise. Power is given to those who can see more than just themselves. It is for people who can feel pain that is not their own. Bonding is for two people who can do more together than apart. More than that, I cannot say.

Knox stopped, the horse jerking the lead in his hand and prancing back over to the herbs. A bond? Like what the masters had tried to do with Lia? All those old stories about special circumstances . . .

No. Calsta was responding to his very thoughts. *Your old masters remember that bonds existed, but not much more. That was what the shapeshifters destroyed. And what you need to destroy in order to save your sister.* Corrupted *bonds.*

The feeling of Anwei at the back of his head flared, her thoughts and feelings too far for him to divine. The moment down in the tomb flashed through him, when their magic had somehow twined together. In that split second he'd seen the rocks, the plants, the *world*, as if they had been made of flaring color. Knox's throat squeezed tight. "Are you telling me that what is happening with me and Anwei—that's normal? Something that happened all the time before the shapeshifter wars?"

Companions. Like the old times, before they tried to kill my love.

"Thief!" Gulya's voice buzzed around him like a swarm of flies.

Calsta's love? *Companions?* Knox's heart sped up. "Basists and Devoted used to work together?" he whispered. "That's what has kept us hidden? And that's what . . . hides this shapeshifter? No one can see his aura because he has some kind of corrupted bond? That involves my sister?"

I cannot tell you any more, Knox. Your sister can speak to more than just you. It is only ignorance that has kept her murderer from rising like Patenga did.

Knox couldn't concentrate on the words, extra information that didn't make sense. *I can be with Anwei and still keep my oaths to you. Is that what you are saying?*

Soon— But Calsta's voice cut off. Knox opened his eyes to find Gulya standing in front of him, her mouth pinched into a snarl.

"You are going to leave," she instructed.

"No," he said back, too unmoored to keep a polite, Gulya-approved tone. "I mean, yes. We are. I could never leave Anwei." The words blistered on his tongue. Forbidden. But Calsta's fire still burned bright inside him.

"You are a child. You think you're in love with my Anwei? Children don't know what love is, Knox." She shoved something toward him, a long, thin bundle he hadn't noticed she was holding. Knox's mind froze, the one last pinhole Willow had through Anwei's warmth in his brain zeroing in on the shape in Gulya's arms. "You don't know what Anwei could be without you. You're dragging her down."

You found me! Willow's voice was suddenly too loud, battering its way in.

"No!" Knox put his hands up just as Gulya pushed the bundle into his arms, the sword's hilt slipping free to touch him. It burned like ice, sticking to his skin.

Willow's voice cut through everything inside his head, a cold that was somehow hotter than Calsta's had ever been. *We'll be able to fix everything now that we're together again.*

Anwei tried to cover her nose, to breathe through her mouth, but it didn't block out the nothing smell, so thick that the air felt like water. She'd argued with Devoted, with maids and servants, then finally with the valas himself, who turned an angry red when she listed the symptoms of gamtooth poisoning. "She doesn't have any of those symptoms, and I do not appreciate you pushing your way into my house."

"She didn't at first, but in the last few days she started having a rash," a little voice piped from upstairs, the little girl behind it fire-haired and not as brave as she was trying to appear. She shot a sideways look at the Devoted lurking at the other end of the hall. Lia had said her father was in some sort of political trouble. "If she's got the plague from the lower cays, then you can make her better, right?"

"Fine," Lia's father blustered. "*Fine.* You think you can do better than the Warlord's own aukincer, then go ahead." He stomped up the stairs, gesturing for Anwei to come along. The nothing smell clotted around her as she ascended.

Anwei! a voice tore through her, stopping her feet.

It was Knox's voice.

Panic, pure *panic*, welled in her mind as she followed the bond in her head to the apothecary. She could feel him there, shouting for her like that day on the wall.

"Healer?" The valas had turned to look at her. "Don't waste any more of my time than you already have." He walked to the first door and unlatched it.

A wave of nothing sloshed out through the door, cascaded down the hallway, and broke across her as it crashed down the stairs. But *Knox*. Knox was somewhere in the direction of the apothecary, the lines bonding them together stretching, turning fiery white.

One snapped. Then another. *Twang, twang, TWANG.*

A Devoted at the bottom of the stairs came to attention, looking around until his eyes found her, a confused expression crossing his face.

Anwei's hands began to shake, Knox's cry turning into a wordless roar. She couldn't answer. She couldn't *move*. The bond between them was a bundle of strings, and they were pulling free.

The Devoted's eyes narrowed on her. Knox's panic swirled around Anwei, joining with her own. If she was shielding Knox's aura and he was somehow shielding her in return, then what did it mean if the bond in their heads was breaking?

TWANG. Another thread snapped.

"Healer?" The valas was staring at her too now.

"Yes. I'm coming." She had to get out of sight. Then she had to *run*. Get to Knox and whatever terror was happening.

Suddenly Knox wasn't standing still at the apothecary. He was moving fast toward the Sand Cay ferry. The wordless roar cut off abruptly, leaving Anwei feeling as if she'd missed a step. The lines between them went still. Not snapping anymore, but cold, like the night before in the tomb.

Anwei reached out to touch the valas's shoulder as she passed him, drawing him into the room after her. If Lia was in this house, he'd know where she was, and Anwei didn't want him randomly spewing that information until Devoted weren't listening. The Devoted who had been at the bottom of the stairs was halfway up, following her. She closed the sickroom door behind them. "What did the aukincer do, exactly?" Anwei asked quietly.

"Made her medicine. How am I supposed to know? My wife started getting better, so I didn't ask too many questions."

Valas Seystone flinched when his younger daughter followed them into the room. "She got worse, though. After she got better. She sort of went . . . empty."

Anwei moved quickly, touching a maid at the bed-curtains with her gamtooth venom. The Devoted she'd touched at the gate should already be showing symptoms, but she wasn't sure if she'd touched the one coming up the stairs behind her or not. "Not all sicknesses are suited to aukincer methods," Anwei said quietly. "And if I'm right, then you could all be in danger of—"

The Devoted slid into the sickroom just as she opened the bed-curtains. The nothing smell rushed out at her in a choking flood. The woman lying on the bed linens seemed to be made of paper and air— her humors, her energy, *everything*, drained to nothing but a flimsy husk that mocked life.

Anwei sank to her knees at the bedside. The Devoted hovered behind her, but she couldn't look away from the wasted skeleton lying in the bed. Lia had said her mother was sick. That she'd need a healer to help move her. But this? A faint rash marked the hollows under the woman's eyes and down her neck. Gamtooth poisoning, like Jecks's family and the other Fig Cay victims. But where they had only been pockmarked with little holes of nothing, this woman was a chasm, as if her very soul had been hacked free. "She's . . . she still lives?"

"Of course she . . ." Lia's father trailed off when his eyes fell on the Devoted hulking in the doorway. "There is no reason for you to come in here. I'm not going to climb out the window. The Warlord will find nothing against me, and I have no reason to run. Take your hand off that sword immediately."

"Healer." The Devoted's voice made Anwei's skin prickle. "You will stand, then turn to face me. Slowly."

Tears pricked hot in her eyes. Knox was still a web of icy strands in her head, but he was fading away, as if the bond between them was dying, its body nothing but carrion in her head. She couldn't tell if he'd gotten off the ferry, if he'd jumped in the river, or if he was directly behind her, holding that sword of his. But she'd never find out if she didn't get out of this room.

Anwei stood and brushed off her knees. "Bar the front doors. Don't let anyone out of the house. This woman is very contagious." She pointed to the door when the Devoted didn't move, not the least bit taken in by her show of confidence. "And would you please check for symptoms among your fellows. A rash. Glassy eyes. Hot skin. Any odd, unnecessary honesty. We have to protect the Warlord. I can treat her before it spreads."

The Devoted unsheathed his sword. "Don't move."

"Now see *here*!" Lia's father was in full bluster, but his only weapon seemed to be his red face.

"Daddy, his hands!" The little red-haired girl scuttered back into the corner, hands over her mouth. Glancing down, the Devoted flinched. He *was* one of the ones Anwei had touched, a blistering rash marking the backs of both hands.

"I can help you." Anwei whispered it, pretending she couldn't see the sword pointed at her chest. The bond between her and Knox was still there, icy cold and biting at the back of her head—dying, but not yet dead. Didn't that mean her aura was still protected? Whatever the

Devoted had seen, it had to have been isolated to those moments when strands had broken or he'd have already run her through. "I promise, I can help you."

As Lia's scarf fluttered to the floor, Mateo's eyes bugged comically, as if the sight of a girl's face would be the reason he fainted this time. Air on her skin felt like the whole world was opening to her. Filling her lungs to their fullest, Lia gloried in the fact that nothing had sucked up against her nose or mouth. She was free.

In that moment flickers of light condensed at the edges of her mind. Pale glows compared with what she would have been able to see before, but they were there. Auras.

A maid upstairs. A cluster of hostlers just outside in the court-yard. And Mateo in front of her, his aura a pale, guttering glow that looked . . . wrong somehow. Not diminished, the way Devoted who had broken their oaths would be, but glassy and small. Starving, like a Devoted with wasting sickness.

There were no golden flecks in it. Not even one.

"You're not a Devoted," she whispered.

Mateo startled back, knocking over his chair, the half-eaten sweet roll still in his hand. "You have your aurasight back."

"A little." She looked sideways at him, as if a change of angle would make a difference. "How can you see auras, how can you have *wasting sickness* if . . ."

Mateo ducked down to set the chair right, something desperate in his face. "Lia, I . . ."

She tamped down her aurasight, remembering the way Knox's golden glow had vanished into nothing on the wall that day. Mateo had seen her aura, something only Devoted could do. He obviously had wasting sickness. It had to mean something.

But it didn't really matter what it meant, Lia supposed. She didn't need Mateo anymore. And now that her family should be safely tucked away in Gretis, she didn't need Tual either. She just needed to hide until the Warlord was gone, the way she and Master Helan had discussed, then run to Lasei. Past the northern border to Trib land. Or maybe to the Broken Isles, or to the barred lands where sailors took their empty ships and came back laden with spices, gold, and silver, speaking in tongues no one had ever heard and of gods who promised new kinds of help.

Or she could wait here. Stay. It was an odd feeling, this peace of having no one watching her, telling her what to do. "I'm sorry you're sick, Mateo," Lia said. "I wish I knew how to help. But it's so good to . . . to *see*." Laughing still felt like she was breaking some oath, as if becoming a Devoted had meant she was supposed to be sad all the time. But now she was happy, and she had her aurasight, so that couldn't be true.

Mateo's eyes were glued to her face once more, tracing the bridge of her nose, the line of her chin. It felt exposed, and odd—almost the way Lia thought people must have felt when she looked into their thoughts. So many years of no one looking at anything but her sword, and then only her veil, and suddenly Mateo was looking at *her*. As if they'd been friends for years and he'd always been able to see her face. Because that's what normal people did. Looked at each other.

Mateo replaced the sweet roll on his plate and wiped his fingers on a napkin before offering her his hand. "You want to see something interesting about Calsta?"

Lia stared at his hand for a moment, then reached out and let him pull her up. The memory of taking off her glove to touch Ewan flashed across her mind. That touch had been a weapon. An act of violence that Ewan had taken as his own and turned on her a hundredfold.

But this felt like a choice, one Mateo wouldn't throw back at her like a spear. Mateo helped her up, then let their hands drop as if it had been nothing—and probably had been to him. Lia followed him up the stairs and across the entryway to a door she hadn't seen behind yet.

Every step he took seemed tired, as if there were some god who took energy from people instead of giving it. Mateo opened the door, and inside were dark shelves, a desk coated in sheets of vellum and ink, and piles of dusty books, pots, herbs, and glass bottles. It smelled of spice and stale rot all at once, the dust of old pages twined together with the dead. Lia leaned on the edge of the desk while Mateo went to the shelves and extracted a heavy book, the pages inside uneven.

"This is your father's study?" she asked lightly, eyeing the messy pile of correspondence. She moved to let Mateo slide by her with his big book. "Why did he bring all this with him?"

Mateo pushed aside some of the papers to set the book on the desk and began thumbing through it. It was full of handwritten notes, copies of paintings and reliefs, all bound together by hand. "You saw how prominently Calsta is featured inside Patenga's tomb. Odd for a shapeshifter, wouldn't you say? Then something my father said made me remember this." He opened to a page with a large depiction of Calsta. Her mask was uncracked, and she held a sword in one hand and a paintbrush in the other. At her feet there was a collection of people—some bringing food to an emaciated woman with two small children in her lap, some with swords, defending an old man from what looked like a robber. One person was veiled, sitting with a group of people listening at their feet. He turned the page, and the next drawing caught Lia by the throat, her fingers clenching around the desk's edge.

It was the nameless god, a darkness to counter Calsta's light, vines twisting around his arms. There were people in front of him, too, growing plants in neat rows, healing. One looked as if he was mediating some sort of argument between two men with their fists raised. Mateo pushed the book toward her. "I think there's a lot we don't know or understand about Calsta. Maybe the nameless god, too—it is hard to tell, what with all the records about him being destroyed. Most gods—Falan, Artena, Jaxom, Castor—they are all trying to help people become something better, even if those people use their teachings to do bad things instead."

Lia bit her lip, staring down at the earthy tones of the nameless god's hands and feet, flowers growing from his head like hair. "Where did you find this?"

"Does it make you uncomfortable?" Mateo sat down in his father's chair and put his slippered feet up on the desk.

She slid from the desk, looking at the painting more closely. It did make her feel a little uncomfortable. But Mateo was right—things weren't as simple as she'd been taught. How else could Lia have her aurasight now, so far from a seclusion? How could Master Helan help her escape and still keep his power if everything were as she'd thought? Her foot knocked against something glass under the desk as she bent down to touch the painting. "Where did you see this?"

Mateo leaned back in the chair. "I copied it from a cave on the eastern coast across from Beilda. It was closed up—forgotten about, probably, long before the first Warlord began destroying depictions of the nameless god. In the original, Calsta and he are on the same wall—all of the Basists and Devoted together. He and Calsta are reaching for each other." He flipped to the painting of Calsta, her hand outstretched with the paintbrush, then to the nameless god again, his hand outstretched and full of stones.

Lia smoothed her hand across the page. "It's hard to know what is right and what is wrong about this."

Mateo shrugged, looking up at the ceiling. "Not really. I think it's more difficult to believe that *people* know the difference between right and wrong." He spoke slow, as if he wasn't sure how Lia would take what he was saying. "You thought Calsta wanted you all bundled up inside a seclusion with . . ." He licked his lips, the studied nonchalance in his tone giving way to something jagged. "With Ewan. But now you're with me instead of your scary auroshe, which—can we please circle back to the fact he's named *Vivi*?"

He paused, the smile returning. Lia pressed her lips together, thinking of beautiful, powerful, sunbright Vivi with Ewan's hand yanking on his mane.

Mateo seemed to sense the change in the way she felt and hurried on. "And Calsta's just gifted you aurasight again. So, was it her or the Warlord who wanted you to stay at the seclusion?"

Master Helan had made it clear what he thought on that point, but Lia shrugged, not sure what to believe. "Does it matter?"

Mateo mirrored her shrug. "Does it?"

All the worry Lia had been keeping bottled up about what Calsta would do to her for breaking her oaths had loosened a little with Master Helan. Now it sank to the bottom of her mind, as if she'd been moving too quickly for her thoughts to settle until that moment. It did matter. It was one thing if a person tried to make you do something and you disagreed. Quite another if it was divine mandate from a goddess and disobedience meant you'd be destroyed, now or in some afterlife.

"That is a very interesting question that I guess I need to think about some more." Lia stood up from the desk, picking up the book. "You did all the paintings in here? And the ones there, too?" She pointed to the stacks of vellum, the top of which had a depiction of Patenga she recognized from the tomb.

He sat up, letting his feet drop. "Most of them."

"They're lovely. You must have spent years . . ." She turned the page and found a Devoted with a sword. The shadows were bloody, the lines harsh. "Wow. You don't care much for Devoted, do you?"

Mateo's mouth pinched shut.

"It must have been nice to walk into my father's house and find out your father meant to marry you off to one."

The pinched expression receded, Mateo's face going carefully blank. "It isn't a social call I look back on with great pleasure, I suppose."

Lia couldn't help but smile at his aggressively neutral tone. "You know, if I were to stay here like your father said, we could figure out some kind of middle ground, couldn't we?" She'd follow Anwei and Knox, find her father, Aria, and her mother. Bring them back. It wouldn't be dangerous with Master Helan pushing the Devoted away from Chaol. She shuddered at the memory of Ewan's off-kilter fervor in searching for Knox. The way his voice had sung out threats against her, reveling in the idea of her cowering and afraid. But Master Helan had said he could stop Ewan from wanting to find her. "Some kind of middle space, one where you aren't stuck under the Warlord's thumb but also don't have to marry your worst nightmare. . . . What are you looking at?"

He was staring at her face again. "You know, I wasn't prepared to say it before, but it's true. If you hadn't been wearing a hood, I would have been at least a *little* tempted to let things move forward that day."

Lia snorted. "I could kill you with two fingers, you know."

Mateo seemed to weigh the possibility. "It's a good thing you like me enough not to."

She frowned at Mateo's odd tone. He'd turned to stare at the bookshelves, his eyes darting back and forth across the titles too quickly to be reading them. "You wouldn't consider staying here and . . . just seeing what happens, would you?" He still wouldn't look at her. "I mean, we'd tell my father it's all off and to maybe go jump in the cape while he's at it. But . . ."

"But what?" Heat flushed in Lia's cheeks and she shut the book. "I let you see my face, and now—"

"No." Suddenly he was looking at her, his eyes focused. "I didn't need to see your face. And I don't mean to start anything between us now, or *ever*, if it never . . . seems like something you're interested in." His cheeks reddened as he grappled for words. "I already told you I like you, Lia. And I'm telling you again now, but in the most tentative, whatever-you-want-please-don't-hurt-me kind of way." The next words came out in a rush. "And I don't mean wreaths or permanent . . . anything. I just thought maybe later when everything has calmed down . . . ? You're going through a lot right now and technically I'm sort of dying and now I'm realizing this was not the right time or place to say this and I'm sorry and—"

"Mateo!" Tual's voice cracked through the air, puncturing the breath trapped inside Lia. "Mateo, where are you?"

Mateo turned toward the door with a bit too much force, accidentally shoving some of the cleared odds and ends under the desk with his feet. Something under the desk fell over and shattered, pieces of glass skittering out into the dim light. The door burst open and then Tual was there, out of breath, his hat in his hand. "We have a problem." He pushed aside the mess of papers on the desk, sending them fluttering to the floor to make room for the roll of paper in his hand.

He glanced over Lia, his eyes catching on her uncovered face in a surprised stare. "Hello, Lia. It's . . ." He shook his head. "I hope you slept well. I'm glad you and Mateo are . . . well, you can help us with this too."

Lia felt as if she were moving in slow motion, Mateo's words still hanging in the air like fireworks. He was wearing pajamas. And furry slippers. And her face was uncovered, and Ewan had *attacked her* what seemed like yesterday. . . .

There were a lot of "ands." Maybe that's why Mateo had said there was nothing to talk about until everything calmed down. He was now staring very intently at the sheet his father had brought, a flush in his olive cheeks that said he could feel her watching him. "What is this? A list?"

"There was another incident at the excavation. Artifacts missing. And scorch marks on the burial chamber door."

"*What?* These are all the things that were taken?" Lia couldn't help but see the way Mateo's eyes jumped from item to item, flinching as if each loss stabbed at him. Knox and Anwei had done this, whatever it was.

"And there was damage done—the Warlord is going this evening to open the chamber and evacuate the rest of the items. She's staying with your family, Lia."

"My family?" Her family was supposed to be in Gretis by now. Anwei was going to help move her mother. They hadn't left?

Tual was still talking. "The thefts and damage are definitely the work of someone associated with the dig."

Confusion roiled in Lia's chest as Mateo and Tual exchanged a look Lia didn't understand. Mateo had said he and his father were after some kind of healing compound, so the damage couldn't affect him too much once he'd gotten over the loss of art and history. Knox had said he and Anwei were only going to steal a sword.

Still, Lia couldn't help the jab of worry at the way Mateo eyed the list, one hand to his chest.

A spider skittered out from under the table, dodging bits of broken glass, headed straight for Lia's ankle. Tual froze, staring down at it. "Lia!"

She crushed it with her heel. It squirmed a little as it squished, as if it was still trying to bite her.

"Director Van will be a part of the evacuation, I'm guessing?" Mateo scrubbed his hands through his hair, letting the list roll back up as he looked at his father, who was still staring down at the spider. "How much time do we have before he gets there?"

Mateo kept on his father's heels as they rode into the excavation compound, the gates hanging open. Lia sat behind him on Bella, pressed against his back as they rode. He still couldn't believe what she'd done, taking off that scarf in front of him. It had burned through him, watching her take off each layer, baring her face to him.

That wasn't what she'd meant by it. Mateo knew that. He'd looked away, or he'd tried. But the first sight of her face had been . . . *right*. As if he'd already known exactly who she was before actually seeing her. It really didn't matter what she looked like, anyway.

He liked seeing her face. Liked it a lot. But he liked *her* more.

Mateo dismounted and tied Bella before offering a hand to help Lia dismount. She smiled, then slid down herself with a fancy kick over the pommel, but it didn't feel like a slight. Her eyes widened as she looked past him into the compound. "Where are all the workers?"

Goose bumps erupted down Mateo's neck as he followed her gaze. The dig was completely empty, a discarded shovel lying in the abandoned path that led to the tomb.

"Van ordered the entire compound be cleared to ensure the Warlord's safety." Tual strode past them, heading for the tomb opening. "Devoted will be here soon to guard the gates. I managed to delay messages so there would be a gap between shifts. We'll be able to go in unobstructed. Unless Van is already here, trying to empty the tomb of anything he can before the Warlord gets here."

"Is . . . he doing that? Why?" Lia asked.

"He's after the same thing we are. We think. He might be . . ." Mateo had to look away from her direct gaze. She hadn't said anything about the . . . whatever it was. Invitation? Plea for an open door? He shook the thought away. Caprenum was his best plan. His surest plan. That's why they were here.

She hadn't said no.

But she hadn't had a chance to say no either.

"He might be what?" Lia asked.

"A shapeshifter." Tual lowered his voice. "Caprenum is a substance that can be crafted only by Basists. I stumbled on hints of its healing properties entirely by accident—Basist capacity was so much greater than any healer now. We think he might know its value, maybe more of what it can do than we do."

"You truly believe it will work?" Mateo asked. Lia stayed close behind him, her attention itching across his back. He couldn't ask about the letter, not with her listening. "Hunting for it wasn't you just trying to keep me busy?"

"Of course I believe caprenum will heal you." Tual shot a frustrated look at the sky. "I mean, I'm as confident as I can be. Just because I have more than one plan doesn't mean half of them are lies."

"What do you need my help with?" Lia asked.

Tual didn't look back. "You'll see."

When they got to the ladder, Tual gestured for Lia to go down first. Mateo couldn't tear his eyes from the fiery warmth of her hair blowing in curls around her face as she descended. Her eyes found his just before she went under, but she immediately looked down.

Mateo went next, the darkness closing over him like water, the familiar smell of stone and dirt comforting even with the taste of poison in the air. More mirrors had been set on the floor in preparation for the Warlord's visit, enough light beaming through the cave that it almost seemed as if the sun had followed him down the ladder. Mateo took Lia down to the statue room, the light striking across Patenga's face in a harsh stripe. At the statue's feet, one of the little souls had crumbled away, as if someone had purposely crushed it.

Mateo darted over to get a better look at the damage, pulling out his hand mirror to redirect the light. A bolt of fury stabbed in his chest at the broken-off stone, the little worshipper nothing but jagged edges and stone dust.

Lia's hand touched his shoulder. "Are you all right?" she murmured, Tual still coming down the ladder.

"Do you see this?" He jabbed the mirror at the destroyed figure. "There was no reason to do this. They didn't even try to take it with them. It's just destruction of something beautiful for no reason whatsoever." He flashed the mirror up the wall and found black streaks across the top of Patenga's head. "And who would bring a *fire* down here? Don't they know how easy it is for smoke to destroy—"

"We can be angry about the destruction of history later." Tual hopped off the ladder and started toward the stairs. He glanced up at Patenga, a shadow crossing his face. "We don't have much time."

Lia's head swiveled to look at Mateo, her eyebrow raised.

"Right. Yes." Mateo turned away from the relief, forcing his anger down. "I'm fine." He followed Lia and his father down the stairs to where Calsta and the nameless god faced each other, their little charges like children in their laps. Tual paused by the doorway, touching the rope tangled around the columns. He sighed, picking up a few uncleared rocks, and threw them across the nameless god's carving. The ceiling, higher than the last time Mateo had been in the room, began to inch down.

"I'll do it. You have to put weight on the column for the floor to open, yes?" Lia grabbed the rope's end, then ran to the column rising from the nameless god's mouth. She climbed up on top of it, looped the rope around her foot, and held on to the length with both hands. When the floor fell in, she gave a whoop that sounded significantly more like joy than Mateo thought appropriate. Once the spiked columns had crashed into one another, then ratcheted back into the ceiling, he followed his father to the edge of the hole to peer down at Lia swinging back and forth on the rope. "Are you going to come down or not?" she called.

Mateo could now clearly see the door below with Patenga's face glaring up at them from the stone. There were scorch marks along the base, but it seemed intact. Tual climbed down once Lia had swung over to the platform. Once he was safely standing by the door, Mateo braced himself, hoping his arms were up to the job of climbing, then lowered himself down onto the rope.

"I've been left here to die." A song in his head. Mateo's fists burned on the rope, his fingers loosening as he looked down for the voice. A child, he thought. *"I've been sick so long, and they finally left because it was too hard. Will you help me?"*

A child abandoned because it was too hard to care for his sickness. Mateo let go of the rope with one hand, peering down into the darkness. "Where are you?" he called.

"They're narmaidens, Mateo!" Lia's voice cut through the song. "Swing over . . ."

A light bloomed into existence, and suddenly Tual was there, reaching out to Mateo, a lamp in his hand. "Son. You want to live. Think about that. Don't listen to them. Think about what *you* want."

"I'm alone. No one wanted me. You wouldn't leave me here, would you?" The song slithered inside his head.

Mateo closed his eyes, trying to shut it out. *I want to live.* The voice in his head seemed too slow, almost going backward. But then it recited the words back to him. *"I want to live. I want to live."*

"What did you . . ." Lia's voice was confused. "They aren't singing to me anymore. How did you do that, Mateo?"

Swinging his body forward, Mateo reached out to grab his father's hand. Lia helped him onto the platform, looping the rope onto one of the rocks.

"Narmaidens behave in the right circumstances." Tual placed one hand on the black wall, turning his head to look at Mateo. "Most things will. Come closer, son."

Mateo couldn't help but glance down into the darkness, wondering what his father had done. He inched over, not liking the black drop, the chorus of *"I want to live, I want to live"* echoing in his brain. Forcing himself to focus on the light newly burning in his father's hand, Mateo tried to find some indignation to cut his fear. "You brought a lantern? You know how much damage that will cause."

"We're in a bit of an extreme situation, Mateo. We'll just have to hope the Warlord forgives us for staining the reliefs." His father grabbed his hand and placed it against the stone.

The rock was unnaturally warm under Mateo's palm, the feel of it pulsing in his mind, making him feel dizzy. He snatched his hand away.

"I think you are the only way we can get in, son," Tual murmured.

His meaning took a second to sink in. "You want me to . . . Father, I *can't*," Mateo hissed. "Even looking for auras breaks everything inside me. You said it was dangerous for me to try. That I'd be a drain."

Tual patted Mateo's hand and took a step back. "Stone doesn't speak very loud to me. But it does to you. We'll have to chance it this once, or risk . . . plan B."

"What is going on?" The sound of Lia's voice sent a cringe through Mateo's gut. She didn't know. When her aurasight had come back, she'd looked him over and found nothing at all.

Why couldn't she see it in him? In his father? She'd said herself that Basists had something special to their auras, so where was his marker?

Why hadn't he ever thought of that? What were Devoted looking for, if it wasn't auras touched by the nameless god, the same way he could see Devoted shining with Calsta's light?

He'd always thought he and his father were different somehow. Or perhaps that his father had done something to hide them. But what could he have done?

Tual had stopped the narmaidens from luring them in. What else could he do?

"What do you see, Mateo?" Tual whispered.

Mateo touched the stone. The wall in front of him seemed to push against his mind.

"Focus," Tual breathed. "Focus on what you want."

What do I want? It was a hodgepodge of things that didn't fit together. They filled Mateo's mind, for once clear of anger and bitterness. If he could get through this door, he had a chance at life. A chance for a healthy body. A chance to finally use his powers without hurting himself. A chance for his father to see him as a worthy investment, an asset. Irreplaceable. The true companion his father had been hoping for when he saved Mateo, not a stone pulling him deep into the ocean of politics and war.

And Lia. Mateo wanted her to see *him* as worthy too.

And this wall. He wanted it to break.

The list seemed silly, but as Mateo breathed in, the makeup of the wall began to crystalize in his head, a curtain of tiny pieces that had somehow been laced together when they shouldn't have been, energy at each of the bonding points. Created with the nameless god's power to form something that wouldn't break without the right tools.

The right tool being him.

Tual stepped back from the wall, and Mateo could feel his worry and reluctance. But he put his hands on Mateo's shoulders. "This is dangerous, son. I didn't want to do it this way, but we're in a bind. What do you *really* want? Think about that—only that—and *take it*."

Mateo reached inside himself and staggered, almost losing contact with the wall. The light inside him, the understanding of the wall and all its parts, started to drain.

Tual's hands tightened on Mateo's shoulders. "Lia, come closer. Quickly, now."

Mateo felt Lia's hand on his arm, and suddenly the spinning and dizziness stopped.

"Now do it, Mateo."

In that moment, between his father and Lia, Mateo felt . . . solid. Not like a butterfly caught in a gust. He finally felt like his own person with his own feet, his own lungs, his own stamp on the world.

In his mind Mateo caught hold of one of the knit strands of stone and began to pull. The knots of energy that held the stone together began to unravel, falling apart into little granules that scattered to the floor.

Lia gasped, her hand on his arm tightening. "You're a . . ."

He *pulled* the string again, and the whole wall came undone, falling to sand from the center out like curtains suddenly opening.

"A Basist." Mateo let his hands drop and looked at her, elation singing through him when before there had only been weakness. He'd climbed into the tomb with his feet dragging, but now he felt as if he could crash through walls with his bare hands. What had his father done to turn his sickness to strength? It seemed impossible—there hadn't been any oaths, no sacrifices. Just wanting, and then the world had changed. "I'm a Basist, Lia." He said it too loud, the words echoing out past the narmaidens and the chant they'd stolen from Mateo. *I want to live. I want to live.* "Both of us are."

Lia fell back from him a step. The hand that had been touching him reached up to cover her mouth. "I would be able to see it if you were a Basist. And you could see my aura. Since when can Basists see auras?" She was choking on her words, her breaths coming too fast.

Mateo reached out to her, flinching when she recoiled. "Father has been using his magic to heal the Devoted suffering from wasting sickness. The Warlord was the one who sent us here to find caprenum. If we don't find it, then he won't be able to fully cure wasting sickness, and the seclusions will fall."

"But—"

Tual pushed between Mateo and Lia to the narrow doorway, brushing the bits of sand from his coat. "We'll explain later—just know right now that we're on your side. We need to get the caprenum and then get you far away from here before the Warlord sees your aura, Lia."

Lia physically wilted, a pulse beating in her throat. Her face looked altogether too pale in the mirrored light. She put a hand to her head. "I'm feeling a little faint."

That seemed odd. Lia wasn't really the fainting type.

"Is it really that big of a deal to you?" Mateo whispered. "I was born to see stone the same way you can read thoughts. My father was born to heal—he can see the properties of growing things and medicinal elements, of sicknesses and how to fix them." He swallowed, watching her closely. "Meanwhile, I saw you stab a man with my drawing pencils. You're scared of *us*?"

Lia blinked, her fists closing and falling to her sides. "Absolutely not."

Mateo pressed his lips together, hating that the answer was obviously for the latter question, not the former. "I've never stolen a single soul. I'm not a shapeshifter."

Lia's aura flickered around her, stronger than the first day they'd met, threads of gold veined through it.

"It's unfair to believe that every single person who the nameless god chooses will become a monster the way Patenga did." Mateo willed her to listen, to actually talk about it the way they had in his father's study. "As it is to believe every Devoted is made of gold and sunshine just because the seclusions burned Calsta's oaths into their skin. You know that more than anyone. It's what we choose to do with our power, right, Lia? Remember the painting?" His throat seemed to squeeze around the words. "The cave?"

Lia blinked again, the tendons in her neck taut from how hard she was clenching her teeth. A tear slid down her cheek.

"You don't have to have anything to do with me." He lowered his voice even further, hoping his father wouldn't hear the raspy echo. "I'll make sure you can get away from my father. And from me. If that's what you want."

One of Lia's feet slid forward, and Mateo tensed. "You said you were scared of me earlier today," she whispered. "You were being sarcastic, but it's true, isn't it? You're scared of what I can do."

"Of *course* I'm scared of what you can do. But I'd like to believe you won't do any of it to me."

Her hand brushed his arm, and suddenly she was only inches from him, her warmth seeping through the air to touch him. Mateo shivered. Held very still as she looked up at him, wondering if he'd been wrong to hope she wouldn't hurt him. Maybe she'd stab him straight through with her bare fingers. She'd said she needed only two.

But all she did was nod once. "Let's find the caprenum and go, then." Her hand slid down his arm and she pulled him after her into the opening.

The chamber inside was narrow, the ceiling twice as tall as Mateo. A huge relief painted in bright colors covered every inch of all four walls. The room was empty—no sword, no coffin, no caprenum.

Footsteps rang out from above, filling the empty chamber behind them. The narmaidens hissed.

Mateo's stomach contracted at the empty room. "Father, what . . ."

"This is just the antechamber." Tual's neck craned to look toward the narmaidens. "Find the door, Mateo. I'll deal with whoever's out there." And with that, his father was gone.

The Warlord looked worn and shrunken inside her armor from where Anwei stood in the procession, hovering just outside the ring of Devoted Anwei hadn't managed to poison. Knox still pulsed with cold inside her head, nearby but out of sight—the connection between them a fuzzy, many-legged thing that writhed in pain.

The Warlord stepped up to the gates, the shaved sides of her head flashing oath scars that appeared faded and old. It was hard for Anwei to look at her, the woman who'd twisted Knox all around his oaths to a goddess that probably didn't exist. What she'd done to Lia, handing her over to Ewan like a cream-filled roll.

Not that Devoted ate cream.

Anwei inhaled, steadying herself. Grateful they were out in the open air. Now that they were away from the house and the awful sinkhole Lia's mother had made in the air, Anwei could smell shapeshifter on all the Devoted just as Knox had said, as if he'd touched them all one by one. The Warlord herself seemed the most drained, her steps a little slow. She'd listened to the Devoted who had run panicked to the bottom of the stairs, showing her the rash on his hands. To the others running outside at the first sight of the boils, trying to protect their leader.

The Warlord had instructed him to take Anwei's herbs without question—to test it just in case she, too, became infected, Anwei supposed. The Devoted had blinked blearily at Anwei as if looking for the darkened aura he'd seen around her, only to find it gone. He, of all the Devoted who had been poisoned, had been brought along to the tomb so that his reactions to her cure could be observed. Anwei had been brought to help just in case the Warlord broke out in a rash, but Anwei had come because of Knox.

He was close. Somehow, even with the bond a mess, she could still feel him. He was waiting for something.

Anwei followed the retinue through the compound gates. The Warlord halted just inside and gestured for her Devoted to circle around her.

"I need Tual," the Warlord said, her voice quiet. Infused with a lifetime of being obeyed no matter how loud she spoke. "He was supposed to be here. He's the one who found this dig and the one who told me it was his best chance. . . ."

Tual? Isn't the director named Van? Anwei clenched her fists, as if holding on tight enough would stop the world from spinning around her. Shale had said the man with the snake on his tooth had been the one to bring the digging crew to Chaol.

"Are the rest of us going to wait?" another Devoted asked. The slick oil on his armor and the hint of murder in his eyes matched the smells she'd detected over the wall that day with Lia. Anwei held herself still despite the anger uncoiling inside her.

"If Tual doesn't come, we'll empty the tomb ourselves, and he can pick out the prizes later."

"What about Lia?" The Devoted kept his head bowed, his voice compliant, but an ugly undercurrent pulled at each word, raising the hairs on Anwei's arms.

"No one can hide from Devoted. We will find our runaway spiriter." The Warlord's pronouncement bristled with certainty. "For now, we do what we came to do." She started toward the hole in the ground.

Anwei braced herself, ready to run. Noa's cue to set the wall on fire had been the Warlord's entrance into the compound, but if Noa was the snake-tooth man, Anwei wasn't sure what to expect. The Devoted fell in line behind the Warlord, hands on their swords as if they expected some kind of trouble from a dead king and a bunch of dirt.

"Stop." The last Devoted in line barred Anwei's path as she tried to follow. "I don't think any of us are going to need herbs shoved down our throats in here."

An explosion erupted from the southern end of the compound, flames spurting over the top of the wall. Anwei's eyes widened as the timbers immediately began to char, the barracks' straw roofs going up in flame. Noa had done more than sprinkle oil on the wall and set it on fire. Maybe she'd kept some of the explosives Anwei had given her for the ghost distraction the night before.

The Devoted divided, some running for the back wall, some bursting back out the gates, the Warlord herself standing alone in the path that led to the tomb opening. With her hand over her shoulder, fingers grasping her sword, she looked like Knox, only years older, shrunken inside an armor of power both from Calsta and from the Devoted who followed her without question. The Commonwealth who feared the sight of her double-auroshe crest because it meant shapeshifters were being hunted in their midst.

It was fear of *dirt witches* that had gouged scars down Anwei's arms and legs. Fear created by the Warlord and her Devoted and the last five hundred years of hatred for any the nameless god touched, whether they wanted him to or not. It was this woman who'd made sure Anwei would be on this hunt alone for so many years.

And now the Warlord was standing all alone too.

Anwei shoved a hand inside her bag, gloved fingers finding the calistet.

The Warlord launched herself toward the blazing wall, drawing the sword in one fluid motion. Letting the calistet and her moment of anger fall, Anwei ran for the tomb's entrance. That was where she'd told Knox she would be, so perhaps that's where he'd gone.

Because that was where the shapeshifter would be. Eventually.

"What is all this?" Lia looked up at the carvings that took up the whole wall. The lantern's light flickered across an image of Patenga in a crown, his sword point through a man's armored chest. Next to the man, a golden shield lay on the ground. Patenga plunged the sword with one hand, the other hand to his head as if he was weeping. "I thought this was where Patenga's body was supposed to be."

Mateo's eyes were wide, tracing over the figures. He turned to look back toward the doorway. Over the door, Patenga stood under a trellis hung with flowers, the man with the golden shield standing across from him, their hands joined. All around them people held an abundance of fruit and baskets of grains, their paint bright. There were other paintings too: Patenga and the man giving food to hungry children. Patenga in battle, the golden shield raised by the man to protect him. The colors became darker, angrier, farther from the flower-covered trellis, paintings of hunger, famine, battle. Until it ended with Patenga's sword through the man's chest. Over Patenga's head there was an eddy of golden paint swirled together with a muddy purple that seemed to be coming from the fallen man.

The shape of the sword was familiar. "It's styled after Calsta's?" Lia pointed to the weapon. She'd seen so many depictions of the goddess's sword over the years—her own sword had been made with similar lines.

Mateo's back went straight, his eyes wide. "And the haze around him. Gold. Like an aura." He bit his lip, turning to Lia. "And he was in Calsta's lap in the last chamber. Do you think . . . no, that's impossible. Patenga was the shapeshifter."

"What's impossible?" Lia looked at him.

"He's got gold all around him, Lia. Could he be . . ."

"Are you trying to say Patenga, the shapeshifter king, was a

Devoted?" She started shaking her head. "How could that—"

"No, look. How did I not see this?" Mateo put a hand to his head, gesturing to all the carnage depicted between what looked like Patenga's wedding day and the end with his sword through his partner's chest. "He *was* a Devoted. Which means he couldn't have been a shapeshifter, unless . . ."

Lia looked over the carvings, trying to find whatever it was Mateo was looking at, but his lantern light slid onto the angry swirl over Patenga's head, the colors muddying and mixing together in a horrible storm. The shapeshifter's face was contorted with agony, as if he'd murdered his only love. "Unless what?" she whispered.

"Calsta is holding Patenga in the room above us. His sword is styled after hers, just like you said. And here her power, the golden aura, is coming out of him to mix with—"

"A Basist," Lia breathed, looking at the muddy purple. She'd seen auras just like his all across the Commonwealth. "His shield is in every room."

"Patenga killed him. Power requires sacrifices." Mateo's voice shook. "The legends say Patenga was a Basist. But in this relief it looks like he's *stealing* a Basist's aura from the man with the shield."

Lia licked her lips. "That's not how it works."

"How do you know? Basists are almost all dead because history books say they have potential to become shapeshifters, and the risk of a shapeshifter was more destructive than killing an entire segment of society. But what if that's not what really happened?" Mateo turned toward her so forcefully that she flinched, her muscles ready to fight before her brain could take in what was happening. He stretched his arms out toward her, his voice breaking. "My father said there's a way to bond. That if we—"

Lia shrank. "Like what the Warlord . . . Ewan . . ."

"No!" Mateo's hands came up, as if he could push that thought away. "I would never!" He shook his head. "No. Those bonds aren't real anyway. They *break* the oaths Devoted make instead of bonding them together. The bond Father was talking about was supposed to be like . . . in the drawing I showed you. Calsta and the nameless god working in concert. That's why my father threw us together. He said together our powers would balance. That the bond would fix me. Like . . . them." He pointed to Patenga and the man with the shield above the door. "Two halves of something whole, working as one. Until . . ." He looked up at Patenga's sword sheathed in the man's gut. "Until it wasn't enough for Patenga. Power comes from sacrifice. What if sacrificing a person, a person you *love* . . ."

Lia pointed up toward the dead Basist in the relief, her hand shaking. "Your father wanted you to do *this*?"

"No." Mateo started to laugh, a dry, useless thing that echoed all around them. "He told me to love you. And to hope . . ."

"So that's what all that was about earlier? You were just trying to fix yourself?" Lia hissed.

"No. It was me telling you the truth. And hoping you would feel the same way someday. Yes, I want to get better, but I don't have any claim on you, Lia, and I know it. No one does." Lia stared at him in the shaking light, his face pale as he took a step toward her. "I'd *hoped* that maybe you'd be interested in getting to know me better. That maybe after we were friends . . . well, it doesn't matter."

Lia looked up at the carvings, suddenly seeing a ghostly wraith of Calsta in the golden aura over Patenga's head. "We *are* friends. I like you just fine, Mateo."

He let out a breath of laughter that sounded almost like relief. "That's a lovely thing to hear. Especially next to this"—he glanced up at the painting—"rather gruesome depiction of a murder." Pressing his lips together, Mateo put a hand up. "The power-balancing stuff isn't important. I don't *need* you. Caprenum will be enough to fix me. His sword is made from it."

"A healing compound made into a sword?" Lia pointed at the swirl of gold above them. "It doesn't look like it's healing anyone here, Mateo. Devoted *can't* become shapeshifters. Basists were the ones who . . . That's why the first Warlord . . ." Her breath caught in her throat, and suddenly she wanted to throw something at the carvings, to negate what was up there on the wall. "That's the only reason she could have had for trying to eliminate them all."

"The only information I've ever found about shapeshifting oaths is that they were an abomination. That they allowed shapeshifters to wrest power from the gods and steal souls to make them stronger." Mateo was shaking too, the light from his lantern skittering frantically across the stone. He stepped up to the carvings, hesitating before pressing a palm against the stone wolf's paw. "I have to get through this wall. Whatever all this means, I need caprenum, and it's inside. Maybe—"

"Wait." A clatter of stone falling caught in Lia's ears, her arms prickling as if she'd been stuck full of pins. She reached out with her aurasight, but she couldn't seem to see beyond this room. Mateo was too still, as if he was about to collapse again. "There's someone down here with us."

Anwei stepped off the ladder, trying not to think of all that had happened here the night before. Knox had to be down here. But now that she was underground, she couldn't feel which direction he was in, the bond throbbing soundlessly at the back of her head. Like Knox had said—these walls blocked magic. Auras. Everything. She breathed in and gagged.

The scent of the void was here. Worse, a *thousand times* worse than Lia's house even. That meant shapeshifter was here, too.

Maybe.

Anwei moved as carefully as if she were walking on gamtooth web. The smell thickened, twining around her when she got down to the stairwell. The mirror light flickered in the room ahead, but there was no way to see what or who it was—she couldn't smell anything but *nothing*. No rock, no ancient paint, no leftover char from torches. No metal, no glass. She was walking into an alternate world sucked dry of all life. *Made* of nothing.

Slipping into the room with Calsta and the nameless god, Anwei found the floor already open and the burial chamber door below ruptured, orange light leaking from its slack mouth. Anwei clutched the serum, sweat making it slick between her fingers, as the voices of two people floated out from below.

"I *can't* wait," a young man's voice whispered. "I have to open it." A shadow moved, and suddenly Anwei felt something about the cave change, the wall inside the burial chamber folding together in front of the young man's hands as if it were paper, not stone. A draft of air blew up from below, and Anwei gagged again, the nothing smell drowning her. The stone around her began to groan, the floor tipping under her feet.

"I want to live," a narmaiden's voice sang up from the darkness, the tone jarring and wrong, setting Anwei's teeth on edge. Even the creature sounded confused.

The walls shook again, bits of the ceiling crumbling to rattle across the floor. Anwei dodged away from the storm of stone shards even as the floor fractured under her feet. Suddenly she was falling, then flat on the ground, and everything hurt. There were stones in great heaps all around her, the nameless god's black eyes staring at her from a slab of rock that had fallen just a few inches shy of her arm. Anwei groaned but sat up quickly when she saw lantern light overhead, realizing she was at the bottom of the narmaiden pit. A rush of water sloshed by, wetting the bottoms of her skirts as she frantically looked around, wondering where the nest was, if the mother was there. She clutched the glass tube of serum, checking for cracks. It hadn't broken in the fall.

But as Anwei pulled herself up from the ground, something rose in the darkness to meet her, far too large to be a narmaiden. Anwei fell back a step, but not before one of the thing's clawed hands had snagged her arm, the other hand holding a blade to her throat.

"Don't move." Its voice was nothing but wet leaves and scales. "Or it'll be a dead thief instead of a live one I hand over to the magistrate."

Mateo's whole chest seemed to contract as he stepped through the hole he'd made in the wall. The room inside was dark, the sharp feeling of wrongness he'd felt every moment in this tomb bearing down on him. He felt strong. Stronger than he ever had in his weak fainting spell of a life. When he inhaled, the air seemed to shimmer with power.

Lia was saying something, but his mind was full of magic. Dust filtered through the air, enough to almost block the raised platform in the center of the room. Artifacts crowded around its base, and there were intricate reliefs on the ceiling and walls, but it was too dark to see them clearly.

Now Lia was tugging on his arm, trying to pull him toward the door, but the stone box on top of the dais pulled harder, drawing him in. Mateo climbed up the stairs leading to the dais to stand at the side of the box, its stone lid pushed askew. Inside was a body.

No, two bodies.

The one closest to Mateo had its arms crossed, a bronze shield over its chest that bore a symbol Mateo vaguely recognized as northern Trib. The feel of the metal rang sharp in his head, unnatural, but clean and honest, unlike the rest of this tomb—definitely fabricated with a god's power, but it wasn't . . . corrupted.

Based on the size and shape of the skeleton's pelvis, it was male. The preservatives his clothes had been treated with had long gone sour, leaving rotted piles of fabric around him in the coffin, stuck between his ribs and spine.

The other skeleton . . . Mateo's breath caught in his throat.

"Mateo!" Lia was pulling hard at him now. "Mateo, whatever is down here is *coming*."

But Mateo couldn't look away from the bones. They were wrong. Too large and too tall to be human, and yet Mateo couldn't explain them as anything *but* human. There were human femurs and a pelvis, but the lower legs were elongated and warped, as if they'd been stretched and reformed to fit a monster mold. Claws jutted from the parchwolflike toes and feet, and the skull boasted a distinctly inhuman snout. The fingers, clasped across the chest, were broken, bits of bone and long claws littering the bottom of the box around the body. The skeleton was sitting slumped forward with a long, ugly sword skewered between its ribs, as if it had purposely fallen on the weapon, the hilt long rusted away. Mateo slid a hand into the coffin but couldn't bring himself to touch it. Not without the proper equipment.

He stared at the bodies, the two skeletons practically entwined. Why would a shapeshifter king, a man who stole a thousand souls and reigned in terror until he faded away, give another person so prominent a place inside his tomb? A place of reverence. Respect. Love.

Regret?

All power required sacrifices.

"Lia, we were right. Patenga killed the person he loved most and that's what changed him." Mateo's mouth was dry, full of five hundred years' worth of rage. "Shapeshifters aren't Basists who have gone too far. They're . . . a combination of powers. A perversion that starts with *murder*. That's why everything in here except the shield feels wrong. The shield was made with Basist magic, and the rest of it is corruption. Power stolen by a shapeshifter and twisted into submission." He took in a shaky breath. "Patenga was a Devoted. But the first Warlord tried to pin all shapeshifting on Basists. She only needed one kind of magic gone, and she chose the one that wasn't hers. Is that why she destroyed all the records, the histories, and the art? So no one would know what she sacrificed in order to stop shapeshifters coming back?"

Mateo looked up to ask Lia. "You're a Devoted. What do you know about this?" But she wasn't there, nothing but dusty effusions of light cluttering the air all around him. "Lia?"

Arms prickling, Mateo suddenly felt how very still it was inside the tomb.

Steel jabbed against Anwei's throat, the scaled arm dragging her toward the open burial chamber. Jewels glinted in the beam of mirror light, Calsta smirking down from high above. The thin vial of gamtooth serum felt fragile, close to breaking in Anwei's fist.

"You're going to rot in prison, dirt witch." The voice in her ear curdled with anticipation. "If you make it to prison. When Shale told me what you did with those explosives—"

Anwei tore the stopper from the vial, crushed the glass lip between her fingers, and stabbed the jagged edges into the creature's arm. He hissed, its grip loosening long enough for Anwei to duck away, plunging one hand into her bag for the calistet.

The thing—no, the man?—swore, paint on his face smearing as he tried to wipe away the blood. He was large, his muscles bulging and his face shadowed by a hood with beads of glass sewn onto it like eyes.

The *nothing* had diminished enough that Anwei could smell the sour green of old palifruit, sweat, and the oily yellow of paint. The man pointed his knife at her as she drew out the calistet. There was a very thin line of nothing spiraling out of him, as if it were a wound almost healed. "Who are you?" she whispered.

"I'm . . ." He frowned, stumbling forward one step, his knife falling a few inches as he looked at the bits of glass embedded in his arm, the serum sticky on his skin. "I'm the director of this dig, and you have been stealing from it. Or at least, that's what I'm going to be telling the magistrate once I've tied you up. You escaped last night, but—"

Something jumped down into the fallen floor with them. It ran straight at Anwei, and suddenly the nothing smell was back. Anwei threw herself out of the way, trying to understand. This man . . . the director . . . he was wearing a costume, his face painted just the way Anwei's had been the night before when she'd been playing the shape-shifter. The new threat sprinted right at the costumed man, slamming a fist into his jaw.

It was Lia.

She spun past him, plucking the knife from his fingers to turn the weapon on its owner.

"Don't kill him!" Anwei yelled, staggering toward them. "Are you the man who killed my brother? Show me your teeth!"

Lia fell back, holding the knife between her and the dig director as he put up his hands.

"I'm not a murderer." He coughed, one of his hands snaking up to touch his mouth, but he couldn't stop the words. Not with gam-tooth serum from the shattered vial on his skin. "I took this job so I could steal the artifacts and sell them. I had to come up with a person to take the blame."

"You got Shale to hire me. A thief." Anwei let her hand holding the calistet packet fall to her side. "What was his part in all this?"

Even as the man—Director Van—backed toward the far wall, his mouth spilled open. "Shale wanted the sword. I caught him digging near the tomb to find a way in, and instead of turning him in, I came to an agreement with him. I promised to give him any sword I found in the burial chamber, so long as he found someone to take the blame for the rest of the valuables I took from the dig. Everything is so closely monitored and reported on the dig—there was no way to hide anything I found, so I had to find a way to make it look like someone else had stolen it. It was taking too long, so in the end Shale helped me dig a tunnel down to these lower rooms together so we could get artifacts out of the dig before the Warlord got here."

"All the thefts were done by people dressed as ghosts after we dressed as ghosts at the governor's ball."

"Nobody even suspected me for a moment, except for those Montanne people, I guess."

"You're not a shapeshifter?" Lia hissed. "Mateo said they worried you were. But . . . you're just dressed like . . ." She snorted. "What are you dressed as?"

All of Anwei's limbs wilted. "It was *you* in the tomb last night, the voice and the wind and . . ." She touched her side where the wheal of red skin was raised from the crack of his whip. He must have planned to capture them, but she and Knox had gotten away. "You couldn't get into the burial chamber, so you let us attempt it for you. Then, when it didn't work, you tried to knock me out so you could blame me for everything *you* have been stealing?"

The director darted away from Lia's knife, running to where the huge slabs of stone had fallen from above, propped up against the wall like a bridge. He climbed up to the upper room and disappeared behind the guttering sheet in the corner. A tunnel, he'd said. To the outside. Shale had helped him dig it.

A coat of fake scales and a hood with teeth and glass eyes, a tail trailing behind him. A costume to scare off any workers who interrupted his last bid to extract valuables from the dead shapeshifter's tomb. Lia eased over to Anwei, her chest heaving. "Are you all right? Why are you here?"

Tears pricked in Anwei's eyes. "I don't—"

A liquid scream shattered the air, and Director Van stumbled out from behind the fabric to trip forward, taking the dirty sheet with him. Behind it there was a hole gouged into the stone, a passage filled with bags of jewels, painted pots, and gold.

Knox's space at the back of Anwei's head suddenly roared back to life, the frozen pain of it bending her forward. Anwei gasped, clutching her head in her hands.

"Anwei?" Lia's hand was on her shoulder even as she raised the knife. Because someone was coming out from the darkness of the passage.

Knox was supposed to find Shale. And Shale was probably somewhere up there in the tunnel.

But it wasn't Shale who came through.

It was a familiar outline, and he was holding a terrible sword.

CHAPTER 38

Grow

Anwei's stomach roiled at the nothing smell welling around her friend like a bloody wound. The bond between them flamed to life in her head now that there weren't shapeshifted walls between them, but it was stuck through with needles and pins, as if there were something else inside him violently trying to sever their connection.

"What is wrong with him?" Lia shouted as Knox barreled toward them. "Knox, it's *me*. What in Calsta's name . . ."

Knox's eyes seemed black in the mirrorlight, the sword swinging in a perfect arc toward Anwei's throat. The world slowed around Anwei, her gloved hand full of calistet.

Lia burst into Anwei's line of vision, deflecting the sword with her knife. Everything sped back up, only faster. Lia spun before her, dodging another swipe from Knox's sword, to lash with the knife's heavy hilt. He slid away like water, his eyes burning coals, ever on Anwei.

"Climb up to the burial chamber! It's open. Run!" Lia roared.

"Get the sword away from him. It's the sword doing this!" Only it wasn't the sword. It was the *thing* Anwei could feel in their bond, grown strong. The sword only made it stronger.

His sister, the ghost.

Anwei clutched the calistet, reaching out to Knox inside her head. She could feel him underneath this alien mask, a panicked warmth trapped inside a cage made of sharp thorns and a void.

Knox slammed the sword down toward Lia's shoulder, the Devoted barely able to turn him back with her little knife, and yet she stood firm between Anwei and Knox. Every strike brought Knox closer to Anwei, his eyes nailed to her as he fought. Anwei took a step back, then another, then she was climbing, the sound of that first cry inside her head echoing over and over.

Anwei! he'd screamed. She hadn't gone quickly enough, and whatever it was inside him had taken over.

Anwei pulled herself up over the ledge where the burial chamber door had broken in, a plume of dust billowing from inside. There was a raised dais, a coffin, bones, and a boy on the ground, shaking, shaking, *shaking*. . . .

"Anwei!" Lia screamed, like an echo to Knox's voice in Anwei's head.

Scrabbling on the rock below her set Anwei's feet running, Knox's monstrous presence in her head flared with victory and *hunger*. Anwei tore open the calistet packet and spun around, the cloud of powder erupting from her fist before she could even think, jetting toward the opening just as Knox burst through it.

No! She didn't want to kill Knox. She didn't want him to kill her, either.

The flaring cinnamon red of calistet was in the air, Anwei feeling every speck of it as Knox ran toward her with his sword raised. She could feel the shape of the poison cloud in her mind, each granule in the air.

Stop. She screamed it inside her head, her mind wrapping around each particle. And . . . they did.

Knox charged toward her, but something inside him changed the moment his foot crossed the broken door. He stumbled, falling to his knees, one hand grasping at his chest. The sword clattered to the ground next to him, shining in the dead lantern light.

Lia charged in after him, her eyes wild and the knife clutched in her hand like an extra limb. She skidded around Knox and almost fell into the cloud of poison Anwei was holding in place.

"Back! Get back, Lia," Anwei cried, not sure if she was warning Lia away from Knox or the calistet.

Knox gasped, and then again, as if he couldn't get any air. For a moment Anwei worried she hadn't stopped all of the calistet, but the bond between them seemed to stretch thin, the coldness inside him growing thick. All Anwei could smell was the burning fire of calistet warring with the wave of nothing that gushed from Knox.

"Mateo!" Lia kicked the sword away from Knox and ran to the dais behind Anwei, where the boy lay shaking by the coffin. "Calsta above, this is bad. Where is your sky-cursed *father*, Mateo?"

Anwei couldn't rip her eyes from the haze of red in the air and Knox beyond it. A tear burned down her cheek as she tried to hold the cloud in place, the little bits twitching here and there. The calistet wanted to move. It wanted to be breathed. She was locked in place just as it was, unable to shift an inch without it breaking free. "Knox," she whispered. *"Move out of the way."*

Knox's eyes were shut, one hand reaching for the sword, the other at his throat as he tried to suck down air through his blocked airway. The nothing around him seemed to deepen and bleed off him in patches, moving like a wave to attach to the dais behind Anwei, then to come back again.

Not the dais. The *boy*. The collapsed boy. He and Knox were swapping energy and nothingness back and forth, and somehow it was killing them both.

Anwei tried to look at the boy, the shape of him familiar. All of a sudden she could smell the *something* she'd detected up in the tomb, the scent that had confused her, made her stop and wonder how she knew it. Under the weight of all the nothing, she finally realized what it was, a smell she hadn't detected since her days as a girl back in Beilda. A memory flashed across her mind of a boy's fingers tying one of her braids into knots. . . .

The boy jerked up from the ground. His hair was cut short like a servant's, but his clothes stopped any possible misconception about where he fit into society. The colors of him, the shape of his face, even his long fingers, were exactly as Anwei remembered.

When he opened his eyes, something inside Anwei broke.

It was impossible. She'd seen those long, thin fingers lopped off like extra bits of hair, lying in pools of blood under his bed. So much blood that no one could have survived.

A new void opened up inside Anwei, bloodier, deeper than the scars her parents had left on her skin, more terrible than the nothing so thick in the air around her. *He* didn't smell like nothing.

He smelled like home.

Like the boy she'd been searching for since she was twelve.

Like someone who was alive and shouldn't have been.

Like someone she'd spent her *life* trying to avenge, only he wasn't dead.

Like someone stealing energy first from Lia. Now from Knox.

Like a *shapeshifter*.

The calistet muscled through the air. Anwei tore her eyes away from Arun, Knox kneeling only a few inches from the cloud. Tears streamed down his cheeks—

And a dark shape appeared behind Knox in the stone opening, blocking silvered mirrorlight that was creeping in from above. The shadow cast long and wide, much too large for the man standing in the doorway.

"Lia?" the snake-tooth man said. Anwei's skin trilled with memories of blood soaking into the hem of her dress. He'd laughed as he'd escaped through the window, leaving nothing but blood in her brother's room.

Anwei couldn't move, couldn't even breathe, or the calistet would envelop Knox.

"What have you done to Mateo?" The snake-tooth man's eyes flicked over Anwei and the cloud of calistet, over Knox, and then to the pockmarked sword. He hardly blinked, scooping up the sword and walking past Knox and Anwei as if they didn't matter to where Arun lay.

Mateo. That's what he'd called her brother. Lia had called him that too.

The snake-tooth man's face was different from the one in her memories. Pleasant. *Bearded.* It was the aukincer Anwei had met in the apothecary, not a single whiff of nothing to him. How had his voice sounded that day? Anwei couldn't remember.

Her eyes crumpled shut even as she concentrated on the calistet, willing it to drop to the floor. A cry escaped her lips when the granules twisted in the air instead, wafting toward Knox's face. Knox's mouth contorted, both hands wrapped around his throat. Tears streamed down his cheeks in pained rivulets. A bright spark shone in her head, deep inside the frozen pit their bond had become, as if he were trying to fight his way out of the darkness.

"You have to help him. Is it another attack? I don't think he's breathing." Lia was saying it from behind her. "And Knox. He's my friend, and something's happening to him, too. Is it the tomb? Something in the air? Tual—wait, where are you going?"

The man reappeared in Anwei's line of sight, Knox's pockmarked sword clutched in his fists. "I know this sword." He held it up toward Anwei. "And you." He smiled. "Who did you kill to hide your aura, little Beildan?"

Anwei's stomach clenched. *I didn't kill anyone to hide my aura. Knox and I hid each other. Our bond hid us.* Did that mean whatever it was that hid shapeshifters required killing instead of . . . whatever it was between her and Knox?

Love?

Anwei's mouth was full of blood. Her mind full of calistet. And the air full of a seven-year-old murder she had meant to avenge and found contorted into a new shape instead.

Her brother. Her twin. He'd been alive all these years she'd been searching for his murderer. Not only alive, but he'd become a *shapeshifter*.

Had *he* looked for *her*? With all of a shapeshifter's power, it seemed as if it wouldn't have been hard to find his sister, starving, hiding, stealing, and poisoning to fix the wrong that had been done.

The distilled gamtooth serum was spent on the floor, shards of glass in the dig director's arm. No weapon. No herbs. No breath to breathe. Anwei had nothing. "Help me, Lia," she croaked.

Lia's voice: "You think Anwei killed someone to hide . . . ? Because of the relief outside?" Her voice slowed. "Knox's aura was hidden. And shapeshifters kill someone as part of their oath. They steal another person's aura. Does that mean the two auras cancel each other out?"

"Knox and I didn't kill anyone," Anwei croaked. "We worked together and it hid both of us."

"Keep Mateo still, Lia." The shapeshifter was walking toward Knox now.

"*He's* the one who's been doing all of this, Lia." The words choked out of Anwei's mouth. "He sucked your mother's life away. She's dead." The calistet swirled and burned. Glossy, poisonous, deadly red. Anwei's brain began to crumble at the edges, exploding in little spurts at the effort of holding it away from Knox. "He's a—" A *shapeshifter*. He and Arun both were.

Before the word came out, the snake-tooth man bolted forward and kicked Knox over. Knox fell backward, his head hitting the floor.

Then the man raised the pockmarked sword and stabbed Knox through the stomach.

Agony exploded through their bond, and a wordless scream filled Anwei's head. But it wasn't Knox's scream: this one belonged to something *else*. The ghost, prickly and rotted and foul. Dead already and somehow dying again.

Anwei's mind blanked with the pain, and suddenly the calistet cloud was flying at the snake-tooth man where he stood over Knox. The shapeshifter stumbled to the side, eyes on the poison spiraling toward his face. But then, in a flash, it was gone. Reduced to ashes as a jolt of unnatural energy thrummed through the air, telling the poison to unmake itself.

A hiss of *nothing* oozed out of Anwei, coming from a tiny void newly opened inside her. A piece of her stolen to destroy the calistet, smelling like death in the air.

Knox's whole body curled around the hard metal stabbing him through. One moment he'd been standing in the yard with Gulya, and now—

And now—

His whole mind was frozen with Willow's unholy scream. There was a cave, and hard rock underneath him, and a sword, that horrible sword, and Anwei kneeling on the ground, and Calsta's voice raging like a bonfire, trying to melt the winter of his sister's ghost. All of it was fading at the edges. Narrowing. Darkening.

NOW, Knox! Reach for her now!

His eyes caught on Anwei. The spark of her in his mind blazed. Like the last night they'd been in this tomb, the two of them stronger together.

He reached.

Anwei surged to her feet, her hands clawing toward the snake-tooth man. He'd taken her brother. Her parents. Her village. Her home.

Now Knox? She tried to charge him, but her feet stumbled, her energy sapped.

"So strong. I should have taken both of you." The snake-tooth man's grin was casual, his hands still holding the bloody sword jammed in Knox's stomach. "I did try, but I couldn't make your mind stick."

Anwei couldn't speak, remembering watching her mother's blank face, her mind stuck on something that wasn't reality. He'd made everyone else's minds stick.

"I'm surprised you survived. You were so much more timid than he was back then." He smiled, a full-mouthed, genial sort of happiness gushing out from him even as Knox twitched at his feet. "You can come now, if you want. Now that your brother is fixed, we'll be able to disappear."

"Fixed?" Anwei's hands clenched, Knox limp at her feet.

"Those purging rituals that almost killed you and your brother came from somewhere. I'm cutting away the bad magic."

"Tual!" Lia's scream filled the chamber. "What are you doing? Is that why I can't see your auras? Because . . . you killed someone to become . . ." Lia ran forward, knife in her hand. "How could he be a shapeshifter too? Mateo's *dying*. He said you told him the two of us together would stabilize him. Like Patenga and his partner."

"I'm afraid that when I changed Mateo, I had less information than I do now. He was very badly injured, and the only thing that would have kept him alive was . . . this."

Badly injured. Anwei couldn't stop seeing the blood. Arun's scattered fingers.

"But it didn't work the way it was supposed to." Tual eyed the pockmarked sword where it stuck up from Knox's stomach. "When I turned myself, the weapon I used disintegrated. When I changed Mateo, the same thing happened, or so I thought. And yet, here it is. All these years I wondered if blending her with Mateo hadn't worked because she had survived." He looked down at the sword. "Not exactly the case. It seems as if her soul survived—and latched on to this sword."

"Tual, the caprenum, *all of this was to*—"

"Save Mateo. I'm afraid I don't know much about caprenum other than the fact that it can change someone from gods-touched to shapeshifter. There's so much to learn."

Anwei couldn't follow the conversation. *Who did you kill to hide your aura?* The snake-tooth man didn't know about bonds. Only about killing.

"I'd guess this boy found the girl's body soon after she died, and the sword . . . came back somehow because she latched on to it. And that linked him to my Mateo. She's been draining both of them ever since. Mateo was a shapeshifter with no way to access power because she took it all. And this boy . . . I guess he was a Devoted who managed to take enough power from Calsta to stay alive."

Knox wanted to kill me every time he picked up the sword. Because the thing inside him needed more power? Because she knew that if he killed me, it would . . . complete her, maybe? A Basist and a Devoted. One taking the life of the other.

The snake-tooth man looked to Lia behind Anwei. "Luckily, the sword will kill . . . Knox, you said? He was dead the moment he picked up the sword, so this is a mercy, Lia. It'll end this parasite that's been latched on to him for so many years, and Mateo will finally be complete."

"You said you needed *me*." Lia was breathless, her chest heaving as she held up the knife. "You said he had to love me. Just like Patenga loved the man he sacrificed. And you . . . you must have loved the person you killed."

"This drama is unnecessary, Lia." The shapeshifter smiled so very kindly, as if it were not yet another shape he wore. "Help Mateo up, and let's go."

"Help him? Tual, get *away* from . . ." Lia's voice was like an arrow behind Anwei. Far away, farther than the sky, farther even than the moons up above, flying slowly, oh so slowly . . .

Knox's hands quivered, jerking up to touch the sword where it protruded from his stomach. The spark in Anwei's head flickered. Dimmed.

Screaming filled the cave, and she didn't know where it was coming from: Lia, or Arun, or maybe it was from her own mouth. Knox's head twitched in Anwei's direction, one hand reaching toward her.

The snake-tooth man pulled the sword out in one violent jerk, then pointed it at Anwei, though the blade seemed to be collapsing, dripping in steaming rivulets to the ground as the thing inside Knox bled away. Knox looked at her, his eyes suddenly fierce and hot and wholly his own.

Anwei took one step toward the shapeshifter. Then she was running, Knox a surge of power inside her to replace the energy the snake-tooth man had stolen from her. The world around Anwei focused as if she were seeing twice, with Knox's Devoted eyes alongside her own. Lia was a flare of gold behind her, knife out and running toward the snake-tooth man. Arun still lay struggling to breathe, he and the shapeshifter both haloed in a white that seemed a little too perfectly plain. Anwei could see the rock all around them, bonded together at angles that screamed in the pain of magic that shouldn't have existed. And she could feel life in the dirt above, so many seeds and plants and trees. Just like the day of the storm, the day that had left her whole village dead and her half-drowned at sea.

Instead of wrapping her hands around the snake-tooth man's neck, Anwei slid to her knees at Knox's side. His breaths were coming in gurgling spurts that spoke of blood and ruptured humors and ends. The air around Anwei came alive. She could smell every bit of Knox, the spots where his bones were dry and broken, the wet russet smell of blood, the slashes in his skin, his humors as they mixed. Only it was more than that, more than she'd ever seen before because Knox's power was inside her too.

The energy pulsing from her sent shock waves out, power reaching into the soil for miles, as if Anwei were some kind of goddess, trying to draw life from the sky, the stars, the sun itself, to put it back inside her friend.

"I can fix this." Anwei hissed it at Knox, even though she knew she couldn't. Bodies didn't grow back together any more than plants would if you chopped them off at the stem. But what about the plants that had pulled the bricks apart in the wall at the governor's house? The poison she'd drawn out of Knox that night that should have killed him. The explosive powder she'd created that should have been impossible, the tang of calistet holding still in the air. *I am not doing this for myself. Nameless god, whoever you are, Calsta, may your sky throne forever be covered in wet paint, this boy believes in you. If you exist, then DO SOMETHING.*

Her hands on Knox's ribs were on fire, her whole mind was on fire, full of Knox's power, her power, *their* power, and voices and vines and plants, and there was too much, too much.

But he had to grow. She wasn't letting him leave her, not like this. Knox had to stay. He had to grow back together.

Lia flailed back as the ground between her and Tual began to buck and roil. Over on the dais, Mateo's eyes burst open, air wheezing from his lungs. "Lia," he gasped. "Lia help me, I can't breathe."

But Tual was holding a bloody sword, and chunks of rock were raining down from the ceiling, and roots were bursting through the ground and growing along the walls like snakes. Tual dropped the sword and ran to his son, gathering Mateo up from the ground. "Help me, Lia. I know this looks terrible to you, but you don't understand all of it. Mateo needs to get out of here now, or he'll die. We need you, Lia. If you care for my son at all—"

"You killed my friend. My *brother*." Lia couldn't even hear herself speak over the rumble of rock. The knife in her hand felt slick, but for the first time in her life, she didn't know what she was supposed to do with it. "You . . . she said you killed my mother."

"You're going to believe a Basist? A shapeshifter who enthralled your friend? He was dead long before he walked into this tomb." Tual hoisted Mateo up off the ground, dragging him toward the coffin. "Help me carry Patenga's sword. . . ."

Lia stumbled up the steps onto the dais and peered into the coffin. There, between the slumped skeleton's ribs, was the sword this shape-shifter had fallen on. He'd dealt his own killing blow. With a sword made of caprenum.

"Take the sword, Lia." Tual's voice hummed. He was already trudging down the stairs. "And come. Quickly!"

Lia stared at the sword. The ceiling groaned, the stone cracking in explosive bursts. A healing substance that would save Mateo. A bond between a Devoted and a Basist. *Who did you kill to hide your aura, little Beildan?*

And the depiction on the wall of Patenga shoving a sword through the man who meant the most to him in the world.

Shapeshifters *weren't* Basists. There was a bond between Basists and Devoted formed through love. And if one of them destroyed the person they loved to gain their power—*that* was the abominable sacrifice that created a shapeshifter. That was what distorted them into something no longer human.

Lia picked up the sword and swung it to touch Tual's throat, pointing the knife in her other hand at his face. Her arm shook as she tried to hold it up, her whole body crying as if she hadn't eaten in a week. "This sword? The one you want Mateo to murder me with, Tual?"

Tual backed away, holding Mateo close.

"Lia!" Mateo gasped, his eyes fluttering shut.

"They say shapeshifters can do more than any Devoted or Basists on their own, and they steal people's souls to do it. Like . . . like Mateo did when he opened the wall." Lia's stomach dropped, her voice curdling. "Using energy he stole from *me*. That's why I can hardly lift this sword."

It wavered in front of her, fragments of rock raining down from the ceiling all around her. Anwei was by Knox with her hands clenched, a power wafting off her like waves crashing into the shore.

"Mateo isn't going to be better because you killed off the thing draining him. The first sacrifice didn't take, so you need a replacement. You need *me*." She whispered it, but Tual could still hear her. She could see it in his eyes, the way they bulged when the tip of her sword touched his Adam's apple. "Or he'll die?"

Tual's eyes went hard, the pupils seeming to thin into slits. "All three of us are going to die if you don't let me take Mateo out through the tunnel, Lia. Is that what you want?"

"Does he know?" she asked. "Does he know what you are? What *he* is?"

"Who are you to judge, Lia?" The words slicked out of Tual's mouth like a snake's long tongue and his face seeming to elongate, his nostrils flaring. "How many innocent Basists have you killed in the name of a goddess who doesn't even speak to you?"

Mateo lay limp, his eyelids fluttering as if he were trying to stay awake.

"Help us, Lia. There is much I can explain, and much you don't understand—" Tual dove to the side, a boulder-sized chunk of the ceiling crashing down where he'd stood. It shattered, tiny pieces zipping through air, peppering Lia's arms and legs with burning lines of pain. She stumbled back, raising her arms to shield her face.

The sword yanked from her hand, and suddenly Tual was standing over her, Mateo still in his arms. "We aren't the villains history wrote for us. Come with us, Lia. Come *now*!"

Lia's body shook, the knife still clasped in her hand.

"Remember my promise when we discussed what would happen if you tried to go against me?"

Tual's nostrils folded back against his cheeks, his nose flattening, jaw opening to spill a mouthful of jagged teeth. In one sinuous movement, his neck stretched up, his arms coiling too long around his son. The sword arced toward Lia's leg as if he meant to wound her, then drag her along after him, but Lia lurched toward him, too close for the sword to reach, and stabbed Tual's ankle with the knife. He hissed, skittering back.

The ceiling caved, chunks of rock cascading down between her and Tual. Stone pummeled the ground, and Lia curled into a ball, the whole world falling around her.

It took years, an entire lifetime, for the noise to stop. For the rocks to stand still and the ground to stop heaving. Lia coughed, rock dust grainy in her mouth and down her throat when she finally raised her head. Sunlight pierced the tomb—vines, roots, and flowers choking the opening. The coffin on the dais had tipped over sideways, the floor strewn with bones.

Still shaking, Lia forced herself to stand. Where were Tual and Mateo? Buried in the rubble?

There was a perfectly empty ring in the mess of fallen stone, Anwei and Knox at the center. The Beildan's chest was heaving, tears making muddy trails in the dust on her cheeks. Streams of blood ran from both of Anwei's nostrils, and her tears were tinged red. Knox was still lying in a pool of his own blood. There was no sign of Mateo or his father.

Lia could hardly breathe as she stumbled toward Knox and Anwei, trying to understand the space around them, the rocks on the ground, the vines twisting down from the ceiling. She collapsed onto her knees next to Knox's body, nothing making sense. There was a long, bloodstained tear in his tunic where the sword had stabbed him, Anwei's hand fisted around the bloody material. But underneath it, instead of a gaping wound opening Knox's stomach, there was a nasty, bulging scar.

Pitching forward, Lia checked his breathing, his pulse. Anwei didn't move, her eyes shut as if she couldn't bear to look at the world ever again. "He's breathing," Lia gulped. "What did you do?"

"I don't know," Anwei gasped, tears streaming in earnest down her face. Her fistful of Knox's tunic didn't move, as if she were firmly holding him in this world. His hand circled her wrist, the two of them breathing together.

Lia thought of the painting from the cave that Mateo had copied, Calsta and the nameless god reaching for each other. All the ones they'd touched, working together. *Bonded,* like Mateo had said.

And Patenga bonded to a Basist, then destroying that love and bond for power. She closed her eyes, thinking of all the shields in the tomb, the painting of Patenga crying despite his crown. He'd regretted it. Designed and built this tomb. Killed himself instead of extending his own life and power like most other shapeshifters.

Killed himself . . .

Lia stared down at the sword Tual had stabbed into Knox, the end now half-melted and dull. There had been a sword through the shapeshifter king's ribs. A sword Tual had taken with him, wherever he'd dragged Mateo, made of that stuff Mateo had said they needed to heal him. *Caprenum.*

Patenga had been made by that caprenum sword and then had died by it.

She moved to pick up Knox's half-melted sword, but Anwei's eyes sprang open. "Don't touch it," she rasped. "She's still in there. She's still in Knox. If she goes, he will too. While he stays . . ."

Lia swallowed, pulling her hand back. "The . . . ghost. His sister?" She'd grown up with Knox. Played with him. Fought with him. And never once had she seen the sword. How could she not have known Knox had another person living inside him, feeding off him like a tick? He'd said Calsta had spoken to him, gotten him to a seclusion, where she could feed him power. And then when that hadn't been enough anymore, she'd brought him to Anwei.

The thought made her clench her eyes shut. Calsta had brought Knox to Anwei. A Basist. Because a bond between them would balance him. Just like Mateo had said.

"If Knox is still alive and his sister hasn't . . . gone, that means Mateo is going to get worse," Lia whispered, opening her eyes. "Which means Tual is probably already on his way back here for me."

Anwei's eyes burst open, the whites of them spidered over in red. "He doesn't have to come back for us because we're going to go to him. My entire life has been wasted on finding that piece of silenbahk dung."

"Tual?"

"I thought he killed my brother. It destroyed me. My family. My whole village. So I was going to destroy him. All for a murder he didn't commit. Arun's calling himself Mateo now?" Lia's skin pebbled at the razor edge to Anwei's words. "All my life fixated on avenging my twin, and he never gave a second thought to me." Her fingers were still clenched in Knox's shirt. "He turned into a shapeshifter himself."

"Mateo isn't . . ." Lia stopped. She'd known Mateo for only a week, and most of it had involved him spouting off insults, tearing things up, and hiding his head while she fought for her life. But he couldn't help what Tual had done to him, could he? He'd been kind and funny and just ridiculous enough to make her forget what was hanging over her for whole minutes at a time.

Of course, so had Tual.

Lia took a shaky breath and looked down at Knox, finally asking the question she'd been too afraid to voice. "Is he going to be all right?"

Anwei's eyes drifted shut again. "I don't know."

"We have to move. The Warlord was supposed to come."

"She's already here."

Anwei's whisper scraped through Lia. She frantically sent her aurasight up to the circle of light above them where there once had been floors of statues, artifacts, and reliefs, and where now there was nothing but a jagged hole clear to the sky. Lia's heart jittered in her chest, and she fancied she could already hear auroshe cries, the brash sound of Ewan's cocksure laugh. "Can we move Knox?" she asked.

"I don't know."

Lia shoved the bloody knife into her pocket. Tual and Mateo had run in the same direction as the man who had been wearing a shapeshifter costume. She didn't want to follow them to whatever was waiting at the end of that tunnel.

Instead Lia went to the cascade of vines and roots that had ruptured the ceiling, growing in sticky swirls all the way to the floor in thick bands. A bridge to the surface.

Once she'd climbed out of the tomb, Lia stared at what was left of the compound, feeling as if she had fallen asleep in one place and woken up in a new one. The structures, the walls, the baskets, the pavilions— they were all gone. A gargantuan tree had grown up in the center of it all, spilling into the hole Anwei had made of the tomb. Crackles of fire caught in Lia's ears, hidden in the lush new growth. She couldn't feel any auras nearby, but she was too afraid to push far enough for it to matter. The Warlord could be within shouting distance, waiting to snap up anything that came creeping out of the ruins.

Lia and Anwei couldn't carry Knox a long way and couldn't walk back to Chaol hoping no one saw them on the road, so they needed a horse. Lia picked her way toward where Mateo had tied Bella.

Mateo. Lia didn't like the way her thoughts stuck on him. He'd probably stolen pieces of her every moment they'd been together. Even when he'd stood between her and Ewan. When he'd ridden to her father's house, the Warlord bearing down on him. When he'd sat with her in his father's study, saying "maybe later when everything has calmed down . . ."

He'd been so embarrassed and earnest, so apologetic when he realized what a stupid thing it was to say to her.

But there was no over. Not when Mateo's very existence depended on draining the life from people around him. He'd reached into her and plucked something straight from her center, from her *soul*, leaving her exhausted and grasping at the stone walls just to hold herself straight.

It was different from what Ewan had done, but it still left her feeling dirty, violated, wishing she could wash away the feeling of foreign hands clutching at whatever it was that made her Lia.

When she got in sight of the gates—where the gates had been, anyway—Lia stumbled, stubbing her toes on a discarded shovel hidden in the knee-high grass. Where the horse tie-ups had been there was nothing, no roof, no hitching post, and no Bella. She closed her eyes, pulling on her aurasight once again, then letting it go in a panicked flurry when auras popped into existence at the very edges of her mind. Golden ones.

One was coming toward her, the gold flecks so diminished she could hardly see them.

Ewan.

A reptilian scream split the air, the familiar call filling her chest until Lia thought she would burst. He was still riding Vivi, as if he owned the both of them. She pulled the knife from her pocket, wondering why Ewan was coming when the others hung back. Could he see her despite his diminished aura?

Did Calsta accept sacrifices from a would-be rapist?

Vivi's familiar form tore through the sugarcane, ripping holes in the earth with his claws and screaming as Ewan manhandled the reins. He leapt the last timber, the Devoted throwing himself from the auroshe's back, rolling out of it to come toward Lia at a run. He was all steel sword, oiled leather, and white teeth in one ugly blur.

Lia had frozen the last time she'd seen him. She'd frozen and let a sky-cursed shapeshifter with no more muscle than a little child stand up for her. She couldn't freeze this time. She groped in the grass for the shovel she'd tripped over. Knife in one hand and shovel in the other, Lia fled back into the ruins of the dig.

Ewan's aura blistered in Lia's head as she tried to keep track of it behind her. Ewan had greater strength, a longer reach. A sword instead of a shovel. Lia was faster, but her legs were already shaking, her insides hollowed out. The gold-splattered aura chased after her, weaving through the newly grown trees, the broken remains of buildings, and the piles of dirt now hidden by flowers. Lia's heart hiccuped in her chest as she looped back toward the spot Ewan had left Vivi rearing, praying to Calsta he was following the trail of broken grass she'd left in her wake, not her aurasparks. She was so *tired*, all her energy sucked out of her.

She slid to a stop behind a tree, Ewan's aura darting around the other way as if he couldn't see her. So it wasn't aurasight. He'd heard the noise, heard her voice, or perhaps he'd just hoped all this destruction had belonged to her and had come running.

Lia broke from her cover toward where she could still hear Vivi's cackling calls, only to hear Ewan's dry laugh behind her. Muscles screaming, head screaming, all of her screaming, Lia ran.

"Lia," his voice came in an unhinged yell, all too close. "The Warlord already saw your aura. She sent me to collect you."

Vivi's long, choking scream echoed across the compound, as if he could smell blood. It chilled her, wondering if he'd still recognize her now that Ewan had forced him to receive a new master.

Planting her feet, Lia twisted around, swinging the shovel toward his head. The blow barely glanced off the side of Ewan's skull, and when she swiped at him a second time, he blocked it with his sword, then wrenched the shovel from her numb fingers.

"Look at you with your pretty red hair." Ewan was still laughing, his grin so full of bile that she didn't need to see his thoughts to know what was inside him. His sword hung loose in his hand, and he circled her, herding Lia toward the edge of the compound. Lia kept the space between them, darting in a few times to jab at him with the knife, but he knocked each blow aside with a lazy swipe from the sword, the last catching her hand with the flat of the blade in a painful slap.

"To think you thought you could take me in the training yards. Everyone said what a good little Devoted you were. Powerful. Special." He swiped at her with a sneer, forcing her to stumble back. "Now look at you. Cowering. You can start pleading any time now, I'll listen." Ewan grinned when she stumbled again, then changed the angle of his sword so Lia had to retreat toward the broken wall. Toward the Warlord. Toward the end of her life, where there would be no escape. Roots and grass pulled at Lia's ankles as she tried to remember where the breaks in the wall had been. If only she could get to Vivi.

She could hear him keening, though perhaps not for her now that Ewan had tamed him. Going to Vivi could end this fight with her guts on the ground.

"I've taken your auroshe. Your shovel. The knife will go next." Ewan spat on the ground at her feet. "And then once the Warlord gives you back to me—"

Stabbing pain shot through Lia's ankle as a rock skidded out from under her foot, and suddenly she was on the ground and Ewan was on top of her, grinding her into the hard dirt, pinning her knife hand.

"I'm so disappointed, Lia," he breathed into her ear. "I know you can fight better than this."

Lia's whole body writhed at his breath on her face. She tried to roll to the side, jabbing at his eyes with her bare fingers, but he only laughed, shifting his weight to hold her other arm down.

"Maybe you played this easy. Hoped I'd find you," he whispered. "It's okay. I understand."

The knife felt damp, hard, too heavy in Lia's hand. But Ewan's shift to hold her down had left that arm barely pinned. She tried to inch it out from under his weight, but it wouldn't budge, the blade pressing against her own ribs.

"Maybe I don't even need to wait for the Warlord. She's too scared to come back here. It's just you and me—"

Something whistled through the air, slicing into the back of his neck. In his split second of pain and confusion, Lia tore her arm free and stabbed the knife into the slit between leather plates in his armor under his arm. Ewan's eyes bulged, his breath all coming out in a pained wheeze.

Just in time for Vivi's horn to spear him through the side.

Ewan's mouth gaped open, his hands flailing to find the twisted horn piercing him through. One hand flopped toward Lia's knife, but Vivi was too fast, shaking Ewan loose of his horn, then darting toward him with a gaping mouth, jagged teeth finding Ewan's neck.

Lia rolled away, pinching her eyes closed at the awful sounds, her arms creeping up to cover her head. She didn't move until Vivi—still *her* Vivi—had gone back to nickering, coming to nudge her head with his inky-red muzzle.

Arms and legs shaking, she stood, hugging Vivi's face to her chest. "I missed you," she whispered. "I needed you. This whole time."

The auroshe nipped at her, smears of blood marking her dress where he lipped the fabric.

Ewan's aura blazed brighter than the sun behind Lia, then drained away into the sky until there was nothing left.

Lia didn't look at his body on the ground. Holding tight to Vivi's neck, she stumbled away a step, her foot catching on something stuck in the grass. Lia bent to pick it up.

It was a wooden hair stick, the end decorated with a pretty flower. The two prongs were sharpened to wicked points, each of them marked with blood.

Something had hit Ewan before Lia had stabbed him. Before Vivi had come. Lia looked around the jumbled mess of plants and found an aura hovering behind a thick tree that had grown so fast, it had split its own bark.

The aura was white, not a trace of Devotion inside. Vivi squealed, starting for the tree, but Lia grabbed his reins, holding him back. "Hello?" she called.

A girl peeked out from behind the tree, soot marking her nose and cheeks, knots that looked as if they belonged on a high khonin snarled in her hair. "Aren't you going to run?" she whispered, her eyes on Lia's blood-soaked front. "That thing—"

"He won't hurt me." Lia's voice shook, but she put up her hands to stop the girl when she retreated a step. "Or you. I'm not with the Warlord. You . . . you helped me just now." She couldn't bring herself even to gesture to the pile of flesh that was Ewan. "Thank you."

"What monster wouldn't? Are you all right?" The girl edged backward, her eyes on Vivi's bloody teeth. "I know a healer who might be able to . . ." She looked around, the dirt streaks on her cheeks marked with tears "I mean . . . I did know a healer. I don't know if she . . ."

"You came with Anwei?"

The girl's eyes widened. She nodded but still hung back.

"Come on. We need to get out of here before any other Devoted come." Lia turned toward the tomb, hugging Vivi's neck as she walked. He let her, and an awful laugh that might have been a sob burst up through Lia's throat when he began nosing her pockets, looking for treats. No other golden sparks flickered across Lia's aurasight as they picked their way across the compound. Perhaps the threat of a risen shapeshifter king was enough to shake the Warlord herself.

Every inch of Lia felt bruised, dirtied, touched. But Lia was still breathing. Lia had Vivi back. And Lia wasn't done.

. . .

Something shifted in the darkness behind Anwei. She closed her eyes, her mind swollen and protruding. Knox's chest moved up and down, the blood soaking his shirt wet against her cheek.

The sound came again, rhythmic. Footsteps. Anwei jerked up, grabbing a rock. Images of the aukincer's snakelike face drummed through her head, but when a shadow emerged from the gloom, it wasn't the snake-tooth man. Altahn stumbled out of the rubble, his long tail of hair disheveled. His eyes found Knox's sword where the shapeshifter had thrown it on the ground, the melted end black with blood. He bent to pick it up. "All this over a sword . . ."

Altahn's whisper barely reached Anwei. She gripped the rock, her fingers rubbery and useless. "That's not Patenga's sword." She couldn't sense a change in Altahn despite the fact that the sword was in his hands. He still smelled of horse and leather and salpowder.

But she *could* still smell the sword on Knox. The ghost who was eating him. The shapeshifter had said Knox had been dead from the moment Willow latched on to him. But Knox had said Calsta could fix it somehow. That he and Anwei could fix it together.

Altahn looked down the length of the melted sword, then set it back on the ground. He stepped over it and extended his hand to her instead. "I didn't know there was a shapeshifter here, or I wouldn't have gotten my father involved."

"You know now?" It was hard to bring up words to answer such a declaration when Anwei's world was already punctured.

"He came out our tunnel. The shaking, all of . . . this . . ." He kicked at one of the roots that had swollen up from the ground. "My father . . ." He swallowed. "He's dead."

Anwei blinked, the plants that had come at her call finally registering in her mind. Something had unfolded inside her when Knox's power swirled through her. She'd reached farther, felt more, done more than she ever had before. The magic in her wasn't broken.

"Here." Altahn stepped up to Knox and pulled his legs straight. Anwei flinched, ready to swat him away, but the Trib put his hands up. "The Warlord is up there. I can help carry him out."

"You want to help me?" Anwei hurt everywhere, her other hand refusing to come unclenched from Knox's tunic. He still held her wrist, his fingers leaving lines on her skin. "You don't want to, say, hand me over to the magistrate in exchange for a magic sword?"

"I'm sorry that we lied to you. I had no choice. That sword was stolen from us. Used to murder the very man who'd forged it, then buried with the murderer. It's powerful, and we need power right now." Altahn shook his head. "And Van needed a scapegoat."

"You could have warned me."

"It wasn't the most honorable thing I've ever done. But you drugged me and left me underground for two days, so I suppose none of us are blameless." Altahn flexed his hand once, then held it out to her. "You were in this because of the snake. He's killed my father and taken the sword." He raised an eyebrow when she hesitated. "Why don't we go find him together?"

Anwei let the rock in her hand fall to the ground, then wrapped her fingers around Knox's wrist. His heart was still beating, his space in her head warm. Less separate than it had been before. He hadn't stirred, though she couldn't smell anything wrong with him.

She untangled her fingers from his tunic long enough to feel for the pulse steadily beating in his neck. His body seemed fine, but that didn't mean his mind was still inside.

She looked up at Altahn. "Why did you come down here for me?"

Altahn glanced up at the vines that had broken through the rock, before letting his hand fall back down to his side. "Because I think I'm going to need help, and I've seen what the two of you can do."

Knox's eyelids flickered. Anwei sat forward, watching. Not wanting to think of everything Altahn must have overheard in the apothecary.

"We can't afford to be caught down here." Shadows twisted in the darkness behind Altahn, resolving into a man and a woman with Trib leathers and ponytails. "So it's come now or wish you had."

A light *tap, tap* of split hooves echoed down from above. Bile rose in Anwei's throat. It was too late, the Devoted were already here. An auroshe peered over the edge of the hole in the ceiling, its single twisted horn jutting toward them like a sword. Blood dripped down its muzzle.

Gathering everything she had left, Anwei forced herself up from the ground, her mind a gaping hole of fear as she dragged Knox back from the light and the thing's line of sight. Altahn was there next to her, groping for the nothing sword.

"Wait! It's me!" Lia's voice filtered down. The creature's black eyes followed Anwei hungrily as Lia's face appeared alongside its neck. "I have a present for you out here. She may have helped save my life just now. The Warlord is hanging back, but I don't know how long it will last. Can you get Knox to Gretis?"

Anwei's mouth was dry, nothing more than a croak coming from her throat. But she glanced at Altahn, who nodded. "Where are you going?" Anwei asked, craning her neck to peer up at Lia.

"I have to get my family. I'll meet you after nightfall."

"Lia, go to the apothecary for me. Tell Gulya . . ." Thoughts of the old woman who had taken Anwei in felt stale and tired in her head. The old apothecarist had liked the customers Anwei's braids had brought in. She'd cared about Anwei, too, though. "Tell her I'm sorry. And get everything she'll let you take. Herbs. Money. Anything."

Lia nodded. "I'll do what I can." Then the auroshe snorted and withdrew its head, Lia disappearing with it.

Another head stuck out over the gap, blocking the sun. "Sky Painter protect you, Anwei!"

A spark of something bright erupted in Anwei at the sight of

Noa waving at her from above, though she was too far away from herself to know what it was. Relief? Joy? "May she send her storms far away from us," Anwei mumbled, not loud enough for anyone to hear.

Noa grinned. "Was that a big enough fire?"

CHAPTER 39

Promise Kept

The thick fog that had settled over Mateo wouldn't lift. His head pounded. When he opened his eyes, the world seemed to have been made small, nothing but a tiny room that rocked back and forth. A carriage.

His father sat across from him, a long sword on his lap. The air smelled of burning, and there were black smudges decorating Tual's shirt and sleeves.

"What . . . what happened?" Mateo's voice crackled painfully in his throat. "I was down in the tomb, and all I remember are flashes. And Lia . . . Lia with a sword." It had looked so natural in her hand, as if she'd been born to be a Devoted.

"We were attacked." Tual set the sword on the seat next to him. "You know how dangerous it is for people like us. You opened the burial chamber and it caused an episode, but I managed to get you out before they got to us. We have the caprenum." He patted the long, twisted weapon. Mateo had seen it among Patenga's bones before he'd blacked out in the tomb. Now, in the better light, he could see the northern curl to the hilt, the shadow of a horse in the design. Trib-made.

It had been in Lia's hand, the tip at his father's throat, but those thoughts were slippery, as if they wanted to wash away. Mateo blinked, looking down at his hands. Remembering the way it had felt to want something and then to have that thing stream into him from the very air. The burial chamber wall had fallen because of *him*.

"Caprenum isn't going to help me." Mateo whispered it. Finally understanding—why caprenum, why Lia, why the two had to go together. After all, like Lia had said, what healing compound would be crafted to look like a *sword*? The sword Patenga had used to become a shapeshifter had been a specific kind, made by a Basist.

Maybe that's why it had been so easy to blame Basists all those centuries ago. Why the images of caprenum had been scratched from history. It wasn't just anyone who could turn shapeshifter. You had to have the right tools.

Mateo scrubbed a hand through his hair, turning toward the window. "Everything to do with shapeshifters had been destroyed, so you didn't know how to do it, exactly. You didn't know until it was too late why turning worked for you and not for me."

Tual breathed in, the sound loud in Mateo's ears. "How did you . . ."

"I heard what you and Lia said. I saw . . . I saw enough. What you can do—what you did with the narmaidens, what you did with our auras . . . that's not something Basists can do, is it?" Mateo closed his eyes even before his father could nod. "You knew the change had to be done with caprenum, but not that the person sacrificed had to be someone I loved." Mateo forced himself to open his eyes, to make sure the nightmare he was spinning for himself was true. "You tried to turn me, and it worked . . . but not all the way. So now you want to use Lia to finish it."

"You would have died if I hadn't done it when you were younger." Tual's words were small. Not apologetic, but quiet, as if the information would be softer if he used the right voice. "You are my son."

"Your son. I thought you took me when I was a baby. So much of my life is a blur. . . ."

"Your life is blurred because it was easier to make it that way. Easier for you to forget."

"You took my own memories away from me. My own thoughts. Silenced them like you did with the narmaidens?" Mateo swallowed the gall in his throat, an image of a young man with a sword through his belly frozen in his mind. He groped for this one truth, this one thing he knew. Tual loved him. All the notes he'd found on the desk about Tual looking for someone . . . had he been looking for that boy? When he'd walked into the tomb with that sword—another sword of caprenum, just like Patenga's—Mateo had felt the void inside him grow teeth and claws, rear up into something that thought and felt and *hungered*. He was connected to both of them, his soul being eaten away because they existed. His father had been looking for *them*, the source of his wasting sickness, not a new child to replace the faulty one he'd taken on. "Why?"

Tual's head bowed. "I didn't get to you in time. You weren't in good shape. The town council had assembled to cleanse you—they pretended it was for something else, a final braiding ceremony for your sister—after some incidents in the town made it clear you and your sister were better at healing than any herbs could make you."

"I was old enough to be a healer?" Mateo choked on the words, fumbling through his memories to somehow place this life that wasn't his. "And what do you mean, *'sister'*?"

"You were also aware of your power and saw what was about to happen, so you snuck away. Some of them followed and tried to cut your aura themselves. They started with your fingers because of your art. That's where they thought you kept your magic."

Mateo flexed his hand, whole and unbroken. "If they cut off my fingers . . ."

Tual swallowed, looking down. "It *wasn't* just your fingers. I got you away, managed to keep you from dying, but it wasn't enough. It took a while before I found a suitable candidate to change you, and *that* healed you he rest of the way." He swallowed again, leaning forward to rub his hands across his face. "And your sister . . ."

Mateo leaned forward too, every inch of him aching. "Yes?"

"I tried to make them all forget that she was like you. But she was so upset by your disappearance that they didn't need their memories to know what she was. They tried to kill her right after I took you. She is strong and managed to escape. But no one else in your village did."

"What do you mean?"

"I mean she lost control. Like she did today."

"The girl from the tomb?" Mateo's brain was a horrible fog, ghosts of what had happened down in the tomb dancing in and out of his consciousness. A Beildan girl crying. A murdered boy. Lia with a sword. "She's my sister?"

Tual nodded again. "She is dangerous. Her life has been stealing and lying, starving and hiding, where yours has been safe." His eyes closed. "I have regrets, Mateo. So many regrets. But I have you, and I wouldn't give you back for anything. I was so alone before, but the two of us together . . ." He looked down. "You are my family."

Mateo swallowed, sitting up as he remembered the reliefs, Patenga bowed over in grief even as his sword stabbed another man through. "You said it took you a while to find a suitable candidate. Who did you kill to change me? They must have had something to do with that boy and his sword."

"Yes. His older sister. The Devoted were coming for them. Her family—"

"Would have liked her to be alive, probably?"

"Probably. But why should they get a few extra days with her rather than you getting a whole life?"

The words sat on Mateo's chest, a lead weight.

"She didn't melt away like she was supposed to, though. I believe she must have latched on to her brother, and he's fed her with Calsta's power all these years. Your episodes should stop now that she's gone.

With her brother dead and you too far to feed on, she'll be unmoored and will fade. But the hole she made inside you isn't going to go away."

"So this whole time, what I thought was wasting sickness was actually some spirit draining my energy away? Especially when I try to use extra energy like a Basist should be able to. Except for in the tomb." That feeling of exultation, of strength, of *power*—

Tual's head was already shaking, his hat gripped in his hands. "You're not a Basist anymore, Mateo. You haven't been since you were twelve. And you still can't use your power until we fix this. When we weren't close to the sword, she didn't notice you enough to actively steal from you, but you were still sick. I've had to feed you slowly all these years."

"Feed me slowly . . ." Mateo gripped the door's handle, trying to anchor himself in this new version of his life. "So what is wasting sickness? I got sick because my energy was draining away, then got *really* sick when this ghost thing started actively feeding on me. So what is wasting sickness for Devoted?"

Tual smiled, a fatherly, soft expression.

"You've been stealing energy from them? Just like the ghost was from me?"

"I've been keeping you alive, Mateo. It took so much to keep you from fading away—energy from a *goddess*. And when no Devoted were available, I had to take from her more casual worshippers, the little drips of power she leaves in people."

Mateo's head lolled to the side, hitting the window. "Like Lia's mother?"

Tual's smile dropped away. "She was going to die anyway. My healing is magic, but there are some sicknesses I can't fix."

"So wasting sickness . . . *all* wasting sickness—it's only cropped up in the last decade. Because of you? No, because of *me*. You started draining Devoted to feed me, then set yourself up as the healer who could save them." The truth was black and deadly. It must have been easy for Tual to convince the Warlord he could cure Devoted. All he had to do was stop taking their lives.

No, not their lives—their *souls*.

Soul stealers. That's what shapeshifters were.

"*I* changed by accident. It's . . ." Tual's eyes went to the sword. "Not important right now. But there's no information on any of this, Mateo. No records. It's all been destroyed. I didn't realize that regret, *pain*, were important to the sacrifice. It has to be someone you love. But after years of study, years of searching through old reliefs and tombs and paintings, I saw hints of what I'd gotten wrong."

Mateo closed his eyes, suddenly feeling as if he were nothing but a clay figurine, fragile, and empty inside. So many things they thought they knew about the past came from tombs and paintings and books. But the reliefs with Patenga and the love he'd killed seemed clear enough. A bond made just like Tual said, Basist and Devoted working hand in hand. And then Patenga had taken that bond and destroyed it.

"I hardly know Lia," he whispered.

"But you like her."

"Yes, I like her *alive*."

But an ugly truth peeked through behind it: *I want to live too.*

Mateo opened his eyes. He was hollowed out, as if now he could finally feel the void sucking at him from the inside. "What about a normal bond, like the ones you said used to exist? It's obvious Patenga and the Basist in the tomb . . ."

Tual shook his head slowly. "Mateo . . . you aren't a Basist anymore, so how *could* you bond in that way? No, I don't think half measures will do."

"There aren't *any* measures left to take," Mateo interjected. "There aren't any other Devoted for me to cozy up to and then stab. And Lia's not going to come skipping after us." She had seen the reliefs. She'd been the one to say it out loud: "shapeshifter." And even if she hadn't, Mateo wasn't . . . he couldn't . . . the idea of connecting himself to her was still so new. Adding her death as a foregone conclusion was impossible. Monstrous.

I want to live. The words snaked through his head, a truth even the narmaidens had been able to agree was his most terrible.

Tual patted his arm, glancing out the carriage window to the wagon behind them. Mateo's brow furrowed, and he looked too, but there wasn't anything he could see in the wagon worthy of his father's interest.

"I have a plan to bring her to us, Mateo. This will all come to right." Tual smiled, pointing out the window. "Did you see I brought Bella? I knew you'd be sad without her. She'll help you to feel better."

Mateo looked where his father pointed, ashamed to feel tears pricking in his eyes, because with everything so very amiss, the sight of his horse walking along in front of them did make him feel a little better.

But his stomach twisted tight when he saw the shape just beyond her, ranging between stalks of sugarcane, there but not really there, like a thief or a spy. A much taller beast, skeletal and fanged. As if Lia herself were running after them through the fields, a sword in her hand and Mateo's name like a curse on her lips.

It was Rosie, the broken auroshe.

You like her.

Mateo put a hand to his head at the thought that was not exactly *his* thought, cold prickling through him.

You like that auroshe, don't you? If you like her, I think you will like me, too.

Lia left Vivi tethered in a field outside the markets that spilled through the trade gate. She traded Noa's hair stick for a scarf wide enough to cover the blood dribbled down her front. The seller looked askance at the brown staining Lia's dress but asked no questions. It seemed no one asked the questions they should.

It took the better part of an hour to sneak her way past guards, looking out for Devoted glows and ducking magistrates to get to the apothecary. The doors and windows hung open, and it didn't take Lia's barely budding aurasight to feel the prickling emptiness of the place. She slipped through the back gate and into the workroom.

It was in complete disarray, the table overturned, herbs torn from the ceiling and trampled on the stone floor. Cabinets were on their sides, their contents of spines and petals spilled out like entrails. Lia pushed open the door to look in the store and found glass shards coating the floor like salt. A jar with a heavy clamp stood in the center of the pandemonium untouched, the one stalwart after a massacre on the battlefield.

Upstairs, Knox's bed was on its side, copper and silver rounds strewn across the floor like hailstones, each feeling as if it weighed more than it should as Lia collected them into her purse. Anwei's room was too still. Completely untouched, except for the old woman sleeping in her bed.

No, not sleeping. She had no aura.

Gulya, the apothecarist. Lia walked to the bedside, hands shaking, and grasped the woman's shoulders, hoping she was somehow wrong, but the old woman's head fell sideways, her arm flopping lifelessly out of the bed. The old woman's skin was pockmarked with a blistering rash, just the way Lia's mother had been.

The plague. The plague that Tual had sent down on Chaol.

And Gulya was still a little warm.

Lia startled back, a thread of fear pushing through. She retreated to the doorway.

Horrible certainty flooding through her, Lia ran to the skybridge that would take her toward the Water Cay. Tual had said so many things. So many things. But why would he have come to the apothecary to kill this old woman and trash everything left in the store?

To upset Anwei? He had to know the Beildan would be coming after him.

But it was what he'd said to *her* down in the tomb that set her feet running. *Remember my promise.*

He'd promised her that going against him would destroy her.

Smoke hung over the drum tower as she ran past, an acrid fog of ash coating her throat. It thickened as she ran across the bridge toward her home. It wasn't until she was a few streets away that Lia started seeing scorch marks on gates, on the walls and rooftops, a plume of black smoke rushing into the air as if it meant to battle Calsta herself. Lia couldn't make herself stop to look, running with every drop of energy she had left, hoping, praying. *Calsta!* she sang in her heart. *Aren't you merciful? Aren't you on my side? You didn't return Ewan's aurasight.*

A horrible ache erupted in Lia's chest, as if the goddess wished she could answer. Her aurasight blazed, finding no one in these scorched compounds.

She ran into her own street. Came to her own gate, the high wall blocking sight of the house beyond, that fantastical place of paintings and silly jokes and arguments with Aria. The smoke was coming from inside.

The gate wouldn't open when Lia barreled into it, the latch tied shut with a length of twine, a little paper fluttering like a gift tag on its end. Lia tore the twine from the gate, shoved it open, and found . . .

She found . . .

Lia collapsed onto her knees, staring up at the blackened, dead thing where her house was supposed to be. A body lay in the charred, open doorway, nothing left but bone. Lia combed the house for auras, but there was nothing alive inside. Nothing.

The paper that had been attached to the twine at the gate blew in a gust of wind toward the house, catching for a moment against her shoulder before fluttering toward the red embers still glowing hungrily in the wind.

Had they all been at home? Locked inside because of Mother's illness—no, because the Warlord herself was enacting justice on a disobedient valas. Mother, who had lain in her bed not even knowing Lia had returned. Father, who had just barely accepted her. And Aria, little Aria.

This is not my doing, Lia Seystone. The voice burned in Lia's head, *burned* until she couldn't think, couldn't feel, leaving no room for anything but certainty that Calsta really could speak. It left her staggering, one hand to the compound wall, her muscles all quivering. *I cannot control you little humans, only hope you will listen.*

Wind turned the paper over and over, whisking it toward the flames. There was something written on it.

Darting forward, Lia skidded on her knees to grab hold of the paper before it could disappear forever into the embers left of her home. Her name was on one side. On the other:

Your sister misses you.

Lia dropped the paper like it was on fire, every breath burning in her lungs. Aria was alive. Aria was *alive.*

You are the only one who can stop him, the voice whispered. *You and Knox and Anwei. The Commonwealth has long been unbalanced. You three can set it straight. Or you can fail, and shapeshifters will rule again.*

Forcing herself to stand, Lia felt her knees wobble. Flames poured from her home's windows and doors. Eating at the roof. At the tile and stone.

Was it only that morning she'd thought of bringing Mateo here as a guest instead of an interloper? Of living here herself as a person instead of a commodity to be traded? Was it only this morning she'd marveled at being free?

What do you want to do, Little Spot? Her father's voice echoed in her head. And Master Helan's: *This power is a choice.*

A choice that was no choice, not with Aria in Tual's grip. Lia pulled the hood of her cape up over her head. Tugged her sleeves down so they covered her hands, sheltering her from the sun. The wind. The bite of flame on the air. Lia let the long drapes fall around her, hiding her hair, her cheeks, her lips and eyes.

Like a veil.

CHAPTER 40

Group Effort

Anwei sat next to Knox in the wagon, her eyes running back and forth across him. The horse pulling the wagon snorted and jolted forward, the driver swearing in Trib as Lia rode up on her awful, bloodstained mount. She wore her hood low, completely obscuring her face.

"We know which way they're heading?" she asked.

Anwei nodded, despite the confusion cottoning the inside her head. Altahn's men had been watching the shapeshifter's cliff house, and the whole household had set off only hours before. "I'm going to kill him."

The auroshe squealed, dancing to the side to nip at the horse's haunches. It darted forward, the driver swearing even louder, though Anwei doubted Lia understood the words.

"Only if you find him first." Lia reined her auroshe to the side so he couldn't nip the horse.

Smoothing a hand through Knox's hair, Anwei couldn't find it in her to smile. "Let's call it a group effort. We'll need all the help we can get. It took me seven years to find him last time. He's not going to sit out in the open, waiting for us to cut his throat."

"What is your plan?"

"I don't have one yet." Anwei pulled her gaze up from Knox's closed eyes, the bend of his back, the sweat that had dried salty down his neck. The sword was bundled up next to him, the hilt looking charred against the blanket wrappings. Instead she watched the grass as it rippled alongside the road, smelling of dew and jade. Lia smelled of blood, salt, and tears, like actions ready to be taken. "All I know is that to make a rich man come out into the open, you take what matters most to him."

Lia's face turned, still lost in shadow. "The sword?"

Anwei shook her head, looking down the road to where the snake-tooth man had taken her brother. Of all their plans today, all the things they'd wanted to accomplish, they *had* found out one thing: how to kill a shapeshifter. "A sword like that is what started him, and it'll be what ends him too. But what did *he* steal it for?"

He'd stolen it to save Arun. Mateo. The son he'd filched, the brother he'd murdered and made over into a new creature that belonged to him. The snake-tooth man had taken Anwei's twin, half of her soul, and warped him into a person who'd left Anwei to face their village alone. To starve, cheat, lie, steal, and hunt alone, to try to exist as the shredded half-thing that had been all that was left of her after he was torn away. Arun—no, *Mateo*—had left her to ruin. Lia said he'd spent his life eating sweet rolls, studying rocks and old bones at the fancy university in Rentara, and telling tailors to add extra lace to his coats.

Mateo was the one thing that mattered most to the snake-tooth man.

And Anwei was going to do what she did best: *find* him.

Acknowledgments

I had a nightmare nearly ten years ago that resulted in this book. I can't say there's any crossover between my weird spotty dreams and the story as it ended up, and you and I can thank these lovely people for that blessing:

Sarah McCabe, my unfailingly patient editor. She took this book from goat rodeo to a slightly more normal rodeo (are there normal rodeos?), or at least a rodeo that made sense. I mean, I *think* rodeos are supposed to make sense. Sarah finds all the holes and extra words, then points them out in the nicest way possible. If she decides to edit these acknowledgments, there will probably be less in them about rodeos.

The entire team at McElderry is such a privilege to work with. There are so many people who are involved in editing, setting, styling, and so many other things that I don't have the vocabulary to properly describe the sorcery that happens behind the scenes. It's so cool to watch my story turn from words on a page to something so magical that when I was a kid I didn't believe books were written by people like me. I know it isn't magic; it's lots and lots and lots of hard work. Thank you so much to Justin Chanda, Karen Wojtyla, Anne Zafian, Bridget Madsen, Elizabeth Blake-Lin, Lauren Hoffman, Caitlin Sweeny, Alissa Nigro, Lisa Quach, Savannah Breckenridge, Anna Jarzab, Yasleen Trinidad, Saleena Nival, Emily Ritter, Annika Voss, Nicole Russo, Jenny Lu, Christina Pecorale and her sales team, and Michelle Leo and her education and library team. Last but not least, I'm so lucky to have lovely cover art from Carlos Quevedo (close the book and look at it. Seriously. It is beautiful.) and design from Greg Stadnyk.

Thanks go to my agent, Ben Grange, as always. The Wellies: Hillary Homzie, Rebecca Grabill, and Elizabeth Schoenfeld, you were there to talk to when I needed it most even though I only sent you half the book. Kristen, Cameron, and Aliah deserve more thanks than anyone else, because they read my drafts and merely nod sedately when the entire plot and all the names change halfway through rather than getting annoyed at me for not warning them or providing any context. I couldn't ask for a better writing group. Thank you very much to Chelsea Mortenson who beta-read for me when she was supposed to be taking finals. Also, thank you to Sherri and Allen Sangster who listened to me read the first chapter enough times to memorize all sorts of words that they probably wish they could forget. Thanks to Morgan Shamy and Jenna Moulton for last minute reads and timely feedback. Thank you also Tricia Levenseller who is not only a lovely friend, but who helped wrangle the beginning of this book into something that made sense.

Thank you to my eight-year-old neighbor Evie for giving me the lovely title "Finding Mateo." It ended up not quite fitting, but I appreciate the effort on your part to help me come up with a compelling title so I could stop working. Playing outside definitely does seem like more fun than writing books.

Thank you Grandma and Grandpa Recht for lending me space when I really needed a spot to write, to my parents-in-law for holding the world together when it could have so easily come apart at the seams. Hopefully your neighbors won't always remember me as that girl who lived in your attic and never slept.

My immediate family deserves the most thanks of all. There aren't words for the year this book was written. All I know is we all pulled each other through it. I wrote the story, but it's only because of the people holding me up that I managed to get a single word on the page.

Turn the page for a sneak peek
at the captivating sequel!

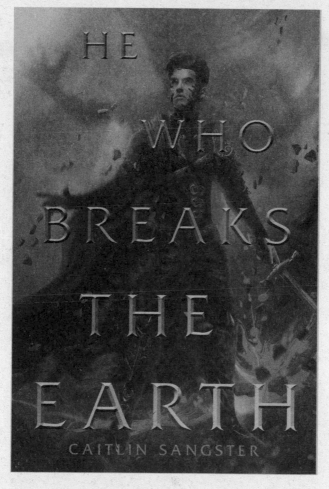

When Mateo stepped out of his room at the inn, all he could feel was death. It was a scent coming off the scuffed wooden walls, from beneath the floorboards with their threadbare carpet runners. Death was a shadow in the chatter of servants emerging from their rooms and a sour note in the scent of honey and cream-filled sweet rolls coming from the kitchen.

He took in a deep breath, as if he could latch on to the fleeing details of the world where he was alive instead of slowly rotting away into nothing. If he ignored it, maybe it would go away. His father had always made the nothing go away before.

I'm not *going away*, the nothing said. *I only just found you.*

Mateo started down the hallway, his humors churning with discomfort at the hollow voice. The nothing hadn't always *spoken* to him. It had started with a hiss just after he'd woken up in the carriage with his father, the dust of Patenga's collapsed tomb still on his coat. Now, even walking down the inn's narrow hallway felt as if he were trapped in a spotlight on a stage, hundreds of little eyes peering up at him from a darkness that had gnawed at his humors, his muscle and bone. Mateo had always believed that slow drain of energy had been wasting sickness burning through his aura, but now he couldn't un-know.

It was . . . a thing. A *nothing*.

A nothing that was suddenly aware of him, watching him, occasionally commenting on his choice of dress, and pushing energy *toward* him instead of sucking it away, lacing the air around him with rot.

Mateo wasn't sure it was a fair exchange if it meant he was already dead.

Mateo's toe caught on the stained rug just before he got to the stairs, almost sending him down them headfirst. Heart racing, he blinked at the narrow passage, harsh beams of morning light touching each stair he would have hit—his knees on that second stair, then his head and neck on the fourth, his spine on the tenth, as if the light itself wanted to break him into little pieces. Calsta, the sky goddess, set on destroying an abomination.

Chin thrust forward, he started down, shrugging off the light as it washed over him.

A month before Mateo had been at the edge of a new beginning, a new *life* to replace the one that had been gnawed to pieces. He and his father had finally located an undisturbed shapeshifter tomb with the specially Basist-made healing compound, caprenum, sitting at the bottom, just waiting to heal the wasting disease that plagued him and half the Warlord's Devoted.

They'd dug and dug, dodged traps, lost workers. Then his father had introduced him to Lia. And Mateo had brought her down into the tomb with them the night they'd broken into the shapeshifter's burial chamber to get the caprenum—which turned out to be the shapeshifter's very own sword.

Are you stomping? the voice asked. *Did the stairs do something to you, or are you always this delightful?*

Mateo caught himself stepping lightly onto the last stair, then made himself stomp the rest of the way to the kitchen, reveling in the feel of energy bursting inside him, then disgusted with himself because he knew where that energy came from. He slammed open the kitchen door, the last barrier between him and the heavenly scents of Hilaria's cooking, and couldn't stop his mind ranging out to touch the bits of metal and stone in the room, like even more potential energy just waiting for his signal.

For the first time, using his power like this didn't make him dizzy. He didn't stumble, didn't faint. His feet were there, squarely in the world, and suddenly nothing could stop him from doing what he liked.

Not even the hole inside him come to life.

I'm not *a hole,* the voice whispered. *And I wasn't going to stop you eating your weight in sugar anyway.*

Even the sweet rolls smelled like decay.

Mateo gave the maid a dignified nod, then grabbed a plate from the rack of dishes she'd been drying, surprised when she gave a perturbed squeak and jumped out of his way. As if somehow, for the first time in his life, he was someone to be wary of.

"I'm so sorry, I didn't mean to frighten you." He gave her a flourishing little bow that would have made Lia smirk at him.

"No, of course not, sir." The maid shrank back against the wall, keeping one eye on him even as she continued drying dishes.

Odd. Mateo carefully checked the wide kitchen for Hilaria before stepping in any farther and only found raw fowl trussed and ready to be roasted on the wood-topped island at the center, the back counters filled with vegetables and roots for stew. Hilaria's tray of sweet rolls were shoved onto the counter just by the door out to the stables, topped with snowy cream and glistening with raspberry glaze.

Mateo sidled up to the tray and slid two sweet rolls onto his plate.

Just as he began to lick his fingers, the door swung open and whacked him in the back of the legs.

"Mateo Montanne, you *entafolin*!" Hilaria was on him before he could run for the stairs, the maid blocking the door with both hands clamped over her mouth, looking between him and the terror Hilaria had probably made of her life for the two days their party had been camped at the inn. Hilaria swatted at Mateo's plate, knocking one of the sweet rolls back onto the tray, narrowly missing his shoulder. "You get your grubby hands away—"

Mateo ducked the next swat, pushing past her through the courtyard door, gratified that he'd managed to keep hold of the one sweet roll. Hilaria's food was to die for, but sometimes it seemed as if death was the only payment she'd accept for consuming it.

Once he made it through the door, Mateo snaked into the hubbub of servants carrying trunks, saddling horses, and hitching wagons and carriages. He ducked behind their head hostler, Harlan, even as Hilaria shouted from the kitchen door. Harlan cleared his throat, pushing Mateo down an inch lower as he scanned the organized mess with an absurdly casual air, as if he weren't trying to hide a young man and his stolen raspberry cream behind his spindly legs.

"She's going to gut you one of these days," the old hostler murmured once Hilaria had shouted her way across the courtyard, letting Mateo stand up. "But not today if you get into the carriage quick."

"You'd think she'd be flattered." Mateo lifted the roll to his mouth to take another bite, freezing when he caught sight of a small carriage out front, the door hanging open. A shock of coppery hair showed through the window, the occupant arguing loudly with the servant trying to close her inside. "Where's the other carriage, Harlan?"

Harlan's face didn't change, a little too close to read. "Master Montanne sent it on ahead of us the day we got here. Didn't you notice?"

Mateo swore, shoving another bite into his mouth and looking around for a place to hide. His stomach lurched as he looked down at his coat, the lacy front dribbled all over with glaze, the bright raspberry red dripping from his buttons like blood.

There had been a lot of blood down in the tomb. All from that boy on the ground, a sword in his gut, impaled just the way the shapeshifter's skeleton had been.

Knox, the voice hissed.

A sword just like the one they'd stolen from the tomb that Tual had bundled up and dragged behind his carriage in its own special wagon—a sword that was supposed to save Mateo's life. Mateo wasn't sure why the caprenum sword they'd stolen from Patenga's tomb needed a whole wagon to itself, but Tual had kept him and everyone else in their company from peeking under the tarp, as if touching the sword before the right time would ruin everything. But his father *couldn't* expect him to share a carriage with Aria Seystone. She was just like Lia, only smaller and slightly less good at violence.

Mateo shoved the last of the roll into his mouth, icing dribbling down his lip. "Saddle Bella for me, would you?" he mumbled to Harlan around the lump of pastry.

Tual appeared at the inn's main doors, his sun hat tipped. He was all smiles and banter as he crossed to check under the tarp covering the wagon where the shapeshifter sword was. Once he'd resecured the canvas, Tual walked toward the little carriage, Aria's growled insults from inside actually quite impressive. Mateo ducked down even farther, his stomach swirling with bile.

". . . riding alone probably isn't the best option." Harlan was still talking, and Mateo hadn't heard a word. "Didn't they tell you about the attacks, boy? That's why we stayed at the inn for two days despite your father being in a fury to get home. Even he couldn't brush off finding bodies in the road."

"Bodies?" Mateo turned to look at the hostler only to catch sight of Hilaria storming from the kitchen yet again, both her fists clenched around the tray of sweet rolls to offer to the company. She made straight for Tual despite servants grabbing at the tray left and right and presented him with the last one, which Tual took with a bow, then handed it in to the carriage's single occupant.

It flew back out quick enough, landing in the dirt at Hilaria's feet. Mateo cleared his throat, turning back to Harlan, vaguely horrified about the waste of a coveted sweet roll. "What do you mean they've been finding bodies?" His mind flicked back to the terrifying girl who'd been at the bottom of Patenga's tomb, the one who'd made vines burst out of the earth and grasp at him like snakes. Had she managed to follow them somehow? Father had said she might.

"The first night, it was . . . well, a *Devoted* of all things. On the road."

"Something killed a Devoted?" Mateo paused.

"Yes. Completely white and shriveled, he was, like he'd been drained of blood. And there were bites. . . ." Harlan looked down. "We thought it was a coincidence coming across him on the road. But then we started seeing animals in a similar condition near the camp. And then last night . . ."

"Last night *what?*" Mateo leaned forward.

"Well, Master Montanne's getting us out quick enough, but it won't bring back the kitchen boy."

Mateo's chest clenched a hair tighter. He looked just beyond the inn out into the dense wall of foliage, the road cutting through it like a wound. They'd be safe soon. They'd be back at home where no one could get to them.

No one except Lia, who'd stop at nothing to get her sister. A shudder trilled down his back. Lia Seystone was not above killing. The Beildan girl he'd seen at the dig wouldn't be either. Mateo's mind flashed again to the shadowy figure in the tomb, energy singing like poison in the air around her, Tual answering with a terrible magic that stank of murder . . .

No. Mateo's jaw clenched. *No. She isn't my sister, and I'm not . . .*

You're not what? the little voice sang. *You're not like your father, the one person who loved you before I found you? If you weren't like him, then you'd be dead.*

Dead. The thought echoed in his head. He hadn't chosen to turn shapeshifter. He hadn't wanted it, didn't want it now. But that couldn't *change* the sacrifice Tual had helped him make, killing an innocent girl to save his own life, even if it had made him into . . .

A monster.

Mateo breathed the word in and then out again. People were the choices they made, not the labels other people gave them. He was what he was. He was alive. And he would make do with what life he had left.

No one could fault him that.

"Are . . . you all right?" Harlan's voice was concerned.

Mateo looked down to find the plate in shards between his two hands, blood on his fingers. He dropped the broken pieces like a dead snake, recoiling back a step. Hilaria was very animatedly speaking to his father by the carriage, and the barely contained glee on Tual's face made Mateo fairly certain that it had to do with a stolen sweet roll. His father turned a fraction and caught Mateo's eye across the courtyard, a guffaw so painfully held in that Mateo knew Tual would be cackling about it later.

He'd thought his father had finally decided to be open with him, to *stop* keeping secrets. How could Tual have known about these killings and not told him?

"Mateo?" Harlan was still standing there, worried.

"I'm fine." Mateo wiped his bloody fingers on his coat, flinching when red smeared across the fabric to match the raspberry. This coat had been his favorite back at the university—just the right number of ruffles to be interesting without being too much, the shade of green perfectly complementing his light brown skin. He started toward the stable, Harlan twitching along behind him as if he'd been attached with string. "I'm going to ride, Harlan. Nothing is going to attack us in broad daylight."

"They look almost like auroshe kills," Harlan murmured.

Mateo's stomach roiled, the sweet roll threatening to come back up.

"With the first body being a Devoted and . . . well, I think we both know auroshes don't roam free this far south. Honestly, I'm surprised we don't hear more tales of those monsters killing their riders. If you are determined to take Bella, keep your eyes open. There could be more of them following us."

"Devoted or feral auroshes?"

"Either." Harlan shrugged.

Mateo turned toward the open stable doors. It wasn't the Warlord he was worried about. She would at least try to talk to them before gutting him. The Warlord thought they had something she wanted: a cure to wasting sickness. Auroshe kills and dead Devoted on the road sounded more like Lia with her foul steed prowling after them. It wasn't enough that her actual job . . . magical calling . . . gods-given *purpose* in the world was to kill people like Mateo and his father. Tual had gone and kidnapped her younger sister.

Because he wants me to live. The words unspooled inside him, his own this time. *I want to live.*

Mateo strode into the light-starved stables, straight for Bella's stall. She gave an excited whinny when she saw him. He ran a hand down her neck, grateful when she buried her nose in his chest. His heart slowed a beat. But only the one.

If the kills out there weren't Lia's doing, he'd eat his own oversized sun hat. A sick feeling of betrayal welled deep in his chest.

Tual had blackmailed her into an engagement, encouraging Mateo to get to know her, to give her a chance. And Mateo had accidental-ly done it. He'd talked to her, almost been killed with her, stolen an auroshe with her, saved her from the Warlord, and then he'd thought that maybe . . .

He'd *wanted* to . . .

He'd even thought that *she* might want . . .

That someone could see past the many deaths of Mateo Mon-tanne to *him* had always been an impossible thing until that day in his father's office with Lia. She'd stayed. She'd talked to him. She'd listened. She was smart. She was funny, she was beautiful, she was exactly what he . . .

Mateo forced the thought of Lia's burnished hair, her freckles, her blue eyes from his mind, turning to take the saddle from a hostler and place it on Bella's back. The maybes that surrounded Lia had been so new and unexpected and *hopeful* that they'd felt forbidden, secret, delicious. But then she'd seen the reliefs in Patenga's tomb the same moment he had.

She'd been Tual's plan all along—Lia *plus* a caprenum sword. All magic required sacrifice, and the sacrifice that had made Mateo into the creature he was had been botched, tearing a hole inside him instead of filling him to the brim with power. The magical caprenum he'd been searching for with his father for years was just the vessel—the knife, the sword, the ax to seal the sacrifice of the person you loved most.

Because that's what Mateo needed to survive—a new sacrifice to replace the old one that hadn't worked.

But that put him in a difficult place. How could he fall in love with Lia Seystone knowing it was all to keep his own heart beating at the expense of hers? And how could he persuade her to love him back as the oaths required when she now knew *exactly* what the end would look like for her? Dead on the end of a shapeshifter's sword.

But without Lia, Mateo would continue to die bit by bit from the hole the transformation had left inside him, a hole that had to be filled with something. Some*one*.

All magic came from sacrifice. It was only in the last month that he understood it was sacrificed love—a love realized, bonded, solidified, then torn asunder—that could make something as powerful as a shapeshifter. And if Mateo wanted to live, he had to make that sacrifice himself, the right way.

Mateo finished pulling the buckles tight and stood. Lia would come, but it wouldn't be with an open heart. Maybe she'd already gone back to the Warlord and would come with an entire Devoted army.

She's not with the Warlord, the little voice giggled. *She's with your sister.*

Halfway to sticking his foot in the stirrup, Mateo faltered, falling forward. Bella snorted, her head twisting back to look at him reproachfully. *Lia's with . . . are you sure?*

I think they've formed the first official "I Hate Mateo Montanne" club.

Mateo's insides went cold. *Gods above, couldn't you have said something earlier?*

Why does Lia scare you so much? it said, ignoring his question. *Lia Seystone is just a girl. She's made of muscles and energy and toenails and hair, and worms will eat her face just as quickly as they would anyone else's. As fast as they would have eaten you, if I hadn't been there.*

I didn't ask for my father to make me kill you, he thought furiously at the nothing, but then turned the fury back on himself for engaging with it at all.

I'm not nothing, and I'm not an it, the little voice hissed, and Mateo could feel the shape of her underneath the helpless whisper she'd been using with him, like a monstrous mass of sinew, bone, and claws flexing from behind its little-girl mask. *My name is Willow. And if you know what's good for you, you'd be worrying more about the other one.* Her voice broke. *Knox never would let me have her, even when I starved. She would have fixed everything, but she ruined it instead.*

I am worried about the other one. Mateo mounted Bella and steered her out into the courtyard, past the little carriage, the wagons, the life that had been so kind to him these last seven years. Running from the one he'd forgotten. Tual had told him in the carriage as they'd ridden away from the tomb that his sister had spent her whole life looking for him.

But even if that were true, how had *Willow* known?

Mateo cleared his throat, kicking Bella even faster, pushing the name away. The thing in his head didn't get a name. It didn't exist.

I'm so hungry, Willow sighed. Her voice quieted, shriveling down to almost nothing. *You're hungry too, so you know how it feels. You'll feed me, won't you, Mateo?*

Mateo shivered at the sound of his own name made from thorns and ice. Because he did know how that hunger felt.

He did want to live.

And nothing was going to stop him, not Hilaria and her sweet rolls, not blood in the cuts on his hands, not Aria Seystone swearing when she thought people could see her and sobbing into her pillow when she thought they couldn't. Not his sister, whatever monstrous thing she'd become.

Not Lia and her red curls, her auroshe, and her sword.

If I tell you more about what they're doing, will you stop calling me a thing? Willow asked.

But Mateo couldn't let himself listen to a ghost—who even knew why she was inside him, what she wanted, and what she'd take from him? Because that's all people ever did. Take.

Keeping his eyes open for the rocky formations that marked the hidden path to the caves that would take him home, Mateo kicked Bella out onto the road, thinking only of the wind in his hair and the sun on his face because it was touching him, making him as real, as important, as *alive* as anyone else in the company, no matter the scent of death in his nose.

He wanted to live. If that meant loving Lia, then killing her, then somehow that was what he was going to do.

Discover the spellbinding worlds of *New York Times* bestselling author Margaret Rogerson

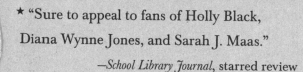

★ "Sure to appeal to fans of Holly Black, Diana Wynne Jones, and Sarah J. Maas."

—*School Library Journal*, starred review

★ "An enthralling adventure . . . and a world worth staying lost in."

—*Kirkus Reviews*, starred review